t

Also by Nicola Griffith

Menewood

Menewood

✠

Nicola Griffith

MCD ⊗ FARRAR, STRAUS AND GIROUX NEW YORK

MCD
Farrar, Straus and Giroux
120 Broadway, New York 10271

Copyright © 2023 by Nicola Griffith
Maps copyright © 2023 by Jeffrey L. Ward
All rights reserved
Printed in the United States of America
First edition, 2023

Library of Congress Cataloging-in-Publication Data
Names: Griffith, Nicola, author.
Title: Menewood / Nicola Griffith.
Description: First edition. | New York : MCD / Farrar, Straus and Giroux,
    2023.
Identifiers: LCCN 2023012554 | ISBN 9780374208080 (hardcover)
Subjects: LCSH: Hilda, of Whitby, Saint, 614–680—Fiction. | Christian women
    saints—England—Whitby—Fiction. | Christian saints—England—Northumbria
    (Region)—Fiction. | Women—History—Middle Ages, 500–1500—Fiction. |
    LCGFT: Historical fiction. | Novels.
Classification: LCC PS3557.R48935 M46 2023 | DDC 813/.54—dc23/eng/
    20230317
LC record available at https://lccn.loc.gov/2023012554

Designed by Abby Kagan

Our books may be purchased in bulk for promotional, educational, or business use.
Please contact your local bookseller or the Macmillan Corporate and Premium
Sales Department at 1-800-221-7945, extension 5442, or by email at
MacmillanSpecialMarkets@macmillan.com.

www.mcdbooks.com • www.fsgbooks.com
Follow us on Twitter, Facebook, and Instagram at @mcdbooks

1   3   5   7   9   10   8   6   4   2

For Kelley:

everything, always, for all the reasons

Contents

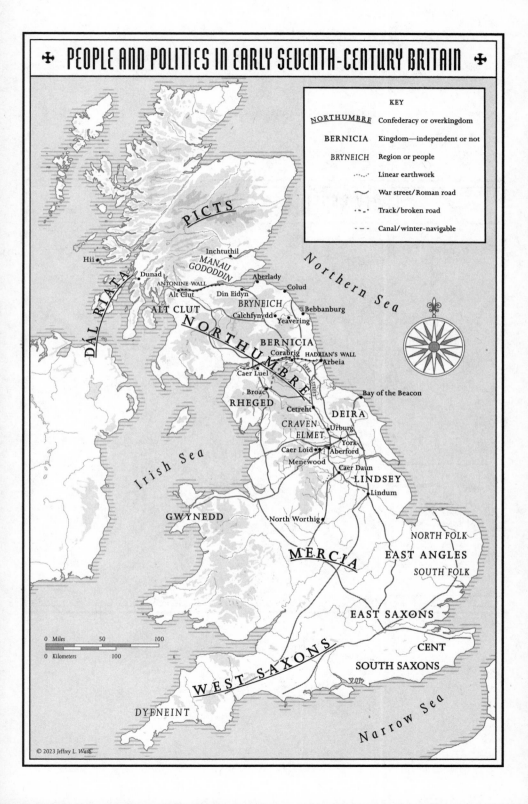

PEOPLE AND POLITIES IN EARLY SEVENTH-CENTURY BRITAIN

KEY

NORTHUMBRE — Confederacy or overkingdom
BERNICIA — Kingdom—independent or not
BRYNEICH — Region or people
······· — Linear earthwork
⌒ — War street/Roman road
·–·–· — Track/broken road
– – – — Canal/winter-navigable

PICTS

Hii

MANAU GODODDIN
Inchtuthil

Dunad
ANTONINE WALL
Alt Clut
ALT CLUT
Din Eidyn
Aberlady
Colud
BRYNEICH
Calchfynydd
Yeavering
Bebbanburg

DÁL RIATA

NORTHUMBRE

BERNICIA
Corabrig
HADRIAN'S WALL
Arbeia

Caer Luel
Broac
RHEGED
Cetreht
Bay of the Beacon

DEIRA
CRAVEN
ELMET
Urburg
Caer Loid
York
Aberford
Menewood
Caer Daun
LINDSEY
Lindum

Irish Sea

DERE STREET

Northern Sea

GWYNEDD

North Worthig

MERCIA

NORTH FOLK
EAST ANGLES
SOUTH FOLK

EAST SAXONS

WEST SAXONS

CENT
SOUTH SAXONS

DYFNEINT

Narrow Sea

0 Miles 50 100
0 Kilometers 100

© 2023 Jeffrey L. Ward

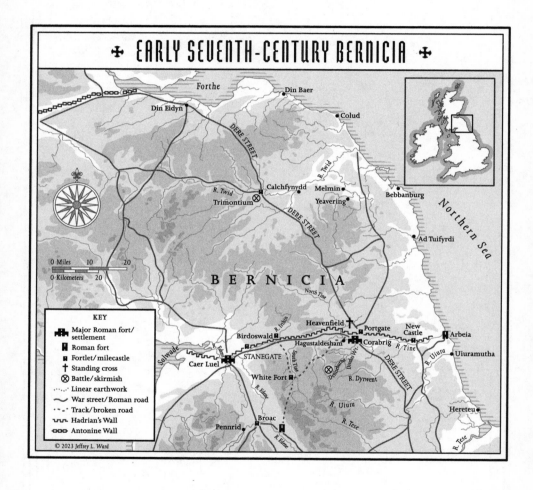

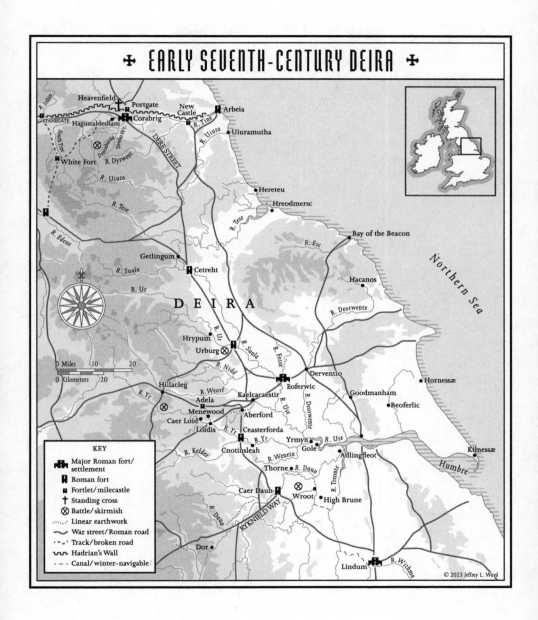

☩ EARLY SEVENTH-CENTURY DEIRA ☩

KEY
- Major Roman fort/settlement
- Roman fort
- Fortlet/milecastle
- † Standing cross
- ⊗ Battle/skirmish
- Linear earthwork
- War street/Roman road
- Track/broken road
- Hadrian's Wall
- Canal/winter-navigable

DEIRA

Northern Sea

Humbre

Heavenfield
Portgate
New Castle
Corabrig
Arbeia
STANEGATE
Hagustaldesham
R. Irthin
South Tine
R. Tine
R. Uiura
Uiuramutha
Denisburg
Diuelis W.
White Fort
R. Dyrwent
R. Uiura
DERE STREET
R. Tese
R. Edene
Hereteu
Hreodmersc
Bay of the Beacon
R. Esc
Getlingum
Cetreht
R. Suala
R. Ur
Hacanos
R. Deorwente
Hrypum
Urburg
R. Ur
R. Suala
R. Fosse
Derventio
R. Nidd
Hillacleg
Eoferwic
Goodmanham
Hornessæ
R. Yr
R. Weorf
Kaelcacaestir
Adela
Menewood
Aberford
R. Use
R. Deorwente
Beoferlic
Caer Loid
Loidis
Ceasterforda
R. Yr
Yrmyn
R. Use
Kilnessæ
Cnotinsleah
R. Yr
Gole
Adlingfleot
R. Kelder
R. Weneta
Thorne
R. Daun
Caer Daun
Wroot
High Brune
R. Treonte
RYKNIELD WAY
R. Daun
Dor
Lindum
R. Withma

0 Miles 10 20
0 Kilometers 20

© 2023 Jeffrey L. Ward

NORTHUMBRE

Deira and Bernicia began as separate kingdoms ruled, respectively, by the Yffing and Iding family dynasties. At the beginning of the seventh century, Æthelfrith Iding conquered Deira, forcibly married one Yffing, killed or sent into exile the rest, and merged the two kingdoms into the overkingdom of Northumbre. For the next few decades, kingship followed the fortunes of war.

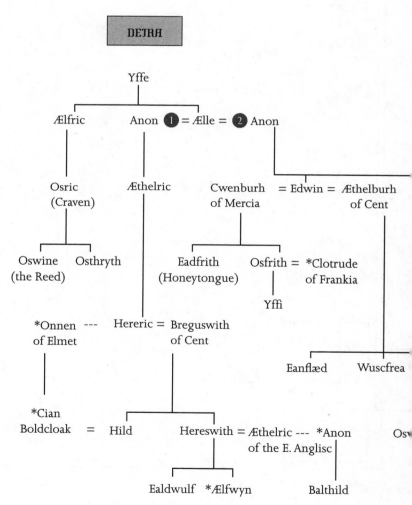

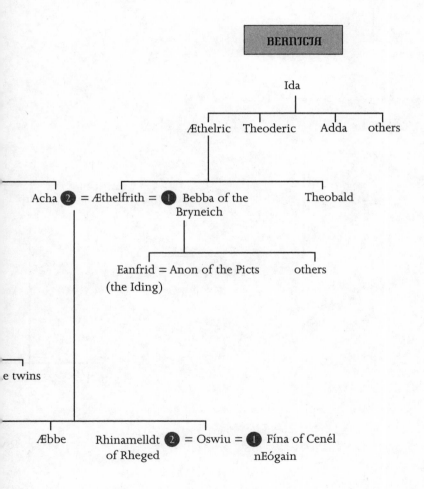

Cast of Characters

✥

Four ruling dynasties feature prominently in this book:

Idings	Bernicia (and occasionally Northumbre)
Oiscingas	Cent
Wuffings	the North and South Folk of the East Anglisc
Yffings	Deira (and occasionally Northumbre)

However, in early seventh-century Britain, power and loyalty (to religion, king, or family) rose and fell with the fortunes of war: exiles fled and returned, rivals married, kings and priests converted and apostatised. Affiliations were fluid. Consequently, the best way to list the characters of *Menewood* is alphabetically.

Name (dynasty, kingdom, or title)	Bynames and relationships
Acærn	Cian's warhorse
Acha (Yffing)	Edwin's sister, second wife of Æthelfrith, mother of Oswald, Oswiu, and Æbbe. Dead.
Adair	swordsman and son of a Bryneich chief

Æbbe (Iding)	sister of Oswald, twin of Oswiu; in exile with her brothers in Dál Riata
Æthelburh (Oiscinga)	Queen of Northumbre; Edwin's second wife, sister of Eadbald of Cent
Æthelfrith (Iding)	aka Flesaur, Fflamddwyr; first king of Northumbre, father of Eanfrid, Oswald, Æbbe, and Oswiu
Æthelric (Wuffing)	aka Short Leg; lord of the North Folk of the East Anglisc; married to Hereswith Yffing
Afanc	daughter of Eirlys and Pabo on Ynys Bwyell
Aidan	Irish priest of Hii; admirer of Oswald Lamnguin
Aldnoth	spearman-in-training of Elmet
Aldred	young, indecisive priest from York; previously one of James the Deacon's choirboys
Almund	earnest priest from York; one of James the Deacon's choirboys; Hild's scribe
Artorius	aka count of the Wall; British chieftain, lord of Birdoswald fort
Balthild	natural daughter of Æthelric Wuffing by a lady of the South Gwyre
Bassus	captain of swords to Queen Æthelburh
Bavo	Frisian trader with many relatives
Bearn	stripling spearman-in-training of Elmet
Begu	Hild's gemæcce, daughter of Mulstan of the Bay of the Beacon, beloved of Uinniau
Beli (Alt Clut)	king of Alt Clut; father of Eugein
Berhtnoth	gesith, one of Hild's Hounds; brother of Berhtred

Berhtred	gesith, one of Hild's Hounds; brother of Berhtnoth
Blæcca	Coelgar's deputy in Lindsey
Blodfoot	Leofdæg's mare
Bone	Hild's grey gelding
Bote	milkmaid at the Bay of the Beacon; sister to Cædmon
Breguswith (Oiscinga)	Hild's mother, daughter of King Æthelberht's first wife, widow of Hereric Yffing
Brona	butcher's daughter, then butcher, in York
Bryhtsige	gesith, Fiercesome
Cadwallon (Gwynedd)	aka Bradawc, Treacher; sometime king and always war leader of Gwynedd
Cædmon	cowherd at Bay of the Beacon, plays harp and lyre
Ceadwin	Hild's foster son, son of Saxfryth of East Farm, Elmet
Cenhelm	master of the *Curlew*
Cian Boldcloak	beloved of Hild, son of Onnen; lord of Elmet; rumoured to be son of Ceredig, last king of Elmet
Ciniod (Picts)	Pictish overking, newly dead
Clut	Ceadwin's cat in Menewood
Coelfrith	Edwin's reeve; son of Coelgar
Coelgar	lord of Lindsey; father of Coelfrith and Coelwyn
Coelwyn	gesith, one of Hild's Hounds; Ceolfrith's little brother
Coifi	former priest of Woden in Goodmanham, now in Craven
Coledauc (Bryneich)	prince of the Bryneich; father of Cuncar, husband of Langwredd
Cormán (bishop)	priest of Hii, Irish, newly made bishop to accompany Oswald

Cuncar (Bryneich)	aka the piglet prince; son of Coledauc
Cuthred	stripling spearman-in-training in Elmet
Cygnet	Hild's mare
Cynan	gesith, one of Hild's Hounds
Dieuwke	powerful Frisian trading captain
Domnall Brecc (Dál Riata)	king of Dál Riata
Druyen	a farrier in Craven
Dudda	gesith, Fiercesome
Duv	steady woodworker of Menewood
Dwmplen	Dumpling; Rhin's lazy pony
Eadbald (Wuffing)	king of Kent; brother of Æthelburh
Eadfrith (Yffing)	aka Honeytongue; eldest son of Edwin Yffing by Cwenburh of Mercia
Eadric the Brown	gesith, one of Hild's Hounds
Eanflæd (Yffing)	daughter of Edwin and Æthelburh
Eanfrid (Iding)	eldest Iding, son of Æthelfrith and Bebba of the Bryneich, half brother to Oswald; ætheling-in-exile among the Picts
Edwin (Yffing)	aka Snakebeard; overking of Northumbre; Hild's great-uncle
Eirlys	mother of Afanc; respected landholder of High Brune in Ynys Bwyell
Eugein (Alt Clut)	son and heir of King Beli ab Neithon of Alt Clut
Felix (bishop)	Burgundian bishop, bishop of the East Anglisc
Fína (Cenél nEógain)	Irish princess; companion of Oswiu Iding and mother of his first son
Flicker	Wolcen's filly, twin to Whisk
Fliss	Eirlys and Pabo's territorial dog
Fllur	mother of Geren; milk mother to Wilfrid; young refugee who fled to Menewood

Flýte	Hild's mare; big, with a wonderful gait
Fursey (bishop)	priest, perhaps bishop of the North Folk of the East Anglisc; Hild's first tutor
Gartnait (Picts)	Newly made king of the Picts
Gladmær	gesith, Fiercesome
Grimhun	gesith, one of Hild's Hounds
Grina	shepherd of Elmet; arrived in Menewood with Brona
Guenmon	Onnen's right hand at Bay of the Beacon; runs the kitchen
Gwladus	Hild's bodywoman, and more
Heiu	Irishwoman; Breguswith's right hand at Aberford textile works
Hereric (Yffing)	Hild's father; ætheling of Deira; poisoned in exile in Elmet (probably) at the behest of his uncle Edwin
Hereswith (Yffing)	Hild's sister, married to Æthelric Wuffing, mother of Ælfwyn and Ealdwulf; lady of the North Folk
Hild (Yffing)	aka Cath Llew, Butcherbird, Baedd Coch, light of the world; lady of Elmet; daughter of Breguswith and Hereric, beloved of Cian Boldcloak
Honorius (overbishop)	overbishop in Cantwaraburg (archbishop of Canterbury)
Honorius (pope)	bishop of Rome (the pope)
Huelwen	farmer; daughter of Jonty; one foot
Hunric	a sly Bernician thegn; father of Yrre
Innis	swordsman of the Bryneich
James the Deacon	previously songmaster in York, now deacon in Craven; Hild's sometime mentor
Janne	Linnet's daughter in law, first wet nurse to Wilfrid

Jonty	old man, singer of depressing songs in Ynys Bwyell; father of Huelwen
Laisrén	Irish priest and Oswald's man
Langwredd (Bryneich)	lady of the Bryneich; married to Coledauc; singer and harpist
Lél	Leofdæg's bay mare, stolen from Osric's messenger
Leofdæg	gesith, Fiercesome; brother of Leofe
Linnet	woman who lives near York with her old mother
Llweriadd	old woman (though younger than she looks) in Menewood; aunt of Sintiadd and Morud
Luftmær	scop, Breguswith's bed mate
Maer	orphan girl from Cnotinsleah; Hild's foster daughter, sister of Tette
Mallo	priest and spy
Manfrid	gesith, sister-son of Tondhelm, father of Wilfrid
Morud	Hild's runner; brother of Sintiadd, nephew of Llweriadd
Moryn	bard of the Bryneich, cousin of Oran
Mot Oer	chief swordsman of Rhoedd of Rheged
Mulstan	thegn of Mulstanton/Bay of the Beacon; father of Begu, husband of Onnen and father of her twins
Oeric	Hild's first sworn retainer; swordsman
Onnen	mother of Cian, lady of the Bay of the Beacon, married to Mulstan and mother of his twins
Oran	sword captain of the Bryneich; cousin of Moryn
Osfrith (Yffing)	lord of Arbeia; son of Edwin by first wife Cwenburh of Mercia, brother of Honeytongue, father of Yffi

Osric (Yffing)	aka Whiphand, Trembleknee, craven of Craven; lord of Craven; father of Oswine and Osthryth
Osthryth (Yffing)	daughter of Osric Yffing, sister of Oswine
Oswald (Iding)	aka Lamnguin, Brightblade, Whiteblade; son of Acha Yffing (Hild's great aunt) and Æthelfrith Iding; ætheling in exile in Dál Riata
Oswine (Yffing)	aka the Reed; heir to Craven; son of Osric Yffing, brother of Osthryth
Oswiu (Iding)	son of Æthelfrith Iding and Acha Yffing, twin of Æbbe, brother of Oswald
Pabo	husband of Eirlys of High Brune, father of Afanc
Paulinus (bishop)	aka the Crow; bishop of York, senior priest in Northumbre
Penda (Mercia)	war leader, then king, of Mercia
Rhianmelldt (Rheged)	daughter of king Rhoedd of Rheged
Rhin	British priest, steward of Menewood
Rhoedd (Rheged)	king of Rheged; uncle of Uinniau, father of Rhianmelldt
Ronan	swordsman of the Bryneich and bodyguard of Cuncar
Rulf	young Anglisc wood worker in Menewood
Sandy/Memps	Begu's pony
Saxfryth	sheep farmer at East Farm in Elmet; mother of Ceadwin
Sigeberht (Wuffing)	king of the North and South Folk of East Anglisc
Sintiadd	niece of Llweriadd, sister of Morud, bodywoman-in-training of Hild in Menewood

Sitric	older recruit, spearman and bow hunter of Elmet
Stephanus the Black	priest of York, amanuensis of Bishop Paulinus
Suibne (Fir Thrí)	ambitious Irish priest of Hii
Tette	girl of Cnotinsleah; sister of Maer
Tole	bowwoman recruited to Menewood
Tondhelm	Deiran thegn; uncle of Manfrid
Uinniau (Rheged)	prince of Rheged; sister son of king Rhoedd, beloved of Begu, cousin of Rhianmelldt
Whisk	Wolcen's colt, twin of Flicker
Wilfram	gesith, one of Hild's Hounds, brother of Wilgith, son of Wilgar
Wilfrid	Hild's gift son, son of Wilgith and Manfrid, grandson of Wilgar
Wilgar	thegn and substantial landowner near York; father of Wilfram and Wilgith
Wilgith	Wilgar's daughter, mother of Wilfrid
Wilnoð	gemæcce to queen Æthelburh of Northumbre
Wolcen	Uinniau's mare, dam of Flicker and Whisk
Wulf	gesith, Fiercesome
Wuscfrea (Yffing)	youngest son of Edwin and Æthelburh
Yffi (Yffing)	only son of Osfrith Yffing and Clotrude of Frankia
Yrre	swordsman of Bernicia, son of Hunric

One

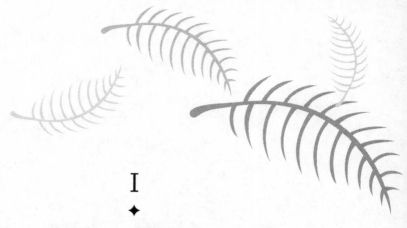

I

✦

Butcherbird and Cath Llew

Elmet—York—Menewood—Twid Valley—Bay of the Beacon

(End of Wulfmonath 632 to Litha 632, 15 weeks)

1

✛

ON THE HIGH MOOR OF ELMET, ghostly in the pale winter light, wind hissed like grit through frozen bracken. Hild eased Cygnet to a halt, loosened the reins, and hooked one foot up across the saddle to wait. The big mare turned her rump to the wind, but Hild drank deep of the cold, clean air, unbreathed by any but lost sheep and soaring birds.

Below her, seven riders picked their way up the slope: six striplings, alike in coarse grey cloaks and plain leather caps, and Wilfram, her Hound. In this world of silvery lichen and snow-dusted rock, Wilfram, in the gleaming glory of a warrior gesith, was the only splash of colour: blue cloak, silvered war hat, and great shield, its leather cover painted half in green with the hazel tree of Elmet and half in purple with her own Yffing boar. He was keeping the younglings to a deliberate pace, no doubt to give the lady time to whisper with the wind, or walk with the wights, or whatever else her Hounds thought she did to gain uncanny knowledge. So many songs, so many stories: Hild Yffing, light of the world and godmouth; hægtes and freemartin; Butcherbird and king's fist.

Old songs, all of them. Time for new ones.

She turned in the saddle, gauging the distance to the top of the moor. From there she could see for miles, and, as new-made lady of Elmet, everything she saw was hers—or would be when she had the spears to defend it.

Three months ago Edwin Overking had given Elmet to Hild and Cian Boldcloak to hold in his name, much to the rage of Osric Yffing, who now must be content to hold only Craven, to the west. This much was known. What was unknown, or as yet undecided, was where Craven ended and Elmet began.

Nothing could be done in Wulfmonath, when sensible folk bided by the fire to make and mend until the world turned back towards the light and the land unfroze. And she wanted nothing begun until she commanded more spears. What better time, then, than now, with no one abroad but the wolves, to train those spears?

Today was their first trial. She and Wilfram should be enough to test these few, though she could wish she had at least Oeric here. But she had left him in Caer Loid, the great vill, because with Cian and her other Hounds gone south to the Wolf festival—glittering with gold and the gear of war, all the better to lure restless and trainable young men—she had no other spears to watch over her folk.

Her group were close now, close enough to see how tightly young Cuthred clutched his reins, how closely he followed the others, how he startled when they passed the mouth of a stony gully and the wind stirred bare saplings taking hold there to eerie creaking. Small saplings, none of more than five years' growth, they spoke of a land too long without a lord, a land whose folk feared to bring their herds to graze such a lonely place. As lady of Elmet she would change that.

Wilfram called an order for them to spread out and one of the striplings made a cheerful reply—still cheerful despite the cold; still proud of his new spear. She glanced at her Hound and raised an eyebrow. Without moving his hand from where it rested near his sword hilt, he gave her the one-shouldered gesith shrug: Here was as good a place as any.

She motioned them ahead. One of them turned to look back, wondering if she would attack from behind: Bearn, lighthearted and eager, always ready to burst into song. Well, she would change that, too.

Over the rise, out of sight, a peewit's call rose and fell and rose again, fading into the distance. A gust of wind lifted Cygnet's mane, and the mare turned to give Hild a mild look. Hild patted her neck. "I know." Too cold to sit out here and think. Time to begin.

She secured her staff and gathered the reins, watching a throstle's brisk wingbeat as it climbed up and up, south and east. It was cold out for such a bird. They usually—

The world snapped into enamel-bright clarity, every grass-blade sharp: not a throstle, a pigeon hawk; not flying low after the tasty peewit but rising, rising out of danger.

She kicked Cygnet into a run and whistled, the liquid trill of a blackbird she had trained her Hounds to recognise. Wilfram turned, sword already half-drawn, and she pointed at her eyes, then, with a chopping knife-hand, south and west: *Go!* And to the youngsters—gaping as Wilfram's horse disappeared over the rise—the exaggerated fist-clutch and pull of *Hold!* For a wonder they did, and then she was among them, towering over them.

"Spears!" Cuthred and ever-eager Bearn already had theirs halfway out; the others were hauling awkwardly, excited that the challenge was begun.

"This is no trial." Her voice was harsh. "South of the rise, someone comes." Nothing hunted a pigeon hawk on its own moor except people—but it was the wrong time of year for drovers, and any shepherd's dog would have barked. "We are the only blades between the vill and those who would do our folk harm." Bearn's grin faltered. She nodded. "Today you're spearmen of Elmet in truth."

The striplings swallowed, stiff and serious. Only one was dangerously pale. Oh, for the rest of her Hounds now . . .

"Follow my lead."

She led them uphill, but at a slant, on a track that would keep them below the skyline, to a gap between the boulders just below the top. At their backs the wind was turning northwest. When the clouds dropped their burden she doubted it would be rain. No sign of Wilfram.

Keep them busy.

"Check your mounts," she said, and watched as they laid their palms on the ribs to feel their breathing, tugged at the girths, and tested the bits as she had shown them.

"Spears."

They held them out for inspection, still-new and unblemished ash shafts gripped tightly in still-new and unblemished hands.

"Bucklers."

The small round shields were best for mounted work, and it would be a long time, if ever, before these barefaced boys were ready for the shield wall.

She hefted her staff—bound with iron at each end, and longer than most men were tall—and loosened her slaughter seax in its sheath. Cygnet knew that sound. Her ears pricked forward and the great ribs between Hild's knees moved faster.

Hoofbeats. Coming at a run. Wilfram.

He skidded to a halt. "Half a mile," he said. "From the west. At a walk. Eight."

Bandits?

"Good mounts. Good blades—"

Not bandits.

"—but no banners, no colours."

Men who did not want to be known. "Gold?"

"Not much."

A warrior wore his wealth. These men were not the best, not king's gesiths but lord's men, though not here to talk or trade. "Craven," she said. Osric, testing Elmet's defences—testing her. And all her Hounds but Wilfram gone with Cian Boldcloak somewhere south of Ceasterforda.

Eight. Well-armed and well-mounted, against herself, Wilfram, and six striplings not yet half trained.

She looked at her Hound, then his shield, tilted her head. His slow smile was answer enough. He slid the shield onto his arm, gripped the bar behind the boss, and waited at her word.

She caught the striplings' gaze, one by one. "We face men who've dropped their colours." She grinned, sudden and savage. "So shall we."

Wilfram tore off the Elmet colours to show chalk-white planks daubed in bloody red: a man spiked on a stake like a warning. Totem of the Butcherbird.

The striplings paled, knobby bones showing white at wrist and jaw. They looked up at her with eyes huge and dark: a song come to life.

She led them east, below the summit, until she found the gully she was looking for—the steep run south down to the river. It was covered in a thin blanket of snow, but she could tell by the ripples and bumps, the soft flat and rounded humps, what was water, what was reed, and where marsh lay. "Follow exactly."

She picked out the narrow track winding alongside the fenny beck, then let Cygnet find the way.

The great Yr's deep vibration grew. When it rumbled in her bones she reined in, signalled them to hold, and slid from the saddle. Staff in hand she crept forward around the last curve in the gully to where trees clustered on both sides of the mouth of the beck, thicker to the east than the west.

From behind the still-red berries of a rowan, she listened. There. Over the deeper note of the river, the jingle of unwrapped harness. Either fools or they had never raided before.

She whistled softly. Wilfram appeared at her shoulder. "They're close. Take four striplings back into those trees." She pointed behind her. "Send two to me, here, quick as you like." She watched the scudding cloud. "At my signal, fast and loud. Drive them back." Back west through the Gap. "Kill if you must"—no quarter for nameless men—"but drive them."

Some would die—she could not afford to be careful, not with untested striplings—but not too many. Nameless or not she was not yet ready to risk open war between Craven and Elmet.

They were barely in place among the trees on either side of the beck when the men of Craven came around the curve in the river. The one leading was turned in his saddle, laughing with another. Only one, riding closest to the river, had his shield on his arm and spear forward. She marked him in her mind, knew Wilfram would, too.

She studied how they moved. She looked at the sky. Another two hundred paces and they would be in place. Behind her a horse shifted its weight and she smelt the sudden stink of fear sweat from its rider. Cuthred.

"Steady," she said.

One hundred paces.

"Ready . . ."

She felt herself swell, blood coursing rich and thick in her veins, and her heart rose like a great bubble.

A pause and swirl of wind brought sleet slanting in from the raiders' flank and the man in the lead hunched down against the pearl-grey streaks. His mount slowed and the horse behind him turned to avoid bumping them, then they were milling in confusion. One man jumped down to tug a cloak from the bundle behind his saddle, another was turning from the sting as sleet hardened to hail.

"Now!" And with a sharp whistle, she kicked Cygnet forward, charging the raiders down the path of the wind.

"Butcherbird!" Wilfram bellowed behind her. And *Butcherbird!* his striplings screeched, and the raiders, astonished, turned into the slash of sleet and jerked their reins in shock at the sight all Craven dreaded, the shield of the Butcherbird. Their panicked horses reared, and she smashed into them.

She moved without thinking, staff punching, short and hard, out and back. Out and back. One man unhorsed and scrambling to his feet, another lolling over the neck of his mount. Feint against the standing man's head, reverse to sweep his legs. Down. No time to drive him. She leapt down. Punch, punch, punch.

Screaming erupted closer to the bank as Wilfram's charge hit.

She wiped the blood from her face with one hand, saw Bearn trying to lever the half-conscious raider off his horse with his spear. "Leave him!" The stripling did not let go of his trapped spear fast enough and nearly fell. Cuthred just stared in horror at the bloody mess she had made of the other.

"Leave them!" She jerked Bearn's spear free. "Bearn!" She threw it to him. "Cuthred!" She pointed at the milling chaos now a little upriver. "Drive them! Drive them!"

She whistled for Cygnet and dived forward, belly down, onto the mare's back. Cygnet, well-trained, was running even as her rider swung upright, dropped her legs down either side of the saddle, and took the reins.

The riverbank was a whirl of shouts and horse screams, curses and flying blood. The raiders had not run as they should. Even from here she could see one man, cool and steady, moving in to spear a stripling, swaying away from another's wild thrusts, moving back in. Two of the striplings were unhorsed, and one unmoving, and Wilfram, the pale mane and tail of his mount twisting and plunging, was hemmed in by three mounted men.

She set Cygnet for the man with the shield and charged.

Bearn died that night in Caer Loid, teeth bared in a hideous grin through the gaping wound in his face.

Hild sat by him on a stool, both hands wrapped tight around his forearm so he knew he did not die alone. Cuthred and the others had mumbled their farewells and fled to the bright warmth of the hall. Fighting men were all the same. Stripling, grizzled spearman, or sleek gesith: They did not like to see the results of their work. They wanted only the songs of gold and glory; to eat the hero's portion and drown memory in mead; to forget that death was their wyrd.

When the rattle of his breath quieted at last, she lifted her hands and shook out the ache. She leaned back and let the wall take her weight. In the greasy, wavering light of a single tallow dip she studied the wound. A good blade, well-wielded: The tip of the sword had opened the cheek just under the bone, parting skin and muscle like water, then the heavier part of the blade had sheared through the upper teeth and the lower jaw, splintering and cracking the bone, wrenching free and scattering a handful of ruined teeth. The bone and teeth that remained were already drying and dulling.

If he had not lost so much blood from the torn vein in his leg, the wound itself might not have killed him, or not quickly. If he had survived the fever, he would not long have survived others' horror as he tried to eat; the shying away as he spat and drooled when trying to speak.

They had brought in his saddlebag and left it. As his oath-keeper, she now owned all that was his: spear, horse, even the cloak on his back. She lifted the bag onto her lap and took out a leather roll and a small hemp sack. The roll held one comb, antler, plainly carved; an ear scoop; a spare hair thong. So little. In the sack were a fistful of nuts, coarse grey salt, and two boiled eggs still in their shell—always carry eggs, she told them; they were the perfect war food: always fresh in their own wrappings, easy to eat with one hand . . .

She saw again his quick look back on the high moor, his eager face, her resolve to cure him of the urge to sing. And so she had.

She took one of the eggs—Bearn would not miss it—crunched and shelled it, and stretched out her legs. She ate slowly, aching all over, as she always did after pouring out strength so hard and fast.

In the distance the songs began. Wilfram would be telling the tale of how the lady had seen through the rock—the solid rock!—of the summit and spoken the doom of nithings from Craven; the striplings would chime in with her call to the gods to sweep blinding ice into the eyes of the enemy; of taking the enemy champion with a single blow . . .

As a child she had needed her reputation as hægtes and godmouth; it made men listen; it kept her safe. She no longer needed it, but reputation was not something to mend in a night. For now she could, and had, ordered Wilfram to cover the Butcherbird totem before they reentered the vill: in Caer Loid she was lady of Elmet; her men, men of Elmet.

She sighed. Bearn's body would not wash itself. She finished the egg, wiped her hands on her skirts, and reached to light another dip. The wavering light glimmered on the hairs of her forearm, stiff and bristling with blood—blood smeared past her elbow—and she bent over and heaved up everything she had just eaten.

She stared at the stinking mess on the floor. No. Wiped her mouth with her shoulder. Not now. Not yet.

By the next day her belly had settled. Perhaps she was wrong.

In the hall at middæg, she took Cuthred's chin and turned his head this way and that. "More scrape than cut," she said. Gwladus, her body-woman, handed her the bee glue. "Still, you should have let me see it yesterday."

"I didn't even feel it!" He sneaked a look at Gwladus, standing tawny and gold as an autumn leaf to Hild's left, and deepened his voice. "A man doesn't feel such things in the heat of— Ow!"

Hild daubed his forehead briskly with the bee glue.

"There. Don't fuss with it, and don't get it wet, and a week from now you'd never know it was there."

"Oh. So it won't scar?"

"My poor hero." Gwladus gave him what any hopeful young man might mistake for a kind look. "Would you like a big snowy bandage for your great war wound so all folk will know it was you who singlehandedly defended the vill?"

He blushed, and stammered, and Hild, taking pity on him, said, "Hush. Listen." Horses, loud voices, a booming shout: one of the brothers Berht.

"Boldcloak's back!" he said, eyes shining, and rushed away to greet his lord.

Gwladus brought food to the bower, then left them, for Cian was still not always easy in her presence.

Hild watched him as he ate. Most people saw his cloak first, red and black checks—a big cloak, for he was a tall man, almost her height—rather than his hair, chestnut, very like Hild's own, or the shape of his bones, like hers only thicker. What she noticed was his smell, salt and iron, though it was his eyes—blue, like hers, but where hers were green around the rim his were grey—that showed his feelings. Today they were pale—his pupils small, for he had been disappointed at Ceasterforda—and getting paler as she detailed their losses against the men of Craven: Bearn dead; Wilfram with a gash on his sword arm, though that would heal clean in a fortnight; the stripling who had lost his left thumb.

"Though he's strong—he'll be holding a buckler again before the new moon."

He ate some cheese. "If he's not raving."

"It was a clean cut, and honey and bee glue work well." She took a pull of small beer. "And the one who fell stunned into the Yr coughed up all the water as soon as we pulled him out. I doubt he'll catch lung fever, but we'll know by tomorrow."

He cut another wedge of cheese. "So, of the eight we fielded, one is dead and three damaged."

"And one horse lamed. Though in exchange there are five Craven men dead or close to it. Including one at least who had been a valuable man."

"Their losses won't help us defend our southern border."

She ignored that—over the last months they had talked the thing half to death—and turned instead to the news he had brought back, got from a king's messenger at Ceasterforda. "So. Ciniod."

He shrugged. "What does it matter? The Picts are no concern of ours. And he was old."

It was true, the death of the king of the Picts was not unexpected, but it did matter. With Ciniod's death, all oaths sworn to him died, too. So now his hostages were free of obligation, free to go where and when and as they wished. And chief among the Picts' hostage-guests was Eanfrid Iding, eldest ætheling-in-exile. And that could be a worry. Though Cian would only say: Not Elmet's worry.

She poured herself more ale. "Tell me of the recruits you brought."

"You saw them. A sorry lot." Just eight, seven striplings, only two of them likely-looking, and one greying spearman with a bow.

She had warned him it might be so. As Edwin's chief gesith, leader of the war band of the overking of all the north, Cian Boldcloak had won much gold and glory for his men, and many clamoured to follow him. But as lord of Elmet, he could not offer glory.

"Your uncle will just have to give us more."

"He won't." Cian knew that, but thought it was because he was the son of Ceredig, last king of Elmet. The truth was more dangerous.

She was tired of skirting truths and tired of gloom. She smiled. "This morning I heard Wilfram call Cuthred a Pup."

He looked blank, then laughed. The Hounds and the Pups.

Four weeks later she rose with the morning star and passed through the gates of Caer Loid, seen but unremarked. They believed she went to a hidden grove to talk to the gods; she let them.

The bark of the old oak, pollarded in the long ago, was damp and cool to the touch—easy to climb, for now. She pulled herself up and settled astride the great bough that stretched west over the valley, her valley. Menewood. Two miles from the bright gold and bold light of Caer Loid; hidden and quiet, its system of becks and ponds wreathed in dawn mist. A safe place to think of patterns and promises.

The oak had no leaves yet, not even buds, but they would come. Every year, as the world turned from dark to light, the ancient pollard unfurled with green as fresh as any sapling. Old trees and new alike knew how to do that. It was their pattern.

Kings, too, had their pattern. Their pattern was summer war: the never-ending battle for gold to reward those who fought in their war bands in order to defeat other war bands in bloody skirmishes and win their gold. Edwin Yffing, overking of all peoples north of the Humbre, even as far as the second wall, was rich in men and gold, so much richer that lesser kings gave him gold in tribute, and he grew ever richer without war. But for fighting men, a comfortable king in a warm hall offered no chance for glory gained in the red raids of summer, no songs sung of their bright blades. Eager young men no longer flocked to Edwin Overking's hall; they gathered at the hearths of the young kings, the hungry kings, and one day those lesser kings would seek common cause, and join together to tear Edwin down, then fight among themselves to become overking in turn. One day, as surely as the oak would sprout leaves, war would come.

As lady and lord of Elmet she and Cian Boldcloak had sworn to Edwin king to ward the southmost of Northumbre's lands; to feed and judge the people; render tithe to the king; and strengthen their borders. Elmet was the shield against which the weight of any army heading north would fall first, and she had promised Elmet would hold. But if that weight fell soon she did not have the men to keep her promise: Counting herself, Cian, Oeric, the Hounds, the Pups, and the new youngsters, Elmet had barely a score under arms. Not enough, and Edwin would not give her more; as godmouth and Butcherbird she had gained too much power. He had made Paulinus Crow his godmouth, and now he was done with her. Which was why here, in her hidden valley, she was building a bolt-hole, a place to hide and hope the war, if it came before she was ready, would pass over and leave them untouched.

At least there had been no more attacks from Craven. Osric was licking his wounds; he could not even claim weregild because the men had not fought under his colours—just as Hild had not fought under Elmet's. He would try again, no doubt, but Osric was a known part of the pattern. He did not worry her. The news she had had late yesterday through Rhin's priest network did worry her: It did not fit the pattern.

Below, a water vole cut a widening crease across the silvery pond. Swimming home to safety, or away in search of adventure? She knew how she would choose if she were free—how she had always chosen: always on, always out, learning the new. But Edwin had penned and pinned her with an oath to Elmet. Now, as lady of Elmet, she must stay and hold.

A blackbird sang, liquid and unhurried. They always sounded unhurried, and they nested anywhere, seemingly without thought or planning. How would it be to not have to plan, not have to always think faster than anyone else, just to stay alive?

She had watched many women big with child. For some there was a time, just before they dropped, when they did not think well. For her that would be Winterfylleth, as the world turned its face from summer and light slipped like yolk between the fingers and there was always so much to be done. Winterfylleth: a time, now and then, of bitter war, winter war.

Winter war was the ruin of the pattern.

Near the beginning of a new weave, if she felt a flaw through her hands—the hitch in the flow, a tension on the loom as she threaded the shuttle through the warp—she could stop and unpick one row: a moment, a blink, and it was mended. But if she ignored it, if she pretended it was nothing, she would begin to feel each pass of the shuttle, each beat of the weft turn more wrong, until she slowed, closed her eyes, and stopped. Then she must tally the time it would take to undo the weave, and weigh that against the rest of the work to be done. Then she must choose: live with the wrongness of the cloth as the years turned, or unpick and begin again while the unwatched child fell into the fire and the pig wandered off.

Yesterday's news could be that flaw, and she could not take too long to make a choice. For once winter war, real war, began, none could unweave it, not even her. She had to choose: stay lady of Elmet, with a scant score of men, standing or falling as Edwin king stood or fell—with only Mene-wood to hide them if the north failed—or go back to the king as his god-mouth, and fight to unpick the flaw and reweave the pattern to protect them all. If he would let her. She had to choose, and the time was now.

She watched the vole swim. Home or away? Which would it choose?

She rested her hand on her belly. Nothing showed. Not even Cian knew. Gwladus knew better than to speak of it—though four days ago, as she wiped Hild's mouth, she had suggested it might be time to send to Mulstanton for the lady Begu. Hild shook her head. Once her gemæcce knew, everyone would, and the choice would be made for her. The king would not listen to a woman great with child.

The blackbird began again. She turned her head this way and that: there, hidden in the understorey. If it was making its nest low to ground perhaps it foresaw, in the way of birds, high winds. Here in Menewood, too damp for adders, in such wind the ground would be safer than any tree. But even Menewood, hidden from the knowledge of most folk, un-known to kings and their armies, might not be safe in a winter war.

She turned back to the pond. The vole was gone; she did not know which way. It had chosen its path, and now she must choose hers.

She was in a hurry to get back so she went to the unwalled shelter that passed as Menewood's byre. She lifted the rope halter that hung on a nail and clucked. Rhin's shaggy pony lifted his head from the tiny shoots of new grass in the meadow and ambled over, hoping for a lick of fruit leather. She slipped the halter over his neck and swung herself onto his back. He sighed at her weight but was used to it, and to the short trot to Caer Loid, where he could at least be certain of a treat.

His unshod hooves were muffled on the sod; the halter did not jingle. The morning was still and quiet.

Timing was the thing. She could ride to York now to talk to Edwin; her belly did not show. But any woman who had given birth would know what it meant when her face turned pale at the smell of food in the morning. No, there was too much to weigh before she freed that news—if she ever did. She might yet have to choose to take pennyroyal. Until then Cian could not know—his face had always been too easy for others to read—and he did not understand the true threat their child could be. She did not want him to understand.

It was full light when she came on a cloud of breath over the rise. Below, the bread ovens were already cooling, but smoke seeped from the eaves of the main hall and drifted north and east over the palisade—beginning to weather, no longer raw—to the new orchard. She would like to be here for the first apple blossom. Perhaps she could be. After all, morning sickness would be done soon enough, one way or the other, and Rhin's news was fresh. Perhaps she could afford to wait.

If only she could know if she carried a boy or a girl. A boy would be the death of them all: an Yffing heir, a double Yffing, grandson, on both sides, of her father, Hereric, the Yffing ætheling. Edwin had killed him—one of the many he had killed—to begin the last winter war and become king. Her uncle stayed king by not suffering threats to live.

If she got rid of it, there would be others.

She guided the pony down the slope at a walk, then reined in, hard enough to make the pony jerk his head in protest. In the yard stood a gelding with oiled hooves, the mount of a king's messenger.

2

✦

HILD AND CIAN TOOK ONLY GWLADUS AND OERIC, and they rode hard after the messenger. *Now*, the king's messenger had said. *Edwin king demands the lady of Elmet attend him in York now, this day.* They arrived in late afternoon.

Inside the gate, Hild slid off Cygnet, handed the reins to a byre boy, and pulled free her staff. She stood still while Gwladus tucked a strand of hair back into its braid, and said to Cian, "Find the queen." Then she and Gwladus and Oeric headed for the heart of the fort, and the great hall.

After a winter among nothing but the Anglisc baulk and beam of Elmet, the brick and stone of York smelt cold and wrong, and the gaunt new church in the courtyard of the hall loomed behind her like a threat. The doors of the hall were open and even in the coolth of a Hrethmonath day it reeked. She breathed through her mouth, and swallowed, and the nausea passed.

The doorward held his spear at an angle across the doorway. A new man. Oeric stepped forward to demand his lady's rights, but the warder's spine was already straightening as he took in Hild's height, her hair, her gold. Her staff. The slaughter seax at her belt. He seemed to brace himself and risked a quick glance back into the shadowed hall. "Lady—"

From the hall snaked laughter, the ugly laughter of a group of men tormenting another. A shout, a crack of hand on cheek, and a priest, holding his face, stumbled unseeing into the doorward's back. The doorward lunged to catch him and Hild stepped through the gap—and nearly ran into Edwin striding to the door.

The king stopped and his gesiths eddied around him.

"So." His gaze was unwinking, then he held his hand before her for inspection. "You'd better not tell me to wait, too."

Three months ago, at Yule, in York's great hall, all shadow and flame and torchlit glitter, Edwin had glowed with the ruddy health of feasting. But in the courtyard the Hrethmonath light, colourless as water, was pitiless. It showed hair, sprouting around the thick gold at his knuckle, wrist, and throat, now salted with grey, and skin winter-pale, wight-pale. For a moment even the great carved garnet on his right hand seemed like the jewel of a barrow king.

Hild turned his hand this way and that. It felt like hacked leather: a stripe of sword callus across his palm, spear callus just above it along his knuckle pads, and a thick scar from some long-ago blade that began at the base of his thumb, twisted across the back of his wrist, and eeled under the gold cuff.

She doubted that the man who gave Edwin that cut had lived long enough to try again. For the swollen, bilberry-blue nail of his pointing finger, though—at least according to the messenger—Edwin had no one to blame but himself. Though, being king, he blamed the unmortared stone from the church's unfinished gateway that he had dropped on it, and then the priests who had told him God would mend the nail in time.

Nausea stole over her like mist. She let go of his hand and turned away, swallowing. "Take the token off."

The dozen warrior gesiths and thegns who had trooped outside with her and the king flinched—anyone, king's niece or no, who spoke so to the king was likely to go the way of that long-ago swordsman—but she just swallowed and swallowed and fought to not bend, not heave.

She made herself keep turning, said to Gwladus, "Find the smith. Ask him for a scrap of leather." She swallowed again. "And a piece of wire, so long." She held her palms about a foot apart.

Gwladus, who knew when to hurry, did.

"Ask, you say," Edwin said, and the air turned as slippery as blood. "*Ask* the smith. Yet you *tell* your king."

She kept turning, until she faced him again. She did not straighten to her full height and she did not meet his gaze—kings were like dogs, they rose to anything that could be a challenge—but nodded instead to Wilgar, father of Wilfram, a thegn familiar since childhood; Wilgar, who stood with his bottom lip caught between his teeth, cup dangling forgotten and spilling ale on his foot. "Tell the housefolk we'll need two tapers, good wax ones, and the use of one of the boards by the door." The nausea began to lift. She breathed, and again, and put a banter and smile in her voice. "Please."

Wilgar, whose daughter was only two years older than Hild, grinned— the lass had not lost her mind after all!—and stumped off into the hall, shouting for a houseman, and for ale, by Woden's balls, ale!

Only then did she look at the king. "No doubt your finger throbs, Uncle, but three breaths after I get that wire hot I'll make it stop. Let's go inside."

After a moment he said, "Three breaths, then. But that woman of yours better be quick."

Hild sat on one side of the elm board with her back to the light, such as it was, and Edwin, with his men gathered about him—Oeric stayed by the wall, as she had taught him—took the other. The board was clean: The household was running smoothly, then, always a sign that all was well with the lady of the hall. She hoped Cian, when he got back from Æthelburh's apartments, would give her some news about that.

Edwin lifted his cup, drank. Studied her. Held out his cup for the houseman to fill. He studied his swollen fingernail. "Paulinus Crow said the Christ would make it well in three days."

"Three breaths is better." His fingernails were well-shaped and cared for, not too horny, and she had drilled nails half a hundred times. The houseman filled her cup. The ale smelled clean and fresh. "Where is the good bishop?"

He ignored her. It was not a king's job to satisfy anyone's curiosity. "Æthelburh agreed with the Crow that her god can put right anything he upset in the first place. But then she wondered how Boldcloak was doing. She said the children missed him."

The queen liked Cian well enough, and the children loved him, but Æthelburh was happier with Hild out of the way in Elmet, where the people either were fooled by their lady's Christian cross or did not worry one way or another about her reputation as hægtes, uncanny giant, Butcherbird. And no one in their right mind would send for the lady of Elmet, godmouth and light of the world, for a blue nail that anyone could drill. Whatever the king wanted, the queen, in her roundabout way, agreed. Hild did not ask what that might be: If she was once again the light of the world, she was supposed to know. The king was already restless; he felt the change in the pattern though he did not know what it was that he felt. And she knew her uncle; he was already looking for a way to lay blame for the ills he sensed coming.

She looked at him over her cup, nodded at his token. "I meant it, Uncle. It will have to come off."

He narrowed his eyes.

"Just to your other hand, where it won't get in the way."

The gesiths stirred, their attention lifting and settling somewhere behind her. Gwladus was back, corn-coloured hair swinging bright beneath her headcloth and body swaying luscious as a pear. But then their attention shifted to the east end of the hall as the queen and Cian Boldcloak entered from the apartments.

Hild turned and leaned back, elbows on the board. She smiled at Cian, nodded at the queen, hair smooth and sleek as sealskin, and turned to Gwladus, who handed her a scrap of undyed pigskin, a length of wire— gold wire, for the king—and a square of beautifully dyed brown linen. Hild had forgotten she would need linen. She tucked it under her belt and was glad, again, of the three pæningas she had paid the Frisian slaver eight years ago. Glad, too, that she had struck off the slave collar six years later.

The king slid the token from his injured finger and onto his left hand.

She pulled one taper closer and gestured for him to lay his hand on the table. When the light that seeped through the doorway lit the nail just so— the boundary between blue and pink as clear as a priest's ink stroke—she nudged the second taper back a little and to the left. Cian came to stand at her right, not close enough to be in her shadow but close enough for her to smell the iron and salt of him. The queen sat at her husband's left.

Both ends of the wire were bright and clean but one was cut at a slant. She wrapped that in the pigskin and bent the rest in an easy curve with a sharp hook an inch from the tip, which she held in the closest flame.

"Three breaths," the king said.

She turned the wire a little. "Or fewer."

The men craned forward.

She looked up. "Any takers?"

"Fewer than three? I'll take that!" Tondhelm. He always was a betting man. "Riffa's headstall." Riffa was his gelding, as stout as he was and twice as mean but lavished with more gold than any ætheling.

"Coelfrith to count," Cian said. They all nodded except Coelfrith, who looked worried—but the reeve always looked worried. Cian grinned. "Don't fret, man. I know my wife. And so . . ." He looked around, making them lean forward even more. "I bet two breaths. Or fewer."

There was a roar as half a dozen men took him up on it. The tip in the flame glowed red.

"It's hot," Tondhelm said.

"When it's white, then it's hot," said Wilgar.

"You're a smith now?" Tondhelm said. Then, to Hild, "You want to be careful. It can get too hot."

General agreement from gesiths. One volunteered that he'd heard of one horseshoe that got so hot that when the smith had picked it up it melted his tongs. That's nothing, said another. His wife's uncle had once had his nail drilled by a man who'd not got the wire hot enough, so the man had to—

Then there it was, the smell of hot gold and burnt air. "Ready?" she said. The crowd fell silent.

"Oh, get on with it," Edwin said, voice bright with tension. No matter how many times a man had faced the roar of battle, holding still for a piece of glowing wire was unnerving. She nodded at Coelfrith and, without hurry, touched the hot wire to the king's nail.

"And one," said Coelfrith. The room breathed in and then out in the familiar rhythm. The wire sank through the nail as though through butter. "And—"

Hild lifted the wire and blood welled, sudden and satisfying, rich red in the candlelight. Garnet red. Royal. The crowd admired it. Before it could fall from its perfect globe into an ordinary smear, she wiped it away with the cloth. Æthelburh leaned forward to look, and the scent of jessamine wiped away the faint smell of burnt nail as neatly as Hild's cloth had the blood.

Edwin laughed—the pain was gone!—and flexed his hand. Cian moved away to claim his winnings—something always best done quickly.

Hild pulled the wire through the cloth, cleaning and straightening it while she watched Cian laugh with his former men—thump a shoulder there, slap a fat belly there—then handed them to Gwladus. Her body-woman took her time to the doorway, swaying and ripe.

"Come north with me," the king said. She wrenched her attention back. "Time to stop rutting. I want you in Yeavering."

He wanted her back, and in the north? It was the death of Ciniod, king of the Picts, he was worried about, then, and the freedom of Eanfrid Iding to now make his move.

Æthelburh smiled. "You've been married half a year. I'm sure . . . Cian can spare you."

Hild did not miss the faint pause. The queen had a way of veiling threat as friendliness. But Hild had been away too long to tell which mattered most. She needed to talk to Cian.

"The Crow is useless," the king said. "He thinks of nothing but baptising ceorls, and that woollen shawl he wants from the bishop of Rome—"

The pallium of an overbishop. In his last letter, James the Deacon had told her Paulinus was feeling his age and fretful with it: The Crow thought Pope Honorius should have sent him the mark of his promised rank a year ago.

"—and with the Iding about to stir up trouble in the north, and Penda and Cadwallon scheming together in the south, a king needs more than prayers." He pulled off the great garnet, weighed it briefly, then slid it back to its rightful place. He propped his elbow on the bench and clenched his fist, token facing Hild. "I need my seer. I need my Butcherbird."

Gwladus let go of Hild's head and wiped her mouth. "Perhaps now you'll let me send for the lady Begu."

Hild panted. "No."

They waited for another heave, but Hild was done. Gwladus draped the cloth over the bowl. "Well, it'll have to be mint again, that's all I had time to snatch up before we left. Unless you want me to ask the kitchen for something else?"

Hild shook her head. If she asked the royal kitchen for any of the usual herbs they would know, and then so would others.

Gwladus handed her the bag of dried mint and picked up the bowl. "You'll have to decide, lady. The later you leave it the worse it gets."

Hild said nothing, and after a moment Gwladus took the bowl away.

Hild dipped her thumb in the grey-green powder and rubbed it on her gums. She loathed mint. She wanted to spit, but there was no bowl. She dipped again, sucked at her thumb. Elm seeds would be better. Something to chew until she decided one way or the other.

The door hanging rippled with the opening and closing of a door far down the passage. She stilled the ripple with one hand, imagining Gwladus treading the same corridor she herself had first explored a dozen years ago. Broken, then, full of rubble and angled shadows, so strange to an Anglisc child, so wealh. Rendered and limed now, smooth and well-lit, re-roofed and braced with warm wood for the queen and king's guests. But under the bright colours, still hard brick, still alien, still wealh.

The hanging, at least, felt like home, a dense weave dyed deep yellow, the colour Begu was so fond of. Woven in her own Aberford, where her mother had put the Irishwoman Heiu in charge of the cloth workers.

Breguswith would be back soon from the Bay of the Beacon to plan the year's trade goods. There would be no hiding it then.

"You look like a carving," Cian said. "Where—"

Hild had one hand on the hanging and one on her belly. She dropped them both. Not fast enough.

His face stilled. His pupils grew and his eyes, usually so blue, now seemed grey. "You don't like mint."

Here it was, then. She moved to the bed and sat down.

"You don't like mint but this is the second time in a week I've smelt it on you."

He turned away, his back rigid, but Hild saw his shoulder move and knew he was rubbing his knuckle in the groove between nose and mouth. She had seen that gesture a hundred times, a thousand. *Please*, it said. *Please*. Her heart squeezed.

He took a deep breath, turned, and squatted before her. He took her right hand with his. His hand was big and callused on the palm—like hers, like the king's. And like hers, but unlike the king's, it was still soft at the fingertips. He braced himself, as though before a shield wall he had always known he must face. "Tell me."

She looked away, and in the corner of the room imagined she saw a child with blue-grey eyes rubbing her lip like Cian, and one with blue-green eyes resting his hand on his seax like her. Their child. Made from them both. Inside, something shifted and rang, like a corner post thumping into its hole in the ground.

She turned back and met his gaze "I'm not ill. But I'm young, I'm strong. I'm not Angeth."

"Your spew smells the same." Bleak as a winter beach. She had not heard that voice for a year, not since Angeth died giving birth to what would have been his daughter. "She was sick. All the time."

She wrapped her left hand around his. "Yes. But later. Not at first."

He thought about it. "No." His hand stirred.

She nodded. "This is the morning sickness." She shook his hand gently between hers. "It's healthy. It's normal. Our son just wants to be noticed."

"Son?" he said.

Why had she said that? *Never say the dangerous thing aloud.* She put her finger to his beginning-to-curve lips, stood, checked behind the curtain to make sure no one was there. "Where's your shield?"

"My . . . ?" In a blink he moved from father-to-be to gesith, and straightened, ready.

"Lean the shield against the passage door." It was yew, heavier than most, iron-rimmed with a silvered boss. It would make a lot of noise on the hard wealh floor.

He moved, the way she loved, pent, like a cat, into the passage.

When he came back she patted the bed for him to sit, and took his hand.

"Sons often make their mothers more sick in the first weeks than daughters. And I've been sick enough for a war band after a feast. But I can't be sure." It would make the choice so much clearer, to be sure. "Now is a dangerous time for a son. But I'm young and strong, and it's early enough. There could be other children. But we have to decide now, today."

"Decide?"

She caught his jaw in her hand. "Ceredig, last king of Elmet, acknowledged you as his son. Edwin would not welcome another son of that line."

"But it could be a daughter."

"It could. But we can't know. And my uncle would not wait to see; he would not suffer an heir to an alliance of two great British kingdoms."

"Elmet's no longer a—"

"Think," she said impatiently. "What does Edwin fear most? Cadwallon of Gwynedd. He dreads Gwynedd and Elmet as allies: Yr Hen Ogledd come again." The Old North come again. As a boy with his first wooden sword he had loved "Y Gododdin," the great hero song of the last British lords of the north. He knew the power of that dream.

"That would never happen. Cadwallon wants me dead—he's already tried to kill me once."

"He wouldn't need you, only the promise of your son. That's all it would take to raise the banners."

He said nothing.

"I know my uncle. He's overking still because he gets rid of even the smallest risks before they grow." And their son—Yffing, double Yffing in truth, and rumoured to be an heir to Elmet—would not be in any way a small risk.

"So to stop the king killing our child, you would kill it first?"

Why couldn't he see? "To stop the king killing you and me, my mother, your mother, even Begu, I'm thinking of taking a few herbs and being ill for a day."

"Our child—"

"Our lives."

He rubbed his lip. "Don't you want our child?"

"Of course I want him! Or her." She reined in her impatience. It wasn't his fault he could not understand the real danger; she had kept it from him all these years. She put his hands on her belly. "In a month I'd feel her heart flutter, right there, under my ribs. I'd feed her with milk from my breasts. She's already part of me. She'd grow up with your eyes and your mouth and my laugh. She'd be tall and strong and proud. But first she'd be small enough to tuck in the crook of my arm and her cheek would be smoother than butter." She could feel the weight of her, like a newborn lamb; she knew how she would smell, the catch and gurgle of her laugh, the way she would wave her fists in the air. "Of course I want her. But there'll be others."

"Will there? You said war is coming. I'm a gesith, thegn now. In war gesiths die. Dead men don't father children."

So many of them would die if she sat at home and did nothing but swell with this child. Her mother had warned her, so many years ago. *The king will have no use for a swollen seer, and you'll be more interested in your belly than anything else in the world. Oh, yes, even you.*

He stroked her hair. She kissed his neck—thicker than hers, with hair where she was smooth, a neck that, unless she could change the pattern, might be split with an axe before the year turned. But she had felt that ringing, the post thumping into its hole, settling, and she understood what it meant: Despite the risk, she had already chosen; she would have this child.

She sighed and nodded.

His smile was brilliant. "She'll be beautiful."

"Love, don't smile like that. Please. Don't smile for the rest of our time in York if you can help it. No one must know. No one. Not yet." She needed time to find the middle path, to save them all.

"I won't." He put his hands on her waist and sat back. "You don't look any different." His thumb brushed her waist and his fingers cradled the curve of her belly. "And you feel the same." His voice warmed, roughened to a cat's tongue.

"Yes," she said, and she wanted to taste his skin, lick the salt from it. She pulled him to her, and pushed his hand lower.

Linnet and her mother lived far enough outside the wall to be beyond the halo of people-stink—eight hundred bodies made too much night soil even for pigs and compost—but they made their own smell, enough to be followed with her eyes shut. Hild found Linnet sitting in the early-morning light on a log, winding yarn with another woman who, by the looks of it, was six months along. She was very young—younger even than Hild—but her freckles were swollen and, when the slanting light caught her face just so, Hild saw patches on her cheek and forehead like a mummer's mask. It happened to some women, and some got spots, and broken veins . . .

The younger woman, when she saw a giant wearing clothes fit for a queen and more jewels than a king, an enormous staff in her hand and a slaughter seax at her belt, gaped and started to let go of the yarn.

Hild dropped the sack she was carrying and slipped her right hand inside the skein before it could fall. "I'll take it."

"But your dress!"

Linnet said, "Give it to the lady, Janne."

Janne stood, and Hild, without letting the tension in the yarn slacken, slid into her place on the log. Gwladus would be unhappy about the dirt on her dress, but Gwladus was used to it. She propped her staff against her knee.

"Go feed the pigs. Go on." Linnet waited until the reluctant Janne, glancing back all the while, walked behind the hut, then turned to Hild. "My son's. I know, he's hardly grown enough for face hair, and she still smells of her mother's milk, but there you are. Besides, with Mam getting woolly, it doesn't hurt to have help."

"She's inside?"

"Napping." The old woman was probably wide awake and watching through a knothole, but she would not hear much; she was more than half deaf.

As Linnet unwound the ball of nettle yarn Hild swam her hands through the air to take it up. After a while they caught their rhythm.

"Good colour," Hild said. Somewhere between rust and brick. Not a colour she would wear, but nicely done, for such a yarn. "I'm going north." The ache of the saddle, leaning down to be sick . . . "While I'm gone, there might be no one by for the messages. Keep them for my return."

"And if someone is by?"

"It would be Oeric, who you know, or Morud, a lad with a mole like a tadpole right here on his neck. Anyone else must say—" What must they say? She thought of the hedgepigs Cian had carved in her travelling cups, for her and him and Begu. "Three in one." Cian would remember that. And Rhin, of course.

Linnet nodded. "Three in one."

When the nettle yarn was skeined, they started on hemp. They talked for a while.

The sky had brightened to midday when Hild rose, stretched, and picked up her staff. She left the sack of beef shins and sheep's cheese—the kind of food Linnet and her mother would never see otherwise—and walked out past the sty. It stank, though not as badly as the hall midden. Janne was scratching the back of a sow snout-down in the trough. Even the sow was pregnant.

Hild passed through the scrub of elder, hazel, and blackthorn, stepping over tangles of branches and the occasional fern without thought or attention. No one in their right mind would annoy a swelling sow, but they did not treat a swelling woman the same way, and sows did not suffer the fig and morning sickness or find everyday smells as overwhelming as an armed horde. Or perhaps they did. Perhaps that was what made them so dangerous and quick to anger.

The north, though, would smell clean. The north where Edwin was sending the Butcherbird, who could terrify a man with a look. But who was afraid of a woman throwing up on her boots? She needed time for the sickness to pass. She needed help to gain that time.

In the shell of Paulinus's stone Anglisc church, in the courtyard of what had once been the Roman principia and was now Edwin's great hall,

Æthelburh and her gemæcce Wilnoð sat on either side of a brazier. It had not been lit long enough to throw off much heat. Hild ignored it. They wore thick mantles, and gloves. Their breath hung in the still air.

"There are more comfortable places to meet," Æthelburh said.

The church had an untended feel. Columns still ungilded and the massive foundation blocks of Roman stone, taken from a collapsed temple across the river, showing a jumble of unconnected carvings: letters perched above birds who flew upside down and vines twining around nothing. Paulinus, James the Deacon told her, had been too busy with his feverish baptisms and his hope for the pallium to pay attention to the church. At least it now had a roof. "The cold keeps other ears away," she said.

"I'd forgotten how little it affects you." Æthelburh tilted her head, looked Hild up and down, took in the muscled arms and clear eyes, the smooth skin. "You seem well."

"I am, lady."

"But you seemed . . . unwell earlier. They say." The queen's matte-brown gaze was as unreadable as ever. Not like Cian's. He would do his best, but his life always shone from his face.

If Hild wanted the queen to help, she would have to know. "I'm with child."

Wilnoð beamed and held out both hands. "Hild!"

Hild squeezed them briefly without taking her eyes from the queen. Æthelburh under her mantle was as slim as a sapling. It had been two years since her newborn twins had died. Perhaps Eanflæd and Wuscfrea would be her only children, though perhaps the queen wanted it that way; there were no rumours of miscarriage. "But for Cian you're the only ones who know."

Æthelburh nodded. "But that's not the news you wanted to give us away from others' ears."

"You know already of the death of Ciniod."

Æthelburh nodded and waited for more. She knew Eanfrid Iding had no men, and the Picts—far in the north and east, beyond even the second wall—had no reason to support a powerless exile. "On his own, the Iding is not dangerous."

"I have news of his half sister. Æbbe Iding is to marry Domnall Brecc." King of Dál Riata—young, hungry, and with a powerful war band.

Æthelburh's face stilled as she turned the news this way and that: Æbbe, daughter of Æthelfrith Iding, who as king of Bernicia had slaughtered the

Yffing king of Deira and driven the æthelings Edwin and Hereric into exile. "So. Not only Eanfrid Iding among the Picts in the east, but in the west the king of Dál Riata joined with the sister of an ætheling-in-exile, Oswald Iding."

Hild nodded. "Though as yet Oswald has no war band because, as yet, his sister remains unmarried."

"Why?"

She did not know. A delay made no sense—just as the marriage itself made no sense. The king of Dál Riata should be marrying the daughter of a powerful king and the Idings were impoverished exiles. *Why* was what she needed to understand; and to understand that she needed to go north.

Charcoal shifted in the brazier. "It will be made plain soon."

"Good. When?"

Hild hid her surprise—those who believed her a seer and godmouth were afraid to question matters of wyrd—then saw Æthelburh was looking at her belly. "Oh. Winterfylleth."

The queen folded her hands in her lap and thought for a while. "Will we have time?"

Even if the Iding half brothers at opposite ends of the wall both raised men and marched, their joined war bands would still be nothing compared to Edwin Overking's. They knew that. So they would wait for Penda and Cadwallon to march from the south, which would not be until after the harvest. "We will, lady."

The queen leaned forward. "But you will make Elmet safe before then." *You will make Elmet safe before the swell in your belly eats your sense and you become nothing but a doting mother.*

"We will. We are sworn to it. Elmet will be the north's south wall, its rock."

But she had to understand that missing piece. She had to go north.

She held her hands over the brazier—not because she was cold but because it made her seem less different. "Cian can oversee Elmet's defences." She rubbed her hands together, as though they were warming. "I will be happy to accompany the king to Yeavering."

The queen raised her eyebrows and looked pointedly at her belly. "Happy?"

"The sickness will pass before Œstre Mass. Before Yeavering."

"But once he has news of this other Iding, this marriage alliance, my husband will not want to wait that long."

"No. Which is why I need your help."

"I see." The queen had never been slow. "By Œstre Mass, you say?" After a moment she nodded. "Bishop Paulinus. I will suggest to him that he and my husband celebrate Œstre Mass with the lady of Elmet and Boldcloak."

The queen's influence with the bishop was not what it had been. The favour would cost her something. "Why?"

Æthelburh did not pretend to misunderstand. "We need you and your— We need you to do what you do. And for that you must be strong."

Hild nodded but wished, just once, that it was because Æthelburh cared, because she wanted to shield a friend from sore breasts and queasiness on a rough sea or moorland track.

"Happy to go north, you said," Æthelburh said, and smiled. "You're the only one of us who prefers high places to a green valley."

Hild, wary of that us, said, "I like to see what's coming."

Wilnoð looked from one to the other, sensing the change in mood: It was sorted, time to be done. "And like any girl who's to be a mother, what she sees coming is an aching bladder and groaning back."

Hild was startled to find herself referred to as a girl. She forgot, sometimes, that she was barely older than Cuthred.

Wilnoð stood. "Come now, my lady. This young giant might not mind the cold but I'm tired of it. And we've the feast to dress for."

Before Hild got back to her rooms to dress, a houseman found her: The king demanded her presence.

The housefolk had not yet set torches for the feast and the hall was shadow-thronged, lit only by the firepit dug down the centre of what had once been a hard Roman floor. The flames had just settled to coals and begun to warm the air. She smelt meat roasting, but faintly—Edwin's household was now so big the kitchens were under another roof—for which she was glad.

Edwin twisted restlessly on his bench as Coelfrith recited the number of cattle and sheep owed by each chief at spring's Yeavering render. The king scowled as he listened. That had not changed, at least: The king always scowled over his tithes; they were never enough. Coelfrith, who knew that as well as Hild, kept going.

Edwin stopped listening mid-sentence and turned to his niece. "Tell me news."

The queen could not have told him, there had been no time, but Hild was his godmouth; of course she had news, or what use was she?

"Æbbe Iding is to marry Domnall Brecc."

Edwin stared at her. "Is he mad?" He did not mean Brecc.

Hild said nothing. She knew her uncle, knew that tone: He didn't want an answer, he just wanted to shout. Coelfrith, who knew it too, sighed and began to gather his tally sticks—there was no point talking numbers once the king started to shout. Hild wondered where Stephanus and his boc full of names and numbers were. With his bishop, no doubt, scribbling down baptisms instead of tithes, totting up souls.

"Oswald, Acha's boy. To come against me. My own sister-son . . ."

Hild had heard it all before. Edwin talked of Acha as though his sister were a sacrifice he had made personally: given to Æthelfrith Iding in marriage as peaceweaver between Deira and Bernicia to save all their lives. Edwin, a lesser ætheling, had never had that power. Æthelfrith had taken Acha on no one's say but his own so that his children by her would be as much Yffing as Iding, æthelings to both Iding Bernicia and Yffing Deira; the first æthelings of all Anglisc north of the Humbre. But the marriage had not stopped Edwin killing Æthelfrith—and probably Hild's father, his Yffing rival—when he'd had the chance, at which point Acha had understandably been so unsure of family feeling she had taken her children north to the protection of her mother's brother in Dál Riata.

Edwin was still shouting. "And why now?" He slapped the board before him with one hand—the nail was already fading from ripe bilberry to a mottled red and blue; old or not, he healed fast—and fretted at his cup with the other. "Eanfrid Iding, yes. He's no kin of mine, all twist and cunning, just like his father—like his treacherous mother, Bebba."

Bebba, the same blood as Morcant the Traitor. Morcant. Now there was a story still rippling through the weave, Morcant the Bryneich who—ah . . .

She didn't realise she was nodding to herself until Edwin's attention fastened on her. She should know better. She did know better. Never think aloud before royalty, never speak until you're sure. Too late, his eyes were already crawling, the black centres spreading, eating up the blue until all that was left was glistening, crawling green around the edges.

"What? What do you see?"

She had never seen, not in the way he meant. "They don't like each other much, Oswald and his half brother, the Iding." Edwin waved his hand: Everyone knew that. "But they watch each other. And Oswald is getting ready." That was the only explanation for his sister's marriage to Domnal Brecc: the Dál Riata war band. "He must know something." Oswald might not plan to go against his uncle directly but he would be ready when his older half brother did. "Perhaps that Eanfrid is plotting with the Bryneich." Yes. It fit. "But Oswald thinks . . ." She found a careful half truth. "Oswald thinks the Iding will fail—"

"But I'll be weakened and easy pickings? Me? The overking of all the Anglisc? Weakened by the Iding and his pitiful war band of children and old men? Christ's useless balls! The Iding is nothing! His war band is nothing! He must be mad. But why? Why now? Why would he think—"

He stopped mid-run, like a dog that swallows a bee and sits hard.

"Oh, that worm! He's reaching past them, past the Bryneich to that nithing of Gwynedd. Cadwallon! He's behind all this."

"Perhaps," she said. Her uncle saw Cadwallon lurking in every shadow and behind every twig. The rivalry went deep: foster-brothers who had become rival kings with rival priests and rival trade webs speaking rival tongues. "But don't forget Mercia, Gwynedd's ally."

But he was fixed on Cadwallon. "Penda only allies with that nithing while it suits him." He sat back. "But, ha! I have more gold and more swords than all of them together. Enough gold to persuade Penda that alliance with Gwynedd no longer suits. Ha!" He slapped the board again, this time with both hands. "And I have just the man to persuade him: Eadfrith Honeytongue."

Honeytongue. Edwin's eldest, the Yffing ætheling, was a man eaten by worms. Hild did not trust him. Even his own men did not trust him.

Edwin scratched his chin. Shadows writhed in his beard, like maggots. "And don't think I've forgotten you, Butcherbird. You'll go north, but not to Yeavering. Oh, no. The Iding might have used Gwynedd's gold to take the Bryneich to his side, but you're going to go take them back again."

She lifted her hand to her belly but, just in time, rested it instead on her seax. Edwin could not know until the baby was well-seated and it was safe to travel. Æthelburh must buy her time.

3

✧

A MILE SOUTHEAST OF CAER LOID, just past the roar of the weir that ended clear passage into the heart of Elmet, the Yr flowed smooth and stately. It smelt of winter still. Hild chewed a heel of bread and shifted in the saddle to ease her bladder. Her staff, fastened at a slant across her back, bumped Cygnet's rump and the mare sidled, unused to this restlessness. Hild thumped her on the shoulder: This was how it would be for a while.

Cian squatted by the edge of the low bridge, frowning. His hair, just washed and not yet greased, blew this way and that as he peered at the linseed-soaked elm faggots jammed among the supports.

He poked at the firewood. "It's not enough," he said, in British, their way when alone under the sky.

"Then add more." They had precious little time alone left, and they had talked about this more than once.

Æthelburh had bought her time, and in the three weeks since York they had pondered the strengths and weaknesses of Elmet. To the west, Caer Loid, new and strong, timber freshly seared and proofed against fire. East and running south, the great fold of Brid's Dyke, now partly redug. East of that was no worry: The whole of the flatland out to the coast and beyond were Edwin's; nothing would come that way by road or river. North lay Aberford, their plug across the old redcrest road, now strengthened with five extra men and Grimhun in charge of defences. And, running south, the war street to Caer Daun, the ruined redcrest fort they had cleared but could not begin to rebuild until the weather improved. And the trackless waste beyond. If they had threescore men, if they had time . . .

They did not have time, they did not have men. The striplings would not be ready for a year, and by autumn they would no longer be able to count on her; she would barely be able to sit a horse.

Cian shoved a stick farther under the bridge. "We'll have to pull it all out and redouse it after a month. Every month. And we might not even need it."

"Yes." And blades had to be sharpened every day and beer brewed every week. It was the way of the world.

"But what if it rains all summer?"

"If when they come it's too wet to burn, we'll cut the supports. We have axes."

"But what if there's not enough time?"

"Then we'll use the fire barrels." Stuffed with grease and tinder, rolled out to the middle of the bridge and set alight, they would be as good as a shield wall.

"But a fire barrel doesn't last long."

"Long enough to take an axe to the supports."

"But what if—"

"What if all the kings in all the world marched to our door, and hosts of the dead rose up and joined them?"

"I know, I know." He rocked back on his heels, hands dangling over his knees, and shook his head. "I'm feeling the weight."

Hild knew about weight, she had carried it all her young life. But Cian had grown up listening to hero songs, his dreams were of the sword path, of gold and glory and his band of brothers. As a king's gesith, even as chief gesith, his goal was to move ever forward. Gesiths thought in straight lines. The best—and luckiest—fought an enemy just once: kill, cripple, or conquer, then step over and on, ever on. She had grown up as light of the world. Her life had always been a thing of watching and adapting, of turning aside, slipping back as well as forward. And beyond that she knew a world that was an endless river of work, where life was to sow the field, reap its harvest, and thresh its grain; the same field. To breed the flock, rear its lambs, shear its wethers; the same flock. To feed the families, birth their children, and mend their hurts; the same families. Over and again. That was the story of life.

But now life, for them both, meant to hold and protect, perhaps on a muddy riverbank and in wind that was not quite done with winter, unseen, far from gold and glory.

She reached down and laid the back of her hand on his cheek. He leant into her touch. "Elmet is strong. It will stand. And I'll be back before midsummer."

They stayed like that a while as the Yr poured—as it had poured time out of mind, to the Use, from the Use to the Humbre, and from the Humbre to the sea, sometimes carrying trade, sometimes war—then Cian slapped the timbers, straightened, and stood.

Acærn had found a patch of wiry winter grass and was not happy to be taken in hand and mounted.

In the saddle, Cian looked this way and that. "If they lose the bridge, the ford is staked," he said.

She nodded: good elm, iron-shod.

"And men are watching the roads."

Boys. Just boys. But this bridge was not the problem.

He knew what she was thinking. It was an old argument. "Penda won't come this way, no. But Cadwallon might."

"Cadwallon might do anything." Cadwallon was mad, driven by a deep hate of Edwin and everything Yffing. "But he's not the worry."

He turned Acærn in a circle. "I just wish I could be sure . . ."

"We are sure."

He tucked his hair behind one ear, then the other—always one hand free for a weapon; it was how gesiths were trained—and shook himself, like a drake rattling its feathers into place. "On to Aberford, then."

"Aberford," she said. It had always been Aberford.

In the small, informal hall Hild ate her mutton and Cian nodded blandly across the board at Grimhun.

Grimhun, spoon clenched in his fist, faced his lord and lady but aimed his words at Heiu, sitting next to him. He said, with exaggerated patience, "We can fret about cloth once we're sure we're safe. And if we dam Cock Beck nothing can get past. Nothing. Then we can talk about making your cloth."

Heiu made a face at her lord and lady—*You see what I have to put up with!*—and put down her knife. "Ah, but the fleeces will be here before midsummer and they will need washing. Time and enough then to turn this lovely laughing rivulet into a stinking pool. For surely not even mad Anglisc will march north in their great war boots while the sun beats down and the corn grows high?"

Heiu was Irish, like Fursey, and, like the priest's, the tip and tilt of her voice danced like a provocation. Fursey was in East Anglia with Hereswith. Hild missed him. She missed her sister, too, especially at this time of year.

She ate steadily. She was rarely sick now in the evenings—though mornings were another matter—and besides, today it was Cian's turn to listen and judge. It was plain he already had some path in mind. She tore off another piece of mutton.

"No war band in its right mind would try to cross the beck in spring at the height of its flow," he said to Grimhun. "Not if the ramparts were held against them. Would you?"

"Not in spring, lord, no, but—"

"No, because you've built well, man. Trust it. It'll be spring a while longer." He turned to Heiu. "When will you have the fleeces washed?"

"If I have good, strong, *flowing* water, *clean* flowing water? Before Meadmonath."

"And between now and then you would not complain if Grimhun were to begin staking the water's edge and cutting trees, ready to build the dam as soon as the fleeces are clean?"

A triumphant look at Grimhun. "Not if he kept downstream until we've rinsed them well and well. I don't want that great oaf getting mud—"

"Good. Then it's settled." The lord Boldcloak popped a piece of carrot in his mouth.

Grimhun glared at his spoon, then plunged it into the jellied eels—his favourite—as if he wished it were Heiu's gut. But Cian reached over, thumped him on the shoulder, and grinned, and the gesith could not help but grin back, and soon the three of them were talking about the beck, its salmon—the run had finished in Solmonath this year, a good run—and whether they should go east or west to cut elm. The east woods were closer, but if they went west the current would be with them . . .

Hild stripped the layers of fat and gristle from her mutton belly and thought she might talk to Grimhun later about building a gate in that dam. She had spent many walks with Rhin talking about water, and mills, and sluices, and she had an idea . . . Later. For now she studied Heiu, who was a find of her mother's, brought here to be mistress of wool and weave. Hild didn't know her well. But she knew Fursey, and she saw a kinship, not of blood but of voice and mind: well-born, but with a tangled story. She would enjoy getting to the root of that, in time.

When she had finished her meat she ate the stale bread it had been served on, sucking out the wet dough, then gnawing on the crust, which was like wood. Next perhaps she'd have some of those eels. Everyone liked eels, except Begu—

Morud was signalling from the doorway when a small woman burst past him in a hurry and flurry, shedding her travel cloak, already talking. "I said to Winny, you know how it is for newlyweds and those long winter nights, she'll be needing me early. Here," she said to Morud, and handed him her cloak. Hild smelt the dusty perfume of the lavender Begu had told her Uinniau liked on her so well. "Have Gwladus see to it, there's been rain and mud. On the moor the lambs were out early, too, so I said to Winny, Aberford will be busy early. So I came. Winny's with Oswine. Bread?" she said, looking at the remnants of Hild's trencher. "Is that all you're having for dinner? Starving yourself won't work! It'll be a boy if it wants to be a boy. He'll just come out thin and cross."

Hild chewed fast and swallowed. "How—"

"I tried Caer Loid first but Pyr said you were here. Winny went on to Craven, to Oswine. Can I have some of that mutton? Never mind." She turned to Morud. "Wipe that grin off your face and go tell the kitchen—" She remembered this was a small hall, without a kitchen, and reset herself without pause, raising her voice to the woman by the hearth: "Bring something decent for the lady, more than bread! Beef tea. Cheese. Porridge. For Eorðe's sake, she's eating for two. And I make three. You should all be whipped!"

Morud, still grinning—in his memory Begu had never whipped anyone—bowed and ducked away.

"Well?" Begu said, looking up at her gemæcce through wisps of escaping hair, very like a goat trying to decide whether or not to butt a wall. "How are you?"

Hild blinked, realised she must have smelled that lavender before Begu even entered the hall, then laughed and stood and held out her arms.

Begu stepped into them, and though the small woman barely came to her breastbone, Hild felt that rush of warmth and comfort she had known since their first meeting on the edge of the sea when she was shocked and silent and haunted by bloody dreams.

Begu hugged her fiercely, held her at arm's length, said, "You really must eat more!," and hugged her again. "But I'm here now and we'll soon fatten you like a winter goose." Begu leaned back. "What? Is it because I mentioned geese? You really should get over that. If—"

Hild, falling back into the habit easily, as though Begu had never left, simply talked over her. "There won't be time to fatten me up. I'm leaving for Menewood in two days, and then York, for Œstre Mass."

"Then it's a good thing I'm still packed. It will be lovely to see the queen."

It was drizzling when the four of them set out for Menewood. Begu did not like the rain and she fussed, telling Gwladus to cover this and Morud to carry that—and why did he still prefer his own two legs rather than riding, like a sensible person? Morud just ran ahead, and Gwladus, wearing russet brown and sitting on a pretty little bay mare, as perfect as an apple that might fit in Hild's hand, sighed. But they were all used to Begu's fussing; after a while she would settle down.

"So I'll finally get to meet your mysterious priest in Menewood. I hope he's not like Paulinus."

"We don't call Rhin a priest."

"What does that mean? Is he a priest or not?"

"Not while there's any danger Paulinus might hear." To the Crow all wealh priests were heretics and spies. Rhin no longer shaved his forehead; then again, he no longer really needed to. His hair was retreating in a line over the hill of his head, though he was not old. "Rhin is . . . Rhin is Rhin." He was in his prime: the right man to head her hidden family of Menewood in her absence, at home with the beekeepers and goatherds, the maltsters and brewers, the children who pulled the weeds and each other's hair—and with her network of bishopless wealh priests who came and went at night with news from all over the isle.

"But what's he like? What's the whole place like? I don't even know how many people there are."

Hild felt a great reluctance to talk about her special place outside its bounds. But slowly she told Begu of the becks and ponds, the glades and trees, the hives and patchwork of hidden fields; the long house—not grand enough to be a hall—the single huts tucked under trees, purposefully easy to overlook. Three dozen people, hidden in her haven, secret and safe.

"How long has it been there now?"

"Five years."

"I don't understand how you've kept it hidden."

"You'll see."

The trees began to thin. Begu's mount strayed to the left and its hooves made a sucking sound.

"Stay on the path," Hild said.

"This isn't a path." Begu craned her head this way and that. "This is nothing but bog." She flicked at a fly. "A fly already! What a miserable place."

"Miserable?" How could she think that?

"Sorry, it's just—wait. What are you doing?"

Hild swung a leg over Cygnet's neck—easily, still—and slid off.

"Oh, no. Not here. You're pulling my leg, surely. Not here. It's nothing but mud. Is she pulling my leg, Morud?" She looked about. "Now where's he gone?"

"He's letting Rhin know we're coming. Careful when you get down. It can be a bit soft along here."

Begu leaned forward and clutched her gelding's mane as she slithered down, belly to his solid withers, and instantly sank ankle-deep in mire. She shook her foot crossly. "No wonder Cian doesn't come. This priest of yours better be worth it. And where's Gwladus going?"

"She'll cross in another place. We don't want to make a path. Especially when it's wet."

"It looks as though it's always wet."

Hild pointed. "Cross there. It's not as bad as it looks. But be careful to tread where I do."

She stayed ahead, leading Cygnet through the trees, but at an easy pace, stopping to listen every few steps, sometimes helping Begu over a suspiciously green patch.

She stopped.

"Now what are you smiling about?"

"Just breathe."

Begu breathed in dramatically and her face changed as though rung like a bell. "Oh!"

It was a scent that lay on the cheek of the morning as delicate as a newborn's lashes; the smell of home in spring. Hild looked about, found the low bush of naked stems each topped by a purple flower. She bent, breathed deep. Apart from the smell it was not remarkable, and when the rest of the understorey leafed out it was hidden.

Begu reached to pull in a stem close enough to sniff.

"Don't." Hild laid a hand on Begu's arm. "It'll give you a rash."

Begu blinked. Her gelding tugged at his rein in protest. She loosened it a little, but not enough to let him nibble at anything. "What is it?"

"I don't know its name."

"What do you mean? You're supposed to know everything." Begu pushed back the hair that had escaped her veil band—a new one, Hild saw, sewn with amber, but as useless as any of the others when it came to keeping her tidy. "What does it do?"

Hild shrugged. "Nothing that I know of, just that it smells like a good dream you don't want to forget, and fruits red berries in late summer. But they're poison."

"Poison. You should pull it up. Little ones love putting pretty things in their mouths. It's silly to keep something dangerous just because it smells good for a month."

"Not even that," Hild admitted. "Less than a fortnight. It might all be gone tomorrow."

Begu looked about. "Are there other dangers I should watch out for, like broken hives you stir up against intruders every morning?"

"I didn't think of that."

Begu burst out laughing, and Hild laughed, too, her creak that turned into a bittern-like boom, nothing like Begu's light tumble, but the sounds fit together just as they always had: warp and weft. Gemæcce.

Morud had already stirred Menewood, and Rhin was waiting at the door of the modest long house, built on wood sills laid on flat stones, that stood for a hall in Menewood. He greeted them quietly, as he did all things, and followed them inside.

Gwladus was in the bower with Sintiadd, laughing and talking in British—it struck Hild how seldom she heard Gwladus laugh—while they prepared the bed the lady would share with her gemæcce. When she heard Hild's voice she popped her head through the hanging, and said, "If the lady Begu would come and tell me if the bed suits . . ."

Begu went.

Hild turned to Rhin.

"Two letters from East Anglia," he said, and lifted them from the purse at his belt. It had been five years since he had worn the tonsure and skirts, and though he wore his tunic and breeches with ease, she might still have guessed his calling. Perhaps it was the way he stood, no hand reaching to rest on the haft of a weapon but folded in front of him, as though tucked into his robes. Perhaps it was his eyes, brown and set deep in their stained pits, like a goshawk's.

She turned the folded and sealed squares of parchment. She recognised both hands: Hereswith and Fursey. "When?"

"Yesterday."

"Anything else I need to know?"

"Nothing that won't wait for a warm fire and a cup of ale." He smiled. "I'll see to your mounts."

When she was alone but for the chatter, in Anglisc now, from the bower, when she was sure she would not be overheard and, if she were, the eavesdropper would not understand Latin, she broke the seal on Hereswith's letter and read it.

Hereswith's spelling was better than it had been, the letters more strongly formed, but the parchment was flawed in patches and the ink had spread, and her sister's Latin was odd and inside out. Hild had to repeat the words several times before she understood what Hereswith was trying to say. Æthelric Wuffing, prince of the North Folk and Hereswith's husband, had hopes he would soon be king of all the East Anglisc, North Folk and South; he had given Cnobheresburg to Fursey for a church—

The two ideas were clearly connected in Hereswith's mind but she had not explained how.

—though she might still not forgive him for bringing the cuckoos into the nest.

It took Hild a moment to understand it was Hereswith's husband who had brought the cuckoos, not Fursey.

Hild folded the stiff parchment along its creases and turned to Fursey's letter; perhaps he could explain.

Fursey's hand was sure and fluent—he had been writing longer than Hereswith had breathed—and she could read it with barely a murmur. While the words were clear, here and there he fell into an elusive code they had agreed on long ago.

Sigeberht, king of the East Anglisc, had endowed the church of the South Folk with not one but three tracts, one of which Felix—lately from Burgundy, and, by the grace of God and His representative in Cantwaraburg, Overbishop Honorius—newly consecrated bishop, was to turn into a school where children might be taught their letters. Lately, the most pious king seemed more and more inclined towards cutting his hair, cutting it so short that it might, in fact, reveal what he, Fursey, was quite sure would be visible, a bald patch on the crown of his head—

She held her place with her finger. Sigeberht had spent time among the Franks, where the custom was for only kings and kings-in-waiting to wear their hair long; for a man or boy to cut off his hair was to signal he would not be king. Sigeberht was thinking of giving up the throne—and shaving the crown of his head in a Romish priest's tonsure. She had never heard of such a thing. Why would a king want to become a priest?

—and now there were murmurings among the thegns: Felix and his priests were to be exempted from any tithe or service, and the land was to belong to the church forever in exchange for eternal prayers for the king's soul. There was a great charter—binding on the heirs and their immortal souls—with a seal, and oaths before God, and witnesses. The new church would hold the charter and use it to prove that it was God's will, higher than that of any mortal, that the church stand forever, even if the giver no longer held his power—

A charter: an impressive version of bocland meant for display, and binding on the donor's heirs—though its value would depend on those heirs being able to read, believing in the Christ, and caring about their immortal souls. Clearly this Felix—of Burgundy, a Frankish kingdom— believed that to be so. Felix had been raised to bishop by Honorius, the Centish overbishop.

Edwin, as overking of all Anglisc, would not like that news. The king of the East Anglisc should have appointed as bishop a man who was raised to that station by Edwin's overbishop, Paulinus—only Paulinus still did not have his overbishop's shawl. But perhaps Edwin would not hear of it for a while.

She went back to the letter.

—Felix, in name bishop of all East Anglisc, North Folk, and South, was, in fact, building his great churches in the south—and if the South Folk were to have a mother church, a see, why should the North Folk not? He, Fursey, had represented as much to her sister's husband, who had understood: If the north were not to be overshadowed by the south it must match it. So he, Fursey, was hence to be known as Bishop Fursey, or at least almost-bishop Fursey, there being the small matter of consecration, which Felix might take some time to arrange—

Fursey was telling her that he had explained the matter to Hereswith's husband, Æthelric Short Leg, prince and underking of the North Folk, and that when Sigeberht stepped down, Æthelric intended to step up and take the kingship of both North Folk and South. And he would appoint his own bishop: He would not be looking to Cent and, through Cent, Frankia. That was a piece of good news to offset the earlier, unhappy news—for Edwin would assume Æthelric would look to him as overking and his bishop, Paulinus, as overbishop.

—and, finally, he, Fursey, was well, Hereswith was well—though not pleased about her husband's wildflowers, his by-blows, who, it seems, had been brought into their household—

Ah.

—and Hereswith's children were blooming, though little Ælfwyn had been unhappy lately in the matter of teeth. He hoped God would set a flower upon Hild's head.

Food at Menewood was plain—pottage of foraged greens, the last roots from the cellar, and shreds of mutton, all scented with dried herbs—and conversation quiet. There was small beer but not mead at the two long boards at which all sat. They were crowded. After Sintiadd and her fellow housefolk had served they sat with the rest, and the benches become more crowded still.

Begu plumped her fist on the board, spoon sticking straight up, and looked around. "The time of year's wrong," she said, "and there are many men, but otherwise it reminds me of that summer when we first set up the cloth, when I spent so much time at the fold." She smiled to herself, thinking perhaps of the shepherd she had spent time with. "Do you remember?"

Hild's nostrils flared and she forgot all about Hereswith and the Wuffings, and priests and tonsures. She was back in those long summer days thinning at each end until she walked through a dream, waiting, waiting for what she did not understand. She remembered that first kiss of plum-soft lips, the hand on her back . . . Gwladus, sitting down the board talking to Sintiadd, looked up.

"Oh, how I wished Winny had been there that summer!" Begu said. "And now, well, it's hard. Just when I most want to—well, then I can't. Other things sometimes just aren't as good. I wish they'd hurry up with Rhianmelldt. I wish she weren't mad."

If they had not talked about it so often Hild would have had no idea what she meant. Begu wanted Rhoedd of Rheged to join his daughter Rhianmelldt to some prince or ætheling strong enough to rule Rheged when Rhoedd died. But Rhianmelldt as a child had been quite mad, and as a woman—though said to be beautiful—was still touched; no prince had stepped forward. Until his kingdom was safe, Rhoedd would not allow his sister-son, Prince Uinniau—otherwise his heir—to pledge his allegiance anywhere else, certainly not to Begu, the daughter of a country thegn, who could bring no hearth troop or gold to strengthen Rheged's precarious position, balanced as it was between the kingdoms of Gwynedd, Alt Clut, and the Anglisc north. And until Begu and Uinniau were finally and formally joined, they could not play the kind of bed games that made babies, the kind of games a woman wanted most when she was ripe to kindle. For that, they always had to wait for the times of the month when it was safe.

"It's getting harder," Begu said. She dug her spoon into her pottage. "You don't know how lucky you are." She stared at the spoon as though it held stones, sighed, and put it in her mouth.

This was why Begu and Uinniau spent so much time apart. "It won't be for much longer," Hild said.

Begu swallowed hastily. "Have you heard something about Rhianmelldt?" She looked at Hild, saw her gemæcce had no good news, and her face—eyebrows, cheeks, mouth—sagged.

"Change is coming, because war is coming."

"But when? When is change coming? A fortnight? A year? Ten years? And will it be good change—for me, for Winny? Just tell me something, gemæcce. Anything. Please. Just guess."

Guess? Alt Clut and the Gododdin, the Gododdin and Bryneich, the Bryneich and Æthelfrithings, the Æthelfrithings and Dál Riata, the Æthelfrithings and the Picts, the Picts and Cadwallon, Cadwallon and Penda . . . A shift in the balance of any and Rheged would be swallowed as cleanly as Elmet. And the balance would shift, it always did. And it could be anytime.

Begu's hazel eyes were steady: *Please, for me.*

Hild looked up and down the bench: women and men and children eating, some talking, some too tired to talk. Tired because they were working in service to her vision. *Never say the dangerous thing aloud* was one of the first rules. But speak of it or not, it would happen; nothing could change the shifting pattern. "Two years," she said. "At most."

Later, when Hild and Begu were the only ones left at the board and Hild was rereading part of Fursey's letter, Begu said, "Why are you speaking that strange, spitty language?"

"Because that's what the letters are written in."

"Yes, but why? You sound like a scalded cat. Why not write it in Anglisc?"

Hild stared at her. She had no idea what Anglisc might look like.

She woke in the middle of the night to Begu's soft snores, trying to imagine what Little Ælfwyn has lately been unhappy in the matter of teeth. May God set a flower upon your head might look like in Anglisc. She fell asleep with strange letters dancing in her head, waving swords and shields.

The next morning Hild's nausea was brief, and instead of the vile mint there were elm seeds.

It was raining again, but lightly, and the doors were open to let the light in. A step past the curtain between the bower and the main hall, Begu turned in a circle, frowning. "There's something odd . . ." She turned again. Tilted her head. "I can't decide. Something."

Hild just smiled. She was in no hurry to explain Menewood; she wanted its secrets to unfurl slowly.

They sat at the bench. Gwladus, followed by Morud and Sintiadd, brought them cheese and bread—Begu's favourite breakfast—porridge, hazelnuts, two jugs and two cups, baked bacon and onion, honey, and more. Hild poured from one of the jugs and sat back to let her belly settle while her gemæcce helped herself. She sipped.

Begu cut a slab of cheese and frowned. "It's goat cheese."

"You like goat cheese."

"Yes. But—" She tore off a piece of bread and sighed at the grit. "You need a mill."

One day they would have one, built on the old Roman channels that needed clearing. But a mill needed wheat from outside the valley, a mill meant no longer being secret.

"Wait, wait," Begu said, bread still held in the air. "Cows! That's what's odd: I don't smell cows. Did they die?" Begu reached for the jug Hild had poured from, and frowned. "It's water."

"We have a lot of water. And honey." The oatmeal began to smell good at last. She dragged a bowl towards her, sprinkled it with hazelnuts and drizzled it with honey, then took her spoon from her belt. "By the time we've eaten maybe the rain will have stopped. I'll take you on a tour and you'll see why there are no cows."

It did stop and Begu followed her around the steading on a maze of paths packed hard with little stones. Lots of goats, some chickens and a few pigs, but no cattle, no sheep, no geese, no horses except Rhin's pony: no animals that were too big or too noisy to hide, or that smelled too much. Lots of hives, lots of garths. And everywhere the sound of water: trees dripping from last night's rain, breezes ruffling the pond and sending the edges lapping at the sedge, the trickle of brooks, and, in the distance, the rushing beck.

Hild propped her staff against the doorway of a hut on a small rise and they went in. It looked like a smoke house—the planks of the walls pegged tight against mice and other thieves—though with no hearth.

The roof was low enough that Hild had to stoop or risk tearing loose the herbs drying in bunches under the rafters.

"Woundwort," said Begu, reaching up to finger the herbs. "Garlic. Com—" She abandoned the comfrey and picked up a carefully wrapped lump. "What's this?" She sniffed and jerked away. "Ugh!"

"It's bee glue."

"Bee glue? All this? There's a lot. A lot of honey, too." She looked at the jars in orderly rows with their wooden bungs and wax seals. "A lot."

"Double strained."

And tubs of drawn butter. Goose grease. Small waxed-leather sausages of salves. Vinegar. Begu stopped at the piles of torn rags, clean, bundled neatly. She touched one bundle with a fingertip, prodded another. "You said you had fewer than three dozen folk."

Hild nodded.

"This is enough wound care for an army."

"Yes." Hild slid her belt to the left a little, so the seax haft came to hand just so. "It's our bolt-hole." She had not told this clearly to anyone but Rhin, not even Cian, and she wanted to get the words exactly right. "It's our den. Our last place. From here, there's nowhere else. Nowhere."

Begu opened her mouth, paused, shut it.

Hild wrapped her fingers around the haft of her seax, slid it an inch from its sheath, then back in, so it hissed slightly with the release of air from the wooden casing. "This time, the king isn't going away to fight. This time, the fight comes to us. To our moors and woods, our byres and fields, our halls, our hills. And if the king falls—when the king falls, because he will—he's a boar ringed by dogs. Bigger than any one dog, yes, but they're all around, there are too many. When Edwin king falls, Aberford falls, too. And this will be our last place."

Begu was shaking her head. "But Aberford's strong. You said so. And we have a score now, twoscore, three when you call ceorls from the land—"

"Even threescore king's gesiths couldn't hold Aberford against an army. And the men of the land aren't gesiths. Willing, yes, and strong, but how many know war?"

Butchering a pig was not the same. Pigs did not fight back. They did not shove their spear in your face or gut your brother.

"Even if we had five hundred, Aberford isn't a fort like York or Bebbanburg, it's a line. If we have people at our backs, we can hold, but if we have enemies on both sides—and if I fail in the north, that's what will happen—we will have to run, we will have to hide. If it were just you and me and Cian and Uinniau, and Gwladus and my mother—if it were just us, we could." They could run to Hereswith and Æthelric in East Anglia. "But it's not just us. There's too many." Pyr and Saxfryth, Saxfryth and Ceadwulf, Heiu and Grimhun—all her Hounds and the Pups—Llweriadd and Sintiadd, Oeric and Morud, Rhin . . . Onnen and Mulstan would be safe by the bay, for a little while. But in the end Cadwallon would hunt and kill them all because they were hers and she was Yffing. He killed like a young dog among lambs: because it excited him, because he could, and because once he began he could not stop. "Some of the folk"—the ones no one knew were hers—"they can scatter. The rest, we have to hide. We'll hide here." Here, in what most people thought was empty bog. And those who reached Menewood would be hunted. They would be burnt and bruised and bloodied. She looked at the stacks and jars and bundles. Not enough, not nearly enough. "If I fail in the north we'll need all this, and more."

Begu said nothing.

"Have I frightened you?"

"No. Well, yes, but not with all that." She flapped her hand at the coming fall of the Yffings as though it were no more surprising than the death of a lamb born too soon. "It's more—" She sighed. "Let's go outside."

Outside, Hild took up her staff gratefully and stretched.

"I hate seeing you bent over like that," Begu said. "All trapped and held down. Let's walk. Now, when you go north who are you taking with you?"

"Don't worry. I'm leaving the Hounds here with Cian. You'll be safe."

"It's not me I'm worried about. You said it yourself, you can't fail. We can't afford you to. But you're with child. You'll need someone with you who understands what to do if the baby slips."

"But I know what to do," Hild said.

"You might not be the best judge if it happens, if it happens to you."

"I've delivered a hundred babies."

"Yes. And you need someone with you whose baby has not slipped, who has not lost blood. Someone you'll listen to. A woman. Take Gwladus at least."

"Gwladus?" She shook her head. She would need someone of standing to get them help if she could not.

"Then take me."

"You?" Begu, who had never seen war or lived on twice-baked bread, who had never had to make a bed of rain-soaked fern or kill a horse with a broken leg. Begu riding into the camp of a suspicious northern chieftan . . .

"I'm hardier than I look. And—"

"You don't even speak British."

"I understand a few words. Besides, they speak some Anglisc, surely. And—"

"No. No, listen to me. For now, the Idings don't know your name. Cadwallon doesn't know your name, or Penda. But if you come north with me they will. By the time we get off the boat all those princes and chiefs will know you. They'll know the name of your father and your father's father, the dam of your mount and the woman who swaddled you at birth. They'll know you like yellow and can't resist anything that glitters. You won't be hidden anymore. Don't you see? I won't be able to keep you safe."

Begu's laughter spattered about them like sunlit raindrops. "You're right!" She thrust her arm through Hild's as they walked. "You're always right! As soon as you get on the boat they'll find out everything about you, everything that matters—if they haven't already. They'll find out even the name of your gemæcce, whether I'm there or not. So, you see? I may as well be where you can keep an eye on me."

Hild kept walking. She did not know how else to respond.

"You mustn't fail, gemæcce, you said so. And if I'm there, you won't."
She bumped her forehead on Hild's shoulder and looked up with a hazel-eyed grin. "Besides, I know about boats. And it's not yet the best time of year to sail north."

They walked a bit more.

"Oh," Begu said. "I wonder if Winny will have time to get to Caer Loid before we leave. He'd like to see your mother."

Hild stopped dead. Begu slewed to one side. "My mother?"

4

⊕

THEY SMELLED YORK long before they saw it: that midden stink of hundreds of well-fed people and their mounts. The sky was deepening to twilight when they got to the bridge. The torches had just been lit, hissing and spitting and sending shadows swaying over the dark water. Their hooves rang on the bridge and Hild closed her eyes, lost in the scent beyond the midden—the burning pine and old river, broken brick and stone with the overlay of a recent malting—and then they were passing through the gate. One of the gesiths who straightened at the gold glinting at their necks and belts, at the gleam and jingle of their mounts' harness and rich work of cloak and scabbard, was new. The other, Glædmar—missing one ear and the tip of his nose after the last terrible fight at Long Mountain, though you could hardly tell at night, from the front, when he wore his helmet—began to bow to the king's seer, then recognised his former chief gesith and began to salute him instead. Hild smiled and shook her head, and Cian called, "How's that ear?" and then they were past and turning right into the byre yard. She gave the nod to Morud and he ran ahead to the kitchens.

She slid from Cygnet and handed the reins to a byre boy: someone else she had never seen before. Half a year ago she had known and been known by everyone; knew the names of the men's mothers and the women's children; that the butcher had a daughter; which of them ached, and where, when the damp cold blew off the river. She knew the fears she could use to terrify them, and exactly what kindness would make them willing to die for her.

Around her, Cian and Begu, Oeric and Gwladus and the brothers Berht were dismounting and slapping dust from their clothes—but at least it was dust and not mud, the gift of an unusual week without rain. She stretched and breathed—rain tonight, perhaps—and looked around. The stables were half full already, a mixed lot of mild-mannered priest mares, shaggy brutes still in their winter coats, and sleek mounts with oiled hooves and trimmed manes, tall and strong, fit for war or fast travel.

Gwladus was already telling the housefolk holding torches which bundles to bring first when Morud appeared at Hild's ear. "Your mam's here, and that scop of hers. In the hall. Himself isn't expected til moonrise."

Hild glanced at the sky.

Begu patted her on the arm. "There's time. Hold on." She thwacked dust from the front of Hild's dress, stood back, shook her head. "Oh, well, as long as you've got your cloak on people will know you've been travelling."

"But I don't have my cloak—"

Begu handed it to her. "And leave that staff here. You'll give them enough of a turn showing up looking as though you're in a hurry without carrying that big stick as though you're hoping for a chance to hit someone. Go on. Go get it over with."

It was rarely cold enough for Hild to wear a cloak; she disliked feeling covered up. Gwladus, long since used to her tendencies, made sure that the linings of her cloaks were more magnificent than the outside. Even flung back, this one gleamed and rippled and shouted that here was someone to be reckoned with. Hild checked that her seax was to hand and her cross glittered on her breast, and strode into the hall.

The hall was jammed with the great and good who had come to celebrate Œstre Mass with the overking, to see and be seen, to ask a judgement or reward, to bask, to complain. When someone entered the roar dropped a note before swelling again when the crowd saw it was not the king. But the lull for Hild spread like a stain. She waved off a houseman offering her a cup and moved deeper into the crowd. Men and women glanced at her, then away. It was not lucky to meet a hægtes's eyes, especially if she was in a hurry, and she had obviously come straight from the byre; what bad news did she bring this time? Those in her path edged to one side. Then Tondhelm—deaf to subtleties—standing by one of a row of pillars running down the right side of the hall, bellowed a greeting: something about Wilgith, Wilfram's sister. Hild nodded at him and his sister-son, Manfrid, but didn't stop.

She had known this hall most of her life. In those early years, the priests had worn green, not black, but the Anglisc voices and Anglisc gold were much the same. They did not make her feel at home; she had never felt at home here. The muscles under her skin jumped and tightened at the stir of shadow gathered behind pillars and under boards. *Wrong*, her feet told her, as they trod the cold, unyielding floor. The dozen black-robed priests looming among the bright tunics and dresses seemed uncanny, and the tapestries softening the hard Roman stonework felt like lies. Danger drifted in on the unfamiliar spices wafting from the kitchens, slipped among them in the phrase of an unknown tongue—she turned her head but could not pin that down—and trembled under the conversation that should have roared like a river but instead broke around hidden rocks.

Then there was her mother, standing at just the right distance from a torch burning against the wall, far enough away to avoid the gobbets of pitch that dripped and spat at intervals, but close enough for the light to catch the magnificent garnet and gold at her breast. The sight of her sparked familiar wariness. Breguswith smoothed her dark green dress, touched Luftmær on the arm, and turned to greet her daughter. Her lips were curved in that slight smile, the smile that could warm you like sunshine or cut so clean and fast you wouldn't know you were hurt until blood sheeted to the floor.

Her mother's eyes snapped brighter as she took in the hollows under her daughter's cheekbones contradicting the darker weave along the seam where Gwladus had let out her travelling dress.

"Well," she said. "I see."

It had been a long time since her mother ruled her, but she stood still while Breguswith walked around her, appraising her as though she were a bullock. No one was watching but one of Paulinus's priests, Hunmar, and he was no one to worry about; he frightened easily.

"Three months?"

Hild did not bother to respond. Her mother knew more about childbirth than any woman breathing.

Breguswith kept circling. There was a hitch in her gait, slight but noticeable to someone who had watched since the day she was born.

"Well, if you're going to cover it you'll need to eat more so the rest of you keeps up with your belly and breasts."

She had thought her breasts seemed less swollen—they were much less sore—but about this kind of thing, her mother was never wrong.

"Still, you look well."

Breguswith tucked her arm in Hild's; those watching would think it an affectionate gesture.

She steered Hild away from any listeners. "Does the king know?"

"The queen does." It was her right leg. Her hip? "But she wants me to help him. Wants me to go north."

"Let's hope she's said nothing. It would be best coming from you."

"If he's to know before I leave."

"Oh, he'll know. Your woman's done a good enough job with her needle but any mother will know in the light of day. Some will know already if you walked close to the torchlight. We'll discuss it on your way to change into more suitable clothes. There isn't much time."

When Hild and her mother arrived—with Begu and Cian—at the feast, the king was already there, and he ignored her. He held his neck and shoulders with a whip and tension she recognised: He was livid. Someone had told him, and who else but Æthelburh. For the first time since she had claimed the mantle of light of the world, Hild's party was led to a bench far from the king. People noticed—they blinked, or frowned, or turned their smooth faces away—but none spoke of it: Never say the dangerous thing aloud.

She took her seat, blood pooling hot and thick in her chest and the veins in her neck swelling.

"The Crow isn't happy, either," Cian said. Paulinus Crow sat at the right hand of the king and seemed to suck light from the hall. His skirts were newly dyed black—expensive stuff—and the only colour about him was the enormous amethyst on his hand and the gold and amethyst cross at his chest. His hair was still black, but it had the look of being helped with ink.

"Oh, he's never happy," Begu said. "But who could be, with this fish? Fish at a feast!"

Hild's throat was too tight to talk.

Begu looked at her bread trencher and made a face. "Mullet." She popped a chunk in her mouth. "Well, it tastes good. For fish. So why are you so cross?"

The king was a fool. He needed her. But like a sullen child he was punishing her, and people would die because of it.

"Don't," Cian said to Hild. He was smiling and his tone was ordinary, but his eyes were not. "Don't let them see." His hand lay warm and light on hers, and his skin seemed dark against her thumb knuckle, which glowed white with the strength of her grip on her meat knife.

She breathed, relaxed her jaw, and eased her knife grip from fighting to eating. "I'm fine," she said. She put the knife down, reached for her cup, and drank, smiled. She forced her attention to the fish and chewed, imagining it was Edwin's liver.

In the morning, she felt thin-skinned and snappish. The rage had gone but it had left behind its poison. Cian, after trying twice to make her smile, patted her on the thigh and took himself to the hall to eat. Gwladus brought breakfast but for the first time in a fortnight Hild did not want to eat. Even Gwladus's tansy scent, and the rich promise that wafted from beneath her skirts with every rustle and swirl of cloth, made her turn her head away.

"Agate earrings to meet the king today," Gwladus said.

The king would not care what earrings she wore while he nailed her ears to a post and explained why the Crow was his godmouth once again and she was no longer needed. But she let Gwladus dress her in finery.

Cian came in just as Gwladus was fussing with her hair. "Edwin's houseman's on his way," he said. He saw the untouched food. "You must eat something before you talk to the king. Here." He tossed her a wrinkled apple. "Take a bite."

After the houseman left with Cian, Gwladus, not sure what to do, brought Breguswith, who took one look at Hild standing in her finery, hands dripping with apple pulp, and said, "What did that apple do to you?"

"He shut me out—"

"The apple?"

"The king! He shut me out like I'm nothing."

"So you took it out on an apple."

"He needs me!"

"Strangling an apple won't help."

Hild looked at her sticky hands. Gwladus handed her a cloth. Hild wiped her hands. After a moment she said, "He asked for Cian, not me."

"And does Boldcloak know Elmet's defences?"

"Yes, but—"

"Then let him report them. You have another task."

But did she? The king had refused her, as though she were no more than any other mother-to-be. Did this happen to all women? Was this how Breguswith had felt? And Hereswith? "Today's her birthday."

Breguswith followed her thought effortlessly. "You've heard from your sister?"

"I would have told you last night."

"But you were too blinded by rage. Like today."

"You have no idea how—"

Breguswith smoothed her dress. "Shall I come back when you've finished pouting?"

"Why is everyone treating me like—"

"Because you're behaving like one." She sat on the stool by the bed. "Tell me of your sister. She's well?"

"She's— Sigeberht is becoming pious. Hereswith and Fursey are encouraging him."

"Truly pious?"

"Fursey thinks so."

"I don't trust that priest."

"His aims and Hereswith's join. With his help, Hereswith will be queen."

Breguswith's eyes burned. Queen. She had always wanted that for her daughter. "When?"

When. That was all anyone asked her. "How should I know?"

Breguswith just looked at her. "Well enough. If you are nothing but an empty head and swelling belly, we will talk of nothing. Did you know that Wilgith is with child?"

"Everyone is," she said. "Even the sows."

"Ah. So you no longer feel special."

"No! I mean, that's not it." Not all of it. "War is coming. I can see it. And I could help." And she longed to go north, to smell air she did not know and see trees she could not name. "But not now. Because Æthelburh told him."

"Well, of course she told him. The whispers have already begun and she would be deaf to not hear them. She's his wife, the king relies on her to tell him such things. So she had to."

Deep down Hild knew that, but it still hurt. Breguswith flexed her leg once or twice, waiting. Was the limp yesterday a ploy? Even if it were, it did not make her mother less right. She sighed.

Breguswith nodded. "Now, did you eat any of your breakfast or just punish it? While Gwladus brings you something—which you will eat—you can take that finery off. So. You surprised the king. He feels made game of—humiliated, just as you felt last night. He'll take time to come up with a suitable punishment and I doubt you'll like it. While he decides, you will use the time to find a way back to the centre."

Her mother had taught her long ago that when a wheel hit a stone it was the rim that suffered, not the hub. Perhaps it was true but the edges were where she learnt things. Edges were where she felt free.

"Meanwhile, don't brood."

"I'm not—"

"Get out in the fresh air, it'll be good for you. And take the children."

"The children? They're best left to Cian. They like him better."

"But Cian is talking to the king. Those children will one day be kings and queens. We need friends. Teach them to like you."

Outside the wall, the mound in the fork between the rivers Use and Fosse was a chaos of timbers and piled dirt where the king's men had pulled down the old tower and cleared the ground. After Œstre Mass tomorrow they would begin the new tower, bigger and better, to guard the wīc and docks. Today the site was deserted but for Hild and the three royal children.

She knelt by the great hill of earth and pebbles and sticks the children had spent the late morning turning into the isle of Britain. They had happily pushed piles of dirt to and fro under her direction, made mud sides to hold up mountains. Hild brushed her hair from her face—she had taken off her veil band—and felt freer than she had for a month: not sick, not careful of her appearance, just happily sweeping great mounds of earth into shape.

Yffi, Edwin's grandson, pushed another twig into the forest of Elmet (six twigs; he'd even managed to find a mix of elm and oak), Wuscfrea sat plop-bottomed on the damp grass wholly absorbed by whatever he was trying to ferret out of his left nostril, and Eanflæd peered at the packed ridge Hild was shaping.

She frowned. "What's that?"

"The second wall, to the north."

"There's only one." So certain.

"There are two," Hild said. "Look. Here's our wall, the first wall, south of Bebbanburg." She pointed to the row of pebbles and sticks running from Tinamutha all the way west to the other coast, to Rheged. "Think of it as being the gather line of a woman's dress, running under her armpits and breasts. And here's the second wall, north, like a necklace under this long chin."

She showed them how the east end of the northmost wall split the Gododdin and Bryneich from the Picts, and how the west end divided the Britons of Alt Clut from the Irish-speaking Scots of Dál Riata. At the west end she stuck a pale pebble in the cleft of the Clut to show Dun Breatann, the Irish name for the fortress on the rock that towered over the river.

Eanflæd frowned some more. Her cyrtel was rolled at the front and the back kilted up between her legs and through her belt. Her legs were sturdy, scabbed at the knee. She stuck out her chin. "Have you seen it?"

"I have. I was eight. Only a bit older than you."

Eanflæd looked as though she did not believe Hild had ever been eight. Hild did not blame her; it was only ten years ago but seemed like something that had happened in another age.

Eanflæd had never been north of Yeavering, never had to look a king in the eye and use the language of dreams to make him save her family. Never been alone. This future Yffing peaceweaver knew only her small world, a world in which she was the first child of the overking of the Anglisc and his Centisc queen, the strongest, the loudest, always speaking her mind. She knew nothing but safety.

Hild rested her hand on her no-longer flat belly. She wanted that same safety for her child—work she would begin in the north. For now she would give these children what she could.

"Pass me that," she said, pointing to a splinter of elm left from the torn stockade, and Eanflæd handed it to her. "Scoot back," she said to Yffi. She patted the mountains running like a bony spine down the middle of the country, from the wall they all knew to the waist of the isle before it swelled at the hips. "Britain, the whole isle, is split in half by the Spine. Imagine it's a boat belonging to two brothers, one Anglisc, one wealh, who turn their backs to one another and cast their lines on opposite sides."

She held her left arm out, pointing east.

"We Anglisc throw our line east and north, to the Frisians, the Norse, sometimes the Franks. Our priests face east, all the way to Rome, and shave—"

"Snivelling skirted priests," Eanflæd said, in exactly her father's tone. "With shaved pates."

Yffi touched his head. "Like Father Stephan—"

"Paulinus is more important, he's a bishop!" She was eldest, she was first; she knew more and best.

In a few years Æthelburh would train this child to listen more than speak; when she did speak to do so softly—and then only to suggest, not state; and never, ever to interrupt a man. It was how Æthelburh survived: persuade her husband to a wiser course and pretend it was his idea all along.

She would do what she could to teach Eanflæd how to see power and perhaps one day she might find her own. "Paulinus is a bishop, yes, and he is important. Even so, he must look to the overbishop."

"Who's that?"

"In the east of Britain, bishops look to the overbishop Honorius, in Cent."

She made a scornful noise. "My fa is overking of the Anglisc. His bishop is overbishop!"

"Not yet. But one day soon, yes, because your fa is so important, and if Paulinus Crow pleases his lord—the overbishop of all the bishops, the pope in Rome—he will be raised to overbishop of all the Anglisc, over-bishop of all who kiss the hand to Edwin king."

Eanflæd looked satisfied: Even the overbishop of all the bishops thought her fa important.

"Now, in the west"—she pointed with her right arm—"the wealh kings of Gwynedd and Rheged have priests who shave their foreheads—"

"Foreheads don't have hair!"

Hild pointed at her hairline. "Back from here." They had never seen a British priest because Paulinus had driven them out before they were born, and now east of the Spine they were only seen by those, like Hild, they knew as friendly.

"Do they have bishops, too?"

"They do." Or they used to—though they were an odd sort of wander-ing bishop. She had not met one for a very long time. And she had no idea if they looked to Rome, or whether kings chose them. "These priests—all the wealh, priests and kings and princes—look south and west for trade and marriage: Ireland, Less Britain, and Iberia and lands farther east that they in turn trade with. Warm lands, full of sun and grapes."

"We get wine," Eanflæd said. "That's from grapes."

Hild nodded. "But only wine that's travelled north, from those hot southlands."

"What are southlands like?" Yffi said.

"James the Deacon could tell you," Hild said.

"James isn't here," Eanflæd said.

"That's true," Hild said. With her stick she scored a great valley south of York to the North Sea. "Do you know what that is?"

Yffi opened his mouth but Eanflæd beat him to it. "The Humbre."

They had all been on the Humbre many times.

She drew all the rivers south of their wall that fed into it. The great Treonte, which flowed up through Lindsey, north and east into the Humbre. The Daun into the Treonte. Her own Yr, which moved south and east to join the great Use, which, in its turn, joined the Humbre. The Deorwente, which flowed south to the Use—and then to the Humbre. The fast-flowing Swale, the Weorf, the Ur, all into the Use and on into the vast Humbre, and so to the sea. And above the Swale, on the northern edge of Deira itself, the Uiura, with its great mouth opening directly into the sea.

Then the rivers north of the wall: the Tese, the Tine, the Twid. They, too, all flowing east to the northern sea that linked the Northumbrans to the never-ending web of trade and favours between the kingdoms of Britain and beyond.

She poked holes by the rivers and they named the forts and vills one by one, sometimes with help: Caer Daun on the Daun. Caer Loid on the Yr. York on the Use. Derventio on the Deorwente. Arbeia on the Tine. Galashiels and Calchfynydd and Berewic on the Twid. Stoctun and Heretue above Uiuramutha . . . She had travelled them all, more than once, and many others besides.

Eanflæd was frowning again, restless, bored by too many names. Even Yffi was looking wistfully at his twigs.

She stood, brushed her hands free of dirt, and picked up her staff. She swung it, enjoying the low swoop as it cut the air, and the smooth fit in her hands—she'd had this one for months now. Her hands were still gritty. She scrubbed them one by one on her skirts. Better, though Gwladus would not be happy. "Who wants to know how to make a gesith with a sword drop his shield?"

They leapt up, even fat little Wuscfrea. She rummaged through the ruined spars and timbers for wood to make a staff for each of them, showed them how to balance them and feel the heft, then to hit with a swing or a punch. Then she told them the story, with demonstrations—Wuscfrea chortled as she mimed splashing in the stream, climbing a tree, running away—of how she had at last worked out how to get Cian to drop his shield.

Then they all had to have a go. Wuscfrea was too small but tried anyway and hardly cried at all when he fell over and banged his elbow on a stone. Hild told him what a fine gesith he would be, how brave. Eanflæd bellowed and thumped and charged like a maddened bull, and did not cry at all when Hild cracked her across the shins—that would leave a bruise to boast about. But it was Yffi who learnt fast, whose moves with the heavy staff were tidy and contained, Yffi whom Hild thought might one day be the warrior of the three. But Yffi was the child of Osfrith, Edwin's second son by his first queen, Cwenburh. She would make sure James spoke to this boy of the sunshine and grapes of the southlands, of Frankia and Iberia, of Rome. To live through what was coming, little Yffi would have to leave; he might be safe in Frankia. Eanflæd was safe—safe from any victor but Cadwallon, who hated Yffings beyond reason. No matter what happened to Edwin she would still have worth as a peaceweaver. But little Wuscfrea, only son of Æthelburh and Edwin? No king would suffer the heir of Bernicia and Deira, and cousin to kings of Cent and the East Anglisc, to live.

"Sit." They were tired and happy to obey. She knelt, swapped her oak staff for the splinter of elm. "How do you think gesiths, with their bitter blades and slender spears, their high hearts and stout shields, get to the battle?"

Eanflæd frowned. She always went by boat, or in a wagon. "They ride," she said, chin stuck out, sensing something unsatisfactory with her answer but not sure what.

Hild scored two great lines, north to south, one in the west, from Alt Clut through the wall to Caer Luel then down along the coast to Chester; and one in the east, from Din Eidyn through to Corabrig, and York, and then right through Elmet—and Yffi's careful forest—to Lindum. She cut not only through the Roman wall but also through the rivers in the east and the mountains in the west.

"What are those?" Yffi said, glancing at Eanflæd: Perhaps he could at least be allowed to be first to ask a question?

"War streets. Here, along the south of our wall." She slashed a line from Corabrig to Caer Luel. "And here." A deep swag, hanging from Lindum on one side to Chester on the other. "Redcrest roads, hard and fast, good in any season." There were other paths, good only in warm weather, or dry weather. "Now watch." She cut a V, its left arm running south and east from the center of the swagging belly, its point, Londinium on the Thames—another great river that flowed east—and its right arm slicing back up, north and east, to Lindum. "Do you see?"

Eanflæd nodded, though Hild knew she did not. Not yet.

She stabbed the swag where it met the left arm of the V. "Tomeworthig," she said. "A royal vill. Now do you see?"

The river was loud.

Yffi tilted his head to align with the V. "Mercia," he said at last. "Penda son of Pybba."

Wuscfrea looked up at the quaver in his cousin's voice. They were æthelings. Penda was their bogeyman, the one who would come for them, roast them on spits.

"No!" Eanflæd said. "My fa's war band is bigger than Penda's!" She planted her sturdy legs wide and her fists on her hips.

Hild said, "Your father's war band is very big."

"The biggest!"

"The biggest by far of any single war band. But Penda's war band won't come by itself. To Penda's men, add Cadwallon's, from Gwynedd." She showed how close Deganwy was to Chester, then traced a line from Chester to Tomeworthig and up through Caer Daun to Aberford. "To that add Domnall Brecc's from Dál Riata." A line from beyond Alt Clut all the way south to Cetreht. "And then add the Picts." A line from beyond Din Eidyn.

Eanflæd lifted her chin stubbornly.

For a moment, Hild imagined laughing, saying No! Not really! and ruffling the child's hair. Then they would all squeal and giggle and tell stories of who would be in the most trouble from Arddun. But then she smelt the dirt under her knees: old dirt, tired dirt, dirt turned many times, by many kings, who had all fought to hold this fork in the river, to stay safe against the ever-rising tide of other kings. Walls never kept you safe. These children were Yffings, and Penda was coming. They had to know.

"Do you see?" she said again, but gently.

Eanflæd blinked furiously. "But Fa's the overking. Those other kings swore an oath!"

Hild said nothing. She had not even mentioned Powys, and Dyfneint. Perhaps even Rheged and Alt Clut. When the boar grew old, the dogs gathered.

"They won't all come at once," Yffi said. "Will they?"

"I won't let them." She scored two of the lines, over and over. She could stop them only if she went north.

"You're spoiling it," Eanflæd said.

Hild looked down. Dere Street, coming south from Din Eidyn to the wall, south again to Cetreht, south again to York, was now a rutted mess where she had dug so hard she had torn pebbles out and spoilt the lines. She smoothed it carefully. If Edwin let her go she would keep this route safe, at least from the north. But the other half, the left arm of Ermine Street that ran up from Lindum, north across the great mire, to Aberford, that was out of her hands. That was up to Cian while she was in the north.

Wuscfrea gurgled and pointed. Two housemen were heading for the mound. She could tell by the way they walked—small steps, toes turned in, chins down—that they knew she would not like their message. The king had decided, then; and as her mother had said, she doubted she would like it.

She dropped her elm splinter in the ruined road, took up her staff, and stood.

It had been so long since she had seen any expression but worry on Coelfrith's face that she did not at first understand the look he gave as they brushed past each other in the doorway to the king's outer room. Pity, she realised as the curtain fell between her and the two gesiths on guard outside. Pity, and not for the dirt on her hands or the state of her dress.

Her uncle was alone. He gnawed a leg of goose but did not offer her any or suggest she sit. He flung the bone to the board and wiped his mouth.

"Who ever heard of a king's fist with child? I'll be the laughingstock of the north."

"No one laughed at Grendel's mother."

He blinked. "Who?"

"That song you like. Liked. Grendel was the enemy's son."

"What—oh, that tale sung by Rædwald's ungrateful scop." He frowned—just like Eanflæd—and flicked at the leg bone, and again, until it fell to the floor, at which point he lost interest as kings do when something is resolved to their satisfaction. "Wherever did he go?"

"To Cent, lord. According to Luftmær." Who tracked other scops jealously.

"Luftmær? Who the fuck is Luftmær?"

"The scop who wrote Wuscfrea's praise song." My mother's bed mate.

He nodded, remembering. "Song of Wæbeg, son of Woden, king of kings! I liked that one, too. I liked it better; no one died." He chose two walnuts and cracked them in his hand. Inspected the meat. "Well, you won't have my token. That goes south, with Eadfrith and his honeyed tongue."

She stood very still. She was going. North, into the wild, where the sky was wide and she could see for miles. A great bubble rose under her breastbone. There would be punishment, too, oh yes. But she was going. "No token? Then I'll need gold. Gold and men."

"I gave you men as a wedding present. Have you lost them?"

"Cian will need the Hounds. For Elmet."

"I'll give you . . ." He tossed the nut meat into his mouth and the shells over his shoulder. "Five."

"Give me a dozen." She felt reckless, unbounded. North: where she could breathe.

"A dozen? No. The fewer who know about you and your womb turd the better."

Womb turd. He wanted it out. And he was a king. He could watch them tear it from her while he sipped wine and played knucklebones.

He was watching her.

"Who will you send with advance word?"

He laughed, the laugh with the twist and slither in it that meant he was about to be vastly amused at someone else's expense. "Advance word? You are my advance word." He seemed pleased with himself. "Yes. A dozen is far too many. Five will do."

"Five?" She met his gaze as steadily as she could. Into the north with only five men. "Then make them fearsome."

"Fearsome?" His eyes glittered, and then he smiled.

She rolled Cian's hair between her fingers. It felt fat and slippery and satisfying. Cian, skin still damp, lay on his back with his head across her thighs, eyes closed. The tiny lines around them, lines made by squinting against sun and wind and rain every day of his twenty-four years, were smoothed away in the ruddy glow of rush light.

"So after he told me Honeytongue was getting the token for his travel to Penda, he agreed: gold, and fearsome men. But only five."

His breathing was so slow she thought he was asleep but he murmured, "And then?"

"Then he smiled."

He opened his eyes, focused. "You aren't worried?"

"I saw that look on Coelfrith's face, and I know my uncle. Of course I'm worried." She laughed, and stretched. "But five men is more than enough for this. And gold. Coelfrith is a worrier. The king needs me too much to do anything too terrible."

"He hates to be surprised, and you surprised him."

Yes, and he had punished her with public humiliation at the feast. But he needed her. And now, right here with the smell of Cian all over her, in her, and hers on him, she felt wholly alive, better than she had for months, strong and ready.

Womb turd. She had not told Cian that. He did not need to hear the king's contempt for their child. She would not dwell on it. She was going north, to wind and hills, to places she had never been and people she had never seen. Once again in a king's name and with king's men. And her man was here, marked with her scent; he would make Elmet strong in both their names.

She ran her palm over the curve of his shoulder, hard bone under taut muscle, and skin as luscious as run honey but for the ridge of the seax cut. She traced it with her fingertip, felt the grain of it, the shift of muscle beneath. The heat in her belly began to build again.

His stick stirred. "When do you leave?"

"Tomorrow? The day after?" Her hand moved to his chest; the vein in his neck began to thump. She leaned down. "Not just yet." She cupped his breast and tugged on his hair, urging him, until he rolled onto his elbows.

She followed Coelfrith's man to the undercroft, smoothing her clothes with one hand, carrying her staff balanced like a pole in the other. She patted her jewellery. Gwladus had handed her piece after piece so fast there was no time to think. When the king called, you came, even twice in one day.

Cross, rings, beads, matching earrings. All there—Gwladus had already laid them out for the feast. She did not need to check her seax; she was aware of the subtle difference in how it hung from the new belt made to fit her growing waist.

The man stopped outside the outer chamber of the treasure room, bowed, and gestured for her to go in. She paused—a room with only one door—but the clear light spilling from the door meant it was a room lit by wax tapers. Not even the king would waste beeswax on an ambush.

Edwin, combed and brushed for the feast and wearing his heaviest gold belt and baldric, hardly looked at her. He nodded to Coelfrith, who coughed and handed her a small bag. Hild weighed it in her hand: gold, but less than she had hoped. Coelfrith coughed again, the cough that meant he was preparing to say something she would not want to hear. She slipped the gold into her purse.

"What the reeve is trying to work his way up to saying is, I expect you to bring most of it back. I don't have enough to fling about."

All around them the shelves were heaped with ingots, chests, and sacks; the floor piled with furs, ivories, and glass. But for Edwin there could never be enough. Gold by firelight was what woke the dragon in every breast, and the dragon weakened will and sense. Once greed woke it goaded its bearer to risk what they would regret the next day, swear oaths they would wish unsaid. Gold broke a person open. And gold was easy to smuggle, easy to run with, easy to carry into exile. Gold spoke every tongue.

Coelfrith held out a bigger bag, a sack, with both hands. She nodded for him to put it on the floor. He put it at her feet. Without taking her eyes off the king, she bent and hefted it an inch or so with one hand—not easy—then squatted and untied the hemp twine at the neck. Even the twine was good quality: long-fibred, strong. She folded back the thick cloth: hacksilver, oily and awkward. She retied the twine, thinking. She could get around the bulk; she had ingots of her own. Cian could take the hacksilver back to Caer Loid for their hoard. The thought of Cian's warm hands cradling the rounded sack brought a rush of heat to her belly. She pushed the thought away and stood. But something must have shown in her face.

Edwin raised his eyebrows. "My silver doesn't suit you?"

"I'd rather have ingots—" His face shifted, like curd just before the whey slips out from under it when you tilt the jar. She said lightly, "Just as I bet you would rather own the stallion of the wind and all the gold of middle earth as yet undelved, uncle."

After a heartbeat, he said, "And just what do you bet, niece?" He smiled widely. "You haven't asked about your men."

"What about my men, uncle?" Her heart began to thump.

"They're waiting for you. Five fearsome men. You're a bit overdressed for the occasion but I'll take you there on my way to hall."

Overdressed.

He watched her, in no hurry, a cat with its paw on the mouse's back. "Even you, niece, can't be two places at once." She had lied to him, made a fool of him. Now he would exact his price. "You have work to do. Bring the Bryneich back to our side, and do it before the render at Yeavering. I want Coledauc to kiss my ring without secrets behind his eyes. Bishop Paulinus wanted you at the Mass, he wanted to show the folk a hægtes is nothing to fear, but I need you in the north, so the Crow can whistle. Make sure of the north before Oswald marries his sister to Domnall Brecc. Your men are waiting, and the tide is turning."

She would not be at the feast.

He stooped and pulled a fur from the heap on the floor. "Here, this is more in keeping with your task."

He flung it at her. She caught it. Heavy, dense, and soft: lynx furs, dappled black and grey, sewn in a hooded cape. A rare thing, and precious, but uncanny, smelling of fear and legend and ill wishes. Cath Llew. Who had given it? Just like a king: get rid of a difficult thing and make it look like a boon. Just as this hurry was both hastening his goal and punishment for her. Kings liked getting two things for one price, especially if they weren't paying.

She slung it over her shoulders, accepting the double-edged gift.

She stepped onto the deck and turned in the light thrown by the wharf torches, such as it was, to face them. Five gesiths, no more than dark shapes against the torchlight flaring and swinging in the breeze. The boat, a big one, rocked.

No one said anything. Sound carried oddly in the damp that hugged the river: horses moving uneasily in the stern, the creak of hull against the wharf, the slap of the river, and the king's laughter hanging in the air—though she knew she was the only one who still heard that.

The dark cloud of fur added inches to her shoulders. Beneath she flashed with gold. One hand rested on a slaughter seax, the other held her staff. She felt the weight of their attention. For the next two months she was their lord and could command them to anything. Let them look.

The deck tipped, tilted, and steadied under her feet. The tide was moving west; the river was still in flood. There was time, but not much.

"Who captains the boat?"

A man stepped forward and even in the dark she could tell by the way he moved that he lived on the water, not land. Short, unbowed legs, bare feet. "Cenhelm, lady." A voice like cracked oak. "This is my boat. *Curlew.*"

"Crew?"

"Fifteen. Sixteen when we pick up my man downriver."

Introductions would wait. "The tide?"

"Flood's good for a bit yet."

"More, man." Her voice was harsh.

"Tide turns as æfen turns to niht."

"Do we need the flood?"

"Depends."

She breathed deep. Patience. "On?"

"Wind and weight. I was hired for five men and five horses, who are on board, plus you and your woman. Anyway, ebb'll run til úht. But we won't run with it. We'll put into Brough when the moon sets, tie up til undern, middæg." When the flood had passed and the next ebb would take them out to the sea. He tugged on the cable tying them to the wharf, nodded to himself. "That's where we'll pick up my man. He's—"

"The weight. Do you have room for four more, and horses?"

"The king said you and your woman. And nothing about horses."

"I have four people. Two horses." She could barter for ponies in the north. Begu and Gwladus would not mind what they rode, and Morud preferred to walk, but she and Oeric needed warhorses.

He shook his head. "Even with the flood, shoals'd rip our bottom out. If you keep all these men?" She nodded. "Then you, and either your woman or your horse."

"I need both." But which? Gwladus could speak British; Begu had standing and knew more of babies. "Leave your man at Brough. My people can row."

"It takes more than muscle to—"

She turned to her men. Her voice sliced across the captain's. "Which of you can row?"

One stepped forward. All she could see of him was wide shoulders, thick thighs.

"Good man. Name?"

"Oh, Wulf doesn't speak," another shadow said.

"And you are?"

"They call me Dudda." He stepped forward and the light fell on him. He was bone thin and his face hideously burnt.

"And you speak for Wulf, Dudda?" Dudda: round. Not his real name.

"It's Wulfnoth to most. And he speaks for himself, once you get used to his ways." He gave her a grin, or what would on any other face have been a grin. "When you can see him."

She looked at Wulfnoth. "But you can hear?" He nodded. "Show me your hands." Rower's horn under the sword stripe and shield ridge.

The boat shivered. Time was running with the water. Time enough when she got back to see what the other men looked like. Fearsome, no doubt.

"I'll be back with my horse and woman before the tide turns." She pointed to a sailor. "You. Bring—" A flutter under her ribs surprised her. She clapped a hand to her belly, breathed. Straightened. "Pick up that sack and come with me."

Hurry, questions, more hurry. The surprise on Begu's face, and pleasure. Telling Gwladus, "Look after my mother." Changing her shoes as she ate the bread Gwladus, after a long pause, handed her. Gwladus giving Begu instructions and Begu saying, *Yes, yes, I know.* Sliding ingots in her saddle-bags. To Gwladus, "Where's Cian?" Then to Morud, "Only Cygnet. But bring the best harness for us both. We have to ride over the brow of every hill gleaming like sunrise. That first—" And another flutter.

"The baby!" Begu said. "Already? Oh, so that's why you want me. But why you didn't say—" In a whirl of yellow she turned on Oeric, who was just catching up with the fact that he would be left behind. "Don't even *think* about whining. Gwladus isn't whining. Sort the horses. Horse. *Now*, Oeric. Oh, stop fussing," she said to Hild. "The baby's fine. You're fine."

Hild breathed carefully. Something inside, alive. She needed Cian, needed the smell of him. Their child.

Around her, people whirled like leaves. Her mother, lighting every-thing, so they could see. Gwladus, in the flare of wicks, issuing a flurry of orders to housefolk, whipping together bundles. Her mother touching the lynx cape. "You're strong. The baby is strong. Remember: We need friends." Hild telling her, "Three in one. Linnet. Gwladus knows her." And then Cian was there. Cian's buckle hard against her belly. His hands, his voice, his strong red mouth.

A turmoil of people, voices, wind ruffling the fur on her shoulder. Torchlight. River light. The splash of rope, creak of steering oar. Cian's words floating from the wharf but falling into their wake before she could catch them, and Cenhelm moving the Curlew into the steady flow midstream. The wind shifted to the northwest, and cloud unwound from the just-past-full moon. Its blue-white spill was bright enough to weave by.

While Begu did her best to organise the small shelter—no more than a tent, really—in the middle of the boat, Hild, chewing a strip of dried meat and trying not to think of the roasting ox she had smelt in York, the honey cakes, the wine, found a free patch of deck just aft of the mast and leaned against the rail. She lifted her face to the moon but its light was cold. The water smelt brackish, unlike the clean iron and salt of Cian.

She called her men to her one by one.

Dudda had combed his hair. It would be yellow in the sunshine. His burn was more than a year old. His eyes were sound, and his teeth. He smelled of sharp sweat and smoke. She offered him a piece of meat, which he accepted readily enough, and ate, though with much mopping at the corner of his mouth with his shoulder. His thinness was not because he couldn't eat, then. She clasped his arm, clapped his shoulder, and told him to send Wulf.

Wulf would be hard to knock down. Although his width made him seem short she overtopped him by only four fingers. His knees were thicker than trees she had climbed. "Do these other men understand your signs?" she said. For a moment he gave no hint he had heard her—his face could have been cut from rock—then he made a tipping sign with his hand: some do, some don't. When he saw she understood he held up two fingers and nodded, and then again, this time with a headshake. That seemed clear enough. In the morning she would find out who was who.

Next was Glædmar. She realised she was grinning and stopped. "Take off your helmet and let's look at you." The ear scar looked healthy enough, but the skin over the newly blunt tip of his nose . . . She reached as though to touch it and he flinched. "Tender?"

"A bit."

She nodded. "Eat more greens."

"I don't like—"

"You don't have to like them. Eat them. That skin's too thin. I'll make a salve for you but meanwhile, eat more greens."

She knew Leofdæg, too. He was small, like his sister, with the same wave in his hair and fine hands, and one shoulder so much higher than the other he looked as though he were always rubbing his ear to get rid of an itch. "How's young Fortheric?" His sister-son by Forthere, the giant gesith who had died on an assassin's blade that terrible Easter day five years ago.

"Big," said Leofdæg. His clothes smelt of beer, new and old. He never had said much but he fought like a mad dog and she would trust him in a shield wall.

And last there was Bryhtsige. In the moonlight his hair looked like tarnished silver. He was tall, but not overly so, and strong, with muscles that looked new and fresh. His skin was clear and he had all his teeth and fingers. She could not tell how old he was.

"You're wondering what's wrong with me," he said. His voice was light, and Hild found herself listening for what might be hidden there.

She said nothing. Silence could pry men open almost as fast as gold.

"I will not father children."

She considered. "Nor will I."

He laughed, a laugh as whippy as a hazel switch. "A West Saxon arrow took my balls."

"When?"

"I was seventeen."

Geld a horse or a bull late and it still knew how to use its stick. But it could never be lord of the herd. Its smell changed, and after a while its look. It was not shunned, not driven off, but it was not seen, not part of the group. But this was a small group; she needed every one.

"Look after my horse, Bryhtsige. Her name's Cygnet. She's used enough to boats but she'll miss her friends." A mark of favour the others would pay attention to.

In the leather tent, a tallow burned in a dish hanging over a bowl that swayed on a rope from the roof line. Begu seemed such a creature of the field Hild forgot sometimes that her gemæcce had grown up by the sea.

Begu thumped their bedrolls into shape.

"That looks like a lot of work."

"You'd rather be miserable for two days? If you're trying to say thank you, just say it. Here."

It was too dark to see but Hild smelled cheese. She sighed.

"Oh, don't worry. Gwladus packed plenty of meat and bread and fruit leather. But cheese won't keep you awake. And hang that cape outside. It smells."

Hild sniffed it. "It's well-tanned."

"Not rotten, just wrong. Untrustworthy. As though it might leap on me in the middle of the night."

Cath Llew of the tufted ears. Smiler in the dark, tearer of throats. Hild slipped it off—the skin really was beautifully tanned, supple and smooth—and stroked the fur. So dense and soft, so well-matched.

"No one will steal it."

"I don't want it rained on."

"It won't rain tonight I shouldn't think."

Hild hung it on the outside of the tent.

Begu chattered about nothing in particular as they ate, not expecting a reply.

Hild's task was to break any Bryneich alliance and shift it instead to the Yffings. She had a paltry amount of gold and few men. That wasn't what worried her. What worried her was finding the Bryneich in the first place. They would begin at Colud, if the weather held.

"It's becoming a habit," Begu said. She nodded at Hild's hand, cradling her belly. "I can tell when you're worrying about the small one."

"Edwin called her a womb turd."

Begu gaped, then barked with laughter, hard laughter, not the usual tumble, a side of her gemæcce she did not get to see often. But then she softened and patted Hild's arm. "What do kings know?" And Hild was glad she was there. They chatted about Wilfram's sister Wilgith, and the proud father-to-be Manfrid—the even prouder Tondberht and Wilgar: "You'd think Tondberht had invented babies!"—and that Begu had reminded Cian to make sure Wilfram got to visit his sister in York when her time was due, though they would most likely be back before then . . .

They were bedding down when the boat began to slope and the rope running overhead from the top of the mast to the stern creaked. The wind was changing direction. Not to the east, as they'd hoped, but directly from the west.

5

✦

I T RAINED. The *Curlew*, fifty yards from the shingle beach just below
Colud, rocked at shallow anchor. Cenhelm, eye pits stained with lack of
sleep, eased his grip on the steering oar and stretched. The wind had been
against them all the way; his men were exhausted. He would not go in any
closer. He did not want to be embayed for a week. If they wanted to get off
here, the horses would swim and his passengers would off-load by skiff.
They were just waiting for the tide to turn, so they would at least not have
to fight the current.

Sailors tossed saddles and rolls to the two men in the small boat alongside. Begu was already in the skiff, tiny and brightly coloured next to the
men, sitting on a thwart guarding their tent and trunk. Leofdæg and Bryhtsige, who would swim with the horses, were weaponless and without arm
rings.

She felt the rock and sway under her feet change a little. The tide was
turning.

"You will unhook your swords before you get in the skiff," she said to
the other three.

"We're not the ones swimming!" Dudda said. He was going in the first
relay with Begu and the bulk of their gear.

"All it takes is the skiff to go one way and the boat the other as you step
across." She had seen more than one man drown because he missed his

footing and sank like a rod, weighted by iron and gold. "Your swords will stay unhooked until you're on the beach."

Dudda unhooked his scabbard and began to strip his arm rings. "Hey, don't throw that!" he said, as one of the sailors picked up his blue-and-green shield. The sailor grinned and threw it, hard. Dudda scrambled aboard, still shouting.

Hild saw Begu wag her finger at him, and Dudda grin, then subside, then the rest of their gear was aboard, along with two more sailors, and the skiff pushed off. She and Wulf and Glædmar watched it, tipping up and down on the slope of the waves, impossibly small and fragile against the grey. Begu, she knew, swam like a porpoise, but Dudda looked too thin.

"The horses aren't going to like this," Glædmar said.

None of them would. Not the horses, who had to jump from an unsteady platform into a cold sea. Nor the men who had to bully them to take the plunge or who swam with them. But they were all trained to it.

The skiff was almost at the shore.

Bryhtsige led Cygnet to the ramp. The golden bay following the mare was Dudda's young gelding. He and Wulf brought two more, she had not heard their names, handed the halter ropes to Leofdæg, went back for the last two. The last was a roan stallion, Strayberry, Bryhtsige's own.

The prow of the skiff ground on the shingle. Two sailors jumped out to their waist.

Hild pointed. The mare and the stallion first. If they jumped, the others would follow. Bryhtsige took the roan's rope in his right hand, Cygnet's in his left. Two sailors poured sand on the slippery ramp, stepped out of the way.

On the beach, Begu hopped out of the skiff. Dudda did the same but fell face first into the surf. Sailors on the deck behind them hooted. Begu hauled Dudda up. Everyone from the skiff started throwing and catching, Begu pointing, Dudda carrying.

Hild patted Cygnet on the shoulder, stepped away, and nodded.

Everything happened at once. Slap on haunch, great hoof crashing on the ramp, white of eye, bright noise as the stallion shrieked, then an enormous splash, and another, a boil of water, then two horses and a man swimming to shore.

Then the next two horses. The last two. Six horses and two men heading for shore. The skiff heading back.

She unhooked her seax and added it to the bundle at her feet that she would carry herself: her jewels, Edwin's gold, her wound roll. She hadn't swum since she had started to swell. Would that make it harder or easier to float?

"Cenhelm," she said. She clasped his free arm. "The Yffings honour you. We'll meet again."

"Maybe," he said. But he did not sound too worried one way or the other. A man with a sound boat and good crew would always have business, no matter who called himself king. "Good luck to you."

The shingle was wet and slick and cold. Bryhtsige checked his sword, squinted at the walls of Colud on the cliff. "There's not much smoke."

"No." One small spiral rose from the fort, enough for a handful of men at most; Coledauc was not there. Whoever he had left behind would have seen the boat—if he had left them. She did not remember there being much to guard. But things change.

Colud sent a boy down to the beach, no doubt to look at them and report back. But the boy, a youth barely old enough for his spear, almost fell off his stubby little pony when he saw Hild. No doubt she was taller than anyone he had seen in his life, swelling with child and weapons, and wearing what seemed the coat of a demon. She was surrounded by hideous gesiths who were something from a nightmare. For him they would turn the beach from a place he knew to a treacherous uncanny landscape. When she beckoned him to come down to them, he did not want to, but could not help but obey.

"You've shocked him rigid," Begu said—in Anglisc, which of course the boy did not understand. He looked wildly about, blinked when he looked down and saw the little woman standing in front of the giant, not the least frightened, hair slightly askew, and smiling. His death grip on the spear eased a little.

"I am Hild Yffing," she said, in British.

"My da—" He cleared his throat. "The lord of Colud, in the prince's absence, welcomes you on the prince's behalf."

———

The lord of Colud—a grand name for the man with the badly set leg left behind to keep the bats out of what, even nine years ago, had been perilously close to a ruin—told her, with many sideways glances at her hideous retinue, that Prince Coledauc had taken his household and war band two days' ride south and west to Calchfynydd for the gathering of the Bryneich. He could offer no guide; there was just himself and his boy, Keir. And he needed the boy.

Hild was sure there were other people about but she said nothing: She did not blame the man, Vaughn, for his caution; her Fiercesomes would be enough to make anyone hesitate. Besides, there was only the one pony, and Begu would need it.

But, Vaughn went on, she would not need another to speak for her. While he himself had not been there on the day nine years ago when she had made the prophecy of eternal friendship between Bryneich and Yffings, she was known. She would need no introduction. And the way was not hard.

He agreed to sell her the stubby pony—she gave him silver, not gold, and bargained hard, because despite protestation of friendship only fools overpaid—and told her the best path through the hills. She refused his offer of food—she guessed he and his son had little enough to see them through the month—and shared theirs, instead. By the way the boy scoffed the fruit leather it had been a while since he had even smelt something that grew on a tree. Colud was a bleached place: salt-stained stone, grey-green grass speckled with pale flowers—white, and silver, and a yellow like old teeth. *We need friends*, her mother had said. Silver was useful, and prophecy, but food was what people remembered. She would remember the names of Vaughn, the lord of Colud, and his son, Keir. They would remember her.

They crossed the Eye Water into what seemed another world. The greens were greener and flowers more yellow. She felt her mind turning and winding and thinking in British, the tongue of secret ways.

They came to the Whiteadder Water at dusk. Behind them, the hills were lit by the last of the sun. South, beyond the Whiteadder, the Twid valley stretched like a dream, broad and welcoming. She had ridden that road before, but in the company of a large war band. She sat on Cygnet and pondered. Being in the open on the smooth valley floor all the way to Calchfynydd would be easier on them all, and faster, but a well-travelled path was filled with risk, and empty of game, and she was still thinking of food and friendship.

She called for Leofdæg. Away from the mead he was her best scout, quick, quiet, and clever, well-mounted on the mean, wiry mare Blodfoot.

"See if there's a less open way."

He flicked a glance at Begu.

"Don't worry about her. That beast's better in the hills than ours." Memps, Coledauc's man had called it, though Begu had said, *Memps? What sort of name is Memps? If he and I are to be friends it will be by another name!* A good hill pony, though it would not be able to keep up if they had to run in the open. She would have to make sure they did not need to run. "Not too hard a path, but more hidden than this. Be back by moonset."

He nodded and kneed Blodfoot across the ford, and faded into the twilight.

They dismounted and loosened their mounts' girths and slipped their bits, but did not unsaddle them. Glædmar picked up a flat river stone for a hearth. "No fire," she said. He sighed and tossed it aside. "Perhaps later, if Leofdæg finds us somewhere more sheltered. You take the first watch."

Dudda laughed, probably at something Wulf had signed.

"Quietly," she said. It would be too dark to sign soon.

It began to rain. They pegged out their leather sheets and crouched beneath, eating a little while their horses stood nose to nose, hunched against the rain.

Bryhtsige and Begu talked softly. Already the Anglisc fell oddly on Hild's ears and she longed for Cian to talk to, or Gwladus. Begu's pauses grew longer. "Don't let her snore," she breathed in Bryhtsige's direction and felt rather than saw his nod.

She drifted, part drowsing, part alive to the water and the things in and on it; Cygnet's weight shifts; the flick of new grass. A whiff of elderflower, not close . . .

When the quarter moon was low and hidden by cloud she came alert as Cygnet tossed her head in greeting and a hoof splashed, no louder than a leaping salmon. Then there Leofdæg was on Blodfoot, not looming from the dark as others might but small and taut, like a bent bow. "No one close," he said. "Good place to rest a mile along Blackadder Water."

"This side?" The clouds looked set; crossing in the dark was never easy.

He shook his head. "But not too hard, dismounted."

Dismounted meant getting wet above the knee. But if there was no one about they could dry by the fire. A fire meant hot food, too, always heartening, and what was to come was as much a thing of the heart as of the blade.

Two mounted Bryneich watched from the finger of hills that reached south and east from the join of the Whiteadder and the Black into the wide Twid valley towards Calchfynydd, standing turned a little away from each other to cover a wider angle, but just in sight of one another, their backs to Hild and her men. If they scanned north it was to the west, where a track moved alongside the redcrest road from Din Eidyn, but more often they looked south and east, to the path men might take from Ad Gefrin and Melmin, along the Til, their eyes narrowed against the morning sun. Hild signalled her men forward.

She rode easy, at the leading edge of a curve of men and Begu, all with their blades scabbarded and their shields slung, and when they came out from behind the finger of hills she nodded at Dudda, who began to sing.

They rode slowly so the Bryneich had time and enough to turn and marvel at the sun shimmering on their mail shirts, winking from the jewels on their harnesses, gleaming on their war boots, glowing on the rich colour of their rolled and padded warrior jackets—yellow, blue, green, striped—and Hild's dark, dappled furs. Begu wore her veil, though Hild rode with her head uncovered as Bryneich women did. In the land where her prophecy was known, Yffing chestnut was not something to hide; it burned like bronzed copper against the cape slung about her shoulders, under which her arms were bare. They rode slowly, too, for the sake of Glædmar and Bryhtsige, who behind them pulled a triangle of downy birch, its reddish bark even redder with splashes of blood from the butchered roe deer, a just-budding buck whose hooves looked very small all bunched together. A good bit of venison. Food, for making friends.

Begu, on her pony, was hung about with sacks: sorrel leaves, and elderflower blossom to fry with the venison. If it were later in the year there would be tubers and roots, juniper berries and more, but venison and elderflower and the good mead they carried would be a beginning. Plus a brace of hares, on either side of her saddle bow. And Hild had gold, though it was hidden.

Hild lifted her hand, palm out, when she knew the Bryneich could see, and rode, still slowly, as though assured of welcome. The men rode to each other first, and put their heads together—if they were her men she would whip them for such carelessness; she could have hidden men with bows—and then one rode away south and west to Calchfynydd. Four or five miles.

The one who came towards them was at or just passing the flower of his strength, older than any in Hild's party, and his mount, though small like those of all hill people, was well-shaped and -groomed. Not well-trained, though: It saw Begu's pony and whickered at it and nodded its head. Its rider frowned and held his reins with only one hand. "What do you with Memps? Oh, whist, Gerritt. Whist." He patted his pony's neck.

"His name's not Memps!" Begu said crossly, though in Anglisc. "Well, yes it is. But it's a silly name. It doesn't even mean anything. He's—he's Sandy." She bent and scrubbed at a smear of hare's blood on her boot. "Yes. Sandy. Oh, tell him," she said to Hild.

The man frowned more, but did not think to put his hand on his sword even though he did not understand a word Begu said, because she was as small as he was, and carrying food and no blade. Then he looked at Hild, and blinked, and became aware of his sword hand, though he did not lay it on his hilt, quite.

Hild looked down at him, letting him see her gold, her height, her blade. Hearing Begu's Anglisc had changed the turn and angle of her mind. Talking about a stubby little pony was not how she had foreseen this meeting. Fate goes ever as it must.

"The pony is Memps, yes, though now in our tongue it is named Sandy." Terrible name. "We left Lord Vaughn"—she did not miss his blink at the honorific—"and young Keir happy and healthy and richer by a fistful of silver. In exchange they pointed us here." We did not kill anyone or torture directions from them. "His rider is Begu. These are my men. I am come in the name of Edwin king to speak with Prince Coledauc, who once gave me this in friendship." She nodded down at her seax, which lay quiescent on her rounded belly. "I am Hild Yffing, light of the world. Also called Butcherbird."

He sat as tall as he might. He had heard the stories. As a child she had glamoured the prince: made a prophecy of friendship between their two peoples and addled his mind, taking as her reward a knife worth more than a sword. She was no child now, and, oh, those hideous men . . . "We will ride together to meet those who Prince Coledauc will no doubt send to honour you."

He hoped the prince would send a dozen. A score.

Hild rode beside him keeping to his smaller mount's pace exactly. Her men rode behind them in a crescent, as before, and his neck crawled. He wondered if they were fingering their blades, or laughing at his faithful Gerritt, or thinking of ways to cut him, cook him, and eat him.

Calchfynydd was a camp snugged inside an elbow of the Twid opposite its join with the Tefeged. An island midstream slowed the water in one channel and skin boats could put in easily on the bank. Between the two rivers was flat land, very green: marshy, no doubt. Their escort—nine altogether, weapons at the ready—were watchful even as they gestured for them to dismount on the outskirts of the camp where cattle lowed and half-naked children ran about screaming in delight at having so many others to play with.

"The children seem happy," Begu said, stretching and looking around. "And well-fed, for wealh."

"Don't use that word here," Hild said. She straightened her seax. "They are Bryneich."

"That one called us *seas*," Dudda said, pointing with his chin. He understood British well enough, though spoke only a little.

She had heard that, and also noted the captain's scowl at the man. Oran, the captain was called; he reminded her of someone. "To our faces they'll call us Anglisc. We call them Bryneich whether they can hear us or not. No," to Glædmar when he dusted off his breeches and reached past the cantle for his spear. "Leave the shields slung and the spears stowed."

"Your men stay here," Oran said to Hild. "We will take you two to the prince." He made no move to dismount.

Coledauc's tent—or at least the big one flying the Bryneich eagle banner—was close to the river, a good walk for weary travellers. She leaned on her staff. "In Northumbre we do not herd guests like cattle. Should we mount or will you get down?"

Dudda signalled Wulf and they closed up. Leofdæg caught on fast, patted Blodfoot, kept patting her, hand near his spear. Glædmar turned casually to look behind them. Bryhtsige stood very close to Begu.

One of Oran's men hefted his spear—the same man who had called them *seas*—and Oran barked at him. After a moment he swung down. "My apologies, lady. I will walk with you to the prince."

"My thanks. Once my men have seen to our mounts I would ask that you see to their comfort. We have brought food to share, as you see." He nodded. She said, in Anglisc, "Wulf, make sure no one kills anyone until I get back. All of you, follow Wulf."

Oran asked politely after their journey as they walked. He even managed to smile to Begu and say, "Welcome," in Anglisc, and was disconcerted when she beamed at him and chattered back. Hild, glad of Begu's deliberate distraction, looked about her. The camp had an air of purpose and decision, more than a gathering and render. And more women than she expected. She began to count.

Oran ushered them into the tent and stopped, disconcerted: Coledauc was not there. Two women turned resentfully—they had been arguing, Hild thought—a third folded her arms at them, and in the shadows a fourth shushed a squalling child.

"Oh, now, aren't you a pretty thing!" Begu said, and stooped to scoop up a toddler crawling intently for the glowing brazier. She beamed at no one in particular and dandled the child on her hip, then wrinkled her face and held the child away. "Don't you need a good wipe! Ah." She tucked the child against her shoulder—where it promptly stuffed a bit of her veil in its mouth—swiped a cloth from the stool by the fire, tucked it into her girdle, and put the child back on her hip. It twisted, wanting to get back to the tasty veil. Begu bounced it a couple of times until it forgot about the veil, and gurgled, and held its arms up. "Who are you reaching for?" She smiled at the women around her. "I'll swap the little one for a cup of that mulled wine I smell."

It was like watching a pile of logs tumble and spill every which way. Hild doubted they understood a word Begu said, but despite the visitors' Anglisc clothes and Anglisc voices—and Hild's outlandish furs, great staff, and prominent seax—between one breath and the next they were no longer intruding *seas* but women like them. Or at least Begu was, and Hild, who was silent, was with child.

"Sit, sit," and "Ach, that one will be the death of us all one day!," and "Let me take her," only all at once.

Oran, with a muttered ". . . should go find Prince Coledauc," backed out of the tent and fled.

The woman with the strong face, arms now unfolded, said, slowly and clearly, looking from one to the other and waving at the now-naked stool by the brazier, "You'll be wanting to sit." She snapped her fingers at the others and pointed, said, fast, into the shadows, "Denw, shut him up, for pity's sake," and held her arms out for the child at Begu's hip.

While the other two women dragged stools over, and moved aside the hand harp that had been warming by the hearth, Begu handed the child over with a smile and a pat, along with the cloth. The woman—the chief among them—handed the child to one of the others, settled herself on one of the stools, and said—again, slowly—"You'll be wanting some food, and a cup of wine." To Hild, "You can drink wine?" She had great dark eyes, deep blue like twilight.

"I can," Hild said.

If the woman was surprised at Hild's easy British she did not show it, but when she spoke again it was much faster. "You're lucky. I couldn't, with my first."

"Just two weeks since nor could I."

"A miserable time," the woman said.

"This is better," Hild agreed, and everyone laughed, even Begu, who had caught the sense of it. She laid her staff on the floor, some kind of coarse matting. "I am Hild Yffing and this is Begu ferch Enynny, my heart friend."

"I'm Langwredd. This is my tent. No doubt you've come to see himself. He's off killing things as usual but he's been fetched and will be here as soon as he may."

The wine arrived in assorted cups. Begu got the best one—a horn thing with gold mounts—while Hild and Langwredd took matching silver. Hild sipped the warmed, spiced wine—it reminded her of Guenmon's, and she was surprised at such spices in this place—and studied her host. Gold wrapped her finely muscled neck and a blue-grey stone nestled in the hollow of her throat. Gold and tortoiseshell held back her smooth dark hair. Wide gold banded both wrists, and pinned to her breast was a gold Pictish brooch. Though some of the gold was yellowed by smith trickery, it was not a small amount that she wore. Langwredd was Coledauc's wife, then, though not the wife Hild had met nine years ago, not the mother of Cuncar the piglet prince, in whose name she had given the brooch and, in turn, received the seax. Too young. But with a mind as lively as her eye.

Coledauc entered the tent in a swirl of cloak and skitter of claws, a pair of sight hounds before him, and his bard—Hild would have known him anywhere, the man who had given her the seax she wore—at his back. He froze at the sight of the tall stranger, seax at her belt, sitting dangerously close to his wife and son.

Hild stood and moved a step away. His muscles relaxed. The dogs—young, perfectly matched; handsome beasts with leather collars woven in a combination of difficult-to-dye colours she had not seen before—stood tall, one at each hip.

"Is all well?" he asked Langwredd, not taking his eyes from Hild.

"Well enough, husband. Was the hunting good?"

He scowled.

Nine years ago he had been an inch over Hild's height, now she over-topped him by a head. He was stouter than he had been, his hair deader and darker (oak gall?), and his arms more knotted. He hooked both thumbs in his belt, not at his knife but near it, and stood square.

"Yffing," he said in British.

"Coledauc ab Morcant," she said. "The years have been kind."

He wore gold, a lot of it, more by far than she had seen nine years ago, more than would be expected of a prince of a dwindling people. And this was heavy gold, the true weight.

"The years pass," he said. "The world and our place in it changes."

She touched her seax with a knuckle. "Does an oath sworn in friend-ship change?"

"Friendship, when sworn before a war band two hundred strong?"

The bard stirred but said nothing.

"I come with a handful of men, not a war band."

He nodded, fondled the ears of the left-hand hound. "What do you offer?"

So, they were to be blunt. She nodded at Coledauc's belt with the thick yellow strap end, the gleam of gilded hilt. "What were you promised?"

The bard cleared his throat.

"Shut up, Moryn."

Moryn; she had never learnt his name. He was why Oran looked so familiar: the same round nose and pointed chin, the same peaked hairline, though Moryn's was receding into more of a spearhead than wide hunting arrow. Brothers, or cousins in whom family blood ran strong.

Coledauc fondled both hounds, tugging their ears absently. The right-hand hound did not like it but made no sign other than lowering its tail. "Let us leave your friend here with my wife, and walk."

Moryn opened his mouth as though to speak.

"We'll leave my sweet-tongued bard, too, for the women's amusement." With a pointed look at the seax at Hild's belt he said to Moryn, "Try not to give anything away this time."

"We could see to my men," Hild said. "They guard some small tokens of Edwin's esteem."

Coledauc nodded.

She said to Begu in Anglisc, "Stay here. I'm going with the prince to see to Wulf and the others. Moryn, here, will wait with you. I believe he speaks our tongue." She knew he did, and much better than Coledauc. Look at his harp, she said with her eyes. He's a bard, unarmed. "Perhaps he and Langwredd will teach you some British." *You are with other women, and children. Learn what I cannot.*

The path Coledauc took back to the horses was a roundabout one: north, along the loop of the river, and then east. A light wind blew from the west, ruffling the water and the ruff of hair along the dogs' backs. It smelled of new-dug mud and there were reeds bitten off at the tell-tale angle: water voles. The dogs ran this way and that, as though questing for scent. They seemed eager but young.

"So how was the hunting?" Hild asked.

He snorted. "We found the tracks of a doe and a buck. We should have had them. We were close enough to make them bark." She knew that roe-buck alarm. "But these, these lolloping lumps ran right at them, tongues hanging out, as though they were chasing squirrels." He spat in disgust. "They're noble-looking beasts but useless."

"Ah."

"Yes, ah. Their collars are worth more."

"They're young . . ."

He waved the conversation away. "What do you and Edwin Snakebeard want?"

He wanted bald talk, unswaddled by a bard. "You. You and the Bryneich."

"You speak for the overking?"

"I do."

"You have his token?"

"I have his gold."

"So. What will you pay?"

He already had gold, though for princes, as with kings, there was never enough. "Tell me what it is you want."

"Din Eidyn. That's what the Iding offered. And the gold."

Din Eidyn. A rocky fort reoccupied by the Manau Gododdin, clients of Ciniod—Gartnait now—king of the Picts. "The dogs are from the Iding?" He scowled, as good as a nod. "Then if the dogs are not all they appear perhaps this part of his offer also is not."

He scowled again—it seemed to be his favourite expression—and kicked a stone in the path. One of the dogs pointed its ears at the grass he had disturbed. Coledauc looked as though he wanted to kick the dog. But he said nothing, and let her think.

Nothing would move the Manau Gododdin from their rocky fastness but an army. The Iding was a landless exile in the court of Gartnait, and Gartnait would not back an Anglisc ætheling if he was likely to lose—and, against Edwin, he would lose. So the Iding was making promises he could not keep. Unless he had rich and powerful allies.

Edwin Yffing had an army, more men than the Iding—more than the Iding, Manau Gododdin, and Gartnait together. But she knew what her uncle would say: What do I care which petty princeling holds what hill? Let the miserable rag-tags fight it out and leave fewer for me to worry about.

"It's a serious thing, to take another king's fort."

"It's not another man's, it's mine! Din Eidyn belongs to the Bryneich by rights. It is our seat, time out of mind. It was Ciniod who made it possible for those Pictish puppets to cross the firth to our side, Ciniod who lent the men and the blades. Those—" He mastered himself. A covey of ducks floated serenely past the camp, and one of the hounds set up a baying. "Useless things!"

She had never been to Din Eidyn but knew it stood on a great rock by the Leith. "Is there a well?"

"There is."

Like Bebbanburg. Water made a siege a drawn-out thing. Fire might work on the palisades, depending on wind . . . But no, she had only five men; she could not take Din Eidyn, but perhaps she could offer Coledauc a reasonable chance to do so in exchange for his loyalty. Not lasting loyalty, just enough that he would tell her what she needed to know: Was Eanfrid Iding allied with Cadwallon, or Penda, or was he deluded enough to think he could do this alone? "How many men hold Din Eidyn?"

"Enough."

He did not know. She turned the picture of the north this way and that in her head. She guessed the Manau matched the Bryneich: twoscore blades. But they had the rock. Here, now, with what she had to hand, they could not take it. Unless Alt Clut and Rheged would help? No, not Rheged. Since Morcant there had been bad blood between Rhoedd's kin and Bryneich. To buy Rheged's help would cost Edwin more gold than he would be willing to part with. "Tell me of the rivers and roads to the west."

"Moryn could best do that."

"Then after we have seen to the men, and gathered Edwin's gift, we will talk to Moryn."

A different tent, smaller, plainer, full of the stuff of war—hidden under sacking, but Hild could smell it: iron and turned wood and grease. Coledauc and Oran, with Moryn. Young Cuncar—ten, if that—and his man Ronan, whose knife sheath was well-worn and well-oiled. Hild and Wulf.

Moryn ran through lists of rivers and roads in a singsong voice, their distance, measure, and repair. Twid to Lyne to the redcrest road that ran south from the north wall; then ten miles to Din Eidyn through hidden hill paths.

"How hidden?"

"Hidden. And hard."

"Could you do it?"

"I could do it!" Cuncar the piglet prince said.

Hild looked at Ronan, who gave her a flat stare: His princeling said he could do it, so he could do it.

Coledauc smiled indulgently. "She was asking the bard, brave one."

"Perhaps I could, on a good day," Moryn said. "But off the war street Lombormore would not be kind to our mounts."

If the Lombormores were too hard for tough Bryneich ponies then they were hard indeed. Three against one for sure success, two against one if mounted Angles against mounted Bryneich. But unmounted in unfamiliar hills? Wulf gave her a long, slow blink: no. An assessment that matched her own.

The other way was through eastern Lleudiniawn at the coast. When Moryn had finished she did not even have to look at Wulf.

"It can't be done," she said. "Not without an army."

"Edwin Snakebeard has an army," Coledauc said.

"The hills are hard in this weather. And in summer the army will be busy." In autumn even more so. She nodded at Wulf, who passed her a saddlebag. "But . . ." All eyes fastened on her hand, which weighed something inside the bag. She brought out a plump sack. "We offer you friendship." She put the sack in Coledauc's left hand. The weight caught him by surprise: He had to use both hands. "As a token of friendship to come we offer you this paltry sum. And we will help you block the western war street where it joins the North Esce, and at the Twid." They could not pry the Manau Gododdin from Din Eidyn but they could make sure they could not enter Bryneich territory in any numbers. And the work would set Yffing and Bryneich men on the same side.

In the falling light Hild was squatting by a fire with Wulf and Dudda and Glædmar—Bryhtsige was with Begu, and Leofdæg was walking the camp unobtrusively—when a small band driving cattle to Calchfynydd from above Aloent Water arrived in a great stink and lowing. Hild stoppered her linseed oil, tucked the wool in her purse, and sheathed her seax. Such a lot of noise for such small cattle but she knew the way of it from Yeavering: The beasts had been on the drovers' track for leagues with people they were familiar with but now were surrounded by people they did not know, and new beasts, a great heaving mass of them packed close in the corral. Noise and shoving were just how it was. Not unlike people.

Dudda was detailing the stowage of their gear when Leofdæg appeared from the small shadow thrown by their leather shelters. "News," he said, and nodded over to the newcomers. Hild stood. Dudda and Wulf followed; Glædmar stayed; it was his turn on watch.

Strangers, the chief drover, a barrel-chested man with a red beard, was saying. He leaned against the fence and gulped beer as he answered questions. Just two of them, west of Eildon Hill, moving east. No, not Bryneich, not any people he knew. On the redcrest road south of the river. On foot, and not armed, but strange. He couldn't exactly put his finger on it, but not right. Uncanny, even—

He saw Hild, standing like a giant in the half-light, furred like a beast and glittering with gold, and faltered.

Then Coledauc was there, with Moryn and Oran, trailed by Cuncar and Ronan, and the drover, at a nod from his prince, wiped his chin, stole a glance at Hild, and told it all again.

Coledauc listened. "Two? And how far from here, did you say?"

"At the rate they were moving?" He took another swig of his beer and passed the bowl reluctantly to one of his companions. "Five leagues, if you take the north path."

"We'd take the south," Oran said to Coledauc. "In case they move down Dere Street."

Hild stepped forward. "Would you take company?" She wanted to know what stranger would walk unarmed into Bryneich territory.

"It's a hill path to Dere Street," Oran said. "Not easy. And you and your mounts are not rested."

"We're well enough."

Hild looked to Coledauc, who squinted at Oran, at his son, at Hild. "I'd thought to let Cuncar lead his first party."

"Even better," she said. "Me and four men to aid the men you choose. For what better safety than numbers?"

Coledauc chewed his fingernail, then flicked his hand. "Aye. Why not? Leave your friend here with us, in safety, and why not?"

Begu as surety against Cuncar, and five strapping Anglisc to do his work for free.

"Why not," she agreed. She would leave Bryhtsige, who was more than equal to any three Bryneich and could charm the rest.

6

✧

I T RAINED OVERNIGHT and the air was damp and fresh. Nine of them set out: Hild and four of her men, and three Bryneich with Cuncar. Eight mounted blades, nine if she counted the boy, against two unarmed strangers. Coledauc wanted his piglet prince back safe and Hild would make certain of it: Begu was surety.

When Begu had understood her position, her expression had momentarily turned itself inside out, then she managed a brave smile, and Hild had to fight to not hug her until she bruised. Barely as big as Hild had been as a child, not toughened by the world, in a camp of strangers speaking an unknown tongue, knowing that if Hild did anything wrong, allowed anything to happen to Cuncar, her life could be forfeit. But not for one breath did she suggest Hild not go, not leave her. She would be fine, she said. After all, Bryhtsige was there.

Bryhtsige was there, yes, but he could not fight all the Bryneich. And his task was not just to look out for Begu but to charm Langwredd, charm her in an altogether different way than Begu already had. She was a woman very high in standing among those of Calchfynydd, once a people independent of the Bryneich. She had her own influence, as well as the ear of Coledauc.

As they rode west the valley began to narrow and climb. The morning cooled. Nine miles from Calchfynydd they crossed the river at a stony ford before hills only thinly clad in green. Even lit by the midday sun, their folds could have hidden a war band. They rode now in three pairs, with Leofdæg roaming at the rear and Innis, the Bryneich who had called them *saes*, ahead. Wulf and Dudda, riding with shields unslung but swords sheathed, then Cuncar and Ronan—silent, as always—and Finiodd and Glædmar. Those two were of a kind: bright with youth, springy as saplings, though Glædmar already knew hurt and Finiodd, she thought, did not. Hild, on Cygnet, easily the biggest mount, rode at their southern edge, away from the rush and pour of the river, listening. Three or four miles to the west, on the far side of Dere Street, stood a great hill, Eildon.

She was aware of how the others looked at her, tall on her massive dappled grey; darker dapples across her own shoulders, dense and uncanny; glittering with her beads and cross, rings and harness; belly swelling with life and topped by a slaughter seax; staff in her hand. She was everything in one body: death and life, fame and fortune, woman and wyrd. Glædmar had already told Finiodd of her slaughter of a dozen, a score, a hundred bandits in Elmet, her ride to rescue the ætheling from Long Mountain, her prophecies . . .

She had heard the stories a hundred times; she listened instead to the air. There were few birds: spring came later here in the hills; the migrants had left and the visitors not yet come. Far away the kiiii of a buzzard; closer, the chiff-chiff chiff-chaff of a siffsaff, like a tiny drummer marching before a war band. At Yeavering the siffsaff would be laying eggs. Here, it sounded like a mating call, yearning and yet to be fulfilled.

A mile from Dere Street unease settled over her. She turned in her saddle to see what had tickled her senses: nothing but hills, grey skies, the river on their right, and Eildon rearing before them. Then she saw them, the picked-over carcasses of sheep for whom the new grass had come too late. They had been there some time; their smell was faint.

Over the rise she breathed deep: nothing now but fresh grass, as sharp as newly forged iron, and the scent of Cath Llew from around her shoulders.

Just south of a lively burn they rode past a branching track that recrossed the Twid and ran on its eastern bank, parallel to Dere Street. On her own she would have considered it—the urge to edge unnoticed along the skirts of the eastern hills was strong—but Cuncar and Ronan did not signal a halt.

They splashed across the burn; on the other side the path began to climb another hill.

Her belly fluttered: The child was awake. She was getting stronger, more definite, and she seemed to like midmorning. Cygnet's neck was arched, her pace and breathing steady. If Hild reached forward and put her hand just behind where the shoulder moved smoothly, back and forth, she felt her heart thump slow and strong. Her hair and skin were dry. She was nine—about the same age as Cuncar. Perhaps she would breed her this year. Rider and mount both in kindle at the same time . . .

The greenery smell changed and she heard the metallic whistle of a harrier. Wetland somewhere near. In the distance, a roe deer barked in alarm, then another. Wolves?

She kneed Cygnet alongside Finiodd. "Are there many wolves in these hills?"

"West and north of here maybe," he said. "Where the valley widens and the trees grow thick."

"But not here?"

"Cath Llew owns these hills."

Lynx hunted at dawn and dusk—and the harrier cried again, and not in alarm. The deer's alarm was not for a cat. She whistled—she hoped Leofdæg was close enough—leaned low over Cygnet's neck, and kicked her into a gallop. Ahead, Wulf and Dudda were shortening rein, unsheathing swords. "They're close," she called as she passed Cuncar and Ronan. "Four or more."

Deer did not startle for one person, they did not startle from two different places for the same people.

"Innis?" she said to Dudda.

After a moment he shook his head. "Not since the ford."

Where was he? Perhaps he was already lost. If so it had been quick and quiet. "Four, at least. Two groups." Or more. She scented the wind blowing from the north, loamy and moist. "There'll be soft ground over the hill." A quarter of a mile? Less. "Stay this side of the slope. But listen, look."

She wheeled Cygnet.

Ronan had his reins under his thigh, shield ready to protect his lord, and a spear balanced in his hand. Cuncar was white around the eyes.

"There's soft ground over the hill," she said as Glædmar and Finiodd cantered up. "And another burn?" Ronan nodded. "Are there rushes enough to hide men for an ambush?"

"Ambush?" said Cuncar, and his pony edged closer to Ronan.

"Hiding places?" she said again.

Ronan nodded at Finiodd.

"Enough for one, maybe," Finiodd offered. "Two if they're—"

Thudding: hooves. It was Leofdæg. She could tell by the way he looked at her, alert as he galloped up, that he had nothing. She pointed ahead, said, "At least four. Find them. Report back."

"Innis?"

After a moment, she said, "If you can." If he must choose, information was vital and Innis was not. She turned to Finiodd. "Anywhere close we can guard the prince or hide him?"

"I won't hide!" Cuncar said. Hild kept her gaze on Finiodd, who shook his head. "I said, I won't—"

"Quiet now," she said. She flicked a look at Ronan: If he doesn't close his mouth, close it for him. After a moment, he nodded.

A group of eight at most, she thought, more would be too many to hide. Probably fewer. And good at staying out of sight: a handpicked band. But who had picked them, and for what? She left that as she would a shiny thing spotted by the trail on a hunt: something to ride back for after they had trapped their quarry. She had four men with arms and armour as good as, better than, any in the north; king's gesiths. Their mounts were fresh enough, and faster and bigger than anything they were likely to meet up here. The Bryneich, though; she did not know them. Ronan could fight, or he would not be guarding his lord's son, but how did he fight? And Finiodd, how steady was he?

"Leofdæg will find them," she said to Ronan. "We stay here. Look to your weapons." She unstoppered her water skin, said to Finiodd and Cuncar, "Now's the time to drink, to piss, to drink again, and eat if you can."

In their short time together, she and her men already had the habit of taking it in turns to piss while others watched their back. She would go first, watched by Wulf and Dudda, who in turn were watched by Bryhtsige, then Glædmar and Leofdæg. Bryhtsige, like her, always pissed alone, and because Leofdæg rarely seemed to need to empty his bladder, Glædmar often did, too, as he would today.

Her piss smelled different now, and was a darker yellow.

While she ate, Ronan watched Cuncar's back, and allowed Finiodd to watch his. If Ronan trusted him, perhaps young Finiodd was not so raw after all. She drank small beer, ate pork, and sucked on fruit leather. Cuncar, she saw, was not eating his bread. She squatted next to him, held out a strip of fruit leather. "Suck it slowly. Easier to eat than bread." No matter how many times she got ready to fight, her mouth went dry. A gesith saying she had heard many times: Dry tongue before wet blade. A dry mouth meant you were filling with battle readiness.

The baby fluttered again, but lazily this time. She breathed around it. Cuncar said, "Will you—will you be all right?"

"I'm not ill, I'm having a baby."

"My sister tripped a lot when she was big with hers."

"I'm not very big yet."

"Is it different, fighting when . . ." He gestured at his own belly.

She thought about it. "The weight is different. Higher up." Soon she would have to learn to change how she held her staff, so she didn't bang her belly. But not yet. "Eat some more if you can."

Leofdæg took a long time, and when he came up it was from behind them, legs scratched and Blodfoot lathered.

"Five," he said. "Two under the bridge where the war street meets the path. Less than a mile north—" Hild turned to Finiodd with raised eyebrows. He nodded: He knew the place. "Pictish," Leofdæg said. "Two at the east end of the bog over the rise. One at the west, by the street—tall, that one. For a Pict."

Anglisc in Pictish gear? West was the position she would choose, to see all her men. The tall one was in charge. "Innis?" She already knew the answer: How else had they known where to wait?

"They have his horse. It's bloody."

Cuncar paled. Hild did not have time to worry about him. Ronan would keep him quiet. "And you?"

"Blackthorn is a good screen."

She squatted, drew her seax, and cut the turf from a patch of soil. "Finiodd, draw the path. Leofdæg, show me."

When she was satisfied she understood their situation—Leofdæg had not seen bows; the Picts, or Anglisc in Pictish gear, were not dug in, just hiding—she beckoned Ronan and Cuncar closer. Ronan was the one she had to persuade. "If we go back to Calchfynydd now, they won't catch us."

Cuncar, his pride stung at being ignored, said, "Run from Picts? On our own land?"

"Not run. Leave men here to discourage them. Bring more men. Three to one are the safe odds. At almost even numbers, your father would not thank me for risking you." As soon as she saw Cuncar's face she wished to call the words back.

"You may run," he said. "But I am a Bryneich of the blood. I decide my own risk." He drew his knife: Irish work, intricate haft and poor blade. His hand only shook a little. "I am Cuncar ab Coledauc, I say we go on."

She had not reckoned on Bryneich pride, that of a dwindling people who still sang songs of the three hundred, marching to their glorious death. She looked at Ronan, but he looked back: He would not gainsay his princeling.

"You are brave, prince. But Innis is already dead, and it's five against seven—that is, against eight of us. Too, they are hidden, sheltered. We won't be. And we'd have to split our forces."

"My father gave me charge, not you."

"Your father sent nine blades against two unarmed men. Now we are eight, and they are five, and armed." If Begu were not in his father's hands, she would not even talk to him, just club him on the head and fling him over her saddle.

"Good odds. A Bryneich is worth two Picts."

"On level ground."

Wulf and Dudda did not move but she knew they were with her however she decided. Leofdæg, too, and Glædmar would follow the others. Between the five of them they could take Ronan and Finiodd safely enough, if they had to, and fling the child over his saddle, but once they carried him to safety there was still Coledauc, holding Begu. Coledauc, though, was a reasonable man, and he wanted the overking's gold. But it would be easier to persuade Ronan to be sensible, she just needed time to—

With a screech, Cuncar kicked his pony forward over the brow of the hill and then there was no time.

Eildon stood proud of the river plain like a bubble of rock, a giant's bubble, sprouting three tops, more rounded than peaked. Cloud mist shrouded the northmost top, and though Hild stood on grass she could feel the hill's bones through her soles. The mist hid the river, snaking north and east to the sea, and smelt of rain and the edge of forever.

"My father will rebuild it," Cuncar said.

Hild looked down at the river and said nothing. This child's pride had killed two of their mounts, and cost Leofdæg a broken arm and Glædmar a bang on the head that dented his helmet and addled his brains. They had tracked the last of them halfway up the slope of Eildon Hill, where Ronan skewered him with a spear, slid down from his spattered pony, and slit the man's throat. Ronan had a slice down the muscles of his shield arm that would take time to heal and Finiodd would never be carefree again. Five men in Pictish gear would not be going home.

And they still had not found the two unarmed strangers they had set out to meet.

She ached. She had skinned her knuckles on a Pictish shield and her shoulders had driven her staff through a man's skull. She ached for her men; ached for her own rashness—always think before speaking to royalty, always, even prideful children who live in the hills—and ached even for those Picts they had gutted like deer. One had cried for his mother, or a Pictish word that sounded very like mam.

What was the nature of pride that it drove them all to such deeds? Pride had sent her north believing she could protect them all. Pride drove the Iding and his alliances and perhaps led him to betray it. Pride had driven the redcrests to built their forts and roads like chains across the world. There was a fort just west of the river bend, or so Finiodd said. Perhaps the mist would thin once it rained, which would be soon, and then they could see—

"The fort," he said again. "My father will rebuild—"

She whipped around. The boy stumbled back, from her snarl, from the smell of blood, and the stink of Cath Llew. He had seen her kill those Picts, faster even than Ronan, fast as a cat. *Cath Llew.* She did not need to be a seer to predict her new name with the tribes of the north.

We need friends. And none of her men had died.

She eased the grip on her staff. "Your father will rebuild this place? Why?"

He recovered himself. "Because he is king!"

The fort was nothing but slumping rampart and broken stone, a redcrest beacon stabbed into its heart. What she could see of the hillside seemed more brown than grey. It would be cold in winter—was cold even now with the wind yowling and prowling.

He flung his checked cloak back as though men of the north—for he was a man now, blooded in battle—paid no attention to such things. Foolish child. Even after the death he had seen he still thought that once the Bryneich were back in their rightful place, all would be sunshine and soft air, and clouds would shower them with gold.

She turned, propped her blood-tipped staff against the redcrest beacon, then turned back to face him. The light, what there was of it, would cast half her face in shadow and her furs would be a dark cloud looming over him. Her shoes were stiff with blood and brains—though there was more on her hose where she had kilted up her skirts. She drew her slaughter seax with a slither. He paled, then flushed, and—as she had known he would, as a prince of any age must, because of pride—he pulled his own knife, ready to defend the honour of his people.

That Irish work—no, a Pictish copy of Irish work, she saw now. She lifted her seax so that the edge ran with light and the silver-copper inlay winked like gold in the bed of a rushing burn. She remembered the first time she had used it, the slippery blood, the shock; she had been mute for days.

"Your father gave me this when I was younger than you are now." When he had been three months old, sucking his toes by the hearth. "Do you like it?"

He had seen her slide it into a man's belly and probe for the great vein and flood the bog with red. An Anglisc scop would call it a hard and bitter blade. A Bryneich bard, though, would sing of a blade like water with an edge to cut air, and Cuncar was British to the core, head ringing with high deeds and honour, even now. So now she would use his pride and his honour.

"It was given in your name, Cuncar ab Coledauc. Your father and my uncle swore friendship between their houses, our houses, for all time."

He gripped his knife until the bone of his knuckles shone through the skin.

"Why? Because I made a prophecy. I saw it, Cuncar. Your house and mine." She had seen a knife she wanted, and smelled a feast the war bands were impatient for. They had been ready, more than ready, to eat rather than die. Most men are if they are shown a path past their pride. "I still see it. Do you?"

She flipped the seax, caught it by the blade, and laid the black hilt on her forearm.

He stared at the offered knife, shifted from foot to foot—his shoes had been new and bright, dyed the green of new leaves, a difficult colour for leather; another gift from treacherous Pictish allies?—and drew a long breath. If he had spoken aloud his thought could not have been more clear: He was Cuncar ab Coledauc, prince of the Bryneich! Frowning, because grown men frowned at weighty matters, he swapped his knife to his left hand, and took the seax.

"It's an Anglisc knife," she said. "And that day we swore an Anglisc oath. The Anglisc don't break oaths. My uncle has not broken it. I will not break it."

Has your father, Cuncar? We killed your allies today. Perhaps your allies were betraying you, and perhaps they were not, but now they are dead, and we cannot ask them.

"I am your friend, princeling. I've sworn it, by that knife. But these are dangerous times. The Bryneich will need their prince to lead them. A prince who has chosen his own path. So choose, Cuncar ab Coledauc. If you would be my friend swear with me now—we will both swear—the unbreakable vow. Here on the hill. A vow of blood." More blood.

"But this is a fairy hill!"

"It is."

Last night at Calchfynydd, by the princeling's father's hearth—only five leagues east but another country, one in which he had been a child—they had sung of the lord who slept by day in the hollow hill, his uncanny warriors about him; the music that seeped in the dark from the earth; music that might twine about your ankles and steal your heart. Now he was faced with this giant who filled the air with the shadow and scent of Cath Llew and wanted him to swear by blood, while beneath him fairies slept. So much death so close thinned the veil between the otherworld and this. Who knew what might step through?

"Anglisc oaths are proof against the magic of ælfe." She used the Anglisc word deliberately. It stood plain as a pebble among the tumble and splash of British. "You are safe with me. Lend me your knife, Cuncar."

He started to hand it to her blade first, caught himself, and reversed it clumsily.

He had done his best to sharpen it but it was poor metal, and after stabbing the belt buckle of a Pict it was jagged and uneven. Without giving him time to consider, she took it and sliced along the side of her hand, hard enough to be sure. A ragged tear filled with blood. "Your turn." The air thickened with the promise of rain. "Now, Cuncar, before blood drips through this rock and onto the face of the fair lord, and he stirs."

The thought of a fairy waking to the taste of blood widened his eyes. He hacked wildly and it was only luck he opened a two-inch gash on his palm instead of taking his hand off. Hild took his wrist before the gash filled—he looked as though he might faint if he saw his own blood—and pressed the two wounds together. Hers was not deep, but it stung.

In Anglisc, she said, "I, Hild of the Yffings—" She repeated it, this time with his name, for him to say after her.

"—vow on my blood and my bone—"

The Anglisc words fell awkward and sharp from his mouth.

"—that your blood will be my blood—your bone my bone—we will be as one—we are kin."

Cousins of the knife. Cuncar looked very young, an otter kit torn from the teat and flung from the den to lie dazed under a pitiless sky. But he was a prince of the Bryneich, one his people would one day follow, and the Yffings needed friends.

At the foot of the steep slope, still high above the smaller hills but below the mist, the men waited at the head of the burn with their own mounts and three extra: Innis's, now draped with Innis, rolled in saddle cloth, and two Pictish ponies, loaded with the spoils. Wulf was facing their direction, Ronan the other, one hand on the bridle of his pony. He had suffered her to daub his wound with bee glue before she climbed the summit with Cuncar, and by the way he favoured it now it was stiffening.

Dudda and Finiodd leapt to their feet, Dudda stuffing something in his tunic pocket. Knucklebones, Hild guessed. She hoped he had not won too much. She was glad of it, though; Finiodd needed something to think about that was not death. Glædmar was pale, and stood slowly, but he was not spewing and he did not sway; he would be all right to ride. Leofdæg was also pale, his arm splinted; but it was his mount Hild watched. Blodfoot was exhausted. They could not afford to lose her; they had already lost Dudda's mount, and a gesith needed a well-trained horse.

At the sight of her and Cuncar's matching wounds both Wulf and Dudda kept their faces smooth—though Wulf always looked like that—as did Ronan. Finiodd looked puzzled and opened his mouth but shut it again at a hard stare from Ronan. Glædmar and Leofdæg were too taken with their own hurts to notice.

She nodded at them and pulled her wound roll from Cygnet's saddlebag. Her knife was clean but Cuncar's own knife had been filthy—she would talk to him about that later—so she smeared a little bee glue on both cloth strips. Cousins of the knife must be treated the same. At least in the beginning. She wrapped Cuncar's hand quickly and cleanly, then held her hand steady for Cuncar to do the same for her. Her belly was so empty the walls felt stuck together, but she held still as the first rain drifted over them, did not move as he tied an inexpert knot. She would redo it later, but the first binding was tradition.

The ponies were small enough that the Bryneich could vault into their saddles. On the way all four had delighted in showing off before the Anglisc but now the three remaining, even Cuncar, waited quietly as the Anglisc led their mounts to a cairn.

She swung into the saddle, and she was tired enough that for the first time she felt the extra weight of her belly.

The path down the north slope to the eastward track was short but steep enough they had to be careful of the horses. No one spoke. No one looked at Innis's burdened pony. The rain began in earnest. Hild raised her hood. From beneath its soft overhang the rain sounded personal, private. Her rain. Not unlike the rain the day they buried Bassus's little son and the other children by Ad Gefrin, the mothers wrapped in their private grief.

At the eastward track they all relaxed a little except Dudda, whose turn it was to ride first, on his Pictish pony, sword loose, his dead horse's salvaged harness behind what passed for a saddle. Luckily he was not a heavy man.

It was not far to the redcrest road that would take them to Dere Street and the fort, then north across the river and along a good hill path to Calchfynydd. They would stop for the night halfway, in a place Ronan had told them of on their outward ride: a burn, woods curving along a sheer dropoff to the south, and a bare hill to the north, with good lines of sight in all directions—they still were on the lookout for those strangers—and there they would make a bier to carry Innis the rest of the way home. For now the living needed warmth and rest.

The track approached the ruin of the redcrest fort. Hild kneed Cygnet alongside Cuncar's pony. The wet brought out the smell of blood and her furs, and the pony snorted and rolled his eyes. Wolf, lynx, bear. She doubted this princeling's mount had met any of them, but he knew their smell. They all did. Cuncar patted his neck, then hissed and shook his hand.

"It'll make a fine scar," she said.

He brightened. "It will, won't it?"

She showed him the mark on the back of her wrist. "I got this shearing a wether that kicked at the wrong time."

"Did you kill it?"

"As my mother might say, sheep don't grow on trees." Breguswith would no more say such a thing than fly. "But I half strangled it to keep it still after that."

"I have a scar on my foot, where I fell off my da's pony when I was little—"

She swept the line of the horizon, back and forth, back and forth, and did not point out that to some he was still little, for now he had been in a fight and among the Bryneich would be reckoned a man.

"—and fell onto my father's spear, which I'd borrowed." He grinned and his teeth seemed huge. Hild thought he might grow tall for a British prince, with one of those wide faces that spoke of stupidity or violence depending on the path. "My mam smacked me hard enough that I stopped crying, but my da was proud, I could tell. He—"

Ronan shortened his rein. Wulf moved up. In the ruined fort, two men moved among the stones. They were on foot, unarmed, but something about the way they moved . . .

"Wulf," she said, and he dropped his shield to his arm and waited for her. Together they turned from the track.

The two men saw them coming and waited on one side of the ditch. Hild slowed Cygnet to a walk and pushed her hood back. The rain was easing. The only trees were small things rooted on ruined rock whose leaves were still new and soft enough to whisper rather than hiss. Between the thunk of each of Cygnet's hooves on the turf she felt the slight tremble of the river's power. No other sounds but birds intent on dragging worms from the grass.

The two men wore long cloaks and hoods. Both carefully, deliberately folded their hands before them: visible and empty.

Wulf kept to her left, ready to thrust his shield between her and harm.

"Greetings," she called, in British, across the ditch. She smelled smoke.

They were clean-shaven, with dark eyebrows and steady eyes. One older than the other, though not by much. In their prime, but not fighters. They had a similar look to them, but not kin.

"I am Hild, a visitor to these hills." Their cloaks were woven in a style she did not know. Not Pictish. "Like yourselves."

"Indeed," said the elder, and from that word, even before he pushed back his hood, Hild knew he was Irish and a priest, but nothing like Fursey. More like Paulinus: used to weighing consequence. She watched him do so now, taking in her clothes and horse, Wulf, the men coming behind her. "I am Suibne moccu Fir Thrí." Suibne, kin of the men of Thrí. A man of tradition and importance, at least among the Thrí, whoever they were. "This is Aidan mac Ailbe." Aidan son of Ailbe, who did not speak for himself but did not act like a servant.

A rush of hooves: the boy pushing to her side. "I'm Cuncar ab Coledauc." He had his hand on his knife. "You are on Bryneich land and we have just killed other trespassers."

Aidan, the younger one, stirred briefly at the tone, then, like Suibne, he bowed. If Suibne took fear or offence at Cuncar's words, he made no sign. "We mean no trespass, Cuncar ab Coledauc." His voice was unruffled in the way of superior men who knew that their superiority would soon be evident.

"Prince Cuncar," the boy said sharply. Perhaps he heard it, too: the patience offered to an ant because it pleased the giant to stay his hand.

Another bow. "We are new to this place, prince. Perhaps we could make amends by offering you shelter at our fire."

Hild flicked her gaze at Wulf, who nodded. He would ride with Dudda around the bounds of the ruined fort, to be sure.

It was a well-chosen corner, across the river from a steep rise that would protect them from north wind, and against the remains of a wall that would shield them from the east or south. Roomy for two, but small for five, for Ronan would not leave his prince's side; he did not know these men.

They ate a cold meal of hard bread, strips of dried meat, and a fragrant cheese the priests had brought. Hild did not recognise the taste but Begu would have loved it. Cuncar, a boy who had just taken a blood oath atop a fairy hill, soon forgot the strangers' arrogance.

She chewed a piece of fruit leather—she was hungry all the time—as the boy entertained the priests with a long tale of a glorious hunt over hill and heath: chasing a stag, a king among stags, a stag from the dawning of the world! From the way he spoke—he called neither Father—he was not much used to priests. And she could tell by the way the priests nodded in the wrong places that they had never hunted deer in their lives. Not like Fursey, who had grown up a prince, or Coifi, for Anglisc godmouths began their god training only when they came of age and could choose to make their god vows or to receive instead girdle or weapons. These men had been taken earlier, as children. Like the Crow. She doubted either had ever hunted, or trained with a blade. If they rode it would not be well.

She did not like Suibne, did not like his smoothness and clear belief that he was worth all of them put together. That, too, was like the Crow, who believed he had the power of something vast behind him, not just his god but an earthly power. And Suibne had that same look of someone with their vision fixed on a far horizon, set for high office. But where? Irish, yet not Irish. And Aidan. Not of the same aristocratic lineage, by the name, and clearly not schooled to the same height or with the same care as Suibne, but just as arrogant as Fursey, probably just as clever, though not as sure as Suibne, or not in the same way, and she did not dislike him.

She tore off another piece of fruit leather and sucked it to make it last.

Their names were Irish, and their voices, but she had seen something in the way they moved, the way Suibne spoke and Aidan nodded . . . Ah. Paulinus and Stephanus in Derventio and York, poking about the ruined wings of the principia. These Irish-not-Irish were surveying the fort: quartering the ground, noting the quality of the stone, the aspect of the fortifications, the roads and river. For what, and whom? The Picts—or four Picts and one Anglisc in Pictish gear with a hammer on a thong around his neck—could no longer answer questions. These men could.

Cuncar was waving his hands about, approaching the kill, always the longest part of any hunting story. She stepped away from the fire to check on the others: they had a fire, too, and were drinking mead. Leofdæg told her Blodfoot was resting and eating. He slurred a little; for once she did not begrudge it. Wulf would watch him. Glædmar was asleep, but it seemed a good sleep, and his face by the fire was pink. She took Finiodd and Dudda the mead skin, so they could drink while they kept guard and vigil over Innis, now laid flat on the turf along a wall, mostly sheltered under what remained of eaves.

Cuncar was finishing as she returned. Ronan fed another branch into the fire, and Aidan complimented the prince on a fine hunt.

"You didn't say where the hunt was," Suibne said. "Near here?"

"In the hills east of here," Cuncar said. Hild imagined tracking through the heather and gorse, the flash of white rump at dusk. But if you saw that heart-shaped flash, you were too late and would never catch the doe. "They don't come down to the river. Because of wolves."

"Wolves?" Aidan said. "Are we in danger here tonight?" His British was passable.

"Wolves hunt by day," Cuncar said, and gave Hild a sidelong look. Where might these men be from that they didn't know about wolves?

"Cath Llew hunts with the morning and evening star. We don't go into the hills at twilight when she is hunting to feed her young."

The branch caught with a crackle and stink—elder. She leant forward and selected a hazel twig from the pile. She began to strip it. "You didn't say where you're from," she said.

"No," Suibne agreed. For a moment their wills crossed, like two staffs, testing.

She leaned back, picking her teeth, letting him see the dried gore on her hose, the wrapping on her hand that matched that on Cuncar's, prince of the Bryneich, and giving him time to remember they were on Bryneich land.

"We are from Hii."

She didn't know where that was, but she knew where there were few wolves. "An island."

Aidan nodded. Suibne sighed. "To the north and west. And you?"

There were two ways to persuade another to give more information than they were given: say a lot about nothing important, or choose things that don't match. Her name, her men, and her mount were Anglisc, she wore Anglisc clothes, Anglisc gold, an Anglisc seax. But her cross was Centisc work and her beads Roman, her British was faultless and she was cousin of the knife to a prince of the Bryneich. "I am from Elmet."

Suibne guarded his face well; Aidan, though, was younger and less practised.

So was Cuncar. "Where in the north and west? Who rules your island of Hii?"

"It is a holy place, prince."

"Yes, but who is its king? Who do you kneel to?"

"God," Suibne said.

Hild tossed her twig in the fire, letting her cross swing and glint in the light. All priests knelt to bishops, bishops to overbishops, and overbishops to kings. "Your bishop—"

There was no warning. This flutter was a kick and it took her breath away. She hissed. The two priests froze. Then the child kicked again. Oh, she was fierce tonight—and early. Perhaps she'd grow up like Eanflæd: prone to tantrums before falling asleep.

The priests were staring at her as though she were possessed. Clearly, on Hii they did not have much experience of childbirth.

Cuncar handed her his cup of small beer. "My sister told me it's like having someone wring your insides like washing but it passes, like a coughing fit." She sipped. He took the cup back when she was done.

"So," she said, when her breathing had steadied. "Your bishop."

Suibne was looking at her as though she were a pig rooting on his altar.

"Your bishop," she said again, this time in the Irish she had learnt from Fursey, Irish a prince might speak.

"Abbot," Aidan said, stung by her tone. "The isle is under the rule of Abbot Ségéne mac Fiachnaí, of the Cenél Conaill. He bows to no man."

She was not sure what an abbot was or whether these priests of Hii even had a bishop. But she knew of the Cenél Conaill. Irish allies of Domnall Brecc of the Dál Riata. Domnall Brecc, shield brother of Oswald Iding, and betrothed of Æbbe Iding. And Oswiu, the youngest brother, had married Fína, the daughter of an Irish king.

The party riding back to Calchfynydd was not the same as the one that rode out. They were a band now; they had ridden shoulder to shoulder, been marked by the same enemy, and had lost one of their own.

Innis was on a bier cut from birch and alder, pulled by his own mount. The spoils, such as they were, were heaped on the saddle before Suibne: two Pictish cloaks—plain two-up, two-down plaid—draped over a bundle of stained tunics, poor jewellery but for one piece she had kept, and three swords barely worth their scabbards. The priest had nearly objected to sharing his mount with dead men's goods, but Hild had smiled at his hesitation and said that of course he could walk if he preferred, and he turned his complaint into a remark about the sunshine as he mounted. He did not think to offer to carry Aidan's bundle.

The others were about to mount when Aidan, his bundle still between his feet, said, "Will I bless him?"

Ronan put his hand on his sword hilt. They did not know this strange priest.

"No," said Cuncar. Definitely not much used to priests.

Aidan nodded. "And how far is it we travel?"

"Four leagues." Ronan did not let go of his sword.

"Not far," Cuncar said. "But once across Leder Water the path is steep. It'll be dark when we get back. But don't worry, priest. We'll keep you safe. All you have to do is keep up."

Again, he nodded, then slung his bundle to his shoulders, the others mounted, and they set off.

The redcrest bridge across the Twid was still sturdy, but when they came to the Leder Water they found the ford deep enough that the bier would have to be carried. The four uninjured—Hild, Wulf, Dudda, and Finiodd—dismounted and waded through the stream with the weight on their shoulders. As they reharnessed the bier and mounted, it began to rain.

The northern path to Calchfynydd was steep, but they were all on horseback except Aidan, and he, like Morud, was used to walking. Wulf and Dudda rode ahead, and Suibne edged his mount alongside Cuncar—alongside the prince, in what he no doubt felt to be his proper place. Gladmær seemed well, though his helmet was uncomfortable enough that he hung it on his saddle horn; he was no longer shy about his ruined ear. Leofdæg was surly, though given the pain of his arm and the likely mead headache, Hild was unsurprised. Ronan and Finiodd took it in turns to ride last.

After a while Hild dismounted and walked with Aidan, matching the thunk of her staff to his pace. He kept his distance from Cygnet and where the path narrowed to single file she let him walk in front and stayed between him and the mare.

"Will you tell me something," he said in Irish.

"I might."

"Why is the dead man trussed like a roasting fowl on that bier? It is not . . . seemly."

Hild found it difficult to believe a man could be so ignorant. "The man's name is Innis, his loved ones will be waiting, and it is four leagues we travel." He seemed none the wiser. "He must be wrapped tight so his arms do not slide free and hang down or his face turn sideways." He seemed puzzled. Had the man never seen a body? "When a man is dead, his blood pools after a time and his skin turns black. Would you have Innis's mother or his little ones see their man black-faced and black-handed to haunt their dreams?"

He shook his head.

"You'll see, too, we tore a dead man's cloak to make padded strips to hold his legs together and straight. Bodies, do you see, stiffen after a time." And after a while they fell loose again, but by then they were also smelling and swelling and she hoped to be back long before that. "At Hii, who cares for fallen brethren?"

"The priests say the blessings before burial—"

"But who washes them, and tidies them?"

"I suppose . . . I should think it is the laywomen who live beyond the walls, the servants of the monastery."

He supposed. "And are they the mothers and wives and sisters of the fallen?"

"I—" He frowned. "I don't know."

She tried to imagine her body being handled in death by a stranger. "I would want my body taken care of by those who knew and loved me."

"It is women's work."

"So?"

"We have no women religious at Hii."

She stared at him and he stared fixedly at Innis's pony with its drooping head, dragging the bier. Even talking about women seemed to offend him.

"You've seen Pictish work before?" she said.

"I might have, so."

She nodded at the cloak. "Do you know these colours?"

"I do not."

"Do you know, though, where these men come from or who might have sent them?"

"Know? I do not." The path grew steep. There was no breath for talking for a while. Hild held out her hand for his pack. Cygnet would barely notice the weight. She strapped it to her saddle so it would not bump, next to the knife and neck-charm she had taken from the Anglisc dressed as a Pict.

"If you do not know might you venture a guess?"

"The chasing on that hilt." He nodded at the knife. "I might have seen something like. At Inchtuthil."

"Will you tell me of Inchtuthil, now?"

"Will you answer me in turn a question?"

"I might."

"How did you learn to speak the Irish?"

"From a priest I knew." She wiped the rain mist from her face with the sleeve of her staff hand. "His name was Fursey. He did not baptise me. But he taught me a vast great deal. He lives now with my sister, far south of here."

"He was from Connacht. I hear it in your voice."

"He said he was the son of Fintan the son of Finlog, and of Gelges, daughter of Aed-Fin, the king."

"So?" He smiled, a quick splintering like the crack of a bough: The sound of that lineage was what had set Father Suibne on his heels . . .

They walked. He wore sandals, and Hild wondered how he stood his feet being cold and wet all the time. Fursey always hated sandals. "He also said he was baptised by Saint Brendan himself."

"Did he now?"

Her turn to smile. "I didn't believe him, either."

"Quite so. Now then. Inchtuthil is a place I've only been the once. It is the sometime home of Pictish kings."

Cygnet huffed and tossed her head at the jerk on her bridle. Hild patted her neck in apology. The Pictish court, home-in-exile of Eanfrid Iding; that could explain the hammer charm she had found on the tall non-Pict: old and once-fine but now carefully mended Bernician work. And Coledauc had not known they were coming. Her mind rushed.

The path ran downhill, and up again, and below them the Twid looped around a spur of land. They paused to rest the horses. Hild looked down at the bright colours: flowers along the riverbank, a steep bluff. Bright red burnet, blood-red. Two days ago she had ached for red, anything but green and yellow and white, but now she had seen enough red for a year. The bluff was a lovely spot: safe, defendable, easy to put a wall across the narrow neck.

"Almost like an island," Aidan said. "A good place for a church."

South was a good ford, and it would be easy to beat a path west to Dere Street, which led to the heart of the isle. "Is that why you're here?"

His face, which had broken open earlier, closed. "That is for Coledauc to know."

"He will tell me," she said.

"But he will know first."

"He didn't know you were coming."

"That is true," he said after a moment. "But he will be glad."

"Eventually?"

Again the quick smile, as good as a nod.

The path wound now along the north shore of a small lake. Shelducks honked their odd purring honk.

"Are there shelducks on Hii?" She used the ducks' British name; she did not know the Irish.

"Shelducks?"

She stayed with British, the language of wild things. "The big ones, there, with the red beaks."

"And with the band, here?" He pointed at his chest. "The one the colour of your hair? They're not geese?"

"Ducks. Shelducks. Do you find them on Hii?"

"I think so. Yes." So much less sure in British.

"What do they eat there?"

"Fish?"

Hild smiled. A duck eating fish!

He switched to Irish. "Well, and why would they not?" In Irish he was both more sure and less cross. "Are they not creatures of the sea?"

A duck was more a creature of shallow water and its shores, the edge where water met land. "I have seen them eat water snails, so perhaps on the seashore they eat other creatures with shells." Their beaks would be strong enough.

"Shellfish are fish, so. Of a kind."

"Of a kind." She switched back to British. "What other birds are there on Hii?"

She coaxed him to tell her of puffins and terns, sea eagles and gannets. Land birds, too: peregrines and goldfinch, skylarks and corncrake. His British wasn't quite good enough to describe the corncrake, so he did their call, that querulous creak, which reminded her of the priest Hrothmar, which made her laugh, though she was quick to say, in Irish, that she was laughing not at him but near him. As he talked she began to form an idea of the size and shape of the island, where and how it might lie on the routes of birds, and men—and he got used to answering her questions.

"And the Idings, what are they like? As different from each other as birds?"

"Very different. Oswald, he is a great owl. Quiet. Wise. But not meek. Oswiu, though. Ach, he is a puppy, barking and running and making messes. Just as a puppy might chew a stool, or knock it down, or hump it, he will take a thing and not do with it what he should. Not like Oswald, who is continent and thoughtful."

"And Oswiu's twin?"

"Æbbe? She is a woman."

"Yes. But you've seen her? What is she like?"

"Something between her brothers? She can read, I am told."

"Can her brothers?"

"Of course they can read! They lived on Hii, founded by the wise Colm

Cille, not some stinking croft! Oswald has a beautiful hand. Beautiful. And a beautiful mind, clear and deep. Oswiu, though, he is . . . turbulent."

"But Æbbe?"

He shrugged: She was a woman.

As they moved down into the Twid valley and closer to Calchfynydd, she felt her aches again, the extra weight of her belly. She was tired and hungry and wished this priest would ride while they talked. "Tell me more of Oswald."

"Oswald Lamnguin is a scholar who reads with the ease of a priest." And killed with the ease of a hero; she knew the songs of him and his brother. "He loves the book, he loves the word. He could have been abbot. But he was born a prince. That is his curse." She wondered if Oswald saw it that way. Oswald Brightblade, or perhaps Whiteblade, an ætheling-in-exile who aimed to be king. And Aidan was his man.

After the clean scent of the hills the reek of even a way camp like Calchfynydd was clear from half a mile. Ronan sent Finiodd ahead with the news and the others straightened the cloak on Innis's bier, rearranged the bundle on Suibne's mount to look larger, and blinked themselves awake. Cuncar— though now accounted a man of Bryneich, still only perhaps ten—scrubbed his face with his unwrapped hand and sat up straight.

Hild offered him a heel of bread and a sip of mead. "You'll need it, cousin," she said. "They will want you to tell the story. You are their prince."

Though it was not yet full dark by the time they came to the cattle enclosure, the night blazed with torches: the Bryneich had come to honour the fallen and to look at the strangers. Among them were Begu and Bryhtsige, and Hild saw immediately how it was between them.

In the bright morning she and Begu walked half a mile upstream, until they found a spot where they could bathe in privacy but no one could listen from hiding.

The clouds were small and the wind blew in fitful starts from north and east. The sun was out more often than not. Begu hummed as she stripped off her clothes and draped them over a rock. Hild, silent, put her jewels in her purse, then built a cairn of boots, cape, clothes, and purse, seax on top and staff propped to the side. Begu shouted at the cold as she ducked beneath the water. Hild sank slowly, counted to three, and rose.

"I don't know why you're cross with me," Begu said.

"You know why," Hild said, and after two days of nothing but British and Irish, the Anglisc felt like chewed wood. She wanted to spit the words out in an ugly heap, be rid of them.

"But it's not my fault Langwredd wasn't interested in Bryhtsige. He tried."

"Not hard enough. It's only been two days." The riverbed was stony here. She moved a little farther out, up to her waist.

"Two days is enough to know if there's interest. She had none. He sang with her—she plays the harp, almost as well as the bard—and learnt her songs. Even taught her one. But she had no interest in him."

"But you did."

"How many handsome men are there around here who can't get me with child? Besides, he speaks Anglisc. And it was nice to have someone who would listen."

"Moryn speaks Anglisc."

"He's not one of us. And it wasn't bard song I wanted." Begu wrung out her hair. She looked different with it down, quieter, more like a woman. *Understand me*, she was saying: *I was alone, left alone by you and lapped about by strangers.*

But she had had a fire, the comfort of women. She had not had the weight of the world on her shoulders and men's lives under her knife. "We needed him to do this. We needed Langwredd on our side. I needed it."

"And I need to marry Uinniau. I need someone to marry Rhianmelldt and free him! I want, oh, I want . . ." She slung her wet hair behind her. One flick of wind was all it took for a tendril to blow astray. "But this is what I could have, so I took it. I'm sorry, gemæcce. I wanted him and he wanted me, and you weren't here. It happened."

Hild nodded, not sure why she was so . . . She was not even sure what. It was done. Her hand ached. She unwrapped it. The edges of the cut were red, which was only to be expected. She waded to the bank, dropped the curl of cloth by a clump of buttercups, and waded farther upstream. Better. Softer under her feet.

Close to the bank, something splashed. A fish? The thought of the taut muscle made Hild hungry. Hungry for succulent salmon, yes, but also for lying spread in summer sun, for mead, the softness of another's skin against hers. The water coursed over her thighs. She wanted to drink the river, hurl herself at the sky. She wanted Cian: the sound of his voice, the warmth of his breath, the touch of his hands. The weight of him. She imagined Begu and Bryhtsige. The weight of someone who laughed, who did not burst and run red under her hands.

"Bryhtsige was never going to suit Langwredd," Begu said. "You, now. You might be more to her taste."

Three days later Coledauc walked with Hild around the cattle pen, gesturing with his toothpick at a particularly finely muscled bullock. "Your uncle will be pleased, I think." There were a goodly number of the hairy little cattle, and all in reasonable health for their journey tomorrow.

"Only if you don't wear all your gold."

Coledauc grinned. Greed was the way of kings and princes; the more they saw, the more they wanted. Tribute was a game he understood well. For all that losing the game could be deadly it was still a game. And he was winning. Yes, he had just lost a man, a good man, and learnt of a faithless ally whose promises were not worth the breath they were carried on. But he had good yellow gold from the Anglisc king, a renewal of a prophecy, a blood friendship for his son with this strange creature, this glittering giant, dealer of death who burgeoned with life. Added to that, he was two ponies richer and his wife had been unaccountably cheerful these last three days. Oh, yes. He was winning.

"I've a mind to give those priests what they want." The older one, Suibne, had made a long speech last night to a meeting of the high men and women of the Bryneich, a meeting to which Hild, as representative of the overking, had been invited. He had talked of friendship and the grace of God, the blessings of the church, and had asked leave for him and his companion to wander Bryneich land and talk to its people about suitable sites for a church—future foundations that would spread light and prayer and kindness far and wide. They would report back to their abbot, a wise and godly man with nothing in his heart but charity.

"To give them what they say they want? Or what they really want?"

"Does it matter?"

For Coledauc? No. For herself, she was not yet sure. What Suibne said he and his abbot wanted was to move unmolested into Bryneich territory to live and preach the word of their god. The abbot, Aidan told her, must name his heir soon. And who better than the man who had brought God to the godless? That was what they said they wanted.

But Aidan served Oswald Brightblade, and what Oswald wanted was a smoothing of his path to the heart of Northumbre: for important men to know his name and think well of him when the time came. What Hild did not yet know was when that would be, and what he might give in exchange.

"My wee prince doesn't like Suibne, and would say no. Langwredd likes the other one of the priests and would say yes for his sake. Moryn is a bard and can say yes or no, and say it at length, depending which way the wind blows."

"And Oran?"

"Oran is my captain. He ventures no opinion. Ronan, though. He does not like them."

Ronan's thoughts were easy to read: The search for the two who had wandered onto Bryneich land without leave had cost the life of one of his men. He would never like them. "And you, do you like them?"

"Like is neither here nor there." He flicked his bone splinter into the corral. "I suffer the wandering priests but they are fewer than they were; they have no bishops and speak for no king; we are none the worse for it." He had no bishops, for a king chose the bishops who chose the priests, and he was not a king. "I would have your thoughts."

Her thoughts as Cath Llew, blade-cousin of his son, maker and keeper of prophecy? Or her thoughts as the mouth of his once-again ally and lord, Edwin Overking, the man who chose priests? And if she spoke as herself, what might she say?

She thought about it from Coledauc's vantage. Edwin's chief priest, the Bishop Paulinus, had no great love of British priests. He would not like the Irish kind any better, even if they did shave their crown rather than foreheads. They were all rivals—all spies, he would say. But she doubted Paulinus or his priests would venture farther north and west than Yeavering. The Crow was not young, and he wanted to convert the Anglisc. It was the Anglisc his pope was interested in, the Anglisc who mattered for his pallium. Coledauc would not suffer and might profit if his Hii priests stayed outside the Crow's knowledge. "For now don't let the priests wander south of the Twid or east of the Til and there will be no clash of priests." And now Aidan and his lord, Oswald Brightblade, would owe her.

The cattle and their drovers left in a cloud of filth and noise. Only a portion of the Bryneich would follow with their prince to Yeavering; most, having brought the cattle for tribute and goods for trade, having gossiped and mingled, would now return to their holdings, where there would be many new children born after the turn of the year.

Aidan stood with his bundle between his feet and watched Suibne bid farewell to their hosts. "I will remember and speak well of you, Hild Yffing."

Hild nodded. "Remember to stay north of here, and not too far east."

"I shall. And should you ever have need to send a message, sign it . . . Sign it with a cat."

Sign it. Written messages were as natural as breathing to this priest and Oswald Brightblade. She tried to imagine it: an ætheling who was a scholar. Book and blade. Like her.

7

✦

THE *HOMETUN* was a barrel of a boat, nothing like the *Curlew*. Hild and her Fiercesomes wallowed along the coast from Tinamutha, heaving through every sunlit wave. But by the middle of the afternoon the Bay of the Beacon was in sight.

It was as she remembered. The sky was the blue of twice-dyed linen, the sea the same grey-blue as the flint arrowhead she kept at her belt—the one she had found at Yeavering just a week ago—knapped to whitecaps by the wind. Her belly was now too big to lean against, so she propped her hip against the gunwale and watched the familiar haven draw closer.

She rubbed at the scar on her hand. Edwin had been pleased about Cuncar—though not enough to let her have the *Curlew*. "Do you know how much a boat like that costs?" But pleased. She was not. She had shared blood and an oath and now this scar would always remind her. There was now a wide-faced, big-toothed boy who could call her kin. Perhaps she should have found better last words to him than, "Make sure Ronan gets the dressing on his arm checked."

Ronan had been lucky, the blade had not parted any sinews. But he was one of those men who liked to admit no feeling, no weakness. Being weak drew predators, and Ronan wanted to keep his princely charge safe. And he was too proud to complain. So it was up to Cuncar, his lord, to look after him. Someone had to tell him that, just as Guenmon had said to her of Gwladus: *That lass is yours. Protect her.*

She wiped spume from her cheek and swayed with the boat. So many people to protect now. Not just those of Elmet, her household, not just her family and Begu, not just the child growing inside her, but now all those others. The Fiercesomes: Leofdæg, whose arm had been broken in her service; Gladmær, whose head still sometimes rang with strange noises—she could tell by the way he would suddenly blink and look up that he'd heard things that weren't there, but this would pass—though he, too, was too proud to say anything; Dudda, for whom she had bought a new horse in Arbeia, a gelding as mean as Blodfoot, but taller; Wulf, whose signs she understood now; and Bryhtsige. They were hers to lead until they reached Elmet and she sent them back to the king in Derventio.

From behind, the smug rattle of knucklebones in a cup followed by a shout of triumph from Dudda and a groan from Gladmær. It was Wulf, this time, taking their gold. They were drinking, but only beer; even Leofdæg was mostly sober. Bryhtsige was barely paying attention. He was instead listening to Begu with a look on his face Hild recognised: bemused by the endless eeling of words, but fond.

After they got back to Caer Loid those two might not see each other again but she did not worry for Begu's feelings. Her gemæcce could pick people up and put them down again as a child does, without a thought, though any toy she picked up was put down undamaged, and happy to have been played with. How did she do that? Did Langwredd feel happy to have been played with? She had been happy at the time, as had Hild. But Langwredd had her place with Coledauc, just as at Caer Loid Uinniau would be waiting for Begu, and Cian for her. But first there was Onnen to—

The boat smashed through an errant wave and fell at a steep angle on the other side. Hild held on to the gunwale.

"I'll be glad to see the back of this boat," Begu said, standing easily on the plunging deck. "Are you nervous?"

About Onnen. Hild had sent messages by every priest, bard, and scop they met on their travels. News would have travelled with the king—Cian would know she and Begu were safe, and that they were coming home by way of the Bay of the Beacon—but most news reached Mulstanton by boat, and the weather had been favourable enough that Edwin's boats would not have had to seek port between Tinamutha and Brough. Onnen would not know she was coming.

"It's been a long time. Don't worry. I think she's over it. Mostly. Fa said your mother mellowed her. About you and Cian, anyway."

It was hard to imagine her mother spending a winter in Mulstanton, on the edge of things, and even harder to believe she could mellow anyone. But Breguswith and Onnen had been gemæcce in all but name.

Men began reefing the sail. The boat steered for the river mouth between the cliffs, then was between them, coasting in on the tide. On the east cliff it looked as though the redcrest signal beacon had lost a few more stones. "Do you remember the first time I tasted the spring water up there?" She still remembered the shock of it. "It was so—"

"Cold, yes. Winty had hurt herself on the thorns. And Cædmon was cross when you nearly panicked the other cows. I remember, of course I remember. But it's different now. Well, a bit different. A lot different for you."

Hild rubbed her hand again, realised what she was doing, and put her hand on her belly instead. Begu shook her head but left it unsaid: Onnen would not be happy.

The boat glided to the floating dock.

She did not wait for Cygnet, did not wait for her men, but as soon as the bow rope was thrown she leapt for the dock.

"Was there word of our coming?" she asked the man and boy hauling on the cable.

They gaped at her—her height, her furs, the seax on her swelling belly—then the man recovered himself. "No, lass. Lady." He shook his head. "They'll not be expecting anything like you."

She nodded absently. On a day like this, Mulstan was most probably at the summer stacks: the unwalled roof that covered the store of goods at the south end of the dock that, from spring to autumn, grew and shrank with the carriers going north or south up the coast, each time paying a little something into the coffers, a little for Mulstan, a little for the king: a pig of lead, a tun of honey, a pretty ring, a bolt of cloth. But Mulstan was for Begu to look to; her business was with Onnen. She took the path south and east to the hall.

A hall on a sunny day was a drowsy place, cool and shadowed, smelling of old smoke. The woman sweeping the floor started when Hild strode through the door. Hild thought she knew her but could not recall her name. "The lady Onnen?"

The woman stared. Hild shifted her hand from the hilt of her seax to her belt, leaned her staff against her shoulder unthreateningly, and smiled. The woman blinked. "I'm looking for the lady Onnen."

"You've grown," the woman said. "You won't remember me. I'm Bote."

"Cædmon's sister." The dairy maid.

Bote nodded. "Onnen's in the garth. The new one." She gave Hild and her belly a shrewd look: She had heard about her and Onnen's son. "I could fetch her, if you like."

"Just tell me where it is."

It was just off the path by the beck, a bit upstream of the smithy. The path was wider than Hild remembered but the gurgle and burble of the water was the same, and the whisper of trees. That was the birch whose leaves Cian had eaten that tasted like—

She heard the quick, light steps she would know anywhere and then Onnen came round the turn in the path, saw Hild, and stopped as though she had run into a wall.

They looked at each other. Onnen was holding greenstuff: banwort, elfwort, eyebright, mint. Hild wanted to throw down her staff, rush into her arms, and be wrapped about by her smell, wool and woman and toasted malt. She did not move.

Onnen looked down at the greens as though she had never seen them before, moved them to her left hand, then looked back at Hild, at her belly.

In the hall, Onnen sent Bote for small beer, and bowls for the herbs, and then they had the hall to themselves.

"Begu's here. She's with Mulstan."

"Keeping him busy while I tear your eyes out?"

"While I say sorry."

Onnen picked up the bunch of mint, began stripping it with expert sweeps of her thumbnail along the stalk. "When are you due?"

"Winterfylleth."

"And he's well? He's safe?"

"He's well." None of them were safe. She reached for the eyebright.

Onnen seized her fingers. "I told you you couldn't have him, and you didn't listen. You didn't listen."

"I had to. I had—"

Onnen's look silenced her. "You've never done anything you didn't want to do. Oh, I know, your mother told me why it had to be. But I know you; you have the mind of the world, you could have found a way." She gripped Hild's hand harder. "But you must keep him safe."

Hild stared at their hands resting on the board. Onnen had caught her as she fell from the womb, wiped her free of blood, wiped away her tears over the years. She had been more of a mother to her than Breguswith. Now her hand was so much smaller.

"If I closed my eyes it could be his hand." Onnen was looking at their hands, too. "I wish he was here." She sighed. "But I'm glad I have you." She squeezed gently and let go. "Now, how long will you stay?"

Forever. Here with those who would love her for who she was. High above the world where she could see things coming, with a woman she could pick up with one hand but who had always looked after her, always protected her as she could. "Until we can find a better boat to take us on. Begu would kill me if we got back on that barrel."

"Then we have a day or two." She picked up the mint again. "While we finish these you can tell me everything."

They talked the afternoon away as they cut and stripped and pounded. The light began to yellow as they worked, and the patch of sunshine crept farther into the hall through the open door, stretching like a finger across the floor, up the legs of the trestle, over the wall. The tapestries glowed: very clean; Onnen ran an efficient household. The golden light shone on the great medallion Mulstan had given her when they first came there, nine years ago. The changing light showed no grey hair escaping from Onnen's veil band, some reddening but not yet thickening of the knuckles, and her breasts not yet begun to billow with age. But her face was softening and settling and there were lines around her eyes and mouth. She must have been very young when she caught Hereric's eye.

"Tell me of my father," she said.

After a pause Onnen said, "It was long ago."

"Did you like him?"

"Is the wildness that leaps like salmon between two people like?" She huffed down her nose, sifted the mint through her fingers for no reason Hild could think of. "What do you really want to know?"

"Was he a good man?"

"Does a good man get his wife's friend with child? He was a man: tall and strong, shining. I was young. He had a lovely laugh. He was lordly. He liked to hunt, to laugh, to throw his daughter in the air and catch her."

Daughter. Not daughters. He had always liked Hereswith more.

"All men have favourites, little prickle. And all mothers."

Hild stared at her.

"Didn't you know?" Onnen laughed, a rare sound. "Then you were the only one. Hereswith always did; she was jealous. Your father loved pretty, but your mother liked bright. And that was you: quiet mouth, bright mind."

Her mother's favourite. Her mother had never given any hint to her. "She limps sometimes now."

"Her hip gets stiff. There are worse things. She'll outlive me."

"But you're younger."

"I was fifteen the summer I had Cian, and she was twenty-two."

She was not yet forty—young, still. But the herbs before them— banwort, elfwort, eyebright, even mint—were herbs for the old, for the weakening heart and lungs.

And then the hall was full of tumult: Mulstan with the faithful Swefred, Begu, the twins and their dogs, the Fiercesomes. Laughing, talking, shouting for ale. And then Mulstan was bellowing a greeting, and one look at his purple-red face told her who the herbs were for.

Hild found Guenmon sitting outside the west door enjoying the last of the sun, half an ear cocked in case those inside needed anything, happy to do nothing for a while. Hild handed her a cup of ale—just as Guenmon had given her many cups in the past—and sat.

"You've grown," Guenmon said.

"That's what Bote said."

"Even Bote can see through a plank in time."

They sipped. Guenmon's ale was still the finest in the north.

"That lass of yours, Gwladus. She's with you?"

"She's safe in Elmet. Safe, well, and well-looked-after. And free."

Guenmon nodded: just as it should be.

They said nothing for a while, enjoying the feel of the air moving past them on the way to the sea, soft as Langwredd's breath on her skin. Someone was tuning a lyre, then stroking out soft music. Bryhtsige, playing one of Langwredd's songs.

When she stood to go, Guenmon said, "Those furs are a horror. You should burn them."

Back in the hall, Mulstan and Swefred, Dudda and Gladmær were playing a complicated game that involved throwing dice, slapping the board, and drinking. Leofdæg was brooding over his ale, and Wulf, to whom large groups could be wearing, had slipped away. Begu was talking to Bote while Bryhtsige played, and the twins were asleep with their puppies by the hearth.

She sat by Onnen in the corner and picked up the bone she had been gnawing earlier.

"Even a dog couldn't get much more out of that," Onnen said. "The baby hasn't kicked away your appetite."

"Earlier tonight I think she was dancing. She must like Swefred's tune about hearth and home; you know the one I mean."

They both smiled. Mulstan loved that song. He called for it every time. Hild had tried to talk about Mulstan's health but Onnen said only, "It comes and goes, like the tide."

"Tides ebb as well as flow."

"When it's his time, it's his time, he says. He doesn't like to talk about it. And he's some time yet."

"Begu hasn't mentioned it."

"He's her father."

Hild wasn't sure how to take that.

"Ah, little prickle. We all know. Everything that can be done, I'm doing. But we can't change his wyrd. Put it from your mind. Tonight is a feast."

So Hild threw her gnawed bone on the pile in the middle of the table and they settled in over their ale. Onnen had questions about Hild's health, the state of her nipples and cunny, bladder and joints.

"My back hurts," Hild admitted.

Onnen held out her hand and pointed to Hild's. She put down her cup and gave it to her.

Onnen laid it palm down on the board and spread Hild's first and second fingers, then again on her left. Nodded to herself. "You're fine."

Some women's sinews stretched like rawhide as they swelled and their bones grew loose. Hild had seen them take a year after birth to knit.

"Don't worry about every little thing." She poured them both more ale. "I don't—"

"Yes, you do. You've always tried to protect the world. You can't. But you'll have a family soon. Protect them." They drank. "A daughter you said? Protect her."

"A daughter I hope." Neither needed to say more. "I wonder what she'll be like."

"If she's anything like her mother, prickly. A little hedgepig."

"Cian's like you, sometimes."

Onnen smiled.

"His smile, especially." She nodded over at the twins. "Do they take after your mother, perhaps? Or one of Mulstan's forefathers?" Mulfryth and Onstan looked nothing like the stout, blue-eyed Mulstan with his fox-red hair, nothing like the neat and contained Onnen. They could have been changelings: long-limbed, ash-blond, and grey-eyed, more like Bryhtsige than anyone else.

"They're beautiful," Onnen said. "But I feel as though I had nothing to do with it. It makes no difference, though. Yours will be beautiful, too. Your little hedgepig will come out looking like a crushed turnip, they always do, but you'll love her, you'll love her more than anything on this earth. You'd give your life for her and hope, hope that she marries someone who will love her as you do, and will protect her as you would."

Hild found Cædmon by the ruined signal tower, still freckled, still shock-haired but now a young man whose impatience had darkened to a banked anger evident in his tight muscles, the creases by his mouth, and a missing dogtooth.

They sat in the shelter of the last stones of the signal tower and shared his cheese and the pasty Hild had brought. He winced when he bit, then moved his mouthful to the other cheek.

"A fight?" she said.

He nodded.

"You didn't fight, before."

"I was a child. Children don't mind being told what to do."

A cowherd is told what to do by everyone. They listened to the cows tearing at the grass, then the squirt and patter of one loosing her dung, followed by the mewling of a black-headed gull. Hild leaned back on her hands and watched it. "She sounds as though she's complaining."

"Who wouldn't? Imagine flying about up there, looking down, thinking how green it all is, and then, phmmph, dung all over it." They grinned at each other, and Cædmon made up the verse of song, and Hild sang the next, and he said, "No, like this," exactly as he had years ago, and Hild laughed, and listened, and forgot her cares.

When she got back down from the cliffs the sun hung low in the sky. The Fiercesomes challenged Mulstan's men to a game of tug-of-war. Onnen did not let Mulstan play. "After all, Hild isn't playing with her men, so nor should you." He grumbled, but not too hard. And when they had all shouted themselves hoarse—the Mulstaningas won (because Leofdæg could pull with only one arm, Dudda said)—Onnen called for food to be brought outside, and another cask of ale to be broached, and Bote flirted with Glad-mær, who was at first bewildered by the attention but then basked in it, like a cat in the sun.

Hild sat on the bench with Onnen and Mulstan and while the sun set they watched the folk laugh and tell jokes and the children chase each other among the daisies. It was a break from time, for all of them. Today no one would be called to fight or die, to worry about crops or trade, or to scheme how to survive the summer. Edwin and Cadwallon, the Æthel-frithings and Penda, were another world. This place stood shining and open, untouched by care.

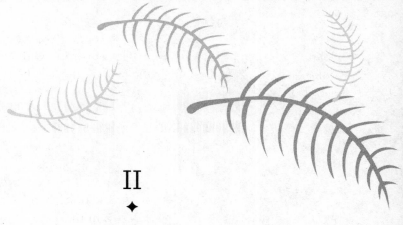

II

◆

Godmouth

Elmet—York—Caer Loid—Aberford—Hæðfeld

(Midsummer 632 to Winterfylleth 632, 14 weeks)

8

＊

IT WAS AN EASY PASSAGE from Mulstanton to Brough, a slower one up the Humbre and the Use to the Yr, and then, once they ate and drank with Cnot and his wife in their new long house at Cnotinsleah and their horses were saddled, it was less than a day's ride to Caer Loid.

It was too warm for her furs, which she rolled and carried before her. They rode helmetless and easy under a blue sky while a light breeze chased itself around the knots of ragged robin and the tiny white garlic flowers gleaming from under the trees. Nuthatches flicked and twittered in the dense understorey. The air smelled secret and satisfied between oak spotted with bright green acorns, hazel no longer springy enough to knot as they had been in spring, and elms, shapely and full, swaying smooth-barked under their robes of leaves, soft and wide as small hands . . .

"I can always tell when you're thinking of tupping," Begu said, as they paused in the afternoon to stretch and water the horses.

"I was not—"

Begu snorted. "Did I tell you? One of Langwredd's women asked me if I was your wife. I said, I suppose I am, apart from bed duties. And she laughed and said, 'Well, it's clear someone's been taking care of that!' The point is, I know you. There's no use pretending. And I know how you feel. Me too. I hope Winny's at Caer Loid when we get there."

"They know we're coming." She had told Cian she would be back by midsummer. And it was two days to midsummer.

Midsummer in Caer Loid, with Cian. Caer Loid where the skeps would be humming, the plum trees beginning to show dabs of colour as the fruit warmed in the sun, and the fish in the beck packed close enough for children to walk across on their backs. The vill would be waiting, sleek and heavy-lidded—

"You're doing it again. I hope Cian's ready for you." Begu patted Sandy. "Winny better be ready for me."

But even as she spoke she watched Bryhtsige, mounting Strayberry, laughing with Gladmær, whose mount was skittish after being snapped at by Dudda's new gelding. Gladmær could wear his helmet again—the smith at Mulstanton had hammered out the dents—and he looked well, they all looked well: well-fed, well-rested, well-mounted, gleaming with gold, though Gladmær was lighter by a ring and a wrist cuff, both no doubt now adorning Bote's arms. Leofdæg's arm was healing; he scratched at it end-lessly. Wulf and Dudda were the same, though Dudda's horse was a differ-ent colour. They were a strange band, but hers: her gemæcce and the men of Cath Llew. At Caer Loid she would feast the Fiercesomes for two days, let them boast of their fight to those left behind, then send them back to Edwin at Derventio.

Her bladder ached but they were almost there. As they climbed the rise, moon at their back, she smelled the river, hewn wood, and a hint of plums, and smiled. Caer Loid. For a strange, doubling moment the roar of the weir, the faint stir of trees on either side of the track in a breeze she could not feel, made her expect to find the Caer Loid of Ceredig king: thorn hedge, orchard bowed with fruit, geese hissing and lifting their wings, silver in the moonlight, and, inside, a hall hazed with peat smoke and bright with bronze-stringed harp and gold torc, Ceredig leaning forward in his wolfskin cloak. But when they topped the rise, below lay the Caer Loid she had left two months ago. An orchard still new and thin; instead of thorn a double box palisade of thick oak; gates open with two men standing easy before it—

She reined in Cygnet. There was only one man, and he was not stand-ing easy. He stood spear forward and she did not recognise his shield.

She turned her head this way and that. No stink of battle fire, nor the particular stench of a horse's opened belly.

Dudda moved up. "Lady?"

A hint of red still tinged the sky on the far side of the river but on this side the grass showed the steep sides of charcoal moon-shadow: divots and drags, gashes in the turf, and what looked like a great dark stain.

Around her, Fiercesomes dropped shields to their arm, loosened swords in their sheaths, hefted spears.

"What's wrong?" Begu said. "Why—"

Hild said, "Stay up here with the others." To Dudda, "Stay out of sight until I call. Make for Derventio if I don't." To Wulf, "With me."

And then she heard it, faint on the night air: a dirge.

The world narrowed to the thud of Cygnet's hooves as they walked down the hill. The spearman at the gate—young, no more than a stripling— saw them and licked his lips. His barely grown moustaches gleamed in the torchlight and she could see the glisten of sweat where his leather war cap did not quite fit. She saw, too, the tear streaks on his face and his knuckles white around the new ash of the spear.

She kept Cygnet to a steady walk, Wulf one pace behind and to her left.

From the singing, lifting clear, Cian's voice, his beautiful voice that usually sang of Branwen and heroes, singing now of death. But not his death.

She heard the river again. She felt her heart, the breath in her lungs, the night on her cheek. She turned in her saddle, and whistled up the rise. Then she kneed Cygnet forward and the stripling scrambled out of the way.

On the grass before the hall singing men stood before two biers. One for a horse with a pale tail and mane, the other for a man. Wilfram. Newly dead: not yet washed, still stinking of death shit, and horse, and mead.

As the singers—Oeric and Uinniau, her Hounds, and the spearmen of Elmet—blinded by torchlight and mead and their own grief, reached the end of their verse, she slid off Cygnet, handed the reins to the houseman who appeared from the shadow, and stepped into the light. "Husband."

He turned, eyes red and face blurred. He blinked: at her belly, at the new scar on her hand. "He died," he said, wiping his eyes and nose with the heel of his hand. "It was my fault."

He was drunk. They were all drunk, even Oeric and Uinniau.

Morud and Gwladus came running from the hall just as Begu and the Fiercesomes entered the vill, hideous faces twisting in the torchlight, new wounds livid still, and hands on hilts.

"Hold!" she said loudly, slowly to the drunken shieldmen and spearmen of Elmet. "These are my men. Men of high honour. There will be no quarrelling."

She looked at Wilfram, remembered him ripping the Elmet colours from his shield, how he had fought on the banks of the Yr. Now lying in his own shit.

She turned to Oeric and did not bother to hide her disgust. "If you can stay on your feet long enough to find Pyr, tell him we have five guests who are hungry and thirsty and in need of meat and drink." To Morud—one, at least, who was not drunk, "Show our visitors to the byre." To Dudda, "Follow him and I'll be with you soon." To Uinniau, a sorry sight compared to the gleaming Bryhtsige, "Begu is here."

To the Hounds and spearmen of Elmet, "Wilfram needs to be washed. Four of his brothers, if there are four who can carry without dropping, bring him."

Eadric the Brown, the brothers Berht, and one-eyed Coelwyn carried the bier beyond the palisade to what had once, long ago, been the priest's house and was now the house of the dead. Cian and the other men, a dozen of them, followed like lost sheep.

In the doorway she pointed. "Put him there. Then go." She looked at Cian, at the face she knew better than her own, bleared with drink. "All of you."

The others turned, some more smoothly than others, some held up by their friends. Cian, with one hand on the wall for support, lingered. "Surely you're tired," he said in British.

She replied in Anglisc, short and hard. "There is no rest yet."

"Surely the other women—"

She rounded on him. "You left him in his death stink, in his—" Hedgepig kicked. She breathed hard, bent around the kicking—Hedgepig seemed to have four feet today—and he reached for her. She stopped him, and straightened, tired now, tired and done. "Go to bed. I have to stay. Wilfram was one of mine. Mine to tend."

"I've missed you."

"And I you. But go. I'll be back sometime after moonset." Saxfryth came in with Gwladus, carrying pails and cloths and a wooden box of salves, and she was glad to turn from this man who did not smell like Cian. "Bring another pail," she told Gwladus. "And a stool." She could at least sit for some of this.

Begu came in, unfastening her sleeves. "Winny is drunk as a sow, drunk and sloppy. All this time away and it was like kissing a dish of spit. Welcome home!" She lifted one torch from its cresset and peered at Wilfram. "Well, it could have been messier. Gwladus, before you get that stool you should probably take the lady's furs, and bring an apron."

They had Wilfram half off the table so they could get to the worst mess down his legs. It was a horse race, Gwladus told them. "Saxfryth made a new batch of summer ale, and it's strong." She nodded at the reeve's wife wiping between Wilfram's toes, who looked up and nodded back. "Or maybe it was the heat. Anyway—"

"Lift his leg," Begu said.

"Anyway, Wilfram, you know how he is. Was." How they all could be, when overfed, overheated, and overwatered. "He boasted his Blæcci would leave Acærn in the dirt on midsummer; he wouldn't stop. Boldcloak turned it aside with a joke the first time or two, but Wilfram kept on needling him: Well, if he was *afraid* to go man to man, if he *preferred* to hide while real men, aye, and real women defended the vill—"

"Drink turns even the best men into boys," Saxfryth said. "Who can jump the farthest—"

"Run the fastest!"

"—piss the highest. Pyr's the same. They get prideful."

"No," said Begu. "They want to belong. They want to be just like everyone else. Only better."

Gwladus shook her head. "Afraid. Afraid their brothers will think less of them."

"Or women will laugh at them."

"Anyway," Gwladus said. "Boldcloak challenged him to a race. I told—"

As they talked Hild dipped her cloth in what had begun as the clean-water bucket, wrung it out over the dirty-water bucket. She wiped at her forehead with a mostly clean forearm—it was hot, the hut stank—and wiped Wilfram's arm, the still darker-than-the-rest scar she had tended not so long ago.

"—not enough light left but they didn't listen. Men were yelling and betting. One breath Boldcloak and Wilfram were riding shoulder to shoulder and the next, just like that, Wilfram was lying white and still, neck snapped like kindling, and the horse thrashing, bone sticking out, screaming—terrible screaming. Boldcloak had to let its blood out right there, the noise was so bad. Enough to put your teeth on edge."

Hild knew that sound, knew a person would do anything to make it stop.

She woke on her back in the dark to find Cian stroking her hand.

"You have a new scar," he said, and he was himself again. She had missed that voice, sure and light and clear as blackbird song, especially when he used British.

"I have stories," she said.

He cupped her breast. "They're bigger."

And veiny, though in the dark he could not see. "My belly, too."

He ran his palm up her arm. "I missed you."

He smelled of sweat and sour mead, but also himself, the smell she had known all her life, overlain with the familiar salt-and-iron man smell. Her breasts prickled.

He lipped her shoulder, her neck. "Did you miss me?"

She had to swallow before she could speak. "Yes." She reached down; his stick was stiff, slippery at the tip. He kissed her.

So different to kissing a woman: thinner lips, harder jaw muscles, stubble against her cheek. She kissed him harder, pressed her breasts against him. Her belly got in the way. She pushed him away to make space to turn on her side, reached back. "Here," she said. "Like this."

Gwladus set wattle screens around the door of their bower and opened the door to let in air and light. Hild and Cian held hands as they ate breakfast. No one else but Cian had hands as big as hers. He gave her his piece of bread dabbled in bacon grease. She reached for it with her left hand.

"That scar," he said, nodding at it.

"Yes." She studied it—pink as the inside of an earthworm, healed. Ragged, though, from the poor blade. Cuncar's, though deep, would have healed clean. "You are now cousin of the knife by marriage to Cuncar of the Bryneich."

He sat back. "The piglet prince?"

"The same. Though he is now as tall as Sandy."

"Sandy?"

"Begu's pony."

He dipped another piece of bread in the bacon, popped it in his mouth. "Tell me, from the beginning."

She told him of swimming to shore at Colud—he remembered Colud, remembered their feast there, ten years ago, "It was the first time I was mistaken for Anglisc"—of the pony, of learning the Fiercesomes and their ways. The smell of elderflower, and how Leofdæg had tracked the deer. Cian laughed when she described the Bryneich captain, Oran, backing out of the tent when all those women looked at him. When she described Langwredd, careful to give her no fewer, no more words than anyone else, something moved behind his eyes but he asked no questions, just as she would not ask him.

He asked her about the fight with the Picts, why she had decided to bind Cuncar to her. "To us," she said. "We're going to need friends." She told him how she had frightened him with tales of ælfe. He smiled. But when she began to tell of Aidan, how he was there on behalf of Oswald Brightblade, his eyes kept sliding away.

"What?" she said.

He shook his head. And from the side she saw that the puffy look was not all mead. He was tired, several weeks tired, and unhappy.

"Tell me, love."

"You have a new scar."

She nodded.

"You have a cousin of the knife. You have a new name and new men. New stories. What do I have?"

Peace. Comfort. A bed. "Me. The whole of Elmet. And hot food." He did not smile. "You've been making us safe."

"Safe," he said, in that tone she had known all her life: Feed the pigs! "And how does the sow's new litter, stronger bracing on the palisade, and a dam in the beck compare to the battles of Cath Llew, to becoming cousin of the knife to a prince of the Bryneich on the top of a fairy hill?"

"A litter of pigs compares well to the piglet prince." Still he did not smile.

"Your deeds would make a song and mine would not." His hand opened and closed on hers rhythmically but his mind's eye was on another horizon. "You've been out there, on new paths, facing the sun rising behind new hills, and I've been here, worrying about yields, the training of unbearded striplings, and stakes for the ford. You've been knife to knife with Picts. I've judged disputes between Grimhun and Heiu and told them wait, wait til the wool is washed. I've told Saxfryth, too, that no, she may not send her son for foster just yet, she must wait, wait until the lady Hild returns. Wait, that's all I've done. All we've all done, except you. Wait. That's not the stuff of song—"

It was for women, she thought. All those songs of women waiting, yearning for their man to return.

"—but I was once chief gesith. Hundreds obeyed my word. Hundreds."

"Not your word. The king's word." She held his face between her hands so that the bristles along his jaw prickled under her palms. "You were the king's hand of war. Here you're your own man, you follow your own word. You are Cian Boldcloak, lord of Elmet."

"Cian stay-at-home. Cian husband. It's easy for you—"

Easy?

"—but I'm not good at waiting."

"No one is. But sometimes it's our path."

"I can't do it anymore."

"Of course you can."

"I can't. You don't understand. You've been out there, lifted your face to new skies. I've been . . . here. You've seen everything, had everything. I've had nothing."

She dropped her hands. "Elmet is not nothing."

"I feel like a hawk in a hood."

"You're safe. I need you to be safe."

"I'm bound and in the dark," he said. "And I'm bored."

Bored? "Children may be bored. But men do what they must."

"Yes. But boredom makes men careless. Wilfram is dead because of it."

She stared at him. "I leave you with six Hounds and come back to five. Because you're *bored*? Perhaps next time I'll come back to four. Penda needn't bother bringing an army. He'll have nothing to do but wait."

He looked away, and anger burst inside her like a bubble of slow-heated fruit syrup. She pushed herself back from the board.

"Don't you have a grave to dig?"

In the still, stifling heat they laid Wilfram on a bier covered in clean beaver pelt, draped him to his chin with wolf, and carried him up the hill to his grave. To go with his polished mail shirt and war hat, his gleaming finery, they heaped the fur with treasure: a lyre for him to pluck at the feast board of the afterlife, a jar of white mead, a walrus-ivory comb inlaid with beryl, a mirror, tweezers, and shears—each gesith had taken something from Wilfram's belt pouch and given his own, his most prized item: a beautiful set of game pieces carved from jet, his shield and sword, two spears, his seax. A drinking horn inlaid with silver, a gold coin, a purse of silver, a tooled leather belt . . . Their brother would go arrayed as a prince to his afterlife. What did their own gold matter to them? They would win more, more gold, more glory. Death was their wyrd.

On their way back to the vill, with grave dirt—the deep, unsunned scent that could be nothing else—still on their hands, they met Wilgar and the four men he had brought from his vale by York. With him were Breguswith and Luftmær and Grimhun; they must have met on the road from Aberford. It was clear Breguswith had already given the grieving father mead, and matched him drink for drink; their faces were cherry-red.

So then, awkwardly, the whole company rode back to the turf-laid mound they had just left, where Luftmær sang a praise song for Wilgar's son. It could have been about any shieldman, but the scop was practised enough to still make men catch their breath and blink. Hild watched as though from another country, eyes dry, unmoved, and thought how like a needlewoman's job that of a scop was. No doubt once Luftmær had listened to Wilfram's shieldmates for a while he would cut the verse finer, shape then drape it to fit the man.

She returned to the hall with the others but felt only hot and restless as they sang loud enough and toasted long enough to claim notice for Wilfram's arrival in the next life: Here was a man loved and respected, a man worthy of welcome and honour. His name would live forever! She watched Luftmær's far-away gaze and knew he was running words in his head, tossing them aside, choosing, changing. She was not surprised when he stood, one foot forward, forehead shining in the heat, and sang again. It was the same shape and rhythm as the grave song but mentioning now Wilfram's fights for the Butcherbird, his tendency to quarrel when drunk, his kindness to the young, the horse he was so proud of and that had killed him. Every man in the hall wept openly; most of the women, like Hild, were dry-eyed. And when he was done Wilfram was still dead, the fire was low, and despite the thrown-open doors, the heat stifling. The evening was thick and still, and smelt of hot tin; over the western woods the sunset, overlain by thickening cloud, darkened the sky to old and bloody liver. She felt the air curdling, tightening, making her bones itch. She longed for the bright strike of Woden's bolt, the flash that would hurl the remains of the day to the ground and sear the air clean.

She turned her attention back to the hall, to her guests. Wilgar was a thegn, he had seen death: his shieldmates and his foes, his first wife in childbirth, two infants and his second wife to illness. He had always seemed to Hild a bull in his prime, well-muscled and heavy, settled in his enclosure with his progeny beyond the paddock growing full and sleek in their turn. But now he looked destroyed. She poured him another cup of white mead.

"What will I do?" he said.

Breguswith leaned forward between them. Her face gleamed red in the twining shadow. "Wilgar, old friend, you will drink that cup, and then another. And if you are still standing, you will drink another. And then Luftmær and Boldcloak and your man here will carry you to bed, and to-morrow your son will still be dead, but it will be a new day, and with the help of old friends perhaps you will bear it."

When Cian left to help carry Wilgar to bed, Hild joined the gesiths around the middle hearth: Hounds on one side, Fiercesomes on the other. Five and five. She lowered herself to the bench with care; she was feeling her belly. She turned her cup around and around in her hand.

"Wilfram was not a good man," she said. "None of you are good men. Being good earns no praise song. You are fierce men." She looked in turn at Wulf and Dudda, Gladmær and Leofdæg and Bryhtsige, the scars on their faces and the wounds on their hearts. "Loyal men." The brothers Berht and Grimhun, the cousins Eadric the Brown and one-eyed Coelwyn. Ten men. Hers. "You are strong, and brave, and mine. All of you. You have fought for me; we have never lost. They sing songs of us: the men of the Butcherbird, the men of Cath Llew. Half of you leave soon, back to the king. Tomorrow we'll feast you, and Luftmær will sing your praises, and then you'll rejoin the king. But you'll always have a place here, with me, with each other. You're brothers. Remember that."

Around the high hearth Begu and Uinniau dozed against each other's shoulder and Luftmær plinked idly on his lyre with that far-away look that meant he was trying out his praise song for the Fiercesomes. Cian whittled at something but his knife paused for long stretches as he nodded in and out. They had not spoken since the morning but the two of them were one; the thing between them mended with every breath. Tomorrow. They would speak of it tomorrow. All around them dark shapes lay sleeping curled on the floor, slumped over the board, or propped against the wall. It was dark outside, the moon hidden behind the gathering stormcloud. The doors stood open but the air was stifling.

Breguswith was still drinking steadily, holding her cup in both hands in her lap, lifting it, staring at the hearth. "You and your hero don't—"

"He's not my hero."

"No? You have seen his nakedness?" That made no sense to Hild. Breguswith flapped her hand. "It's a god story. A story Æthelburh tells the children. Something to do with a garth." She stared into her cup. She was very drunk. After a moment she said, "You had another brother. Before your sister Hereswith."

Another. Hild kept very still. Never say the dangerous thing aloud.

"This one, though, was mine. His name was Ælfric. His hair was pale, like mine. Like your sister's. He lived two days." She took a meditative sip. "Another sister, too. She slipped out dead." Another sip. "Tomorrow would have been her birthday."

Another sister. "When?"

"Two years before you. Midsummer. She had chestnut hair."

Another sister, with hair like hers. "What was her name?"

"Does it matter?"

Hild reached for the sleeping Begu's cup, sniffed. Ale. It would do.

"Drinking helps, sometimes," her mother said. "And it quiets a kicking baby in the womb. Ælfric kicked. He was lusty. He had hair like mine, like Hereswith. Did I say that? Honey hair. His name did him no good. I didn't give you your name until you were ten days old." She peered into her cup again, looked about for a jug.

Hild beckoned a houseman. When he brought the mead Cian blinked, looked at his knife blankly, and fell fast asleep again. Hild waved the houseman away and poured for Breguswith herself.

"It was a night like this that I found out. Hereswith was three months old. A hot night. Thick. Onnen was swollen with child, about as far along as you. Hereswith was crying again, and Onnen looked at the mewling mite in the cradle and she might as well have spoken it aloud: *That child by him will have all she needs but mine will have nothing.*"

Why was her mother talking about it now?

"She nearly died getting him into the world." She sipped. "I nearly let her."

The fire settled.

"But I didn't. I fought for her. I fought death for her, and I won." Her eyes glittered in the hearthlight. "I won. I always win. And she was wrong: That child of hers has everything. He has you." She smiled a flat-lipped smile, like an adder. "It's funny. I could not foresee this. Your child weaves him and me, him and her together. Forever." She wove the air one-handed, the other half holding her cup, half balancing it on her thigh. Hild had never seen her mother so drunk. "Weaving us back into ourselves, tucking the ends in, twining our blood together into one cord, whether we want it or not. Pulling us tight. Tight." She yanked the imaginary cord up, as though pulling a purse-mouth closed, and her cup tipped and spilled and fell to the floor.

Hild bent for it, came up to find Cian looking at her, his face empty as fresh-scraped hide. Breguswith's chin fell forward and she began to snore.

Cian blinked and flowed back to himself. He looked at his knife and frowned, looked at Hild, but before he could say anything a great crack split the sky. Rain sheeted down, rippling like a jewelled curtain beyond the open door.

Little Hedgepig woke and tumbled and kicked. Hild laid her hand on her belly. "Come here, love. Our child is dancing." She pulled him in for a kiss, felt the just-from-sleep softness over the strength. Perhaps he had not heard her mother. "She's strong. We're strong. When she's born, we'll make her a brother, then a sister. And another, and more. We are us."

He laid his hand on her belly. "We are us."

The Fiercesomes left at daybreak to join their king at Derventio. Wilgar did not want to leave. Caer Loid was where his son had last breathed and laughed, sang and sweated, and when he went back to his valley outside York Wilfram's thread would stop and the world weave would go on without him, close up as though his son had never been. But eventually he climbed on his horse. As he said farewell, he begged Hild to come attend Wilgith when it was her time; he couldn't lose her, too. He wept. Men were allowed to weep.

Cian rode out with Oeric at dawn the next day to look at Brid's Dyke.

To Hild it seemed he was eager to get away from her mother. Perhaps it had nothing to do with that drunken conversation.

The following morning, at the vill gate, Hild hugged Breguswith hard. *Don't go,* she wanted to say. *Don't take Begu away. Not yet.* But she did not.

But Breguswith was her mother; she saw and understood. "I'll be back soon enough. And I'll make sure your gemæcce's back in plenty of time for the baby, perhaps by harvest. But I must go. The cloth in Aberford won't dye and cut itself."

Then they were gone, even the Hounds—only as far as the war street with Grimhun: Now that they were so few they were loath to let him go to work on strengthening Aberford further, even though he, too, would be back for harvest.

It was the end of the day, and Hild and Cian sat upstream from the weir. Flies hummed over the dimpled water and a coot paddled back and forth by the remnants of a beaver dam. Hild sat on a stone with her knees wide, so her belly could hang between them; today Little Hedgepig had been kicking with lead boots and what felt like intent. She was quiet now; perhaps she was dreaming. At least she was strong.

Fursey had sent her another letter: Hereswith had been with child but miscarried. Æthelric was encouraging Sigeberht strongly to cut his hair and abandon the throne. Bishop Felix was of two minds how to advise his king because although Sigeberht would endow his own monastery most handsomely, Æthelric would not be a pious king. And so, given that the net gain for God was uncertain, which path would she, Hild, like him, Fursey, to encourage Hereswith to support?

She had turned the parchment this way and that, trying to guess from Fursey's words on the page how he felt. Writing was a miracle, yes, but an oddly empty one. A person was a living, breathing moment, a whole world wrapped around the bones that bring out the sound. A letter was more like seeing tracks in the snow. If the footsteps were deep you could tell a story about a big man, or a small man carrying a heavy burden—which could be a dead child or a pot of gold. But it was just a story, a guess. It was not like *seeing* the man walk in the snow. When you talked to a person right next to you, your understanding of what they were saying, what they felt, what they meant, changed with every heartbeat, every pause, every breath. You could see what they meant, you could smell it.

She brushed a fly from her face—she wished she had not thought of snow just now; it made the hot afternoon feel hotter—and turned the question this way and that. Hereswith as queen, Æthelric as king: How would it tilt the balance? Æthelric had alliances with the peoples of the North and South Gwyre—indeed he had two daughters by a princess of the South Gwyre—who lived interlaced with the Middle Angles. With Hereswith married to a king who was allied to the Gwyre, they could balance Penda's growing weight in the middle of the country. But Hereswith had miscarried; she might miscarry again, and die. Any married woman could die at any time. With or without the throne childbed was as dangerous as the shield wall . . . No. Hereswith was strong. She would be fine. And a sister as queen of the East Angles would make another bolt-hole if Elmet failed. Yes. She would tell Fursey yes.

Her thoughts turned to Wilgith. In three days she would ride to Wilgar's valley for the lying-in. Wilgith was a cross woman, and petty, the kind who would stamp on an ant because she could; they had never liked each other. But she owed Wilgar. But that was not for three days; for now she would watch the coot preen and think of nothing.

It would be a good harvest, but they were driving their people hard: She wanted more charcoal, more mead for trade, more pig iron. More ash poles, more spearheads, more butter, every cow and goat milked to its limit, every field weeded clear so the crops could drink the sun. They could not afford to lose a drop of daylight, a fistful of barley, a cup of honey. If their fields were fired or many men were absent over winter they would need all they had, and more, to survive.

Cian had worked without cease. He rode the walls and ditches with the Hounds, practised with the striplings, and visited the lookouts on the roads west and south. When he was at the vill he was quiet, inward-looking. He seemed far away, turning something over in his mind.

Whenever she probed he turned her aside, deft as when she had first faced him, staff to blade. She did not push. And so she waited, and meanwhile checked the hives, the sickles, the fish smoking over racks. She talked to Pyr—to Saxfryth at the East Farm, to Llweriadd, who had lived in Elmet the longest of them—of building more hiding places to cache food and fodder and fuel. Instructed Pyr to plant more roots—turnips, beets, carrots—in fields far from the vill, where they could grow in the dark, secret and safe, hidden from enemies with torches and retrievable at need. And seed, always seed. She rode to Rhin in Menewood, to tug on the threads of her network, to listen.

Paulinus was still in Craven, feverishly baptising. In the north and west, Æbbe was not yet wed to Domnall Brecc; perhaps she never would be. In the north and east, the Iding was not taking oaths, and the Bryneich showed no signs of gathering. All good things. She heard nothing of Aidan or Suibne, nor hints of other strangers on the road.

The south was another matter. There the signs of war were strong and clear. In Mercia pole coppicing was on the increase, smiths were journeying from their homes, and tanners were working day and night. Corn and hay being carried to Tomeworthig. That was where Penda would gather his men and march east and then north on Ryknield Way, alongside the great earthworks people called the redcrest Rig, to Caer Daun where it met the left hand of Ermine Street that ran from Lindum. Ermine Street, the war street that became Dere Street, where countless armies had marched; the road Edwin himself had marched to take Deira and Bernicia and all Northumbre. Penda was taking the oaths of more gesiths; and everywhere he was buying horses and fodder. If the weather turned dry and stayed dry he might keep to Ryknield Way and cut the corner to join Ermine Street above Caer Daun, but if it rained he would stay on the higher path, through Caer Daun.

Whichever road he took, the signs were stronger every day: When the harvest was in, the hay stooked, and the grain threshed, there would be war. Little Hedgepig would slide into a world of blood and death, though because of Hild's work, they would not be facing war from the north and south at the same time.

It was out of her hands now. Babies came in their own season. So would Cadwallon. He could march early. If he came in summer, he could take the old road, the slanting road up and over the mountainous Spine of Britain, through Craven, land of ironstone and gritstone, through the Gap and into Elmet.

As though he had heard her thoughts Cian said, "Will Osric and Craven be ready?"

Osric listened to nothing that was not to his own immediate advantage. A stupid badger of a man. "James says young Oswine watches the Gap." Oswine was no sharper than his father but he was easier to bend. James, together with Uinniau, Oswine's friend, had on her behalf persuaded him. "Though on his own he doesn't have enough spears to stop them."

"None of us do."

"No."

Cian loosened his hair, closed his eyes, and leaned back on his hands to soak up the slanting sun. Far away, near the vill, children were chanting some song. From the tilt of his head he was listening but his face gave nothing away. When had he learnt how to do that?

She kept watching the coot. "Stephanus brought his boc to Craven and has been writing down who farms what land. James has persuaded the queen to persuade the king that Osric, a mere ealdorman, should not tithe the church in Cetreht, and Stephanus has recorded it in his boc. James is happy."

"I doubt Osric is."

The coot went round and round as though its left foot were tied to an anchor. "A thegn called Cedwin died, but because his hides were recorded in the boc—for some favour he had done the church—Osric could not give the land to another thegn. The land passed instead to Cedwin's wife and her sons."

Cian opened his eyes and looked at her.

"Yes." She nodded. "It makes me wonder: How high does this boc-land go?"

He sat forward and wrapped his arms around his knees.

"Imagine the whole of Elmet written in that boc, written to us," she said. The slanting light turned his jaw from iron to bronze and the brown-black streaks in his chestnut moustaches to the warm brown of old wood. "No king could gainsay the boc without gainsaying the Christ on threat of their immortal soul. Imagine. Little Hedgepig could grow up safe, protected, lapped about by land no one could take when the king died."

Cian thought about it, then shook his head. Ealdormen were chosen by the king, just like chief priests. Edwin would feed Stephanus and even the Crow to the dogs without blinking if either even hinted things might be otherwise.

But it was a lovely dream: that when a king died order would not die with him, that a new king would not drive out the thegns and ealdormen and put in his own men.

He closed his eyes again and she went back to her thoughts. If Osric were written in the boc as ealdorman, would Oswine inherit Craven as a man might his father's sword? When Osric died, Oswine would be a good ally, biddable—he worshipped Cian; and Uinniau, friend to Elmet, was also his friend. But Osric was as strong as ever. Not like Mulstan. She sighed.

"What?"

"I was thinking of Mulstan."

He opened his eyes. "Will he live til the twins are of age?"

She shook her head.

"Then when the time comes, my mother must bring them here."

She nodded. Where else? Elmet was Onnen's home, but leaving the bay would be hard for the twins; it was all they knew. They would miss the sea, as Begu did. Perhaps Begu should take the bay, with Uinniau, once they could marry. Begu's mother had been born there. Begu had been born there. She should bear her children there. There was a spring on the top of the east cliff, a quiet, secret place where mother and daughter should go together.

Cian was watching her. His eyes were as opaque as lantern horn. Again, she wondered when he had learnt to shield his thoughts.

She turned her beads—warmed by the sun—around her wrist. "You know the spring at the top of the east cliff? Begu showed it to me. Her mother showed her. I want a place like that, that's forever. A place where I can take Little Hedgepig and she'll take her daughter. Where each in turn can say, 'Here, here's where my mother brought me.'" Sitting on the bough of the pollard, pointing: *There is where I saw the water vole.* Her daughter saying, *Here my mother told me of a water vole.* Hers in turn saying, *Sitting right here my mother told me about her mother.* "I see it: foremothers and mothers and daughters and their daughters through the ages, standing in a line that reaches the horizon. All the same blood: Here the same eyes or catch in the laugh, there a familiar tilt of the head or snag of dogtooth against the tongue, like an echo. Or like opening a peapod, and inside finding another peapod, and inside that another." On and on, unbroken.

"She would be lucky," he said. "Sons can never be sure of their fathers."

9

⊕

A T THE END OF MEADMONATH, on an early morning already growing hot, Hild sat next to Linnet on the log outside her hut. This time she sat not astride but with her feet spread and belly hanging like a fat thegn's. Her arms were bare—bloody sleeves hung from her belt—and her mood low and thick. She had slept just four hours in two days. Linnet herself was hard and drawn with the long-standing weariness of work and grief. Her son and his wife, Janne, were in the wood burying their first-born, who had died the day before of wet lung, sinking from life along with the evening star at twilight. It was why Hild was here, why she had sent Gwladus and Oeric into the woods to fetch Janne, as soon as the burial was done.

She explained to Linnet about Wilgar's motherless new grandson, though right now Linnet cared nothing for the thegn's dead daughter or her hungry son.

"He came before dawn. He suckled, and Wilgith smiled, then died. She smiled. It's the only time I ever saw her smile."

Linnet nodded. Wilgar's valley was less than a mile away; she knew the thegn and his daughter—she had always been a sour thing.

Hild stared at the bowl of beer in her bloody hands. It was bitter, but she sipped. She had not slept or eaten. There had been so much blood, a flood of blood as though someone had pulled out the sticks in a beaver dam. Gushing, rushing blood, blood that would not stop no matter what she did. So red. "He kept suckling—Wilfrid. Even as his mother paled and died. He sucked, harder and harder, like he was sucking out her life."

"So. Janne's to be his milk mother."

Hild nodded tiredly. "She'll only be a mile from here."

Linnet's smile was bitter as the beer. "But she'll be living in a thegn's hall, eating a thegn's food to keep her milk in for the thegn's grandson. Soon she'll be too good to come visit us."

Hild said nothing. It was most likely true.

"The boy is strong?"

Hild nodded.

"If he dies Janne won't suffer for it?"

"She will not. And for now she'll have a child to suckle, and as you say, food in plenty, and a warm bed."

Janne came alone to Wilgar's valley, sitting sideways on the horse before Oeric, hollow-eyed with grief. They were halfway there when the king's messenger found them: Hild was summoned to York.

She blinked. York? She had thought the king was at Derventio. She was bone-tired, unwashed, and hollow with hunger. All she cared about was getting Janne to the newborn Wilfrid.

The messenger—the same brown-haired, brown-eyed one who had come for her in Hrethmonath—had already ridden to Caer Loid and been told she was at Wilgar's valley; had then gone to the valley and been told she was at some ceorl's hut. The king would have the messenger's ears if he did not get her there soon. He read the refusal on her face and without thinking reached as though to grab Cygnet's headstall—and found the tip of her staff an inch from his throat. He stared in shock.

Gwladus laid a hand on his arm but spoke to Hild. "Lady, let Oeric take Janne to the thegn."

At midmorning the York gate was still in shadow, which suited Gladmær. It was going to be a filthy-hot day and he was stuck on guard duty with Boertred, who after about an hour would start complaining. Probably his arm: He'd scorched it in that arm-wrestling last night. Shouldn't have challenged Bryhtsige; the gelding was a lot stronger than he looked. Boertred was as thick as two short planks. Not the only one. The Bryneich had fallen for that boyish look, too; when they'd been up there he and Dudda and Leofdæg had won a lot of bets.

Bryhtsige was fighting a lot. More than he had before. Maybe it was because he now had shield brothers to back him up. It had been different since they'd come with the Bryneich to Yeavering with Cath Llew, and the king had been so pleased. There'd been no sword ring from it, but there were those Pictish spoils, and his wound scar, and the songs. Even better had been the way the other gesiths looked at them. The nose and ear didn't matter now. He was special: Fiercesome, not deformed. He was one of the chosen. One of her chosen. And if Cath Llew, who could see through a mountain and predict ambushes, thought he was special, then he was.

If only she were here now. Honeytongue was back, they said, which made everyone twitchy. And there was war coming, which was good, because gold was good, and the chance to make a name, but Leofdæg was drinking more and talking less—his brother had died at Long Mountain and the sight of Honeytongue was more than he could bear—and Dudda looked thoughtful. Which he didn't like one bit.

Four horses on the other side of the bridge. Something about that grey . . . He peered. His eyes had not been quite so sharp since that bang on the head. But yes, it was. It was her. What was it his ma always said? Naming calls. And here she was, Cath Llew. He'd recognise her anywhere, even without the furs.

"Is that the king's freemartin?" Boertred said.

"Call her that and she'll butcher you like a calf." Not that he'd mind seeing her open Boertred like she had that Pict. Such an arse.

"Doesn't look like much to me. Not like that other tasty piece."

"Her bodywoman? You *really* don't want to touch that."

He'd heard rumours. More than rumours. The fool with Cath Llew—Oeric? Yes, Oeric; his horse was looking more sweaty than it should—told them that night in Caer Loid that the bodywoman had been the lady's own once, and any man who touched her got turned into a toad and their eyes folded inside out, any man who even *thought* about touching her, he said, because the lady always knew. They'd all nodded at that, Fiercesomes and Hounds both. Cath Llew always knew your mind. Hounds—stupid name, but that's what they called themselves: Hounds of the Butcherbird. They'd seen some things, Oeric said. They were lucky they hadn't seen what he'd seen . . .

You've no idea what we've seen, mate, Dudda had said.

We've seen Cath Llew read the wind, said Bryhtsige in that voice he could do sometimes, the one that made you think of wights drifting along boundaries in the moonlight. *She knew about that Pictish ambush, right, mates?* And it was the Fiercesomes' turn to nod and look wise.

Ah, that had been a night. The songs at Caer Loid. For the dead man first—Wilfram? Wilstan?—then boasts about Butcherbird. Then their songs about Cath Llew . . .

They were crossing the bridge now. Herself, next to the king's messenger, in front. She looked tired. What did that portend? He'd seen her after days of hard marching and she'd been untouched. And that belly of hers was so big she looked like she was in kindle with twin foals. Wonder what kind of baby grows inside Cath Llew. Red fangs and claws. Eyes yellow as a wolf's . . . Stood to reason she'd been tired, hosting that.

He straightened as they approached and out of the corner of his eye he saw Boertred go rigid and expressionless. *Ha! Different isn't it, mate, when she's close up and fixes you with those eyes?* Then she was right there, and he could see for himself the blood drying stiff and brown on the sleeves through her belt, and he swallowed the beginning of his grin.

The messenger raised his eyebrows. Better step aside and wave him through. "I'm going straight to the king," he said as he passed. "Make sure she follows. Alone."

As if he could make Cath Llew do anything. He turned back to her and smiled tentatively. "Welcome, lady."

"Your nose looks better."

"Been eating my greens."

"Happy to hear it." She didn't sound happy. "The others?"

"About the same."

"Keep at it."

At what? Oh, eating the greens. Might be tricky come winter.

"The king. Where is he?"

"In the Christ temple."

She did not even correct him, tell him to say *church*, as she usually did. He was conscious of the cross around his neck, the same weight as the hammer he'd worn since he got his first wooden sword. He understood the old gods who fought and boasted, drank and cheated like men. He would never understand this milksop who bleated about peace and turning the other cheek. The only cheek a gesith should turn was his bare arse, waggled at the enemy. But the king wanted them to wear a cross now.

"He's with the Crow—" Boertred cut his eyes at him, all proper all of a sudden. "That's to say, with the overbishop Paulinus, lady. And the reeve."

"Overbishop," she said.

Was that a question? She scrubbed at her face like an ordinary person who was tired beyond bearing.

"How many messengers went out?"

"Just the one, lady." Didn't she already know that?

She nodded her thanks and kneed Cygnet past. He tried to watch her without turning his head. No doubt the king wanted to send her somewhere to bring another prince to heel. Well, they'd have to be quick. Her belly was huge.

If she thought she could get away with it she would ride Cygnet all the way to the church door but in York the only animals allowed past the gate must go to the byre. She slid down into the rutted main street, once again feeling her weight, and straightened slowly. Perhaps this was how it was to be old.

Gwladus leaned back to swing her own leg over her mount's neck.

"No." She handed Cygnet's reins to Oeric. "Get them in the shade and loosen their girths but don't unsaddle. I want us back at Caer Loid before dark." Back behind Caer Loid's strong palisade and defended by her own spears. And to Oeric, "You should walk your mount first." He had hurried with Janne to Wilgar's valley and then back to her, as she'd asked. The horse was lathered but there was no bloody foam at its mouth. She tried to think. Said to Gwladus, "Find Arddun. Find out what you can."

She walked north and west. The road was rutted: Carts carrying heavy burdens had been this way in the last month. York stank. The king's household now numbered at least ten hundreds, and traders to the wīc added their waste to the rivers. The air was so greasy and many-layered that she wanted to wipe her tongue on her sleeves. Except her sleeves were filthy with Wilgith's blood.

Outside the church she made sure her cross hung outside her dress and slid her seax to a less prominent position to one side of her belly. She had no idea what the king wanted, or why, and she was late; the king hated to be kept waiting. Even so, she took a moment to draw together what strength she could.

The church door opened and Paulinus stepped past Stephanus into the light.

They saw each other at the same time.

The Crow was thinner and beginning to stoop. His nose now was as sharp as an axe. He wore a new hat of embroidered silk. The milky hint of age around his black irises looked like ash on burning charcoal. His eyebrows and the hair sprouting from his nose were no longer black.

Stephanus pulled the door shut with some effort and stood behind his master. His face—pale except for the dark shadow around his chin—was dewed with sweat.

The Crow's mouth spread in what others might have considered a smile. "I see your sins weigh heavily on you, daughter." He looked at her belly.

"Losing a woman's life in childbed weighs on me."

His eyes glittered like a spider's. "Sins have a way of finding the sinner. And, God knows, yours is a heavy burden."

They had been enemies a long time, and he was still dangerous to her, and to Cian, but his time would end with Edwin's. She faced more immediate dangers. "Yes. God does know. But only God." She laid a hand on her belly. "And this is the fruit of a marriage blessed by you. A marriage of Hild Yffing to Cian son of Ceredig, announced as such by Edwin Overking." A statement of parentage not to be gainsaid by any on the isle while the king lived. Not even a newly made overbishop.

His lips thinned and stretched, then he held out his purple-spotted hand. His ring was new: a bubble of sapphire. She took his hand—she could break the bones like sticks, and perhaps one day she would—and bent over it briefly but did not kiss the ring.

He lifted his other hand in the Christian gesture of blessing. "May God one day relieve you of all your burdens, child. One day soon." Then he beckoned to Stephanus and swept past her towards the hall.

Less a threat than an ill wish, and more blunt than usual, but she was too tired to care. A more immediate danger waited in the church. She laid her hand on the great bronze door ring and breathed in, then out, and out again until there was no air left. Then with another great breath she turned the ring and stepped inside.

The church was shadowy as a cave and should have felt welcoming after the heat, but the chest-high carved and painted candles by the steps to the chancel, the gilded wooden panels, and the altar reeked of Paulinus's new power. In one long, slow look from right to left she took in the altar, draped with a sleek white cloth that shimmered and seemed to glow; a mixture of silk and linen, embroidered in gold and scarlet with the name of Saint Peter. The massive ivory and gold cross studded with beryl and sapphire, crystal and garnet standing on it, throwing light like a sun-struck weir onto the great gold cup before it.

That cup. She knew it, remembered how the muscles of her seven-year-old spine had flexed and her thighs swelled as she straightened under its weight of thick yellow gold. Trade must be good—better than good—and Paulinus high in the king's favour for Edwin to offer such a treasure to the church. He must be pleased about the pallium: Now he had an overbishop who could match any godmouth on the isle.

But where was the pallium, the mark of the Crow's new status, of his new-found willingness to ill wish her? Why was it not displayed here at the heart of his power?

Three men sat at a table on the left of the nave against a plain, unplastered wall. They were lifting their heads and turning towards her. In the chancel beyond, a monk was painting a panel—he stared at the blood on her sleeves (he would swoon if he knew it was the blood of childbed)—and against the right wall, also rough and unfinished, two housemen stood, eyes on the king.

The monk turned his attention back to his panel. At the table, Edwin leaned forward and the light from the high east window raised the pattern in the subtle, compound weave of his tunic. Blue with a hint of green. *With our hair colour, blue is better:* Her first advice to a king. In the gloom he seemed like the king she had first met. His grey hair was masked by the gleam of chestnut, and the small muscles above his elbows, below heavy gold rings, moved easily under skin whose blemishes were smoothed by diffuse light. Shadow emphasised the wide, satisfied cheekbones of a man who had just won a dangerous game or a great race. His token was back on his finger.

The man next to him wore red. He could; his hair was silver gilt, like that of Cwenburh of Mercia, his dead mother. Eadfrith Honeytongue, the ætheling.

"My king," she said.

Edwin wrinkled his nose. "Did we interrupt you killing something?"

She looked at her sleeves. She should have left them with Gwladus. "Wilgar's daughter died in childbed."

Edwin shrugged. He did not care about the daughter of one fat old thegn whose only virtue was his valley farmland. He could always find some other thegn to make sure it produced and sent the milk and butter, wheat and barley he needed. "You look weary, niece. Coelfrith, bring her a stool."

She did not want to sit in this place, but nothing a king said was a suggestion.

Coelfrith brought the stool, and she sat, watching Honeytongue.

"My son brings word from Mercia: Penda offers an alliance. Tell me, if I make alliance, will it turn out well?"

Everything turned out well for someone. She looked at Honeytongue, eldest son of the king. Honeytongue, who ten years ago had called her a hægtes in a cyrtel. Honeytongue, who two years ago had abandoned his men to the allied armies of Penda and Cadwallon at Long Mountain. Honeytongue, whom Cian had saved after Long Mountain at the cost almost of his own life—and hers.

The silence pooled between them.

Eventually she said, "Did Penda send a token?"

Honeytongue flicked a dead fly from the table. "I didn't know freemartins could kindle."

There was a lot he did not know. "Did he send a token?"

"Am I to answer this woman?" Honeytongue asked his father.

"For now," said the king.

Hild and Honeytongue regarded each other. The scar on his forehead where he had been kicked by a horse on the flight from Long Mountain was as pale as shelf fungus. His hair was well-groomed but when he smoothed his moustaches she saw that his fingernails and the skin around them were ragged.

"There is no need of a token." He addressed a space just above her left shoulder. "Penda gave me his word."

"And will he keep his word?"

"He will keep his word to me. To kin." Cwenburh had been the daughter of Cearl, the dead king of Mercia.

She did not know Penda, but no man's alliances could hold if his word did not; she was inclined to trust his word—if he had indeed given it. "He sent no letter, no token?" Nothing to support Honeytongue's claim.

Honeytongue looked as though he would like to slide his knife under her tongue and saw slowly. "I say Penda wants friendship between all the Angles. Any man—or freemartin—who gives me the lie must prove it with their body."

This was a challenge, clear and simple, aimed right at her. She was weary to the bone, she had not slept, and her weight was all wrong. Even so, if it came to it, she could take Honeytongue. She overtopped him, overreached him, and she had seen him fight; unlike him she would not flinch.

But. Oh but. Not only was Honeytongue Edwin's eldest son, she had learnt long ago that a man, even a king, believed not what he said he wanted to hear but what, deep in his secret heart, he yearned to hear. Edwin's hatred of Cadwallon was deep and abiding; he yearned to crush him, to win. He yearned to be undisputed overking of the isle with all men and women bending the knee. He would believe whatever might make that possible. With Penda as ally, it was possible.

How long had Honeytongue been in York pouring his honey in the king's ear? She should have asked Gladmær. "My king, Penda once tried to kill your own son—his kin. Could you trust such a man?"

The garnet on Edwin's hand winked as he waved away her question. "That was Cadwallon."

Cadwallon when allied with Penda. But he did not want to hear that. She chose her next words carefully. "If Penda takes your part against Cadwallon, his ally, what will he want in return?"

Edwin slitted his eyes like a cat in the sun. "He has a daughter."

"I see."

Edwin was telling himself a story. Penda's daughter was just a child, a byblow from a woman of Magonsæte—Mereburh? Mereswith? Edwin was telling himself the hero-song Honeytongue had fed him: that Penda as ally would bend the knee to Edwin as undisputed overking of all the isle. Like all kings he believed he would win every battle, live to a good and great age, and never lose the glittering edge of his shrewd mind or the strength of his mighty arm. But if he did by some mischance one day die, comfortably in his bed, then the heir of his body, Honeytongue, ætheling of Northumbre—also grandson of King Cearl of Mercia—would, if he were husband of Penda's daughter, be in line for Mercia, through blood and through marriage. King Honeytongue, overking of all the isle. And Edwin's line and Edwin's name would live forever. The Edwingas would rule for a hundred years; even after death men would sing his name. Men would sing his name for generations.

Honeytongue had whispered in his father's ear exactly the story Edwin wanted most to hear. But was it a story Honeytongue also believed—

had Penda made such an offer—or was Honeytongue lying for his own purposes?

She knew in her heart he was lying. But Edwin was a king, and he wanted her to agree with this story, his most secret yearning. But agree as godmouth? As Butcherbird? As niece? To disagree could mean death, and she was too tired to puzzle it out.

She said carefully, "Yffings will be overkings of the isle, Uncle. All folk, east and west, north and south will bend the knee."

"Ah." He leaned back and put both hands on his thighs, satisfied.

Before he realised she had not said which Yffing or when, she added, "And, Uncle, I hear now that the overking has an overbishop to match."

"You saw that ring, then?" *That* ring, not *The ring I gave him*, or *The ring the pope sent.*

She nodded. "But, Uncle, he wasn't wearing his shawl from the pope, his pallium." She made a show of looking around.

"The pope did send one, supposedly. He also sent one to the Centisc overbishop, along with a letter saying the two overbishops were now equals. The overbishop—the Centisc one—sent a copy of his popish letter to the Crow a fortnight ago. When the Crow read it he glowed like a new-forged sword, told everyone his letter and shawl were coming, and put that blue ring on—he's probably been carrying it around in his pocket since he left Cent—and insisted that his priests call him his grace." His chuckle was fruity with malice. "But yesterday we had news that the boat with the Crow's own letter and shawl sank. The bishop in Rome will have to send a new one. Meanwhile, the Crow's got that copy, and the ring." He yawned and stretched. Hild fought the urge to yawn, too. "He'd kill his own mother for that piece of cloth."

A badge of rank was no good unless those who saw it understood it. James had told her that the pallium was a white shawl. No one who had not listened to the Crow rant about it would care: It wasn't made of gold or precious jewels so how important could it be?

Edwin certainly did not look worried. The Crow might still be his godmouth, and the church well-endowed, but if anything he seemed pleased at the thought of the Crow smarting from a tap on the beak. Good. A pleased king was a generous king.

She put her hand on her belly, huffed as though in pain, and swayed on her stool. "I . . . Uncle . . ."

Honeytongue drew back as though he might catch something, but

Edwin rolled his eyes and said, "Don't make a mess in the Crow's precious church or I'll never hear the end of it." He turned to one of the housemen. "Take the lady to the queen."

Beyond Bassus and his two men, who stood discreetly out of earshot of Hild and the queen, the river's tide ran smoothly towards the sea. Two ships had already left. When the tide turned, more would arrive, laden with goods. The Rendlesham wīc might boast more precious goods in stronger colours from hot lands, and more slaves, but here in York there were goods from the north as well as the south. Ivory—tusks and teeth—horn, furs, ingots of silver and gold, chunks of precious stone, the fruits of warm weather, such as figs—a small boy fanned away wasps—jars of wine, pairs of hunting dogs.

The man selling the dogs held their collars as the queen looked at their teeth and fondled their ears. Hild imagined the feel under her hands, silky and soft. But she did not trust dogs.

The hounds—bitches—panted at her in the heat, tongues lolling, gums pink and teeth white and strong.

"They look like they're grinning at us," Æthelburh said.

They were scenting Wilgith's blood on the sleeves still tucked in her belt.

Æthelburh shook her head at the seller and they moved to the next pen. Another matched pair, but smaller, more nervous. "These look likely."

"For what?" They were like Coledauc's beautiful hounds, good only for being admired.

"For Wilnoð. A gift. Coursers."

"That's right!" The seller, a genial man with the plaid trews of the Manau Gododdin. "They're bred for running. Fast as hares. Now this one—"

The dog followed the man's hand with its ears down, and shifted its weight from side to side when it came too near.

"He'd make a fine lady's dog. Gentle and sweet."

The queen laughed but Hild thought the glint in her eyes was not amusement. "Gentle and sweet." She looked at Hild. "He doesn't know who he's talking to."

Hild said nothing.

"Set them aside, man. I might send for them later."

They moved on. They passed a man selling carved whales' teeth, and a woman with a display of amber and beautifully thick pelts—one looked like bear fur, but it was white and she was too tired to look closely—showing another trader, a Frisian, how, if he rubbed a lump of dark amber on his sleeve, he could make the hairs on his arm stand up. Glass didn't do that, she said, only amber.

And jet, Hild thought. But jet did not come in the shade of yellow that would make Begu drool. Jet was not flecked with what looked like frozen bubbles that glittered in the sun.

The queen said to Bassus, "We'll walk across the river."

On the other side of the Use the air was no cooler but it was less complicated with smells, and quieter—at least in the orchard; beyond, in the long-abandoned redcrest settlement, crews took down ruined buildings with the ring of chisel and the crash of masonry, crack of ox goads and creak of carts. But the dust was swallowed by the trees and the noise was muted. Bees hummed. A lark arced high across the blue. The muscles over Hild's ribs began to ease.

Æthelburh waited for Bassus to lay his jacket on the grass under a tree and retreat with his men to pace in a protective circle, then sat. She said something but to Hild it seemed to come from underwater. She was so tired she was not sure if she was asleep or awake. She lowered herself carefully and looked at the tree. Perhaps it was that very tree that she and Uinniau had climbed after she was baptised . . .

Æthelburh sighed. "Very well. I'll go first. Honeytongue. I don't trust him or his news."

Hild blinked herself awake. Honeytongue. Yes. He was like a dog that has been tormented for years, then been washed and brushed, fed, and given a fine new collar. He looked fine, like those Gododdin dogs, but he was not. You could not always predict a dog but she could predict Honeytongue. He could run away with his tail between his legs and then come back looking as though he had slain the wolf. He was a man without shame.

For a moment she thought she might have said all that aloud. Then the queen said, "He'll steal anything and hurt anyone to get what he wants. And what he wants belongs to my children."

Northumbre. In the queen's mind it belonged to Wuscfrea, even though he was a child.

"We must stop him."

By which the queen meant: *You must stop him.* But Hild did not see how.

Poison his wine? With Paulinus watching her every move the queen could do that more surely than she could. Slit his throat from behind when he was squatting on a pot? Not inside walls surrounded by people. Outside the walls, though . . . "How long is Honeytongue in York?"

"He would be gone already if my husband had not sent for you—if I hadn't suggested he send for you—"

From the ruins, a bellow of pain and shouting—someone had dropped a stone on their arm or leg—followed by others' laughter, the kind that meant, *Thank the gods it wasn't me*.

"—talk sense into my husband. He's pleased with you, since the Bryneich."

"The Crow's his godmouth now." She was glad of it; she wished only to be done with Edwin.

"But my husband isn't afraid of Paulinus—he hasn't seen the Christ work wonders. When you speak with the voice of wyrd, he has seen what happens. He listens to your word. He called you here to tell him he will be overking of all the isle. Because if you tell him he will believe you."

Hild said nothing.

"Did you tell him that?"

"He thinks I did."

Sooner or later he would see what she had left unsaid. She had to get away. But first she had to deal with something, someone . . . She was so very tired. The world seemed to slip sideways and she almost slid into sleep. She blinked again, harder. Honeytongue. She had to deal with Honeytongue.

"How many men does he travel with—Honeytongue?"

She should not have had to ask; she should have gone to the byre and counted horses before she ever set foot in that church. *Always remember, scout the ground*. She could not remember who had said that, but she remembered the smell of lavender, a bee . . .

"Hild? Are you all right?"

She rubbed her eyes. "How many?"

"A handful. Bassus could tell you."

Bassus, who had told her about bandits years ago. Bassus, whom she could trust only while his queen trusted her. But the queen was the one who had told Edwin she was with child.

"Hild?"

She shook her head, trying to wake up. Half a dozen gesiths. And their men. Too many. "Honeytongue won't kill his own father." Not if he thought he would get caught. He would get someone else to do that. Penda. Or Cadwallon. Cadwallon would kill all the Yffings. All the Yffings in North-umbre. What did that mean? She didn't know. She wanted to lie down and sleep, like Wilgith . . .

"We all die in the end," she said.

The bees hummed. Honeybees. Lighter, paler than the bumblebee that time in the garth, with Fursey. Fursey. It was Fursey who had said *Always scout the ground*. This one time she had not.

We all die in the end. Had she really said that aloud?

Æthelburh's face was set like calf's-foot jelly. "Can my husband be saved?"

She had. She had said it.

The blades of grass between her fingers seemed outlined in crystal, and the red and black of a ladybird climbing the grass glowed like enamel set in blackened silver. Æthelburh was queen; the queen needed to know. "No. Penda will kill him. He will kill him soon, with or without Cadwal-lon. With or without Honeytongue."

Æthelburh was pale but composed. "How soon?"

"A month." Honeytongue had a plan. But plans took time to implement. "Perhaps two. Take your children to Derventio—no, to Sancton. Have a boat ready at Brough. A boat for Cent. Or Frankia." It would cost, hiring a boat to do nothing but wait. But the church was full of gold.

"And you?" Light, unconcerned. She might have been talking about dye colours.

"Caer Loid is strong."

By the time she got back to Caer Loid the night was whispering. Colours and shapes slipped in and out of the dark's edges: Clouds scudding over the half-moon became banners, wind rustling in the understorey seethed like a cauldron. Roots writhed. Once, a broken-boughed oak caught the light in such a way that it loomed like the face of a laughing fox, one big enough to eat her horse. Gwladus was dozing in the saddle—as she had at the York byre after talking to Arddun—and Oeric, who had slept while Hild and Gwladus battled for Wilgith's life, led her horse.

Hild dreamt with her eyes open. *We all die in the end.* Wilgith. Angeth. The sister and brother she had never met. *Can my husband be saved?*

In a blink the stripling at the gate was bowing. She could not remember his name. He said something. Torches flared, sending shadow figures up the wall and over the turf. Another blink and Cygnet was finding her way to the byre. Someone was saying something but the sound had no meaning. Cygnet stopped by her stall; shifted her weight and twisted; rolled her eye trying to see why her rider did not dismount.

She should pat the mare, reassure her, but she could not move.

The byre boy said again, "Lady?"

With an effort she slid down.

Another blink and she found herself standing, saddle at her feet, hands against the post by Cygnet's stall and head bowed while the byre boy, currying the mare's flank, twisted every now and again to look at her, just as Cygnet had. Tears dripped on the straw. *We all die in the end.*

Behind her, Cian's tread was soft but heavy. Slow. It stopped four paces from the stall. "Did the king's messenger find you?"

She lifted her head slowly, wiped the tears from her chin, and turned. He took half a step forward, saw the blood on her sleeves, and stopped.

"What did the king want?"

It was too late for the king. And Wilgith. "She died."

"What—"

"The baby thrives. She called him Wilfrid. I thought she'd live but then she just . . . died." And then she could not bear it anymore. "Tell me," she said. "Tell me what you heard that night."

He looked at her so long that she thought he would pretend he did not know what she meant. But then he said, "Why didn't you tell me?"

She lowered herself slowly on a sack of oats. She could lie and say, *I didn't know.* She could tell the truth and say, *I was afraid.* She could say, *I love you, you love me, what does it matter?* But words felt like strangers in her mouth.

With deliberation he knelt before her, put both hands on her shoulders. "We grew up almost as brother and sister. But I was treated as wealh. In my heart I thought, I could be son of Ceredig king! But it—I felt . . ." He rubbed his lip with his knuckle. "Outside. I felt outside."

"Even when you were chief of the king's gesiths?"

"No." He sighed. "Yes? I always felt watched and weighed. Always a part of my story hidden. And now I wonder: Did everyone know but me? Were they laughing?"

"They weren't laughing. They didn't know." Except the king, the queen, and Paulinus. And her, and her mother, and his mother. And now, finally, Cian. He knew. She no longer had anything to hide from him.

A great weight, a chain about her heart, lifted and broke. She trembled like a beast of burden suddenly unshackled.

"Love?"

She did not have the words. She pulled him towards her until their foreheads touched. "We are us."

They breathed for a while. "This," he said. "This is what feels right. This is home. We are us." Then he sat back. His face was naked, wholly unguarded. "And I'm afraid. Life, death, luck. It runs through families. My child died—and Angeth. Your mother's children died and my mother very nearly did. And now Wilgith."

Childbed was as dangerous as a shield wall. That was not what he needed to hear.

She forced her back straight and her voice firm. "I will not die in childbed. It is not my fate. I'm Hild Yffing: Butcherbird, Cath Llew, hægtes, and light of the world." She put her hands on his hips, settled the thick bones snug in her palms. "Listen to me. I will not die. Not now, not while you live. The rest we will learn the shape of in time."

She pulled him slowly, inexorably, to her, and he came.

It was raining as though Harvestmonath were already Winterfylleth.

"Something's wrong," Cian said. "Something else that you're not telling me."

"Nothing's wrong." Her legs ached for no good reason. And now her head. Perhaps she should not have started this conversation on a day when the bull had gored one of the stockmen and almost got Cian. The stockman's leg was torn to tatters. He had bled almost white before she tied it off. He still might die.

"Then why do you want a wet nurse to hand? You want her because you know there's something wrong."

She stood, pressing her hands on the elm board because pressing her back did no good. "There's nothing wrong, but Manfrid and Wilgar will be gone with the army soon. I just think Janne will be more comfortable with Wilfrid here."

Cian turned her around, rubbed her back. "And that's it? That's everything?"

"No." His hands were strong and sure on her muscles. "Cian, I won't die. I swear to you. But what if my milk doesn't come? Little Hedgepig might need a wet nurse."

"Truly, there's nothing wrong?"

Her womb gave a practise squeeze as it had begun to do a week ago. "I hurt all over and I'm as big as a hut. But no, there's nothing wrong that another three weeks won't cure."

Little Hedgepig was pulling every joint in her body out of true. Everything was harder than it should be. She was three stones heavier than she had been at Yule.

"You're sure you're well?"

"I'm sure!"

He held her from behind. "Then we'll send for Janne."

She felt his ribs move in and out, in and out.

"Come for a ride with me."

Ride? She turned round but before she could speak her womb squeezed again, though more gently. She sat down. Waited. "Maybe when the rain stops." Or maybe never. Would she ever again have a flat belly and small breasts?

"It might rain for two days."

"Then the ride will wait two days."

He rubbed his lip with his knuckle and picked up her hand, turned her wrist this way and that so the rainlight lit her beads. "Little Hedgepig might wear these, one day," he said. "And she might give them to her daughter. But they're on a string that could break—out riding, crossing a stream. They could catch on a branch and fall—"

Purling into the water. Gone.

"—a piece of you, lost. But I've made something for you to give Little Hedgepig, something from both of us. Something that she can't lose. Come and see. We'll be back before dark."

She rode Cygnet. The first time she had seen Menewood, the sun was shining and Morud running alongside. This time, the jackdaws had already moulted, it was just the two of them, and the rain tasted of leaf-fall. But something of that same spirit filled her and despite her aches she kicked Cygnet to a canter. After a startled moment Cian kicked Acærn and they rode, laughing, north and east to Menewood.

This time, though, it was Cian who led the way, Cian who slid off first and began to climb the old pollard. He climbed as though he had done it many times. Halfway up he leaned down and held out his hand.

She was glad of his help. The bark was slippery and she could not see past her belly to set her feet. When she got to the top he wrapped his arm around her waist and she found her balance. They listened to the rain pelting down on the leaves; they were green still, but by the leathery sound not for long.

He shifted a little and pointed with his chin to a knot on the trunk. "Look."

There, carved from the lump, was a hedgepig, life size, sitting up, alert, as though scenting the wind. The rain glistened on its coat, shone on its nose, winked from its eye.

She twisted, trusting he had her, and touched it with her fingertips. The prickles were sharp.

"For you. And Little Hedgepig. And her daughter in turn."

She touched it, touched it again, imagined generations of girls and women running their finger over it until the prickles were smooth. This was his promise, his way to make their survival real: She would live, he would live, their child would live. He had planned this, lying in the dark while she slept, hands behind his head, imagining. Riding out to the valley, day after day, climbing the pollard, carving a little here, a little there, looking out over the valley but not seeing it, seeing instead her showing his carving to Little Hedgepig, and Little Hedgepig showing it to her child. Child, maid, woman, an unbroken string running into the future.

10

✥

The first day of winterfylleth, the harvest in and tallying done; seed sorted, apples laid in barrels and pears in straw; honey strained and flax weighed. Alone, under the trees, Hild pulled wild garlic, shook the dirt off, and laid the stalk-and-bulbs in a basket. There was garlic still to be picked in the Caer Loid garth, but it was good to be away from the vill where there was room to breathe. She straightened and shaded her eyes against the white glare through a thin shaw of cloud and watched a hawk on the other side of the Yr spiralling down like an ash key, its beak gleaming flint blue where it caught the light. She knew which clearing among the oak and elm he must be circling, watching whatever had strayed too far from cover in search of food.

Food. The race to gather what they could before the world turned its face to winter filled the days of all living things. Yesterday she had watched a slow-worm—her head and neck scarred from years of mating, like an old war hound's, if ever war hounds grew old—flicking up slugs and snails in the long, wet grass near the Caer Loid midden, taking her last meal before sleeping until spring. Children had to guard the sacks of seed waiting to be loaded onto carts against flocks of chaffinches feeding for their long journey south across the water to the sun.

It had been a good harvest—barrels full and sacks straining at their seams—but still she drove her people to find what they could: the last of the blackberries before they mildewed and soured; even mouth-wrinkling blackthorn sloes. Listen for the goldfinches, she told them; they will lead you to the sloes. And more, she told them; find me more. It was too late in the year and the sun too weak to make fruit leather but they dried the berries in the fading heat of the bread ovens after the loaves came out. The bread ovens were in use more hours because she wanted extra bread, and baked twice, to keep against need.

Cadwallon's army was gathering. Perhaps his men were fractious or must be persuaded, and there would be more time. More time meant worse weather for the invaders and more readiness for Elmet. She had sent messages to every farm and steading in Elmet: Bury food hoards. Bury what would keep: mead and honey, butter and dried peas, a barrel of sound apples packed in straw. Hide the hoards as though your life depends on them, because it might.

Her mother, recently arrived from Aberford, was a great help though Hild tried not to let her do too much. Otherwise, when she was besotted with Little Hedgepig, Breguswith would take the reins wholly into her hands and it would be an effort to take them back. Begu was still at Aberford, waiting for Uinniau, but had sent word that if he was not back from Craven the day after the full moon she would set out for Caer Loid.

She would be happier when she had all her people under her eye.

Little Hedgepig shifted—as though trying to burrow out, out!—and kicked, less dancing now than ramming the walls of her prison, though it would be a fortnight yet before she made her escape. And the pressure on her bladder was suddenly urgent.

Behind her, the endless *yewtic-yewtic* of an old female whinchat—the young had already left—dropped into silence and a wheeling, quarrelling flock of rooks rose, scolding some intruder. She could tell without thinking that the intruder was someone the birds knew. She had seen this sharp awareness, or something like, in other mothers-to-be and new mothers; even previously stupid folk could now read a face for intent and distinguish threat in a footfall. Even so, just in case, she changed the grip on her staff and turned to face whoever was coming.

Morud trotted into the open. "Visitors, lady! Ceadwulf and his lady Saxfryth." He grinned. "With the little ones. Both of them. One has a bindle."

Before she married, she had agreed to take Ceadwin into her household to foster but had found reason after reason to delay. And just after Wilgith died, when she again told Saxfryth's messenger that, no, no she could not possibly take the boy this year, Cian had folded his arms—so like Onnen—

and said, "He's a likely-looking lad. And his sister Ceadfryth will one day make a good companion for Little Hedgepig."

No, she said, and laid out all her reasons, including the fact that war was coming. He unfolded his arms, laid a hand on the muscles behind her elbow, stroked with a sympathy that was not apparent in his voice, and said, "All the more reason to take him and keep him safe."

She could feel that hand still. And because she knew he wanted this, wanted a boy he could treat as a son, and because, after all, long ago she had said she would, she gave in. And now here the boy was. She could not even remember what he looked like.

"Stay here." She thrust the basket of just-pulled garlic at Morud, walked into the trees to a rivulet, where she hiked up her skirts, and squatted. Her piss smelt clean and strong and warm. It smelt of Little Hedgepig. She wiped herself, rinsed her hand in the rivulet, rubbed it dry on a tussock of grass, and rejoined Morud. "Tell me about the boy and his sister as we walk."

He was eleven and she was four, Morud said in British as he trotted to keep up with her. He always spoke in British when he trotted or ran; she had given up correcting him. Acorn-brown hair, he said, both of them, though his maybe lighter than hers. She looked like any other dot of a thing; they all looked the same at that age. The boy, though, he could tell him from any child breathing. He was thin, leggy as a cranefly, but with hugeous teeth, like a beaver—

She listened with only half her attention. They would stay for the Hlaf-Givers' Feast, to which every head family in Elmet was invited—three days at least. In that time she was sure she could find a way to put Saxfryth and the boy off. She could send the boy with the men to clear and deepen the drainage ditches to the north of the vill. Yes. It was hard, muddy toil— breaking roots, digging out stones, pulling out fibrous weeds—that must be done before winter to keep the vill, its garth and byre and orchard, snug and dry during the endless rains.

As they drew closer she heard the reassuring sounds of a vill hard at work: the hammer of the barrel-wright thumping the iron hoops over his casks, the chuc-chuc of a planing axe, and the complaint of a cow who did not want to be byred. Turning and rinsing cheese, stacking charcoal, re-thatching roofs, spinning wool, heckling flax, chopping mushrooms, re-pairing fences, closing down hives, sorting the ash poles . . . Endless work but not enough, never enough to be safe. War was coming. They might have to scatter and hide, and the main stores could be taken or burnt. Like squirrels they needed hidden caches, each full. And if something should happen to Cian, something to her—but nothing would happen to her. She had sworn it.

Ceadwin did indeed have big teeth but they were small compared to the amount of pink gum above them, and, even so, nothing to stare at—unlike the rest of him. He looked stretched to breaking, a dab of honey drooling from a wand. His arms and legs were thin as reeds, and his fingers impossibly long. His face was long, too, and his shoulders narrow. His feet were hidden in boots, but by the look of them they were as long as his hands. His eyes, though, were the brown of calves' eyes, rich and warm, his smile—his pink and toothy smile—shy. He held his sister's hand (tiny in his) and looked at Hild with wariness but no fear. Something turned and settled in place in a corner of her heart, and the future unfurled before her: She would teach this boy.

She glanced at Saxfryth and Ceadwulf, at Cian—who was whittling a long piece of elm and smiling to himself as though he knew what had just happened—then squatted before the children. "Do you understand why you're here?"

Ceadfryth shrank against her brother's side but Ceadwin looked at her—looked down at her—then at his mother. Saxfryth nodded encouragingly. "To stick to you like a burr," he said in a light, silvery voice. "I'm to be nice so you like me, and your glow will rub off on me, and I'll one day be a thegn and Mor and Fa will be easy in their old age."

Saxfryth flushed dull red and gripped her husband's arm. The poor man would carry a mark for days.

"Just so," Hild said. "But you will have to leave your sister at home. Will she be all right without you?"

He looked at the little hand in his and thought hard. "I think so. She's brave. She'll be sad, though. Can she come visit?"

Later, after the mortified Saxfryth, the somewhat bruised Ceadwulf, and the two children had been led away by Gwladus, she said to Cian, who had not stopped whittling the whole time, "What are you making?"

"His first sword." He held up the wooden blade. "Elm, because it's lighter. We can switch to oak when his muscles come in."

Hild rubbed at her back, though that was not where the ache was. Their fosterling might learn to handle a blade but one look at his reediness told her he was not built for the shield wall. She would teach him to read.

On the morning of the third day of Winterfylleth, the day of the feast, just as the dawn star was fading, a runner brought a message from Rhin: *Cadwallon marches on the salt trail through the peaks with eightscore men. Penda's banners fly in North Worthig.*

Hild's morning passed with her mind unyoked from her body. She seasoned the ox and pig for the spit, crumbled dried marjoram into the broth of soup bones, and ordered the opening of mead and ale casks hardly knowing what she did. Cadwallon on the salt trail, the road east rather than north, with 160 men. Here in ten days at most. He would pick up more on the way, young and eager, with untried swords and unscratched shields. But now at least she knew he would not come through the Gap.

Penda had planted his banner at North Worthig, forty miles north of Tomeworthig. When his men were gathered he would march north. The two groups could meet south and east of Caer Daun, by the redcrest Rig on the south border of Elmet.

Cadwallon's murderous band would be ready to burn and destroy, like eightscore bandits. Would Penda be joining them or opposing them? It depended on Honeytongue.

Gwladus dressed her in silence. The blue dress with the panels let in to accommodate her belly. A stiffly worked belt from which hung the magnificent purse Æthelburh had given her. Her carnelians and seax. Agate and gold earrings to match the rich embroidery; the agate and garnet ring that was her favourite; smaller rings, set with red and white enamel, and blue and white glass; the pearl and agate veil band to match both cross and earrings. A dab of the precious jessamine. Once Æthelburh was gone that would be hard to find . . .

Her mind flew on as Gwladus chose and fastened.

The feast hall was warm and colourful and smelt richly of roasting meat and rosemary—the new cook was fond of rosemary; no doubt she had added a double fistful after Hild went on to the next task. Her guests' chatter was loud and cheerful; they did not know war was already in motion. No one but Cian knew what the message said—though no doubt some had guessed. Tomorrow was soon enough to tell them. Everything that could be done was being done. Let them have their feast—for some, their last.

Her people. Safe, and warm, and happy.

Breguswith wore a new green dress with russet sleeves and all her gold; she had gained a little weight and there was a hint of discontent about her that meant she was getting ready to do something no one would enjoy—Luftmær probably least of all; the scop did look a little paler than usual. Llerwiadd seemed more wrinkled than a woman who had been a goosegirl only fifteen years ago should be, but wrinkled like a sound apple; she had lost another tooth sometime in spring, but her clothes, at least, were now thick and whole. If she lived through the war she would be all right. Her niece, Sintiadd, though, was now in the early flower of her womanhood. Her eyes were like Langwredd's of the Bryneich: deep, deep blue. No doubt some young man or woman had already made a fool of themselves for those eyes but their lively snap would not survive a meeting with Cadwallon and his men . . .

A stir at the door. The stripling door guard—Cuthred today—had one hand up and the other on his seax hilt facing someone outside. Then he dropped his hand and stepped aside. A king's messenger.

No. No, no, no. Her people deserved one last time—she deserved one last time. The king could wait. She must head off the messenger, move him away out of hearing. But as she stood up Little Hedgepig kicked and turned and she could not move. "Cian."

He looked up from his conversation with Ceadwin, alerted by her tone, and followed her gaze to the door. Then he was on his feet and halfway there. Too late. The king's messenger was through and he called out in that voice that messengers have, the voice that cuts through din like a cheesewire.

"Lady! A message from the king!"

People began to turn and Cian was reaching him—reaching out to clap him on the shoulder, urge him to wait, just wait, then steer him to Hild while gesturing for a houseman—when the Fiercesomes came in.

Hild looked at them. They looked back, faces carefully blank. The brothers Berht stood, then Grimhun, reaching for swords that weren't there. Hild waved for them to sit. "An unlooked-for pleasure," she said loudly, and smiled. "Set aside your weapons and join us for mead!"

Wulf, after a moment, nodded to the others and they began to unhook sheaths and lay them against the wall. Bryhtsige scanned the benches but Begu was still in Aberford.

Hild looked at Morud, who hurried to bring them cups. Gwladus was already bringing mead. Their guests shrugged and turned back to their food. The king was sending messages but their lord and lady were not alarmed: Nothing to worry about. And meanwhile the food was hot.

Luftmær, who was not practised at hiding his interest, was watching, along with others such as Breguswith and Oeric, who were more skilled. She breathed carefully until Little Hedgepig settled to a lazy swim, then leaned back as though this were a welcome and long-awaited message.

The messenger—the same one who had come to summon her to the king outside York—perched on the edge of the stool Pyr brought. The Fiercesomes arranged themselves along the wall, holding cups. Hild caught Gwladus's eye: *Keep those cups filled.*

She turned to the messenger and smiled. He, too, held a cup, but would not drink until he had delivered his message.

"Lady, from the king, for you, in his words." He cleared his throat.

"Softly," she said.

He paused, put down the cup. "Hild Yffing, we require the light of the world at Aberford before noon on Frig's day after the first full moon of Winterfylleth."

He did not say, *And the Fiercesomes are here to escort you.* He did not have to.

Frig's day after the first full moon: six days from today. And the message was for Hild, light of the world, not Hild, lady of Elmet, nor Cian Boldcloak, lord of Elmet, and their spearmen. A simple blessing, then, a good word to speed their way—*He does not fear the Crow. He listens when you speak with wyrd*—and then she would, at last, be done with Edwin king.

She pulled off her smallest ring, the red and white enamel, and put it on the board. "Talk to me."

"The king has called his thegns—"

She had never seen the call go out but knew how it would be. Horses ridden to their uttermost carrying the king's bidding to Osfrith his second son and ætheling at Arbeia. To the Tine valley and the Twid. To the Deorwente valley, and to Craven; to the coasts and the rivers. Men with spears gathering in small groups on hilltops: the farmer with three hides and his sons and neighbours, their saddlebags bulging with twice-baked bread and fruit leather, which the more provident had been gathering since harvest. One of each group—perhaps the one with the extra mount carrying oats or beans for the horses, the one who thought ahead—choosing when to put out the fire, turn their face to York, and march. Each group marching down cattle trails that became paths where they would join other groups, and the one with the banner—or the most packhorses or the storied sword—would choose how to order his men and when they should stop drinking and follow. These bands then flowing along the old ways, where they would meet other bands to form troops, and the troops pouring down the old roads into the eddying pool that would swirl and resolve into Edwin's army, gathered under his boar banner sewn with its gold-thread cross—Æthelburh's addition—and garnet eye. Some come to reap gold, some to defend their farms, some for need to do as others do and hold their heads high in years to come, or for the adventure—but they come. They have to; their king calls.

"—boats to resupply at Caer Daun—"

"Caer Daun?" Cian said.

"Yes, lord."

She imagined Edwin with his captains—the ones with bright mail and inlaid helmets, with their banners, and followed in turn by men with their own banners—while Coelfrith, worried Coelfrith, supervised the loading of boats with forges and anvils, flitches of bacon and tuns of ale, casks of arrows and spare spearheads and bandaging, lots of bandaging. Organising timing. How long would it take to sail down the Use and then into the mouth of the Treonte? Was the Daun navigable yet to big vessels or would they have to transfer to smaller ones . . .

Meanwhile, Edwin and his spears would march south down the war street to Aberford. Then south again, to Caer Daun, the Roman fort on the south bank of the Daun, once the edge of Elmet and now part of the waste between Lindsey, Elmet, and Mercia.

"Supplies for how long? And for how many?"

"I don't know, lady."

She thought for a moment. "Have all the thegns answered?"

"Yes, lady." He met her eyes boldly, as men do when they try to hide something.

"Who stays?"

He hesitated. She tapped the ring: heavy gold, bright enamelwork. It was a good ring. "Ealdorman Osric, lady. In Craven. To guard the Gap."

But Cadwallon was not coming through the Gap. Osric wanted Elmet while the king was gone.

He picked up the ring. "I also have a private message, for you both.

From Lord Wilgar. He says he and Manfrid will bring the babe and his wet nurse when they come with the king."

One less worry. Janne could come back to Caer Loid with her once she had seen Edwin.

Pyr appeared at her shoulder, a houseman by his side holding the mead jar.

It was time for the toasts. She stood. "Stay and enjoy the mead." She looked at Cian, *Get what you can from him*, and Pyr nodded for the houseman to pass the mead. But when he gave her the jar she weighed the jar, thinking. She handed it back. "Bring the white mead."

The houseman looked at Pyr. White mead? This toast was for the folk, for those who came to be thanked by their lord and lady. Not the kind to drink white mead, or to even have dreamt of such a thing.

"White mead," she said to Pyr. "There's enough. Use the best jug." He nodded at the houseman. "Now sit and be my guest."

It took a while to find the silver enamelled jug and fill it, but eventually she walked down the boards and poured the fiery stuff with a steady hand. Pyr and his lady Saxfryth, Llweriadd and Sintiadd, the other Saxfryth and Ceadwulf from their East Farm. "Drink to all our healths," she said.

She smiled at the young ones. "Perhaps they will give you a sip."

She poured for Breguswith and Luftmær. "Sing well," she told him. "Sing as though it may be the last time." She said nothing to her mother; she did not need to.

Down the boards she went, slowly, with a word for each.

Oeric and Morud. The brothers Berht, and Grimhun, Eadric the Brown and one-eyed Coelwyn. The new striplings whose names she knew but could not bear to recall, striplings who already mirrored the manners of those around them: teasing like Coelwyn, singing like Eadric, wearing the gaudy colours of the brothers Berht. Would any live long enough to find their own way? She took a breath, went on.

Then the Fiercesomes. She caught the gaze of each. "However fate throws her dice, you are always welcome in Elmet." She poured for Gladmær. "See that you eat your greens." And Leofdæg. "You should join the Hounds later. They will welcome you." To Bryhtsige, softly, "The lady Begu is in Aberford. One way or another you will see her soon." And to Wulf and Dudda: "Enjoy the feast. I would speak with you later." Edwin held their oath; they must carry her to Aberford, by force if necessary, but they might also talk to her.

Back to her seat, where she raised her cup. "The lord Boldcloak and I give thanks," she said. "To Elmet, the rich land that sustains us. To you, to you all, for your work, and the work that is to come."

Her people. And she would sacrifice them all, every one, to keep Little Hedgepig safe.

The summons to Aberford, fifteen miles from Caer Loid, was for Hild Yffing, light of the world, to pronounce victory before they marched south. He had not asked for Cian.

"Of course I'm coming with you," he said.

"Stay," she said. "The vill needs one of us here."

"I will see you properly escorted."

"I'll take the brothers Berht to make sure we all get back safely." Herself, Begu, Janne, and Wilfrid.

"Three women and a baby in a time of war? No. You will go properly escorted by the lord and spears of Elmet."

If he was going arrayed as a lord of war, she would go not only as light of the world, wearing her beads and rings and cross, jewels and gold crusting even her horse's harness, but as Butcherbird, with her seax and staff; as Cath Llew in her furs; and as Hild Yffing, lady of Elmet, wife to Cian Boldcloak and mother-to-be, with her big belly, her bodywoman, retainer, runner, and Hounds.

Gwladus, wearing her own travelling dress and best bracelets, dressed Hild with care in all her tokens, even the three nested travelling cups Cian had carved for her from the old thorn hedge. Partway through, Breguswith came into her bower and, without a word, put her own seeing stone with its hanger on the bed, gave Hild a stern look, and left. Gwladus added the seeing stone to her belt, rearranged the other tokens to her satisfaction, studied Hild, moved her veil band slightly, and finally nodded.

Cian, in his finest fishmail, seax on the same gold-buckled belt she had given him years ago, and inlaid helmet under his arm, walked her through the still-dewed path to the byre. They did not speak. Rooks wheeled overhead, showing off.

At the byre, dew sparkled on the tips of the thatch, and a dozen mounted figures waited: Gwladus and Oeric, and every single Hound, all polished to a high gloss. Coelwyn carried the banner of Elmet—the green hazel tree of Ceredig and the purple Yffing boar. The Fiercesomes, who for the last days had mingled with the Hounds in a single brotherhood, now sat in their own group, scars livid in the light and Bryhtsige shining like an ælf. Morud, wearing a new hood and belt, stood grinning with five spearmen, none of them striplings. Pyr led out a high-stepping Cygnet and Acærn. In the low morning sun both horses gleamed—even their hooves had been oiled—and their harness was dazzling.

She turned to Cian. "All these men. The vill—"

"Will survive a day," Cian said. "Cadwallon can't be near yet, no matter the road he takes. And we'll be back before the evening star. You will be properly escorted."

He understood. This might be her last meeting with her uncle the king; this was a campaign Edwin most likely would not come back from. It should be honoured with all their splendour.

The dew had burnt off when, from the trees ahead, they heard a trotting pony and saw a flash of yellow. Hild reined in and rested both hands on her pommel.

When she saw them, Begu kicked Sandy into a canter, which he held for just a few strides. "What are you doing here?" Her voice was tight. And Sandy was slightly lame. "Oh," she said when she saw Bryhtsige.

Before she could say anything else, Hild reached out for the pony's bridle. "What happened to Sandy?"

"A gesith's dog bit him. I thought— There were so many. They were so big."

Hild did not know if she meant war hounds or men. It made no difference. The dogs would already have started fighting, taking their lead from the men. The men would be loud and dangerous and have that stink about them, the stink of war. They were riding towards a battle that would make their names or bring their deaths. Perhaps both.

"You shouldn't be here," Begu said. "I told you I'd come. You should have waited." She twisted this way, looking behind her, which set Sandy tossing his head. He might have bolted if Hild had not had a firm grip on his bridle. "And Cian. All these men . . . You're not joining the war band? You can't. You have to go back."

Sandy was sweating and wild-eyed. Cygnet stood still as a carving. "How many?"

"Men? I don't know. They were marching in as I left. Hundreds of them. All singing, but not happy singing." Hounds and Fiercesomes exchanged looks. Begu did not notice. "Come back to Caer Loid with me. Is Winny there yet?"

"No. And I can't. The king summoned me."

"But the baby could come anytime!"

"Not today."

"Do you have to go?" She looked at the Fiercesomes, at Bryhtsige. Something passed between them but Hild did not know what. "Yes, yes, I suppose you do. Well." She fretted at her lip, twisted again, patted Sandy. "Then I'll come with you."

"Not this time." Begu in her bright yellow on her little pony, ringed by men with swords who thought they were marching to red ruin and had no reason to behave. "Go on to Caer Loid. We'll be back before dark."

In the bright sun Aberford smelt like a cauterising iron, the air sudden and dangerous. They walked their horses past groups of men and lines of picketed but still-saddled mounts, towards Edwin's banner, purple, with the cross and the Yffing boar and its garnet eye sewn in white and outlined in gold. Hild looked for the Crow's white silk banner sewn with a red cross. She saw Osfrith's banner—the Yffing boar with a ship—and a host of lesser sigils, but not the white silk. Nor did she see Honeytongue's boar and axe. Wilgar's brown and yellow banner hung with Tondhelm's and Hunric's just north of the beck—or what had been the beck but was now a ribbon lake. Grimhun's dam was holding.

The Fiercesomes moved into a box formation—one in front, one on either side, two behind—with her and Cian at the centre.

Edwin's banner, so heavy with jewels and gold thread that its stitching was sewn in four rows, hung limp on the pole; it and his tufa standard were driven into the bank of the pond. Or what had been the pond. In the space of a morning the turf had been torn to mud and the water fouled, drunk from and pissed in by men, horses, and dogs so now it looked more like a slurry pit. Opposite the banner stood the tufa, its glass ball glinting blue, with the king's chair beneath it.

Edwin sat with Stephanus standing at his left shoulder and his second son, Osfrith, at his right, with Dewal, the heavyset chief gesith—the third since Cian—a pace to his right. Coelfrith would be with the boats. But where was Paulinus? Where was the king's chief priest and godmouth?

Stephanus bent to murmur something in Edwin's ear as the king watched her approach; she couldn't tell if Edwin was listening to his priest or not. He moved from side to side, as restless as on that awful Easter day after Eamer had tried to kill him, though this time, at least, his sword was sheathed. Still, when he snapped his fingers at one of the housemen everyone flinched.

Dudda took Cygnet's reins and Wulf turned his mount to block Cian. The two men locked eyes. Without expression, Cian rested his sword hand on his thigh, ready to move. He looked at Hild. She shook her head. His sword hand remained on his thigh. She caught the gaze of the Hounds one by one: *Hold.*

She slid down with care.

Edwin said, loudly, "I see you have your dogs as well-trained as I have you. Now come to heel."

She kept her face smooth and her hand away from her seax. She could kill him, none could stop her from so close, but she would not survive it. Penda would do it for her, sooner or later, while she was safe in Elmet, behind the stout palisade at Caer Loid.

"Oh, you don't like that, do you?" Edwin said. Hild recognised the tone: goading, wanting to provoke something he could control. Stephanus smiled slightly but Osfrith, too, knew his father. An uncertain king was a dangerous king, dangerous for everyone.

"My king."

The houseman handed Edwin a horn travelling cup. Without taking his gaze from Hild he lifted the cup to his lips and appeared to sip but Hild could tell by the strained swallow that he had taken nothing. Still loudly, he said, "I am Edwin Yffing, overking of the isle. I always win. All know this. And the part of a king is to satisfy the gods on behalf of his people. But I'm tired of these skirted priests of a skirted god who bleat from hiding about meekness and turning the other cheek and rewards in heaven. Men want to hear they will get their reward here on middle earth."

Stephanus leaned forward. "Lord king, we are not hiding. While the overbishop selflessly watches over the queen's safety, I myself—"

"Shut up." Edwin did not lift his gaze from Hild. Another false sip. "The Crow hides with the queen in Sancton. Probably with all the church treasure—my treasure. But we don't need him. Just as we don't need the craven from Craven, do we?" He looked at Osfrith.

"No," Osfrith said, steadily enough, but the sip he took from his own cup was more like a gulp.

"Cadwallon alone rides with eightscore men," Hild said.

"Yes. And I have four times that many."

Osfrith looked into his cup; Edwin was overstating his numbers.

"Christ is on our side," Stephanus said.

"One more word," said Edwin. To Hild, "Honeytongue sends to say only four hundred march under Penda's banner."

"To the Christ numbers are as chaff in the wind," said Stephanus. "Our cause is—" He stared down at the bubbling slash in his belly.

Edwin wiped his seax on Stephanus's sleeve and sat back down. He tilted the blade in the sun, beckoned one of the housemen close, used the man's tunic to polish away a smear near the hilt, and sheathed it. Behind him, Stephanus, cradling his coiled guts in his hands, folded onto the torn turf.

Every rustle of cloth, every crunch of hoof on stone was distinct as the men behind her stiffened. A long way off, ravens creaked. A gust of wind lifted the Yffing banner so it snapped once, twice, then was still.

Two housemen dragged Stephanus away. A loop of intestines, like a bloody blue sausage, trailed beside him, leaving a smear so bright it seemed to glow.

No, she thought. No. I am done.

Osfrith held out his cup for a refill.

"So. Now we need a new godmouth. That's you, niece. You're coming with us."

He was not done with her.

The world slowed. Behind her Acærn tossed his head and Cian patted his neck slowly, one two three. She knew that sound; he was thinking, gathering himself.

Don't move, she thought at him, at the Hounds, at Oeric. Don't move. But did not take her gaze from the king. "My time is almost upon me."

"So? If you have to squeeze out your womb turd by the side of the road, kick dirt over it, and be tied back on your horse, you will come. You are my godmouth."

"I have never spoken for any god."

"Wyrd then. Even gods bow before wyrd. Foresee our victory. Proclaim that winning is our wyrd. You're Cath Llew, Butcherbird, light of the world. Make them believe." *Make me believe.*

Because he did not believe. He was going down in red ruin, and he knew it. But he must march; a king must lead his army when another king threatened his rule. To do otherwise meant being forsworn, branded craven and nithing, a man with no name. Edwin Yffing would march his gesiths and thegns, his spearmen and beardless striplings to war because he would not kneel to greater numbers, would not bow his head and call another man lord. He would lead them all to slaughter so that his good name would live on. But for his name to live, the fight must be worthy of song. And to make such a fight his men had to believe they could win. Fate goes ever as it must. But nothing was certain until the last throw. He was Edwin Overking and she was his cup-and-knucklebones.

Her life split like a raindrop hitting tent leather: two paths, four, eight . . . All ended in blood. Most with Cian at the centre bound and burnt and broken, begging—both of them begging.

Most but not quite all. Very well. He was not done with her yet. She would dice with wyrd.

"One of my men, this one"—she pointed at Oeric—"will return to Elmet. And he will take five spearmen for their defence."

Edwin shrugged. Farm boys and spearmen were not the stuff of songs. "Fewer to feed."

"We have no food with us."

"I'm sure there's plenty."

Hild was, too. Coelfrith would have made sure before he left. "Thank you. Uncle." A reminder to Dewal that she was the king's niece and would expect no argument later about food. "I'll need something for the horses before we leave."

"You'll have to hurry, then. We march for Ceasterforda before the end of middæg."

"Rest while you can," she told the five spearmen. One was the greybeard Cian had recruited at Ceasterforda in what seemed another life. "You march at noon. Be glad; you're going home with Oeric."

"Lady—" Oeric said.

"Feed your mount," she said to him. "I'll be back soon."

To Cian, "We ride to war but we don't stay for it. Meanwhile, remember you were once their chief." She nodded at a group of gesiths beginning to tighten around two others—some kind of fight brewing—and another throwing knives at a tree.

He understood: Pick up the threads of friendship and command, it might save them both.

War. Its stink drenched the camp, the scent of men preparing to fight and die, of hearts turning like axles and breath tearing in and out, of muscles knotting and clotting, veins distending, stomachs closing and guts loosening. You could smell it ten miles away.

Horses rolled their eyes and did not settle to their feed. Dogs snarled and snapped and tore at each other. A witan of ravens, easily a score, glided in, croaking, and settled in the wych elms to the west. They were drawn by the glitter of spearpoints, jingle of harness, and shouts of men that promised a feast.

The brothers Berht, as they walked before Hild towards Wilgar's banner, deeper into the stink and clamour, began to sweat lightly. Hild watched as they—like her—grew more aware of the heft and balance of their weapons, and began to turn their heads back and forth, back and forth, eyes and ears, noses and the very hairs on their skin attuned to danger: walking in a state of arrested violence.

Under the limp brown and yellow banner, Wilgar, shoulder to shoulder with Tondhelm, was showing Manfrid and his wispy-bearded friend how a pair could defend themselves if they were cut from the shield wall. Janne sat on a log nearby with Wilfrid in the crook of her left arm, watching Manfrid. Hunric, perched on a stool and sharpening his sword, was the first to see her. He rested the naked blade across his thin thighs. "Well," he said loudly enough for his hearth troop to turn and look. "Aren't we honoured."

Hunric was an ally of Paulinus, and the king's weasel.

Wilgar turned, saw her, and lowered his shield. Manfrid's friend, wholly intent on showing this old man that his time was past, walloped him in the face with the hilt of his seax. Wilgar roared, banged the gesith's shield aside with his own, and stabbed at his belly. Hild lunged and deflected the blade. The brothers Berht, spears in their hands but not levelled, stepped between them. Berhtred shook his head at Tondhelm and Manfrid.

"Well, that was exciting," Hunric said. He squinted down the edge of his sword.

Hild itched to hit someone, anyone, especially the weasel.

"Pup needs a good whipping," Tondhelm said, glaring at Manfrid's friend.

Hild relaxed her muscles, one by one. "Wilgar, Manfrid. A word." She gave the brothers Berht a look: Watch them.

Wilgar clapped Manfrid's friend on the shoulder harder than necessary, shook him a little, and followed her to Janne's log. Janne stroked Wilfrid's head—crowned now by the same tawny tangle as his grandfather—and did not look up.

"Janne."

Stroke, stroke.

"Look at me."

She lifted her head but her gaze slid away.

"You and the child will go with Oeric to Caer Loid. I'll follow as I may."

"I don't know Caer Loid," Janne said. Her voice was as thin and wispy as Wilfrid's baby hair. A voice with no root. She looked at Manfrid. "Can't I stay with you, lord? You'll protect me."

Manfrid swelled. Hild kept the impatience from her voice. "Manfrid will soon have important things to worry about. He can't be distracted by trying to keep a pretty girl and a baby safe." The girl set her face and feet like an ox. Hild did not have time for this. "Then come with me. I'll be leaving for Caer Loid soon enough."

Janne blinked. "With you?"

"Now, Janne."

The gelding had almost finished the feed in its nosebag. Oeric unhooked it slowly, reluctantly. "But, lady—"

"You must."

Gwladus crooked her finger at Morud and pointed to Janne: his responsibility for now.

"Lady, no. Please. Send the Hounds, send—"

"Take the spearmen to Caer Loid. You are their captain now. When you get to Elmet obey my mother's word as you would mine. Tell Pyr that, too. Tell Begu to look after Ceadwin, and to remember Menewood. She'll know when it's time."

She turned to Gwladus, who had her back to her, checking the girth on her saddle. "You should go with him."

Gwladus tightened a buckle and did not turn. "I stay." She lifted her heavy corn-coloured hair over one shoulder, paused, and turned. "I'm your bodywoman and an army needs a godmouth who looks the part."

Hild had sworn long ago she would never force Gwladus against her will. She swung abruptly back to Oeric. "Go."

"But what about—"

"Now, Oeric."

It was past middæg when they left Aberford. Without Coelfrith there was no one to sort the carts and the horses, no one to patiently point out to the chief gesith what must be done. Dewal's voice was heavy, and so was his gold, but his authority was not. He shouted and gesiths shrugged and went back to their conversations and their bets: Ceasterforda was only two hours' march; there was plenty of time.

Mounted—they would leave with the king in the front; no breathing others' dust for Edwin overking—Cian stroked Acærn's neck and watched the men, and Hild watched the birds.

A great flock of mistlethrushes skimmed overhead: The wind was fresh and from the north and west. "At least it won't rain today," she said.

Cian nodded. That was good; they had brought no tent.

Somewhere she heard a single rook kaa-ing, and the deeper, quicker notes of gathering carrion crows.

"Tonight we'll camp at Ceasterforda," he said. "Tomorrow we overnight on the lea at Scanton." He stroked Acærn's neck and mane, looking to any observer as though their talk was of nothing in particular. "But we'll make at least one stop between them. Probably just south of the Weneta."

She stretched casually, thinking. There was a place where the Kelder ran close to the source of the Weneta, four miles or so of it hill country. A good place to slip away. But it was too dangerous in daylight. Her womb squeezed. "He'll want my speech before we march from Scanton."

He nodded. Just as the sun rose—if he were king that's how he would do it.

She looked around; no one could hear them. "It will have to be midniht." The night before a battle men would drink, and be too tense to do more than doze lightly. But the army would be restless, constantly stirring. Men would be watching for the enemy and might not be so careful of a friend. "We'll—" Her womb clenched, no soft squeeze but hard, convulsive.

She bent. He steadied her with his right hand. She leant into him a moment, then straightened.

He saw the aftershock on her face. "Will there be time?"

She nodded. But not much. Little Hedgepig would come soon, ready or not. She tried to remember their ride to Caer Daun right after they gained Elmet, just a few months ago. "There's a path north of the hill by Scanton . . ." No. Even Dewal would watch that path. There was another hill—or was that on the other side of the Daun? She couldn't remember. Maybe they should ride east. But that was mire and marsh. Not land she knew. But there would be boats. Coelfrith was bringing boats.

"Well, well." Behind them.

They turned as one: Hunric, mounted on a magnificent black. He was heroically helmed—in the middle of a host, and far from battle.

Hunric looked from one to the other and scratched under one of his silvered cheek plates, setting it winking in the late-afternoon sun. "You two look more like Freyr and Frig every day."

Cian's hands kept stroking and patting Acærn but his face rippled. Then it stilled and he nodded blandly to Hunric, as though he had heard only the compliment, the likeness to gods, not the insult.

Hunric made a few more remarks, she did not know what. This was Cian's fear: *Did they know? Were they laughing?* But he was laughing now at whatever Hunric said and speaking in turn to make Hunric snigger—just as he would have a year ago.

"—and I'll ride with Hunric," Cian was saying. To her.

She reran the words in her head: She would ride with the Hounds—and Fiercesomes if she could—while Cian rode to Ceasterforda alongside Hunric. It was what she would have suggested if she were not so close to her time—they needed friends—but she had seen that look on Cian's face. And she wished he would for once not be proud, not try to prove he feared no man's scorn.

Hild and the Hounds crossed the Kelder and got to Ceasterforda with the leading group an hour before the evening star rose. Hild sent Gwladus for Janne and the child, who had ridden in one of the wagons, and scouted a good camping place: under the stand of oak to the west, deep in leaf mould with no nettles, molehills, or tree roots to poke in her back. High enough to be well-drained, upriver from the main camp. To the east of the camp, the ravens were already settled in the alders. By the time the main body crossed the river, followed by the stragglers and carrion crows, the moon was hidden behind gathering cloud.

It rained before dawn, light and brief, just enough to lend sparkle to twigs as they set out. The sun came and went and the scent of late woodbine made it seem like an autumn jaunt to gather mushrooms. Edwin's drummers struck a rolling pace, their birchwood stretched with deerskin punching out a fine rounded note as they marched. On the southern moorland they passed grey-green mounds of juniper, and the gorse was still gold. There would be no fighting today, just marching; they knew how to march. They might march forever. They laughed and sang.

The songs were light and high-stepping with words to match: songs of fish who swam backwards up a waterfall, of meat and mead, an unbreakable sword that could bend to improbable shapes. She knew most of them, and sang along. Then as they crossed the Weneta, the wind veered to the northeast and a skein of geese—too high to tell what kind—crossed under the belly of darkening cloud. When they stopped to eat and rest, the horses lowered their heads and turned their rumps to the wind.

The march from the Weneta to Scanton was slower. As they began to cross the edge of the great marshland, wind cut at them from the side, and here and there the road was muddy and broken. Instead of harriers and kestrels skimming the rise and fall of the moorland, small songbirds among the marshgrass—linnet and wagtail—fell silent as they passed, leaving the rearguard to walk nervously through silence. Hild, with Gwladus and a trotting Morud, moved now at the centre of the Hounds and Fiercesomes with more men edging closer as they marched south. Ahead lay Caer Daun, the redcrest fort on the south bank of the Daun, and at Caer Daun they would face Penda. Edwin had never lost, but nor had Penda. And Cadwallon would be marching from the west, Cadwallon who carried death in his heart for them all. But against Penda and Cadwallon they had the Butcherbird, they had Cath Llew, against whom no enemy could move unseen or stand. She was the light of the world, their guide and way, weigher of wyrd. They wanted to be close, to breathe her air, be inside her light and her wyrd shield.

They rode past the broken shape of a redcrest burgh. It looked melancholy in the rainlight. Someone began a song about the ruins of giants but none took it up, and after a verse or two the words trailed into nothing.

The sun was sinking and the moon, waxing crescent, rose behind cloud as thin as campfire smoke. Gwladus and Morud, escorted by the brothers Berht, were getting water. Hild fed another twig into the fire, hazel this time. All around her, men watched. Everything she did now was an omen.

Behind the cloud, the sun slipped below the hill to the west and the sky began to dim. The air to the east was misty with rain and the moon haze spread like melting wax.

Cian squatted by the fire, whittling. To anyone watching he looked relaxed, but he whittled and threw the wood in the fire, began again, whittled and threw, whittled and threw, and he never once turned the grain to the light to see it better or adjust his stroke. In the distance the sound of axes meant the king's men were felling one of the sheep pasture's last pollards. This was where armies from north or south had camped since the long ago. And now there would be one less tree, one less shelter for man or beast in days to come.

Another gesith, one she didn't know, came with an unlit torch, said, "Lady?" and on her nod dipped it in her fire.

She watched him walk to his shieldmates reverently with the sputtering torch—or as reverently as a man in heavy war boots could—and sucked air through her teeth. "Look at them," she said. "They watch everything I do." A dozen men, a score, two dozen men had watched as she struck fire from flint on the first try—a good sign, they said, and came one by one to borrow her fire, borrow her luck. Soon there would be twoscore, watching every twist of her head and stretch of her hand.

Cian tossed the half-whittled thing in the fire, picked up another, and this time turned it this way and that as though looking for the grain. But Hild knew he did not see it. "They'll get bored," he said.

She knew they would not.

Morud trotted to the fire and knelt between them long enough to murmur, "The king has a visitor. Honeytongue." Then he was up and gone again.

She closed her eyes. Honeytongue.

"What? It is the baby?"

"Not yet." But she felt different, nervous as a foal, and she was thirsty. She understood why so many women talked so much just before the pains came. It would begin soon. And they would be surrounded by gesiths. They could not get away; she knew it now, had known it deep down since they crossed the Weneta. They were watching her. They would not get bored, they would not stop. And now Honeytongue was here.

The moon on the marsh underlit the sky, like a cold, pale sunset on the wrong side of the world. A sunset for the dead.

"Lady." A man she had seen before—one of Dewal's. "The king wants you."

She picked up her staff and stood and Cian followed. At that moment the light from east and west was perfectly balanced; for one eerie heartbeat she cast no shadow. Dewal's man stepped back a pace and a murmur ran through the men like wind in the corn: Cath Llew casts no shadow. Cath Llew walks with the wights.

The night thickened fast and it was dark before Hild and Cian got to the felled pollard ringed by torches and men—thegns, Dewal, his captains, but no Honeytongue.

Edwin sat on the thick end of the trunk, his sword jutting forward across his hip, a silver-rimmed travel cup in his left hand and a rowan stick in his right. Red and yellow torchlight rippled on his gilded war shirt and glittered from the jewelled eyes of the boar on the helm by his right hip. Before him stood an unarmed man, delivering news of some kind. Edwin's eyes were half closed, he seemed barely to listen but sipped and every now and again leaned down to prod the dirt at his feet with the stick. It was a map, like the one she had made for the children in York, but cruder, and the proportions wrong, or perhaps hills in the wrong place. It was hard to tell from this angle and with the torches sending shadows this way and that.

As Edwin leaned his hair lifted and stirred in the wind; Hild glanced at the sky. So did the unarmed man—a sailor, used to reading the weather.

"Am I boring you?" Edwin said to the man, eyes still half lidded.

"Not much." Not a man used to the savagery of kings. "But a change in the wind . . ." He pursed his lips, whistled silently to himself, thinking. "Nah, it makes no odds. Or not much. Not enough to matter, I reckon."

"You reckon, man, or you know?" said Hunric. He looked less ridiculous without his helm. Several thegns, even those who did not much like Hunric, such as Wilgar and Tondhelm, nodded.

"Should know if the boats'll be there or not," said Tondhelm.

The sailor eyed him with disdain. "I said so, didn't I? Lord Coelfrith and his boats will be at Caer Daun by morgen. Or close enough." He turned back to the king. "If that's it then I'll be off. We've ground to make sure of at Caer Daun."

Edwin waved his hand and the sailor left with no more ceremony than a nod to a man standing in the shadow beyond the torchlit ring, who followed him into the dark.

Edwin mused on his stick for a moment, then turned to her. Face-on, he looked haunted, a man who says one thing and believes another, looking away from his feet so he did not have to see the chasm before him. His eyes, what she could see of them, were blood-shot. With a shock, she realised he was drunk.

"No turdling yet?" Even his voice sounded old, like rope, twisted and fraying. "Well, don't plan on tomorrow. Unless you want to squeeze it out in front of the men. You'll speak at first light. Then we march for Caer Daun." He poked idly at the map.

"And our enemy?"

"Honeytongue is on his way back to his men at the fork of the war street, here, at the barrow fort on the other side of the river—"

There was no barrow at Caer Daun, only one north, and one hard by the—

Little Hedgepig kicked, just once but etin-strong, a warning of what was to come. She leaned on her staff and cradled her belly with one hand. Turdling. Tomorrow at dawn.

She blinked, trying to force herself to pay attention to the map and not her belly. The king was pointing southwest, to the redcrest road that ran along the Daun's south bank and linked Ryknield Way to Ermine Street. The Rig, the earthworks that in the long ago marked the limit of some Elmet king, ran on the north bank, west of there. And there was a barrow.

"—warn us when Cadwallon approaches."

"And Penda."

Edwin took another slow sip. "Penda comes as our ally."

She waited but Edwin said nothing of Honeytongue bringing a token as proof. She pointed to the north bank of the Daun on his map. "We need men on this hill." Men who could be trusted. You could see for miles from there: Ryknield Way, the Rig . . . clear to the river Roder on a good day. It would not matter then which side Honeytongue took, they could see and decide for themselves.

"Why?" Dewal said. "Even if there was anything to see they couldn't get to us with word in time."

"They wouldn't need to," Cian said, understanding what she meant. "They wouldn't need to," he said again, this time in his chief gesith's voice, Lord Boldcloak's voice: cutting and clear and Anglisc to the core. "A beacon there." He pointed with the blunt toe of his war boot to the hill on the map due west of them, just this side of Ryknield Way. "And a beacon here." He nodded southwest, to the hill they could all see—the one where the last sunset had died. "With the beacon, and a fast rider on the south side of the river to run to Caer Daun, we're covered."

"There isn't time to get beacon wood to both," Dewal said.

"There is," Cian and Hild said together, like mirror images.

Hunric sniggered, and mouthed at the man next to him: *Freyr and Frig!*

Edwin tilted his head as though trying to decide nothing more important than whey or buttermilk for his cup. "Oh, very well. Never let it be said I ignored my counsellors. Two of Dewal's men will ride to the hill tonight." He waved at the hill to the southwest. "But no more talk of beacons."

Two men with no beacons in the middle of a triangle of roads, four miles from the nearest. Two men who would be able to do nothing but stand by helplessly and watch. No one said anything. They had all watched Stephanus be dragged away.

"Good. Tomorrow we march for the redcrest fort at Caer Daun. Coelfrith's boats will be there with food for a month. Penda will come to us bearing green boughs not banners but if he changes his mind we'll have strong walls to shield us, water at our doorstep, and command of all roads."

She looked at Cian. Who had repaired Caer Daun's walls? And you only had command of roads you could see, roads held by men you could trust. Only Honeytongue could see the roads to the west.

Edwin threw the rowan stick into the dark behind without a care for who might be standing there. "Good," he said again. "Now we'll have a drink. Tomorrow we'll win, as our godmouth will tell us."

They all turned to her, some, like Wilgar, with a wary look.

"Tomorrow is soon enough for speeches," she said. "Tonight you drink with the king."

Wilgar brightened: Drinking! That was something a man could understand.

They walked back to their fire in a silent ring of watchers who kept pace just beyond earshot. They said nothing for a while as they walked. "A man who tries to hunt two deer at once will lose both," Cian said softly.

She nodded in the dark.

"Why not put men on both those hills, send a dozen to the barrow, and stay here?"

She did not bother to answer. He knew why: Edwin was telling himself the story in which he believed Honeytongue when he said Penda would bend the knee. Besides, a dozen might not be enough. No one knew how many men Honeytongue had at the barrow, whose side he was on, or what Penda would do. All she knew was that tonight they could not slip away, and tomorrow she had to find a way to persuade an army that they were not marching to their death—or at least persuade their king that she had persuaded them—just long enough for them to escape before the slaughter.

The daylight, such as it was, grew behind her. She faced the host: seven hundred mounted men, drummers, and spike-collared war dogs. At least the wind was blowing the stench of loose bowels away from her. She sat on Cygnet, reins loose and tucked under her thigh, staff in her left hand, and right hand resting on top of her thigh. Banners streamed, bits chinked, and dogs panted. Her furs lifted in the wind. Seven hundred men; scores had slipped away in the night. To the left, halfway back, but not as far back as she would like, Elmet's hazel tree shone white against green.

She breathed, in and out, in and out, deeper, stronger, then raised her right hand, palm out. When she moved it, right then left, she drew their gaze to her. She lowered her hand to her thigh.

"You know who I am," she said. Her voice rang.

Front and centre Edwin's banner rippled and snapped so the great boar of the Yffings ran in the air over them.

"The Yffing boar." They looked at it. Its red eyes glowed, its muscles seemed to swell. "The Yffing boar is strong. The Yffing boar is powerful. The Yffing boar never backs down. You are sworn to Yffings. The heart of a boar runs through you. Men fear the boar. They fear you."

She felt their attention as clearly as the fur brushing her cheek.

"Men fear a single boar. You are dozens, scores, hundreds. You are an army of shield brothers. Nothing will stand against you."

Edwin's eyes glittered. The hand on her thigh was clenched in a fist. She forced it open.

"Cadwallon brings eightscore men but Cadwallon is a nithing. No nithing can hold men to their oath. His eightscore will break against the Yffing wall like a hide boat against the rock. You will overwhelm them. You will crush them. They will scream as you crush them. They will drown beneath your fury. They will drown in their blood."

She began to feel very strange.

"You know who I am," she said again. "I am Hild Yffing, lady of Elmet." The Elmet contingent shouted; even from there Hild could pick out Cian's bell-clear voice. "Hild Yffing, Butcherbird." More shouts: Hounds and others. "Hild Yffing, Cath Llew." A wordless bellow from Wulf and an obviously practised Cath Llew, Cath Llew, Cath Llew from the Fiercesomes and those close by. "I am Hild Yffing, light of the world." Light of the world, light of the world! "At an age when a gesith takes up his first wooden sword, I took up wyrd. I wield wyrd. And I say to you: I am never wrong. I say to you: You are strong. And I say to you: Yffings will rule the isle from sea to sea. We will prevail."

Something softened and gave inside and, Oh, she thought, Oh, and knew that in the drawers of Cath Llew, of Butcherbird, of the light of the world there would be a tiny smear of blood as the plug in the neck of her womb gave way. Now she was launched into a current over which she had no control, one that would follow its own course and carry her to whatever shore fate decided. None could stem this tide, not even her.

"We stand together. We are Yffing! We fight like boars and trample any who stand in our way! We march!"

She nodded to the drummer, who raised his sticks, licked his lips, and rattled out a roll.

"Ho-o!" Dewal called.

"Hu!" They shouldered their spears.

"Ho-o—"

"Hu!"

And with the trill of a whistle the Yffing host moved forward. Hild turned Cygnet and led. Cygnet sidestepped—she knew something was wrong—but Hild dug her heels in, and she steadied.

It was three or four miles to Caer Daun. They moved at an easy walk. Gradually, she fell back and to her left. Not far from the Elmet banner now, and the banner was closer to the edge of the host. Bryhtsige, she saw, was falling back with her. Then she saw Leofdæg and Gladmær. Like boys not wanting to be sent from the hearth to bed they looked anywhere but at her; if they didn't see her, they were not there.

She looked around: Wulf was there, and Dudda. And that gesith Gladmær had stood guard with at the York gate, Boertred, and another.

A squeeze, a real one this time, spread from her belly to her back, and she panted and tried not to bend. On it went, on and on. A score-count, longer. She wanted to rest, to lie curled on her side in a tub of warm water.

She doubted she could stay on her horse past noon.

All about her, men sang. Mud songs and blood songs, reckless gore and wild glory. And now the songs grew ugly: war was bitter, war was waged in horror and pain, war was death. She fell back with the brothers Berht, who sang with the rest. They fell back through Hunric's men, and then Cygnet's haunches were level with Acærn's nose, Acærn's neck, and Gwladus's gelding wanted to match her pace for pace, as was usual, but Gwladus was leading a horse on which sat Janne and the baby Wilfrid. She had forgotten all about them; her thoughts were turning slippery; she couldn't catch them. Morud ran at her heel. He was not grinning. At last she drew level with Cian.

While the others sang he leaned in. "We can't run with them watching."

"Must," she said.

But before the squeeze eased enough for her to explain the urgency, they approached the rush and pour of the river, the Daun, named after the mother goddess of long ago.

The riders crowded together to cross the bridge and the Elmet band was hemmed in; no way out but forward. The Elmet banner Berhtnoth carried, the hazel tree of Ceredig and the Yffing boar, moved farther away. Behind them the songs turned uglier.

> Your sister's your mother
> Your father's your brother
> You fuck one another
> Now we'll fuck you!

She looked at Cian just as another squeeze—so strong it felt as though her body were trying to turn itself inside out—bent her over. She could only pant while Cygnet, confused, stopped and tossed her head. Cian and Acærn were pushed forward.

He turned back as he was pushed forward, and she saw the look on his face: blank, armoured against the hurt.

> You fuck one another
> Now we'll fuck you!

Their gazes met. His face shifted, he saw he was trapped, and she fought to straighten, to move forward, but could only watch as he saw there was no way out until he was over the bridge, put one hand on his heart, and mouthed *We are us!* and was carried away in a tide of horse.

Meet at the boats! she shouted to him, or tried to, but she had no breath.

Someone shouted for them to get out of the way, get off the fucking bridge, and Cian moved farther away.

Someone—Gwladus—had her bridle; they were moving. A hand rubbed her back. "Lady, how long? Morud, stop gawking and run for Coelwyn and Eadric. Lady? Where's Boldcloak?"

But all she could do was pant.

A flash of white face and a shiver in the Elmet banner ahead, far ahead now, as Berhtred craned to see if he should stop.

"It's a ruin," she heard a man say. "And where are the fucking boats?"

No boats. Where was Cian? *We are us.*

Then Morud was there with Coelwyn and Eadric. No boats: no supplies. No one had rebuilt the walls—one of Honeytongue's lies. She straightened as much as she could. The pain was easing, and her breathing. No boats. "Food," she told them. "Coelwyn and Morud. Get as much as you can as fast as you can. Steal it, kill for it, anything." They left. "Eadric, you're with Gwladus. Get Janne and Wilfrid safe into a wagon. If you can get the wagon here, do. But don't dwell on it. Then—" She straightened more. "Then food, any food. And fuel. Bring it . . ." Bring it where? She turned in her saddle. The banner, and the brothers Berht, were approaching. "Bring it to the banner. Now go."

Gwladus was about to protest but then the brothers Berht were there and she bowed and left.

"Boldcloak. Where is he?"

"At the fort." Berhtnoth scratched his thigh. "It's a mess. Grimhun said he didn't like the look of things."

Berhtred nodded. "He said somebody'll catch it. Let's hope it's not Boldcloak. The king's man dragged him off to look, to explain himself. Grimhun, too. But even from here we could see the walls all higgledy-piggledy—"

"And no boats," Berhtnoth said.

"—no boats," Berhtred echoed.

No boats meant no food.

"No anvil, no arrowheads, or spearheads—"

"King's got a portable forge on one of the wagons."

"But just one. And not much charcoal. Not enough for an army."

No boats. No food. The fort the same ruin it had been when she and Cian had checked at the turn of the year. Barely three courses in some places, no gates.

"What else?"

"Else?" The look on his face, both their faces, said, *That's not bad enough?*

She sat straight in her saddle. Cygnet was taller than most and she was taller than any rider. But she was not tall enough to see over the seething mass of men.

"I have to get to the landing place."

"But there's no boats," Berhtred said.

"Nonetheless." She had to know if Coelfrith's sailors had ever got there or had been delayed. It might make all the difference. Soon, very soon, the only way she could travel would be in a cart or by boat.

The landing place had been built by the redcrests from elm and a dark, gritty stone. Much of the wood had been replaced over the years by this king or that, but even the newest was old. She remembered being there with Cian, listening to the slap of the water on the pilings, the wheeling cry of seabirds, and one black-headed gull perched on a great jagged piece of elm, watching her.

The elm was gone and instead of gulls overhead here came the ravens. Beyond their croaks all she could hear were the calls of gesiths dipping for water, and their trampling had masked any signs she might have found.

She needed Cian. At the fort with Grimhun, Berhtnoth had said. With the king. Trying to explain Honeytongue's lies. He would have to find his own way back. He better do it soon.

She turned in the saddle, trying to think. Even without pain her thoughts squirmed, frantic as eels in a bucket, because she knew more pain was coming. And she needed Cian. Needed his size and his steady weight and his smell.

Think. Coelfrith had come and fled, or been waylaid, or perhaps delayed by weather. Or he had joined the enemy. No way to know. But there would be no escape on a boat. Think.

Ermine Street ran spear straight from the southeast gate of Caer Daun, raised high above soft and dangerous ground, over the Torne and the Idle, to Balltreow ten miles away, deserted since the redcrests left, then up over a slight rise and down again to Lindum. No help would come from Lindum; Coelgar would be guarding his own walls. From the opposite gate the war street ran back across the Daun to Scanton, the Weneta, the Kelder, the Yr. They had just come that way: nothing to worry about but no help, either. That left the road Honeytongue watched—but for whom?—the road east along the south bank of the Daun to the Roder, where Ryknield Way, the road that Penda travelled from North Worthig, met the salt road through the Peaks, bringing Cadwallon.

The rearguard watched the bridge and the road north. The enemy were coming on the western road. The south road led through miles of mire and waste to Lindum, where Coelgar, assisted by Blæcca, still held sway. Coelgar had never liked her, but they had an understanding. Lindum was a possibility, if she could get there.

It was not yet noon but the day began to dim as the cloud thickened. The wind picked up, fluffing her furs.

Another squeeze, stronger than before, began at the small of her back, but she was ready for it and did not groan, and when she bent it was as though to look more closely at the bush for sign.

The pain started sweat on her scalp and made her want to scream and curl on the muddy stone and not care about anything but wailing and wanting her mother. She hung on grimly; it would pass. Ten breaths. She could endure that. But her waters would break soon, and then she would have to get off the horse. She would never get to Lindum before then. Unless she was on a boat. But the boats weren't here. Her thoughts swam after each other, round and round, like a ring of otters.

Where was Cian?

Not north, not south, not west; and east lay nothing but mire and trackless waste, a maze of marsh and mere, miles of marshgrass and bog and hidden traps where peat had been dug and slowly filled with black ooze. But there was half a mile of solid ground between Caer Daun and the fenland, and the river for water if they had fuel to boil it. Yes. By the time the squeeze eased she had made up her mind: east of the landing place. Plant the banner for Cian to see. If the boats came, they would be first on.

Grimhun found them as she was filling Cygnet's nosebag and telling Coelwyn and Morud where to pile the food they had brought. There was a tiny smear of blood on Coelwyn's shield rim, and Morud's knuckles were raw, but she had no time to care who had suffered. "Where's Boldcloak?"

"With the king."

"Where?"

"He's taken the soundest room in the fort. West corner."

There were no sound rooms. "Stay here, with the banner. Make the best of this place—or find a better, just make sure it's this side of the fort and not far from the bridge. Tell Morud, when there's time, to start looking for another way to cross the river. Downstream." Upstream was enemy territory. "When Gwladus returns keep her here." She took a grip on her staff, beckoned the brothers Berht. "We go to the king, to get Boldcloak."

They were moving towards the northeast gate when the cry went up: Penda! Penda to the west! She ran, or tried to, one hand on her belly as though to hold Hedgepig in.

Outside the west gate was a scout's horse trembling and heaving, its wind broken. The news was not peace. No messenger bringing news of peace needed to break his horse's wind. But no woman had given birth on a battlefield, either, and that might yet come to pass.

Edwin stood sideways in the press by the gate, hunched like an old man facing a strong wind. He squinted shrewishly at his baldric, settled it twice, and called for his helm. A way behind him, Cian stood in the front rank of the king's thegns and their hearth troops; so few thegns. Osfrith the only ætheling and Cian the only ealdorman. No prince of the Bryneich or Gododdin; no Osric of Craven or his son Oswine; no nobles of Rheged or Lindsey.

Edwin saw her. "Banners!" he shouted to her, cross as a fishwife. "Penda bears banners not boughs!"

War banners, not the green boughs of peace. Bitter war, winter war; the ruiner of the pattern.

His helm came and two bodymen began to buckle and tie.

Cian saw her and raised his hand, but his face was calm: There were no more choices to be made. He was surrounded by armed men on the brink of war; he could not leave if he wanted to, for now any man leaving the line would be forsworn, and killed as an enemy.

He gave her a faint smile and that one-shouldered shrug. This was his wyrd. Not Cian who waits. Not Cian husbandman of Elmet. He was Cian Boldcloak: gesith, sworn to the king; oath-bound to defend his lord until glory or death. First, foremost, here, now, this was his place. He bumped his fist to his heart: *We are us!*

No, she thought. No. Your place is with me.

She needed a plan, a way to pull Cian from the battle. She looked around for Leofdæg. The broken-winded horse had not been his, but if he knew the scout she could ask him: Is it Penda himself, or only Penda's banners? Are those that bear them experienced men—lords of war glittering with gold?—or young fools looking for glory? How fast are they moving—do they march willingly and with high heart? How many are archers, how many spearmen? How many mounted? But he was standing with the other Fiercesomes to Edwin's left, where the tufa bearer, called before he had expected, was hastily lacing his breeches.

She filled her lungs. "My king! Where is Cadwallon? Any news of Honeytongue?"

With his helm fastened she could not read his face, but she saw his body change as the weight settled in place, just as Cian's had. Saw his spine lengthen and his feet plant and his shoulders go back. The king she had known all these years was canny and cunning, careful in his anger. Now she watched him throw aside that care. There were no choices left. He was king. His enemy approached under the banners of war. His wyrd was to fight and if necessary to die; it was what kings did.

In one of those odd moments between the breaths of the world, silence settled between them.

"Honeytongue?" she called again.

"My son?" Even his voice seemed strong again, strong and wide. "Honeytongue is lost to me. But I have another son." Silence. "Two other sons!" And he began to laugh, the huge mad laugh of a man whose dice are thrown, who has an army at his back and an enemy at his door, and one clear and simple path. He laughed on and on, and the laughter spread, until the whole war band howled and bellowed, even Hild's men behind her.

After a while it died, and Edwin turned to Dewal. "There!" he shouted past his cheek pieces, and pointed to the slightest of rises to his left topped by a mulberry bush. When Dewal hesitated Edwin seized the tufa, strode to the rise, and thrust the shaft deep into the dirt. "Here," he cried in a great voice. "Here's where the boar of the Yffings will stand. The fort at our back and our face to the enemy!"

Berhtnoth began to step forward but she grabbed his arm. The world turned to a boil of dogs and men pushing and punching to make way, to find their shield brothers, their place in the line.

"No," she said to Berhtnoth and Berhtred. "No!" Once in that line no man could walk away without shame.

"Lady——"

"Your oath is to me; me, not the king. To me! Back to the river, to our banner."

She could not wait; they would come or not. Another squeeze was gathering deep inside her belly. Between two armies was not the place for it. She needed a high place to see, but there were no high places this side of the river. They followed.

Coelwyn and Eadric were mounted when she got back to the banner. "No," she said. "Not yet. We have to——"

The clamping squeeze was earlier than she expected, and stronger. She panted, Gwladus rubbed her back and said to the gesiths, "What are you looking at?"

The four of them turned the other way and formed a square around them.

"I can feel the ripple," she said to Hild. "Soon now. No more riding for you."

A spatter of rain. Hild panted some more. She might have to ride. "Where's Grimhun?"

"With Morud, scouting for a river crossing."

Hild squinted downriver past Berhtnoth's broad, armoured back and saw nothing but flat green stretching to the leaden sky.

"Not that way," Gwladus said. "Too wide downstream, Grimhun said. Too boggy."

"But——" South and west was where the fighting would start, where they did not want to be. "We have to get up high. We need the nearest hill. We have to climb it." Or she couldn't see the battle, wouldn't see the path to getting Cian out.

Gwladus wiped the sweat from her face with an expressionless look that nonetheless Hild knew well: The lady might as well be asking for the moon, split and buttered and served with plums. The nearest rise already had a war band standing on it. The next was across the river. The next was in the direction of the enemy.

"South, then," Hild said. "We'll go south. To Lindum." If they hurried they would be across the Idle before there was a victor. If she could ride. Surely she could ride? "Find the horses. Gather . . . gather the—the food." Her thoughts flicked one way, then the other, like a silvery shoal of fish. "No. Wait." Not Lindum. She caught Gwladus's hand. "It's— I'm not thinking well." They would never get to Lindum. "Think for me."

Gwladus stilled.

"I need—" She panted and her thoughts darted apart, flying in every direction. "Boldcloak, he's gone. For now." There might be a way— She could not grasp the thought. Her belly was readying for another squeeze. "I don't know. Stay or go, south or north, I don't know." And that was terrifying: She did not know. "You have to decide. I can ride if I have to." Could she? "For a bit." She hoped. But soon she might be squeezing Little Hedgepig into Gwladus's hands in between two clashing shield walls, and long before then she would not be thinking of anything beyond her belly. It was up to Gwladus.

Gwladus said nothing.

"We must . . ." But she did not know what they must do. She wanted Cian; she wanted her mother. She wanted to lie down.

When Gwladus was thinking her face did not soften, it sharpened— softness was the mask she wore to survive—and now the sharpness hardened. She nodded once. "Stay there." Even her voice was harder, denser, definite. "Rest while you can." She stood and called something to someone in that new voice, the one that could not be turned aside. Then talked at speed to the gesiths. They looked at Hild. She nodded, though she could not follow the words and had no idea what Gwladus planned but her body-woman knew how she thought.

Her thoughts skipped and stumbled. When she looked again Morud was trotting away and all five gesiths were busy: Coelwyn lifted his patch and rubbed at the ruined eye beneath, then wheeled his horse and cantered off, Morud at his heels. The brothers Berht furled the banner and slid it in its case. Eadric started packing food.

Hild's heart raced like a frightened horse. She wanted to pace; she wanted to sleep. She was being steered by something she did not understand

and could not persuade. She had no more say in what would happen next than a leaf caught in a current. But there was something, something else she had to do. Something . . .

"Here."

She stared. Coarse bread dipped in pork grease.

"Even just a bite. You've real work ahead. Drink this."

Something . . . "Cian."

"Lady, you can't help him now. Drink."

Hild sipped obediently at the thick wooden cup thrust into her hands—ale, a little musty—then she realised how thirsty she was and gulped despite herself.

"Morud and Coelwyn have gone for Janne. I told them not to give her a choice; Manfrid will be in the shield wall by now. When Eadric's done with packing he's to go watch for news."

News. News of what? She couldn't remember and she did not care. Whatever it was was no longer her task. Her task lay ahead.

Gwladus tapped the bread in Hild's hand. "So eat. Rest. Nothing will happen until—" She glanced at the sky, but it was so heavy with cloud it was hard to tell the hour.

The latest squeeze had come and gone and Hild's thoughts were slow and heavy. Grimhun and Morud returned with a surly-looking Janne and baby on an old gelding, and the report that there was no river crossing upstream to the west. Grimhun thought they could ride north, talk their way through the rearguard on the bridge, and make a run for Elmet. Coelwyn wanted to risk the mire: His brother's boats were somewhere.

"Cian," Hild said, but could not attach anything to that thought.

"Boldcloak must look to himself. You need to be on the other side of the river," Gwladus said.

Reluctantly, Grimhun nodded. "Lady, it's the only way."

"We could get you to the other side and then come back for Boldcloak," Berhtnoth said.

"And get caught between two shield walls?" Grimhun said. The brothers Berht looked at each other unhappily. Janne opened her mouth to say something but Gwladus quelled her with a look.

"We get the lady to the other side," she said in that remorseless voice. "Help me get her in the saddle."

Grimhun mounted and set his roan on the far side of Cygnet, then Gwladus pushed and Hild did her best to haul while Grimhun heaved, and she was up. Once she was in the saddle Cygnet stayed under her like a cradling hand, catching her, keeping her on. Hild would have lain over the mare's neck, just to be bent in the middle, just to rest in the company of a friend, but the swell of her belly would not allow it. Gwladus slid Hild's staff through the loops behind the cantle, tugged to be sure it was tight, and mounted her own gelding. A shirr of rain blurred the air and the roar of the river made the air tremble. Ahead was nothing but road, behind was road, to her left was road, to her right grey-green fenland, flat as a killer's face.

The brothers Berht rode first, followed by Hild with Gwladus on one side and Grimhun on the other, then Janne and the infant Wilfrid mounted on the gelding led by Morud, with Coelwyn and Eadric coming behind.

A quarter of a mile behind them the sound of hundreds of marching men and horses swelled, then broke into another, greater sound: the thunder of spears on shields, the throat-bursting song of men taunting each other.

> Your sister's your mother
> Your father's your brother
> You fuck one another
> Now we'll fuck you!

The rattle and boom of drums. The shield walls were working themselves up to attack.

> You fuck one another
> Now we'll fuck you!

The rattle and boom of drums.

> Fuck you!

Cian, she thought, and she remembered what it was she had to do. Cian. And it seemed as though Little Hedgepig twisted inside her, turning her face to her father like a flower to the sun. Cian. She had to . . .

. . . Had she fallen asleep? What was it she had to do? Cian. No. Going back meant being caught between a thousand men trying to kill each other. But she had to. Didn't she? She didn't know. She couldn't think.

Before her, the brothers Berht swayed in the saddle like twin bears. She could tell by the hunch of their shoulders that they hated riding away from a fight. War was their purpose; war was what they lived for. They were gesiths; they yearned to be shoulder to shoulder with their brothers, shields locked, faces red and shining in the rain, laughing at fate, ready for the muscle-bursting, throat-tearing, and blood-soaked thrust and slip of the wall. Instead their shields were slung at their back, bright green and yellow in a world of greys . . .

Hild blinked awake, became aware that Cygnet had halted and the air had changed and turned. Gwladus was tugging behind, at the saddle—at her staff, pulling it free of its straps. Grimhun was now ahead of her with the brothers Berht and all three had their shields unslung, on their arms, and spears poised; Coelwyn and Eadric crowded close behind and their breathing was fast and harsh.

She stared stupidly at the bridge. Where were the rearguard? The bridge should have been blocked by thirty men—steady men, strong men, men with wives and children, men who did not care to make a name, but men who would hold. But they weren't there guarding the south end, keeping it free for Edwin.

The rearguard were in the middle of the bridge, facing the wrong way, facing north; six men across and five deep like a great glittering beetle, spears pointing like feelers north, pointing at the enemy, a mounted horde, a war band bearing down on them under a red and gold banner.

A red dragon. The red dragon of Gwynedd.

Cadwallon.

She licked the rain from her lips. Cadwallon, with more than a hundred men—many more. Even from here she could see a thicket of bows. How were they here? And then she knew, knew as surely as night followed day: After colluding with or killing Honeytongue's men he had cut the triangle, hidden behind the hill, waiting there even as she made her speech to Edwin's men.

Her mind cleared. "Back! Back! South, for Lindum!"

It was the only path. North and west were closed. They must ride back through the ruins of Caer Daun and to the war street running south. Ride and hope Cadwallon's men would choose glory and gold, fall on the rear of Edwin's war band rather than chase a ragged, unknown band fleeing for Lindum.

She leaned forward as best she could and sent a silent plea to Little Hedgepig to wait, just wait, and kicked Cygnet into a gallop.

The mare leapt forward, and after a moment the others followed. Crashes and shouts behind her faded into the thunder of hooves, and she took the jar and thud in her thighs, rising and falling as the great beast found her rhythm.

They tore through the north gate of the fort just before the shock of Penda's and Edwin's shield walls clashing slammed through the air around them. It was such a buffet that Cygnet's hoof slipped and for a moment Hild thought she would go down, but then they were upright and into the fort proper. Through the centre of the fort. Reaching the south gate.

But a wagon, horses frantically whipped by the driver who was trying to look four ways at once, eyes starting from his head, careened through the gate and slewed sideways on the road ahead of them. One of the horses went down and thrashed itself into a tangle of harness. The wagoner leapt free of the wreckage and kept running, straight for them.

"Stop!"

But he did not hear; he was mad with fear. Hild nodded at Eadric, who leaned from the saddle, swept his spear shaft low to the ground, and sent the man tumbling.

The wagoner jumped to his feet, heedless of the blood running down his face, and turned to run again. Eadric's horse blocked the way. "Let me go! They're coming!"

"Who?"

He just gave a terrified look over his shoulder, to the south, then was off and running again, heedless.

Hild shook her head at Eadric—let him go—and then men and women, wagons and carts and horses, a river of horses, horses that should have been picketed, were streaming past them trying to get north, get out, get away from whatever was coming.

"Close up." The Hounds formed around her and Gwladus and Janne. She knocked a man down—a wet tooth gleamed as it flew—and the brothers Berht methodically lay about them until the crowd split and streamed to either side of their group. "South. I need to see."

They fought and pushed their way through the press until they were past the south gate looking down the war street.

Massed clouds turned the light as dark and wrong as a sick man's piss but even so, the heaving mass half a mile south over which banners flew winked with spear points. Too far away to count the spears, too far to see the symbols on the banners. Coelgar, she hoped. Coelgar from Lindsey. But as her eyes adjusted to the strange light she saw not the bull brown and carrot red of Lindsey but a sea of sky blue and yellow: Penda's colours.

Screams now from the north, where Cadwallon's men were on the bridge. Another air-shattering clash of shields from the west where Penda's men were already. Penda's colours coming from the south. Then the rain started.

Gwladus turned her gelding in a tight circle. "Shit," she said, and the gesiths reined in and cursed along with her.

Around Hild the world seemed to float away in silence, and under her breastbone a tiny star of energy lit. She looked at the staff in her hand, at her knee where her dark blue hose were turning black in the rain, to the coarse greys and blacks of Cygnet's mane falling to the left as it always did.

Today. The Yffings would fall today. But not all of them.

The rain poured. Grimhun was talking to her but she ignored him. She was listening to the thing gathering beneath her breastbone, feeling it swell.

"With me," she said, and turned Cygnet. She did not look to see if they followed; they would. Her words were living things, twisting through the air, winding about the necks of any who heard and pulling them with her.

She felt huge, a thunderhead of power. Nothing touched her but the rain.

Even Cygnet seemed to float over the ground as she rode down the steep slope of the road, onto the tussocks of wiry grass, and due south to the rise, to Cian. A thousand men with a thousand wounds, a thousand swords, and a thousand shields, but she would find him.

The king moved at the crest of the rise like one of the figures Cian might whittle for Wuscfrea, tiny, insignificant, dancing about behind the shield wall under his little tufa. Before him figures lay knocked here and there as though flicked down with a finger, some with their stuffing falling out. And there he was, Cian, checked cloak ragged, red and black crest on his war hat torn and filthy, *Red and black, to not show the mud and blood,* and the world snapped back sharp and clear and noise crashed in on her.

Cian stood shoulder to shoulder with the ætheling Osfrith and Dewal—Dewal's leg was the wrong colour. Just to the west and south of them

Gladmær, Leofdæg, and Bryhtsige fought back to back. Cian's seax was red to the hilt, and his shield, that heavy yew shield, was hacked and splintered. He was laughing, they were all laughing or snarling or screaming: They would die, they would die in glory, doing what men did, what gesiths did. They were sworn to put their bodies between the king and hurt, to kill or be killed. Some sang, but different songs.

But she saw what they could not: a wedge of Penda's men cutting towards them, fresh men who wanted the ætheling.

"Yffingas!" Her voice was a forge. "Ware Penda!" And she pointed.

She was a bolt of lightning wrapped in a body. Her words cracked through the air, bright enough to blind. All men looked. "Fiercesomes!" She pointed again, just for them. Then, snaring the Hounds behind her with a look, she charged.

The Elmetsæte were strong, they were fresh, they came from the flank with no banner, and the woman at their head was a giant. They scythed through the edges of Penda's war band. Strength poured through her, and now she steered Cygnet with her knees, punching left and right, left and right, and Cygnet's ribs moved like a great bellows, in and out, in and out.

"Cian!" And behind her, "Elmet! Elmet!" and Penda's war band rippled and turned. Men fell like corn before their bright blades, but there were many, and more, and the Elmet blades began to dull.

She slid off Cygnet. "Kill," she told her, and a hoof lashed beside her and a Mercian fell with a shattered face, choking on his own blood and bone, and her staff whirled so fast it looked like an unmoored mill wheel rolling down the hill, biting a little farther ahead with each turn: a head, an elbow, a knee; a jaw, a rib, a neck. Deeper she cut into the war band, deeper. Behind her men screamed. A horse screamed.

A pulped eye; a finger landing on her boot; the red of a man's mouth smeared sideways across a patch of stubble where he had missed a patch shaving; dirt in the crease of another's neck, crushed; split and sharp bone bursting through the shin where the guard was missing—

And then the Hounds and the Fiercesomes met and merged, but now there were only seven of them, and Hild's staff chewed on, on towards the sound of blades thudding on yew.

Now her arms were made of lead and stone, and she was slowing, and every time her left arm moved blood splashed red about her. But she paid no attention—later, if she lived—and kept her eyes on the dark flicker and red flash that was Cian's shield, another of gleaming yellow—hair, Osfrith's hair; where was his war hat?—surrounded four-deep by men, Penda's and Osfrith's. Three-deep. Two. None of them Osfrith's. Then . . . gone. Then a howl: *Osfrith is down! The ætheling is down!*

"Cian!" The shout tore her throat. It was muscular enough to lift the dead, but it lifted nothing.

She spat blood, swung blood, blood flew all around her. Her seax was out now, punching in and out, in and out, a spike of steel, thrusting through the gaps between chinstrap and fishmail shirt, between shield and war boot, slicing a collop of muscle, shearing bone and gristle, putting a hinge in a man's face where his mouth had been.

And now she was standing over Cian, who lay with his face pressed in bloody mud, helmet twisted to one side, shield shattered. In and out, in and out.

A horse screamed, screamed again. Her hip flared in white pain, then she forgot it. Something was wrong with her foot. And now she was screaming, a long ululation that went on and on like the birth of the world.

And shouting went up behind and to her left, a howl: *Get him! Get the Yffing!* And the men before her swayed like kelp and turned, drawn away by a riptide of bloodlust, to where the great boar banner was falling.

Her ears were ringing. She bent, took Cian under the armpits, and began to pull.

She was pulling, pulling—but Cian wouldn't move, not even an inch—and someone was pouring lye into her wounds, her legs were wet, everything was wet, and her belly quaked like calf's-foot jelly. *Lie down*, her belly told her. *Don't stop*, said her heart. *Never yield*, said her bones. And so she pulled, like trying to pull an anchor from the bank when the whole ship tugged the other way. She set her feet, set her will. One inch, two.

Breathe. One inch. Another. Breathe.

The world became a long dark tunnel with no light at the end and sound slow and muffled. She wasn't sure if she could see at all, yet she did not trip. She dared not stop to wonder. If she stopped the world would stop. One inch. Breathe. Another. Breathe. On and on.

Whoever was screaming she wished they would shut up. Shut up. Shut up.

"Shut up," it came from a long, long way; a small sound you would have to stoop to hear. Her throat hurt. Her hands felt like claws. And then someone was fighting her for him.

Rage scorched through her, but dry, so dry. Even her teeth were dry. And pain in her belly, pain turning like the world.

"Let him go, lady. Let him go. We have to run." His hand on her. "We have—"

Her seax was at his throat, the blade resting on a mole like a tadpole. Mole: Morud. The world blinked back. All around her the roar and clash of armies ebbed and flowed but as though on another plane.

"No," she said. It came out as a whisper.

"We'll all die." Gwladus, behind her. Sounding like her mother. Moving forward now that she knew Hild was of this world again.

"Then we die." She looked across into those grey-green eyes, eyes she had seen black with fear, black with pleasure, tight with rage. Across, not down. That was odd. Across, because she was bent, one hand still in Cian's armpit. His face was white, smeared with mud and blood. And still. So very still. She reached her other hand to take him, but it just hung by her side, holding the seax. She stared at it. Willed it to move. It would not.

Gwladus reached slowly for the seax. Hild let her. Gwladus lifted it for her to see: the blade thick with clots of blood and other things. She bent, stabbed the tussock at her feet. "We only have two horses." Stab. "Mine." Stab. "And Janne's." Stab stab. She held it out to Hild, who was too tired to reach for it. Gwladus slid it into the sheath for her. "We have to get to the bridge."

"Not without him."

"But your b—"

Bairn. Belly. Blood. It was all one; she would not leave without him. She shook her head, and the world slid to one side and began to turn.

"Catch her!"

Then there were hands all over her: lifting, plucking, tightening. Lying down. Then on a horse, not Cygnet, not the smoothness and size and pent power. Just a horse. Now they galloped. She had to hold on. Hold on. She was cold. The world closed.

The world blinked back: shouts, curses. A great splash. She was draining away, drifting away. More pain, a strange tugging. More splashing. Turning. Galloping again. Someone seemed to be forcing her insides into different countries.

Another blink. Closed. Open. She twisted in her saddle—Gwladus held her—and squinted into the slanting sun. Another horse ran behind theirs, eyes starting, Cian slung over it, Morud perched sideways behind him, clutching something close. The smell of marsh.

Blink.

The rain had stopped and the world was flat and green and gold and oddly churned. Their shadows stretched before them. "This isn't the bridge."

"We had to run east."

The mire. Churned by hooves and feet. The banner falling, the howl . . . "The king."

"He ran. They all ran. Cadwallon and Penda followed. Listen." Far away, shrieks. "They caught them."

Blink. Their shadows were longer. This time she was shivering.

"Give her back those furs," Gwladus said to Morud.

"If they see us . . ."

"Then we're all dead."

They were all dead anyway. The Hounds. The Fiercesomes. Osfrith. Cian. Oh Cian Cian Cian . . .

Then they were running again. Then slowing. A horse stumbling, foundering. Falling. Sliding, then standing, thick light in her face. The wrong way, she thought. I'm facing the wrong way. The purse at her belt was heavy as a millstone.

Her eyes were sticky. She tried to wipe them but her right arm wouldn't move. Her left hand lifted slowly, scrubbed blood crust from her eyelashes. She tried to blink them clean. Janne's horse lay on its side, kicking slowly. But there was no Janne. Cian lay in a heap. No helm, no sword, mail shirt torn open. She did not have the strength to howl. Morud dragged him like a log, propped his body against the dying horse: There was nothing else to lean against.

Around them stretched the mire, green, with long brown shadows reaching from every tuft of marshgrass. In the distance, behind them, parallel to the horizon where the sun set, ran the path. There was no one on it, no one following them.

Her whole body felt as tight as a swollen leg about to burst, hot and wrong. Someone had bound her wounds in haste.

Beyond, in the northwest, a small rise crawled with figures, black against the bloody sky. Dragon banner, red on white, to one side; Penda's wolf on blue and yellow to the other.

Far away a figure knelt, glinting with gold and hair burning with the setting sun: chestnut. A tiny man, far away. A poppet built of sticks. Unreal. Edwin Yffing, overking of the Angles.

A great voice, booming out. Too far for the words, but she knew the tone: triumph. More shouting, rhythmic now, and men shouting with it. Bigger, louder, ecstatic. Drums rolling, building.

A man stepped forward. Light ran like molten gold on his axe as he lifted it. A flash, a long roar, like the waves at the bay beating on the cliff, and again, and the headsman stooped, grasped a round thing by its chestnut hair and lifted. Another flash. Another roar. This time an arm held aloft, bright with gold. Another, and another, and now the roar went on and on as the red sky darkened.

Sunset of the Yffings.

"We have to go." Morud, to Gwladus, standing by Gwladus's hanging right leg. A little bundle squirmed by his feet. "We should take his gold and leave him."

Cian Boldcloak, Cian Yffing, lying propped like a puppet against a dead horse.

Behind her, Gwladus moved as she nodded. "I'll do it. Watch that bairn. Watch them both. Lady? Lady, can you hear me? I need your seax, and I need you to hold on. Just for a bit."

Hild nodded vaguely. She heard the words but had no idea what they meant. Gwladus slid down, seax in hand, and knelt by the puppet. She began to strip it of rings and necklet.

Where was Cian? Who had made the puppet that looked a bit like him but not really?

Gwladus was working at the puppet's legs now, prying at the gold inlay on its shin guards. A pity. The puppet was prettier with its gold. They should leave it something. Gwladus began to unfasten its belt.

No. Not that.

"Lady!" Morud had her arm.

Gwladus turned. "Get back on the horse, lady."

"Don't touch him."

"We need the gold."

"Not the belt." She remembered buying that buckle, at the same place she had bought Gwladus. "It's his."

And just like that it was Cian. Cian stiff as a wooden puppet. Cian who would never hold her again. Cian who would never see their daughter. Cian who had fought for his king and not for her.

"Give me the seax." She took it, sheathed it, and waited until Gwladus stepped away. Then she turned back to Cian. "You are a fool," she said to him, and knelt. "You should not have died." She lay her hand on the tear in his mail, right over his heart. She felt nothing. He was cold. The world was cold. It was raining again. "We're taking your gold. I'm sorry there's no sword, or shield, or helmet." She stroked his face, cool and hard as wax except where the bristles on his chin prickled her palm. The left side was mangled and swollen but the right side looked like him. She tugged his cloak over his broken body and empty sheath, wiped his face with both hands, and turned his head slightly so she talked to the whole side. "Your mother will be angry." *Love him*, she had said. *Protect him*.

"Lady . . ."

"I have to go," she told him. But she could not leave him with nothing in this waste. "I'll leave your belt, so no matter what you'll have that buckle. A knife where all else fails." Her first gift to him. She stroked his hair. Her left hand was numb and she was glad; she could ignore the coarse filth and remember how it should feel.

The buckle was not enough.

She fumbled at the straps on her purse with fingers like sausages, then had to upend the purse to see rather than sort by touch. She picked up the nested travel cups. Perfect and beautiful, each carved with a little hedgepig. His first gift to her.

She tipped the smallest into her palm, or tried to, but her right arm did not move. She picked it up with her left, weighed it. Remembered him stooping low over the roots of the hedge torn out by Edwin, the hedge that had been old in the time of Eliffer of the Great Retinue, searching. The red-gold hair on his arms gleaming in the firelight as he carved, night after night. For them. She lifted it close and smelled it—it smelt only of rain—then tucked it under his cloak. "So we can drink to each other, wherever we are. Me, you, Little Hedgepig. We are us."

It was dark. Her feet were wet. She wasn't wearing shoes. She was not wearing much of anything except her furs and wound wraps. No weight at her belt or her wrist, none at her fingers, only the cross around her neck.

"It's coming," a voice said. "It's coming." She knew that voice, that smell. Gwladus.

Another mewl, that child again.

"Shut him up," Gwladus hissed to the dark.

"He's hungry—"

"Morud, shut him up. We'll all die."

Small sounds she could not quite hear. Singing?

". . . your feet. Get up, lady. Now squat."

"Hurts." Her leg, her arm, her left hip—and her belly, oh gods there was a wrap slung low around her belly and stained dark and leaking.

"Yes. Push. Good, that's it. Push. I can see her head—" Pain, tearing her open.

Singing. Morud was singing. A lullaby, one she had heard as a child. British.

The singing stopped. "She's bleeding," he said.

"I know she's bleeding. Tighten the wrap."

"Which one?"

"All of them. Push, lady. She's coming, she's coming. We can't stay here. We can't. Morud— That's it, lady. That's it."

Movement somewhere in the red dark. Morud's British whisper, "There's something out there."

The pain ripped through her, a gush and rush. She grunted. She would have screamed if she had more breath.

"Be quiet, oh gods be quiet. She's coming, lady. Here's her forehead." Pain, pain, but she must not bellow. "Mouth, yes, yes, you beauty. Chin."

Death was coming. She could feel it. She could see it, a writhe in the dark, a change in the air. Cian was coming; he was coming for her. Another whimper from the child. No, she was not even born yet.

"Keep it quiet!"

And then even though pain took her in its hand and began to crush her, her mind settled and cleared like a pot of water. She shrugged her furs off.

"Lady, you need—"

"On. This. The boy." And after a moment Morud's shadow bent and put something that squirmed on the furs.

Gwladus was feeling between Hild's legs. "I need light." Soft cursing but too far away. "The cord's in the way. I can't see—we need light. Don't push, lady. Dear gods, don't push."

But she had to push. She could feel the muscles tightening.

"Morud, find the lady's purse. Flint and birch fungus. For fire. We—"

Death drew closer.

"Hello," she said to it, and then it stepped closer and it had a hand, a torn hand. Not Cian's hand. A hand that held her belt and purse. "I know you," she said. "Leofdæg."

"Strike a light," Gwladus said.

"They'll see!" Morud.

Hild shook her head, began to gasp as she fought to keep her muscles from squeezing down.

"By now there're mostly dead or drunk," Gwladus said. "Do it, Leofdæg. Give me light. Morud, get me twine and a knife. Now!"

Then there was a monstrous whirl of pain and crying out, and more blood, and bright pain, pain like nothing she had known and did not think she could bear. She screamed with what was left of her voice, enough to wake the dead, but her dead would never wake, never. He was gone. She had left him.

For a moment, above her hoarse panting, the marsh night began to breathe. Something slithered and plopped, the long grass hissed. An aromatic waft of bog myrtle.

And then the child slid into the world with hardly any fuss like a long, bloody eel, and was caught by Gwladus. But she could not see her because Morud was fussing again, tugging, tightening, and when she struggled Leofdæg held her, solid as a badger, while Morud tightened.

"She's bleeding!" He sounded very young. "I can't make it stop."

But Gwladus was kneeling in the flickering pool of light, working frantically with Hild's wound roll, wrapping the baby.

The light began to shrink and she could not see. *Let me see her!* But she made no sound but a long wheeze. Then a moving thing, warm. She stilled. Morud's tugging went on, but she ignored it. Her attention was wholly taken with the tiny mouth, lipping its way blindly up her breast, fastening on the tip, and sucking.

And her face was wet, and it did not matter if it was blood or rain or tears, it did not matter, because here was Little Hedgepig, sucking, sucking hard, and if she had had a voice she would have laughed, and if her eyes had worked she would have shut them, and then her belly squeezed again: another, longer slipperiness.

While Gwladus was busy, and she was trying not to get drunk on the honey scent of Little Hedgepig, she whispered into the void, "Leofdæg." She could not see; she did not know if she spoke aloud or if he listened. "Leofdæg, take my cross. Go. Go to Elmet . . ."

11

✣

SHE SMELT BLOOD and that sweet meaty scent of open bone, and she swung her staff again at Mercian knee and Gwynedd elbow. Osfrith the ætheling dead. Fighting her way through to Cian, only to see him go down again. Then white pain, black pain, red pain, and setting her will, dragging him, dragging, turning to look, seeing the banner dip and fall. And later, as the sun set, the wink of that other blade swinging back on the ridge, the roar as Edwin's head fell. Sunset on the Yffings. Perhaps she was dead, perhaps she would fight this battle forever, never come back. But every time she began to float away down the dream stream something snagged her.

Somewhere a baby whimpered and she wanted to call to it but could not move. She felt a vague tugging. Was she dead, too, like Cian, being stripped of her gold by Penda and Cadwallon's scavengers?

"No," he said, and she knew that voice but it was thin and wrong and far away. The voice of the dead. She must not go to it. She had to stay. There was a reason she had to stay. "What are you doing?"

"What I must," said another, a woman. Much closer. She knew that voice, too. More tugging.

The tugging changed and the thin whimper stopped. Hild's world rushed to a point and she welled, filled with a gathering, thrusting hunger. And a scent she knew but could not name. And something else, something that should worry her. She drifted on.

What snagged her this time was the remembered smell of fresh bread, tearing it open, delighting in the moist give in her hands, then dipping it in the meat juice and grease, telling him, *Yes, all of it, and then more. Begu is always nagging me to eat for two, and there might be precious little to eat soon*, but laughing, not believing it. She was the lady of Elmet, the light of the world; there would always be enough . . .

"She's going again. Lady!" *Crack.* "Help me."

Crack. Hild did not like that.

"Don't!"

"Then help me!"

Hands on her shoulders. "Lady!" *Crack.* No, she did not like that at all. "Lady!"

"Don't." And this time it was her own voice, though wandering and weak. She opened her eyes to slits. The light was dim; rain dripped through the gaps in the roof. And there were the hands—his hands, big-boned and hard-knuckled, like hers—on her shoulders. "I was dreaming," she said. "Of before you died. When you weren't my brother."

The hands jerked back, and now she saw them: small hands. Not his. He was lying alone in the mire, stripped and shorn.

Hild looked down at the bundled child at her breast and that round, rich thrusting love crowded out everything else. A smell of little head and damp skin, like bread and honey, and sleep, and morning dew on a fresh-spun web. A tiny breathing thing. Little Hedgepig. Little Honey. Here, outside herself, made real. The perfect weight, the axis of her world. She wanted to kiss every toe, feel every bump in the tiny spine but she was bundled up tight.

Her right arm was wrapped and clumsy, and she had no strength. She could not resist as Gwladus took the child. She could only follow with her eyes as Gwladus laid her in the fur nest, next to Wilfrid.

She remembered: Janne was gone or run. Wilfrid would starve. "Give him," she said. It came out as mush, but Gwladus understood.

"Lady, you've not enough milk."

"Give him," she said.

Gwladus lifted Wilfrid, bigger, stronger than Little Honey, from his nest of clothes by the broken hearth and put him to her right breast. Wilfrid began to suck, uncertainly at first, then greedily, endlessly, sucking the glue from the world until it broke again in pieces.

———

Morud pushed through the leather flap that served as a door. "It's all there was," he said in British, and showed Gwladus the half-full pan of milk he had sheltered as best he could from the rain. "The goat ran away and the cow's near dry. Or as dry as anything can be in this place. How is she?"

Hild could move nothing but her eyes. She followed some of what they were saying but not all. Mostly she watched a beetle crossing the floor waving its feelers.

"Quiet now." Gwladus took the milk and poured half into the biggest of the lady's last two travel cups. Hild imagined milk filling the third cup, Cian sitting up, eyes pecked out by ravens.

Morud wiped his face with his arm, though one was as wet as the other. "No one's out in this weather."

Gwladus set the cup on the shelf. It looked wrong, out of place in the filth. But it was wrong, all of it. "Help me."

Something in the tone told Hild that Gwladus had said that more in the last four days than in ten years put together. It will be all right, she wanted to say. But there seemed to be a caul between her and the world; she could not move, could not speak.

Between them they hefted Hild to a half-sitting position with Morud holding her up by the shoulders—hers so much wider than his—until Gwladus could sit next to her on the makeshift bed and cradle her head in the crook of her left arm. "Pass the cup."

He did.

She set the beautifully carved little thing against Hild's mouth and tipped just enough to wet her lips. Hild licked them. Gwladus tipped in earnest. Just before the milk spilled, Hild, eyes still only slits, reached up with a hand that seemed to belong to someone else, steadied Gwladus's hand with hers, and drank. When the milk was gone, her hand drifted down and the caul between her and the world thickened. Everything dimmed and seemed very far away.

They laid her back on the cot—it was awkward—and Gwladus tugged at the blanket to cover her but settled on tucking it round her waist. A sigh. "She never did feel the cold."

"Will she die?"

"I don't know," Gwladus said. "Her leg's stopped bleeding, and her arms but for that deep cut over her elbow, but that hip wound . . . and her belly."

Belly?

". . . were anyone else I'd say, 'Call for the priest'—"

"If there was a priest."

"—but the lady, she's strong."

"How long can she feed two bairns, though?"

Gwladus said nothing, but Hild knew what she was thinking: You needed food to heal, and food to make milk, and in all this mire and waste at the end of the world there was none, only torn grass and dead gesiths.

In the distance, carrion crows cawed and squabbled. You would think there would be nothing left. Or perhaps they were fighting over who would get the people in the bothy when they starved to death, or after the nithings slunk from the shadow.

Had Leofdæg reached Elmet? She did not even know if he had been real. She tried to think, to count, but the grey tide was washing over her, tugging her away again.

Morud came back with fresh blood on his tunic, and it was that smell that woke Hild. Her heart slammed: Little Honey was not by her side. But in the same heartbeat she smelled her and knew she was sleeping next to Wilfrid. She did not move but watched Morud through slitted eyes.

He carried a sack. It was soaked through, like him, like the world. He tipped it onto the broken stool that served as a table. Two apples, one worm-eaten, one whole but bruised. An onion. The kind of thing a gesith might carry to war. A handful of withered nuts—last year's hazelnuts—and a hunk of greasy bacon, with the ragged edge showing where it had been hacked from a hanging flitch. A day or two ago by the look of it. Hild knew from his face that he hadn't the faintest idea what to do with any of it.

He looked at Gwladus, who shook her head. She was a bodywoman, not a cook.

"I'll try," he said. "If I can find something that will burn in this wet."

When Hild woke fully to herself, propped at an angle on a half-rotted pallet of reeds, it was past dawn. Grey light seeped through gaps and chinks in the wattle, and she could see Morud asleep in the corner. It was a small hut; she could have reached out and touched his foot, but she did not move. Gwladus was asleep by the babies. The hearth, such as it was, was thick with ash, not all of it wood by the smell.

She knew where she was—the abandoned lean-to she had pointed them to as the fever came upon her—but not how long they had been there.

The shadow over Gwladus's eyes had changed: She was awake. They regarded each other for what seemed an age. So much to say, but they could not. Morud, when he slept like that, would sleep like the dead, but she did not want to wake the babies. She already knew that the scent of Little Honey, the tiny mouth fastening around her nipple, would drive all sense from her.

Hild put her finger to her lips—her right hand was working again— nodded at the babies, and raised her eyebrows. "How long?" she mouthed.

Gwladus held up four fingers.

She nodded. Even that effort made the air in her lungs feel thin and useless. If she breathed deep into her belly it hurt. She panted quietly. Four days old. And she already had a brother, for Wilfrid was hers now—all his family were dead. The Yffings were dead. Cian was dead. Penda and Cadwallon would be burning Elmet. What of Osric, Osric-hide-at-home, the craven of Craven? And Honeytongue? She would get well and if Honeytongue were not dead she would kill him.

That was for later. For now, they were alive. She must keep them that way.

She gestured for Gwladus to pass her Little Honey. This once she would hold only the one she had grown inside her and carried for nine months. His last gift to her. The last of him.

Gwladus pulled back the tacked-together horse blanket and sacking that passed for Hild's bedding and laid the child carefully along her less-injured left arm, close to Hild's heart.

Hild lifted her breast and held it to Little Honey's lips. Sleepily, eyes still closed, the tiny mouth began to suck. Again, Hild felt that echo of a squeeze in her belly and she smiled, which hurt her jaw where it was bruised. She rocked Honey a little as she sucked. She was lighter than she had been. But babies often lost weight at first.

She nuzzled her head, the only part unwrapped, breathed her scent, and let those first few moments after birth flow through her unchecked. A terrible day in all ways but Honey. Her arm, her hip, Cian pacing alongside them, dead; the rain, the mud, the water running out; the streams, the dykes, the bog stinking with rotting bodies; crossing a river; and nowhere to shelter to make a fire. Then Leofdæg refusing, at first, to leave. Seeing the lean-to, far away, in the mire. Driving them to it. Leofdæg leaving.

Morud wanting to leave with him, to run—it was what he did best. But *Stay for me*, she said. *I need you, these babies need you.* And he had. And she was healing. And here was Little Honey.

Three whole days: If he had found a horse, Leofdæg could be in Caer Loid, if it still stood, with her cross as token. If Caer Loid were gone or taken he would find Menewood; he was good at finding things, and she had whispered the way. And then he would be back, with help, if there was help to bring. Unless he had run to Lindum, sold the cross, and pledged to Coelgar.

No. He was the last Fiercesome. He would follow his oath. They had only to stay alive another two days, three at most. All would be well. Little Honey would gain weight and grow.

But already Little Honey had stopped sucking, and she was not squirming as she should. She was too tightly swaddled.

"No, lady," Gwladus said, so quietly that Hild, ear just two feet from her mouth, could barely hear. "Keep her wrapped."

It was not the words that got through to Hild but the set look on Gwladus's face. Fear sliced through her and she began to fumble at Little Honey's swaddling with fingers that would not obey her.

Gwladus reached out and stilled her hands with her own. They were narrow hands, much smaller than Hild's but stronger today. She had managed somehow to keep them mostly clean, and her face, but mud and blood caked her hair and clothes. Her lips seemed dark and full still, but her cheeks were sharp, fatigue stained under her eyes, and the reed pallet hardly bent under her weight. They were all starving.

She stroked Hild's hand.

"Lady . . . Hild." Her name. Gwladus never used her name. "The child . . ."

The whisper went on. But Hild was looking at their hands, hers and Gwladus's. She could not understand why they looked so wrong. It wasn't just the filth, or the great crusted scrape over Hild's left knuckles or even the cracks in Gwladus's fingernails—gold. Neither of them wore a scrap.

"Where's our gold?"

"Safe. Buried. But, lady, you must listen . . ."

Buried where?

". . . your leg, your arm, your hip. Your belly."

Something crept in the wattle of the wall. That beetle again?

"Lady?" And now Gwladus took her jaw gently in one hand and brought them face-to-face. Her eyes were in shadow. "You must listen." Hild did not know what to do. She should strike her hand away. She should lean into it and let go. "The child, she looks whole. But she doesn't move. She doesn't thrive."

Death had many smells. She knew them all. Outside, beyond the hut, the swollen smell of rot grew daily. It was stronger now than it had been even in sunlight. It would soon grow overpowering. But the scent of approaching death, the death that crept in on cat feet, was different. It disguised itself as many things, always smiling, always promising ease and comfort, the death of thinning and fading and letting go.

"No," Hild said. "I'm well. Honey is well. She'll thrive, you'll see."

She still could not see Gwladus's eyes but the shadow moved when she turned to look at Morud. He was still asleep. Gwladus slid off the pallet and knelt on the muddy floor. Mud, Hild thought. That should worry her, but she did not know why.

Gwladus eased aside what there was of Hild's blanket.

Beneath, Hild wore nothing but bandages. Gwladus pointed to the wrappings on her belly and the shadows on her face flexed: She was raising her eyebrows. Hild nodded.

Gwladus, with those beautiful, nimble fingers, loosened the bandages— what was left of her blue hose, Hild saw, and bits of a tunic—and waited. Hild took a breath and looked.

A thin red line along the sagging curve of her once-full belly ran between the gape on her hip—she did not want to look at that—to the curls of hair in the centre. But the red line was nothing—it was already healing—it was the great, swollen bruise she had to see. She remembered the white-hot pain of her hip and tried to make it make sense.

An axe blade catching her hip? A dulled axe, or she would be dead. The handle slamming into her belly, into Little Honey . . .

She looked at the tiny, unmoving bundle cradled against her ribs. "Help me," she whispered.

She felt Gwladus's breath on her skin—she knew that breath smell; the bitter scent of starvation—and then Honey was naked. She did not wave her fists or kick her feet. She simply lay there, still.

She was perfect, unmarked. All her fingers, all her toes, lashes long and dark and thick lying like brushstrokes against her cheeks. Hild wanted to feel them flutter against her skin. She kissed the fingertips—soft and limp as sleeping kittens, fingernails like pearl shavings—and then her nose. It was tiny, and warm, and it wrinkled under Hild's lips. She moved! Hild wanted to laugh aloud, but it would hurt and it would wake Morud and this was not be shared. She kissed the little belly—not round enough, not plump—breathed in that new-baby smell, her honey smell, the smell that would never belong to anyone else. Blew a tickling breath. No kick, no squeal. Kissed her knees, her toes. Nothing. Nothing nothing nothing.

Hild tilted her gently to see her spine. It should have been clothed in plump newness but seemed instead a fairy necklace of bones, each tiny and distinct and, halfway down, the shadow that was a bruise. It was already fading. It had done its work.

Honey opened her eyes, pale as winter, and Hild's heart rippled. She filled to the skin with the song of Honey, Little Honey, her marrow thrummed with it. Little Honey. More precious than myrrh and briefer than the dew.

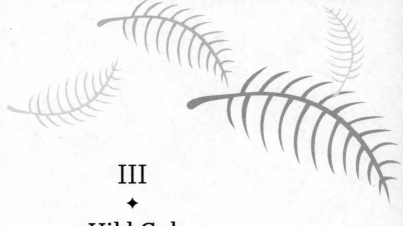

III

✦

Hild Gul

Ynys Bwyell—Adlingfleot—Cnotinsleah—Elmet—Menewood

(Wulfmonath 632 to Hrethmonath 633, 11 weeks)

12

✢

IN THE INSUBSTANTIAL LIGHT OF WULFMONATH, Afanc thought the Anglisc woman wading for mallows at the edge of the marsh looked like the alders down Haksey way: tall, silent, stripped for winter, scarred by generations of cattle rubbing against them, but graceful, each in its own way. Even with a child strapped to her chest and that great big stick at her back. She had been watching her since Blodmonath, piecing together clues. The woman's dress—too big for her, but you could see it had once belonged to someone high; the weave was very fine—was kilted up to her waist and showed the deep gore on her thigh. It was hard to miss: dark red, with the skin all rucked up like a pushed-back sleeve.

There were scars on her arms, too—the hands almost untouched but the right arm like a writhe of pink snakes from shoulder to wrist, with one above her elbow, thick and jagged, still red—though Afanc guessed they didn't hurt anymore because she mostly moved well enough. The woman was strong, too: she had heard from Eira up by Belton that she'd caught and held the ram easily when he charged at her as Eira was trying to mark the ewes just after Yule. The woman had walked the length of the isle, more than once. At first, she had crept about like a crippled child. Afanc asked toothless Jonty—from the northeast point of the isle, so far north it was practically Crowle—one of the few who had talked to her, what she talked about. Nothing, he said. She never spoke, but she did like to listen. Especially to news, and his songs of course. His daughter Huelwen had shaken her head at that, and Afanc agreed. Who would want to listen to the old man's songs? They were always sad.

Afanc asked other folk around the isle and they said the same thing: She listened but she did not speak. They all thought she listened particularly to them: to their news, to tales of their crops, to endless lists of family doings. Duer, the priest, said she knelt for a blessing when he offered, though she wore no cross.

As the weeks then months passed the lean woman's creep had become a slow walk, then a fast walk, and now a stride. She seemed to have healed, mostly. There was at least one scar Afanc had not seen because the woman sometimes pressed her hand against her hip and belly, as though something had stabbed her. If the one on her thigh was anything to go by it was bad. Still, she looked a lot better than when she had found her at Blodmonath.

That morning had been like most mornings in the dark of the year when the waters came and the world stretched grey and wide and weighted with wet. She had gathered her net and favourite eel spear and her mother warned her again that if she saw strangers she was to pull into the reeds, stay out of sight until it was safe, then get back as quick as she could and tell the men on the farm. As usual Afanc only pretended to listen. The battle out by Ynys Coed had been nearly a month ago; any survivors had long since starved or fled. It had been a great battle. They had heard the screams of the dying drifting on the wind. A hundred, two hundred, a thousand men died that day, they said. Afanc could believe it. The screaming lasted two days. Even here in Brune on Ynys Bwyell the stench had been terrible when the wind was in the west. A month later they still got a whiff every now and again; a ghost of what it had been, but still there.

She had been sculling over the mere towards the knoll—the high point of the meadow in summer and, in winter, the only thing above water west of the farm; sometimes eel gathered in the slow eddies in the lee of the current—when she saw a very strange thing: a man sitting on the knoll cross-legged next to a bundle of rags, cradling a bairn. A young man, a boy even. And then she saw that the pile of rags was one woman—very bright hair, paler than anything she knew of—trying to spoon something into the mouth of another woman.

She was outraged. "Ho the knoll! That's my land!"

The bright-haired woman lifted her head and Afanc caught the stink of what she had been trying to feed the other one. They must be desperate.

You had to have a good stomach to get down figwort root at the best of times, it smelt like something rotting, and clearly the other woman—if it was a woman; now that she was closer she could see how big she was, even lying down—was far from good. Thrashing about and murmuring nonsense. Mad with fever. But then she half sat up, looked directly at Afanc, and shouted in a voice that rang like a dented gong—only Afanc couldn't understand a word of it. It was important, though; she could tell. And such eyes! Blue and green in a world of greys. Another shout, this time more of a command. Maybe she should scull just a bit nearer . . .

Her mother had not been happy, but Carwyn's hut was free til he came back with his new wife in spring and, well, now here they were. The bright-haired one, Gwladus, was often up at the farm, and sometimes that Morud, but never this one, this tall silent woman. Afanc had no idea what went on in her head. And she wanted to know; she was the most interesting thing to happen since Huelwen's brother ran off last year, so she had taken to watching when she thought the woman would not see.

Today the woman was up to her thighs, staring intently at the water, a handful of mallows dripping from her right hand. And now she was moving away. That made no sense: If mallows were what she wanted there were more mallows right there. What was she doing?

She twitched in impatience, which made the marshgrass rustle. She seized in place, like fish glue. Breathed carefully. Had the woman seen her? She did not dare move to look. She had forgotten that the marshgrass got stiff and dry in the cold, and it was cold, though the tall woman seemed indifferent to it. Afanc turned her head very slowly. If the woman had heard her, she gave no sign.

The woman moved twenty paces east along the bank of the channel and Afanc followed, staying bent behind marshgrass and reeds. At least it was too cold for creepy crawlies. And now she was staring again—at nothing. There was nothing there but water. Perhaps she was a bit touched.

The bairn made that cross noise he often did. He seemed a crotchety thing, like an old man, but little. Not so little as he was, though. Five months, her mother reckoned. And clearly not the woman's—his hair was tawny gold brown. Then there was the way the woman looked at him sometimes, not like any look she had seen a mam give her bairn.

The woman put a hand—it was a big hand, and bony—under his bottom and jogged, then touched her fingers to the inside of her wrist in that habit Afanc had seen often. She crept closer, ankle deep in a muddy pool, and parted the cold wet reeds to see what the woman was looking at. She craned her neck.

"You'd see better if you stood up," the woman said.

Afanc ducked and turned her face away. Was she talking to her? But she never spoke. Maybe she'd heard wrong.

"You have a question, Afanc Bychan. I will answer it, if you come out where I can see you."

No mistaking that. Clear British, plain as rain. Her face burned. How— wait. That was a Bwyell accent. How was that so? And how did she know she was there? Was she just guessing? She didn't sound like she was guessing. She sounded certain, certain as rising water. Rising water did not care whether you were there or no. It would rise, and if you ignored it, you would drown. Perhaps the woman had stepped through the mist from Annwn. But no fairy was so bony. Oh, why had she followed? She should not have followed! But she had.

She cooled her burning cheeks with her hands, breathed deep. She was Afanc, daughter of Eirlys and Pabo, owners of the biggest farmstead in Brune; the highest, best point of the isle. She was not afraid.

She stood. The woman turned and looked directly at her. Afanc looked down to flick from her kilted skirts the mud that was there, and some that was not. But the woman was waiting. She looked up. Those eyes were no less strange than they had been that first time. Mostly blue with bits of green, like the mere when the sky was summer clear and weed scum gathered at the quieter edges—though that wasn't what made them strange. It was the way they just . . . looked at you, as though what you thought, and how you felt about being looked at, did not matter. Or maybe mattered more than anything else in the world.

Afanc burned hotter, and knew the woman would see it, see her bare legs trembling and understand it, and the knowledge struck sparks of anger from her fear. And how dare she use her pet name? "Don't call me Little Beaver!"

"It's the name I heard your mother use. Is it not your name?"

"No. That is, yes, Afanc is my name." For the beaver furs her mother laid her in as a baby. "But only my mother gets to call me little."

"Then my apologies. You had a question, Afanc ferch Eirlys."

"The mallows—" She gathered her courage. "The mallows were right there. Before. Why didn't you take them?"

The woman looked at her for a while, then moved left, back to the mallows. No glance, no beckoning to follow, but her intent was plain. Afanc followed. The woman waded into the water as though it were summer warm, and pointed down.

Afanc edged closer, closer still. She did not want to stand next to this stranger; she didn't want to stand in the freezing water, either. But there was no help for it. She stepped in.

The water was so cold it hurt but she made no sound beyond a gasp, then waited for the silt she had kicked up to settle. It took a moment for her eyes to adjust. A hole, drowned by the rising water. "A water vole burrow?"

The woman nodded. "They'll be back in summer. They'd miss those mallows."

She did not understand. It was just a water vole.

The woman watched her with those unfathomable eyes, then bent and scooped a handful of water. "Look."

Fairies did magic with water. She should not look. She looked. Silvery water reflected a brown-haired girl who came to the breastbone of a chestnut-haired woman.

"I can hold you, hold us both, in the palm of one hand."

Afanc had never heard such a wintry voice. No, not wintry, because in winter you knew things were alive, finning slowly in the depths, or curled tight under the mud, or dormant under the dirt, just waiting. But this woman was as bare as burnt stone.

She tipped her hand and the water poured away. *See?* her eyes said. *I release the power I have over you.* "Afanc ferch Eirlys, I am Hild." She seemed to stumble over her own name. "I am in your debt."

Afanc wasn't sure what to make of that. Debt? A fairy debt? A kingfisher dropped from an overhanging willow and the woman's eyes flicked to follow it as it came back out with a little whitefish and flew back to another tree to eat it. They never ate on the perch they hunted from.

That gaze fastened on her like thorns. Then the woman, Hild, nodded, for all the world as though Afanc had spoken aloud. "They eat under shelter," she said. "But they hunt from the edge."

How dare she tell her about her own marsh?

Hild was looking at her as though she knew what she thinking. Afanc heard again what she had said, and the way she had said it, the offering, the lesson, and she was curious. Were questions like fairy food? If you took the answers, took them into your heart, were you drawn slowly into the fairy world?

"If I answer your questions, perhaps you will answer mine," Hild said.

Surely that would be safe. But Afanc knew even if it wasn't she would agree. Perhaps that was a spell, too, but she was no longer afraid. She had no idea why she ever had been.

Two days later Hild stood at the edge of the mere. Behind her morning mist twined like a scarf through the trees, and small things watched from the dark understorey behind her. The vines, with other creepers and climbers—she refused their Anglisc names; let them be nameless—drank the light and kept that bit of woodland thick and impenetrable to woodsmen. Boats did not come here because there were few fish. Out here she could be alone.

Her right hip felt unbalanced without Wilfrid, and the front of her dress was stiff where her milk had leaked. He was eating her alive; she was shrivelling and drying, a nurselog fastened and fed on by a windblown seedling not her own. Wilfrid was her burden, she had given promises to the dead, but sometimes she could not bear the weight. This morning she had left him with Morud; Gwladus had been bitter and unhelpful of late.

The water before her was a pewter plate under a silver and tin sky. A stone's-throw out an old swan's nest rose like a mountain of sticks from the water. It was brown and grey: old, ten years of sticks and reeds, feather and down, broken eggs and leaf litter, layer after layer. All dead now. But it was a good spot, safe from foxes at least. Herons were another matter, though as the water here was thick and peaty there were not many fish to attract them. There was no sign of otters, either: no mud slides, no drenching sweetness of fresh spraint; if otters came here, it was not often. But they would come; like kings they always came. Otters always burned with hunger. There was never enough.

Yesterday she had seen a pair of swans, shining white as starlight on the water, and, paddling not far behind them, three slightly smaller, greyer versions of themselves. Apart from the black bump on the adult male swan's beak their bills were smooth and unnotched, not marked as anyone's property. The shining pair were not yet ready to breed. When they were, they would drive away last year's brood and then they would come back to where they had been successful before, to this nest.

Three swanlets. Perhaps they started with half a dozen. Carried the cygnets on their backs, sheltered them with their wings, only to see them lost, one by one. Better to lose them right away if they were to start again—and they could; they still had each other.

She turned her face, turned her heart, turned her mind from the sudden void howling before her. Nothing. She would see nothing, feel nothing, remember nothing. She closed her eyes and emptied herself of all but her breath, in and out. In and out. Felt only the wide nothing of the water; stepped aside from the past, all of it.

After some unknown time she became aware of the lap and plash of the mere and the faint scent of rot arrested by cold. She heard the distant, falling call of a reed bunting, then the rattle and hiss of something easing through the sedge and grass. She opened her eyes.

She touched the inside of her wrist, felt the blood beat through the blue tracery of vein. She was alive. Cian was dead, Honey was dead, but she breathed, her blood beat.

"I am Hild."

The spear-straight Anglisc cut blunt and brutal through the shifting marshland. It did not belong here. It was a name and sound from the heroic world, one in which the owner, clad in furs and gold, might raise her blade to protect her people. But that world was gone. This was her world now: wild and wary, a shifting, watery land of mist and birds where she walked barefoot, toes squeezing the mud, owning nothing, belonging to no one, fading into the reeds at the approach of another. Here no one knew her past; here she spoke only the webbed and darting British of the mire with its strange paddle-and-dive rhythm she had absorbed from the fishers and fowlers and farmers of the isle.

She was Hild. Hild not-Yffing, Hild not-wife. Not Butcherbird. Not Cath Llew. Hild nothing, Hild nurselog. Hild-who-lost. Hild the lean—Hild Gul, a stranger staying in a cowherd's hut at the pleasure of Eirlys and her man, Pabo of High Brune. Hild Gul who walked the spine of Ynys Bwyell with her big stick and small child, who would nod if you gave greeting and always listen but never speak. Those first weeks she had crept like a broken-backed dog, so unsteady that islanders nearly forgot their wary habit and reached out to help. She did not want their help; she took nothing from them but their way of speaking. As she grew stronger and faster, and came more often, they got used to her stepping silently from some shadow they had not known was there, to listen to gossip and news; to watch the hedge priest, Duer, speak his Christ prayers by the cross. Sometimes she would lend a hand with some task or other. They grew so used to her that they talked in front of her as though she were a cow or a tree. But there had been little to learn.

She took the small turned pot of goose grease and marsh nettle from her purse. The purse was made of scraps—some from the extra panel Gwladus had let into her dress in another life and taken out again—of cloth that looked poor but inside was reinforced with sturdy sacking. Her old one, with the gold and ivory strapping, was buried with her beads, with her rings, with her seax and Gwladus's precious bangles. Buried with Little Honey. Hild did not know where. "She rests in glory," was all Gwladus would say, when Hild had finally come to her right mind in the cowherd's hut. Gwladus had kept against need only the scraps of gold gouged from Cian's gear but Hild could not bear to see them; they were now sewn into the seams of Gwladus's dress.

She stripped her own dress—her underdress had long since gone for bandaging—and looked at her scars. The cut on her belly had healed to a faint pink line like the sun-faded edge of leather round a shield rim. Her arms looked less tidy, and tender in places still, but sound. She had been worried about the cut near her elbow, such cuts could be complicated, but she was lucky; the blade had missed the joint and important sinews, and skin mended. Her thigh, well, it would always be ugly, but it, too, had healed well. She imagined someone touching it—imagined Cian touching it . . .

Blank. Breathe. Listen. This time it was the *ploop* of something sliding into the water in the distance, and a waxwing close by that brought her back.

It was her hip that concerned her. She unwrapped it carefully. The dressing was dry and smelt normal; the scab was thick, and coming away at the edges. But it had scabbed before. It had been the source of the matter that nearly took her, that would have taken her if Afanc had not found them and brought them to her mother, Eirlys, who had held her down while she screamed, opened her up again, dug out the splinters the bone was still shedding, and poked in a reed to keep it drained before smearing it with honey and binding it up once again.

It had shed another bone splinter a fortnight after Yule but by then she had been well enough to tend it herself. The hard part was finding enough light. Inside the hut, her hut until the cowherd and his new wife got back from Crowle in the spring, it was too dark; outside it was always raining.

But she knew her own body by touch. The axe, or maybe it was a spear swung at an angle like an axe—men use anything in battle—had sliced off the tip of her hip bone and cut a wedge into the swell of muscle beside it. If it had landed differently the blade could have opened the great pumping vein in her leg, or cut the muscle and sinew that made the leg work. But it had landed where it did and her leg was safe. But Little Honey was nothing now but tiny bones somewhere in the mud.

. The ache to find her, to warm those bones by a hearth, flared as fast as joint fever. She did not want to want. Wanting made her remember. Blank. Breathe. Listen.

She smoothed the marsh-nettle salve on her scar with long steady strokes along the path she wanted the muscles to knit, massaging it deep. It hurt. Despite the pain, she began to stretch up and out to the side. Rub, stretch, rub. She hissed, but kept on. She would never again let feeling stop her doing what she had to. At least she could feel. Little Honey would never feel anything again.

Long strokes, like the grease she had rubbed into Cian's skin on nights after the harvest. Those muscles, his skin, the laugh in his voice, his smile, his smell, oh dear gods his smell . . .

She wiped at her breasts, at the milk leaking from the left nipple. Honey's milk.

"You can't feed them both," Cian had said in her fever dream, in the netherworld filled with the rising stench of the dead. On the mire the reek of carrion had risen hour by hour, until it seeped into her pores and greased her lungs, until she would never be rid of it.

Vaguely she remembered Gwladus pulling Wilfrid away before he was done, his screams. It made no difference. Honey would not suck. She just lay there, did not move, barely breathing. Little Honey was leaving, melting away like dew.

And then her arms were empty. Honey was gone. There was nothing but the marsh and the army of the dead, their stench swelling the air until she could not breathe. The waters rose with the stench, and kept rising, and Gwladus and Morud dragged her south on the blanket, south and east deeper into the mire.

Blank. Breathe. Listen.

More salve. More stretching.

She dipped her fingers into the pot and scraped wood. Empty. Gone.

Gone. Cian was gone. Little Honey was gone. Edwin was gone. All the thegns. The Hounds were gone and the Fiercesomes. Even Cygnet. What was left? She did not know. She knew nothing of anything beyond the watery horizon. Between Blodmonath and Hrethmonath, Ynys Bwyell, circled by great rivers and mire, was cut off from the world. All that reached the farm were broken pieces of news, shouted by marsh dwellers from boat to boat: kings with wings of fire burning all before them as they rode north; strange lights dancing on top of Ynys Coed where a forest of captured spears driven into the hill held up the hacked remains of a king and his son for the crows; the bog dying for half a mile around the battle, poisoned by all the blood.

There was no news at all from beyond the greater mire bounded by rivers on three sides and the road on the fourth. Nothing from Elmet. She had walked the length of the island, listening, and there was nothing.

She pulled her dress back on and picked up her staff: bog oak she had found east of the ore smelters' shelter up past Beltoft. Hard and heavy as iron, dead a thousand years.

A cold wind blew from the east as Hild and Huelwen and the four Beltoft farmers shovelled stiff mudstone dirt into hemp sacks. Old Jonty sat on the hand cart and played a mournful tune on his bone whistle.

Huelwen the farmer rested on her wooden shovel and wiped her forehead with a meaty forearm. "Leave off, Da. It's hard enough work without making us all feel like the night may be black but the day is blacker still. And you should learn something brighter for the light festival."

Two of the neighbours, a young woman and her younger brother, nodded agreement but they did not stop working. High tide was due in two days and the bank needed to be mended or their common pasture, the only one thereabouts for the cattle until the waters withdrew in late spring, would drown.

Huelwen, who had only one foot—she wore a long boot strapped to her left calf that held a carved peg in place—bent and sifted another shovelful into the sack. Hild thought she must have a back like granite to take such weight with only one flesh-and-bone support. "Tell us a story, Awel," the farmer said to the young woman. "Tell that one your brother told me last night in bed." Davy blushed. "The one about the land of lopside."

And so as they worked Awel told of the land of lopside: where roasted larks flew into your mouth, fences were made of sausages, pigs trotted up ready-roasted with knives for carving already dug into their sides. To get there, you had to wade in pig shit up to your chin for seven years, climb seven mountains, cut seven trees . . .

Cian had often told her stories or sung her a song in bed.

In the land of lopside the houses were roofed with white bread and the eaves dripped with butter; the babies fed on clouds of honey . . .

Hild laid her shovel against the cart and walked away.

When she neared the farmhouse, Gwladus was on her knees peering into the thicket of nettles east of the midden. "I swear that Wix hides her eggs just to spite me," she said. And Hild was glad to hear her sounding like her old self. "The hussy. She sees me and gets a glint in her eye . . . Ha!" Gwladus scrambled back holding a big white egg. "Nine today. Your mam will be pleased." She turned, smiling, saw it was Hild, and her face closed.

"Why are you being like this?" Hild said. "What's wrong with you?"

"Wrong with *me*? I—"

Someone ran down the path, in that helter-skelter whirl that meant they were running because the world was an exciting place, because they could.

"Gwladus! Where are you? Mam wants those—" Afanc burst into view and skidded to a stop, spraddle-legged as a colt. She looked from Hild to Gwladus and back again.

Gwladus put the egg with the others in her reed basket, and stood. "Take these to your mam, Afanc. I need clean air."

Hild watched her leave. Hild nothing. Hild-who-lost. Hild-with-no-one-left.

It was raining and late in the day when Afanc found her sitting by the old swan's nest fashioning a fishhook from a heather root.

"Morud said you've not been back."

Afanc sat down next to her.

"It's cold. It'll be dark soon."

Hild sawed at the root a bit more with her knife. It was a poor blade, a piece of scrap iron hammered flat and ground on a stone, one end wrapped in sacking lumpy with knots. The kind of knife even a slave would have shunned at Caer Loid.

"Have you and Gwladus quarrelled?"

In Afanc's world a quarrel would mean a screaming match followed by hair pulling. In the world of the Yffings a quarrel meant the clash of armies, with the winner staking out parts of the loser on a hill.

"Shall I tell you a thing? I learnt it two summers ago. I learnt that one way to mend a quarrel with a friend is to just give in."

Hild looked at her. So small and helpless. Like a dormouse snuffing at the corn stubble, unaware of the owl watching from the trees; she had no idea of the death that could swoop from the dark.

"You're unhappy. I can tell. Gwladus is unhappy. So just give in." She stuck her chin out. "I'm telling you, just give her what she wants."

"I don't know what she wants."

Afanc stared at her. "Then ask."

Ask. What must it be like to grow up being able to just . . . ask? To not have to always know? For lives—hers, her family's—to not depend on always knowing, always being right? But no one depended on her anymore. Except Gwladus and Morud. And Wilfrid.

"It's the fastest way. So just ask."

Ask. She looked at the thorn and then the line and the ugly knife. Hemp and heather and sacking, where not long since it had been gold and jewels and the best blade in the north.

"It's hard," Afanc said. "But it works. Mostly, anyway."

Ask.

"If you won't go home will you come to ours?" Afanc looked about in the gathering dark. "Mam'll be wondering where I've got to."

The only people who would be wondering where she was were those waiting in Carwyn's house. But she had nothing to give.

"That's not a very good fishhook."

She tugged at the line, testing it. It broke.

"Come home with me."

She said nothing, and after a moment Afanc got up. Hild paid no more attention. After a while Afanc left, and she stared at the broken line, the useless hook, the sad knife.

The rain was slowing and the light fading as Hild neared the house. Blue smoke hung like mist above the pointed roof. Water ran from the bundles of reeds that made the roof and dripped from the eaves, cutting another fingertip deeper into the trench formed over the years. She pushed through the deerskin flap, propped her staff against the doorframe, and blinked in the stinging gloom.

In the centre a peat fire burned steadily. It seemed to burn clean, as peat often did, but smoke gathered under the roof and seeped out slowly through the reeds. Here, where the roof was highest, was where the air was clearest. Morud knelt by the hearth, turning wet cloths on a frame to dry. He glanced at Hild, then away.

Gwladus was standing by the great hollowed elm bole that served as a floor mortar, with its upright pestle circled inside the iron ring pegged to one of the wall posts. She stirred and ground and did not look up.

"I would talk," Hild said. Wilfrid made an angry sound.

Gwladus took another handful of greenstuff and trundled the pestle round the bowl. Soapwort. For the endless washing a child entailed. "He needs feeding," she said.

"He can wait."

Gwladus added another handful of soapwort. Morud stared hard at nothing in particular and tried to give the impression he was not there.

Wilfrid shrieked. Hild picked him up and jogged him. He shrieked harder. She unfasted her bodice and gave him her left breast. He bit. She pulled him away and his face turned red with rage, and when he opened his mouth to scream again she held him out to Morud. "Give him a mallow. I would talk," she said again to Gwladus.

Gwladus stooped for another handful of soapwort.

The smoke was scratching at Hild's throat and making her eyes sore, Wilfrid would not be quiet, and now her own bodywoman was making her wait. "You will look at me when I speak. You will tell me what is wrong."

Gwladus looked up, one hand on the pestle, one still holding green stalks. "Will I?"

Hild stared.

"But why would I not? Don't I always do as I'm asked? Even when it should never be asked."

Gwladus looked at the greenstuff in her hand then back to Hild. She tilted her head.

"You. You asked me to think for you while you screamed and bled, and I did. I kept doing it. On and on. I dragged you through the mire on a sack. I buried your child with my bare hands. I did not give up. I have carried you. I am still carrying you. But you are carrying nothing. Your wounds are healed but you act as though you're dead. You're not dead. So what are you doing?"

Silence.

"Are you even listening?" Gwladus threw the soapwort at her.

Hild stared at the limp stalk on her shoulder—it was fraying and sliming and should have been used days ago—then picked it off. It left a green smear on her already stained dress.

"Look at me."

Hild lifted her head.

"Now look at this place." Gwladus swept her hand at the bare lathe, the dirt floor, their filthy and ragged clothes. "This is me and Morud carrying you. We're trying. But this . . . It's not good enough. And it's not safe—not for much longer. And I can't— I can't do it alone anymore. So I will tell you what is wrong with me: I need you, we need you to do something."

"I'm not—" She felt so tired. "I have nothing left."

Gwladus looked at her a long time. "I am nothing? Morud is nothing? Our loyalty, our love is nothing?"

Love. All she felt was empty.

By the hearth, next to Morud, Wilfrid kicked and shrieked. His cries were dull and red and stubborn, like the peat glow. Love. Hild wanted her staff, something to hold, to grip, to anchor herself. Love.

"Tell me—" She stopped. *Just ask.* "Please. Tell me what I can— Tell me how."

"I don't know how! That's what you do." Gwladus's face was painted in emberlight and shadow, the muscles in her neck rigid as cable, and Hild felt at the lip of a yawning pit.

"Not anymore," Hild said. "I did. I tried. I can't do it anymore. And why would you lean on me? I did it all wrong. I lost. Cian died. Honey died."

"You lost. Yes. People died. You nearly died—but you didn't. We saved you. You didn't lose me, you didn't lose Morud. You didn't lose your life, or your mind—so use it. Think. We're safe here in Ynys Bwyell, for now. But Wulfmonath is over and come spring the water will start to go down and news will start to come in, and news of you will get out. So what will we do?"

"I—"

"Don't say 'I don't know.' You are Hild Yffing. Knowing is what you do. So do that. If not for you then for me, for Morud. We need you to not act as if you're dead and nothing matters. We matter, we're here, and we can't stay. We need you to know what to do. For our sake, if you love us. At least try."

Hild looked down at Wilfrid. At Morud, who was hunched and unhappy. Back to Gwladus. *If you love us.* She did not know if she did. She felt nothing at all. But she had asked and Gwladus had answered: Try.

She woke in the dawnlight feeling hollow and fragile as a bird bone. *If you love us.* But she was empty as a drum. *Just try.* She needed to be outside with the wind and the water.

Wind stroked ruffles and ripples across the mere. She stood, letting her mind fill with nothing, but a living nothing—the sound of the water, the brush of air on her cheek—with her staff in her left hand and Wilfrid on her right hip. He was gumming a mallow root and drooling. He had two tiny teeth; judging by the redness of his bottom gum there were more to come very soon. Her left hip was red, too: still tender and thin-skinned after shedding its scab. But Gwladus was right; she was alive and healing. The skin was sound. It would thicken in time, and the bright pink would fade until nothing was left but a pale scar. It would be much less ugly than her thigh; few would guess it had almost killed her. Wilfrid would have all his teeth by then.

Then. A time ahead. A time that was not the endless nothingness of now. It was a new thought, and delicate as a butterfly's wing. Not to be touched yet.

Her nipples were sore from his biting, but at least her bladder was under her control again. She dandled him—he had gained good healthy weight—and he made that small angry sound that meant he wanted her to stop, wanted her to let him concentrate on his root. Roots, when once she had talked with queens of teething on coral and agate.

The past. The place the now flowed from. That was then, and this was now.

Wilfrid was hers now, as surely as her scars. She fed him, she would protect him, but she did not swell with love when he blew a bubble of spit at her, or laugh with joy when he reached for her hair. Not that he reached often. He did not like new things; they made him indignant.

He dropped his root and fell asleep, sudden as a spring rain shower, face turned to one side against her ribs. How would that face turn out? Would he be plump and sullen like his mother, or stolid and steady like his father? At least Manfrid had known his son even if Wilgith had not, and neither, as was proper, had outlived their child.

Just over six months old. Not big for his age, but not small. His hair was still tawny, but with darker streaks now, and his eyes were also darkening.

Perhaps they would end up the same dull stone grey of his grandfather. Nothing like the bright, clear blue that would have been Honey's.

Something that might once have been her heart squeezed. She looked out across the bright water, seeing in her mind's eye the old oak overlooking her valley. Honey would never see it, but the valley was still there. The beginning of Solmonath would have brought a slow easing of the dark—not the sudden tilt towards the light that would happen next month, but noticeable. And next month the tight buds on the old oak would start showing green at their tips.

Over the mere the sky was now more silver than lead, the cloud just a thin film. Perhaps they would see the sun soon. The edges of the marsh were turning pale green, and silvery with bog moss. The wood, too, was changing. Around an open patch, the sodden understorey glowed with a faint sheen of gold from the haircap moss, and something she thought might be pilewort had poked a green finger into the light. Soon there would be horehound, and wolfbane—Anglisc names, she realised. Fellenwort, that was the name of the vine. Fellenwort.

The air stirred. She glanced about, listened, sniffed. Then, there, on the northern horizon: a growing cloud, high up. Tens of thousands, hundreds of thousands of wings beat-beat-beating, rushing, pouring from right to left over her head. As the last of them passed she caught the gleam of white in their tails and wing edges. Skylarks. The land of lopside . . .

Long after they had gone her ears thrummed and fluttered. She turned slowly, thinking. She knew what to do.

As she approached the store hut in Eirlys's farmyard, the dog barked, and Eirlys popped her head out. Her big beaky nose made her look like a finch. "Hush, Fliss. Hush!" The bitch quieted, but stayed at the bottom of the steps, tail and head low and stiff, eyes fixed on Hild.

Eirlys wiped her hands on her apron. "Now then."

Hild looked up at Eirlys and shifted Wilfrid to her other hip. "I would have a word."

Eirlys nodded once.

"I will soon have need of a boat."

Fliss growled. Eirlys snapped her fingers, and Fliss whined and sank onto her belly. Eirlys nodded Hild on.

"I have gold. I can pay."

"You made no mention before."

She had not been able to speak for the first two months. Eirlys knew this well enough. Hild said nothing.

"So. You've some gold." She pressed her lips to a thin seam. "But what will be left when you've paid for these months of barley and cheese and the use of Carwyn's house?"

Living on Eirlys's land, owing Eirlys obligation, had spun the first thread in the weave of connection for Hild Gul on Ynys Bwyell. Exchanging gold for that obligation would cut that thread. She did not know any other way. "Enough," she said.

"Enough for a boat?"

"That's what I would know. You're connected to everyone hereabouts; you know who might spare a boat. Or lend it for a time in spring."

"But why should I tell you?"

Because I am Yffing. Being Yffing had always meant it was enough to simply wish for a thing to be given it. Being Yffing now meant being hunted and staked out on a hill. Why should Eirlys tell Hild Gul anything?

"I was expecting a month or two of your strong back and arms around the farm, now you're healed. Dykes need mending. Fowl don't just walk into the net. Come early summer the cattle'll need moving to pasture, then there's milking."

"Get me a boat and I'll help you."

"Help me and I'll get you a boat." Her eyes were the colour of fibrous peat, somewhere between brown and green. Not warm eyes.

Wilfrid grumbled and stirred. Hild switched him again. "I saw a rush of larks. Not usual here, I think."

Eirlys shrugged: She did not know, she did not care.

"They're giving warning: Cold is coming."

"Cold? Aye, no doubt. That does happen in winter."

"Cold enough to drive larks early and hard?" Now she let a hint of her Elmet accent show, the accent of strong kings of the Old North. "The light festival's in six days. How many will come?"

Eirlys was wary now. "Most."

"Yes. And they'll be caught, you'll be caught by the cold. Killing cold. Those not prepared will die. Those here will be trapped here. If you're not ready, they'll eat you out of house and home."

Eirlys sucked her teeth. "If I did believe you, and I'm not saying I do, mind, why should I worry? We've plenty of cheese to eat and peat to burn."

Hild nodded. "Afanc told me you milked three times a day for longer than usual this summer. But will it be enough?"

"I know my own stores." But the tilt of her head had changed, and Hild knew she was listening.

"The cold will come. Soon." They had enough warning; the larks came from the north, and they flew fast and far ahead of the cold they fled. "Just as the festival starts, perhaps."

"Perhaps?" She fondled Fliss's ears. "Let's say the cold does come, and say it comes during the festival, before folk are safely back in their homes. How long will it stay? Ah, you don't know that either."

Fliss whined again and licked her hand. Again, she fondled the bitch's ears.

"Well, Fliss doesn't like you, but Fliss doesn't like anyone but me and the girl, and the girl does like you. She's a little goose but she's not often wrong." She nodded to herself, thinking. "Some folk don't come to festival. Old folk. But if that cold's as bad as you say, and as lasting, they'll need to be here. They'll need to bide with us for warmth. So. If you help to bring them in, and if the cold comes as promised, I'll find you that boat."

The cloud of precious furs given to her by Edwin as gift and punishment, badge and brand, had been bloodied, muddied, drooled upon, and slept in. They could not be restored in a day. It would take a week more of pounding soapwort, warming water, mixing them to suds, wiping the furs gently with a clean cloth dipped and squeezed to damp. Wiping again with a clean, dry cloth. And again. And again. Over and over. Patiently. Carefully. Attending to missed or stubborn spots. They were soiled but they could be saved. It was just work. She and Gwladus knew how to work.

Hild and Afanc travelled together to bring folk in, rowing here and walking there. Some took longer to persuade than others, but in the end they all gathered their bedding, a pot or two, and the food they could carry, and came to High Brune. All but the smelters on the east slope just south of Huelwen's steading. They were strange folk who held themselves apart. They reminded Hild of charcoal burners, only instead of being addled from days without sleep as they tended their fires, it was suspicion that curled and fumed through their world—suspicion that strangers would steal the secret of the best places to find bog iron, would watch and learn how to dig the muck, what colour the charcoal should glow, how long the chimney should be sealed, the angle at which to pour the pig iron. To them every duck hunter was a bandit lurking in the reeds waiting to scull in, climb the hill, and steal the rusting ingots; every cowherd might read secrets from the very stones. No, they would not leave their fastness.

But others did. So many that Eirlys sucked her teeth and tore the feathers from the feast swans more vigorously than necessary, and every time Pabo, a short, bowed man with a potbelly, showed another family to a floor space of their own he shook his head enough to set his straggling hair swinging like water weed. The air grew thick from the breath of too many folk, and loud with children running about in excitement. Wilfrid was more grumpy than usual and off his milk. At least he had stopped biting.

Hild woke in the dark. She blinked and the black thickened to a reddish tinge. Sleeping folk murmured and rolled closer to one another: They could feel the cold stealing under the door. She sat up. Wilfrid grumbled but did not wake. The fire glowed feebly, shrinking before the cold. She liked the cold better than the press of people. This might be her last chance for a while. She lifted Wilfrid free of the furs and tucked him under Gwladus's arm. Gwladus made the questioning noise of the half awake. "The child," she whispered. "Keep him by you. I'll be back a bit after dawn." She pulled her newly fresh furs around her, felt for her staff, and stood. She stepped over families sleeping in groups, couples in pairs, and children in mounds; old folk wrapped head to foot like the dead.

On the mere, the three swanlets glided from the mist so gradually they seemed to form from it. They passed Hild in silence, without as much as a turn of the head, and dissolved back into the grey. They were asleep with their eyes open. No sign of the parents. Everything was still and silent. She could float away, out into nothing, walk into the water and vanish in the mist . . .

In the reeds, a duck rattled its feathers and settled again. They would all be out of the water, beaks tucked into fluffed feathers, outwaiting the cold. A good time to get out the nets. But even through the thick wool of her dress and her furs the cold sawed into her hip. There would be no hunting today: Today was the festival.

Along the shore, frozen reeds and leaves crunched under her boots. By the time she reached the enclosure the fog, even along the ground, was thinning and brightening—behind the veil of mist and cloud the sun was rising—but the cold deepened. She was ravenous.

Outside the freezing fog thickened with the late afternoon but inside it was warm, bright, and close, like a smaller, less grand version of Ceredig's hall. The hearth glowed high and bright along its whole length; folk, perched at boards, on stools and upturned pails, or on the floor with their arms wrapped about their knees, shouted and laughed and sang, ate and drank and stole the occasional hare leg from a gossiping neighbour. Fliss had given up trying to watch everyone and had settled in Eirlys's bed nook, chin on paws, white brows folding and straightening as a troop of children threw a ball of rags and yarn back and forth.

They had eaten a swan—marked on its beak, Hild saw; not one of her pair—and, when that was gone, a goose. Everyone was in a high state of grease and benevolence.

Wilfrid was with three other infants on old beaver furs at the north end, watched over by an angular woman who had twinkled at Morud and asked him if he wanted to watch the bairns with her. Gwladus sat on a milkmaid's stool black with age, combing Hild's hair. Hild, leaning back against Gwladus's knees with her eyes closed, felt the flex of Gwladus's right leg as it took more weight than the left because the stool was not quite level, the tiny shift and plump of the muscle by the knee as she reached forward, set the comb's teeth, and pulled slowly down.

This was the first time since Elmet that Gwladus had combed her hair.

Set the comb, pull slowly down. Hand again a little farther up. Set, slowly down. Every now and again amid the smells of close-packed bodies, heather beer, the peaty perfume of smoke, the charred turnip someone had left in the embers, she caught the round rich scent of Gwladus. Not tansy, not anymore, but the woman smell that punched through to old memories and made her breasts prickle. The thing between her and Gwladus was in the past, but it still connected them, like the air that held up a bird or the water a fish. For the first time since last summer she felt the muscles around her mouth and eyes ease. Soon enough they would find a boat and leave this place. They would go find what was left of their world. Soon enough, but not now. Here she was not the lady of Elmet, just Hild Gul, tall and quiet but otherwise unremarkable. Here, she had warmth, food, and people she cared for, and no one to ask her to judge this, plan that, or look around corners to foresee what others could not.

A child ran past her, shrieking with triumph, and another hurtled after her, raging red-faced that it was his ball! His! On the other side of the hearth someone began tuning a harp. A real harp with bronze strings. But they were in no hurry to get it right. She kept her eyes closed and let herself sink into the rhythm of the comb.

Awareness of the children, the lilt of the island-inflected British, the smell, the hard board under her sit bones, rose and fell. She drifted, walking among the new stems of wolfbane at the edge of the carr . . .

A shimmering chord, wavering but true, made her blink. Another, louder, sure enough for the hall to still.

A stir. Those around the edges standing to see. Huelwen, one leg stretched out before her, rolling her eyes at her young man who was carrying his upturned bucket to the hearth. The old man, Jonty, sitting down, the harp on his knee. A girl, six or seven—clutching the yarn ball in one hand, the other wiping her nose—came to stand by him and gape.

"I had a girl like you," he said. Another chord. "Shall I sing of her?"

Huelwen groaned. "Not that one, Da!" But the child nodded.

Jonty nodded, too, kept nodding in time to the music he began to stroke from the harp. He seemed in no hurry to get to the words, content to let the music and the bronze shimmer together in the smoky light of the hearth.

He raised his voice to his audience. "Did you like your swan?"

Calls of *Yes!* and *No!* and *Where's the other one?* Gwladus combed her hair steadily.

"Well, I don't like swans. And I'll tell you why." The high bronze shimmer deepened. "I'll tell you of a swan I once knew, and a girl. And what that swan did to her." The shimmer darkened to a moan. "To my girl. My youngest, my best. My heart." The moan began to twist, pull itself out of true.

He sang harshly, with the hiss and rattle of wind through dead reeds.

> I had a girl, killed by a swan.
> The mist was rising—
> green as the growing heart of a secret
> green as unfurling chestnut leaves
> green as the new scum on the lake.

The old man's voice wavered and the note wandered but his bony fingers plucked cruel and sure.

> The mist was rising
> and their wings rose with it
> white, strong-smelling angel wings
> beating
> and them swans blowing and honking
> like the horns at the end of the world.
> It was the end of her world.

Now the chords jangled like a bunch of iron latch-lifters, then sorted themselves, each note distinct, each word falling soft and heavy.

> She picked flowers
> violets
> new and silky, purple as a king's cloak
> and ran ahead
> into that mist
> for more.
> And God's angels flew forth
> from the mist
> and hit her—
> eyes, and throat
> and twice—
> two beats of those heavy
> crocus-coloured bills
> two, I heard them—
> on the drum of her breastbone
> and her little heart stopped.
> And she died.
> And we had swan pie for dinner
> but I ate none of it.

The last chord faded. The turves on the hearth shifted. Nothing moved but Fliss, who lifted her head.

Jonty looked bright and straight as a flower after rain; refreshed by others' pain. He smiled. Gwladus's hand rested on Hild's shoulder and pressed lightly. Fliss turned to the door, cocked her head.

The audience began to stir and murmur like sleepers waking. Two men beat their palms on the board. Fliss growled.

"Oh, for pity's sake," Eirlys said, reaching for her. "Let the old fool have his due."

Fliss rose to her feet like a puppet on hinged legs, and barked.

"Hush, now! There's—"

Fliss flew from the bed, tore over those unable to get out of the way, and flung herself at the door. Those who weren't staring in disbelief at the blood rising on their arms and thighs from the dog's heedless claws turned and gaped.

Hild gripped Gwladus's arm. "Morud and Wilfrid. Get them. Hide. Now!"

Folk were craning this way and that. "What—" "Why—" "Is—" And over their indignation Fliss scrabbled at the door and foamed and snarled.

Hild pulled her staff to her.

The door slammed open. Men, huge with cold and iron. Men in war caps, with frosted beards and hard eyes. Spears pointed around the room. Hild was on the floor, hidden. She gathered her furs, slowly.

One man shouldered in front of the others. Gold gleamed at his belt. "Who speaks—"

Fliss launched herself at his throat.

The man swung the flat of his sword just as Afanc screamed, "No!"

Hild unfolded enough to trip a charging Afanc, belt Fliss unconscious, and catch the swinging blade on her staff. Both rang.

"Hold!" Even after tearing her throat in the battle there was enough left of her Butcherbird voice to command attention. She straightened to her full height.

Around them folk drew back. They did not understand the Anglisc but they understood the gleam of gold and weaponry, and the tone of command.

She stood with the glow of the hearth lighting her left half and her right in shadow. She no longer wore her seax or gold, her hair was undressed and her clothes threadbare, but she stood like a giant with the furs of Cath Llew around her and the tip of her staff unwavering.

The leader took a half step and stopped as though he had run into a wall. "Lady?"

Hild knew that voice. "Show yourself."

He tore off his helmet. "Lady—"

He took another step. Now her staff pointed directly at him. "Stand down, Oeric."

He turned to his men. "You heard the lady." They glanced at one another, then lowered their spears. One tipped back his war hat and scratched his forehead. She knew him; the stripling spearman of Elmet, Bearn's friend. Cuthred. She knew one of the others, too, the greybeard who used a bow. Sitric.

"You." To the last man backing over the threshhold. "Close the door—" He turned. Leofdæg, with a new scar along his jaw. She waited until he had shut the cold out and turned back to face her. "Hard journey?"

He shrugged with that one-shouldered, unwavering-weapon-hand gesith shrug she had not seen for half a year, and sheathed his sword. Then he fished in his pouch and held out the great glittering bauble that was her cross.

All around her, the folk of Ynys Bwyell turned their faces to her like pale, shocked flowers.

Hild sat with Oeric by the hearth on the upturned bucket Jonty had used, with Leofdæg and the spearmen standing between them and the people of High Brune. Afanc and Fliss were on the bed in the alcove, comforting each other, both looking addled and uncertain. There had been no time to be gentle—but neither was bleeding. Eirlys and Pabo were cutting cheese and pouring ale while the people gathered in the shadows murmured and muttered and slid looks at the Anglisc. Her attention was spread throughout the hall: Anger, over there, from the youths. Shock, from the bed. Gwladus and Morud, with Wilfrid between them, folded in and watchful, and Huelwen and Jonty and a small group who seemed more curious than anything. Curiosity, too, from the children.

She turned the cross in her hands. Red-tinged shadow made the holes left by two missing pearls gape.

Oeric saw what she was looking at. "Cenhelm's price. He's waiting with *Curlew* on the Daun out by Thorne."

She turned the cross again. "What else did you promise him?"

"One more pearl for taking us back to Cnotinsleah."

She kept turning the cross. The promise of one pearl was not enough to hold a boat the size of the *Curlew* in a time of war.

"Gladmær's with him. And two spearmen."

Gladmær, then, as well as Leofdæg. She waited but her feelings seemed to be in a distant country she had known long ago.

"We've been on foot since the new moon. Looking for you." She said nothing. "How—how is it with you?"

She lifted her head. "As you see." Her voice was a closed door.

After a moment he sighed, untied his waist pouch, and lifted out a tiny folded packet. He held it out.

After a moment she hung the cross around her neck, took off her furs, and took the packet. "Light," she said in British to no one in particular. She knew the feel of this skin, the nick by one of the folds, and the dimple, the scar on the other side. It was the palm-sized square of old sheepskin parchment Rhin used over and over for notes to her when he did not want to trust word of mouth, worn thin from endless pumicing.

"Light!" she said again, this time directly to the girl standing near Huelwen. Awel, Davy's sister. "Bring a dip."

She unfolded the parchment carefully. Yellow tallow light wavered uncertainly in the girl's shaking hand. Hild nodded to Oeric to take it and bring it closer. Two of the thin patches had worn through completely to holes.

It had been months since she had seen writing of any kind, months since she had heard or read Latin. The brown-black letters looked like worm cast at first, then resolved into Rhin's decisive hand.

It was hard to read, not because Rhin's writing was poor but because it was crammed together without spacing, looped around the holes, and abbreviated almost to nonsense. "More light," she said. She sounded the first line to herself. Light flared in front of her. "Here," she said, gesturing to her right and behind her. "Not too close." The tallow guttered and smoked.

She spelled out the first line again, slowly. Parts did not make sense.

"When did he write this?" she said in Anglisc.

"The day before we left," Oeric said. "The last day of Yule."

Epiphany. The words fell into place.

Epiphany, in haste. Safe and hidden. 71 souls. Safe are your Lady mother and friend and fosterling.

Begu and Breguswith were safe. And Ceadwin. She had forgotten him.

Caer Loid ashes. No room to list dead. Food sufficient to Lent. People restless.

There was a blot by *restless*. He had paused to consider the word. She would ask Oeric.

Reaver and other overwintering in York; latter holds eldest ætheling. Queen and Bishop and children gone. God grant you health. R.

She folded it carefully, nodded to the girl that she was done with the taper, then unfolded it again. Reaver: Cadwallon. She tapped the first word, thinking. Oeric moved his taper closer. She shook her head. "Blow it out."

Epiphany, with food only to Lent. There was food in huge buried caches near Caer Loid that would have survived a burning. Pyr knew where they were.

"Pyr?" she said.

"Dead. Like everyone at Caer Loid," Oeric said bleakly. "I told them to come with me. As you said, lady. But . . ." He shook his head. "Cadwallon is cruel."

And Penda had Honeytongue.

Pabo brought a bread trencher of cheese and wrinkled apples in one hand and a stool to put it on in the other. He put them down, one upon the other, and moved away without a word. Hild folded the letter and put it in her pitiful pouch.

She weighed an apple, and bit into it. She did not understand Cadwallon; she had never understood Cadwallon. He had never shown the urge to conquer and hold, just to kill and burn and torment everything Yffing. Yet he overwintered in York.

She tossed the core into the fire and hacked off cheese with her knife. It was hard and dry. She was used to it. In the corner with Morud, Wilfrid was fussing.

Penda, though, Penda was cunning. And he had Honeytongue—perhaps to install him king of Northumbre or at least of Deira, to make him Mercia's puppet king, once Cadwallon had burned and hacked, sated his lust, and left.

Oeric was staring at the crudely hammered lump of iron and sacking in her hand, and she looked at the oiled sheen of the blade in his.

"It serves," she said. "And the cheese tastes the same." But it didn't. Cheese eaten in the bright gleam of beeswax, rich full-fat cheese cut with a fine knife and laid on soft milled bread tasted better. Her patched dress itched. Her scars felt tight and drawn and every wound she had ever taken ached. She was tired. More than tired.

"What will we do?" he said.

She didn't know. *We need you to know.* So many of them. Gwladus and Morud and fussing Wilfrid. Oeric and Cuthred and the greybeard Sitric. Leofdæg and Gladmær. All of Menewood: seventy-one souls. So many. With food only to Lent. This was what it was to lose.

"Lady?"

Wilfrid's fussing soared into an angry shriek. Her nipples tightened. Another shriek, hard and determined, and her breasts began to leak.

"Lady." Morud this time, holding Wilfrid. It was strange to hear him speak Anglisc again. "He's hungry."

The world slowed. For a moment she was throwing the mewling thing in the fire, hooking burning logs from the hearth with her staff, and walking away while the steading burned, burned them all. She had lost. She would finally be free of it all. Free to ride, to roam the high places, to never have to carry another's weight again.

Then she was sitting in a patched dress on an upturned bucket.

"He's clean, lady," Morud said. "But he needs feeding."

She wiped her knife on her skirts, slid it into her rope belt, and held out her arms.

She settled Wilfrid in the crook of her left arm and unfastened her dress. He grabbed her left breast with both hands and latched onto her nipple like a terrier. That familiar pull, echoed in her womb, then he settled into a steady sucking rhythm. Oeric turned garnet red.

She pulled out her knife and cut another piece of cheese. Morud hovered in the background.

Oeric stood. "I'll— With your leave, lady. It's—"

"Sit, Oeric. We're not done."

He sat and looked at his feet.

"Look at me. Tell me about Osric."

"Osric, lady?"

"Osric. Osric Yffing. Osric stay-at-home, Osric trembleknee. The craven in Craven—if he still is."

"Lady?"

"Is Osric still in Craven? Is he still ealdorman? Report to me!" He blinked. "Morud, bring us ale."

Oeric gathered himself with an effort. "We last had word during the new moon of Blodmonath."

"What word, who from, and to whom?"

"A message to Rhin, lady. From Deacon James."

"Does he send regularly?" A deacon of the Church of Rome and a bishopless British priest. Talking together.

"I don't know, lady." She waited. His colour was calming. He tried again. "No. I don't think so. The roads were not . . . easy."

"Were not. They are now?"

He seemed uncertain. She was the light of the world; she should know without being told. "The Reaver's men roamed the roads in twos and threes while he was at Aberford," he said. "They did as they liked. He encouraged it. It was sport for him."

Morud brought ale. Oeric gulped.

"But then he moved to York for Yule, and it was only the nithings and losers who—" His face deepened to red again. Losers. They were all losers now. "Then it was only bandits. We kept them off the roads within five miles of Menewood, the lady Breguswith told us to go no farther. But we kept it clear past Caer Loid. What's left of it."

"My aunt and Sintiadd?" Morud, not caring that he'd interrupted. "She's old. And my sister—my sister . . ." His voice slid from low to high like a much younger boy.

Oeric looked at Hild, who said, "The old woman who cackles." Wilfrid sucked lazily. He was falling asleep. "And the lissome lass with the mole by her left eyebrow."

"Oh. Them. Yes, safe in Menewood. For now."

Wilfrid's eyes were shut tight and he had stopped sucking. When she lifted him away from her nipple he gummed the air twice, then was still. She handed him to Morud. "He'll sleep a while." She looked over to the corner. "Take him back and wait with Gwladus."

Eirlys and Pabo were coming their way with two trenchers, this time with goose leftovers. "Quickly now," Hild said. "What news?"

"Eanfrid Iding has left Pictland and called the men of the north—and Bernicia, Deira, aye, and Lindsey and the Bryneich, too—to hold themselves in readiness. And Osric in Craven gathers his men, though the deacon thinks not for the Iding."

He had not called Elmet. Why would he? Caer Loid was burnt and Menewood hidden. There was no longer an Elmet to send to.

13

✦

BY THE MORNING the bitter cold had eased and folk began to leave.

"Didn't last as long as you foretold," Eirlys said.

"No." Hild no longer bothered to hide her Elmet accent.

Eirlys folded her arms. "You struck my dog and knocked down my girl."

Eirlys knew well enough why Hild had done it, but she had been frightened and needed someone to blame. Hild no longer needed to ask for Eirlys's help; she could take it, take anything she wanted. But Afanc and Eirlys had saved her life. And Elmet needed friends more than ever. Just ask, Afanc would say.

Hild let the lilt of Bwyell lick about her words again, but lightly. "I owe you a debt. How may I repay it?"

"Leave this place and never come back."

"Find me a boat and we'll leave tomorrow."

"And forget us. Have your men forget us. We want to be unnoticed. It's how we've survived: No one knew we were here to quarrel over."

Knew. Eirlys understood that it was only a matter of time now before others saw what Hild was beginning to see: that Ynys Bwyell—the only solid land by the war streets and water roads between Lindsey, Elmet, and the Middle Saxons—could be the axle around which kingdoms turned.

"I can't command folk to forget, but I can command mine not to speak of it."

Eirlys nodded grudgingly. "My lass saved your life."

"Yes."

"And you hit her."

"I did." To save her life in turn. But Eirlys was in no mood to be reasonable.

"And now you want a boat."

"I do. A boat, four oars. And whatever warm things you can manage for the three of us for travel. Then we'll be gone from here. A boat and someone to guide us."

"Then you'll have to ask the girl's pardon. No one knows the waterways like her and Pabo. You'll need them both."

Hild nodded. "Stock the boat. And send for the priest. We leave tomorrow, and you'll have your gold."

Afanc had just thrown the last bundle to Huelwen, unmoored the rope, and pushed the little skiff into the mere when she saw Hild approaching, Oeric, glittering with iron and gold, following three paces behind and to the right. She turned and faced them, hands on hips. "Here to hit me again? Or lie some more?"

"I couldn't tell you who I was," Hild said.

Afanc's laugh was mean and hurt. "Oh, but you told me exactly what kind of person you are. The way you spoke and expected us to listen. The way you looked down on us all."

"I am tall, Afanc ferch Eirlys. I look down on everyone." Afanc did not smile. "I am sorry. I owe you a debt."

"I should have let you die!"

"But you did not."

The girl's chin trembled, torn between anger and betrayal and hurt.

"I leave tomorrow but the debt remains. You may always call on me."

"I'm to believe that Afanc, fisher, and daughter of fishers and farmers, can call to heel Hild Yffing?"

"Call to heel? No." Never again. "But call? Yes. Afanc ferch Eirlys, I tell you now, on this day, on my name, on this bank, that if you call I will come."

Part of her wished she could sit with this girl who had saved her life, sit and talk as the water moved by, of kingfishers and mallows and water voles and eels, but there were people waiting.

"I've talked to your mother about the best way to keep my presence, and your help, hidden. To keep you safe."

"We don't need your help."

Afanc was still a child. "But I need yours, Afanc. You are free to refuse. But I am asking it. And I will pay, in gold. For your mother says no one knows the western mere like you."

Afanc struggled between indignation and pride. "Pabo does," she admitted eventually.

Pabo and the priest Duer turned the boat while everyone on the bank sorted their bundles.

"We'll be back for you tomorrow," Afanc said to the priest. And to Leofdæg, "If you want to cross to Wroot, take the path upstream. There's a man who'll ferry you. Or you could take the path downstream to a ford."

"I remember the ford," said Gwladus. She looked as though she would rather not.

"The water's higher than it would've been when you crossed. But it's crossable." Without meeting Hild's eye, she patted Gwladus on the arm, tickled Wilfrid under the chin—he shrieked—bumped Morud's shoulder perfunctorily with hers, and climbed back into the boat.

Hild nodded her thanks to Pabo and turned her face to what she had been dreading since she woke in the hut on Bwyell.

In the middle of the mired waste she and Gwladus knelt at the foot of a shattered stump, the only stump for half a mile. The priest waited with Leofdæg ten paces away.

A shirr of rain scudded south to north, brief as a blessing.

Hild stared at the patch of dirt before them. "Are you sure?" But she knew. The grass was sparser than the surround, like a stripling's chin amid gesiths, and the dirt was darker, and shot through with thin, dark threads. Worm tracks. And the smell . . .

They should have brought a shovel. Gwladus must have used her hands the first time. But then it was just dirt. Now it was a grave.

Gwladus handed over her small belt knife. "Once you cut through the sod the ground's soft enough."

The knife was warm from Gwladus's body, and tiny in Hild's hands like a child's toy, the kind of thing that in another world, in another life, Cian might have carved for his daughter to play with. She touched its tip to the grass, the dark green tubular sort that grew in the wet.

Gwladus did not offer to do it for her. It was right that a mother do this one last thing.

She cut into the sod, and shuddered. The grit and glide of the blade through the dirt woke the sense memory of the first time she had killed a wounded man: probing for the soft spot in the skull, thrusting through skin and gristle, and then the sudden slide into the brain. She swallowed, and cut again, and this time the shudder was deeper, a writhe from her marrow.

Gwladus wrapped her arms around her from behind, as a friend supports a drunk leaning against a wall to bring up a gout of ale. And Hild cut again, and then tore and lifted out the sod, and again.

They looked at the naked dirt.

"I didn't have much time," Gwladus said. "It—she's not deep."

Hild dug her fingertips into the dirt and pulled, scooped the dirt out with her hands. It did not take long to reach the maggots.

The only cloth they had had to spare was a square torn from Hild's underdress and laid like a handkerchief over Honey's face. It had fallen in, moulded itself to the corpse's grin. The tiny thighs seethed with white, like a pot of boiling beans. Beetles, she did not know what kind, chewed on the thread-thin sinew around the little knees.

And then she stepped to one side of herself, as though her shadow were walking next to another body, and watched herself reach down.

It was like lifting out a puppet of string and sticks. She cradled the light thing in her big hands. She sang. She sang the song of Honey, Little Honey, who had nestled plump and warm at her breast. Gwladus moved forward to the grave and began to dig for the rest, but Hild paid no attention.

The scrap of cloth fell away, and half her baby's scalp fell with it. The tiny skull glistened. She did not smell like honey and morning dew. Her bones seemed fragile as bird bones. Most of her weight came from the maggots. They only ate dead stuff, then squirmed away in straight lines like ants to pupate and burst into flies that sought another dead thing to feed on. One day they would come for her, they would come, and down she would go into the dark, down into—

"Daughter," the priest said. "I am ready."

Gwladus was wrapping something in the ragged and cast-off cloak she had borrowed from Morud, and the grave was deeper now, and waiting. Leofdæg was watching the horizon.

She felt a shudder waiting but that was for someone else, somewhere else. She turned, said to Oeric's back, to the strip of dark green tunic that hung below his warrior jacket, bright with gold stitching, "Give me your tunic."

He turned, opened his mouth to argue—this was his favourite tunic, the one that made him feel splendid—then saw what she held. He unbuckled his jacket, draped it over the priest's arm, and pulled off the tunic. After one last stroke of the fine cloth he handed it to Gwladus.

Gwladus gave it to Hild. She folded it lengthways so the seams matched, and then again the other way, and laid it in the grave.

"There, Honey. It's still warm. And you will lie in green and gold to meet your fate." She laid the only child she would ever have with Cian in her grave, touched the naked skull, then folded the edges of the tunic over her.

"She will lie in the bosom of Christ," the priest said.

Hild ignored him. "You will meet your father. Give him my love. Tell him—" Tell him what?

The priest waited a moment, but when she said no more he began to speak his blessing. She understood perhaps one word in three, though she did not know if she was stupid with grief or the words were as much non-sense gabble as real Latin. She knelt by the hole and waited but there were no tears. His words went on, then stopped. "I need her name," he said.

Honey was not a real name, but it was all she had. "Honey," she said. "Honey, daughter of Hild—" Even now she could not say the dangerous thing aloud. "Daughter of Hild Gul and Cian Boldcloak."

He stooped and picked up a handful of dirt.

"What are you doing?"

"The final blessing." He lifted his arm. She found herself standing with his robe in her fist. "Daughter, I must—"

"No. Drop it. Drop the dirt. That's for me to do."

And so as he spoke the last words, she poured the dirt back over Honey's feet, Honey's tiny chest, and Honey's face. Her tiny beautiful face. And now the shadow reclaimed its body, and the tears came. She could not see and that, as Fursey might have said, was a blessing. She shoved the dirt two-handed, weeping, weeping while the priest droned.

The grass on the hill and round its foot was yellow and sickly. So much blood had been spilt that soon it would be bald, and it might stay that way for five years or more. Even after the rain the smell was still strong. Ynys Coed, Afanc called it, but for her it was Death Hill, where the sun had set on the Yffings.

They stood and looked at it, at the stakes and their stinking warnings against the skyline. Leofdæg turned to her, ready to do as she asked, but she shook her head. Edwin was no longer her king. He was no one's king now, and his heirs were dead or fled. If they disturbed the warning, Penda and Cadwallon's spies would know someone who cared still lived. Let the ravens have him. She had another task.

Where they had left Cian was nothing but a shallow lake with tide marks at its edges.

"This is not the place," she said.

"It is, lady," Gwladus said.

"No."

Gwladus said nothing in the way people do when they know they are right but are too kind to say so.

"It can't be." She turned into the breeze blowing from the south and west. Her face, already tight with dried tears, tightened some more. "There." She pointed. No one said anything. "Or there. It——" But it was just the water rucking in the wind. Gone. It was more than she could bear.

"I've seen it before," the priest said. "With the storm on it, the water can be strong as the hand of God."

"But there was a horse."

"Even so, daughter."

She could tell by his face that he was not saying it all. Not saying that if what remained, after the scavengers had dragged away and eaten their fill, was still there, they would not find him until the water had gone down. She made herself look again at the water, at the closest bank of the Idle. Imagined the power of a wind-whipped current. He had most likely floated away in pieces on the tide. Perhaps one day someone might find a war boot with its slip of iron cunningly sewn down the front; forty years from now some child might find the rust-eaten point of his spear stuck in a plough ox's hoof, but the man was gone.

He had left nothing, no child to carry his essence.

There was no grateful king to listen to a scop's song of his bravery. Nothing. And she had no place to turn to, to face like the warmth of the sun, knowing he was there. She looked ahead and saw herself always now slowly spinning inside, turning, turning, unable to settle.

The Daun's north channel slipped beneath the *Curlew*'s keel, brown as burdock tea, and the wake creamed out westward from them, turning to dirty foam curling in from the edge. Cenhelm's voice, calling to his men, the creak of the steering oar, and the last lazy flap of canvas as the unreefed sail began to draw, were the same. The furs heavy across her shoulders, and the weight of her cross: the same. Armed men behind her: same. She could be Butcherbird again, Cath Llew sailing north with the Fiercesomes at her back. But the wind in her face was too cold, her hips touched the top strake instead of her round belly, and her seax, hanging like a toy sword from a child's too-big belt, was sheathed in stained leather still crusted with grave dirt. The hands on the rail were ringless and too thin; the ragged scar, where Cuncar's blade had torn more than cut on that fairy hill, edged onto her wrist. No, that was a new one, near the old one.

Thick water, fat water Afanc had called it; water heavy with decay giving life to the people of Ynys Bwyell and the farm at High Brune. All that life from death. Her Fiercesomes and Hounds bleeding onto the blades of grass, blood trickling down the stems, soaking into the dirt. Rain leaching it out, seeping downhill. Shit from ravens who pecked out their eyes and ate their lips and tongues falling on the riverbanks, washing into the Daun and Torne and Treonte, which swelled over the winter fields where the islanders' tree roots steeped in it, their winter wheat drank from it, and the river weeds and reeds swelled with it to shelter the flies that fed the frogs that fed the herons that fed the folk. Someone always profited from war. What was left of husbands, of sons and brothers and fathers, would wash into the Humbre, and from there into the North Sea, where it might feed the seaweed, which would feed the whitefish, which might feed the cod that a fishwife sold to the reeve at Mulstanton who brought it on a platter to the lady Onnen.

Onnen saying to her on that wind-whipped cliff: *You can't have him.* One day she would have to look Cian's mother in the eye and say, *I do not have him. I lost him.* She had lost him, she had lost Honey. She had lost—though not her life, not her mind.

Wind slapped the ribbon of dirty foam in on itself with a clap like that of an impatient mother. The Daun, named for Danu, the mother. British or

Anglisc, it did not matter—gods and goddesses were cruel. She should never have sworn an oath on that fairy hill with Honey in her belly . . .

"Lady." Cenhelm, behind her. "We look to reach Adlingfleot before gelotendæg." She did not respond. After a moment he went on. "If you've a mind, we could anchor there. But it could be, if wind and tide are kind, we manage Gole before dark."

She did not look up from the water.

"She's a good boat, lady." He was not happy. She turned. "The moon's three days from full on what'll be a mostly clear night." He nodded at where it was just up, so pale it could be a ghost moon.

He was a sailor; he wanted to sail, not skulk about in port. And after her sword and spearmen had held him hostage on his own boat he wanted to get her off it as fast as he could. She understood but she needed time. "No."

She had to think before she got back, before she was faced with those pleading eyes and outstretched hands, the shining expectation that she would reassure them, feed them, protect them from Cadwallon's ravenings. How? What with?

Gladmær edged forward. "Lady?" Gladmær, who still had his sword, his helm, his mail shirt, and two arm rings. Who had somehow escaped the battlefield. He held out a bowl of ale and smiled hard, like a dog wagging its tail and hoping not to be beaten for running away.

She considered, took the bowl, drank, and handed it back. She watched Gladmær but spoke to Cenhelm. "How much ale do we have?"

"Two half barrels yet unbroached," he said. "And what's left of a third since your men were at it. I'll want paying for that."

"I'll pay for all three. And I'll pay reparation for my men not trusting you're a man of your word. It won't happen again. I'd like a little more of your time; I'll pay for that, too. We'll drink the ale at Adlingfleot and overnight there." While she sent Morud to gather news. While she got the men drunk enough to admit how they had run, and what had happened. She needed truth now. "But keep your men aboard." The fewer rumours of her the better. "And restrain their drinking enough that we can sail with the dawn." Sailing west on the Humbre, to Gole, and Cnotinsleah; or east with the tide to the sea, then north to Mulstanton, or south to East Anglia. She would decide at Adlingfleot. "And we'll eat. Yes, I'll pay for that, too, if you find something that isn't fish or waterfowl." Something that could not have fed on someone she had loved.

They got to Adlingfleot early. Hild sent Morud out among the small traders but there was not much gossip to be had of distant doings; it was early in the year for foreign trade. They wanted to know where he was from and when he pointed to the *Curlew* they squinted and scratched their noses and said, *Well, that was a gurt big boat for the rivers.* But when Morud only murmured vaguely and asked what meat they had for trade, they discussed it among themselves and thought they might have some sausage, and onions of course. But they had no mead, no. That was something they were a bit fretful about—trade had been right quiet from north of the Humbre this past while. No mead, no, but a mort of lead from the Peaks; no iron, though, leastways not good iron. The best ore was from Craven, everyone knew that, but they'd had none—no, nor none of their salmon, neither. No doubt something to do with kingly clashes? Again Morud expressed vague ignorance—he knew no more than they did—but he'd take those sausages they mentioned and might as well throw in a few onions.

The *Curlew* was tied so tight to the Adlingfleot wharf that she barely rocked. The night breeze was changeable. From the east it carried the cold, ancient smell of the river and half-frozen mud, and the hiss of wind through hoarfrosted grass. No birds. When the wind swung to the west it stank like any port: wet wood, old fish guts, and layer upon layer of human waste, food scraps, and the dung of birds and beasts. Strange gusts of sound—a curse, laughter, the yowl of a cat fight over the right to the mice that ate the spill in the granary . . .

After the sausages and onions Cenhelm had deemed it safe enough for a brazier on the deck midships to warm Hild's eight men—nine if you counted Morud, who held a sleeping Wilfrid—and Gwladus, sitting around a now half-empty barrel, sharing two ship's bowls. The sailors in the bow dipped from the one already broached, with Cenhelm's mate to watch over how they drank it. Cenhelm stood with his own bowl in one hand and his elbow against the taffrail. The moon hung over his right shoulder, low now, but still so big and white that even when a thin shaw of cloud misted it, it was bright enough to trace the embossing on her seax sheath and for her to pick out the dirt with her fingernails.

While the ale worked on them she spoke—though her voice was torn, she found that after months of silence it was stronger, a little less jagged, the rasp sometimes no more than a faint buzz. She began with what they already knew. "Edwin Yffing and the ætheling Osfrith are dead, along with many thegns and gesiths of Deira and Bernicia. They died well." They had died as all men die, in pain, fear, and their own waste.

They waited.

The bowl came round to her. She drank. Harsh and strong, stronger than that brewed on the island—and she had had little of even small beer. She passed it to Oeric on her right. "The queen and youngest æthelings escaped with Bishop Paulinus. We don't know where or when, but I hope to her brother's kingdom in Cent."

"Aye," said Cenhelm. "She's there." Everyone turned to look at him. He handed his bowl to Cuthred, who, after a pause, dipped it in the barrel, and handed it back. He took his time drinking from it. "I took her and the Crow, four other men and two women and the three weans, from Barton to Sceapig. Aye, and a king's ransom—an army of kings' ransom—of church gold and fancy capes." He enjoyed their surprise.

When he said no more, they turned back and murmured among themselves.

The York cross and cup alone would be enough to buy the Crow back into any church. And fancy capes . . . Perhaps his pallium had come at last. But there was already an overbishop in Cent. No matter how much gold Paulinus brought, King Eadbald would not involve himself with Deira or Bernicia, not even for the sake of his sister Æthelburh. Cent looked more to Frankia than to the north. No doubt Eadbald was unhappy about the position his sister had put him in. But he had not refused them. One less loose end for Penda to pick at.

Wilfrid sucked his gums in his sleep, which meant he would wake soon. Gwladus lifted her chin to catch Hild's gaze and tilted her head to Cenhelm. He was looking pleased, like a dragon curled around its hoard.

"What else, Cenhelm?" Hild said. "Tell us the rest."

"I know where your Northumbran boats are, too."

Gladmær looked around so fast he jostled the bowl of ale held by Cuthred's friend, who slopped it on his hose. They were all beginning to get a little loose.

"Coming north from Cent there was a storm. We put into the Wash overnight. Eight boats were anchored at Haven, on the Withma. Northumbran, the word was. Waiting for the tide up to Lindum, and more hands. Cruel short-handed, they said."

Coelfrith had had a fight then. Not treachery on his part, at least. But now he was taking the boats to his father.

"Eight crews!" Oeric said. "Even short-handed that's a lot of men. Northumbran men. Northumbran boats. Northumbran food—"

"Northumbran arrows and spearheads and portable forge!" Gladmær. More than a little loose.

"And food and tents and fodder," Oeric said. "Lady, we could—"

"No," she said. To Cenhelm, "That was . . . before Yule?" He nodded. "No," she said again to her men. "Now they are Lindsey boats, Lindsey men, Lindsey army supplies."

"He ran!" Gladmær said.

"He did. Better to save yourself than die for nothing."

"For glory, you said." Gladmær was drunk. "You said we would win. You said the Yffings would win. But we lost. We lost!"

"Edwin lost. That was his wyrd. I said the Yffings will triumph. And we will. Our time will come."

"How?" said Gladmær.

"They're all dead or fled," Cuthred's friend said. "All gone. And I never even got to fight."

"Perhaps not all," she said.

"Who, lady?" Gladmær said. "The craven in Craven?" Leofdæg snorted. "Honeytongue?"

"Penda has Honeytongue in York and would make him a puppet king. Honeytongue is forsworn. But he is ætheling. So I ask you." She looked around the circle. "Would the thegns have him?"

Leofdæg snorted again. Sitric scratched his grey beard thoughtfully.

"You, Gladmær. Would you follow Honeytongue?"

It would have been an easy question, with an easy answer—no man would follow a nithing—but she had named Honeytongue ætheling, an heir of Yffings, and Gladmær had sworn an oath.

"Honeytongue is forsworn, a traitor," she said, and now her rasp was a saw. "So I ask you again, Gladmær, son of Baldic. Would you support Honeytongue?"

He shook his head.

"No. None will. He will never see a throne." Penda had thought the eldest ætheling could be king. That was why he had joined with Cadwallon, to put his own puppet on the throne of the most powerful kingdom on the isle and make it part of Mercia, make himself overking. Penda would learn his mistake soon enough.

The bowl came to her. She drank, drank again, let the fumes curl around her brain.

"Honeytongue will die quietly and Penda will turn his attention elsewhere. Cadwallon, now. What Cadwallon wants is to murder every Yffing in this world." Did he want Deira and Bernicia, to be king of all Northumbre? She didn't know, only that first he wanted to kill Yffings and wipe their works from the earth. His hatred of his foster-brother ran to anything and everything he had made, or loved, or touched. Why else burn Caer Loid when he could have garrisoned it? He hadn't burnt York but was that because it was still more the work of the redcrests than the Yffings? Or because Penda wanted it? Penda was no fool.

Wilfrid whined. Morud jogged him but he started to huff, always a sign of unhappiness and of screaming to come if he did not get his way. Morud felt his wrapper, and sighed.

"Fill the bowls. Drink deep, then fill them again," she said, and nodded at Morud as he stood up: She would feed Wilfrid when he was cleaned up.

Cuthred filled the bowls and took them round, making sure every man drank; he seemed to have appointed himself cupbearer. People liked to know their role.

"The craven of Craven is gathering his men in Cetreht. And the Iding is in Inchtuthil, calling in his father's old followers, readying to cross the Forth to Din Eidyn in Bernicia and send for the Bryneich."

"But will they go to him, lady?" Cuthred's friend. He was very young. "Wouldn't they side with their own?" He glanced at where Morud was scrubbing at Wilfrid with a handful of tow, and Gwladus was wiping her mouth and passing on the bowl.

"Cuthred," she said. "What is your friend's name?"

"Aldnoth, lady."

She looked at the youngster. "Aldnoth, who's your father?"

"Fenric, lady."

"I don't know you. But know this. In Elmet there are no Anglisc and no wealh, there are only Elmetsæte. Those who swear to me, whoever they once were, become Elmetsæte. I am Elmetsæte. As is Gwladus, my body-woman, and Morud, my messenger—both of whom have done as much to save my life as any gesith."

The stripling looked as though he wanted to dive off the boat and swim, swim anywhere.

"So I ask you, Aldnoth, son of Fenric, who did Penda, Anglisc war leader, side with at Hæðfeld?"

He muttered something no one could hear.

"Did he side with the Anglisc king, Edwin Yffing?"

He shook his head. Cuthred elbowed him. Aldnoth swallowed. "No, lady."

"No. He sided with Cadwallon, wealh king of wealh Gwynedd. And Æthelfrith Iding, the Iding's father, Anglisc from Bernicia, became king of all Northumbre with the help of all Bernicians, including the Bryneich. So which way will Coledauc and the Bryneich fall?"

"I . . ." He looked wildly at Cuthred for help but his friend seemed interested in a stain on his hose. "For the Idings?"

She let him hang for a moment, then shook her head. "I don't know."

It might have been the first time any here but Gwyladus or Morud had heard the lady of Elmet—king's fist, Butcherbird, Cath Llew, and light of the world—say, I don't know.

"I don't know how many men Cadwallon has or where he is, or what he might promise, if anything, because I don't know what he wants. Just as I don't know how many men the Iding has, or what he is promising Coledauc now. I don't know what Rheged thinks, or Alt Clut. And I don't know the size and shape of Osric Yffing's ambition."

If they weren't already drunk some—Gladmær, Cuthred, the spearman by Sitric, perhaps Sitric himself—would be terrified at how much she did not know. But she felt good: sure, light, and clear; herself uncloaked by song. She was no longer a child who needed to walk with the gods and whisper with wyrd to be heard. She was a woman grown. She bled, she breathed, she gave birth. She answered to no one. And she was their lord.

Morud had finished with Wilfrid and was hovering, unsure whether now was the time. It was exactly the time.

She settled Wilfrid in the crook of her right arm. The moonlight was bright enough to show the flicker of Gladmær's eyelashes. All of them, sitting so still and stiff with their heads pulled back like dogs smacked on the nose, all of them needed to understand how it was now, for her and for them.

"I don't know these things because I have been cut off from all news since Winterfylleth. Leofdæg will have told you some of it." She held out her left arm, with the scars like plough marks, then swapped Wilfrid to the other side, and showed the right arm with the livid twist up past her elbow. "These are the small marks, the kind marks."

She unfastened her dress and set Wilfrid to her left breast. "On my belly is a scar that cost the life of my child. On my hip, one that nearly cost me mine." Wilfrid sucked lustily. "I'll answer any of your questions. But first you will answer mine. Tonight, from each of you, every one, I want the story of your Winterfylleth and Blodmonath and Ærra Geola. You will give me what you know—what you saw, what you did, what you heard—and then I will know more." She pulled her furs across her body and over Wilfrid to keep him warm. The eight men breathed a little easier. "So drink up, and Cuthred will fill us up again, because no doubt some of these tales will be grim. Oeric."

He was close enough for her to feel him start.

"Take the bowl, and begin."

He recounted how the lady had given him five spearmen and charged him with the defence of Elmet . . .

Morud and Gwladus exchanged looks but Hild was content to let him shade his account in whatever way made him feel best. She listened and watched.

Oeric had grown, and not just about the shoulders and jaw. Responsibility suited him. As he continued his tale of persuading the ladies Begu and Breguswith to accompany him to Menewood—it was clear to Hild that it was her mother who had hurried them all to safety—she noted the way he eyed the men, including Cenhelm, weighing, assessing their worth to his dryhten, the lady Hild.

Pyr and Saxfryth refused to leave Caer Loid, Oeric said. First, they said the king would win so there was no need to worry. Second, Caer Loid was strong, and they had people to shelter, those as come from Aberford, like Mistress Heiu. Even if by some uncanny chance Cadwallon got past the army, he hadn't hurt them last time, had he, so why would he this? No, they should all stay right there.

"But he agreed to send to the outlying steadings and offer shelter to all who needed it. The next morning, early, the runners went out and we set out for Menewood, me and Lady Begu and your lady mother and fourteen others."

Hild counted back. That would have been the morning Hild faced the host outside Scanton and told them: Yffings will triumph.

Wilfrid's sucking was slowing. She jogged him absently, wondering who had left with them.

They had found their way, Oeric said, led partway by the Lady Begu, then found by the watchers Rhin had sent out.

"Six days later—no, it would have been seven—we heard about Caer Loid."

He drank deep, swallowing, swallowing. Cleared his throat. Hild could see him sifting through his words. "Nine stragglers found their way to us. Two died. Of the others . . . Well, some will never be the same."

Wilfrid complained—he always felt it when she tensed—then sucked again sleepily.

Now Oeric spoke fast, eager to be done. "They brought news as well as horror. Some came later than others. Like young Aldnoth there, come from Colney way. And Leofdæg. They should tell that part."

Aldnoth was young, but even so he carried a spear, and he and Gladmær and Leofdæg would all have to explain why they were alive. Why they had not died defending Elmet or their king.

Aldnoth was slack with drink, but she could tell by the sick look on his face that he would never be drunk enough to talk about what he had seen.

Wilfrid pushed her breast away. She nodded at Morud to take him, then fastened up her dress. It was looser around her breasts than it had been just five days ago.

The moon was sinking, and the men opposite her were dark outlines with the occasional red gleam of eye and tooth and arm ring as they leaned forward or drank. She could still see those closest to her.

Leofdæg had been drinking with steady determination. Unlike Aldnoth, drink did not loosen him but drew him tighter, more close-mouthed and bitter. She knew how to help him to the heart of it.

"Leofdæg found me," she said. "He found me after—he found me. I gave him my cross." She held it up in the fading moonlight, then towards the brazier, so the pearls glowed like ghost tears and the garnets gleamed deep and rich: showing them the heft of the gold, the weight of her trust in Leofdæg. "I charged him with returning to Menewood with bitter news: that the lord Cian Boldcloak was dead, that Edwin king and most others were bones for the crows. I know of no one else who could have carried such bitter news, through land wasted by war and roamed by bandits, to find a place he had never seen." All while holding gold enough to sell for a thegn's ransom and live well. But a gesith was not a farmer. A gesith needed a lord, needed a fight to look forward to, and spoils to win. All she could see ahead was sorrow and struggle. She wanted to fill the bowl, lean back on her hands, and say, *I can't see what will happen or where we're going. This is a good boat. Let's take her and set up as sea wolves* . . .

The ale was working on her, too.

"But I also charged Leofdæg with the news that I lived, and gave him the cross as my token. And he carried that news, he carried it through the mud and mire and murdered men, to Menewood." She looked at the thin, hard man, closed and dense as the bog oak of her staff. "Leofdæg, how many days were you on that journey?"

His voice was like the knotted leather found about the necks of bog bodies. "A moon of nights. More." He looked inward.

Oeric stirred, but Hild shook her head and he subsided.

"How did you evade the enemy?"

"I followed the rivers. A longer path, but winter water birds are loud."

Hild nodded. Migrating waterfowl moved in huge flocks that took days to settle once they landed. The noise and movement of their roosting would hide the sound of one stealthy man. "Food would not have been easy."

Most of the berries would have been gone and the nuts not yet falling. No salmon. But plenty of birds and, with many people dead or running, a wandering pig or lost goat. In the woods, perhaps pignuts and mushrooms; in the fields, buried beets and carrots and onions—but fields were watched.

"I found enough." Above the new scar along his jaw his cheek moved as he ran his tongue over a new gap in his teeth.

Bloated and swelling bodies with hard cheese or an apple in their pocket. And bandits, desperate women and men, children, too, fighting over every scrap. She had a sudden image of Morud throwing an apple and nuts on a broken table, spatters of fresh blood on his tunic.

"Any sign of watchers on the war street?"

"No one but the lame, left-behind, and lost."

And there it was: the melancholy rhythm. Now he would talk. She nodded at Cuthred, who took a bowl from Aldnoth, filled it to brimming, and brought it to Leofdæg.

Leofdæg drained the one in his hand and exchanged it for the full one. He drank, wiped his moustaches, and drank again.

"Apples," he said. "Big sour apples, the kind to fit in a boar's mouth and not a lass's hand, fall later than most. That's what I smelt as I followed the Yr to Caer Loid: the vinegar of apples unpicked and spoiling into Elmet earth. The river was dark, black and strong as a mother's grief, for the moon wanted nothing of the world that night and turned his face. Smell was my guide."

He stared at the dark pool in his bowl but did not drink.

"Vinegar. And burning. Burnt bodies, burnt walls, burnt fowl and dough and hair and skin, charred teeth and child-shaped charcoal . . . Burning, like vinegar, cleanses. Like vinegar, it reeks. And there was nothing of Caer Loid left but burntness and hacked orchard. There'd been no one to come pick the windfall. And the river . . ."

He drank. Remembering the terrible things Cadwallon's men, looking for spoil after a fight, would have done to those who might know where it was buried.

"I didn't want to drink from that river, nor the well, so I camped a mile upriver, past the curve and on the lee of the rise."

Hild knew which bend he meant. There was a stretched loop of river with a still pool where, at the right time of year, salmon laid their eggs and frogs sang.

"The next morning there were scavengers at the bodies so I left them to it and followed the road to Aberford. Aberford was destroyed, but by a different hand: walls not burnt but torn down layer by layer, then drowned. And fewer bodies."

"Fewer?"

"Just one, an old woman. In the pond, or what was left of it."

So Aberford was flooded afterwards. That spoke of a hard mind, a careful mind. "Penda," she said.

He nodded. "Penda went to York to rest his men while Cadwallon was roaming and burning—though he came back to York for Yule. He was there when we left but won't stay long."

Oeric gave her the ale bowl. She took a mouthful, passed it on, and swallowed. "No?"

"Cadwallon's like a murrain," Leofdæg said. "Nothing pleases him more than the weeping of the wounded."

"Except ending the weeping," said Gladmær. "He laughs at both." Then, realising he had spoken aloud, he shook his head and turned his face away.

"I ranged for two days roundabout before I sought out Menewood," Leofdæg said. "The man kills and kills. Man, woman, child, or goose, it makes no difference."

"And then you went to Menewood."

He nodded, a faint silhouette, nothing more. "I followed Rhin's watchers as they took in young Aldnoth there." Aldnoth looked up and stared about at the sound of his name, but he was too drunk to understand. He would puke or pass out very soon. "But I'd already marked where it was."

How? She would ask him about that later. "And the valley itself," she said. "Its people, its heart. How does Menewood?"

"Needs someone in charge."

"Rhin is in charge," she said.

"Aye. And so is your lady mother."

Someone chuckled. Cenhelm. The bow rope tying the *Curlew* to the wharf creaked. "The tide's turning," she said.

"Aye."

"Time to check on your men. Send two of the sober ones back with that third barrel and more charcoal for the brazier."

If Leofdæg would say that of her mother, then he was ready to talk of anything. Gladmær, too.

The wind brushed her left cheek with smells of the night-shrouded east bank and an aromatic waft of bog myrtle. One of Cenhelm's men poured more charcoal into the brazier and stirred it to flame with a fire iron. She looked around their intent faces. It was time for tales of the battle itself. She would go first.

"Listen! I will tell of the battle of heroes, the betrayal of a king, and the bravery of two who saved me when all was lost."

She dreamt of the fairy hill, of her hand dripping from Cuncar's blade, and Honey, tall and sad, wearing ten-year-old Hereswith's favourite dress in green with gold stitching. "I'm here," she said. "Under the hill, bound by your oath." She held out her arms. "Don't you want me?"

Hild cried out as Honey began to fade into the hill to rejoin the fairies. "Stay!" She began to dig frantically with her hands. "I didn't know. I didn't know . . ."

"Hush." Gwladus, on her elbow next to her, stroking her hair.

Hild half sat, looking around wildly. Dark, like being inside the belly of a beast. "I didn't know," she said.

"Hush now," Gwladus whispered. "Hush."

"She's . . . I have to go." Go where? It was all fading.

"A dream. Only a dream."

Hild lay back. That drifting scent of bog myrtle again. Just like Hæðfeld. A dream. Yes. Honey would never grow into a tall girl like Hereswith, never wear a green and gold dress on the Modraniht feast as her sister had, long ago. The real Honey was gone. She was a tiny bundle of bones wrapped in a green and gold tunic and buried at the foot of the stump. The real Honey, not a changeling.

When she woke up again she could just make out the silhouette of Gwladus sitting beside her on the stuffed pallet, holding a water jug. She was in the Curlew's tent with Gwladus and Wilfrid. Morud, drunk as a hero—the hero she had named him—slept with the gesiths.

She listened. Wilfrid's tiny, even breathing from the nest by their feet. Gwladus's deeper, slower breaths. The low voices of sailors on watch fore and aft, and rumbling snores amidship. Inside the tent it smelled of the last hour before dawn when all things are possible.

She sat up. Gwladus passed her the jug. Hild drank, drank again, drank some more. She passed it back, empty. "Sorry," she said. "I was thirsty."

"You told them," Gwladus said, and Hild understood from her tone what she meant.

"They needed to know. You and Morud saved my life as surely as one man saves another in battle."

Gwladus said nothing.

"They needed to know. Things have changed." She turned a little to face Gwladus and crossed her legs. "You were a slave, now free. You were my bodywoman, then my attendant, but now . . . Now, you are your own. You don't need to reflect anyone's glory. You shine with your own."

Gwladus's shape turned to her. Shadows moved as her ribs moved in and out.

"You told gesiths what to do and they did. They did as they were bid. By a woman. On a battlefield. They were not obeying your name, or your blade, or your gold. They listened and did as they were bid because of you. You led them. You led them, you could lead them because you are their equal."

The breath between them was a living thing, tuning them to the same note.

"Am I your equal?"

Hild looked at the shape of the woman by her. The woman she had taken from a slave market. The woman who had taken her to bed—perhaps at Breguswith's instruction, perhaps not. The woman she had freed. The woman who had saved her life. The woman who had stripped gold from her husband—but used it to save them. Who had buried her child when she could not—and remembered where in all that trackless waste she was buried. Who had bound her wounds and kept her alive, kept Morud alive. And when her body was healed had not let her drift away into the mire of despair.

Hild breathed and listened to her body as she would after a blow, waiting to feel what it meant—and, there, rising like bread, certainty.

She nodded. "Gwladus of the Dyfneint, you are my equal."

Silence.

"You are my equal. Look at what you did. So many things."

"So many things," Gwladus said in British. "And I was afraid. So many times."

"I'm sorry."

A thin hard hand gripped her wrist. "Stop saying sorry. That's not what I need. What I need—I need . . ."

Hild held out her arms as she would to a child, and Gwladus tucked against her, thin cheek against Hild's breastbone. Comfort. Plain comfort. That was what she needed now. She wrapped her arms about her and held her, with care and attention. So thin. They were both thin.

"When I buried Honey, it was like losing my own again. Oh dear Christ the smell, the cold skin, and her eyes wouldn't—and there were no stones, I had, I had to—" She made an animal noise. "And I knew that when I went back you would still be raving, and Morud looking at me like I was his mam and the sun rolled into one, and I would have to know, have to decide, all the time. Over and over."

Hild stroked her hair, as Gwladus had stroked hers earlier.

"And at Brune you were like an empty bowl, and I despaired. One morning when I woke and you weren't there I thought, That's it, she's gone, and now what will you do, Gwladus of the Dyfneint? Where will you go? Who will take you in? And I saw a life on my back, burying babies, favouring a broken bone, a lost tooth, until one day I was old and used enough that the latest Lintlaf would beat me in disgust and leave me for dead."

Hild kept stroking her hair.

"Last night, I— It frightened me when you talked about me. To them."

She just listened.

"I don't like to be known. I like being noticed but only when people see what I want them to see. They don't see me." Gwladus's thin face moved against Hild's breastbone as she spoke, faster and faster. "They don't know me. Being known is dangerous to a slave."

"You're not—"

"Being sold in the marketplace like a sow makes a mark. It's like—you've seen scars open and teeth loosen when folk don't get fresh greens?" Hild nodded. "The scar of being owned is like that. A heart wound that can reopen anytime when danger looms. It gapes like a mouth and eats all hope."

Hild kept stroking.

"So being known—being known feels like danger. And I don't know how we can be safe."

Hild rested her cheek on Gwladus's head, but lightly.

"So tell me, how will we be safe? Menewood . . . You heard Leofdæg. It won't stay hidden for long."

"Perhaps that's a good thing."

Gwladus drew back, as though to search Hild's face, but it was too dark. "How is it a good thing?"

"Perhaps some of our people will find us. Who did Leofdæg and Gladmær see fall?" Gwladus was trained to listen and remember.

"Cynan. Eadric. And one of the brothers Berht."

"Gladmær said that Berhtnoth fell, but nothing about a wound."

"But he didn't say he got up, either. And no one mentioned slave-taking."

Cadwallon was more interested in blood and death than money, but what of Penda? There was no way to know yet. "There might be Wulf and Dudda and Bryhtsige as well as Coelwyn and Grimhun. With Gladmær and Leofdæg, and the spearmen, that's a useful group."

"Against an army?"

"No." She could feel some decision gathering but only one small part of it was clear. "No. But when we get to Menewood, we will take stock. First"—her tone became brisk—"what is your mother's name?"

"My . . . ? Heddwen."

"Gwladus ferch Heddwen, I swear to you that from now, today, you will bow to none but those I bow to, and I bow to none but kings. And when I next bow to a king, Gwladus ferch Heddwen, you will have means of your own, gold and lands enough to be safe. I swear this to you now, this night, on this boat, on this river."

And though against the sound of the river she could not hear it, Hild felt the long warmth of Gwladus's sigh on her cheek, and under her hand the soft skin on Gwladus's arm seemed to fill and firm and gather heft.

14

✛

A T YRMYN THEY ANCHORED to wait for the tide to turn. It stopped raining. On the north bank, where the cross once was, stood a totem. The
ground around it held crude bundles, some weathering to grey, some still
painted.

Gwladus came to the rail beside her. "Morud has Wilfrid settled." The
child loved being on a moving boat but was going through another round
of teething. Gwladus nodded at the totem. "That's new."

"It's old." The first she had seen in Deira since Paulinus had ordered
them all torn down and burnt. But with Paulinus and his priests fled, folk
had to pray to something. And here it was, not burnt, rescued from years
spent abandoned and forlorn on some forest floor, carvings crudely re-
painted in the magical totems of her people: the boar and the raven, the
flame and the eagle, the lightning and the sea, and He Who Holds It All:
Woden himself. Not the milksop Christ who had abandoned their king
and whose skirted priests had in turn abandoned their flock.

The river should have been full of boats, boats streaming from York; small
boats casting lines to catch dace and chub, and, on the banks, people waking late after a night fishing for the black-spotted sea trout that tasted best
if caught before they turned brown farther up the river. There were no
boats. The only swimmers were two curious otters that followed them for

a while between Fleot and Beal, then got bored and returned to diving along the overhanging bank for the trout.

The rain started again at Beal, and the oaks on either bank stood bare and mournful. It rained steadily, the endless fine rain of Elmet in early Hrethmonath. Sharp against the grey rain and river, a stand of alders were showing their first small red catkins. Just past the last bend of the river before Cnotinsleah, a half-charred boat rested on the riverbed and blocked the channel. Beyond it, on the south bank, the Cnotinsleah wharf was destroyed: uprights hacked in half and the boards fallen in a body and swept up by some high tide at an angle against the mud. The landing showed green against brown where weeds sprouted on formerly well-trodden paths, and a spindly maple sapling was the forerunner of the wood deciding to reclaim the clearing.

Last time she was here was with the Fiercesomes in their triumphant return from the Bryneich. Just before midsummer, the air thrumming with the rhythmic chanting of a boat sweeping east at slack tide to be the first with fleeces for Frisian traders at Gole, they had off-loaded their horses and baggage here and been feasted by Cnot himself in his long house, comfortable with the stink of twoscore men, women, and children, their fires, and byres, and midden. The buildings now were burnt shells. By the colour of the ash it had been months ago.

Cenhelm reefed the sail and backed oars to the wide bend where he could turn the *Curlew*, a slow business.

There was nowhere low enough for them to scramble up on the south bank. Hild's people began off-loading by threes into the boat's two-seat rowboat—Leofdæg, Sitric, and Cuthred splashing out and scrambling up the low bank first, spears at the ready, then Gladmær with Morud and Gwladus. Finally Hild, holding Wilfrid, saw Aldnoth into the boat and turned to Cenhelm. She gave him the promised third pearl and a fourth—just four left now of the nine she had started with—and held out her forearm. After a moment he clasped it. They nodded; there was nothing left to say.

She set Leofdæg to scout ahead. "See if the ferry bridge is still there. And take a good look around." He nodded and glided away. "Oeric, take Aldnoth and follow us. Stay in sight of one another. Watch our east until we're past the bend, then north and northeast as we move. When we get to the bridge, rejoin."

"What do we watch for?" she heard Aldnoth ask Oeric and they moved northeast into the trees.

"Anything bigger than a fox," said Oeric.

Aldnoth was probably of an age with Morud but without Morud's skills. He would learn, if he lived long enough.

They followed the river north, then east. The trail was muddy and walking with her staff in one hand and Wilfrid on the other arm was awkward; he had gained weight. She would have to sacrifice the hem of her dress to make a sling for him. At least he was quiet, looking about with interest when he wasn't sleeping; he loved being on the move.

The trail tilted and she slipped a little in the mud; her left hip hitched, and lifting that leg high enough to climb a fallen trunk tugged at her scarred belly. But it was not pain, not quite, not anymore.

Half a mile from the bridge Leofdæg appeared from the trees and nodded at Hild: something ahead.

A mile past Cnotinsleah, along what had been a well-rutted track beside the elms, leaves clogged the way; no one had cleared deadfall. Here and there, though, there were subtle signs: a line in the mud where someone had dragged a bough—someone small or injured, or they would have carried it—tell-tale marks where someone had stepped in the same place over a fallen limb; ferns with their new tips cut, not nibbled by beasts. It began to rain again, thin endless rain.

Cnotinsleah itself was abandoned. The smell was not as bad as she had feared. From here she could see only two bodies. Crows and foxes and worms had eaten their fill.

"Find the bones," she said. "Find them all." There was no time to bury them, but this was Elmet, these her people. "Pile them . . ." She turned in a circle, then pointed at the remains of the byre. There would be straw and manure. "Pile them in there with any wood we won't need. Sitric." He stepped close. "Any good cloth or leather, set it aside, then burn them. Burn them well."

The shell of the long house still had a corner with enough of an overhang to build a fire. She set Cuthred to that, left Wilfrid with Gwladus—no doubt he would cry when they stopped but she would be back soon to feed him—and told Morud to make something hot, and soon. She wanted to be past Ceasterforda, then across the war street and making camp before dark.

But before they went farther she needed to take a breath and understand what they were coming home to.

She left them to their tasks, and took Leofdæg, walking silently, alert, listening past the pour of the river and dripping trees. The air had that grey-and-green scent of bare bark and new fern, elm buds still tight but thrumming with life ready to burst forth. But no birdsong.

Leofdæg stopped. They listened. A faint scraping from just past what looked like the root of a fallen oak. Hild pointed: He should keep on, she would approach from the south.

Under the trees she saw the slotted, out-pointing sign of a roe deer. Heavy; a buck or pregnant doe. Hungry healthy folk would have hunted her down long ago. There might be people, but not people the deer were afraid of. She began to creep north, staff in both hands. The scraping got louder.

It was a child, thin as a whippet, scraping black bulger from the dead bark of the oak into her cyrtel. She was sniffing and dripping as she scraped. Her face was covered in an angry rash and her fingers looked as brittle as chicken bones.

Leofdæg was drifting towards her like mist. Hild lifted her hand, slowly so the child would not catch the movement from the corner of her eye, and turned her palm out: *Stop.*

Hild guessed the child to be about seven, but it was hard to be sure from this angle. It was possible that a child so young could have survived a winter alone, but more likely there were others nearby.

The child cocked her head to a tiny sound, high up in the bare elm branches. Hild looked up slowly: a thin squirrel, newly awake.

The child licked her lips, swallowed, then wiped her nose with her hand and went back to scraping.

The child was starving.

Hild stood slowly, considered, and began to hum the "Song of Branwen," very softly.

The child cocked her head again. Hild hummed louder. The child turned, saw her, and froze.

"You shouldn't—" Hild said.

The child bolted into the ferns. Hild took two long strides and scooped her up. She squirmed like an eel and tried to bite Hild, but Hild just held the child at arm's length until she abruptly went limp and waited, eyes staring and still, nose running.

She nodded Leofdæg close but to one side.

"I'm going to put you down." She spoke in Anglisc. But the child showed no sign of understanding. She repeated it in British. Nothing. "I'm putting you down. Don't run."

She put the child down. She ran. Hild scooped her up again.

"I'm going to put you down again." She did, and the child's gaze darted from her to Leofdæg and back.

Hild squatted on her hams. She was still taller than the child.

"What's your name?"

Silence. But Hild was sure she understood.

"My name's Hild. Were you collecting that bulger—the little black buttons—to eat?"

After a moment the child nodded and scrubbed at her inflamed cheek.

"You shouldn't. Your face"—she gestured at the rash—"that's from the bulger." Without taking her eyes off the child she said, "Leofdæg, what food do you have?"

He produced half a cooked sausage from his pouch. The child fixed her gaze on it.

"Cut a piece," she said. "A very small piece, and toss it to me."

He did. And now the child's gaze was fixed on Hild.

She held out the sausage. "Here," she said.

The child jerked in place, as though she had almost reached for the sausage but then made herself stop.

"It's good sausage," Hild said. She brought it to her mouth as though to eat it herself and the child made an anguished sound. "You want it? You can have it." She held it out again.

The child snatched it and stuffed it in her mouth, chewing frantically and swallowing, then looking from Hild to Leofdæg.

"I'm Hild," she said again. She glanced at Leofdæg and nodded fractionally. He cut another very small piece but did not throw it. "That's Leofdæg. What's your name?"

The child licked her lips, which were pale compared to the dark red rash. "Maer."

"Maer? I'm Hild. Would you like some more sausage?"

Leofdæg threw it to Hild, who caught it and held it out.

As before, Maer snatched it, but then she looked at Leofdæg, looked at the pitiful piece of sausage in her hand, glanced east through the trees, and began to shift as though to run—no, to eat—no, to run.

"We have more," Hild said. In her pouch she had cheese, a heel of twice-baked bread, and a smaller chunk of sausage. After her last few months she did not think she would ever again take a step without some sort of food to hand. "We have enough for others. Eat it."

With a sob, Maer did. This time she chewed more carefully.

"Maer, how many others are there?"

A crudely made wattle hurdle heaped with moss and dead leaves and sticks leaned against a stump and was dug out below. There was room for four people to lie down, but only one woman lying on a pile of bracken. Her voice was weak and her eyes wandered, but once she understood that Hild was real, she told her her name was Tette and that her and little Maer's mor was dead, aye, and their brother, too.

Once Hild's eyes adjusted to the gloom she saw that Tette was not old but thin, so very thin she could not understand how she was still alive.

Maer knelt next to her and took her hand. "We have food, Tette. Food! Stay there."

She squirmed backwards and up out from under the hurdle and Hild heard her talking to Leofdæg.

"Can you stand?" she said to Tette.

"I don't know."

"See!" Maer came tumbling back into the den clutching a piece of sausage. "Eat it, oh eat it all! They have more . . ." But Tette had passed out.

If it had been just Hild, she and Leofdæg could have picked Tette up and carried her in turn, but there was also Maer. And in a war-torn land one of them, at least, needed their hands free. But Tette weighed almost nothing. The hurdle, stripped of its detritus, was sturdy enough to take her and her sister, and easy enough for Hild to pull like a sled while Leofdæg ranged.

At first, Maer peered this way and that but as they neared Cnotinsleah she turned pale and smudge-faced; Tette was asleep or unconscious.

"You're safe," Hild said. "Leofdæg and I will keep you safe."

When they came in sight of the first gate, Maer hid her face and crouched over Tette as though to protect her from the view.

Ahead, Leofdæg stopped and called into the trees, and a sheepish Aldnoth stepped out.

"Tell Oeric we'll camp overnight!" Hild called. "And there better be food ready."

Aldnoth half bowed and trotted off up the track.

A gust of wind brought the smell of a fire and the harsh, stinging scent of burning bones. Her breasts leaked, and she realised that past the rumble and snap of the fire she had been hearing Wilfrid's shrieks; it was long past his feeding time.

Maer whimpered and seemed to try to burrow under her sister's arm.

"You won't see anything," Hild said. "You won't see anything, and with us you're safe."

Cuthred and Aldnoth carried the hurdle to the cooking fire. Hild sat with Wilfrid—who spat out her nipple twice before he began to suck with a vengeance, clenching and unclenching his fists as though he wanted to strangle something—and watched Morud dip his own bowl in the pot and hand it to Maer, talking as he might to a skittish horse.

Gwladus was with Sitric by the burning bones; she was sorting through a pile of straps and belt and shoes. Both had cloths over their faces.

". . . hot, so be careful now." Morud held the bowl out to Maer, but she would not take it. "It's fine pottage. I made it myself." He spooned some into his own mouth, chewed, swallowed, smacked his lips. "Better than my mam makes!" He offered it to her again.

She shook her head.

Leofdæg squatted by the pot and dipped himself a bowl. Maer's gaze fastened on him.

One-handed, Hild undid her pouch and pulled out her chunk of sausage. "Leofdæg." She tossed it to him, and nodded to the girl.

Maer did not have to be offered it twice. As she chewed on the sausage she began to relax, but her eyes never left Leofdæg. She was like a hatchling who sees the goosegirl before the goose and now won't follow anything else.

"Well, now," Morud said to Tette. "That's your sister sorted. She is your sister?" Tette stared unblinking at the sky. Hild wondered where she thought she was. "Well, perhaps you would like some of this fine pottage." Silence. "Let's start with names. I'm Morud."

Nothing. He looked at Hild.

Maer swallowed her mouthful. "She's Tette," she said. "I'm Maer."

"Tette needs food, Maer. Will you try?"

Maer looked at the sausage in her hand, at the bowl in Morud's.

"If you put your sausage down, no one will take it," he said. "See the lady there?"

Maer looked at Hild sideways.

"If anyone tries to take your sausage she will hit them with that stick. She is stronger than ten men and fast as an adder. No one can hurt you now. Now you are under the cloak of the lady of Elmet."

Lady of Elmet. With no king there was no lady of Elmet. Maer looked at her sideways, then at Leofdæg, who nodded. She looked at her sausage, looked at Leofdæg again. She handed the half-chewed thing to him.

The child took the bowl from Morud, knelt by her sister, and spooned up a little pottage. "This is pottage." She nudged the spoon at Tette's closed mouth. Nothing. She tipped a little. It ran down the side of her bony cheek. Maer wiped it away, then licked her fingers clean. "It tastes good." She tried again. The lumpy gruel just dribbled down her chin. "Come on, Tette!"

One-handed Hild fished out her bread, her cheese, broke a corner off each. "You'll have to soak the bread."

Maer did. Tette ignored it, ignored the cheese.

Wilfrid stirred. Hild righted him, laid him over her shoulder, burped him. He kneed her, pulled on her ear. She put him down on his plump bottom and he looked around crossly.

Morud dug through his own pack, found a wrinkled apple, cut a piece, handed it to Maer.

This time, Tette licked feebly at her lips. Wilfrid cooed and held out his hand in the sign that in all tongues said: *Want!*

"Mash it," Hild said to them. "As you would for a baby."

This time Tette ate it, and swallowed, and blinked. Morud and Maer both grinned, and Wilfrid chortled.

She half watched the small group in the firelight, thinking, weighing time, and people, and food. She looked at the sky. Late afternoon, but the evening star would be up soon, followed by the time between time, the edge between day and night when animals stepped from the trees and came to the water to drink.

"Leofdæg," she said. "Watch them for me."

Gwladus sat by the harsh glow of the bone fire with two piles of salvage. She pulled down her cloth mask when Hild approached and said, "There's not much."

Hild stirred one pile, then the other with her staff, then stooped for an old and worn leather chest harness with broken straps dangling. "This will do." She pulled free the leather straps, poked her fingers through the holes they left, then took up another, smaller leather patch and set to work making a sling. It was crude, but it didn't need to be beautiful, it just needed to hurl a stone hard and fast, as she had learnt from the camp women on her first war trail. She folded it in half, whirled it, and said, "Let's go hunting."

They came back with two hares and a squirrel, all gutted, plus fern tips, wild garlic, and pignut. In the swaying yellow firelight, even Maer ate the stew. Tette was now sitting up, but she would only eat bread softened in stew juice. There was no salt, no mead, and no lyre, but it felt like a feast.

The fire crackled and the river poured. Cuthred was asking Aldnoth for something, half serious, half teasing. Maer sat close to Leofdæg with Tette on the other side, letting her eyelids droop. Gladmær was talking to Sitric, wiggling one hand: a fishing tale. Oeric sucked a hare bone with concentration, thinking about something else. They were warm, well-fed, and back in Elmet. They were going home.

Home. Menewood: now with more than twice the people it was meant for, and no supplies from Caer Loid—no supplies from there ever again. As a home it had never been big enough to stand on its own for long, even for just twoscore folk. They had had a surplus of honey and hazelnuts, and a good supply of pigs and goats, oats and barley. They could catch fish and birds. But it would take time to clear and sow and grow and harvest wheat. Time to breed cattle and set up a dairy. Time to raise chickens and ducks. A single fat pony who was only ridden two miles one way could manage on a patch of grass but a warhorse could not. Before they left, the Caer Loid meadows had just reached their peak, with the right mix of grasses: vetch and clover, sedge and savory. The harvest had been good, better than good. Some fodder had already gone to Menewood, but not enough, not nearly enough for a dairy herd, a brace of oxen, horses.

Gwladus caught her eye and smiled slightly, looked around the circle: ranged around a fire built of broken baulks and beams; filthy, unkempt, and without horses; they looked like bandits.

No. Bandits had no home. Bandits were hunted, bandits died. She would not allow it.

She cleared her throat. Gradually they quieted and looked at her, waiting. "We are one dozen. We're strong. I need every one of you. We are in Elmet, my land. But before I lead you to the heart of home, we each have to be sure. I have to be sure of you, and you of me."

She looked at them one by one.

"Some of you—Oeric—have already given a personal oath." Her first. "Some—Sitric, Cuthred—have already given an oath to the lady of Elmet." They nodded. "Some of you—Gwladus, Morud—may never have been asked." Gwladus inclined her head, while Morud, startled, looked around before he understood Hild was waiting for an answer, yes or no, and nodded. "Some of you—Aldnoth, Tette, Maer—are young." Maer moved closer to Tette and hid her face, but Tette, arm around her little sister, met Hild's gaze and nodded once, firmly. Aldnoth mouthed *Aye* and fiddled with the lace on his boot. "And some of you"—she looked at Gladmær and Leofdæg—"swore a gesith's oath to the king, a great and binding oath."

Now the flicker of flame and shadow played on wary, waiting faces.

She unfolded her furs and put them on, drew her cross up from under her dress and turned it gold side out so it gleamed, solid and heavy, seamless. "But the king is gone, and all oaths gone with him. I no longer hold Elmet under the king's name. But here, today, I, Hild Yffing, claim it in my own. Elmet is mine, I will hold it." She wrapped her beads around her left wrist. "Menewood needs no claim. Menewood has no lord but me. Wood and water, sky and stone, Menewood is mine." She settled her seax at her waist and pulled her staff to her. "And none who have not sworn to me their personal oath may set foot there. I will have your oaths now."

She stood. From her pouch she took the larger of her two remaining travel cups, big enough for two fingers of white mead. There was no mead. She dipped it in the stew broth. She faced the circle, gold, chased hilt, and beads gleaming in the firelight and furs huge about her.

"Oeric, son of Grim." He stood. "I, Hild, daughter of Hereric Yffing and Breguswith Oiscinga, do swear on my oath, on this cup by this river under this sky, that I will be as your lord. I will protect you and feed you, and defend your name and person while you are true."

She took a sip and passed the cup to Oeric. Despite its size, he took it with both hands, as he had, years ago. This time he was not shaking.

He raised the cup to her. "I, Oeric son of Grim, swear on my oath, on this cup by this river under this sky, that I will be your man. I will protect you and obey you, and defend your name and person while I breathe."

He sipped the broth.

"Finish it," she said, as she had once long ago, though in truth he probably already had with his first sip.

Sitric, son of Sitred, and Cuthred, son of Cuthwulf, rose in their turn and swore their oath, followed by Aldnoth, son of Fenric. Tette, daughter of Bilswith, hauled herself to her feet, and, leaning her weight on her little sister's shoulder, swore for both herself and Maer, *Until she should be grown*. She was grey-faced by the time she sat. Aldnoth leaned over and patted her on the arm: welcome. Then Leofdæg, son of Acwuld, swore to her, adding, as gesiths do for their king, his body, sword, and life. Hild allowed it—though did not hold her blade to his neck as was custom—and Gladmær, son of Gladnoth, followed suit.

Morud ab Addoc received Hild's oath in British and gave his in Anglisc. And last Hild swore to Gwladus ferch Heddwen that she would be as her family. That she would honour and defend her name and person as long as she breathed. Gwladus in turn promised to support and defend Hild, and to honour her name and person as long as she breathed.

If any noticed that she did not promise to obey they gave no sign. They settled in to watch the last of the yellow flame deepen to orange, sitting closer than they had, and, as the embers darkened from orange to red, Aldnoth, prodded by Cuthred, began a song.

We band of brothers . . .

It was a gesith song, one that more often than not morphed into the swaggering, fate-drenched chorus of *We band of buggered*, a song of men marching to their doom. But tonight, Aldnoth's warm, clear voice stayed strong and hopeful and good.

Ceasterforda was built just south of the fork of the Kelder and Yr, guarding the war street on its march north. As they approached, Hild loosened her seax in its sheath.

The gate was splintered and hanging loose but not burnt, the palisade not torn down. Bodies had been nailed to each gatepost and left to rot and fall, bit by bit, into the dirt, and skulls swelled like obscene buds on palisade posts. Daffodils sprouted bright from grey bones at the base of the wall, and one gatepost still held half a rib cage bound by leathery sinew.

The carved and painted cross that had guarded the south wall was torn from its post hole and cast down. Aldnoth looked unwell.

She sent the others on to a sheltered place she knew up near Oulton Beck. "Aldnoth, with me."

Trailed at a distance by Aldnoth she entered the gate and climbed to the top of the west palisade to survey the land. That way, west and north through the valley between the Kelder and the Yr, lay Caer Loid and, a little north of that, Menewood. In other times, a single day's journey. But now she had ten people, one just a babe in arms and two others dangerously weak. They had no reliable food, no horses, and they would have to move by hidden ways.

North, straight as a spear thrust along the war street, lay Aberford. But Cadwallon was overwintering at York and if his men were roaming, there was nowhere to hide on that road.

Aldnoth climbed up beside her. He flinched from the spiked skulls but Hild ignored them and looked out over the valley between the rivers where she could see three steadings. No smoke was rising, no goats grazing, no sheep in the field.

"This was rich, well-farmed country. That steading"—she pointed to the second with the small paddock and row after row of skeps—"they made mead almost as good as Menewood's. Families grew large around here, well-fed; they could farm close and still thrive. A score lived there, more."

She nodded back over her shoulder to the inner fort. "There are not enough bones. There were hundreds in this valley."

"They're alive, out there?"

"Maybe."

"Then why don't they come bury their dead?"

"They're afraid." She pointed down at the water, where skulls, big ones—horses, oxen—rocked in the current. No cattle meant no ploughing. Cadwallon's work. He sowed fear like salt so nothing, no life, no heart, would flower here. He was stamping on Elmet like a child bitten by an ant who shrieks and stamps on the whole line in the grass, then follows the mashed bodies to the anthill and stamps and stamps, over and over, until everything is dead and broken and the child has nothing to show but a red face glistening with snot. But these ants were her people.

At the second steading they found a spade and then a food hoard. Crocks of butter and honey, both good. A wrapped cheese that, under the thick fur of green, might be partly salvageable, and a side of bacon swollen and wriggling with maggots. They dug around some more but found nothing. They shouldered their bundles once more and moved on.

The girls' appetites seemed bottomless, though fixed in different directions. Tette had wanted only apples, bread dipped in broth, and the wizened currants Sitric had been carrying in hopes of taking a deer. Cuthred had finally persuaded her to eat a little of his pottage but now they had honey she would no longer look at it. Maer, though, would at first take food only from Leofdæg, and only sausage. He had persuaded the others to give him their sausage in exchange for Maer's share of stew and bread. But then the sausage was gone. He had eventually coaxed her into trying a little cheese, then a little more. If it was fatty, she wanted it. Once, Hild found her staring at the drop of milk on Wilfrid's lips when he had fallen asleep mid-suck.

They were young. They would manage.

They were now climbing up and down the occasional rise and trees began to thicken. Wilfrid, tight against her chest, struggled to turn his head to look around. "That's oak," she said to him. "Oak. They're bare yet. But the elms, look, their buds will flower soon enough."

Wind rose, sudden and from the south. More rain. They would need shelter. "In Menewood, this wind would set the hazel catkins dancing. You'd like that."

But when she imagined a baby chortling and holding out a chubby hand to grasp a yellow lamb's tail, she was smaller, with hair pale as clover honey, and Wilfrid felt too heavy and smelled all wrong.

The ground was heaved and torn open. A bloated arm lay as though it hauled itself from the dirt by its long fingernails. Another body could be seen pushing from underneath. Both Gwladus and Sitric moved closer to Hild. Gladmær tried to look everywhere at once.

Half under a bramble, what looked like a shin bone poked out between fallen leaves. One mound seemed gouged by a mindless plough. Bare boughs dripped.

Behind them a mound groaned. Sitric jumped and Gwladus flattened herself against a tree, Gladmær swung the spade back like an axe, and Hild dropped her staff into fighting position.

She shifted her staff to one hand and straightened. "Too many buried at once," she said. "And not deep enough."

Bodies, too many bodies, some thrown on top of an already bloating corpse and covered with a bare scattering of soil. As they swelled they heaved up through the soil like monstrous undead things. Scavengers had done the rest. The gouges were tusk marks: an escaped boar truffling up tender remains.

"So many," said Gwladus.

There were at least a score of mounds, and most had two or more bodies. Half, perhaps, looked to have died months ago, when Cadwallon ripped through Elmet, but the others were more recent. A starving, frightened people dying one by one with no one to protect them.

Gladmær looked at their single, broken spade and then at Hild.

"Just search for anything useful."

The first bodies might have been buried with a favourite cup or knife, even a cooking pot. Pitiful objects she might have tossed in the midden a year ago could now mean the difference between life and death.

Gwladus found a hidden charcoal burners' hut with a spade, a rake, iron tongs, and, best of all, tattered strips that were the remains of sacks and the charcoal they had once held. And at the bottom of the tangled hollow, Gladmær found no useful firewood but what was left of a body lying on top of a bow stave with four salvageable arrows. Sitric ran his hand along the long arc of yew, leaned his weight on it, sighted down it, and said, "Useful bow." All it needed was restringing.

A bow and their spears, and that boar was out there somewhere. Hild's face felt strange; she was not used to smiling.

A whole honey-glazed sucking pig, and a buttery stew of pignuts, mushrooms, ramps, and barley: a feast.

They had not taken the boar, but they had found a nursing sow and her litter. Two arrows hurt her enough to snatch one of her litter. Morud gutted it, impaled it on green wood, and set it roasting. It fell into the fire and charred a bit before Morud could fish it out with the huge charcoal burner's tongs, but for starving folk it barely mattered.

They were still dangerously thin, though none so thin as Tette, who was showing Maer how to bend hazel withies into a loosely woven box while Leofdæg pretended he was not hovering over the two girls like a mother hen. First they must survive the cruel season of Hrethmonath and early Œstremonath, when the promise of sun and blue sky persuaded birds to sing and flowers to bloom, but roots were not yet plump, the bees were sluggish, and goats must range far and wide for shoots sweet enough to feed on. It was nearly two months to the fat and ease of Thromilchi, and she did not yet know how Menewood fared. They could be returning to ruin.

Sitting beside her Gwladus wrapped her arms around her shins and rested her chin on her knees, watching Wilfrid. "He seems happy."

"His last tooth is through." At least she hoped it was his last.

Now Tette was rubbing at her forehead and saying something crossly to Maer.

"When we're back you should find him a milk mother."

Hild nodded. Honey would have had one before she started to teethe. Gwladus called out. "Oeric." He looked up. "When you were there, were there any nursing mothers in the valley? We need someone to help with the lady's gift son."

"There was one lass—I don't know much about such things, but she seemed big. So maybe, by now . . ."

Hild nodded. If she were close to term six weeks ago, then her milk now would be in full flood.

"But, lady. The lass—her wits are not—she was handled by Cadwallon's men."

"Where did she hail from?"

"Up Bardsey way."

So far? She needed to know the safest path to Menewood. North across the Yr, staying east of Brid's Dyke, then cutting straight west, bypassing Caer Loid. Or following the Yr valley on the south side, only moving north at its confluence with the beck that flowed from her own valley of Menewood. She did not know what ways were closed, where bandits might lurk.

She whistled. Every head came up. "Leofdæg! We're in need of counsel."

He crossed to their side of the fire. Like Hild, even as he listened he watched the clearing and the people, though his pattern was different. It was a glance at the tops of the trees, then a swift quartering of the group as a whole, then a longer study of the girls by the hurdle—Tette had stopped weaving hazel withies to rub her forehead again—then back to the trees.

"Cadwallon's men have not been seen south of Aberford since Yule?"

"No sign of them west or south of Kaelcacaestir."

"And bandits?"

"Little sign beyond a—"

Across the fire Hild had seen movement that did not belong: Tette's cheeks and forehead darkened and her hand went to her chest. She flailed, tried to rise, and Hild was already moving, but Leofdæg got there first. He caught Tette as she pitched sideways at the fire.

Someone shouted and Maer shrieked. Hild bent to the crumpled child in Leofdæg's arms. After a moment she sighed, knelt, and tugged the tattered cyrtel down over one scratched thigh, already healing as young skin did. She patted it sadly. It would never finish healing now.

Leofdæg looked at her.

She shook her head.

"I don't understand."

Nor did Hild. A strand of dirty hair hung over the child's forehead; she stroked it back. Tette, daughter of Bilswith, should have had a veil band of bronze to keep her hair back; as her loaf giver, it would have been Hild's privilege and joy to provide it on her wedding day.

Morud ran to them. "Here's water."

Hild shook her head. Water was for later, when they dressed her for her shroud.

A little apart from the others, but still in sight of the fire, Hild and Gwladus set up a rough platform of logs, topped by the hurdle they had made in Cnotinsleah, and lifted Tette onto it. She weighed nothing.

Leofdæg kept a bewildered Maer away.

Gwladus washed Tette's hair as best she could in the dim light of the fire. Hild wiped the girl's arms from shoulder to wrist. Even now, after four days of eating, they were nothing but bone, so thin it seemed impossible she had ever held herself upright.

Gwladus combed the hair. It was almost obscenely lush on such a thin body. "It will take a long time to dry."

Hild nodded and washed the fingers one by one. Tiny, fragile things loosely jointed to a wrist not much thicker than a war arrow.

"She seemed better. Brighter," Gwladus said. "She could walk, a bit. I don't understand."

"No." Today was the first day she had felt light inside, almost happy; now this. Perhaps fate ladled out a measure of happiness when you were born, and when it was used up it was gone.

Gwladus weighed the hair across her forearm, thinking. "I should braid it now. It'll be easier."

No one had washed Cian. No one had tended him and combed his hair. She would never again run her fingers through the heavy chestnut and copper. But she could do this for a girl she had sworn to protect.

Hild's breath steamed in the cold, bright morning as she arranged the fresh-cut juniper boughs on the wattle hurdle, now a makeshift bier, to cover the lower half of Tette's body. They hid the dirt and stains, and disguised the already changing, slumping shape of death. She turned over the grimy seams at the neckline to hide the worst wear, and tucked the four tiny hazel blossoms she had walked half a mile to find into the child's hair. It was not much, but at least she looked cared for and smelled now of evergreen not something for the midden.

Leofdæg cleared his throat.

Maer peered out from behind his knee at the shape that had been her sister, then at Hild. Her eyes were shifting and uncertain. "I didn't give her my honey," she said.

Hild looked at Leofdæg but he shook his head. "She had a lot of honey, little one. Every time I saw her she was eating it."

"She liked it," Maer said. "She wanted mine. Last night. She gave me her pork, she said, so I should give her my honey."

"My older sister always wanted my things, too," Hild said.

"Did you give her them?"

"Not always."

"Did she die, too?"

"No, little one. Sisters don't die because you don't give them what they want."

"But Tette did. She died." She looked at what had once been her sister. "You said you would keep her safe. But she died."

The accusation caught Hild under the ribs. "Yes."

"And now you'll put her in a hole with the worms."

"We will bury her where she'll be safe. Where you can always find her."

"But she won't be safe. She'll be cold. And she doesn't like worms—"

The thin threads of wriggling maggots on Honey.

"—please. Don't put her in a hole by herself."

In a country at peace, with a clear river, good wind, and a fine boat, they could have taken Tette back to her mother's grave in Cnotinsleah. But in the time it would take them now, even in winter, the body would stink and swell. "What flowers did—does Tette like?"

"Blue ones that smell nice."

"In spring, we'll come back and plant her grave with blue flowers. So many flowers that bees will come from the hills and the fields and the woods, and birds will marvel. Their sweet perfume will make everyone for miles about smile and feel glad. Tette's Blessing, they will call this place. She will never be alone, because people will come here to hold hands and whisper their secrets."

Maer stared at her as though she were speaking Pictish.

Leofdæg patted the little hand at his belt with the tips of two fingers, each half the size of Maer's fist. "Be brave," he said. "Tette'd want you to be brave."

But one so young should not have to be brave.

15

HILD WAITED BY AN ELM, wenny and swollen about the roots, that had
probably stood among these oak, hazel, and alder trees since the days
of Coel Hen. Purplish flowers were opening high up on its black branches.
The rain was steady but so light that very little got past the branches
overhead. Beyond the elm, where the trees thinned, the road crossed the
Yr, and beyond that lay Caer Loid. So very close now, but this was not the
time to hurry. Now was the time to be slow, to be careful, to think.

A gust of wind made the old tree shiver and a single great droplet fell
on her neck at the base of her braid, and wormed down her back. She
eased her arms from the twisted cloth of the baby pack—Wilfrid weighed
noticeably more than even a week ago—and handed him to Morud.

She did not want to leave the shelter of the trees and face what remained of Caer Loid. But this was the safest way to Menewood and she had
to be sure.

The Caer Loid of her childhood, the Caer Loid of dream and story, had
been a British king's hall, the last of its kind south of the wall and east of
the Spine mountains, so old and one with its place that sometimes it
seemed to be growing from it rather than sinking into it, surrounded by a
skirt of wattle pens for geese and pigs. Edwin had razed the old, torn out
every tree but one, and surrounded his overweening hall with a box palisade, raw and brutal and ringed by bare earth. The first things one had
seen approaching the new Caer Loid were not the goose pen and thorn

hedge of old, but the cluster of workshops near the river: the tanning pits and their stretchers, the livestock pens and butcher huts, the forge and smelter. What awaited her now?

Gwladus stepped to her side and touched her arm lightly. Caer Loid had been her home, too. They would go together.

Morud stirred barley into the pot of water. The fire was too young, too yellow for the water to be hot yet. In the time it would take for this mess to soften and cook they could all be in Menewood sitting by a real fire, drinking spiced ale, eating a bit of mutton—out of this miserable mizzle, anygate. He was sick of rain and cold and damp, sick of birds, too, except perhaps to eat one. He longed to hear anything other than wind in the trees and the drip drip drip of rain. The laughter of his sister—even the scolding of his aunt—would be a comfort. He didn't see why they had to camp here overnight, why they couldn't just go to Menewood. But all the lady had said was, *Beginnings matter.* Which left him no wiser.

Wilfrid crawled about in the dirt, inspecting the old leaf fall with the same pinched disapproval the Crow's priest had when he tallied everything in his book. Well, he'd never see that priest again; he'd gone wherever priests go, with surprise on his face and his guts in his hand.

Wilfrid glared at a twig, said, "Hu!" and tried to stuff a pebble up his nose. Morud was sick of playing nursemaid, too. He understood Gwladus's dislike of children now. Once they were home in Menewood he'd never watch a squalling, drippy—

Gwladus and the lady came back through the trees, moving slowly and with care. He sat back on his heels. No blood, not that he could see, but they walked as though their insides might fall out. They weren't talking, either. And they didn't look at one another, as though they were ashamed to be alive.

Then the lady was walking on to Leofdæg and Oeric, but Gwladus was coming his way. Before he could even open his mouth to ask what on this great green earth—she scooped up Wilfrid and held him hard, and when he struggled she held him harder.

Well.

"Morud!" He whipped around. The lady, standing with Oeric and Leofdæg, waving him to her, without stopping what she was saying.

He scrambled up and trotted over.

"—some bodies are new. Cadwallon's close, and he's used my people to send a message." The lady's voice, a great gritty grinding of stones, made him shudder. "One day we'll meet Cadwallon and make our reply. But not today. Today we stay here, out of sight, while you and Leofdæg and Morud make sure the way to Menewood is clear."

Now she looked at Morud, though she did not seem to see him, and when she spoke she was still talking to the others.

"You'll go carefully. You'll go quietly. They'll need proof that I live—if they're still there at all. So to Rhin you'll say, 'Three in one.' To both my mother and Lady Begu you'll show this."

She reached into her purse for the smallest travel cup, the one he and Gwladus had filled with milk on that terrible day in the waste. He remembered how heavy it was for its size.

"You'll tell them I'll come collect it on the morning of the third day—"

"Two days!" He clapped a hand over his mouth.

"—and they are to prepare the people." And then she turned to him, and this time she saw him. "Yes. Two days. We don't know what we're going home to. You, Morud, will be my living proof that we three who set out still breathe—proof in your body. So keep that body safe. Heed the word of Leofdæg on the way. And take very great care."

We three, Morud thought, dazed, as he was marched away with Leofdæg and Oeric without so much as a wave goodbye from anyone. *We*. And as he walked, he thought, I'm going home. And he thought, One day they will sing stories of the Three Who Lived.

It was dusk, and the rain had eased; the fire burned well. She set Gladmær and Sitric to guard the north and east and to whistle once on every slow count of a thousand. Later, she would take their watch; she doubted she would sleep. Every time the wind drifted from the west she was filled with a dread that could only be soothed by seeing that Maer and Wilfrid were right there by the fire, alive, huddled between Gwladus and Cuthred. And after the dread was soothed, a greasy wave of slow, sick rage.

By the fire, Cuthred talked of Menewood: the food they would eat soon, the bath he would take, the bliss of sleep in a dry bed under a roof. No one was really listening but he did not seem to mind.

Maer asked him about bread and honey, and when he told her there was so much honey in Menewood a person could eat it for breakfast, she said, "Tette would have liked that."

Hild added an oak branch to the fire, and an old damp leaf on the outer edge began to curl and darken, and then caught. Fire ate across it in a dark, orange-edged line—burning out its heart, just as Cadwallon burned the heart from her people.

From the east, Sitric whistled. A heartbeat later, Gladmær. Two more of her people still safe.

Even if they had moved slowly, Oeric, Morud, and Leofdæg would be in Menewood now. They would have shown the cup. Her mother and Begu would know she was alive.

The fire before her became the fire in the long house at Menewood—no, in the private bower that Breguswith would have taken as her own in Hild's absence. And around that fire, Begu laughs at the news, then bursts into tears and badgers Morud to *Sit down, for Eorðe's sake, sit down just this once and tell me more!* while Breguswith pours more mead and smooths her skirts and says, *We should let Morud go to his aunt.* And where is Rhin? But then the door hanging moves aside and Rhin comes in, and behind him, laughing—

Rooks boiled up from the twilit wood in a fury of wings and cawing, and a double whistle from Sitric and the sound of hooves slammed Hild back to the small fire in the wood. Heavy hooves. A warhorse. More than one. For a shining moment she saw Cian, thundering towards her on Acærn, face wet and strong in the rainlight, arms glinting with gold, but even as the dream dissolved she was kicking out the fire and moving at a slant through the trees to protect the last of her people. Because Cian was dead, nothing but bones rocking on the bed of some river, and there was no one to save them but her.

Then the hoofbeats changed, the incomers were thrashing through the trees, and in a flurry and dash and confusion it was Leofdæg sliding from a roan mare—a mare in foal, a mare she knew—behind a round pony dancing about the clearing as a wild-haired figure in a bright yellow cloak managed to half jump, half tumble off, shouting, "I'm here, I'm here! I could—" and barrelling right into Hild so hard that any words were lost to a clutch, a gasp, then a shout, a burst of tears, and a spate of words that slowly began to resolve: Begu, hugging her, then stepping back, holding her wrists, hugging her again, saying, "I could shake you. What were you thinking? Three days?! I was cutting onion when I saw Morud. I thought my heart would stop. I was sure you were dead—except when I was sure you were alive, or sure you were lying mute under a bush. Three days we should wait before you would come, Oeric said. Three days! I couldn't wait another hour. So I brought some things. Leofdæg took Wolcen and followed me. But I'm here now. And everything's going to be all right."

Begu's hair was the same, and the yellow cloak, but to Hild she looked unreal, an uncanny copy of the real Begu.

The hands on Hild's wrists were small and pale and clean. Hild lifted one, smelled lavender, horse, and onion. "Are you . . . ?" But then she realised where she'd seen that roan before. "Wolcen!" she said. "That's Uinniau's mare."

"Yes. He came back from Craven when Osric apostatised—"

Apostatised?

"—borrowed her because Rhin's old pony couldn't keep up even with Sandy."

Slowly, the uncanny copy and the Begu of her memory began to merge and she started to pick meaning out of the spate of words. "Is he—are you well?"

"Yes, yes. He's well, I'm well. We're all well. But that can wait." She turned, called to Gladmær and Sitric. "Bring my bags to the fire before you go back to whatever you were doing. And some more wood. We're going to need light." She turned back. "First, some food."

She led Hild to the fire like a lamb.

"Sit." She dragged the smallest bag into the circle of light. Gwladus made as if to stand and help but Begu stopped her with a look. "You sit, too. You're thin as sticks, the both of you, as thin as Morud—and I thought he'd disappear if he turned sideways." Maer shrank back from the brightly coloured whirlwind and tried to melt into the shadow. "And you, little one. You too. Sit where I can see you and a passing owl can't carry you off."

Leofdæg left the mare mid-tend and moved into the firelight, to Maer.

Begu flapped at him as though he were a goose. "She's safe with me. You go finish—" She saw how Maer looked to Leofdæg. "No. You, Cuthred. You and—Aldnoth, is it? Yes. You two go finish with the horses. Leofdæg, you come sit with the girl." She tilted her head at Maer. "Now, then. I'm Begu. I've brought you some treats. I've brought everybody treats." Maer stared at her cloak. Begu looked at herself and then at the drab mud colour of everyone else. "Well, yes, it is bright, isn't it? Do you like yellow? I do. Wearing it feels like sitting in a patch of sunshine. If you're good and eat your treats I'll let you borrow it."

Maer sat close to Leofdæg, wound about with Begu's cloak, stupefied by the colour and pausing from her second sausage—fresh sausage!—every now and again to lift the thick yellow weave with her free hand and sniff voluptuously. Fresh pork sausage, as much sausage as she could eat, and a honey cake, though she had only eaten half. The other she had carefully put in her ragged pocket.

Begu watched her do it, but said nothing, and Hild saw that although she could not know why, she understood that there was a why. Just as she had not once ordered Gwladus to do anything, but had only suggested she might do this or that, if she was willing, in the way she might suggest to a fractious peer who had been ill. And when she had looked at Wilfrid's dark-streaked hair and the way he pushed himself back onto his bottom and bounced up and down, as no five-month could, then at Hild, her eyes had changed but she said only, "The cloths I brought for him might be too small. But we'll find something."

With their food—good bread, and cheese, as well as the sausage—they drank their first ale since Gole, and the familiar bitter hint of bog myrtle made Hild cradle her cup and her eyes prickle.

Begu nodded. "Your mother's. She's well. Or as well as anyone can be not knowing if their child lived, or whether she might be stabbed in her bed, or if that beast— But that's for later. Oeric will be here tomorrow with messages, and more, but for now she sends these."

She brought out two bundles, one small, one large. She unwrapped the first: Hild's pearl and agate veil band and earrings, a comb, shears, and a small bottle—jessamine—and assorted bits and pieces. The second was a dark blue overdress, one of her best, the finest cloth she had seen since Winterfylleth, with a pale linen underdress and matching drawers, and a pair of sleeves with finely worked cuffs. Beneath that a dark cloak, hose, and a pair of riding shoes of beautifully dyed leather.

Hild touched the linen with her fingertip, and the fine weave snagged on a callus.

The people of Menewood had seen her in work clothes, hair undressed, and hands dirty. But that was when Caer Loid was strong and an Yffing sat on the throne. And some of the folk in the valley were strangers.

"How many in Menewood now?" she said.

"More than fourscore. Nearer to five. Some are . . . uneasy." By which she meant some made Breguswith uneasy; Begu, too. "But that's for later." She turned to Gwladus. "I chose some things for you as well. Some from your chest."

It was both a liberty and a kindness. But it was plain from the look on Begu's face, and Gwladus's, that they understood Breguswith's message as clearly as Hild: You will return to Menewood dressed, and attended, as an Yffing.

Gwladus inclined her head. "Thank you."

"I just hope I remembered to bring soap . . ."

She had brought soap, and much else besides. A great awning—"I couldn't carry the poles but it's Elmet; there's always wood about"—shears, shaving knives and a sewing kit, and more: everything a weary band of travellers might need to look and feel their best.

Hild let Begu and Gwladus dress her under the awning, though for once it was not raining. Begu made a small sound at Hild's scars, but said only, "Do I need to be careful?"

"Not really." Which meant: They hurt, but not as much as they did, and not enough to worry about.

Begu nodded: It could wait, just like Hild's questions about Osric's apostasy. Hild chewed more fruit leather. Her gemæcce could not have gathered all these things in the time between Oeric arriving and her leaping on Sandy. They had been gathered with care and attention, over long, sleepless nights, while Begu imagined this moment and hoped; laid out in her mind what Hild, wounded or frightened or lost, might need; perhaps even gathered objects in a chest, added to them over the months, taken some out as hope and the light waned, replaced them with others as the world turned and a dead world began to green, rising again into hopeful daylight.

As they combed her hair and braided in the fine gold chains Begu had brought—they looked old, Frankish perhaps, or something the women of the redcrests might have worn; she had never seen them before—she chewed fruit leather. Such a small thing, the sweet chewy leather, but such a comfort. Tette would have loved it. The fruit leather was not from her mother. That, like so many little things, was the work of her gemæcce.

"Too big," Begu was saying, tugging the pale linen underdress this way and that. Gwladus paused mid-braid. "Well, no one will see it. But we'll have to do something about the overdress."

Gwladus and Begu pondered the dress, deciding that a V-shaped gather down the back might work. Running stitches would hold it long enough for the feast.

A feast, when the note Rhin sent with Oeric not long after Yule had suggested food was already beginning to run low? But Hild knew her mother's thinking. Hild would ride into Menewood like the lady of Elmet of old—as though backed by a full granary and thronging fold, a busy dairy, and fields under the plough—and a healthy child before her. From far enough away the people of Menewood, new and old, easy and uncertain, would see only the glitter and the high-stepping mare, the gleaming Yffing chestnut hair, escorted by glinting spearpoints and led by king's gesiths. They would not see how gaunt she was beneath her furs, how her dress hung and bagged; they would not guess at the runnelled twisting scar on her hip, the ragged gashes hidden by her fine linen sleeves. They would not know Wilfrid was not hers. They would see only the strong, fertile loaf giver with the male heir they needed, who would protect them, to whom they would gladly swear their oath.

Breguswith was wagering her daughter knew and remembered every food hoard in Elmet, that most had survived, and that they could be retrieved. Feast now, replenish later from the hoards. A risky wager.

They came to Menewood from the east, as she had the first time, six years ago, riding thoughtless and fine on a strong Cygnet. At the ancient pollard she had looked across a hidden valley drenched beechnut yellow with autumn sunlight and glistening with spiderwebs. Between one breath and the next it became hers, in her heart and mind, woven into her wyrd, and she fell in love with the possibility, a place waiting to be tended and loved so that the fruit of its rich and secret land might fall into her outstretched hand, if only she listened and learnt and built with care and attention. And she had. She had made Menewood hers, planning carefully, growing it bit by bit, adding people, pruning away what did not fit, until it was balanced and perfect in her hand.

Now she kept her eyes on Wolcen's poll as the mare moved with conscious dignity up the rise and past the old oak. In the distance one of the two lookouts turned and ran down to the long house where her mother would be waiting. She saw the hornbeam had lost two of its boughs and, even from here, even in the rain, she could see a rutted path where once there had been no sign of people.

Then they were on the path. People came out from their huts and lean-tos, straightened from the thrashing stone at the beck, paused in their woodcutting and grain grinding, and watched. A chicken squawked as someone scooped it up.

The beck was in the right place but everything else was different. There were too many buildings on either side of the path, and even the long house they walked towards was wrong. Too tall? Wide? Something; she could not see it well enough for all the people. The dress gathered between her shoulder blades bunched and chafed. Her furs were too hot. Wolcen kept to her steady pace.

A woman came to the doorway of a hut that had not been there half a year ago, a baby in her arms. She was thin but, like the others, her clothes were mended and her hair clean. The hut seemed sturdy enough but built by a hand she did not recognise.

A white cat with orange and brown patches and a black splash over one eye sauntered across the path in front of them, tail up. Wilfrid stared, then bounced and made the uh-uh-uh sound that meant *That, that, what's that?* And when the cat stopped and flicked the tip of its tail, he struggled and shrieked to be set down.

The shriek sliced across the settlement, shockingly loud. The cat sat right in the middle of the path and stared at them.

Wolcen stopped. Hild looked down at the cat. It looked back unblinking and after a moment deliberately lifted its right paw and began to clean it.

Behind her and to her left she heard a child whisper, quickly shushed, and, just like that, everything snapped back to itself, and it was Menewood again. Hild turned in her saddle, this way and that.

"This is a fine greeting for your lady," she said, using her belly to send the words through the trees to those she could not see but knew were there. "Whose is this cat?"

A stir to her right and from the shadow of Rhin's house stepped a long, stretched figure she knew. Ceadwin the fosterling. Even taller and thinner than before. "Mine, lady."

"There you are wrong, foster-son." She tucked Wilfrid under her right arm as though he weighed less than the cat, swung one leg over Wolcen's neck, and slid down her shoulder. She moved Wilfrid to the crook of her left arm, flung her furs back to show her jewels, and pulled her staff from behind her saddle. A flash of bright colour and the gleam of gold from the long house and she knew her mother was standing in the doorway and had deliberately caught the light so Hild would know she was there.

She stood square on the path in the middle of Menewood and said to Ceadwin, to all of them, to her mother standing with Rhin on one side and Uinniau on the other, in a voice of iron, "This is my cat. She walks on my path, through my land, among my people." Then, with a smile, "But you, foster-son, are tasked with her especial care. Now come and meet your foster-brother, Wilfrid."

She looked along the path to her mother, who was gripping the door-post hard enough to bruise, and nodded, and Breguswith nodded in turn—the same *Yes! Good* and *We live another day* of so many times past—and retreated with dignity to the room where she would gulp mead, and still her trembling, and be able to smile by the time Hild joined her. But first Hild turned to meet her people, the kernel of the Elmet she would grow.

Two

✦

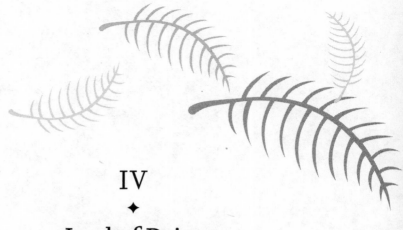

IV

✦

Lord of Deira

(Hrethmonath 633 to Harvestmonath 633, 24 weeks)

16

❖

NEAR THE END OF HRETHMONATH, the world, balanced on the fulcrum
between night and day, tilted suddenly, as it always did, towards the
light and spilled out life. Sap rose and hearts opened, and minds began to
hum, blood to pound, and buds to unfurl. The lady was back in her valley
and all would be well.

Hild walked along the path on the north side of the valley, between the
slope and the rushing beck, listening to the flirr and flute of mistlethrush
and blackbird, the whit-whit of angry robins. Less birdsong than just two
weeks ago, as many birds had left for the north, and those from the south
had not yet arrived. The air was scented and rich with new life. In the
wood south of the beck, in the same wych elm they had nested in last year
and the year before, the tawny owls now had four round white eggs. A soft
wind patted her cheek and sudden need washed through her, need for a
firm, warm hand on her belly, arms wrapped around her ribs, the rhythmic movement of muscle and bone against her, inside her.

Their herd—four horses now—whickered and kicked and galloped
around their new paddock; they felt it, too. Like her, they wanted to run.
She nearly trod on an adder—the first of the year, on the first warm day—
basking in the sunny lee of a rock but half hidden by three-coloured
heartsease. She stepped around it, heading for a shelf of limestone jutting
from the turf farther up.

On the knobby overhang, a robin lay dead, its red breast torn open and tiny apple-pip eyes dull. Killed by a rival over a mate. Spring made fools of them all.

She turned slowly. She was not high enough to see south and west over the rise to the stately Yr valley, but she could look the length of the hidden valley carved by the beck, from the narrow northwest neck with its steep gullies and finger valleys into the upland, down to the plump widening centre now busy, midmorning, with folk stoking the fires of the ovens and smelter, and the small party with spades and hoes raking furrows in the kitchen garth, two women—from here she could not tell who—taking down newly dyed cloth set out to dry in the sun, and on past the pond to the narrow mouth guarded by the old pollard.

From here, it was clear how in the long ago someone, probably the red-crests, had dug a channel to run parallel to the beck, to what was once a millmere—now shrunken to the pond. And there, what was once a wide, straight millrace now blocked by the ruin of what had once been a hand-some mill. Just past that, the thin, rod-straight overflow channel, long silted-up and still. Now, when it rained, the pond flooded and spread, turn-ing the lower end of the valley to a bog. It had suited her for five years to keep it so, secret and safe, but soon she would have to choose whether to keep to that path, or change.

Breguswith poured them both more mead and Hild threw another chunk of applewood on the fire. Extravagant, but now that there was more day than night the world would warm fast and they did not have to hoard every faggot. She dusted her hands and settled back on the padded stool in her mother's bower. They had put the tally sticks away—they were run-ning short of everything but mead, honey, and bee glue—and were talking of how to begin finding and unearthing the hoards Hild had ordered bur-ied late last summer. She knew where those she had supervised herself were, but the rest she would have to guess. They would start with Caer Loid; but Hild did not want to think about that yet.

"I see you took down some of the new-dyed cloth," she said.

"The red. The robins kept attacking it." Breguswith unfastened her veil band—she was the only one of them who still wore one daily—and scrubbed at her scalp with her fingertips. "Ahh." She knotted the long, silver-stranded hair loosely at the back of her neck. "And they're not the only feathers-for-brains wanting to fight."

She was talking about Osric in Craven. That morning one of Rhin's priests had arrived with word that Osric Whiphand, as the Elmetsæte still called him, had sent out a call north and east for all Deirans to rally to his banner, clear their land of meek and skirted Christ priests, and put another proud son of Woden, the last Yffing, on the throne.

Her mother savoured her drink. "It might not have been a good idea to put Coifi and Osric together all those years ago."

While Edwin ruled she had thought the former chief priest of Woden toothless.

"He sees himself as the last Yffing."

"He's forgetting Honeytongue," Hild said. "Though he won't live long." If he wasn't already dead. She had no doubt Penda had hoped to install Honeytongue as puppet king of both Deira and Bernicia, overking of Northumbre. But Cadwallon would never accept an Yffing on the throne, and Penda would soon discover no remaining Bernician or even Deiran thegn was fool enough to swear an oath to a man who had betrayed his father, and his own men before that. Then Honeytongue, ætheling or no, would have outlived his usefulness. Though she doubted Osric had even thought of any of that.

"So," Breguswith said. "How will you reply to Osric's call?"

"He's a fool."

"True. Whoever holds his stick could hold his kingdom." She smiled to herself.

Her mother's main requirement in a man was to be biddable and, before Luftmær the scop, it was Osric who had done her bidding.

Her mother poured herself more mead. "He's a fool with a war band, and gold, and a name. So what will you say?"

"Nothing. He doesn't know I'm alive."

Breguswith's eyes were wintry with calculation. Eventually she nodded: Like Honeytongue, Osric was doomed. "The Iding in Pictland has apostatised, too, they say. And I've heard murmurs even here that Edwin died because a god in skirts is not a king's god but a slave's god. A wealh's god."

"Cadwallon who killed him is wealh, and Christian." Also a king who killed for sport, like a marten. Worse than a marten. No marten could have done what he did at Caer Loid.

"Whatever their reasons, all the north is shedding the Christ," Breguswith said.

Hild nodded. The folk wanted gods like them: Anglisc gods who drank and joked, boasted and swore vengeance, gods who laughed and lied. Gods who lived among the trees and by the springs, who built their halls of wood not cold stone. Gods who made sense. But Edwin had set aside the old gods because Paulinus Crow had promised the power of Rome come again: the power and control of the written word. "If we do have a hammer-wearing king again it won't be for long."

"No?"

"No." The written word would win. She had seen its power.

"But who will be king meanwhile? The Iding or Osric Yffing?"

"The Iding might take Bernicia." If he recruited half of Ciniodd's Pictish war band. If the Gododdin and Bryneich flocked to his banner. If all the old Bernician thegns rode at his side. If Rheged and Alt Clut stayed in their halls. A long string of ifs. "For a while. Until Cadwallon tears out Osric's heart here in Deira and turns north."

If Yffing and Iding would set aside their hate and join together they could defeat Cadwallon and divide Northumbre between them, each ruling one of the old kingdoms, Yffings in Deira and Idings in Bernicia, as they had before Æthelfrith Iding first came south from Bernicia to take Deira and drive the Yffings out. Before Edwin Yffing came back to Deira and moved north to Bernicia to drive out the Idings in turn. But Yffing and Iding were like rival robins; they would fight to the death even in the face of a marten.

And what of Elmet? Twenty years ago, less, Elmet had been ruled by its own king. A small but proud kingdom between Northumbre and Mercia, Northumbre and Lindsey, holding the balance. Could it again? She saw herself riding Cygnet to battle under her own banner, green and white, a boar and a tree: Hild Yffing, queen of Elmet.

She laughed at the thought and her mother lifted her eyebrows. Hild shook her head, drained her cup, and refilled it. "The day of small kingdoms is done," she said. "Our task now is to stay alive."

She thought of Tette.

"Mor, what do you know about starvation? I found a girl near Cnotinsleah. Her name was Tette. She was starving. Her sister was starving—everyone was starving—but only Tette died. We brought food, and she ate. She should have lived."

"I've seen that before. People can die when they eat after starving."

"But why?"

"Perhaps it's their wyrd."

Hild frowned.

"That frown didn't solve anything when you were knee-high and it won't solve anything now."

"But no one else died."

"Wyrd goes as it will."

Hild did not like that answer. "What does our wyrd decide? Are we allotted only so much? So much life, so much love? A measured share of happiness? We use it up and then it's gone?" What if her own was all gone?

Breguswith rolled her cup between her hands, staring into the mead. "Long before I met your father, when I was nose-high to a goat and still running about in a kilted cyrtel, if I liked a boy or he liked me they'd bring me beetles or flowers. Then I grew a little and it was a dripping honeycomb or a round shiny apple. Then I flowered, and the sweet morsels became gold and jewels. And one man who brought me jewels, I loved him. Oh, he was my sun and moon, my dawn and my day—and I thought he loved me back. He gave me a wrist cuff but he chose someone else. And I wept and wailed. I thought, I have wasted my portion of love, thrown it away on an unworthy man, there'll be no more! But, little prickle, there is always more."

Little prickle. She could not remember the last time her mother had called her that.

"Life is what makes love, life is what makes grief and happiness, hunger and rage. While you breathe there is life, and while you live there will always be more. Like the stream, love flows without end. Sometimes strong, sometimes slow, but always coming back." She sipped her mead and smiled. "And that man who chose another woman grew fat and cross and is no doubt dead by now. And I'm still here. I chose another—I chose your father. And after him I chose others. I chose more, and more was given. It will always be given. Never doubt, little prickle, that there is always more, as long as you are bright enough to watch and reach out for it when it crosses your path."

Hild rested a hand on her belly. "Perhaps there will be no more of some things." And despite all her intentions, it sounded like a question.

Her mother moved the jug of mead to one side and put her cup next to it. "Show me."

It had been a while since her mother had seen her naked. Hild stood up and unfastened her dress while Breguswith pulled her stool closer to the hearth and stirred the logs to burn brighter. She motioned for Hild to stand before her, in the firelight, then turn.

"Any gesith would be proud to show such scars only at the front."

She touched Hild's belly gently, with warm hands. With Breguswith's hands against her own springy skin, Hild could see the softness and crinkle of Breguswith's, like the beginnings of the pucker in milk as it comes to a boil. But only the beginnings.

Breguswith ran a finger lightly over the twisting scar that ran from her hip. "Does it hurt?"

"It catches."

"But you stretched it, I think? Yes. And this." She put one hand on the small of Hild's back and the other just above her thatch of hair and pushed firmly. "Does that hurt?"

Hild looked down at her mother's head, the familiar crooked part made unfamiliar by the glints where the firelight turned silver to copper. "No, though it feels different."

Her mother felt around some more, as Hild had seen her do a hundred times on the bellies of women great with child—as Hild herself had done many times. She revisited one place, pushed again.

Hild flinched.

"Hmmm." She turned Hild around and poked at her spine, and then her ribs, then around again and dug her fingers in by the wing of hip bone. She nodded. "It may just need time." She lifted one of Hild's scarred arms into the light. "And these? Any pain?"

"No."

"Do this." On both hands at once she touched each finger in turn to her thumb, and back.

Hild did, faster and more deftly than her mother.

"Good." She nodded that she was finished. While Hild dressed she sat back and picked up her cup. "Keep stretching that scar on your hip. Stretch it every day for another year. Now. Did your cunny tear?"

"I don't remember much. I know I hurt for a long time." Gwladus would know.

"And now? Bed games?"

Hild shook her head.

"No, it doesn't hurt?" She raised her eyebrows. "Or no, you've had none in half a year?"

Another shake.

"That's too long to do without. It's spring. You don't want to be surprised by your needs."

She said nothing.

"You're not a child. See to it."

She just shook her head again.

After a moment her mother said, "Any blood when you piss?"

"No."

"Then you'll be fine."

No blood when you piss: the only praise song for Little Honey, who had not lived a week.

Breguswith put down her cup and held out her arms. Hild knelt at her feet, put her head in her mother's lap, and wept.

Hild and Rhin closed the gate of the temporary paddock on the north slope and watched the horses bend to their fodder. As usual, the new gelding would not approach while they were there.

"His wound's closing," Rhin said.

Hild nodded. She remembered how it felt to watch a wound close, to feel the gratitude. It was when the wound was healed that you forgot what to be grateful for and remembered only what the wound had taken.

When Leofdæg had found the big dappled gelding near Caer Loid he had been nothing but bone and a hideous, festering axe wound on his left flank and haunch. The remains of a saddle had rubbed his back raw and his mouth was swollen with the bit. He would not have lasted another week. Even so it had taken five of them to rope him, and three days before he had allowed Hild to come at his wounds. That had been a grim afternoon's work, after which he would let no one near him. At least now he seemed comfortable around the other horses, particularly Sandy, who would stand between the gelding—who Morud had named Bone—and anyone who approached. And at least he was now able to eat.

If they were careful their fodder would last until the new grass was in. But warhorses needed better-quality grazing. That was for the future. For now they had sown the vetch, clover, savoury, yellowwort, sedge, thistle, and chickweed up the valley and, if all went well, by Thromilchi their herd could run free on good pasture. Their herd: two ponies, a ruined gelding, a mare—so pregnant that soon the only one of them with legs long enough to ride her would be Hild—with bouncy little Sandy their herd stallion. She thought of the pasture and byres of Caer Loid, their three dozen war-trained mounts and the sacks of oat and bran, the score of draught and pack animals; the hunting dogs and rat dogs and bull dogs; the byre cats; the cows and calves, the oxen and asses, the goats, sheep, pigs, geese . . .

"I wish Bryhtsige were here." Then she remembered Rhin had never met the smooth-faced gesith. "He had a way with horses. He persuaded six of them to jump from a boat into the sea and swim for shore."

"You liked him?"

"Well enough." Begu liked him more, and her gemæcce, in full spring tide, was half mad with wanting Uinniau on the days she could not have him. Hild nodded at Rhin's fat old pony. "So. Dwmplen?" Dumpling.

Rhin sighed.

"Your own fault for not naming him." Besides, Morud was right. He did look like a dumpling.

"He likes being part of a herd again. I hadn't realised he'd been so lonely." He turned around, leaned his elbows back on the fence, and looked down the valley to the long house, now even longer, and swollen at the north end with the added bowers, and beyond that, the huts. "He's not the only one."

Hild looked at him.

"Your foster-son—your other foster-son, Ceadwin. He's blossoming here."

She nodded, then stopped. "He wasn't before? He was lonely?"

"More that his family was not what he needed."

There had been no word from Saxfryth and Ceadwulf. She doubted word would ever come. She was Ceadwin's only family now.

A goshawk rolled and tumbled over the oaks, showing off for its mate.

"He'd make a good priest," Rhin said. "I've been teaching him to read."

"A priest," she said, thinking of her conversation with her mother. The goshawk slanted away. She studied Rhin with her full attention. His forehead, pale and fresh-shaved when they met five years ago, was now the same stained oak as the rest of his face because, although for safety's sake he had stopped shaving, his hair was ebbing naturally, exposing his forehead like the beach at low tide. Ceadwin was barely twelve, but if one day he were to be a priest, would he shave his forehead or his crown? As a priest would he look east to Rome or west to the British? "Who would—I don't know the right word. Who would baptise him into priesthood?"

"Ordain. Only a bishop may ordain a priest."

A bishop was a chief priest. Anglisc kings had always chosen their chief priests, whether heathen like Coifi, Roman like Paulinus, or British like Rhuel. Or Irish, like Fursey, and Aidan—whose lord was not a bishop but an abbot who bowed to no one but the Christ.

"We will need priests," she said. She preferred the bishopless British priests of the north who did not spy for any king. But James now no longer had a bishop—though she had always counted him friend. And now there might be other Roman priests without a bishop she could gather and use.

Behind them, the wuffle-tear of a large horse bending to its feed meant Bone was being brave.

"Paulinus and his kind are gone," she said. "There are none left to hunt and hurt British priests now. And the folk need someone to look to for comfort and blessing. Perhaps it's time to shave your head again."

The first day of Œstremonath, three days before Œstre Mass, on a day as sunny as summer, Hild, Rhin, Gladmær, Uinniau, Sintiadd, and Cuthred walked south to Caer Loid, bare-armed and bare-legged through the golden saxifrage and wood anemones. Sintiadd had her skirts kilted up. Cuthred made an unnecessary show of heaving aside a fallen bough—making his biceps bulge—and Sintiadd rolled her eyes at Hild. Birds sang: wheatear and stonechat as well as mistlethrush and blackbird, and everywhere the flick of wrens and the tiny fury of robins. Rhin every now and again touched the plain bronze cross once more hanging around his neck, his inward eye focused on what lay ahead.

As they crested the rise, Dwmplen stopped and shivered, and when Rhin urged him forward he shied like a bran-fed colt. Rooks, disturbed from their new-laid eggs, boiled up from the tops of the elms.

They led him back down the rise and, out of sight of the destruction, wrapped about by the scent of the trees, he calmed immediately. Cuthred fashioned blinkers from fallen bark, and Hild soaked a rag in vinegar. With Sintiadd walking with the rag just ahead of the pony they tried again.

The rooks were suddenly silent. Hild stopped, hand on seax, then heard the strange gull-like cry of the goshawk—eater of rooks—and motioned them on.

This time Dwmplen did not start whiffling and shying until they were past the burnt palisade. This was as close as they were going to get. Gladmær unhitched the cart and Hild told him to lead the trembling beast back to the trees. Sintiadd, Cuthred, and Uinniau unloaded sacks of lime, rope, bundles of rags, spades, and a small clanking cask of assorted iron and wood tools.

To Rhin, she merely handed the soaked rag and tilted her head east along the river. He nodded, and began wrapping his mouth and nose.

Her first stop was the byre. It stank. Only Cadwallon would kill perfectly good horses, but the remains of two—stallions by the size of their hooves—lay where his men had hacked them down in their stalls. Big though they were, there was not much left of them: They had been partly scattered and eaten by scavengers. One leg bone showed clear butchery marks and she wondered who had done that, and whether they were long gone, still lurking, or indeed had made it to Menewood. She nodded to Cuthred to take his axe to the one in the right-hand stall so they could drag it piecemeal out of the way. After that, it did not take long to sweep aside the filthy straw and expose the boards of the byre's floor. Someone had been there before them, before the horse fell—the boards were hacked about—but either they had run out of time or had decided no one would bother going to the trouble to build such beautifully laid and tightly pegged boards if they meant to destroy them to get at anything buried. She had counted on that. She hefted her mallet and knocked out the cunningly laid side sills, then the tight pegs, and levered up the boards one by one.

Beneath the boards the pit reeked. It was littered with the usual byre waste, and bits of broken bridle rings, a file—somebody would have been walloped for losing that; she put it in her belt—and tiny skeletons, mice mainly. Below that was a layer of flat, green-mossed stone once used in the church Stephanus had destroyed. Uinniau looked at the dirt and filth deep between the stones. "They could have been laid in the time of Eliffer of the Great Retinue."

This was the second barrier she had counted on. She fitted the pry blade to the end of her staff, rocked it back and forth, deeper in, levered, and popped those up, too.

Immediately she saw the braided leather handles coiled neatly on top of the barrels of butter, cheese, and salt pork. Undisturbed. "Wait," she said to Uinniau, who had bent to the first barrel. "You'll need help."

Even for both of them it was gruntingly hard to muscle the first cask up onto the floor. Far too heavy for just butter. He looked at her but said nothing. One other cask was equally heavy, but the remaining four were exactly as they seemed: cheese and salt pork and butter. They rolled them over the turf to the cart.

She led Uinniau and Sintiadd to the next cache.

Sacks of salt. Tuns of honey. A plain box of peppercorns sealed in wax. And half a dozen big sacks of hazelnuts, all of which were as they seemed.

In the raised grain shed by the big bread oven, the sacks of flour sewn with silver pæningas were gone. She had expected that; men searching for spoil would not leave until they had found something. Farther west, the stack of lead pigs, two bars in the second-to-bottom row carefully hollowed out and filled with gold bits set in wax, was also gone. Beneath the weaving hut, under the usual rubbish of broken shears and fallen loom weights, half the barrels of roots packed in straw were spoilt—the horses might eat the least spoilt—but the tiny silver bars were still nestled between them. "Don't sort it, just load it all." She would not feel safe until they were all back in the valley.

She showed them the hidden fields of beet and turnip. They would be bitter, left so long, but edible. "And when you're done, wait by the cart. Eat if you can."

She did not stay to help or share the food. She did not want anything in her stomach for what came next. At the palisade, she propped her staff against the stack of tools and boxes, tucked a pair of gauntlets under her belt, and unstoppered a bottle of vinegar, which she poured over a rag that she tied loosely around her neck. Then she took up an axe and two spades with her left hand, and hefted a bag of lime onto her right shoulder.

At the best of times, the tanning pits were vile, reeking of lime and urine and flensed flesh. There were stretching racks of different sizes between the pits for tanning leather.

She did her best to not see what was stretched on them now, from large to small, but dropped the sack of lime and one spade, and went to Rhin, who sat on the riverbank twenty paces west, staring into the river.

He turned to her briefly, face haggard and streaked, but said nothing. She sat next to him.

A swarm of gnats crisscrossed themselves like a badly wound ball of wool. Soon the flycatchers would be back. Perch would swim under that root overhang. In a month or two there would be tadpoles where she and

Cian had once— She looked upstream, away from the memory. The water flickered: minnows. Reflexively, she looked for otter sign. High up, a buzzard *kee-wicked* and slanted away, disappointed. She had no doubt what it had been expecting to feed on today.

She put her hand on Rhin's shoulder. He looked up. "Children," he said. "Just children."

She said nothing. After a moment she offered her hand. He took it, and then the axe, and together they pulled up their masks one-handed.

The pits were big, more than big enough for what the buzzard had not yet eaten. They cut them down from the racks, laid them out as tenderly as they could. It took a long time. They shook lime over them; it began to hiss and fume. Then they broke the racks and piled them for burning. Rhin stepped to the side of the first pit, flask of holy water in hand.

"No." It was not right to leave them like this.

And though she had intended the safest course, to leave the place seeming unvisited—the racks knocked down in some storm and burnt by passersby for a fire—she took her spade, dug up a shovelful of dirt, and sifted it over the pitiful remains. They were her people; they would be buried. She dug another shovelful. After a moment, Rhin stoppered his flask and joined her.

They worked steadily. They worked for a long time. When the pitiful remains were covered there was no mistaking the pits for anything but grave mounds dug by those who cared for the dead. Cadwallon if he came would know there was someone to look for still. Rhin once again took up his flask, shook holy water over the mounds, signed over them, and spoke a blessing.

"Amen," Hild said.

They watched the Yr moving, stately and steely, east.

"May Christ forgive him," Rhin said. "I cannot."

She would not even try. One day she would tear the heart from his chest.

Uinniau scratched Wolcen's poll and she huffed contentedly. Hild felt carefully around the mare's belly, then stepped back.

"Meadmonath?" he said.

"If not Litha." It depended on the size of the foal. "How big was the sire?"

"Big. The chosen mount of Rhoedd's chief sword, Mot Oer."

Mot Oer. Dismal Stick.

He saw the look on her face and shrugged. "It's what everyone calls him."

She had no particular interest in learning why a man might earn such a name. What mattered was that as a king's war leader, Mot Oer would have had a worthy mount, and so Wolcen's foal would likely be a fine beginning for their new herd. Though if she were king no gesith of hers would ride a stallion to war. One ripe mare, especially in spring . . . She thought about timing. "What was your uncle's chief gesith doing in Cetreht, so far from Rheged, in summer?"

"We weren't in Cetreht. Osric was hunting in the iron hills. Digging ore, holding war councils."

Begu had said nothing of this to her, which meant Uinniau had made no mention of it to Begu. She could think of one reason for that.

"Uinniau, what of Rhianmelldt?"

Uinniau sighed. "My father's man was in Craven to meet young Oswine, to gauge his suitability."

"And?"

"If his father takes Deira, and can hold it, Oswine will be judged worthy of Rhianmelldt."

No wonder he had said nothing. If the craven of Craven, Osric Whiphand, became king of Deira, his son Oswine became ætheling. As heir to Deira, a kingdom strong enough to defend Rheged, he would be perfect for Rhianmelldt, only daughter of Rhoedd king. On Rhoedd's death, Rheged would be safe. Uinniau, prince of Rheged, wanted that to happen. With Rhianmelldt married and Rheged safe, he would be free to marry Begu. Yet Begu was gemæcce to Hild Yffing: Osric Yffing's rival for Deira.

She did not bother to ask Uinniau how young Oswine felt about it. Oswine was as pleasant as fruit leather and just as pliant. He would not think to do anything but as his father commanded.

"And James the Deacon. What are his thoughts on the matter?"

"I don't know. He stayed in Cetreht."

A deacon of Rome would not be welcome in hall alongside the newly in-favour priest of Woden. So many gods and godmouths now on the isle. As many factions and power centres as kings and war leaders. She thought of the children's dirt map in York, and wondered how she might describe the priests of Hii and their abbot. Where did they fit?

"But he was well, when you saw him last?"

"He was. And still is, or at least the crav—Osric complained about him often." Wolcen shook her head and Uinniau patted her neck. They watched her amble off. "She needs exercise."

"I'll ride her if you like. So when did you leave Craven?"

"After the Yule feast."

Already in Craven it was no longer Christ Mass. "Tell me of that."

Hild lay with her hands behind her head, musing at the low roof of her new bower. A snug, tight roof—the roof tree was a strong, beautiful curve of elm; which of her new people had done that?—with warmth from the fire still lingering. Gwladus was with Breguswith in the old bower—those two talked often now. Wilfrid slept at the foot of the bed in his cradle and Begu at her left, making a noise somewhere between a soft snore and a sigh, which meant she was dreaming. Chests along one wall, and shelves above them, held their belongings. She could not see it in the dark, but she turned to where she knew that beautifully made but clumsily painted box, a gift from Begu in Mulstan's hall, long ago, still held those eight ivory wafers they had used for their first tablet weaving. The violet silk was long gone, replaced with fine salmon-coloured linen, a gift from Onnen, who now lived by the bay where Begu had grown up.

"You're thinking so loud you woke me up," Begu said. "So what is it?"

"How did you celebrate Yule in Mulstan's hall?"

Begu turned on her side to face her. "How does anyone? Food and feasting and fireside songs. Boasting. Drinking, lots of drinking. The wassail cup with apples bobbing in it. One night for the children. One for the fallen. One for the mothers and the mother gods. Not so different from Christ Mass, only without the Mass. Like it was at York before we were baptised, though not as grand. Why?"

"Something Uinniau said about Osric Whiphand."

Begu yawned and rearranged her pillow. "Winny said? What was that?"

"Osric wore a helmet. A helmet in hall. Like something from the long ago. When was the last time you saw that? And it was his best helmet; Uinniau described it. I've seen him wear it before, the one with the red jewels as eyebrows. Only he had picked out the jewels around the left eye, picked them out so it looked dark. Like one-eyed Woden."

Begu made a vague noise.

"He wanted to look like a king of old whose forebears were gods, a warrior god king giving hero gifts."

Begu began to snore. Hild sighed.

And all the gifts had been swords, Uinniau said. James had not been invited; he had stayed in Cetreht in the church he built. But all the thegns went with Osric, deep into the iron hills, and sang of blades and blood, of the deeds of Yffings and their descent from Woden. She needed to get a message to James, find out what Osric planned. She doubted he was going to wait for summer.

The east door of the long house let in morning light that picked out every scar on the plank floor. Compared to the wall hangings that Breguswith had ordered brought from Caer Loid for safekeeping—hangings fit for the lady of Elmet; made of finely spun and beautifully woven wool of brilliant colours—it seemed the floor of a ceorl. But it was the best floor in Mene-wood, and nearly level.

Sitting on it cross-legged, like an impossible folding of sticks, Ceadwin played with Wilfrid. He set the blocks—Oeric had given them to Hild for Wilfrid as an Œstre gift—one on top of the other and Wilfrid knocked them down. "Ba!" said Wilfrid. "Ba, ba, ba!"

She watched them from her stool as she chewed. Ceadwin seemed listless. He reached his long arms and spidery fingers—so long they seemed as thin as Tette's had before she died—for the blocks.

"Ba!" Wilfrid said again, but this time with an edge.

He was getting hungry. She picked him up and settled him on her knee. She tried the apple mush first; he gave her a deliberate look, stuck his tongue out, and let it drool to the floor. She tried the chewed pork. Wilfrid spat it at Ceadwin.

Ceadwin stared at the mess on his tunic, then looked up at Hild and tried to smile.

She was shocked at his dull eyes and pale gums. "Ceadwin, how are your teeth?"

He looked confused.

"Are they loose? No? Then eat this." She handed him the unchewed half of the wrinkled apple. "Eat every scrap. And the core." She thought as he ate. "Good. Now, go find Sintiadd. She was heading for the fork of the beck to fish for krebs."

He hauled himself to his feet with the same ungainly gangle as a heron taking off.

"And find . . ." She tried to remember the name of Menewood's only new mother, the one who had kept herself alive, foraging, for weeks before coming to the valley. "Find Fllur, too."

What they needed was fresh stuff: the shoots bright and crisp with new life. How many Menewood folk were dull-eyed? Why hadn't she seen it before? She unfastened her dress. When had the radishes gone in? They could harvest the first of those very soon. Meanwhile, they could pull the last of the leeks. There would be turnip greens in two weeks. But if there were more like Ceadwin, they couldn't wait two weeks. She had seen this before: teeth loosening, hair falling out, joints swollen, old wounds splitting open like peapods . . .

Wilfrid sucked greedily at her breast. She winced. He began to croon as he sucked and her heart danced a slow complicated dance: Honey, Wilfrid, bones by a tree, nothing but water . . .

The two young women came in. Sintiadd thin—they were all thin at this time of year—but bright, Fllur folded in, trying to use Sintiadd as a shield and holding her tiny infant as though it were another. Her final shield was her hair, which she wore hanging over her eyes.

Hild spoke British. "How's your bairn? What's the wee thing's name?"

"Geren, lady."

"He looks strong. Your milk must indeed be full and flowing."

Now she could see one bright eye peeking through the hair.

"Fllur, your lady asks of you a gift. Wilfrid is not yet wholly weaned. Perhaps you would consent to be his milk mother."

Fllur said nothing. Perhaps she did not understand. Well, someone would explain it to her.

Hild turned to Sintiadd, stayed with British. "We've need of fresh green stuff. Birch leaves and fern tips. Dock leaves and dandelion. Figwort if they're in leaf yet—but just the leaves; let the roots grow." She never wanted to taste those again. "Fllur will help."

Later, with Rhin, she paced the site between the pond and the beck of what might, when they were safe, become their mill. When they first settled here they had taken down the last of the stones lining the millrace and used many of them as footings for wooden sills for the long house and the first huts. They had built everything in Menewood that way: They could vanish as though they had never been.

But that was not true of a mill. Even now, generations later, you could tell there had been one, if you looked. A mill was a forever thing; it made a mark. It said: *I am here.* It said: *I am strong enough to defend my land and people.* And how to do that was something she did not know, yet.

"We'll need a church, too, soon enough," Rhin said. "But where we'll put—"

"Lady!" Morud, with blood on his hands. "Rulf's axe slipped."

Rulf, the same rawboned youth who that morning had got into an argument with steady Duv, about the right ways and wrong ways to build a new fence.

"Your lady mother says come now, if you please."

The next day Maer walked ahead of her on the faint path that ran along the north side of the valley. Now that the child had gained a little weight and was returning to the unformed look of childhood, Hild saw that she was younger than Hild had thought; she would need teaching everything.

She touched Maer on the shoulder, and pointed down to a slim tree growing in the dip that often flooded when the pool overflowed. "See that birch? How she looks as though she has just thrown up her hands, like the cook when Morud steals another barley cake?"

Maer nodded. She stole barley cakes, too.

She took Maer's hand and led her to the tree. "This is a downy birch."

"It looks soft."

"It does, doesn't it?" But that downy look was a lie. "Here." She picked the child up and held her so she could reach and feel for herself. "See?"

She set her down and ripped off two branches; bent, careful not to loom over the child; and handed them to her. "You pull them into twigs, like this. Little ones to make a whisk and bigger ones for a brush."

Maer immediately pulled a twig from a branch with her chubby hand.

"Good. But let's wait to do the rest until we get back, otherwise we'll be dropping twigs all along the path. One more, I think." She handed Maer another branch. "That's enough from this tree. You never want to pull too many off at one time."

Maer nodded and seemed to be listening but Hild could tell from the way her eyes darted back and forth that she was making sure of hiding places, just in case.

She squatted. "Maer, while I live you will never be hungry again. But if you ever worry that you might be hungry, remember this surprised tree. When you see those upturned branches, remember you can pull the inner bark off and grind it up to add to flour. And they grow good fungus to use to start fires." And the wood was beautiful, fine and pale and smooth-grained. "And this?" She tapped a thin wooden pipe punched into its trunk at the height of her breastbone. "When the sap rises you can drain it. My mother adds it to her beer. It makes people laugh and talk fast."

"Like mead."

"Yes, just like mead. Though—"

"Lady!" Oeric, calling from farther up the path.

For a breath she thought of hiding with the girl until Oeric passed. But there would just be more questions, more quarrels to mend when she emerged. She sighed, stood, and waved, then squatted again and pulled a twist of twine from her pocket. While Oeric thrashed his way towards them she showed the child how to tie the branches together. Then Oeric was there, looking set and hard.

"Leofdæg's at Caer Loid, lady, with a messenger from Craven."

On the rise near Caer Loid, Hild stayed behind the trees, watching. In what had been the orchard, Leofdæg and Gladmær had the messenger off his horse, blindfolded, and, like the horse—a bay mare with black points—very loosely hobbled. His back was to her. She stepped silently into the open.

Gladmær saw her first but she put a finger to her lips. When she was close enough to hear, she nodded to Leofdæg, who took the man by the shoulders and faced him towards the river.

"Now tell us again," Leofdæg said.

"I've already told you. Twice. And my lord, Osric Yffing, the rightful king of Deira, has no kindness for those who try his patience."

Leofdæg did not bother to respond, just slid his seax out of its sheath and back again, loudly, until the Craven man understood: The would-be king would never know his patience had been tried if his messenger never returned.

The messenger cleared his throat, straightened, and said in a voice that had no doubt been impressive the first time but now sounded a little rote: "Osric Yffing, by right of blood king of Deira, and so of Elmet, demands that Cian Boldcloak or whosoever now styles himself lord of Elmet, gather his spears and meet his king at Cetreht two days before the coming full moon. There he will bend the knee, kiss his king's ring, and march with all loyal thegns to destroy the wealh intruder!"

"I like this next bit," Gladmær said in an admiring voice.

The messenger gave him an annoyed look, or, rather, gave a look about half a pace from where Gladmær stood, which made Gladmær laugh, which made the messenger even more cross. But he went on: "The great and glorious giver of gold, Osric Yffing, Osric king, demands Elmet bring ten gesiths and twoscore spears."

The messenger tugged a heavy gold cuff from his right wrist and held it aloft, as a huntsman might the heart. "By this token Osric Yffing demands it! By this token he swears you will be rewarded!"

Leofdæg looked at Hild.

Two days before the full moon: three weeks from now. Did Osric have some word of Cadwallon's or Penda's plans?

After a moment she pointed at Gladmær to stay with the messenger, and then at Leofdæg to follow her.

When they were out of earshot she said, "He may keep his seax and two days' food. We'll take the rest, including the horse. Bring it to me here before you leave. You'll take him to the Gap. Leave the blindfold on until you're a mile or two upriver. Find out, without him knowing that's what you're doing, what Osric knows of Penda and Cadwallon. Does he have word of them leaving York? But, Leofdæg, make sure neither of you tell him anything. Not even lies."

Hild did not want to go back to endless interruption; to feed Wilfrid; decide which ravaged steading to venture to next; try to eke another meal from a dwindling store; hope the slugs had not eaten the pea shoots; and make all the decisions that could only be made by the lady of Menewood. She wanted to be where she could see to the horizon, somewhere to think.

So even though it had started to rain, she rode the Craven mare the long way back, alongside the war street, then west towards the mouth of the valley. Over the hornbeam's fallen bough—which the mare took neatly, wasting no effort. Then cantering between trees, lithe and supple. The mare had an easy stride, and she was fast, a messenger's horse. There was the pollard. She reined in, and the mare came off the boil as fast as a pot swung from the fire: no fidget, no shuffle; stock-still and silent. A scout's horse, too, then.

The bark was damp. Her feet slipped a little as she climbed, but feet and tree were old friends. In a moment she was at the great west-north bough, sitting, focusing directly ahead on the buds bursting and spilling green, vivid as kerchiefs from a sleeve. Birds sang farther up the valley.

Below her the mare moved a step forward, head still down, tearing the grass.

Finally, she lifted her gaze. The hedgepig still sat, nose tilted into the wind, but although its coat was wet, the tips of its prickles did not glisten, nor its eye wink. She reached out. Perhaps her fingers, like her heart, had hardened and set; the hedgepig's prickles did not prickle. Just wood, a lump of carved wood. No longer a hope, a story, a string running unbroken into the future.

Cian was gone. Honey was gone. Honey would have no little Honey of her own to bring here and tell of her mother, and her mother's mother. No one now but Hild could climb this oak and understand who had carved this hedgepig and why. It would become one more forgotten thing. No one but her would laugh when she talked of the hægtes that lived in a frog by the Sancton pool. That part of her that always lit and warmed when she turned towards Cian, wherever he was, was dull and dark. When she sought inside she found nothing but a void, a great hole where half of who she was—all those memories only Cian shared—had fallen in and turned to ash. Hild Gul. Hild the gaunt, Hild the empty.

She lifted her hands from the hedgepig. Big hands, strong hands, meant to hold and protect. Who would she hold, what would she protect? She needed to get away and really think. And she needed to trace the boundaries of the valley she must hold, seek where they might spread and grow. The best way now to lay claim to a place was to know it, to use it, to grow it. And to stay hidden.

17

＋

Four miles north of the pollard, upstream, hidden behind a tangle of new-leafed hawthorn, Hild watched as a vixen sniffed, pawed at a disturbed food cache, and sniffed again. Clearly what she learnt did not please her: She pissed on the empty cache in disgust, sat, and began to lick her chest. She licked for a while, eyes yellow as amber. When she trotted off, Hild stripped a handful of the bright leaves—bright even under the thin cloud—greedy for the green growing life of them, and chewed as she followed the fox across the redcrest road, a narrower road than the war street, with room for only three carts or two wagons to travel abreast, climbing, always climbing. The beck ran faster here, the sides of its valley were steeply sloped and wooded, the grass starred with wood anemones. She passed a ruined fort on the other side of the road. Sometimes interesting herbs grew in the sheltered corners of redcrest ruins; she would check another time.

Still tracking the trotting fox, she followed the beck north and west under the trees, past bluebells budded but not yet open and figwort not yet ready to pull up. The sun slipped free of the cloud and light splashed on the world, washing the fox fur to a blaze of red and the small dell ahead to green-gold. There the vixen went to earth in her den among the roots of a newly leafed rowan tree.

Hild sank behind a stand of ferns where the dirt underfoot smelled rested and cool, untroubled by anything but sun and beetles and green growing things. The sun was warm on her back and for a while she thought contentedly of nothing.

Two vixens brought the den's cubs out into the light to play. As the cubs played she chewed the last of the hawthorn leaves and thought of the hawthorn growing by the cliffs near Mulstanton, the rows of shrivelled butcherbird trophies. By the Bay of the Beacon it would now be noticeably cooler than inland. She imagined Onnen tucking a fur around Mulstan's legs. How was the old thegn?

Before he had sworn to Edwin, Mulstan had been Æthelfrith Iding's man, though he had not followed his king's sons into exile. But now the eldest surviving Iding was making ready to reclaim Bernicia. Eanfrid Iding would have been a stripling when Mulstan knew him. He was a man in full flower now—but was he a man who could wake old loyalties? Would Mulstan declare for the son of his old king? Now more than ever she longed to sit with the old man by the little beck and talk of the water wolf that lived there, and what it was to be brave.

And where were the Bryneich in all this, and the other men of the north? She knew nothing of Eanfrid Iding's strengths or weaknesses. She knew stories of his half brother, Oswald, both the praise songs of the wars of the Dál Riata and the way Aidan spoke of him. And Oswald could write. Were the brothers alike in this? In anything? Eanfrid Iding's mother was Bebba of the Bryneich; Oswald's was Acha, Edwin's sister—Hild's aunt, though they had never met, and never would, for Acha died giving birth to the twins, Oswiu and Æbbe. Both Eanfrid and Oswald were sons of Æthelfrith Iding, but one was kin, the other not.

If Fursey were here she would send him to the bay, as she had long ago. She would trust him to glean what Mulstan knew. If it were not so early in the year she could send Begu by sea, perhaps with Gladmær, and then together they could travel farther north, to the Bryneich, where Coledauc might tell them where his oath lay now. But the seas were unchancy still— and she no longer had a boat; no longer had the gold to spare to send for Cenhelm and the Curlew. What gold and hacksilver they had was for horses and grain, a brace of oxen and a good plough, the pig iron to forge plough blades and sickle blades. And what was left over would be for hunting blades, hunting points, and only then, if any were left, war blades—though she did not have the men to wield them. And even if she did, she did not want to fight in the open.

Both vixens pointed their ears and lengthened their necks, and she thought she heard the faintest cry on the wind. One barked, soft and sudden, then each took the nearest cub by the neck and disappeared into the den. The other cubs followed, yipping and squeaking.

She followed the beck up and up past small freshets that joined it and little rills she guessed in summer might dry to nothing. Up and up a heathland slope on the eastern edge of a cefn, a long, high ridge of gritstone clothed in tussocky heather and gorse and jumbled with jutting rock. The ground steepened as she climbed, up and up until she found the summit, and looked down a steep rock face north into the Weorf valley.

It was almost as high as at Ad Gefrin, but better, because this was the north tip of Menewood; this was home. Wind whipped over the heather and gorse and blew air like spring water into her face. She felt it stir the ashes in her otherwise empty heart, lift them a little, and blow a layer away. She tipped her head back and let it blow.

She turned slowly, shading her eyes against the wind that whipped from the west along the crest of the ridge. Right in the eye of the wind lay the moors near Hillacleg where she and Wilfram and Cuthred had driven away the raiders from Craven. Beyond that, Craven itself. If Osric chose to march from the mines—which was what she would do—he could take either the narrow redcrest road that ran past the cefn or the more southerly trail through the Yr Gap. Either way, from here a watcher would see him.

But he would not march from the mines. He was raising his banners at Cetreht. He would march south on the war street, the great vein that pumped armies in and out of Northumbre. East of here. Perhaps on a fine day in late afternoon a watcher might catch the distant gleam on a polished shield boss. She turned, squinted. No, it was too far. Even for someone with eyes like Leofdæg.

What was Osric thinking? Did he plan to trap Cadwallon in York? How? He could not hope to catch him unawares.

What would she do if she had Craven to protect and Osric's men to protect it? She would split them into two. Set one band across the war street north of where the road from York joined, and another on the redcrest road near Hillacleg. But protecting Craven was not what Osric wanted; he wanted Deira, all of it: Craven and Elmet, then the fertile wolds, and on, east to the sea and south to the great Humbre. That was the rich heart of Deira. That was not all he wanted. He would not be satisfied until he had won back all the gold Penda and Cadwallon had taken from Edwin: the riches of Deira and Bernicia combined.

Penda, what did he want? He seemed a canny man. He would have realised by now that any plan he had to hold the north through Honey-tongue as a puppet king would not work. What would he do? He did not have a name as a destroyer, and the kernel of his kingdom, its centre and strength, lay south. He would go back there. Yes. He would take his share of the spoils and leave Northumbre to Cadwallon, for now.

Cadwallon would move farther north, to burn and spit and stamp on every corner of what his hated foster-brother had touched. And to take everything of worth. There were rich pickings still in Bernicia.

How many men did he have? He had begun with eightscore. Some would be dead. Would any Deirans join him? Perhaps—those who saw him win and win, who did not care that he only burnt crops and ruined land rather than hold and grow it, grow it and share it with his men. Not good men, not steady men. But a blade was a blade.

And Osric? How many men could he call? A hundred, two hundred? With two hundred men she could retake the north. But Osric was a fool, and Cadwallon, for all his faults, was not.

She kept turning, and now she looked south and east, down along her valley. Once Penda and Cadwallon left York, if they moved on any road west of the war street towards Menewood, from here she would see them.

Here, then. Here was where she would build a beacon. Another at the rocks near the bend in the beck. And another at the abandoned fort. That would be enough for now, for the numbers she had.

From here she could see how small her valley was; how alone. When she was in it, it felt too big, too heavy to carry on her own. Here, she knew Menewood was too small to survive without drawing on a wider hinter-land. That, then, was what she must do: build a wider web of settlements. But then how could she hide?

She climbed down out of the wind and found a spot where a rock twice her height sheltered a patch of springy turf and straggling yew. She settled with her back to the rock and ate some cheese.

She had a fortnight before Osric marched with his banners. Was there time? She would have to push and stretch and weave time, dig it, build it, carve it. Make time to put lookouts in all the high places, including the other side of the war street, perhaps no farther east than the farm where Saxfryth and Ceadwulf had kept sheep. Lookouts with horses. Lookouts with beacon fires. Lookouts who would know what they were watching for and who to run to first. If only she had ten men like Leofdæg. She did not. Not yet. But she would find them; she would train the rest. Cuthred had come a long way in a year.

She stood and stretched. Hours yet before dark, and all downhill. This might be the last time she had for herself, to really think, for a while.

18

✦

AGAINST THE GREEN SLOPES above Saxfryth's steading, sheep stood out
like drifts of dirty cloud, many with little, brighter puffs of cloud behind them. Lambs had been coming into this world since the one tree was
a sapling; it was no surprise some had survived even without a shepherd,
though there were more than Hild expected.

"Smart ewe must have led them," Uinniau said.

Hild nodded. The sheep of East Farm grew good fleece, some of the
finest wool in Deira. If the lambs were not yet hefted, they could run with
Menewood's small flock in the finger valleys off the beck. If they could
catch the ram, they might improve their breed. If she had the people, she
could run this steading. All the ifs.

Behind her she heard someone coming. Cuthred. He should learn to
breathe through his nose.

Either way, to run those sheep they would need a shepherd. And a dog.

"Lady," Cuthred said.

Hild turned. "You found them?"

"No, lady. No other graves but the ones you saw."

Nearly a score had lived here.

"Where did they go?" he said.

In the south of Elmet, just past Ceasterforda, Cadwallon had killed
senselessly, savagely, but never everyone, and Rhin had told her he had
heard Penda was careful to kill as few as possible. The survivors they drove

before them to York. The vision of Saxfryth being driven like a sow to market swelled her heart with hot, sick rage.

Hild squatted, tugged her sleeves to cover her arms against the barley's spiky awns, and pushed the stalk to one side. It was a strong green all the way up. Carefully, she worked the seed head; it remained upright. She straightened and brushed her skirts. "Yes. Half-moon at the earliest."

Breguswith nodded. "At least the rain's stopped."

"We're lucky you managed to sow so much. It can't have been easy."

"No." And that was all Breguswith said about forcing men and women who barely knew her to break soil and haul away stones, draw shallow furrows with sticks, scatter seed in rows, bend, cover with more soil, over and over again while the wind when it turned from the south and east brought the stench of smoke and carrion and all they wanted to do was run and hide.

The sharp, shattering whinny of Bone running with the new mare—Morud had taken one look and named her Lél—made them both smile. She would try Bone with a saddle soon.

They walked back down the path towards the long house, and smelled the last of the winter onion and leeks cooking. By the time they harvested the barley, their wheat would have been gone a fortnight and their oats running low. But by then they would be living like queens from the garth.

Hild peeled one more baby turnip, small and sweet as an apple. She wanted bread, but that was something shared sparingly now. Rhin poured for them all: Hild, Begu, Breguswith, Oeric, Gwladus. Hild sipped from her well-turned cup, enjoying the light smooth maple. After the last half year, she would never not be glad to have her own cup to drink from.

"Before men marched from Goodmanham they sowed the winter wheat," Rhin said.

"But did Cadwallon leave any to harvest?" Begu said.

"Or anyone to harvest it?" Gwladus.

"Beyond our honey and oats we won't have much to harvest ourselves here in autumn," Rhin said. "That would leave hands free. And much could change between now and Harvestmonath."

"It could," Breguswith said—*and for the worse*, her expression said. "But if we want to take those wheatfields we'll need to be there long before Harvestmonath—and with more than scythes and willing hands."

Gwladus was nodding. Hild sipped more mead, rolled it around in her mouth. Light, but with the tangy aftertaste of late-season honey: yarrow and asters and witch hazel.

Breguswith looked at her. "How many blades can we field now?"

Blades in the traditional sense, three: Leofdæg, Gladmær, and Oeric. Plus Cuthred, who had some training, Aldnoth and Sitric, who might do in a pinch, and a handful more who could wield spears. And she would bet her bog oak staff against any sword.

"If there are no Goodmanham folk, we'll take the wheat," Hild said. "But if there are, we'll trade."

"And when the mead's gone on wheat, what will we trade for iron?" Breguswith said. "For salt? What will we trade for oxen? For enough wheat seed to sow as well as eat?"

"And then there's wool," Begu said.

"And horses," Oeric said. "We need it all. And all we have to offer is the mead. And silver."

And gold, Hild thought. But the fewer who knew about that the better.

"There'll be hazelnuts at mastfall," Rhin said. "And if we can get to it, there'll be salmon in Cock Beck." But even he was beginning to sound doubtful.

Gwladus was watching Hild. "Our lady is not thinking of mead. Or silver or fish or nuts."

For a heartbeat she thought of walking out, saddling Lél, and riding away. Her plan was a risk, a great risk: to be seen and known.

Gwladus looked at her steadily.

Hild sighed. She put her cup down. "No, I'm not."

She looked at her trusted people.

"We will go to Goodmanham. If there's wheat but no one to harvest it, we'll do it. If there are harvesters, then we'll protect them while they harvest, and take a tithe for our trouble. For everything else, we trade."

Begu frowned and opened her mouth. Hild up her hand.

"We trade on my name. We trade on my protection." It was what lords did, what they had always done. If they went to Goodmanham it would be because Cadwallon was gone and not coming back for a while.

Breguswith looked satisfied, and Hild knew she was thinking: If the folk would not trade a tithe for protection, then they would simply take it all.

"But while we can, we trade." She met their gaze one by one until each nodded, then picked up her cup again. "What else?"

"York," Rhin said. "There's a lot of coming and going. Penda's riders and Cadwallon's, only they've not been killing and burning, just stripping the folk of the foodstuffs thought too poor in autumn, and driving them inside the walls."

"Does your man know why?"

"Couldn't say. I haven't heard from him for two days. Could be he's one of those caught up and driven in."

Three days until the full moon. Osric's banners would already be gathering at Cetreht.

"They know about Osric," she said. "They'll be leaving soon." And they would not want any bright eyes watching and relating their movements: Their scouts might be going out already.

Now there was no time left. They had to hide.

To her mother she said, "Bake half our remaining grain, twice bake what you can. This time tomorrow our fires go out and stay out until they've emptied York. Oeric, send for Leofdæg."

The fires were out. The men and two women Leofdæg thought best were out watching roads and fords, with Sandy at the abandoned redcrest fort to run south, and Dwmplen between Brid's Dyke and the Aberford road to run west, and Leofdæg on Lél roaming between.

On the night of the full moon Gladmær returned on Dwmplen with word from Leofdæg—Penda's advance party was almost at Aberford—then went back out because he had left Sintiadd to watch on her own.

Penda moved fast: The next day his advance party reached the Kelder and crossed at Ceasterforda, and Penda himself and his main band passed Aberford. Then word came from Leofdæg: Swift, lightly armed horsemen—Cadwallon's by the cloaks—were heading north.

So. Penda was leaving, heading south, but Cadwallon had just sent scouts or messengers north; he planned to march to meet Osric's army.

A thick and troubled dream of Cian singing to her as his brains leaked in the snow, only it wasn't snow, it was blossoms, and he had to get up, they were coming, they were coming, and she bent and lifted him like he was a length of heavy cloth, wet from dye, hanging long and long over each arm, and the hooves were drumming, thrumming under her feet, under her back—

—and they were real hooves, many, more than she had heard at once since the tumult at Caer Daun. She pushed her mother aside and was up and out the door, staff balanced in one hand and pointing forward into the late-spring night before she was fully awake. Moonlight shone and dulled and shone again as clouds glided overhead. She could see nothing but trees, smell nothing but sharp new leaves and fresh-turned earth. She listened. Four, maybe five horses, big ones; at least one heavily laden. Oeric came running, tugging his chinstrap tight.

"Who—"

"Shh." She listened again. Four. And coming from the south and west— coming from Caer Loid. No wink of mail through the trees, but there, the well-muffled chink of bit and bridle and, oh, she knew that sound: a gesith's horse-harness wealth. Between one beat and another Sitric and Aldnoth were there, too, spears forward.

The horses slowed, she heard a soft order, then a single horse—a quiet horse, no sound from its tack—moving forward. A shadow on the other side of the beck grew and sharpened; canted shoulders: Leofdæg, with Lél. Just before the moon was hidden again she caught a gleam of dried foam on the mare's shoulders, but she wasn't blowing. The hard riding had been earlier.

She motioned for Oeric to stay, then to Sitric and Aldnoth to fade back to the side, out of sight, and stepped forward. She did not drop her staff.

"Lady," Leofdæg said softly. "I bring an old friend. And three others. Escaped from York."

Three horses and a mule stood, noses together—big horses, well-muscled, their bridles and saddles oddly lumpen; the mule was a big one, too, and heavily laden—tired but not drooping, unlike three of the four riders: two riding double, heavily bundled, and one whose shaved forehead gleamed in the light. Three horses and a mule. Big, beautiful, strong, glossy, well-trained warhorses. One riding bareback, but from the look of the others' wrapped tack, their horses wore the jewelled and gilded wealth of their former owners. Those two mounts also carried heavy packs, and the mule—with long, strong legs—was just this side of overburdened.

She was aware of a question from one of the two riding double to the other—a woman's voice; both women—but she had eyes only for the fourth, who slid off his unsaddled horse and waited.

Bryhtsige.

Bryhtsige had been beautiful before, an eerie mix of fineness and strength, but now in the moonlight he looked unearthly: a drop of cold water fallen from another world.

How did you do it? Hild asked him—not how had he escaped York, but how had he escaped Caer Daun with his life.

He had come to under a pile of bodies while the victors roamed the field stripping the dead, their camp women and slaves killing the wounded. He had dragged himself behind a crumbled wall. "There was no escape, and I had lost blood. But out of sight I cut off my hair, took off my armour and clothes, and dropped them down the disused well."

His face was still and voice tranquil, but the knuckles around his cup were bone white.

"They found me barefoot in a torn tunic with no hose or breeches. And I said, 'I am a slave, lord, a poor bewildered slave, and my master, my beautiful master, is dead.' They took me with them to York. There they sold me to two men, brothers in arms though for different lords."

He seemed to flicker and fade in the swaying light of the tallow.

"It was my choice: die unbowed and proud, or live disgraced."

He had known that any slaver would take one look at his hands and his fine face, at his cut sack, and would sell him as a pleasure slave.

Hild said nothing. Everyone made their choice.

"They used me," he said. "They used me for months, until by Yule all they saw was a puppy eager to be used, to be fed, patted, and forgotten."

They forgot he was there. They talked. He had listened and learnt, befriended all the folk coming and going, and helped as he could.

"And when Penda was readying to leave for the south, and Cadwallon to move north, my—the two—the men were to part, one with each lord, and I saw how it would be: They would use me half to death on their last night, then strangle me together so that neither might keep me for himself and no other have me afterwards. I poured heavily for them, with herbs one of the kitchen women knew. And before they were halfway done they fell asleep. I stripped them, stripped their gear, and left them dead."

His ill-users might never breathe again but she knew that, for him, they would never be dead.

"When five hundred men and horse are drinking and swearing and packing, and groups are riding out every which way, it's easy to slip through the tumult."

She nodded. She knew the chaos of departure.

"I packed their arms and armour, found the others, and ran. But I want none of their gear. Not even their horses, though they are good beasts—they were well-treated and well-trained, at least. They are yours. Though I'll keep the black. We . . . understand one another."

An abused horse allowing a kindred spirit to ride it, though without saddle or bridle. "And the others?"

"Yours, too, lady. Though I hope you'll let the women choose for themselves."

"Why bring them to me?"

"That was not my intent. I didn't know you were here."

No rumours of an Yffing or of Menewood among the men of Cadwallon and Penda. Good. "Then where were you going?"

"Through the Gap."

"To Osric?"

He shook his head. "Through Craven to Rheged." Where they also hated Cadwallon. Where no one knew Bryhtsige. Where, in arms and armour of a southern lord and riding a warhorse, no one would see a king's gesith and wonder how he had survived the death of his king.

Rheged would be a good place for him and perhaps he should go. She was not sure she could wholly trust a man who had been broken. Though he did not act broken. Bent, perhaps, or heated and clarified; changed, yes, but not broken. And she could use his skill with horses. "And now?"

"I'd stay, lady. If you'd have me."

She nodded. "I'll take your oath and you'll have mine."

The moon was set. The world was still and dark. It would not be long before the early blackbirds sang.

"For now, tell me the rest. What of Honeytongue?"

The conversation lasted until dawn, but Hild did not try to sleep. There was too much to do and so little time. While she pondered what Bryhtsige had told her, she and her mother sorted what he had brought.

First, the travelling gear of two gesiths: bedrolls, strike lights, bowls, combs, knives. One bronze hand mirror inlaid in the old style. Then their jewelled belts, arm rings, scabbarded swords. No spears, no shields.

"Well-chosen," Breguswith said.

Hild nodded. Spears and shields weighed a lot for little value. She unsheathed each blade; both shimmered with the hammered pattern of snake steel. Fine blades.

From the style of the scabbards and the rings, one had been a man of Gwynedd and the other of Mercia. Breguswith counted the size and colours of the jewels on the war gear and rings, and cut marks on her tally sticks.

Hild stacked the gear into piles, then lugged in the horse harness, piece by piece. Breguswith's eyes gleamed as Hild slung the first saddle onto the trestle; the second saddle was even richer than the first, as were its matching headstall and tail piece.

Breguswith paused after counting the stones on the first headstall. "How did he do it?"

If Bryhtsige wanted her mother to know, he could tell her himself. "One of the new women knows something of butchery," she said instead. "And Honeytongue's dead. Penda killed him before he rode south."

"Ah." She cut another notch on one of her sticks.

Hild hefted the second saddle onto a bench. She had never seen so many different-coloured stones on horse tack. Edwin and his men liked red stones, garnets, with the occasional blue enamel or glass; not blue like these stones. She touched one of the big matching sapphires set either side of the cantle. Cold and smooth, like the stone in Paulinus's overbishop ring. Good stones. Each worth bushels of seed corn—though she was not sure what seed corn might cost now, or even if it could be found in the north at all. "Penda left Honeytongue's head with Cadwallon. To wave in Osric's face."

Breguswith huffed through her nose: Osric Yffing would not care; there was no love lost between him and Edwin's ætheling. She came up beside Hild, ran her hands over the worked metal and clustered stones. "Will the owner come looking for his property?"

"No."

"So now you are the owner."

"Yes."

"Then choose one saddle to keep splendid, and we'll unpick the other."

"Not yet," Hild said.

She might need more than one splendid saddle. Ten days ago, they had no ridable warhorse. Now they had three. And Bryhtsige could help the other two enough to make five. Wolcen would soon foal, then there would be six. With six well-armed and well-mounted men she had choices.

"Penda's gone south," she said. Leaving the north to Cadwallon. But she was beginning to understand Penda, how he thought; he would be back. "Tomorrow Cadwallon moves against Osric. After he crushes Osric, he'll move north to the wall."

Straight up Dere Street to Corabrig, Bryhtsige said. With no thought to holding, only to tearing out, tearing down any totem and sign of Yffing power. Cow the folk, kill the thegns, take the gold, and burn the rest. She flexed her hands, imagining Cadwallon's neck.

"They'll leave York for us?" Breguswith frowned, tested the edge of her knife.

Hild shook her head. "Forget York." It was too big to hold without a king's war band. She traced the raised patterns of silver and gold on the girth straps, then rested her hand on the smooth leather of the seat, thinking. "They're not even planning to hold Craven—just kill Osric and his war band."

Breguswith raised her eyebrows and put down her tally stick. She unfastened the whetstone from her belt. "Not even to make sure of Oswine?" She laid the blade on the stone.

Hild shook her head and gritted her teeth against the grind of steel on stone.

In Cadwallon's place she would send a strong party, the cream of her men, experienced and steady, to snip the head from what remained of Craven's power. It would not take long. But Cadwallon was driven by burning need, a need that blotted out everything but what lay immediately ahead: getting north, destroying all visible markers of Yffing power. He cared about Osric now because he lay in the path, while young Oswine did not. And after Osric he would care about taking Corabrig. Then Yeavering. And Bebbanburg. He wanted to be seen the victor, seen to have beaten the king more than he wanted to be a king.

But there had been talk, Bryhtsige said, of allowing a handful of young men, hotheads hungry for glory and a name, to risk themselves and try for young Oswine—the sort he could afford to lose.

Six glory-seekers, Bryhtsige said.

Six. Even the youngest and least experienced would ride fine horses. She wanted those horses.

Late morning, Hild leaned on the rail and watched their little herd. Bryhtsige stood next to her, faint shadows under his eyes, like hers, from lack of sleep, but alert enough. His hair glistened, newly washed, and just long enough to tie back with a thong. When it dried, though, it would not stay. He would need to grease it. He was thinner but he did not look weak, more like his strength had been heated, hammered, and honed.

Wolcen, lumbering as a troll, stood neck to neck with the mare the two women had ridden. Like Wolcen she was a roan, but redder; big and hard muscled. In the daylight, the priest's mount, a sorrel gelding, gleamed so like Acærn that whenever he shook his mane against the fly that kept coming in for a bite, Hild's heart caught. Someone had brushed out their coats and they looked fresh and strong.

They had been talking of ambushing the glory-seekers riding to attack young Oswine, but even an ideal trap—where half the band were dead before they even knew they had been attacked—would not be safe and certain without at least equal numbers. And to be safe and certain they would need to be hidden. And for that, they must ride as soon as they had word of their path, and they must get there first.

She nodded at the black, a stallion with massive hooves, tufted fetlocks, and a thick mane, who drank from the far trough. Even from here she could see the weal marks crisscrossing almost every inch of him. They were not old marks. If he hadn't been so magnificent they would have gelded him and cooled him down. "Could these mounts do the ride so soon?"

"We barely stretched them."

"And the others?"

Bryhtsige studied Bone, who stood warily on the north side of the paddock. The grey gelding had gained weight and his ears were pricked forward, but Hild could see the tension in his legs.

"Can you do it?" she said.

"Not in time. Not if you wanted to use him again. But I can ride the black, and others could take the roan and the sorrel."

"And there's Lél."

"Leofdæg's mare? She's been ridden hard."

Hild did not want to hear that. Three or even four was not enough. She needed six to be certain. And with so few resources she had to be certain.

"Tell me of this priest you brought."

At noon Hild had the priest sent to her in the garth. When he arrived she was holding a pea vine with one hand, and with the other feeling pods one after the other, pulling off the plump ones, dropping them in a basket.

He was unremarkable: brown hair, muddy hazel eyes, dusty black skirts. No face hair. A little soft around the middle. Neither young nor old.

"Lady," he said, and bent his head. There was no pale line along his forehead tonsure; he must shave it almost every day.

She stripped two more vines, then straightened, and stood. "Do you know me, priest?"

A pause. "Unless I miss my guess you are Hild Yffing." He spoke like the folk by the wall, flinging his words back into his mouth like an otter tossing back a fish. Not from Gwynedd.

"And you know this place?"

"I know Rhin. I bring a message, and news."

Such careful answers. "Speak your message and your news."

"I would speak it directly to Rhin."

"And I would hear it now." She did not lay her hand on her hilt but the slaughter seax was hard to miss. And if the man knew who she was he knew the stories.

He bowed his head again. "The message is from Coledauc of the Bryneich: Edwin Yffing is dead. And so, dead now, too, is the understanding between Yffing and Bryneich. However, the Bryneich trust not Cadwallon Bradawc"—Cadwallon the Treacherous—"so choose once again to side with the Iding—their kin through Bebba his mother—at least for a time. Though young Cuncar ab Coledauc is mindful of his connection to the Yffing Hild."

She rubbed the scar on her hand, remembering the ragged edge. For a time. Coledauc was always open to a better offer, especially for Yffing gold. "Is the Iding in Bernicia?"

"He is in Din Eidyn." Another beautifully careful answer: Some said Din Eidyn belonged to Bernicia, others not. "With him are a Pictish war band—a handful of younger sons—and some few Bernician lords of old."

Not lords of today, not lords of now but those who had held their lands under the Iding's father and lost them under Edwin. Old men, Mulstan's age, who had gone into exile with their ætheling, with perhaps a few hungry sons. And not the Pictish king's war band but, again, younger sons.

"The Iding has apostatised."

Old news. Like Osric, Eanfrid Iding hoped to rally the remaining Bernician thegns to his banner by calling to the old gods, gods of gold and glory, sword and song.

She surveyed the broad beans. They were beginning to flower; she must remind Breguswith to see that they were kept well-watered.

The priest, she noted, made no sign of impatience. "So. This is all your news?"

"No, lady. Fína of the Cenél nEógain is with child to Oswiu, the youngest Iding."

Just beyond the beck floated the long *twee*, the shivering trill of a wood warbler, the first of the year. A little early—whelping too soon, like the youngest Iding. And this Oswiu was whelping with a powerful clan, though one of Ireland and not of this isle. Oswiu's twin sister, Æbbe, though—if she were to whelp with Domnall Brecc, that would be a worry.

She sat on the old alder trunk gardeners often used as a bench and brushed the dirt from her knees. "What's your name, priest?"

"They call me Mallo, lady."

He was small and, though well-knit, gave the impression of roundedness. His lids drooped a little, yet despite the name she did not think he was either slow or lazy. But she could see he might often find it helpful for others to think so.

"How well do you know the west, north of the wall?"

"I have travelled to Alt Clut. I have seen the great rock."

"And north of that?"

"I speak a little of the Irish," he said in that tongue.

Not as good as her own but enough to be understood by the men of Dál Riata, enough to seek out Aidan. Could she trust him with the message? She would talk to Rhin. She would ask him, too, whether they had any good parchment left.

The evening star still hung in a cool, clear sky when the first messages came from her watchers.

It was begun, Sintiadd told her. Slaves were streaming from York in their dozens, dazed and half dead. They were wandering and uncertain. Many would not make it far.

From Cuthred: Cadwallon was moving, and his war band was bigger than they had thought, twelvescore at least.

Twelvescore. It was a shocking number. "How many mounted?"

"More than half. Aldnoth's gone ahead, off the road like you said, to wait for word from those watching farther north."

Aldnoth came before dawn. In the torchlit dark Dwmplen stood with his head hanging and ribs heaving. "Lady!"

"Tell me."

"Lord Osric and his men left Craven this morning. Moving slowly. Not yet at Masham."

Barely fifteen miles out from Cetreht. "Young Oswine was with him?"

He shook his head. "Not unless his banner was furled."

"Others were unfurled?" Unfurled banners slowed everyone down.

"The banners were bright and their hearts high."

So they were drunk: singing and shouting, banners flapping and gaudy in the wind; no doubt boasting of deeds to come, the slaughter of their enemies. They would march half the night: As the mead wore off, they would notice their sore feet, the weight of their weapons. Their horses would need feeding. The rearguard would start to straggle, trailing back into the cold thin dark before dawn, easy to pick off one by one. The men of Cetreht all over again. But Osric had never listened to a bard like old Ywain sing the hero songs. And he had not been at Hæðfeld. "And Cadwallon?"

"Also moving slowly."

"Slowly?" Not Cadwallon's usual way. "All twelvescore?"

"Lady?"

"Are all twelvescore moving in a body, horse with foot?"

"In a body, most on foot. But, lady, more like sixscore than twelve."

Cuthred had seen twelvescore. Several score were missing, mostly horsed. "Nothing on the west fork of Dere Street?"

"No, lady."

She stared through him. Where were they?

"I swear, lady. Nothing between us and the Nid but those—"

But she was already shouting for Bryhtsige and Leofdæg and Gladmær. Osric would be slaughtered, there was nothing she could do about that.

But when a war band dismounted and prepared for battle, there were always loose horses. Four of them could not face six armed gesiths, but they were more than able to round up a horse or two and return to Menewood with the enemy unaware they existed. But they had to leave now, and they had to ride hard through the day.

In the charcoal dark, just below the crest of the hill southeast of the old redcrest settlement, they heard the muted ring of steel and crouched, motionless. From the other side of the hilltop they heard a British voice, and two quiet replies. Hild reached out a long arm to her right and patted Leofdæg, then on her left Gladmær, and made a pushing motion: back!

The gesiths crawled backwards, low to the ground, while Hild stayed on her belly, listening. The nightingale had stopped singing; dawn was almost on them. Soon the sky would lighten enough that someone close and sharp-eyed might see them. But the wind would rise before the sun. Any cold, hungry, bored man sent with two friends to watch all night would seek shelter from its probing fingers. Yesterday, the wind had been from the north; she would bet it would be again this morning. And bet further that the men on watch would edge to the southeast slope for relief, towards where she waited unseen.

The sun warmed her back where she lay pressed belly down against the hillside, feeling the tremble of the river's roar. Wind hissed over the wiry grass. It stirred the hair of one of Cadwallon's men lying beside her, bareheaded, throat crushed, and eyes staring blankly at the grey sky— bareheaded because Bryhtsige now wore his hat, and cloak and shield, just as Leofdæg and Gladmær wore those of the man's companions. They sat on the skyline. To anyone in the fort below they would be black shapes facing vigilantly south. As the sun rose further it would light the bows at their backs, the familiar colours of cloak and shield, and anyone watching would be reassured that all was well to their rear.

She lifted her head high enough to see over the crest. Nothing.

The other two British men were below with Bryhtsige, still alive she hoped. When she had dragged them down she planned to leave them bound and gagged, to question later, but before she could say as much, Bryhtsige flicked his seax along the inside of one's upper arm, then grasped it in an iron grip, holding the vein closed. "If you move, even a little, if I let go, even for a breath, you will bleed white and die. Do you understand?"

The man nodded.

He cut the rope around the man's wrists. "Hold your arm tightly, just above my hand."

He did as he was told.

Bryhtsige let go, and turned to Hild. "Now, do you see, they will be quiet as lambs, and tell us all we need to know."

He untied the man's gag, wiped his blade on the man's tunic, then turned to the second, who shook his head frantically.

"Nah, nah," Bryhtsige said. "I have heard it all before. Hold still now so I don't cut more than you can hold. For I must go mind the horses, and you must stay here out of sight and silent. It's as one to me whether you do it as a dead man or alive. Choose now."

From the stillness of the faces of Gladmær and Leofdæg they, like her, had never seen the like. They had left the two men sitting quietly against the one tree at the bottom of the hill—left hands gripping desperately at their right upper arms while Bryhtsige murmured to the Menewood mounts picketed out of sight of the road and tended to their needs—and moved back up the hill to wait.

Now the sun was up and the wind blew from the northwest across the river Ur, over the fort, past the hill. None of Cadwallon's men or horses below would smell her men or mounts. All to her favour though not Osric's.

Cadwallon's dragon banner and a host of smaller ones hung from the outer walls facing north and west, away from her. They rippled now and then in the wind and showed where the walls had been roughly patched. Once, like York, the redcrest fort by the Ur had been part of old Elmet, but that had changed in the long ago, before even Ceredig's time. As new-made lady of Elmet she had paid no attention to the old burgh; it was Edwin's to ward.

Now she studied it carefully. Like many redcrest places it was a fort inside a larger walled place. On the outer walls, at odd intervals, towers thickened the ramparts, sometimes at a corner, sometimes near a gate. The intervals seemed wrong, unlike the usual orderly redcrest arrangement. A score of horses were picketed inside the east wall, and men, a dozen at most, huddled before campfires, barely visible in the seeping light. The rest were in the inner fort. Twelvescore of them, according to Cuthred. No more than sixscore, according to Aldnoth.

On their ride north it had been too dark for Leofdæg to read sign with certainty but he thought there were two places where groups of men could have left the road and moved into the trees to the west. At each Hild had stopped and listened and let their mounts sniff: nothing, no hint of a large body of horses and men breathing and farting. Good. She did not want to clash with armed groups ever again.

Below, nothing was stirring, and the few horses she saw were quiet. In the distance a flight of ducks hit the river in a flurry of squawks and rattles. She tightened and relaxed her muscles, set by set, to keep them warm.

The inner fort was in much better repair. It followed the same plan as York, but smaller: four gates, to north, south, east, and west, over four roads; even the same open spaces and principia building and what looked like byre blocks. Smaller than York, but still big enough for hundreds of men and horses. Unlike York, which was built on level ground, Urburg fitted into the north slope of the hill and was defended by it; the outer settlement walls were stretched out of true to encircle more of the flatter northern pasture that sloped down to the Ur. She looked more closely. No, not just for that. One of the rounded towers was at the tip of the bulge, and now she saw that from that height four men with bows might kill a hundred men on the pasture in less time than it would take to sing the bread song. She followed the walls, the towers, the slopes: A defender would not need more than a dozen bowmen to cover every approach except immediately south of the brow of the hill. Exactly where she was; where the dead man had met the tip of her staff.

She crept back, studied the river.

Two bridges crossed it. One, on the road that ran from the north gate, was a spur that moved east to join a road that ran north to the New Castle bridge across the Tine near the end of the wall. But Osric would march straight down from Cetreht, on the war street that ran straight from Corabrig, and cross by the Dere Street bridge, just west of that dark patch of . . . rocks? In the slanting light and shadow of dawn it was hard to tell. No, not rocks, too orderly. Whatever it was, it hid—from her and, she guessed, from the men in the fort—the point where the river Tutt fed into the Ur. If she were Osric it would be there she would water her horses, in small groups, shielded from bowshot from the walls. Though if she were Osric she would not have marched out to meet Cadwallon at all but picked off his men in small groups from the woods along the road. To do that, though, he would need bows. Anglisc gesiths refused bows: Bows were for nithings and bandits, those who skulk in the dark.

She resolved to use more bows. She never wanted a plain clash of equals again. Fighting blade to blade was for fools. From now on she wanted to strike from the dark, and only when she outnumbered her enemy.

Figures by the fires in the outer settlement were stirring now. She stared north along Dere Street, then swept the horizon. Nothing but those low hills north of the river and the two roads twisting into the distance. Where was Cadwallon? She rolled on her back, lifted her head a little, and scanned the southern approach. As Cuthred had said, nothing visible between there and the Nid. Or not moving in a body. Those hills to the south and west might be enough to hide knots of six or eight mounted men, and Cadwallon could be there, with five- or sixscore spread out. Two miles away. A horse could cover two miles in a blink.

Down below, men called back and forth—she could not hear the words but the tone was easy and unhurried—and a moment later there was movement as two disappeared under the arch of the west gate. Then one, bow in hand, climbed the northwest tower, and another, bow propped against the wall, walked open the west gate. Eight men moved out onto the short spur of road that joined Dere Street, which ran past the southwest corner of the fort: north, over the river, and on to Cetreht then Corabrig along the wall; south, to Aberford. Only two were armed. All carried canvas pails.

A loud thud signalled the door beam thumping back into its sill once the gate was closed. Then the second bowman joined the first in the tower.

As if the sound of the gate had been a signal, the inner fort came alive.

The men of Gwynedd ate around cookfires in the bulging northeastern corner in the wide space between walls. Aldnoth was right: nowhere near the twelvescore Cuthred spoke of. Sheafs of arrows stood in pots by the wall, and throwing spears leaned in triangles. The men wore their mail or leather, but were not yet helmed. If Cadwallon were among them, he looked no different from the others, and she knew of no king who suffered to look the same as his men. He was not here.

Down by the tree, one of the captured men had a rope tied around his arm, and both hands wrapped around a water bottle.

The other lay slumped in a pool of darkening blood.

Hild looked at Bryhtsige.

"He would not answer my question. The other"—a nod at the man drinking water—"did. And more besides."

The man was following everything Bryhtsige said with the attention and eagerness-to-please of a beaten dog.

"The lookouts, he tells me, were instructed, in case of an occurrence in the dark, to shoot a burning arrow as a signal. If, as they all believed to be more likely, nothing occurred, then they would be relieved before undern." The curious new rhythms of Bryhtsige's speech were more pronounced. Learnt, like these methods, from his captors?

"No password or secret sign?"

"He says not."

The man with the water nodded vigorously, or as vigorously as he dared. By now he would know that should he prove a liar the unearthly Anglisc would tie his hands together and unbind his arm, and he would be as good as dead before he took a breath.

"He said also that two of Craven's scouts—clumsy fellows, by his account, poorly concealed—watched them enter the fort. But they were left unharmed, for the lord Cadwallon wishes the lord Osric to have word of their number."

As morgen turned to undern and the light strengthened, the jumble of stones by the river became a bigger, wider version of the speaking stage Edwin had built in Yeavering. Much bigger. The wooden one at Yeavering looked like a small wedge of cheese; this was more like the wheel of cheese with a wedge missing. Built in the long ago by redcrests, the risers were still there, but the floor had turned into a giant honeycomb of brick columns and stones.

If they had used such things for speaking, the redcrests must have been giants indeed.

A flicker of colour drew her eye to the road from the north. The rippling boar banner of Osric Yffing at the head of a column of men. The banner was not as big as Edwin's nor as finely sewn, and with no cross, but it was brash and bright and bold. After no more than a short pause he marched the whole group across the bridge. Horse first, a score and more; then sixscore on foot, and they were singing and laughing; followed by a dozen and a half more horse.

No, she thought. No, you fool.

His scouts must have reached him, and reported sixscore men in the fort. Osric now felt himself a fine fellow, almost a king already: His one hundred and seventy men were many, so very many more than the sixscore in the fort. They spread out like a lazy lake on the pasture sloping down to the river. Here and there a thegn would have his men loosely picket their handful of horse, or stand half their spearmen down to eat while the other half watched, but most followed Osric's lead and milled about waiting for something to happen. It was Caer Daun all over again.

Her belly felt hollow.

Osric was a fool, but she had thought even a fool would know better. Even if he believed Cadwallon was in there with so few men, he should have sent half his spearmen down past the fort: one half of those to dig in at the fork of Dere Street and the road to the south gate; the other to the York road from the east gate. The half reserved should be ranged on the north side of the river, between Dere Street and the road to New Castle. The horses should be picketed and the men fed, and settling in to wait: The fort had no water.

But Cadwallon was not in the fort, just as he had not been with Penda at Caer Daun, and Osric and his proud Yffing banner, like Edwin and his, were about to be destroyed. If he had stayed on the other side of the river he might have stood a chance. More to the point, Hild's point, if he had picketed his horse there, as any experienced commander would have, when battle was joined she could have stolen a handful and ridden for Menewood.

There was no hope now of taking horses. And without that hope she would not risk being trapped in a slaughter. Cadwallon could attack anytime.

She turned and hissed to get Leofdæg's attention. *Back*, she mouthed. *Down and back.*

They were less than halfway down when a horn sounded, the east gate crashed open, and men marched forth.

They ran.

Hild did not remember leaping onto the roan's back, only kicking the mare into a dead run just as Cadwallon's men poured from the trees. She crouched low over the roan's neck. Her world narrowed to the space between its ears. Run, she thought, as the hind legs bunched and stretched. Run, she thought as the hooves drummed. Run.

She ran from the clash and choas, the swords and screams. She ran from all things Yffing. She ran and ran. But fate goes ever as it must.

There, ahead of them in bright undern light, six of Cadwallon's eager young glory-seekers, singing, riding to the war street at an angle that would cut Hild's path. They were laughing, cantering without care from the slaughter of the last war band in Deira, for now the way to the heart of Craven lay open, there would be nothing and no one to oppose them, and they were riding to glory, to add the head of young Oswine of Craven to their king's triumph, to kill the last Yffing.

Instead they met the Yffing who no longer wanted to be Yffing. Hild and three men running too fast to change course. Hild who lifted her gaze up, up from the horse's ears to those barely blooded gesiths and saw her wyrd.

Hild Yffing, Cath Llew and Butcherbird, lord and protector of her people, and the three Fiercesome survivors of Caer Daun, smashed into the bright fools and took their dreams, took their last breaths, and then took their horses, gear, and armour back to Menewood.

19

✦

Six stolen horses and their gear made it all the way to Menewood, but on the final rise one, a dun, crumpled among the trees, dead—leaking from a hole in its neck none had noticed. A sturdy, muscled beast that would have made a fine war mount. It was luck that the dun had fallen neck out facing uphill; less luck that it had not conveniently rolled on its back first . . .

Hild dismounted and stood looking at the dead beast. She blinked heavily. No sleep to speak of for two days. Riding to Urburg, hiding, killing from the dark, then this last ride, riding, fighting—fighting as she had thought she would never do again; so much death. She was so tired.

Now this fine beast was dead, dead as a stone, and her men waiting. The world felt different, changed in some way. This fine beast she had risked so much for was dead—but five were alive, and none of her men or their mounts were so much as scratched. Not one. It was a blessing, a gift. It was her wyrd.

But she was tired. Her men were looking at her, waiting. They were tired, too. Think.

Bryhtsige. The new women. Butchery—one of them knew something of butchery. She would send for her, and send her men and the other horses the half mile home.

She did, then she waited. She was stiff and sore after lying still for hours on dew-damp grass, followed by a hard gallop, harder fighting, and more riding. Yet as she waited for the woman, she now felt a vast deep calm, the sense of rightness, of many parts of her brought together and settling, as though she were no longer running.

She stretched. There, in the distance, the woman she had sent for. She was wearing a heavy apron and striding fast, carrying coils of rope and a leather tool roll as big as a bedroll.

As she watched her approach, Hild, with her staff in her right hand, reached up with her left, then swapped the staff and stretched the other side.

And the woman was there, standing, looking at the dead horse.

Hild rolled her shoulders. The side of her neck itched where it was splashed with blood. "You have a name?"

The woman folded her arms around her tool roll. "Depends who's asking. And you'll want to ask nicely."

Hild looked down at her. She was Cath Llew, Butcherbird, lord of Menewood. "This is my valley. You will give me your name."

The woman nodded, turned, and walked away. She was wearing breeches.

Hild stared. "Where are you going?"

Without slowing down the woman shouted back over her shoulder, "Out of your valley."

"I did not give you leave!"

The woman said something without turning around and was now far enough away that Hild did not hear it. She was too tired for this.

Ask, Afanc would say. *It's the fastest way to get what you want.*

"Stop!" The woman's stride faltered. "I ask you to stop." The woman stopped and turned and waited.

Hild walked to her.

"I am Hild Yffing, lord of this valley. I would ask your help to butcher this horse, and I would know your name."

"Brona," the woman said, and held out her arm. Her voice was mild but her eyes were granite: She offered the grip of equals or nothing. Hild clasped it. Corded muscle and hard bone under womanly skin. A bit more meat on her and it would be pleasingly soft.

The woman smiled faintly, and a memory dropped into Hild's head like an unreefed sail: York, a girl, blood on her arms, hanging something on a hook in the back of the lean-to booth; the wet thud-thud of a butcher's cleaver; a slight smile from the shadows as the girl's father cursed at a bone splinter.

"York," Hild said. "You're the butcher's daughter."

"Butcher these last months." Brona turned to the horse. "Pity it fell facedown. Always easier to start underneath." She walked around it. "Good meat on those bones."

"I want the hide whole."

"What for?"

Hild, hungry and tired and itching with others' blood, looked at her and thought maybe Afanc was a fool and she should just kill this woman, throw her in a pit with the horse, and go have a bath.

Brona took half a step back, then her chin went up. "If I know what you'll be using the leather for, I'll know where I can cut."

Hild looked down at her. That chin would fit easily in her palm. Turn it this way and those fine muscles would pull and her throat would be exposed, those plump red lips close enough to—

Hild turned away, shivering with a sudden hard need. "Not leather," she said, more harshly than she intended. "Parchment. To write on. As smooth as a—" She cleared her throat. "As smooth and unblemished as you can."

Brona knelt by the horse, ran a hand down its spine. "Still warm. Shouldn't be too hard to move." Her shoulders were clean and well-formed; as her hands traced the neck, muscles moved where the tops of her shoulders disappeared under her tunic. She turned to look up at Hild, hand shading eyes that were now more sun-warmed grey stone than cold granite. "He's already bled out, shouldn't be too hard between us. Unless you'd rather be in a hot bath being fed honeyed apples and white bread, if you think the lord of the valley should not get her fine clothes dirty." She looked at Hild's blood-splashed tunic, the soil on her cuffs. "Dirtier."

Hild was still tired, and even more hungry, but she wanted that meat and she wanted that hide and she wanted to be near this annoying, abrupt woman. "Show me your hands." No calluses in the right places. "I'll do the roping and hauling." A raw hand on raw meat would come to no good.

The beast was splayed wide, all four legs tied to trees, head higher than its tail. Brona stooped and unrolled her tools. She chose a clean cloth, which she tucked into her belt, and a small sharp knife. Barely bending, she felt the beast's belly for a moment, then pinched up the skin and cut a hole. Then she moved so fast even Onnen, who could gut and clean a hare before you could sing the bread song, would have been impressed: a fast glide just through the skin all the way to the throat latch, then turned around and, in the other direction, another fast, shallow slice down the belly, around the stick sheath, and a fast circle around the arsehole. Gently, surely, like a woman easing aside her lover's open undershirt, she tugged the skin aside, all the way up the seam, exposing a palm-width of pink.

"Always best to keep the hair off the meat," she said. "Do you have dogs here? I've not seen any."

Dogs barked. "No."

"You still want the guts?"

"The pigs will eat them." Pigs were not fussy about their food being clean.

Brona nodded and got back to work, directing Hild to hold this, lift that. She worked fast and well. But it was not a small horse, and by the time they had saved out the bladder—a good one, big—and heaved the mass of entrails onto the grass Hild was beyond tired.

Brona straightened and stretched. "Choose what you want from that. I'll start on the hide." She had a smear of blood on the side of her neck, next to a curious double freckle. She looked at the seax on Hild's belt, shook her head, and bent instead to her tool roll. "Here." She held out a small knife.

The liver looked like a great red-brown brick twisted into a lopsided butterfly by a giant. Hild's mouth watered as she sliced through the veins and ligaments. Plump and luscious, smelling of iron and fat, it would be delicious with onions. This one weighed a stone, more. And the heart, sheathed in white fat, about half the size, still weighed close to ten pounds. If it ate like beef heart then she would serve it with chopped parsley and garlic, the way Onnen had learnt to cook beef heart from Guenmon in Mulstan's hall. Begu would love it.

And as Hild weighed and cut she watched Brona work, watched the muscles in Brona's thighs swell and relax as she leaned forward, easing her fist slowly between the flesh and hide, working deeper and deeper, flexing and pushing . . .

They took three hundred pounds of meat from that carcass, and that night she dreamt of lolling naked in her bath, being served apples dipped in run honey by a glistening Brona.

Linnet sat on the same log she had shared with Hild a year ago. A wood pigeon cooed from the trees, the first of the year. Behind her, two striplings—hard to tell whether boy or girl they were so filthy—sat in the doorway of Linnet's hut, shelling peas. Linnet's fingers seemed thicker and more gnarled than they had been, the creases at the corners of her eyes deeper, and she was thin—they were all thin—but her eyes were sharp. No doubt she had noted Hild's limp, the new scars on her arm, her flat belly and small breasts, but she had not asked. No one did, now. You waited to hear what people could bear to say.

"Ma died when we were making sausage," Linnet said. Blodmonath. She bent and lifted a torn and bloodied tunic from the pile Hild had pulled from one saddlebag and dropped at her feet. She turned it this way and that in the light, fingered the ragged edges where the gold and silver tablet work had already been torn from sleeve and hem. "Good linen." Worth reusing. "At least she never saw that beast and what he made of York."

There were not rivers enough in the world to wash away the charnel reek. Hild had seen it. But she must find a way to deal with it soon. She turned the heavy bag on her lap.

"My son." Linnet stared at the tunic in her lap. "They took him. The beast's men. They took him yon." She jerked her head back at the walls of York, invisible behind the trees and then the great hedge. "Took him along with all them others. When all them starving folk wandered out, I waited. But he never came. Only these two."

Not children, but not quite grown. Twins? Twelve or thirteen. As much burden as help.

"Oh, they'll be strong enough, when fed. And I'd set food by, as you said. And sowed seed. We'll manage." She produced a sharpened bone hook and began to unpick the tunic's seam, flick-flick-flick.

Hild lifted the flap of the second bag and hefted out a red-stained, cloth-wrapped hunk. Linnet's bone hook paused and she fastened her gaze on the meat. Hild plumped it on the log.

"Horse," she said. "Killed yesterday." A poor replacement for a mother and a son, but what she had.

Linnet wiped her mouth with the back of her hand.

Hild flipped the flap closed, fastened the buckle. "Janne abandoned us and the child, Wilfrid. I have him."

"Ah." Flick-flick-flick.

Wilfrid was heir to Wilgar's rich valley, just a mile from Linnet's hut, though the next king would be unlikely to grant it to him.

"A priest came," Linnet said. "Or almost did. But the beast's men frightened him off. He left no letter. But there's other priests among the wanderers."

Hild nodded. She had seen them. They were on their way to Menewood with Morud.

Back in Menewood the day had turned warm, the goats were giving gushes of milk, and every woman, man, and child in the valley had just eaten fresh, hot meat, along with greens foraged by Sintiadd and Fllur, mostly Fllur, and peas, so many peas now, and turnip greens, and roasted turnip. The valley smiled, its people leaning back on the grass picking their teeth, licking their hands, dazed with the first surfeit in more than half a year, ale made from the last of the malted barley, and mead to go with it. A few children had rings of daises or dandelions around their necks.

Bryhtsige had sung them songs, and they had wept good tears at the piercingly sad song of Angharad-over-the-sea he had learnt from Langwredd, and then made them laugh as he and Cuthred sang a song between them of the great shin-kicking contest of Bardsey and the farm of one-legged men.

Now her mother gave a speech praising the lady Hild, their lord and loaf giver: The lady Hild would lead them all to plenty!

Rhin was speaking now, of the valley as family.

"Big family!" someone shouted—Rulf. Duv threw a bone at him and he flung up his hands: The wrapping was off; his wound was healed then, good. She would be needing him soon.

Then they were looking at her. She stood.

"Pour yourself more." She lifted her cup. Cups and bowls, old and new, lifted in response. Still she held her cup out, waiting, and one by one those who could scrambled to their feet. Her people: with all those lately come, nearly sixscore.

"To those we lost," she said. "To our dead." She drank, drank, emptied her cup.

"To our dead!"

Sixscore voices, young and old, Anglisc and British; she heard them all.

Bryhtsige and Fllur who might never be whole again. Ceadwin whose only family now was her. Begu who, knowing no British, had come north with her. Gwladus, Gwladus who had saved everything. Leofdæg, silent Leofdæg who she thought might not drink so much as perhaps once he had, for now he had little Maer to watch for, as she had Wilfrid. Rhin—forehead freshly shaved, like Mallo. And two other priests. Her mother. The two new women. All of them. Her people. Hers to protect.

"Fill your cups again, for today and tonight we will drink our fill. We will talk of those we loved and drink until we are done. But then we turn our faces to tomorrow, for tomorrow we begin our work. Oh, such work! Work to build, to grow, to flourish. We are here. We are Menewood. And so: To us! To Menewood!"

"Menewood!"

While she waited for Begu, Hild hung the freshly waxed bridle over the rail of the new-built tack shed, next to the others; it added to a very pleasing row. A cuckoo called from the wood, followed a moment later by the loud bubbling call of his mate as she left an egg in yet another stranger's nest. It sounded very like the noise Maer made when she blew on her soup. *A princess does not blow on her food in my hall,* Edwin had told her that long-ago Modraniht. *Our food comes to the table just so.* Would they ever have such plenty again, would there ever be a houseman whose only job was to watch his lord and make sure he was served whatever he needed even before the lord knew he needed it?

Who could know?

She ran her hands over the tack. The newest horse gear was not particularly rich but it was well-made, befitting six barely blooded glory-seekers.

"That's a lot of horse tack."

Hild blinked. Begu, sleeves rolled, and, from the smell, come from milking goats.

"We have a lot of horses," Hild said.

"Not if we keep eating them. Morud said you wanted me. I hope it's quick; Nell is bleating and butting."

Thromilchi: the month when the weeds and young grass were so vigorous cows and goats gave milk three times a day. "I'd have come to you but I have a question best asked with no one listening."

Begu nodded, though even her teeth and hair seemed impatient to be moving again.

"I'm sending Uinniau to Oswine, for a week or more. Would you rather go with him or stay here?"

"Stay with Bryhtsige you mean?" She puffed at a strand of hair hanging in her face, a small and sad sound. "Bryhtsige no longer looks at me. He calls me lady, and won't meet my eyes. I thought maybe it was one of those women he brought with him, especially the shepherd—Grina, she's a pretty one."

"Bryhtsige is . . . marked."

"Well, so are you. So many of us now have terrible scars. So why should he be different when you're— Oh. You've not looked at anyone since you've been back, either." She took Hild's hand with her own small warm one. "It's the loss that does it?"

Hild shook her head—she did not want to talk of what she had lost; she did not want to talk of what Bryhtsige had suffered—and squeezed Begu's hand gently to get her attention.

"Bryhtsige is marked, inside and out." No, that was not quite right. "He's lost his way. Lost the heart of who he thought he was." And this might be lost forever. "He may never look at anyone again."

Begu's face set so like that of a stubborn goat that Hild was surprised her hazel eyes did not turn yellow and narrow to slots. She could never understand: She had been here, safe in Menewood. And Hild was glad her gemæcce would never understand. She would do her best to make sure she never had to.

She squeezed Begu's hand again and let go. "Think about Craven. I'll need an answer before we gather this evening."

They ate horse again that evening, this time just the inner group, the grown members of her chosen family. Horse was good meat, sweet and soft. She could see how, if you had all the pasture in the world, fattening horses for food would be a good thing. But they did not fatten as well or as fast as cows and pigs, and to her they were worth far more than food.

Good meat and, with the last of the radishes from the root cellar, the new peas, turnips, and the first sweet carrots, a fine meal. But she'd give half of it for a fresh, fine-ground wheat loaf. She was tired of barley cakes and oat cakes, though soon enough she would long for those, too.

In what had become the sign she would speak her mind now, she stood, went around the table, and poured them each another cup: milk this evening—even turning so much of it into butter and cheese they had too much milk. Better to drink it while it was fresh; mead could be traded and barley seed would keep.

They all sipped except Oeric. Unsoured milk made him rumble and fart and cramp into painful, gushing runs. He chose another young turnip and peeled it with his knife.

She sat again. "Uinniau has consented to go to Craven tomorrow on my behalf, with Begu. With them go Gladmær and Sitric. A good mount each, with as much splendour as will fit on each horse or pony. And they'll take the mule."

"What are we trading for?" Leofdæg asked.

Hild nodded to Breguswith, who lifted two sacks onto the board. "It's not trade," Hild said. "It's a gift of spoil, a reward for an ally, and the expectation he will accept our offer to work together."

"Offer, lady?" Uinniau said, with the careful courtesy of a prince of Rheged.

"Offer. Though one you'll suggest he not refuse. I killed those who would have taken his life. I control the war street from here to Cetreht. I have gold and jewels, horses and men. I'm more Yffing than he is. And, should Cadwallon come marching south, looking to add Craven to his belt and Oswine's head to his spear, there is no one to stop him but me. Us."

"And in return for our help I ask for what?"

"If he accepts the spoil as a gift"—one gave gifts to followers; followers rendered tribute—"we ask for nothing. We explain to Oswine that Elmet and Craven, two lands of Deira, will exchange surplus. We send mead, hazelnuts, and—as our gift—these." She pulled a fistful of the lesser jewels—small, or flawed, or poorly coloured—Breguswith had dug from the horse trappings, and laid them on the table, where they glistened yellow and green, red and blue. "And these." Two swords in gaudy scabbards. The blades were much less fine than their sheaths, and the hilts shimmered with the kind of goldwork the Picts were so good at, that brought the yellow to the surface disguising otherwise poor metal. "In return Menewood will take two brace of oxen, seed corn, barley seed—Rhin will tell you how much—and sacks of ground flour, finely ground flour."

No one said anything.

"Further, Uinniau will suggest to the lord of Craven that he stay where he is; that I have the rest of Deira in hand. He would be wise to be patient; if he tries for Deira too soon Cadwallon will send him to be underking of Hel with his father. Further, he is to suggest to James the Deacon that if he should have an abundance of parchment and fine ink, enough to share, El-met would be most generous in return." It would take until the end of the month to prepare their own and she could no longer wait. "And, Uinniau, ask James to come visit before the end of the year, to stay a while." She looked around at puzzled faces. "I will need his help with some priests."

"These priests," Breguswith said, leaning back, stretching like a cat. The return of the sun, and good fatty milk, or perhaps just her daughter restored, suited her. "Are we to return to those black skirts meddling in what's not good for them?"

"They're no longer priests of Rome. They report to no bishop. And I need them to bind Deira together, and to me. Deira and parts north."

"North? How far north? Tell me you don't aim for Bernicia."

"No. Just enough of the north to stop whoever ends up holding it from threatening Deira."

Breguswith shook her head. "A month ago we spoke only of Mene-wood. Today it's Elmet—and tomorrow all Deira? We're small yet. We should watch and wait, see what—"

"No. I'm tired of waiting." Tired of hiding. "I've seen enough of Cad-wallon's handiwork for five lifetimes. He's heading to Bernicia. He'll take the wall and then move north, to Bebbanburg, to Yeavering. That's what he wants, all he thinks of, to burn and break until he's standing on the last ruins of Yffing. His mind bends north. The time to bind Deira to us is now. I feel it."

Oeric swallowed the last of his turnip. "How, lady? We can mount fewer than a dozen."

Hild turned to Uinniau. "How many swords in Oswine's hearthband?"

He thought for a moment. "Perhaps thirty."

She turned back to Oeric. "With Oswine's thirty we'll have more than twoscore under our command." Oswine had always been happier to follow than lead. "And as we reveal ourselves and word spreads, more will come."

"And when we're so bravely revealed, when all Deira swarms towards us with their hands out, how will we feed them?" Breguswith said. "How will we clothe them, and house them?"

"We'll rebuild Caer Loid. We'll resettle the outlying steadings, and re-occupy Aberford. We'll herd the sheep running wild on the hills. We'll sow the seed corn. We'll ride east to Goodmanham and Sancton, north to Derventio, and protect them until harvest. And elsewhere in Deira the people will sow their own garths, milk their own goats, and rett their own flax, knowing they will live to harvest it, comforted by our strength."

After a moment Breguswith said, "For which we'll take a tithe."

"For which we'll take a tithe. And then we'll send to the Bay of the Beacon to talk of trade—" She nodded briefly at Begu. "Of what they need, what we need. Again, we'll offer our protection. We'll protect the beach wīcs along the Humbre that will come with the warm weather—"

"And take our tithe," Breguswith said, smiling now, no doubt thinking of those Frisian pæningas.

"A small tithe. We want to be welcome wherever we go, not dreaded."

She looked around her circle. Each in turn nodded.

"And then we're going to build a mill."

At the south end of the valley she squatted by the lean-to sheltering the bundles of hawthorn she had gathered at the beginning of Œstremonath. Maer copied her. Her little head did not come much higher than Hild's thigh. In the dappled light beneath the small and still-unfurling leaves, the girl's hair shone clean, showing a hint of gold among the pale brown, and the curve of her cheek was the colour of toasted wheat, smooth and un-blemished. The rash from eating too much bulger was long gone.

Hild felt the bundles. Maer watched. "I'm feeling for dry ones."

"Why?"

"To help make ink."

"Why?"

"So I can write a letter."

"But why—"

"Would you like to help?" Maer was old for asking why all the time, but she had had no one to ask in Cnotinsleah, and Hild had learnt to interrupt the never-ending flow by asking her own questions. The child nodded. "Then choose what you think is the best one and you can carry it home."

Against the rough branches, some shaggy with lichen, her little hands seemed perfect, fresh and new. Beautifully formed fingernails, and the backs unmarked but for the scrapes and scratches of childhood that would melt away in a day or two. An endlessly healing and growing self, like a tree.

And Hild wanted, fiercely, for this child to grow sound and whole, unshaded by others, unformed by any but her own fate, given all the light and air and water she needed. But nothing grew on its own. Saplings needed shelter from larger trees against the wild autumn gales, leaf mould dropped by countless other trees to mulch into the dirt and feed the roots; the company of other grown trees that already drew bee and butterfly, beetle and bird. Fungus to grow at its feet and fox kits to play in its shade.

They walked back along the path with their bundles and found Ceadwin and Rhin by the soaking trough Rulf had built specially for the horse hide. As she drew closer Hild realised Ceadwin was now almost as tall as she was. Begu had sewn him new breeches just a month ago, yet half his shin already showed. She had never known anyone to grow so fast. Nor anyone over her height but Forthere the giant, yet this boy would overtop her by a head, and more, before he was done. But it came at a cost. His arms were too long for his height, too thin, his ribs spindly and his shoulders narrow. When he stirred the hide she and Brona had stripped from the dead horse it was with some effort.

She stacked the wood a stride away and held her hand out to Ceadwin. After one last heave he handed her the flattened pole.

"Take that wood, and Maer, to Gwladus at the house. She'll tell you where to put it. And tell her you're both to eat something. If you see Begu—" But Begu was with Uinniau in Craven. "If you see Lady Breguswith, tell her to do something about those breeches."

Maer put her little hand in Ceadwin's long one—she hardly had to reach; his arms were unnaturally stretched, reaching almost to his knees—and seemed happy to walk with him away from the smell.

The hide had been soaking for three days and was huge and heavy, wallowing like a blowing whale in its thick, cloudy mix of water and old lime. She set her feet and stirred; like most things, once it was at rest it was hard to persuade it to move again, and the pole slipped once or twice as clumps of sodden hair slid from the hide. But once it was moving it did not take much effort to keep it going. "The boy seems to like his tasks. Is he apt?"

"He has a gift. He can form his letters well with chalk on slate. And when we've more ink, we'll try that."

She nodded at the sodden mass. "How long for this?"

He scratched his forehead, something he did more often when he was newly shaved. "The new moon perhaps."

Three weeks. If she started today, her inks would be ready by then. Meanwhile, they still had just enough of the thin, brownish stuff that was all Rhin had had time to make over a terrible winter; enough for one more letter.

She unfolded the cunning sloped board Rulf had made for her and set it up. She smoothed the last of their rough and unevenly shrunken parchment against it. One patch running down the left showed the twisting scar of some wound the sheep had taken—an old shearing scar?—some years before it died. She chose a good feather, and one of the little knives, and sliced the quill at an angle. She whistled through her teeth as she measured in her head the spaces for words, rearranged the words to fit. Fursey would not approve: poor ink, poorer parchment, not fit for the word of God.

She split the nib, bent it against the parchment, nodded, and dipped it in the ink.

Fursey, father dear. Blessings upon your head. He would forgive the brevity she hoped. *We spoke long ago of the mills in your country. I am to build a mill. I have need of your knowledge.*

She hummed as she wrote, hearing the words read aloud by Fursey, perhaps to her sister, in some great hall of the North Folk that she had never seen.

We have a leat, and a millpond, millrace and—overflow channel? spillway?—*spillway.* Or they would when they took the time later this summer to split the stones to line the channels. Then they would have to build some kind of dams, with gates like the one Grimhun had made at Aberford. Perhaps Rulf could do that. He would have to be watched, to make sure he did not get lost in making them pretty.

We have found the great grindstones. But—

Rulf and Duv between them could make the great wheel. But how did it all fit together? Water drove the wheel, yes. But then how did the wheel—

She paused, mid-hum, listening. Blue tits sounding the alarm. Now great tits. Someone coming.

When Morud burst into the clearing she had her staff in hand.

"Lady!" He was grinning like an ælf. "Lady, it's Grimhun! Grimhun's here! And he's brought Heiu. Leofdæg found them at Caer Loid."

Grimhun's laugh, Bryhtsige's quiet pleasure, and even the lady Breguswith's evident satisfaction, together with the back-pounding of Grimhun and Leofdæg, then Grimhun and Bryhtsige, and the bright, rich, unfaded colours of their visitors' clothes gave the path between their huts the air of a fairground on market day—that and the two heavily laden mules, Grimhun's two war mounts, and Heiu's fine mare.

"I came as soon as I knew," Grimhun was saying. "I saw Uinniau and Gladmær, and I knew. I knew even before he spoke. I said to Heiu, 'Mark me, the lady is alive!'"

Heiu, standing with Breguswith, looked up at her name and smiled that side smile that was so Irish, and meant *Foolish man!* and *My heart!* both.

"And I brought tools." He patted the nearest mule, the one with the surveyor's rod sticking from a pack. "To rebuild."

20

✦

THE WOOD THROSTLE LAID A SECOND LOT OF EGGS in the holly tree just
as they planted onion seeds to grow sets for next year. The throstle
eggs hatched just as the children began to lose their war with the munch-
ing caterpillars and the aphids were laying their eggs, and, while the male
churred over the nestlings, the female picked every tasty many-legged
morsel from the tender greenery. Soon the throstles were joined by robins
who fed their nestlings so many caterpillars they turned green.

The birds grew. The carrots and onions, beans and peas, parsnips and
beets, lettuces and herbs grew. The children grew, and Wolcen swelled to
bursting point. Even Ceadwin's cat began to thicken. Young siffsaffs fledged,
and their parents, exhausted, filled their mouths with blue and green flies
instead of song. The vegetables thrived and goats gushed milk.

Hild noted these things with the part of her mind that never slept, always watching, always counting. She knew one morning when she woke
that today was the best day to side dress the parsnips with old dung, but
when she ordered the child picking off the slugs to fetch instead the dung,
Sintiadd appeared, hands on hips: The garths were her charge, the lady had
said so, a moon ago and more. It was her task now to plan, to choose when
to pull the children from one task and set them to another, and she would
do the dung tomorrow; today there were slugs.

Then Hild told Duv to leave building the stretching rack because the horse hide would not be ready yet and, instead, to help frame out the new addition to the long house. But Rhin and Ceadwin, who had judged differently, drained the lime tub a day early, then had to fill it again because the stretcher was still just a heap of pieces. It was the first time she saw Rhin cross.

Breguswith took her aside: Ordering Menewood was no longer her task. There were others now to oversee the daily and seasonal work of the valley; people she had trained herself. They knew their business, and they knew Menewood's needs. Hild's part was their safety, strength, and growth. It was her task to be the centre, the guiding light, to see the path and lead others along it. She should go do that.

Hild climbed the pollard and sat with her face turned north. Her mother was right; of course she was right. But every time the parsnips faltered for want of manure, or the bean leaves showed holes, or she found she must wait an extra day until she had the parchment she needed, she had to fight the urge to take back the reins and push the team to pull in step and to her rhythm.

She traced the spines on the hedgepig carved by Cian in what seemed another age. She had been a child with a quiet mouth and a bright mind speaking seldom, and then only as a godmouth. King's fist—seen by all, giving orders, clear and direct, but on another's behalf. Now she was lady of this single, small valley, giving orders that would keep Menewood hidden and safe. But that was no longer enough. To keep them all safe she must see beyond the valley into all Elmet, into all Deira and even farther.

She could not do that tucked in this one valley. Priests and their news of a man were no match for climbing a hill with that man and watching his face as he looked out over his holdings, being able to tell whether he was content or still greedy. Letters could not show her how well a woman's hall was run or how richly appointed, or who trembled when she passed and who smiled. But she could not be everywhere and do everything. She needed others to do that for her just as now, even here, she would need to have others do the things she once did, not give them orders but trust they would know.

And many of them did know. She had trained them herself. But others . . . She did not even know all the new people. "How?" She asked the hedgepig. "How can I trust they're doing the right thing if I don't even know them?"

The hedgepig slowly warmed under her hand. She imagined it trundling out of the valley with its own young, pointing out the best places for grubs. The warmest leaves for beds.

She wanted to get out of the valley, get up somewhere high. She could do that. Yes. Every time she felt the urge to seize the reins, she would take one of the people she did not know out of the valley, to watch, to question, to learn their skills and their thoughts, to determine their place in her pattern. And to get out and about, breathe different air. Learn more of what lay ahead.

She took Grina to Saxfryth's East Farm on a day that could not quite make up its mind between spring and summer. Grina was brown as a fallen oak leaf, with brown hair, pale brown eyes, and, even a month before midsummer, a bronze cast to her cheekbones and hands. She was tall—almost to Hild's chin—and used to walking hills. They moved fast over Brid's Dyke, across the war street, over the cracked limestone, both with enough breath to talk. Grina answered direct questions with short answers: How long had she watched Wilgar's sheep? These past ten year. On her own? With her brother; he was dead.

They climbed the flower-starred rise to Saxfryth's house and stood together on the hillside, both leaning on their staffs, though Hild's was thicker and shod with iron and Grina's flared and crooked at one end to hold throwing stones, as some shepherds preferred.

Hild studied her as she watched the sheep. Perhaps Gwladus's age, but something about her seemed older, maybe the long stare, the focus on the skyline. Good skills for a shepherd.

Hild tried to remember Edwin's tithe tallies of Wilgar's land. Coelfrith would have known.

"What were your tithes from Wilgar's valley?"

Grina looked at her as though she had asked why the sky was blue: Why would she know that?

Hild waved her hand: Forget it. Tithes were the business of the lords, not the shepherds. "Do you know the cheese yields?"

"Oh, aye. I had charge of the milkers as a maid. They were good, the best. I reckon four ewes gave a wey of cheese. One ewe we kept just for the drinking milk. Best you ever tasted. Oh, she were champion, like to give two sesters on her own."

She smiled fondly, the first Hild had seen her smile.

"Her lambs weren't bad, neither. Maybe because she could suckle 'em for two month and still gush good milk."

Two months. Most milking ewes had their lambs taken away at one month; many lambs died. They made tasty eating but they were not then around to give milk in their turn in a year or two. She looked at the dirty puffs on the hillside. She could see scores of them. That could be a lot of cheese. But Saxfryth's sheep were wool sheep. "And wool?"

"Maybe three dozen for a wey. Depends on the year—and the heft, a course."

Hild said nothing. She should have brought Heiu.

Grina looked at Hild. Scratched her forearm, nicked with many shearing scars, like the faded bow-shaped mark on the back of Hild's own hand. "Look, lass. I mean, lord." She shook her head. "That is to say, lady. I'm not used to talking to lordly folk. Any gate, why don't you just say what you want to know, and I'll see if I can tell you."

"How many sheep could we run here?"

"Well, how big is it?"

Hild was not entirely sure. "Two hides?"

"Walk me the bounds."

Hild looked at her blankly.

"Different land gives different yields. For milkers you'll want good rich land, lowlands with lots of water. Woollers, not so much."

They walked the enclosed land first, and Grina pointed out a patch of grass dotted with vetch and clover. "Good for milkers; you need more of that. It's close in, too. Which you'd need if you milk twice a day. But if it's champion milkers you're after, you'll also want to give them brew grains and green chop." She stopped, looked around. "No orchards? Pity. They like orchards. Sheep keep back the weeds and rotted apples do 'em a power of good."

"Isn't that what goats are for?"

"Eh, this here's too good for goats."

Halfway up the hill they used their staffs to beat back brush and straggling saplings.

"This, now, this is for goats," Grina said.

At the top of the hill the ewes and their lambs were not feeding but were clumped nervously with the ram walking back and forth between the women and his flock.

"Thick-looking wool," Grina said. "No dog and no fold, though, so we can't get close." The ewes all had their backs turned. She walked over to a gorse bush, pulled a tuft of wool off a spine, and rubbed it between her fingers. When Hild followed, the sheep moved away nervously. "Sheep can see you even when you're behind them," Grina said. "They don't like your colour."

Hild looked down at her bright blue dress with the gold and yellow tablet weave cuffs and seams.

"They're not used to it," Grina said. "Did you know who ran them before? What colour she wore?"

Hild closed her eyes, saw Saxfryth sitting proudly on her stool, admiring the flawed yellow ring Hild had given her, turning her hand this way and that against her skirts. "Red-brown."

"There you are, then. Next time, wear brown."

Hild had nothing brown. Gwladus would not let her out of the bower in such a drab colour.

From up here she could see plainly where the bounds might run—and where she might push them out. "If we have four hides, and if we plan on mostly wool . . . Tell me what we'd get from the shear."

Grina rubbed the tuft of wool again, sniffed it. "Some of those sheep look to be five-pounders. Reckon a pound of that is grease. So four pounds." She scratched her forearm again, thinking. "I'd need dogs. Can't run a flock without dogs."

"As many dogs as you want." Up here there was no need to stay hidden.

"And all the land for sheep?"

Hild nodded. "All that's best for sheep, for woollers."

Grina studied the mix of grass and green leaves around her feet, the rocky outcrops north. "Not even a quarter of this. Spring and autumn, maybe six sheep a plough. Summer, no more than four."

Hild, reckoning on four sheep per ox-plough range, moved beads back and forth in her head. "Nearly five hundred sheep!"

"Some'd be lambs. Some'd die, dogs or no. So less a quarter, or more . . ." She half closed her eyes, counting. Four pounds of wool a sheep. "Eight weys. Maybe. I don't know the land, won't know the dangers. Can't tell if the sheep'll settle, with me, or with the dogs. Say four weys the first year."

"And you could move here?"

"I can move anywhere, if I've sheep and a dog. Needs be by summer, though, for the shear."

Four weys of wool and one of grease. They could do something with that. Now she would sit Grina and Heiu and her mother at a bench and let them work out the plan.

One part of the pattern begun.

Hild summoned the priest who had been part of Rhin's web and had walked the length and breadth of the isle, lately come from Lindum. She questioned him closely—on the state of Lindum, Lindsey as a whole, Coelgar, Coelfrith and his ships, news of Penda—then told him to wait a day.

She finished her letter to Fursey. The mill, of course, but, more urgently, Sigeberht. She had changed her mind: Fursey must not let Sigeberht renounce the throne. Yes, she had once told Hereswith she would be a queen, and she would be, but not yet. Hereswith's husband, Æthelric Short Leg, must not become king. *He must not*, she wrote. And again, underlined: *Non oportet*. Not yet. Penda was again recruiting men. He had left the north to Cadwallon and now he would be looking to another prize rich enough for his attention. She did not know when Penda would strike—it might not be this summer—but she knew against whom: the East Angles, North Folk and South. She knew it in her heart. Hereswith must not be queen when Penda came killing; let him kill Sigeberht and his queen instead. Hereswith must stay safe.

She gave the letter to the Lindum priest whom she sent first to Lindsey, with a spoken message for Coelgar, who could not read, then on to Fursey in East Anglia.

With the sky pale blue and the valley stitched with the flicker and call of fledglings—blue tits, chaffinches, robins still speckled and fluffy though no longer green—and wild garlic blooming pinkish white, Hild sat on a three-legged stool by the beck with the remaining five priests in Menewood: Rhin, Mallo, and three from York.

Of the three who had come from York one had the shaved forehead of a British priest and the accent of the west, Gwynedd or nearby; the other two had the uneven hair of a crown tonsure grown out, Paulinus-trained priests left behind when he fled: Aldred and Almund, both very young.

She told them she would ask each in turn to tell their tale of the last year to the group. She began with the two youngsters.

A year earlier they would have been the arrogant ones Rhin and his kind hid from; now they were the hunted ones, marked as priests of the Yffings and so Cadwallon's enemy. And now, bones showing sharp through stretched skin, facing not only an Yffing but other priests, they were talking both at once, stories tumbling over each other's, eager to prove that, no, lady, no, their tonsure was grown out not because they had laicised, no, they had not abandoned their oath to God, only—

"Acted prudently," said one.

"Took some time to think," said the other.

Hild said nothing, looked at Rhin.

"This," he said, pointing to his shaved forehead, "I forsook for some years. For a time I was a man of God only here." He touched his heart. He studied the two young Roman priests with his dark eyes. "I forsook my priesthood to live safe from those like you. Those like you who desecrated our altars—"

"No!"

"I didn't—"

"And turned us out to starve." He looked at them steadily until they hung their heads. "I don't accuse you. You're too young to have even been ordained when I was driven from my parish. I accuse your bishop and his teaching. So. You forsook your priestly vows. Out of fear. Fear only of Cadwallon? Or do you also fear me and my kind?"

The younger of the two, Aldred, shot glances at Hild, at Rhin, at Mallo, at the Gwynedd priest who had folded his arms and pursed his lips. "No?"

The other, Almund, with a big throat apple, shuffled his sandals and cleared his throat. "Not fear. Or fear, yes, but not for my life. For . . ." He too glanced at the priest with folded arms. "I fear you might think me weak and faithless."

Rhin said, "And if we did?"

He looked wretched.

Rhin smiled sadly. "You've nothing to fear from me or mine. Whether you choose to renounce your vows and farm the land, or shave your head again, it makes no matter. Further, it wouldn't matter whether you shaved your crown or shaved your forehead. Here in Menewood, God is God."

Rhin looked at Hild.

They might or might not be useful—the younger was clearly a weathervane, a failing he might or might not outgrow—but the other, Almund, seemed less shallow. "This is my valley. If you choose to stay I will have your oath. And whichever you choose to shave, crown or forehead, on this earth your allegiance is to me first, me before any bishop. You have two days to think. Meanwhile if you want to eat, you must work."

She turned to Mallo, a wholly different bird. "I would hear again your tale of the last year."

She did not explain why she wanted him to repeat himself. After a moment he spoke of his travels in the north; that Coledauc of the Bryneich had given him a message for the Yffing—though not, after a slight shake of Hild's head, its substance—and of the Iding's apostasy. Here Mallo paused, and only at her nod added the news of Oswiu Iding's new son with the Irishwoman.

She appeared to be focused on Mallo as he spoke, but with the edge of her vision, which she had trained wider than most, it was the Gwynedd priest she watched. He listened with a smooth face to begin—either he already knew of the Bryneich connection to the Yffings, and the Iding's apostasy, or neither much mattered to him—but at the news of Oswiu's son by the Irish princess, and the implied Gwynedd-Irish alliance, his body rippled with an alertness instantly hooded.

"Thank you," she said to Mallo. "We will speak of your place later."

Finally, she turned to the Gwynedd priest. His bones were decently clothed in flesh, his forehead shaved a few days ago; his hands were neither broken with work nor soft with luxury. His robes were decent quality, perfectly ordinary tabby, competently dyed. He wore well-used sandals, worn in the pattern of a man who both walked and rode. If she had not seen that ripple of interest he might have seemed exactly what he said he was: a priest of the west who had followed Cadwallon's army to minister to their souls but whom Cadwallon had tossed aside when he decided he did not need the extra baggage of priests in his harrowing of the north. But she had seen that interest, and how smoothly he hid it.

"Now I'll hear your tale."

She listened to his story—of the monastery in Abergele in Rhos; the natural restlessness of a young man; following his king on an adventure—and did not believe a word of it. While the priest spoke of witnessing the horrors of battle, the vileness of the marsh near Caer Daun, she weighed the possibility of a Gwynedd-Irish alliance. She thought back to the banners, the weapons, the war shouts of Hæðfeld. Anglisc. British. No Irish. Nor had she heard mention of Irish from those she'd spoken to of Cadwallon's ravages. She'd seen no sound or sign of Irish at Urburg. No, she doubted there was a Gwynedd-Irish alliance.

The priest was still talking: the taking and sack of York, the shock of being abandoned by his king . . .

She rested her chin in her hand. If not the Irish, then whose interest did this priest represent and why were the doings of the younger Idings of interest? Who was cunning enough, who thought far ahead enough, to plant someone here to learn about the young Idings' possible reach and sway?

Penda. Penda wanted the whole isle and every kingdom in it. He wanted fealty and streams of gold, and, oh, he was patient. Penda. Always Penda.

In the second bower, with the door open to let in the long evening light, Gwladus and Breguswith sat on stools, Gwladus with one of Hild's dresses over her lap, unpicking the seams down the back, and Breguswith holding up a pair of hose, tilting them this way and that in the light, deciding the right-heel darn would do, and tying off the yarn. Hild, in her shift, sat cross-legged on the mat and cracked nuts into a bowl while she thought about the priest of Gwynedd and about Penda, about the Idings, about Oswald Brightblade and Aidan. People and their priests—shave-pated spies, her mother had called them, long ago.

Gwladus shook out the dress and stood. "Stand up," she said to Hild. "Let me see this on you. No, face the wall." Hild stood facing the wall while Gwladus held up the dress, and smoothed it here and there against her back.

Oswald Brightblade, not just Iding but Yffing.

"Still not as big as she was."

"Not too far off," Breguswith said.

"Put it on," Gwladus said.

Hild did. Oswald Brightblade: son of the Idings of Bernicia and Yffings of Deira. Son of both. Cousin.

Gwladus fastened the dress, said to Breguswith, "What do you think? Put in another seam?"

Her mother did not tilt her head when she thought, just as Hild herself did not. They were alike in many ways. She knew how her mother thought. Something like: *The goats and sheep are milking well; Heiu thinks slaughtering half a dozen of Grina's sheep would strengthen the flock; the garth's a riot of green and the weather set for fair. The valley is swimming in food. She'll fill the dress soon enough.*

Her mother shook her head. "I wouldn't bother."

"She needs to look well when we go to Goodmanham in Harvest-monath."

"By the time the grain's gold, she'll have doubled in size." She patted her own, no longer bony belly. "We all will."

Hild tugged at the sides of the dress. It fit well enough.

Gwladus tapped her hand. "Keep still. No, no, see here? It needs to come in just a little." Breguswith shrugged. Gwladus pinned quickly with the odd assortment of pins left to them—bone, bronze, and the last of the fine steel slivers that remained of Æthelburh's long-ago gift—then held the dress by the shoulders for Hild to step out carefully.

Hild went back to shelling the nuts. She knew what she must say in the letter she would send north when the parchment was ready; now it was the rest she had to get right. Wax. She was having a hard time getting the red colouring just right. It was too delicate, almost pink. And the first batch had dried too hard and brittle.

Breguswith pulled the hose over a wooden darning shoe until the left heel was stretched and ready, then picked up yarn and needle. She squinted at the needle with one eye, then the other. "When we're trading again, get me some needles with eyes big enough to thread!"

Hild held out her hand, threaded the needle, and handed it back.

Breguswith nodded her thanks. "Now, where are you with that priest of Penda's?"

"Um? Oh. I doubt he could tell us much." No priest of hers would be able to tell her enemy much, and she doubted Penda would be less careful.

"Perhaps not," her mother said. "But I still say hot iron makes most people happy to talk."

"I don't trust what people say in pain," Hild said.

Gwladus paused in her sewing. "And I don't trust what people say for money. Kill him and be done." Her needle dipped in and out, in and out, leaving behind pale, perfect stitches.

Hild tossed a handful of nuts into her mouth. "He's no danger to us. I doubt he's learnt anything useful to Penda."

"Maybe not yet," Gwladus said. "But what if he does? Best to be sure. Kill him."

"But we could use him. Pretend we don't know he barks for another master, and feed him lies."

Breguswith shook her head. "Gwladus is right. Kill him and be done with it."

Gwladus nodded. "And your mother's right about making him talk first. We've nothing to lose by trying money and pain, both."

Hild remembered Bryhtsige flicking open the arm veins of Cadwallon's men, their white-faced terror. Everything they told him had been the truth, and that truth had made a difference. But was anything the priest might know worth feeling the emptiness she had seen in Bryhtsige's eyes?

She brushed the litter of shells into a neat pile. Whatever she did with him, it would be best if her folk had no notion of just what it took to keep them all safe.

She had Rhin give the priest a sack of nuts and a hunk of cheese, and suggest he take the east path to Dere Street, and, from there, anywhere he chose. Unseen, Hild watched the priest from the brow of the south rise as the priest nodded his thanks, watched him smile as he left the valley—watched as he took note of everything he saw. As soon as he was out of sight of curious valley folk she beckoned Leofdæg and they followed.

Afterwards, they buried him where Dere Street crossed the narrow redcrest road that ran west through Craven. And they took back the nuts and the cheese. She had been right, he was Penda's, but they had learnt nothing more useful.

She took Grimhun to Aberford. What had been a lake was now a bog, the road muddy but passable, and the beck had burst the dam.

"It wasn't made to hold half a year," he said. He paced this way and that, measuring rod in hand. "But I could build something that would."

Aberford was a line, not a fort. Without help at their back they did not have the men to hold it. And even if her letter north was well-received, it would be a year or more before there were men enough. Meanwhile, her people had other needs. "Perhaps we could rebuild enough for a way station and toll point."

He appraised the land on either side. "There's not much to do to stop those on foot or with hardy mounts, but a herd, or carts, and laden wagons? I could funnel them through a toll gate."

"What and how long would you need?"

"Four men for three days. Axes. Mauls. A mule."

So much easier when they needed to only control drovers and traders, not stop an army.

She led him south and west down the redcrest road that passed the beaver dams and their pools between the Menewood beck and Hol beck where they joined the Yr on either side, then upstream along the north bank of the river. He cast a sharp glance at the bridge, asked her questions about the depth of the water on either side, and whistled tunelessly, thinking.

At Caer Loid he took in the ruined palisade, the hacked orchard, the graves by the pits. Without the stench, without the pitiful bodies, it seemed peaceful, ready to rise again.

"If we rebuild it, we need to keep it safe."

He half hummed to himself, thinking. He never could hold a note but as he looked from palisade to river, from gateway to road, the humming grew even less tuneful.

"Can you make it safe?"

"Maybe." He looked upstream to where a cygnet paddled back and forth, too curious for its own good, then downstream to the out-of-sight bridge. Now he whistled through his teeth. Upstream, downstream. Upstream, downstream.

"Could you?"

He nodded, dubious. "I *could* . . ."

Hild waited, the only sign of her restlessness the grinding of her iron-shod staff into the turf.

"I could, lady. Yes. But why—when there's a better place downstream? Where Hol beck and the lady's beck meet the Yr. It's near the road, and strong rushing water. Water's maybe deep enough for small boats—or rafts—to Cnotinsleah. Or maybe not. But the redcrest road south of the river, from Cnotinsleah, is good for wagons. Well, carts—it's only the last bit that's in poor repair. We could mend that. You could mill here, lady, and send flour anywhere in Deira. We'd need to rebuild Cnotinsleah, it's true. But I could build you such docks there!"

Cnotinsleah. New docks. The old Caer Loid. The new Loid. A road. A mill. "You're only one man."

"But, lady, I could build you *such*—"

"One man, Grimhun. And the Cnotinsleah road is fifteen miles." The *last bit* was five miles at least. But she would think about it. He was right. Fifteen miles overland on even a poor road, and then smooth sailing from Cnotinsleah, was better than twenty-five miles by poor road to Aberford, then another twenty on Dere Street, followed by smooth sailing from York—if there were ever to be smooth sailing from York again. And if they could only find ships.

Rhin and Ceadwin watched while she held a sheet of parchment to the light, tilting it this way and that. This parchment would carry the most important letter she had ever written; she needed it to reflect her wealth and power. She stroked it, cool and smooth to the touch, creamy as the parsley blossom spilling over the moss on the overgrown tailrace. She turned it over, and back again, looking for the hair side and flesh side.

"I can't tell," she said. She tilted it and looked along the plane. No sign of hair dints on either side. "This is beautiful."

Ceadwin beamed, showing a shocking expanse of pink gum. "Lay it flat, lady."

She laid it carefully on her writing board: no bend, no cupping of one side or the other. "I still can't tell."

Ceadwin laughed with the pure joy only the very young seem capable of. Rhin smiled with him, and Hild found herself smiling, too.

"Now, if only my ink is as good, Menewood would not be ashamed to write to the bishop of Rome himself. Well done, Ceadwin, very well done. Both of you."

She picked up the next sheet, stroked it idly. Until James came with more ink, she had only what she had made—enough for two letters at most. There was enough parchment here to write to twenty popes—twenty æthelings-in-exile; twenty cousins who might be friend or enemy—but it was too good for everyday.

"We'll need more, but lesser." The pig slaughter was not for months but with so many newcomers the valley needed leather now. "Grina has marked half a dozen sheep for slaughter. And we've a kid or two too many. If Lady Breguswith, and you, Rhin, think we might have hide to spare, talk to Brona. She'll see you get the most out of what there is."

Rulf the wood shaper smiled, arms folded, wholly confident as Hild hefted the cylinder of heart of oak, then tossed it from one hand to the other—it fit her hand perfectly, and the turning made it a delight to hold.

She turned it to look at the carved figure on the base. "You've caught it exactly."

Cath Llew, not snarling, but perhaps a whisker from it: ready to tear and rend, or hunt with a friend. Her secret sigil. *Sign with a cat . . .*

"I'll need two more. A boar, and a hedgepig." One the seal of power, the Yffing boar. The other, more personal, that only those close to her would recognise. One day she would carve them in precious stone, but for now, wood would serve.

Fursey, or even James, would have known the right phrases, and they both wrote a beautiful hand. But she did not know how the Irish priests of Hii got on with the priests of Rome, or whether the Irish of Fursey's kin got on with those in Hii. Besides, they were not here, and they were not the ones who had met Aidan.

As she tested a mix of beeswax and glue and butter to get the right consistency of sealing wax, she tried phrases in her head. Latin, at first. When she cut thyme for the stew of lamb, she scratched words in the dirt, scrubbed them out. And when she tucked Wilfrid up for sleep she drew Latin sentences on the slate hearth with a piece of chalk. And then again, this time in Irish. Ah, yes. Better, much better. The letter would be addressed to Aidan, but others, more important, would read it.

Uinniau returned from Craven riding at the head of a small train: two loaded wagons, each pulled by a brace of oxen; Begu leading an ass; Gladmær leading loaded mounts; and Sitric with one milch cow and one bullock. The ass was hung about with cages: hens and goslings. Hild's mouth watered and her dragon heart gloated over her growing hoard: not only horses and sheep and pigs and goats, but now, soon, cattle and geese and chickens.

Begu would not leave her caged fowl until they were settled, but Uinniau was happy to join Hild for a welcome-home drink, and carried in a small cask of ale for the purpose. It had been so long since Menewood had had a cask of fresh ale to broach she had to send Morud in search of a spile.

They talked first of trade, and numbers. The ale was fine on her tongue with a hint of fizz, and the freshest she had tasted in a year. She did not have to pretend enjoyment as she listened and occasionally asked a question. Uinniau spoke easily, fluently, of the goods, of Oswine's situation—he was looking for a match for his sister, Osthryth—and of Craven. He was six years older than her and had become the kind of man kings valued: solid, energetic, not yet in his prime but already steady. She valued him. But he was not her man. They were bound only by friendship. As a prince of Rheged he could oath to no one, wife or lord or brother of the sword, without the grace and word of his uncle, Rhoedd king. She liked him, she valued him, but she could not trust he would put her interests first.

"Oswine was happy to trade," Uinniau said. "Eager, even. He wanted to come himself but I pointed out that in dangerous times he must travel with his retinue, and riding at the head of a war band would set tongues wagging and messages flying. Cadwallon would think he was setting out to take Deira, and now—as you had suggested—was not yet the time."

"Good," she said. The last thing they all needed was Oswine running about making his own decisions. "And his thegns?"

"Watchful."

"Willing to follow a lord who sits back and waits?"

"If he's waiting on the word from the light of the world, yes. For a while."

For a while, for a while. It was always for a while. To a land-holding thegn what counted was not what you had done, or even what you were doing, but what you would do. What you would do for them. They wanted stability, safety, and profit. They would wait, for now, because the light of the world had always known the path and always pointed true.

Light of the world. She wanted to be done with those old songs, she was tired of having to be more than human. But they could still be useful. Just a little longer.

"Then we must make sure they stay happy with the trade, and feel safe and valued. For a while."

She smiled slightly. He did not notice. He was sitting with his legs stretched long and crossed at the ankle, left on right, dust on his boots and breeches, but he did not look tired. More . . . discontented? Hild realised Begu had still not yet come in.

"And you, Uinniau. How is it with you?" He shifted his legs, right on left. She put her cup down and leaned forward. "You and I share no oath. We each owe nothing to the other but friendship, sealed long ago in the boughs of an apple tree."

He smiled briefly at the memory, but said nothing.

She switched to British. "Is there something you may not tell me plainly, friend?"

"No. That is, not yet. I need to send a message to my uncle, though."

Hild nodded. She knew what about: Osric Whiphand had not taken Deira and so young Oswine would not be marrying Rhianmelldt. Which meant Uinniau could not yet marry Begu. Which meant Begu would be cross-grained and arguing with him about loyalties. "And you would take this message yourself, and be apart from the lady Begu for a time without it seeming to her that you wish it?"

He seemed relieved that she understood.

"I have a favour you may do me that might suit. In two days, when you're rested, I am sending a message north with a priest. Ride with him: Craven to Rheged, give your news to your uncle, then if you would, on to Alt Clut. You are on terms with Alt Clut?"

"My uncle and King Beli had an agreement, though much time has passed. And Eugein and I rode together a while as children." She knew him well enough to understand he had an opinion of Eugein, the king-in-waiting, but it was an opinion formed as a child, and the man might be different.

"Then ride with my priest to Alt Clut, and when he rides farther north to deliver a message he carries for me, stay in Alt Clut a while and talk with Eugein ab Beli. Without him knowing of my interest, I would know Alt Clut's temper, strength, friends, and enemies. What does Beli ab Neithon owe and to whom? Who does he fear or admire, and who his son?"

Uinniau was nodding; he had done this work for his uncle for ten years.

"I wish to know: Would Eugein be a good and useful friend?" She had met him, once, when she was a child and he a stripling Honeytongue's age.

Perhaps it was the matched ages that gave her the impression of him as a bully, but perhaps not. "I ask only that I have word of his heart and mind by early Hrethmonath."

He held out his cup for more. "And Begu?"

"I'll speak to her. And I'll see she's safe." She poured him another foaming cup, and switched back to Anglisc. "When we're done, I'll take you to Wolcen. She'll not drop before you leave, but it won't be long."

Hild and Begu stepped back from the open wicker baskets and watched the hens begin to peck among the rows of herbs in the long-house garth. Peck, swallow. Peck, peck, swallow: caterpillars, ants, beetles, aphids—

"Did that one just eat a slug?"

Begu grinned and nodded. "Only the little slugs, Osthryth says, but if we pick out the big ones, and they eat the small, soon there won't be any. And the more they eat the better the eggs they lay." She grinned again. "Goats don't do that!"

Hild watched with a swelling sense of satisfaction as the chickens pecked and ate. Children freed from a task, greenery growing lush and pest-free, and fine-tasting eggs. These fowl were like the wooden puzzle box with the hidden lock Cian had made her: beauty, purpose, and economy in one harmonious whole. "We'll need a dog to guard them." Another dog. But something would have to keep the foxes away.

"Osthryth uses cats. 'Foxes don't trespass on a cat's haunt,' she says."

"I would not have thought of it," Hild said.

"All this was Osthryth's idea. Well, not her idea so much as her who put the thought in my head when we were eating the best yellow eggs. Oh, such a beautiful yellow! I've been trying to think how we could get that colour in our dyes. Deeper than weld. Osthryth told me the eggs were a different colour since the vill had been swarmed by aphids and the hens ate those instead of the barley. To think they fed their hens on barley when we were dreaming of barley bread! But she had a lot of chickens, a lot of geese, and so here we are."

"What did you trade for them?"

"Charcoal."

"But we don't have charcoal." Not enough to trade.

Begu clucked at one chicken and flapped her hand at it so it moved to a new patch. "We need more, I know. That's why I said we'd take the extra birds off her hands if she gave us a bit of her charcoal for our trouble—and the baskets to put everything in." She tucked a strand of hair behind her ear. "She hates killing them, you see. As part of the trade I had to promise we wouldn't kill these; they all have names." She laughed at Hild's expression. "Don't worry. I didn't promise to not kill their chicks. But even if I had, there's always the eggs."

That was not what Hild was astonished by, but she just nodded. "They're the—"

"Best war food. I know."

"Well, they are. Always—"

"Fresh in their own wrappings, and easy to eat with one hand. You've only told me half a hundred times. And even if there weren't eggs, it was worth it for the charcoal. Winny and Oswine are useless at bargaining. Oh, they know how to ask for what you told them to ask for, but it was me and Osthryth who did the real trading. Now they're happy, and we're happy. You should just send me next time."

Begu was her father's daughter: She understood the sea, and she understood trade. She understood it perhaps better even than Hild, who would not have thought to ask for one thing in order to also be given a second, instead of the usual one thing in exchange for another. A thought began to form in the back of Hild's mind.

"And Osthryth, is she happy in Craven?" She remembered small, pointy teeth, black hair; a smaller, thinner, sharper copy of her brother Oswine. But that was seven years ago.

"Happy? What is happy when your father's been slaughtered and you worry your brother might be next?" She stopped by a rosette of leaves. "Oh! You've planted weld!"

"I know you like it."

"But this soil . . ."

"I know, it might not flower. But it might." The dye yield would be small, but it would smell lovely. "Osthryth," she said again. "What are Oswine's plans for her?"

Begu squatted down by a stray larkspur plant. "This makes yellow, too. But it's very pale." She stood up. "Oswine doesn't yet understand that he needs to have plans. I think he's still waiting for someone to tell him what to do."

"And Osthryth?"

"She doesn't like to think about it."

"Like her brother."

"No," Begu said. "No, they're different. Oswine can't make up his mind about anything—or he can, but then he changes it. He's a reed in the wind. Osthryth . . . If you can persuade her that she needs to be the one to decide something, then she will. She did a lot of deciding while we were there. Oswine wanted to go riding and hunting, and drinking with Winny."

"Does he listen to Winny?"

"Oh, yes. But he listens to whoever is the last to speak to him."

"We can't rely on a reed."

"Then don't," Begu said. "What have I just been telling you? Rely on Osthryth. Persuade her of what's necessary, and she'll decide for him. And she's always there, always the last to talk to him. You worry too much."

"It's not worry."

Begu gave her a look. "Not worry. Just like following that butcher with your eyes is not want?"

Hild ignored that. "It's not worry, it's planning."

"And that sudden colour in your cheeks is wind chap? Oh, just take her to your bed and be done with it!" She stood and laid a hand on Hild's arm. "What is it, gemæcce? Do you still"—she made a sweeping gesture down her front—"hurt? Langwredd—you remember Langwredd? Of course you do—said she was dry and creaky as a split stick for close on a year after hers was born. And she wasn't hacked half to death by swords and spears and starved into the bargain. But there are ways around that. Mind, we are sadly lacking in goose grease. But there's butter—"

"No," said Hild.

"We don't have butter?"

"No! I mean, yes, we have butter. But no, I don't hurt."

"Then what—"

"I'm sending Winny away."

Begu went quiet.

"I'm sending him north."

"To Rhianmelldt?"

"What? No. No, not that." Begu sighed with relief. "To Rheged, yes, and then on to Alt Clut."

"He'll be safe?"

"Cadwallon's in the northeast. Once past the wall I doubt he'll move west of Dere Street. Even if he does, Winny is a prince of Rheged, and no enemy of Gwynedd."

"Rheged. Alt Clut . . . Who travels with him?"

"A priest."

"But he'll be coming back?"

"Yes. Perhaps before winter, but certainly by spring."

She looked at Hild. "And I'm not to go with him. Why?"

"You're needed elsewhere."

"Craven again?"

"No. I want you to go to the Bay of the Beacon." To Onnen. And Mulstan, if he was still alive.

"Da—oh, I would like to see him! But the northeast. Cadwallon. They know I'm your gemæcce."

"You won't go until I'm sure Cadwallon Bradawc is beyond the wall and moving more northerly still." Until she was sure his goal was Yeavering or Bebbanburg. That would give Begu plenty of time, because Cadwallon would not march on one without also taking the other. "That will be later this summer. But Winny will leave in two days, when I've finished my letter for the priest to carry."

When the letter was done, and dry, she folded the parchment three times to make a packet the length of her palm. In the centre of the uncreased side she wrote *Aidan mac Ailbe*. When it was dry she turned it over and held a burning taper to a finger of wax. She had experimented for a week to get the right colour. Beet and dandelion made a satisfying blood-red. She had practised on old leather until she could drip a thick circle that would spread and dry to a stiff wafer, and stamped and stamped again with her wooden block until she knew the right speed and weight to produce a crisp impression each time.

And now here it was, a creamy packet with a perfectly centred blood-red wax wafer, imprinted with the head of Cath Llew.

Then she set about making it sturdy enough for its journey.

She was kneeling in the dirt by a row of colewort when Morud brought Mallo to her. A hen with a black patch on its wing studied him with one eye, then the other.

"Lady?"

She lifted a head of colewort free and set it to one side. She held up her small knife. "Do you have one?"

"One suitable for colewort? I do."

"Then you start at the far end, and we'll meet in the middle."

They did, and both sat back on their heels and surveyed their piles of dark green colewort, pleased at the result. "Fine-looking vegetables, lady."

They were. Since the hens, the holes munched by caterpillars were few, and on the outer leaves only. "I like them with butter and pepper, when we have it," she said.

"Surely there's no better way than fried in pork grease with onion!"

"Sure, it's well enough eaten so," she said in Irish.

He lifted his eyebrows.

She nodded, and switched back to Anglisc. "I have a task for you, Mallo. Travel through Craven to Rheged, then on to Alt Clut, and then farther north. One thing: I would have your oath first."

"My oath is held by God, lady, and I can swear to no other."

She had expected as much. "Then swear to me this: that you intend me and mine no harm. More, that you will tell me of any plans you learn of to harm me or mine." She fished out her cross. "Swear it on this."

He was skilled at making his face do his bidding, but it is difficult when thinking hard, wishing to move from the stony ground under one's knees, and speaking in a tongue learnt long after the cradle. Hild saw the stillness as he weighed his loyalties. But then he nodded. "I will so swear."

He took the heavy gold in one hand and Hild wrapped both of hers around it. And he swore on the cross and his oath as ordained priest of God the Almighty that he meant no harm to Hild and her people, that he would do no harm, and that he would do his best to warn her of any harm planned by others.

When they were done she dropped the cross back down the front of her dress, and took the sheepskin packet from her front pocket. He did not reach for it but watched as she turned the oiled leather with its knotted twine sealed with red wax this way and that.

A bluebottle buzzed.

He cleared his throat. "To Alt Clut, you say?"

"No. This is a letter for a priest of Hii, Aidan mac Ailbe." She held it out.

He took the letter with one hand and pretended to shoo away the bluebottle with the other. But Hild had seen the flicker in his eye.

"You will travel by way of Rheged, and from there to Alt Clut with Uinniau, prince of Rheged. Here is silver for the boats. Leave him there and travel on to Hii. You are to wait for a reply, written or spoken, and bring it to me as directly as is safe. You will be rewarded."

It had to get there. It had to be read in the right frame of mind: as a letter from someone rich and powerful and well-educated, well-supplied, able to command resources even in a time of war. Able to sway others. Those who read it had to believe she could make good her offer.

21

✧

THE WORLD TURNED TOWARDS SUMMER. On the Yr, dirty-cream cygnets glided after their parents, while by the beck, in the old crow's nest on a stump, mallard eggs hatched and a day later the tiny ducklings, heads bright yellow and coats the rich red-brown of just-shelled chestnuts, fell fluffily to the ground and made their first line to the water.

Hild, with Wilfrid on her hip and leading Maer on the ass Morud had named Harian—a white-muzzled long-eared jenny with a rough grey coat like wool—surprised the mallards on their way back. The mother rose up on her thin legs like a beacon, and swelled, and the little ones sank into the grass and looked for all the world like a line of fluffy dandelions.

"Shh," Hild said, and they stood quietly, even Wilfrid, until the mother duck sank slowly to walking height, shook herself with a rattle of feathers, and gave a short, quacking command to her chicks, who rose and formed up behind her, and the line trundled off, tiny little webbed feet whirring like turning ash keys.

Wilfrid pointed. "Duh!"

"Yes," she said. "Ducks. Big duck and baby ducklings."

Maer turned to watch them pass. "I shall tell Ceadwin where they live."

Hild clucked Harian forward. "Why will you tell Ceadwin?"

"So he won't let Clut eat them. Clut's hungry all the time, he says."

"Well, she has four kittens to feed."

"Kittens eat milk, not birds."

"Yes, kittens eat milk, but Clut makes the milk, and to make the milk she needs to eat." As they walked she corrected Maer's seat, her hands, and explained that cats need meat: mice, snakes, voles . . .

Maer looked at Hild dubiously. "Do you and Fllur eat mice and snakes?"

"Do I—? Oh. No. Mothers, people mothers, make milk for Geren and Wilfrid from people food. But Clut is a cat. She needs cat food. Food that bleeds."

Later that day, with Wilfrid asleep under Fllur's care, Hild found Maer sitting on the stoop of Ceadwin's hut nursing a scratched forearm while Clut, smeared in beet juice, licked herself crossly. "She doesn't like beets," Maer said accusingly.

Hild squatted and looked at the arm; nothing a smear of honey could not mend. "No. Clut likes meat, things that bleed."

"Beets bleed!" She held up her stained right hand. "See?"

It was early æfen two days past the new moon when Wolcen went into foal.

"Too early," Begu said. She ran her hands over the mare, bit her lip. "But she's so big. I wish Winny was here."

Hild looked at the thin crescent moon in the still-blue sky and at Wolcen standing with her head down, flanks heaving. As Begu said, she was big, and she was early. This was her first foal, but even though she was early her teats had been swollen for days. There was something not quite right about all this. If the birth went long, and wrong, the moon would not offer much light. They would need help, and there was one obvious choice. But she said nothing. This was Begu's decision. Uinniau had left the mare in her care.

"Go get Bryhtsige," Begu said. "And have Morud bring us food. But you go to bed; you need the sleep."

On the way to the long house, she saw Grina emerge from the trees smoothing her dress and smiling a secret smile. She gave Hild a small bob of the head but the smile did not waver.

Hild walked on. As she passed the thin path into the trees she saw Sitric striding along jauntily, bow over his shoulder like a spear. "Lady!"

"Sitric. Good hunting?"

"Oh, not so bad, lady. Not so bad!"

His bow was not even strung. She would not have expected it of the quiet greybeard.

Hild lay awake for some time, thinking, and fell asleep just as she realised the nightingales were not singing. Their eggs must have hatched . . .

She woke before dawn. Next to her, the bed was still empty. Healthy foaling was always fast; slow meant something wrong. She gathered cheese and beer and nuts and took them to the pasture.

The moon had set and the morning star barely risen, but even in the half dark Hild knew this path.

She heard murmured conversation before she saw the seated silhouettes of Bryhtsige and Begu, both inside the paddock, dark against a still, pale shape stretched out in the grass. The air smelt of blood and sweat. Hild sighed. But as she moved closer the pale shape stirred and the mare nickered softly.

Bryhtsige and Begu turned. Between them now she caught the flicker of movement. Then another.

She climbed the rail, jumped down, and blinked, not sure if she was seeing right in the faint starlight.

Two foals, legs angled like bony tent sticks, suckling from the mare, tiny tails flickering, almost whirring—like the ducklings' feet. Twin foals. Two. And alive.

"They're so small," she said. She handed the cheese to Begu, the nuts to Bryhtsige, and took a healthy swig of the beer. Two foals and the mare, all alive. She had never heard of such a thing. "Are they well?"

"Yes," Begu said.

"No," Bryhtsige said.

Hild handed the beer to Begu, who gave Bryhtsige the cheese, and took the nuts. "Tell me," she said.

A filly and a colt, Begu said. Both with two ears, two eyes, four hooves, four legs, and a tail. They could see and hear, they could stand and suckle.

"But they're unfinished," Bryhtsige said. The sky was brightening from fading black to purple. She saw what he meant: They were thin, and not quite the right shape.

"Will they live?"

"I don't know."

"Twin lambs live," Begu said. "And kids. And how many sucklings did Granmor birth?"

"Horses aren't sheep or goats," he said. "They're too big for twins."

"Twin calves live!"

"Not often, and if they do, only one'll breed." He did not look at Hild and perhaps she only imagined him catching himself in time.

"I heard of one freemartin who calved," Begu said. "These foals will thrive! Look how much they want to live!"

They were both sucking as though their lives depended on it. Neither Hild nor Bryhtsige said what was on their minds: If wanting was all it took no one would ever die.

Hild told Grina she was to go to East Farm and take three others with her to rebuild the steading and herd sheep. The shepherd nodded, and ran her hand thoughtfully over the ears of the two pups she was training.

"Do you know who you'll take?" Hild asked.

"Duv, if you can spare him," she said.

"I can. Who else?"

"It'll take some thinking on."

Hild nodded and kept her thoughts to herself.

Later, when Hild was by the paddock helping Bryhtsige wrap the colt's knees, Sitric came and asked for a word.

"East Farm," he said. "I've a mind to go."

She wiped her greased hands on the grass. "Not much call for spearmen on the fold."

"I've always been more of a farmer, lady."

A poacher, more like. "And Grina would have you there?"

He grinned. "She would, lady. We talked, just now. Her, me, Duv, and Duv's lass." His daughter, a year or two older than Ceadwin. "We'll have the place ready, come shearing. You'll see if we don't. That Grina knows her business." He spoke with pride and stood squarely, a man ready for a job of work.

"At East Farm you'd follow Grina's word. Shear when she tells you to shear, dig where she tells you to dig, and lay your axe as she directs. You'd be a farmer, not a spearman."

"I understand, lady."

She nodded. "Then go be a farmer, but take your spear, too, and take your bow. And remember your oath. If I call, you come."

Midmorning on an unseasonably cool day just before the moon's first quarter, East Farm sent Duv's daughter to Menewood with three sheep for slaughter. Hild studied her for a moment; the girl looked odd but she could not say why. She shook her head, told the girl to leave the sheep in her charge, go find Gwladus, and get a cup of beer and something to eat. Oh, and please to send the butcher up to the foal paddock.

Then she kilted up her skirts and took the sheep herself to the paddock where Harian, Wolcen, and the foals were held. Begu, who was exercising Wolcen, raised a hand. The foals skipped over, and then away; she could smell them, lighter and loamier than their mother, more milky, less grassy.

Hild swung over the railing and into the paddock. Begu released Wolcen with a pat.

"How are they?"

"They like this coolth."

They watched the impossibly long-legged foals with their wrapped knees, pale gold coats, and ashy manes and tails jounce and jump around their mother.

"That's the filly, Flicker. You can see the limp. Not much, but it's there. We wrapped her knees the same as Whisk, but it's not helping as I'd like."

"Wolcen has enough milk?"

"For now. But if these sheep are eating in the paddock as well . . ."

"Not for long. I've put them here for Brona to take a look at. One at least will be gone by the end of the day." The others, well, she had to work out what they must take to Goodmanham, what they would need here; when to move the other pieces on her board. Begu, yes, she knew how and where, and almost when: soon, though not just yet. Thoughts about Breguswith, yes. Gwladus, though. That was less clear. She needed to talk to her. Then she must decide what order—

She shook her head like Wolcen shaking off a fly. Too many things. It was hard to think.

Gwladus came up the path with Brona, who nodded to Hild and swung herself over the rails and into the paddock to look at the sheep. Gwladus said, "A word?"

Hild nodded. "We'll sit over here on the grass. I want to watch the foals."

Brona moved the sheep about this way and that, feeling backbones and haunches, reaching into their mouths for their teeth. Her throat and arms were lightly sheened with sweat, her shoulders strong and golden brown.

They sat on the grass. "I caught the East Farm girl stealing broad beans."

"Duv's girl?" A nod. "Just beans?"

"Actually trying to eat them raw, and stuffing some in her belt purse. I asked why she took them, and she said she didn't know."

Hild realised what had caught her attention earlier: the faint greenish cast of the girl's skin. She had seen that before, but only in poorly fed people, and people with wounds. But she was not long from the valley; like all of them she'd been hungry for a while, but not starved.

"Has she been hurt? Bled in any way?"

"No more than any woman."

"She's started her bleeding?" She seemed young.

Gwladus nodded. "Just before Œstre Mass."

"Heavy?"

Gwladus thought about it. "Heavy for one new to it. But we've all been through that. It didn't turn me into a thief, or you as I recall."

"It's a hunger—for beans, for greens, for liver—I've seen before when people lose blood and haven't eaten well for a while. Hot wine is what she needs. Heated in an iron pot, or with a red-hot poker."

Gwladus raised her eyebrows. "I doubt they've wine in East Farm."

"Beer, then. But it's the heating with the iron that does the trick."

"I'll see to it when we get back." Gwladus leaned back on her hands and lifted her face to where the sun was trying to burn through thin cloud. "Should I punish her in any way?"

"Not this time. Give her a sack of beans to take back with her. Flaxseed too, if we have it. And tell her to ask next time."

Gwladus nodded and closed her eyes, tilting her head back to show her throat and the swell of her breasts, soaking up the thin sun. A year ago she would have been too cold and stayed wrapped up. People change.

"And you," Hild said. "I need to decide what to do for you."

In the paddock, Begu waved her hand at Flicker and said something to Brona, who nodded and followed her over to the foals.

"Before I gave it to Grina, I thought of giving you East Farm, but it's all sheep and wool. And you've never been interested in wool."

"Only to wear," Gwladus said, eyes still closed.

"So we need to talk about you."

"Then talk."

Brona was running her sun-browned hands down the pale filly's leg. "Not here. I can't think here. I need to get away. I feel . . . My head is cluttered. I need to breathe. To get out, get up high."

Brona was saying something to Begu, pointing.

"I'm going up the cefn for a day, or two. If you came with me we could talk then."

Gwladus opened her eyes, looked at Hild, and smiled faintly. "It's not talking you want, and it's not me you should ask."

"But I need—"

"You need, yes." She sat up, serious now. "I know you, none better. While you need, you can't think. But I'm not the one." *Being owned leaves a mark . . .*

Hild knew that. At least for now. But perhaps one day—

"I'm not the one," Gwladus said again. "I will never be the one."

Hild searched her face for any uncertainty but those soft cheeks and lovely lips, the green and tawny eyes were steady and sure: never. *Never?* she wanted to cry. *Never?* Gwladus's mouth softened and her eyes glistened, and that was when Hild truly understood: Gwladus meant it, and it was hard and it hurt, but she would never change her mind.

Hild bowed her head. Gwladus touched her arm gently, then leaned back on her elbows.

Hild watched scudding clouds. She breathed. She had known, she had just not wanted to know. But now she did. It would be all right. She breathed deeper. Then she understood: It would not one day be all right, it was all right now, today. It had been all right for some time.

Gwladus had been herself for months. And not by any favour Hild had granted but because she was Gwladus. Hild had been thinking of how to help Gwladus as a gift. Now she could begin to consider what Gwladus might do. How she might grow, what she might learn. How they might work together . . .

Gwladus, as she always did, seemed to know Hild's mood. She nodded to where Brona was now rubbing the filly's cannon, sun playing on the muscle in her forearm. "You've been taking out the new people, one by one, getting to know them. So how about the butcher? Invite her up your hill."

A cool breeze was kicking up again as Hild and Brona followed Begu and Gwladus down the hill.

"One hogget, three wethers," Brona said. "I'd wait til next year on the hogget, it's only just grown its front teeth, but those wethers'll make prime mutton. Three years if they're a day. Well-muscled."

"How much meat?"

"Twoscore pounds each."

They talked of hanging time, spoilage, driving a wether to Goodmanham to feed harvesters, how much weight it might lose in those three days. "We could crate the wether, put it in a wagon." They would need a wagon for the wheat on the way back. No sense driving it empty.

Brona shrugged: She had no opinion on the wisdom of mutton for Goodmanham. "At least it'll be warm here by harvesttime."

"It'll be warm sooner than that, and not just warm, hot. Hot by midsummer."

Brona looked at Hild: Midsummer was only three days away.

Hild stopped. Brona stopped, too. "Look up." In the north the grey cloud had thinned to almost nothing, and in the south, wisps of white cloud high, high in a pale blue made a thin, streaky veil, moving north. "There's hot air coming from the south." By the end of the day the sky would be blue from edge to edge, and tomorrow warm southern air would fill the valley. "It will be hot. Hotter than Harvestmonath."

Brona looked at the wisps, shaded her eyes. "How do you know? Is it the cloud?"

No one had ever asked her *how* before. They thought they knew: She whispered with the wind, sang to the stars, walked with the wights.

"Well, is it?"

After a moment, Hild nodded.

"Hot you say?" Brona sighed. "I'd have been happier with warm."

"It'll be cooler high up. Tomorrow I'm away north and west, away from people up the cefn. It's high, so high you can see into next week. And the wind is fresh, the wind of the world. Come with me. Come away up the hill."

At the Roman fort where the road crossed the beck they dropped their packs and sat with their backs to the stone wall, facing the afternoon sun. It was hot. They had walked and talked—Hild showing her where the fox lived, pointing to the abandoned nests, telling her of tawny owls—and now they were hungry.

Hild rummaged in the pack Begu and Gwladus had put together for her. Nuts and cheese—two different kinds—eggs boiled in their shell and a little sack of salt. All sensible. But then potted mushrooms in butter; honey-eyed oat cakes; vinegared beet greens; Begu's own lovely flask, filled not just with mead but white mead; and two beautifully turned maple cups to go with it—Rulf's work—all bundled in a square of brightly dyed but coarsely woven linen. She unfolded the linen, laid it down, and set out the food: far more than she usually carried when travelling, and far more beautifully presented.

They ate steadily, drank. Ate more. Settled back to nibble a handful of nuts.

The breeze was faint, the sun warm on her bare legs and grass cool under her toes. Without even turning her head she could see thyme and daisies, buttercups and purple loosestrife, and cow parsley by the hawthorn that was barely leafed last time she was here. Brona sat an arm's length to her left; Hild was aware of her slow, steady breaths, the rise and fall of her gently rounded belly, the flex of her thighs as she leaned forward to pick up a twig to chew into a brush for her teeth.

A fly landed on Hild's thigh. She watched the glittering green of its back, the glimmer of its wings in the light.

"Doesn't that tickle?"

Hild watched the fly investigate her knee. "Have you noticed their wings? The left always the twin of the right, like wood split down the middle and opened. The same veins in the same patterns."

"Like birds," Brona said. She chewed a moment on her twig. "At least the ones I butcher."

"And butterflies, yes. But why? And is it just wings? We have two eyes . . ."

She peered at Brona, and Brona's head moved as she in turn tried to look at Hild's eyes. "No, hold still." She took Brona's jaw—slowly, gently—in her hand, chin in her palm, and brought her own face close. "Your right eye has darker pleats near the bottom." Closer. The bone fit snugly in her palm, hard and solid beneath the warm skin and dense muscle. "The left does, too, but not so thick." The grey was like soft, rich seal fur, the inside of the folds sooty-dark. Brona's breath was warm on her lips, and fast. She let go. "Your hands are different from each other, too."

Brona held out both hands, palm down. The right little finger bent in at the last joint, as did the left, but not as much. She stretched her legs out straight, pointed her toes, pulled them back. "My feet are different, too . . ."

Hild flexed her own feet. Brona looked at them, and Hild felt the butcher's attention travel up her leg and settle, weighty as a hand, on her bare thigh.

"You're so long," Brona said. And now they were close, close as cats who sit with fur just touching. "But not too long, not wrong. Just big. On your own you seem normal size, everything as it should be. It's just next to others that you're a giant. And you're well-knit. I watched you walk. But I can tell you've been hurt, on your left side."

Hild pulled her feet up and sat cross-legged.

Brona nodded at the toes peeking from the underside of Hild's thigh. "A lot of tall people have long thin toes, but yours look like mine." Brona stretched out her foot; they both looked at the strong tendons, the sturdy heel. The butcher used her finger and thumb to measure the length of her big toe, showed how many times that measure fit into the measure from her heel to the ball of her foot. Four times. "Yours will be about the same," Brona said. "It's just that this, the measure"—she held her finger and thumb apart in an approximate measure—"is much bigger. Bigger in the same way as the width of your big toe."

Hild flexed her toe. She had never really thought about proportions, measurements against measurements. She thought of how she looked at people, like Ceadwin, and knew he would be no good in a shield wall. But could you measure a woman's or man's height and the size of their bones and know what they would be good for?

"I've butchered a lot of animals, seen a lot of bones. It's all about weight. You can heft them, feel if they're smooth or rough in your hands. Big animals' bones are different: harder, heavier, smoother. Harder to cut. And they don't bend."

"Like yew shields instead of linden."

"Is yew heavier than linden?"

Hild nodded.

"Then yes. Like yew and linden."

Weight, Hild thought. Weight and relative height. Brona would not be a slight weight alongside her. "The foals," she said. "Their legs are too long."

"All foals have long legs. They grow into them. But . . ." She smoothed the grass, thinking. Looked up. "Have you seen the bones of a calf born too soon? Or any animal come before its time? They're unfinished."

Unfinished. "That's what Bryhtsige said."

"Twin foals were born in York two years since. Dead, of course. I cut them up for the dogs. Their leg bones weren't properly wide and capped."

Hild leaned back on her hands. "What do you mean?"

Brona cupped Hild's left knee. "Here." The warmth of her hand spread through the skin, through the fat, through the muscle, and Hild imagined Brona feeling her bone in her hand. "Where the bone meets the knee, it should be hard, and wider. But when a beast is born too soon, they're soft." She moved her hand down a little, smoothed down Hild's shin, and back, and each time she moved up Hild's chin went up a little, and her breath out.

She bent over Hild's leg, and now added a second hand, so she cuffed Hild's leg in a ring of heat. The blood beat at her throat, and her breasts rose and fell, rose and fell in time with Hild's.

"And here." She moved her hands up, circled the ridge of muscle above her knee. "In those dead foals this bone wasn't spread, wasn't wide enough, and the gristle was too thin. Against the knee it would be like . . ."

"Making an axle of applewood instead of oak."

"And with no grease." They were very close, close enough to breathe each other's breath. "They would rub against each other, back and forth, back and forth." She began to move both hands up and then down, up and down, each time a little higher, until Hild reached up, cupped Brona's head in her big hand, and pulled her close, belly to belly. "Don't stop," she said, and untied the tape of Brona's tunic.

And now their breath tore in and out, in and out, and Brona moved aside Hild's skirts, and Hild pulled Brona's naked belly and breasts down to hers and they began to move in earnest.

Hild sat up, naked, watching a harrier follow the rise and fall of the turf as closely as a woman's hand over another's belly, turning here, there, hunting something. A hare?

She looked down at Brona, spread against the turf, confident as a cat. She put her dark hand on Brona's pale belly, and Brona's smile was slow and rich. "Three more miles to the cefn. Then we'll hunt."

They moved north and west. They talked about the foals: They must keep their weight off their legs as much as possible, until the bones grew right. Wrapping and splinting would help take the weight, but the only cure was for the bone to grow.

The slope steepened, and grew more tussocky, the grass more wiry, and as the sun fattened and swelled, the blaze of yellow gorse deepened to gold. Birdsong began to mirror the rise and fall of the hills, flowers grew closer to the ground, and the scent of the hills dried a little from sweet grass to more aromatic bark, the mineral of stone, and the old, patient lichen growing in its hollows.

When Hild saw the red flash of grouse she laughed aloud, and, for no other reason than that she could, she ran. She dropped her pack and her staff and ran after the grouse, and Brona ran, too, and the grouse dashed this way and that and then leapt, like a pip spat from the slope's mouth into the air, and with a whirr of wings was gone. But Hild kept running, because it felt good. Good to run from sheer joy. Good to feel her muscles work to no purpose other than to delight in what they did best.

Hild laughed, and it felt good to laugh, as though something had been connected up again, like a pipe that was broken was now mended, and the cold bright gush from deep within her could once again flow, fountain up, out into the world, sparkling and clean, powerful, endless.

Wind whispered softly over the rise and fall of the moor. On the south slope of the cefn, in the shelter of a curve of lichened rocks, the hare roasted slowly over the small fire. High, high in the dome of sky, swallows soared and crisscrossed the deepening blue. The lichened rocks grew into looming lumps with long shadows, and the moon, a faint ghost of itself in the slanting evening sun, fattened and sank to the horizon. Brona watched it set. Hild watched the tiny curl of hair just behind Brona's ear spring up as it dried in the cooling air. She remembered the brush of it against her breast, the muscle stretching taut, there, as the butcher threw her head back and cried out. The evening smelt of woman and wood smoke, moor and thyme and slow-roasting hare.

"So low today," Brona said. "The moon. As though it was too tired to climb."

"It's always low in summer." In York there would always have been torchlight at night; she had not needed to know when the moon would be high and full. "It's part of the year's pattern," she said. "In summer, the sun rises early and sets late, and at midsummer it never quite gets dark. We don't need the moon to rise high to light the way; so it stays in a low arc in the south. But in winter, when the sun rises late and sets early and its light is pale and thin, so the moon moves north, rises high and bright, so that when the snow falls it glows like cold silver sunshine, only at night."

She turned the hare, poked it with her eating knife—it glistened pink still—and settled back.

"It wastes nothing, the pattern."

Brona moved next to her, slid her arm around Hild's waist, and rested her head on Hild's shoulder. "It matters to you, this pattern."

"Edwin king named me his godmouth and seer. I'm not a seer, I watch. I name the patterns that anyone could see, if they also watched." She lifted her cross out from under her dress and weighed it, then lifted it off and held it in both hands. "I was baptised in Christ. But who is Christ? Who is Woden, or Eorðe? They are all parts of the pattern. The pattern is in everything. We are all part of it. We make the pattern; the pattern makes us. The pattern is the way a bird's feather grows one way but not another. The fold of a beetle's wing. The—" She looked around, plucked a daisy. "Look. It's the whorl at the heart of the flowers, the pattern of its pollen. It's the same pattern on a snail's shell. Wait. Wait. Don't move." She went to her pack, where her belt lay, and the pouch fastened to it. Brought back the snake-stone. "See? The same pattern."

Brona traced it with her fingertip. "It's like the whorl in a pinecone."

"Yes! But that pattern is just part of the greater pattern. The pattern that's the living weave of weather, of wave and wood, of wishes and wyrd, hope and happiness. It's the breath of the world. It's the tiny seeds on a strayberry, the way the skin of a horse wrinkles in the same pattern as elm bark, and elm bark is like the gold cells we put garnets in on a shoulder clasp, and the little honeycombs bees build from their wax. We all hear it, we feel it, we breathe it. It sings in us. Let the priest have his church and the priestess her pool, my domain is here." She laid her palm on Brona's breastbone. "And here." She touched between her eyebrows. "And here." She cupped her hand between Brona's legs.

The hare was burnt when they ate it but they didn't care. As dusk deepened, shadow lay over the tussocks like felt, settling into corners, smoothing humps and bumps like a blanket thrown over a lumpy mattress. The sky darkened to blue black, paler at its fringes where it draped over the world and owls hunted, while the two women moved together in the glimmer between worlds, running with wild magic.

22

✦

Elmet basked green-gold in the summer morning and Hild felt her blood might also flow golden and full of bubbles, like a rushing beck of mead, rich and strong. She hummed as she walked beside Begu, just back from the site where Caer Loid would rise again, and sometimes skipped a step or two.

"Oh, just run. There's no one to see but me."

Hild broke into a run, loping, leaping, weaving circles around her gemæcce, sometimes mock-charging a tree and swinging her staff with a shout. A rook followed, cawing, and Hild cawed back, and it flew off, offended, and Hild gave chase because she could. The valley was safe, Menewood valley and the Yr valley; her people—well-fed now, and moving to her purpose—worked and walked and watched this land. She had sent messengers west along the valleys of the Kelder and east down the Use, as far as Goodmanham and Sancton, York and Derventio. The messages she got back were wary but folk were willing to listen. For now, this part of Deira was safely balanced. But it was a new balance, and nothing stayed in balance unless endlessly tended.

Smiling, she fell back in step with Begu as they left the road and moved west along the beck. They stopped, as Hild always did, at the pollard oak where she laid her palm against the ancient trunk and surveyed her valley.

Begu bumped Hild's shoulder with her head, like a newborn goat nudging its dam for milk. "What would your folk think if they saw their lady running and jumping like a kid goat?"

Hild only half listened as her thoughts turned to the valley, and the people she must soon send here and there.

"—though I hope the butcher tends to you differently than she did Nell's kid."

Hild blinked.

Begu bubbled with laughter, her freckles stretched wide. "Cath Llew blushes pink as a baby's ear whenever anyone mentions bed games!"

"You're as bad as my mother." Both of them always eager to talk in squirming detail about what one body did with another.

Begu ignored the scowl. "So. It's good?"

For Hild the body made sense only with the body, not with words. But words were what others understood. "It's . . . different."

"Different how? Different from Gwladus, or different from Cian?"

Hild picked at the bark under her hand. "With Cian, our bodies—" Trying to find the words for what bodies did made as much sense as trying to winkle an oyster from its shell with a feather. "The women he played with before me were small. Much smaller than him. But I was as big." Bigger. "Our bodies met in fighting before we wed. And our marriage bed still sometimes tasted of war."

"But not with Gwladus."

"No." But with Gwladus it had not been their bed but Hild's bed. Hild had owned it, just as she had owned Gwladus. "She was my bodywoman. She . . . served me. She tended me."

"But you didn't tend her."

"No. And with Cian, I didn't—" She moved her hands in frustration, as though she were trying to shape words out of the air.

"You didn't tend him? Ah, you didn't tend each other. You only took . . . joint pleasure?" Hild nodded. "And with Brona?"

"We take our pleasure together. And sometimes she gives. And sometimes I give. And it works. For now."

"Now is what we have."

"But how long will this, me and Brona, last? Nothing holds it together."

And she was breathing the air of another summer, watching her mother wipe her hands free of sheep grease. *You need a person to anchor you. Someone whose smell and touch will keep your feet on the ground. Someone no one will notice.*

People can always tell who you've chosen, but if it's someone they can dismiss they won't dismiss you. If they're not your equal, if they don't matter, you will be seen to be you, still.

But that was when she was a girl. That was when there was a king, and they meant men with more power than her. Men she had to sway from the side, to help them think their understanding was their own. Now, in El-met, in all Deira, there was none with more power than her. Now it was what she thought that mattered.

"Brona matters to me."

"Well." Begu looked at her. "That'll be interesting for you."

Interesting. She was not sure she liked *interesting.*

"Oh, don't look so worried. No ownership and no vow? Just two people wanting each other? It'll be interesting. And interesting isn't bad. Well, not always. It's just surprising."

She did not like *surprising,* either.

Begu grinned, patted her on the arm, and they moved down into the valley proper, talking now about the new Loidis that would grow where the beck met the Yr, the old Caer Loid, the East Farm, the food there, and who might be best sent where. But as Begu chattered Hild's mind turned her new discovery this way and that: Her opinion was what mattered now.

". . . how much Whisk and Flicker grew," Begu said.

They passed the women washing clothes by the half-rebuilt millrace; they would have to find a new spot when the mill was— "Wait," she said. "The foals grew? I was only gone two days."

"Of course they grew. They're foals. They'll still be smaller than Wol-cen, but not as small as we thought."

"You were worried Wolcen might not have enough milk."

"She doesn't. But Bryhtsige showed me what to do."

"And how is Bryhtsige?"

Begu snorted. "You mean, how am I and Bryhtsige—are we well to-gether. We are, or well enough."

"So you're . . . ?"

"No."

Hild could tell by the furrow between Begu's eyebrows—so brief it might have been shadow—that there was more to say on that, but they were now in the heart of the valley, passing the huts. And when you were the lady, they listened to everything you said and everything others said to you. And she could already see Rhin in the distance watching in the way that meant he was waiting to talk to her.

"But we're easy again."

"Good," she said.

Begu stopped. "Why?"

"Why? We're gemæcce, I want you to be happy." She tried to move forward.

Begu did not budge. "Well, of course you do. But just wanting me to be happy doesn't make the light of the world, Butcherbird, Cath Llew, lady of Elmet, and lord of Deira—"

Lord of Deira.

"—say 'Good!' and look like you found a lost hoard. So what are you planning?"

It wasn't just Rhin waiting. Past him, Oeric had turned and waved, and was watching. Lord of Deira. "I'm planning many things."

"What are you planning for me and Bryhtsige?"

The sooner she satisfied her gemæcce's curiosity the sooner they would be done. "I want you to go north."

"To the Bay of the Beacon, yes."

"And perhaps more north still." Hild took a step forward. Begu looked stubborn for a moment, then gave in. "I would send Bryhtsige with you. To the Bryneich."

The Bryneich knew them both. Coledauc, and Cuncar the piglet prince, would talk to Bryhtsige, who could listen and not be swayed but could turn a man—or woman—aside with a word as easily as with a knife. And Langwredd would talk to Begu, tell her the things the men might not know, or see, or admit even to themselves. And Bryhtsige would keep them safe.

"When?"

"Soon. I've sent word to Cenhelm for *Curlew*."

"Cenhelm will want gold."

"We have gold." And soon, when they had their mill, they would start earning silver—and more, when the Frisians returned to Deira and found her people tithing at every river landing, beach wīc, and hythe. "But first we need word of Cadwallon." Hard word—word solid enough to stand on if she were to risk her gemæcce on it. "So not now, but soon."

Not now, the magic phrase. Begu immediately stopped thinking about it and they walked on briskly.

As they passed Hild's storage hut, Begu said, "Oh, and I used your lime."

"My lime?" The bag of slaked lime she used for making parchment.

"For the foals."

Hild had a vision of the foals with their manes and tails limed and spiked like the hair of the warriors of the long ago. "I don't—"

"Wolcen doesn't have enough milk, I told you. And Nell's kid is butchered and so not drinking hers."

Hild shook her head, trying to sort the words into some sense.

"I was going to just mix Nell's milk with Wolcen's for foals, but Bryhtsige said they were still so young it would upset their bellies. But he'd fed an orphaned foal once with goat's milk doubled with lime water because he remembered his ma telling him a story about feeding an orphaned calf that way. His foal was older than Flicker and Whisk, almost weaned. But it worked. And it's still working. They're growing like weeds. So, anyway, the lime's all gone."

Lime water. Would it work with— "Wait. Gone? All my lime?"

"Growing foals drink a lot of milk. But don't worry, Grimhun and Ceadwin have been roasting up sacks of the stuff."

And now Rhin was moving towards them, with Oeric not far behind.

Hild told Rhin and Rulf she would have a cottage built on the west side of the curving beck, just under where the hill steepened.

"There is room there only for one small building," Rulf said.

"And it is very close to your house," Rhin said.

"Yes," said Hild. "I will be there often."

And because she was the lady of Menewood, the work began there first.

The doorway was open to the early evening for there was as yet no door, just outer walls and roof, and on the bed—which was still only a rude frame with leather ties draped with furs—Hild flipped her braid over her right shoulder and rubbed a little goose grease into the muscles running along Brona's hip, finding the knots, easing them out. Brona's muscles were different to Hild's, shorter and in different places. Hild pushed with both thumbs over the arch of bone.

Brona hissed and tensed, then let go.

Butchers in York, with its twice five hundred folk, did not use their legs much, but in Menewood, with only fivescore, the butcher, like everyone else, must turn her hand to any work to be done. Today she had been hauling trunks just felled.

"I had no idea trees were so heavy. They kick, too. No, don't stop—just there. The tree jumped when it went down. I had no idea."

Hild eased out in circular motions over the small of her back. "Who was leading? They should have warned you."

"They did, love. Which is why I wasn't hurt."

"Tomorrow perhaps you should work with me."

Brona rolled onto her back. "Do I look like a child?"

Hild looked down at the muscled neck, span of collarbone, the swelling breasts with their sharpening tips, belly rising and falling, and the glisten on the hair between her legs. "No."

"Then why try to protect me like one?"

It was a formless thing, a tightness under her breastbone. She took Brona's hand, put it high against her belly. "I know you're grown, I know you're strong, but when I can't see you I get tight here, just as I do when I can't look around and see Wilfrid. I feel it. The valley is safe, safe as it's ever been, but still, I feel it."

Brona sat up and crossed her legs. "Did you worry about Boldcloak?"

"Only in war." And even then not always.

"And Gwladus?"

"Gwladus was always either with me, or safe at a vill under the care of others." The same for Begu. Safe under the care of others.

And there it was, again: others. Others to take the weight. But now there was no king in his vill, no one to call in her oath, to tithe to, to take charge.

No one. No one but her. The king was dead. The æthelings were dead, and the ealdormen and the thegns. There was Oswine in Craven, but he was a follower, not a leader. "I'm their king," she said.

"You're not like any king I've seen."

Hild stared at her without really seeing. "They look to me." All of Deira.

"People have always looked to you."

"It's not the same." She felt bewildered. "I'm the king. What should I do?"

Brona grinned. "Whatever you want!" Hild did not grin back. Brona sighed. "That's the only thing I know about kings. They do what they want. So what do you want?"

To flee. To ride into the hills, free of all this. But these were her people. They were sworn to her and she had sworn to keep them safe. "To build and make. To grow, to be safe without hiding." To be under no one's sway but her own. To be listened to as herself. To not have to hedge and hide and lead from the side. But also to just . . . be. "To be free." She could not be free until her people were safe. "I need help."

"Well, who helps kings?"

"His counsellors." Who did her uncle talk to? "Edwin sat at York with princes and bishops, thegns and gesiths, and the queen—a daughter of queens. I have my mother, who sometimes can't even thread her own needle."

Brona shrugged. "Could Edwin?"

"It's not about the needle. He also had Paulinus, overbishop of the north and prince of the church. And through him he could talk by letter with the bishop of bishops, in Rome. What do I have? Rhin, a shunned wealh priest."

"Priests don't win wars."

"No. But Edwin king had three hundred sworn gesiths, and half again as many thegns who could bring their own spearmen. And he still lost. All I have is Leofdæg, with his shoulders at different heights and his humped back."

"Leofdæg who was one of those sworn gesiths, good enough for the king. He survived where most of the king's gesiths didn't. Who else?"

"Oeric. Who carries his father's old sword and whose feet are caked with farm dirt."

"And what are thegns but farmers? And their weapons have long stories and were named by their forebears."

"You don't understand."

Brona looked unconcerned. "Then help me."

"Begu then," Hild said. "A girl who looks like a goat and has never seen a man's blood spilt in anger."

"Begu," Brona said. "Who is saving twin foals, which no one has done before, at least no one at the overking's vill in York could."

Hild nodded slowly. "And saved me so many times." Begu, who knew her heart if not always her mind. Whose father took her in when she was lost. Begu, who had never feared for her life, or her next meal. "I'm glad she hasn't seen what I've seen or had to do what I've done. And she never should."

"No."

"No one ever should."

"No, because you'll protect them. Who else?"

"Gwladus." Gwladus of the conquered Dyfneint who as bodywoman and slave kept her safe with news, with gossip she brought and meetings she arranged. "Gwladus, who saved my life on the field of war. Who birthed my child and buried her. Who kept me alive when I would have died. Who even saved my gold."

"Who else?"

"Bryhtsige, who survived, twice, what has driven others mad. And Morud, who is just a boy but has been by my side when I've needed him most. And Gladmær. And Grimhun and Heiu." Her people. Bent but not broken, unbowed and beautiful.

Two days later, Hild came back to the long house hot and thirsty after a hard afternoon with Rulf building the new coppice stack and talking about the trees to fell for the next buildings. At least coppicing the elm stool she and Rhin had begun three years ago was easy: The stems were thin enough to hold in one hand and cut with a hand axe in the other. Elm weave made a good underlayer when building on wet ground. They would need a lot of it; the land drained for the new Loidis would be damp for a year.

They needed more people for such tasks, and others besides. But more people meant more building, more food, more weaving. More decisions. More counsellors to help make those decisions . . .

She unslung the axe from her shoulder, chunked it into the stump by the door, and leaned the billhook against the oak upright. "Morud!"

She sat on the stump and took off her boots. Where was the boy? "Morud!"

And there was still no word from Coelgar in Lindum. She banged her boots against the base of the stump to knock off the dirt, stretched her toes this way and that.

Her axe needed sharpening. She needed a drink. Where was that boy?

She padded into the shadowy house and nearly tripped over a board down from the wall and set on a trestle, and covered in . . . travel clothes? A bedroll. Cloak. Wound roll. A murmur of voices drew her to the second bower, where the door stood open.

"Again," Gwladus said.

Sintiadd looked at a fold of something blue on the bed. "What's wrong with it?"

Gwladus picked up the blue pile and shook it out. One of Hild's good dresses. "Look. See this line? If you put the dress in a saddlebag folded like that after an hour's ride it would look like a crumpled rag. And when you're dressing the lady to meet a king she will not want to look like a scarecrow! Watch again. Like this."

With a lift and a flip, a move Hild had seen Gwladus make a hundred times and thought nothing of, the dress seemed to magically fold itself down into a perfect packet of wool that Gwladus smoothed gently with her hand.

"The lady wouldn't notice if you put her in a sack." Morud's voice from the shadow thrown by the door.

"But everyone else would," Breguswith said. Her mother was there, too? "And she would notice their resulting lack of deference. And then she would look at you."

"Practise more," Gwladus said. "Show me what you remember of her jewels. What would you lay out with that dress and the second-best veil?"

Hild had no idea which was her second-best veil—she only wore such things outside Menewood, when she just wore what Gwladus had chosen for her to wear—but Sintiadd did. She watched through the crack as the girl—young woman now—with the kind of movement that spoke of some practise, found, unfolded, and laid out a veil, then retrieved a box Hild had forgotten she had.

Clearly this was not the first such lesson. Hild backed away.

There was a jug of ale and a whetstone by the hearth; she took them outside to her stump. She sat and set the stone to the blade. *Zzzsst. Zzzsst.* The rhythm was calming. When was the last time she had had to think about her clothes or her jewels? She took a drink. Good ale: Craven barley but an Elmet malting; her mother's work. All those years Gwladus had been her bodywoman and she had barely noticed the work, had never thought about the other skills Gwladus would need to make the right choices. *Zzzsst.*

When the axe was sharp enough she set it aside and took up the bill-hook. After that, there was her seax. She had some thinking to do.

The air was pooling to gold when Gwladus found her in the garth lodging the yellowing onion stalks.

"You will need a bodywoman," Gwladus said. "And Sintiadd will do very well."

So she had known Hild was watching; she saw everything. It was what made her so good at her work.

Hild looked up at her, hair like honey in the sun. "At first I thought to give you old Caer Loid. It's good orchard land, and I remember Gwladus ferch Heddwen is Gwladus of the Dyfneint, cider-makers of the world."

Gwladus folded her arms and raised her eyebrows.

"No," Hild said. "I couldn't see you content mashing apples and pears, either." She bent the last onion stalk, dusted her hands, and stood. "Come with me."

In the bower, Hild propped the door wide to let in the sun, and began to take down box after box, roll after roll of rings, veil bands, ear jewels, neck jewels, cuffs, and bags and spread them on the bed. "Help me."

Gwladus did, both of them stopping every now and again to take delight in the weight of lustrous yellow gold, in the contrast of deep red garnet and dark blue lapis, the pale green fire of beryl, sky-blue sapphire, the sunsets of amber and carnelian, the glowing cloud of pearl, and the sheen of silver and seriousness of enamelled bronze. They covered the bed, and then turned to the bench, and when they had nearly filled that Hild scooped up her carnelians, the heavy cross from Edwin, and the agate and pearl veil band and earrings Begu had brought from Onnen, set them to one side, and said, "Take up and put away anything not gold, then fill the space with the best of the rest."

When they were done they stood back and looked at it all. A dragon's hoard.

"I had no idea," Hild said.

"No, lady. I only kept out a little at any one time."

It occurred to her she did not know how many dresses she had, either, or pairs of shoes or cloaks. But that was not why they were here. "Choose," she said.

"Lady?"

"A king has a Fist. I need a more leftwise . . ." Yes. "A left-handed approach. So choose. You know best what jewels speak of power, the power to bestow favour. When you speak to a thegn or prince, ealdorman or bishop, he must feel your standing, the weight of your wealth. For it will be your wealth, Gwladus ferch Heddwen; yours to keep. You must feel your own power and consequence, and stand tall upon it. Only then will they feel the weight of my power through yours when you speak as Hild Yffing's Left Hand." Silence. "If that would suit you."

Gwladus reached out to touch a thick gold necklet with the long, filigreed wire beads made in Byzantium. "What does the Yffing lord of Deira's Left Hand wear?"

She saw Gwladus standing in the light and the shadow, working equally in both. "Wear something that would shine as well from the shadows as from the light, at least to those who have eyes to see. Make someone like my mother pay enough attention to need to reckon your worth before she speaks."

"You'd have me speak to those like your mother?"

"Sometimes. Sometimes their husbands, sometimes their priests. Sometimes their bodywomen, their housemen, their goosegirls and bread makers." She began to see Gwladus Left Hand more clearly: calculating, cool, willing to step back into shadow or stand forth and shine, ready to guide or lead, speak or listen, and wind a path between opposites with a light tread, soothing where she could and ruffling only when she must, but knowing, always, the path Hild would want to follow, and following it—building it if she had to. "But, yes, most often you will represent me to highfolk, so imagine wearing enough to make them reckon your worth anew every day for a week."

"Wear enough new gold each day for seven days? That's an ætheling's ransom." She stroked a ruby pendant. "It's too much."

It was interesting to watch the echo of the old Gwladus—the new slave who coveted pretty dresses and silver armlets, eye-catching combs for her beautiful hair—wrestle with the new Gwladus, Gwladus Left Hand of the Yffing, the Gwladus she needed.

Gwladus stroked a sapphire, then stepped back and brought both hands together in front of her. "Lady. With Æthelburh gone, you're the richest woman in the north, and even for you I keep only five days' jewels in the small chest. If you ever needed more, then mixing and matching the veil bands and rings, the necklets and the cuffs would be enough for another ten. And, Lady, your Hand must never outshine you."

Outshine. She had thought Gwladus's worry might be not being believed; being seen, still, as Hild's wealh bodywoman, someone who did not matter. But speaking Anglisc, standing tall, dressed in fine jewels, that heavy gold hair caught back under a veil short enough to show the weight and sway beneath, the glimmer of ruby at her throat and ears, a richly woven dress in russet and gold, that waist caught in a gleaming belt, attended by armed men. That Gwladus would never not matter again. And she could have wept for what could have been between them, if they could have begun now.

"Five days' worth, then. No less. And you will need a horse, and its proper gear. Bryhtsige will advise you. And a spearman, of course, and your own woman to—" Gwladus was giving her that half smile. "But I see you know what you will need. I'll say only, don't stint, Gwladus Hand. You'll need to shine."

Gwladus picked up the great ruby brooch again, put it down.

"Red never was my colour," Hild said. "Take the rubies."

Gwladus stroked a red-gold and topaz cuff, Irish work. "And some of the lesser jewels as gifts? As Hand I'll need many gifts."

"Start with something for Sintiadd. She's going to earn it. And when we go to Sancton next week, be sure to trade for good cloth not just in my colours but yours. Use some of the jewels for that if you have to."

"Silver would be better there. They know jewels in Sancton, but with no king there's no goldsmith—no one to rework them."

She had not thought of that. She would need to find a goldsmith, too. "Is that something Sintiadd would know?"

"Not yet. But she will. I'm teaching her how to see, what to see, and how to learn what she needs to know, lady."

Hild smiled. "Then Sintiadd will do very well."

The long house now had a sturdy bench alongside the south wall, facing the beck. Hild and Begu and Breguswith took the bench where they could all soak up the sun while Breguswith span and the two gemæcce worked on a new tablet weave from the vividly dyed thread Gwladus had bought from a Frisian on the sandy river shore down from Sancton. On the grassy slope at the top of the beck's bank Maer teased two of Clut's kittens with a dandelion. Closer to the beck Brona held out her hands and walked backwards while Wilfrid, determined, held one finger in each hand and swung his chubby legs out wide—one, two, three—before teetering wildly and being swept up by Brona, tilted sideways, and zuzzed at the trees, chortling.

"He sounds happy," Breguswith said, teasing and stretching the wool with one hand, stroking, spinning with the other, endless as a waterfall.

Wilfrid's occasional happiness made Hild happy, but her happiness was not an easy or simple thing. She had fed him from her body, kept him alive, carried him in her arms and soothed him when he teethed. He was hers, part of her now. Yesterday as she washed him he had held her braid in one hand and pronounced solemnly, "Mum-mor." And for a moment her heart squeezed, though she did not know if it was for Wilfrid or for

Little Honey, who would never say that. And all day she could not look at him without wondering how it would be for Little Honey to be laughing and trying to walk now, and for Cian to soothe Honey when she fell, and swing her around when she laughed.

The weave she held tugged: Begu, bringing her back to the work at hand. She turned her tablet.

"She chose well," Begu said. "This is a truly lovely green, and look at how it shimmers."

"I hope it didn't cost too much," Breguswith said.

"Oh no," Begu said.

They were not talking about silver—though the silver cost had been less than they had guessed: the Frisians were eager, because dead kings and murdered thegns could not trade. It was the rest of the exchange they wondered about—the carefully chosen information for the Frisians to spread as they travelled north, and, in turn, news from the Frisians who had been trading along the East Angle coast and down the Treonte with Lindseymen and Middle Angles, for there was still no word from Coelgar.

Hild said, "Gwladus made a very good exchange."

Not only that, she had spoken to the head people of every settlement between Menewood and Goodmanham, and the word, now, was that they were ready to listen. Hild Yffing was expected at Goodmanham at harvest, in a month, and many people would be there to listen and bargain. She would have magnificent clothes to wear when she arrived, and be escorted by well-fed, well-mounted, and well-armed men: her own and Oswine's. She would remain there a fortnight, so that others could join after their own harvests, and help plan how they would face winter and the renewed struggles in the spring.

For the last two days, her counsellors had been mulling everything they had learnt, trying to find the best path forward. For Hild it was strange to share thoughts; she had spent her life taking her own counsel, then acting without warning, as though from knowledge snatched from the air. That was what godmouths did. But she was not a godmouth—not light of the world, hægtes, or seer. Nor was she a thegn or chief gesith; it was not strength of arms alone that would save them. And over and over, as she talked with Breguswith and Oeric, Leofdæg and Bryhtsige, Grimhun and Heiu, Gwladus and Rhin, the same missing piece came up: They needed ships.

The Frisians had told Gwladus the ships Coelfrith had taken to Lindsey—

Yffing ships—were still all there, doing nothing. This puzzled the Frisians. Not that they were unhappy—ships that were not trading were ships that were not cutting into their profits—but why were the Lindseymen letting them just sit there?

It had been two months since she sent a message with the priest who carried letters for Hereswith and Fursey, to Coelgar, ealdorman of Lindsey. Coelgar had never liked Hild, though his younger son Coelwyn had been one of her Hounds, and she got on well enough with Coelfrith, who had sailed the ships to Lindsey in the first place. Yffing ships. She wanted them back. She wanted the ships, the gold, the men and horses, but more, she wanted Coelfrith, Edwin's reeve, who held all the steadings' tithe tallies in his head.

She looked at her mother, at her still-nimble fingers and still-handsome face. A counsellor did not have to thread a needle, no. Nor her speaker. "How's your hip?"

"Well enough."

"How well?"

Breguswith, who knew how her daughter thought, said only, "Well enough to travel."

"Then you and Luftmær will go to Lindum, to Coelgar. You will ask him, again, my question. And you will bring me his answer."

She stilled her spindle and her forget-me-not eyes sparked. "I'll do better than that. I'll get you the answer you want." Coelgar had always liked Breguswith. "How will we travel?"

"Frisians are nosing along the Yr. Oeric'll find you a ship. He'll ride with you to Cnotinsleah."

"A trade ship?"

She would be sailing south and east, away from enemies. She did not need a ship of war. Besides, for the shallow summer rivers they would need a shallow draught—that or they must sail out to the coast, down almost to the East Angles, then up the Withma. "Oeric will make sure it's a good one."

After a moment her mother nodded. "But not tomorrow. Tomorrow Luftmær will sing at Wilfrid's birthday feast." She laughed at Hild's expression. "He's your son if he's anyone's. And the son of the Yffing of Deira deserves a feast, and a feast needs a praise song. Luftmær's been working on it a week."

23

✦

By the end of meadmonath the foals were eating handfuls of green chop along with their milk and Flicker needed splints only on one knee. The onion tops in the long-house garth turned brown, and Hild pulled and piled them to carry to the net newly strung outside the small bower.

"Lady."

She turned. Oeric. He should still be in Cnotinsleah overseeing river clearance.

"Lady. Your lady mother is on the boat of Bavo the Frisian, for Lindsey."

"And this Bavo, he's trustworthy?"

"He is, lady. But he also had news—from his brother lately at Arbeia—of Cadwallon. News I thought you best hear quickly. Cadwallon thieved the goods at Arbeia meant for trade"—all the goods that flowed south from Bernicia, and east from Rheged—"and is now past the wall and heading north. And, lady, Bavo gave the news for free, asking only that one day we stop the ravager from spoiling business."

Saying goodbye to Brona was hard. "See that they're well," Hild said, again.

"I will."

Fllur, Fllur's son Geren, and Maer would move into Brona's house, with Wilfrid. "Am I doing the right thing?" Hild asked again. If all went well she would be gone for weeks. They had talked about it many times—or Hild had. Brona had said only *Why talk about it? You'll choose what you choose.*

Now she said, "Has anything changed since you decided?"

Hild sighed. "No."

"Well, then."

Wilfrid was so young, and already she missed Maer's endless questions. "Be sure to ask Rhin if you need anything. Anything at all."

"I will."

"And maybe I'll send for you. When—"

"Just don't let that bag of bones buck you off."

Hild smiled. "Bone's turning out to be quite well-mannered, and very eager to please. You just make sure those foals keep growing, or Begu'll have my hide when she gets back."

Hild's band—a score, half mounted and half on foot—did not enter the city proper but wound their way past the walls and headed east to the docks. In the distance they could see only one boat: the *Curlew*, tied to the same wharf as the first time Hild had seen her.

"I hope Brona will check Flicker's wrapping every day," Begu said. "If she's still not limping after a week she's to take it off."

"She'll remember," Hild said. *Don't make a habit of leaving me to watch and ward small things while you ride about*—but she would do it right. "And you remember what to tell Onnen?"

"She won't like it."

She would not like any part of it, starting with the news of her son's death. "Nonetheless, say it exactly as I told you. And, Begu, please, give her my dear love. Help her hear it. Tell her I would do anything, anything to make it different."

Begu leaned over and patted Hild's thigh. "Yes."

"And—"

"Yes! Yes. You've told me half a hundred times about the dangers of going north to the Bryneich. And what to tell Coledauc if I go. And Cuncar. Yes, I remember."

"And you have—"

"Yes, I have the silver."

Now they were at the river. Where before a dozen boats might have been bowsed tight to the quay, yellow wagtails roosted in the reeds. The air, though better than two months ago, was still thick with the stench of the dead. As the party reined in, they saw that Cenhelm and his men wore cloth wrapped around their faces.

Hild and Bryhtsige dismounted, and Begu slid off Sandy. She passed the reins to Bryhtsige, and hugged Hild. "Now don't worry. I expect to come back and find Deira prospers." She dashed at her eyes; the lashes sparkled. "And remember to be nice at Goodmanham."

"I'm always—"

"Don't frighten them to death. And wear that dress with the new cuffs; they're just right."

"Sintiadd will decide what—"

"I still think you should have worn them for Wilfrid's feast." Begu saw Cenhelm. "Oh, there he is. Cenhelm!" And she turned and walked busily up the gangboard in her bright yellow dress.

Bryhtsige stood with his black and Sandy, waiting. "Keep her safe," Hild said.

"On my life."

"I need you safe, too." She stopped. She had told him all this already; too many times. She held out her arm. They gripped briefly, then Bryhtsige led the pony and war stallion to the boat.

Hild shielded her eyes against the sun, saw Cenhelm leaning on the rail, and remounted Bone, kneed him along the wharf, beckoning the captain aft.

At the taffrail they were almost of a height. "Cenhelm."

He squinted. "Yffing."

"How's the river?"

He balanced his hand back and forth. "This part needs work. This wharf and that"—he nodded to the next one over—"are the only ones worth tying to."

"I'll see to it." She reached up, put a small plump sack in his hand. "If you get to the bay and it's not safe, don't put in, whatever they say. And if you've any doubt about Colud, the same—ignore their pleas and sail them back. I'm the one who pays, and I'll pay well for their safety—more than any other could pay for their harm."

Cenhelm weighted the sack thoughtfully, spat once, and nodded.

"A good wind and kind tides to you then, Cenhelm."

"Aye," he said, and moved forward, shouting. Men began casting off ropes. She turned Bone to move back down the wharf.

"Hild!" Begu, grinning, waving from amidships, pointing back along the deck. "He's got a better tent! Oh, and any special word for Langwredd?" She gave Hild a knowing look. "Shall I tell her *all* your news?"

"Tell her whatever you like, only tell her—tell her I think of her warmly."

The sails began to fill.

"H—" A sudden flap of canvas drowned her words.

"What?"

"—ow warmly?"

Hild just waved, and watched the brave splash of yellow move downriver, around the curve and away.

She rejoined the others. "Grimhun, look to the well first, then the wharves. Oeric, take the hall and apartments; clear them. We'll start a burn in the yard by the stables. The rest, with me."

North and east of York, Derventio was destroyed. The beautiful church that Cian had once found so cold, the blank white that within a year had become glorious with colour and carving, had been used to byre Cadwallon's horses. The paintings of the saints and Mary were hacked and spattered with mud, blood, and dung, the thick wavy coloured glass smashed out from the windows high under the eaves, the floor gouged and shattered. The vill, from where Æthelburh and the children had fled first to Sancton and then to Brough, was worse—vile with the broken bodies of those who had not fled, gnawed bones, and the nests of vermin. They took two days to burn it all. She had Gladmær carve a boar on what was left of the fallen church door, then she and her men rode north, east, south, and west and shouted loud for any to hear that there were Yffings still in Deira and by Blodmonath they would be in York again, and that there'd be work and food for any who chose to come.

They took the narrow redcrest road that followed the valley south to Goodmanham. As they rode through the gentle hills, some still rich with corn, others overtaken by weeds, yet others already scythed to stubble and stooks, she felt the attention of watchers hidden in trees and hedgerows. She saw Leofdæg feel them, too, and gave out quiet orders to ignore any who did not want to be seen. Instead, every two miles she had Oeric, who had a fine strong voice, declare there were once again Yffings in Deira to set the countryside aright. And those who wished could come either to Goodmanham for harvest or, at the end of Winterfylleth, to York. There they could meet, to judge and be judged by, their lords.

"Why not say the lady Hild?" he asked when he galloped back to Hild's side.

"Not yet," said Gwladus. Riding the sorrel gelding with glittering harness, her corn-coloured hair bright against the rich green of her dress, and gold gleaming at neck and cuff, she looked like a lady born, and now sounded like one: clear and certain. Goodmanham was to be her first test as Left Hand.

Hild nodded. "Goodmanham is soon enough." They were putting on a show of strength: a dozen people, including three women and a priest—Almund, freshly shaved—all well-fed and well-mounted, richly dressed and wearing enough gold to fund a war band. This was why she had told her mother not to unpick the horse harness wealth; this was why Menewood had worked to add gold-thread cuffs, to find and share crosses, to bring carts of mead and two penned wethers to roast. A lord who was unafraid to ride the country weighted by gold, and generous enough to share plenty when others starved, was a lord worth following. Let them first see the wealth and the weapons, let them see her person, and let her weigh their hearts.

Goodmanham, with its slow river valley at summer's height, the rolling wolds crimson with flowers and skeps humming, had always been the Yffing heartland. Unlike York with its redcrest walls and protected wīc at the meeting of war streets, or Bebbanburg's blunt might on the searoad, or Yeavering with its massive halls and totems and speaking stage, its corral for the cattle the whole of the north delivered as tribute, Goodmanham was the kernel of the Yffings at rest and play; their home, and the home of their gods. Goodmanham was where kings, queens, and æthelings came to loosen their belts and fill their cups, throw the dice and weave the cloth, watch the sheep and rett the flax. It was here that colts ran with their dams until they were strong enough for war; here where the land provided, where Yffings and the folk of Deira grew strong. Goodmanham was where Deira celebrated the bounty that a strong Yffing king ensured, and where the priests thanked the gods and praised their ancestors for their good fates. Win Goodmanham and win Deira.

From the moment they rode past the nearest fields with the corn being scythed, when she saw the great byre was still standing, unburnt, Hild knew Goodmanham would be theirs: Cadwallon and his reavers had not come this far east; here the fate of Yffings and their folk was whole and unspoilt. At Goodmanham there were no Yffing symbols to destroy, no towering walls to tear down or totems of might to burn. Cadwallon had not understood that this gentle place was the heart of Deira. Once he understood, though, yes, he would come to burn it out. But for now, here they still knew the Butcherbird, king's fist and light of the world. They knew she was Yffing, blood and strength of their land. They were hers before she even slid from Bone's back, staff and blade bright at her belt, her own totems.

Hild left Leofdæg at the top of the rise that led down to the tangled bottomland. He would let no one pass—no matter how great and good, how much they needed to reassure the Yffing of their loyalty.

"The light of the world scries for our fate," he would say, and they would shiver, and back away, and go make their promises to Hild Yffing's Left Hand, Gwladus ferch Heddwen, who, in all her gold and cuffs and polished hair, surrounded by armed men and obeyed by all, bore no resemblance to Gwladus the wealh slave and bodywoman they might once have known.

Hild kilted up her dress and made her way through the dark and damp bottomland, the tangle of oak and crabapple and holly, past the hollow where as a child she had watched the caterpillar instead of paying attention to Cian's game of firing the furze. And then, at last, in the clearing where the air was still and secret and smelled of wood ælfe, was the pool.

She sat on the bank beneath the old cherry that shaded the east end. It had been old even when she first came here, old when she cast her first tooth in the pool and dreamt of the sprite that would watch over it forever and claim part of her. As she had as a child, she watched waterbugs skating across the pool. She leaned forward, laid her palm on the heavy surface, and pushed gently, making the water rock and a spider floating on a leaf thrust out all its legs and hold tight. The afternoon sun turned the surface to a mirror, and when her cross swung out over the water, its great gold reflection moved on the water beneath her. Would the water sprite who had accepted her tooth see it? What would she think—was it the first cross the pool had seen? No. She had been here wearing a cross before. But now it was different.

Goodmanham was where she had understood that her wyrd and her sister's were different, that their mother had been training them for different paths. Hereswith as peaceweaver, Hild as light of the world. Goodmanham was the last place she had felt she and Hereswith were alike. Every breath in Goodmanham reminded her of Hereswith; every breath made her ache.

Except here. She had never brought Hereswith here, nor Begu. This was her secret place, hers and Cian's.

She picked up a stick—cherry; the old tree was still shedding branches— and poked the water. The light was wrong to see the stick break at the line between air and water but she knew it did, knew that in her hand it was now a thing of two worlds, different in each. If it could speak would it be with one tongue above and another beneath?

Elsewhere in Goodmanham she had always spoken Anglisc but here, by the pool, British.

"Wood ælf," she said in Anglisc. "Water sprite," she said in British. "I am Hild Yffing. Will you listen?"

The cherry tree shivered and the pool ruffled, then both stilled.

"My sister." She imagined Hereswith by a pool, under a tree somewhere among the North Folk. Neither sprite nor ælf would understand the word for *letter*. And uncanny beings did not like to be asked plainly to do anything. "May sitting by your domain open her ears to my message."

Words on parchment seemed as chancy as casting wishes into a well. If only she could see Hereswith, take her face in her hands, and say, *Flee! Penda is coming!* But Hereswith would not. Nor even if the message reached her would she heed Hild's plea to not, not let her husband become king. Long ago Hild had told Hereswith she would one day be queen, and her sister would choose to believe that wyrd above all the pleas and messages and visions that followed, because that was the wyrd her mother had trained her to. And it was the wyrd she wanted.

Hild contemplated her stick, then laid it carefully on the surface of the pool, so it lay half in and half out of air and water. The water sprite would look up and believe the stick was hers; the wood ælf would look down and believe it his. Was it both or neither? Could it choose? It would float there until stormy weather sank it or a breeze washed it into the bank. Its wyrd was already woven—but none yet knew what it was.

Harvest was hard work. And Hild—the Yffing, their lord and loaf giver—worked at their side, stride for stride, scythe by scythe. When the others left the field, she followed the older women to the retting pools and listened to what they had cut for fibre and what for oil—mostly fibre this year, because they did not want to leave crops growing to be burnt. And what of next year? they asked. Both, she told them. They needed cloth and they needed oil—she would take part of her tithe in oil—and next summer Cadwallon would not trouble them; she had seen it.

Aye, they said. And *Thank you, lady*, and *Would the lady know if it would be a good winter?*

Hild smiled and said it did not matter if winter was harsh because all was well with the world, with the Yffings in their rightful place; this year's harvest was good, and Yffings loved their folk so would tithe lightly this time in order that the people of Goodmanham could make their settlements snug. And word spread that the light of the world had their wyrd in her hand and though winter might be harsh their tithes would not, and there was time to prepare.

As Hild came back into the hall—sound, still, and now rich with those of Breguswith's hangings Sintiadd had brought from Menewood—Gwladus, on her way out, gleaming like a drop of molten gold after the sweat and dust of the field, told her that one of the biggest farmer's brace of plough oxen had broken its tooth and its jaw was swelling.

"You want me to mend it?" Hild said. Her shoulder ached from swinging the scythe, and after talking to the women her mind had turned to where the world might be next summer. She needed time to think, and though sometimes pulling a tooth was easy, sometimes it was not, and sometimes it made no difference. But it was hard to plough without oxen, and she needed farmers to plough all they could reach this autumn.

"The farmer has a bullock he thinks could be fit for the yoke by ploughing time. I was thinking instead the old ox would be a good tithe—and an even better sacrifice for the feast." She turned to go, then turned back. "Stop working so hard now, lady. Be their loaf giver and lord. Be gleaming, be seen; be heard by many at once, not one at a time in field and garth."

She sounded like Breguswith. She was right.

"Sintiadd is drawing you a bath."

Hild nodded.

"I'm to the dairy shed with two women to talk of milch cows for tithes."

Hild thought of the dairy shed and a summer six years ago or more, a hand in the small of her back and her mind turning white.

Gwladus smiled slightly—no doubt Hild's thoughts were painted plain on her face; they always were to Gwladus—and left Hild to wish Brona had been able to travel with them.

"I'll come by later," Gwladus said. "And I'll bring buttermilk if there is any. I have thoughts to share."

The ox was roasting for the three-day feast, along with the two wethers brought from Menewood. The ovens were cleaned out and refired, mended and fired again, and the first part of their flour tithe was now baking in the form of loaf after loaf of good bread. With the mead also from Menewood, the harvest ale, the butter and colewort and berries and cheese the harvesters had brought, there would be enough to feed those who came to give tribute, those who came to decide, and even those who had planned to watch from the shadows, hidden, and report back to others.

By the second day the number at the boards laid out in the afternoon sun had increased by half. One of them was a man with a lyre, and two others with whistle and drum.

On the third day every woman, man, and child, every thegn, ceorl, and slave had eaten to bursting. Many were half dozing in the warmth. Others had formed small groups at board—neighbours who were comparing their harvests, assigned tithe portions, and thoughts on the Yffing—and Ceadwin was chasing after a rag ball as eagerly as the other older children, as though he had never been through the ravagement and grief of war. Young men were making bets on a knife-throwing contest between Cuthred and Aldnoth.

Hild looked at the daymark elms; it would not be long before gelotendæg turned to æfen. No one was drunk yet; none fighting. She watched them all. Here and there a face would glance up, glance down. She called for more mead. As cups were filled, more and more paused in their talk, or shook themselves awake, and looked about.

It was time. She looked at Gwladus and nodded, and Gwladus leaned and murmured to the red-faced man to her right. He was not young but nor was he old. Stout. A little gold at wrist and upper arm but not much. The marks on his belt where a seax would hang, and the padded left shoulder of one who wore a baldric. A thegn, but not one with many men to take to war. A farmer now, a good one—his wife, a sharp-eyed woman, wore a well-dyed dress, with two strapping sons and two fine daughters to her left—and respected, or Gwladus would not have chosen him.

Burgmod, son of Brugræd, she had told Hild last night when they shared their buttermilk. Husband of Luta. Two sons, two daughters. Farms the most land, with eight ceorls, three of whom had enough land for men of their own.

Burgmod, son of Burgræd, once gesith of the ætheling Hereric, Breguswith's dead husband, Hild's father. She remembered him as young and shining, in war hat and mail, with sword and shield and high-stepping horse. This man looked too short and stout to be the same.

Burgmod stood, lifted his horn, and toasted Hild. She rested her chin on her fist and listened to the rhythm and tone of his voice more than his words.

People were banging on the board, raising their cups. She lifted her own and drank.

Burgmod spoke some more. All turned to her. She rose.

"People of Goodmanham, you are strong-hearted, open-handed, cunning-minded folk. I am glad to have laboured in your company."

Rumbled ayes and mellow yeas.

"This is a good strong valley—good strong land farmed by good strong folk. Here, today, we are Deira, its heart, its home. This is not an Yffing feast, not a Goodmanham feast, but a feast of Deira. When you speak your oaths, you do more than swear to me, you swear to serve Deira. When I speak my oath, I do more than swear to you, I swear to hold Deira safe for all. We swear for Deira, for this land, this bounty—this meat, this mutton, this mead. We swear so that we may sleep at night without fear, sit by the fire untroubled in winter, and reap our corn in summer and hope to keep it."

No bad thing will happen if we do as we have always done: Keep the ancient balance, the pact between land and folk and lord.

"Cadwallon Reaver bypassed this place on his way north; he won't a second time—if he returns this way."

If. Let them begin to feel fear, but not too much.

"Cadwallon Reaver is now north of the wall; he will be there a long time. So sow your crops; sow every foot, every rod, every ell and furlong you can. Your task is to sow and reap. It is the Yffing task to shield the land, allow the crops to grow in peace. And they will grow, and you will harvest your crop. I, Hild Yffing, swear this to you: I will protect your kin and kine, woods and wold, hearth and home. You will be safe; I have seen it. Last time the enemy was many and the Yffings few; this time, it is we who are many and the enemy few."

Or would be by the time the Iding and Cadwallon had finished with each other.

"We are the folk. This is our land. It will stay so, by my breath and bone."

She picked up her cup. Sintiadd refilled it, slowly, solemnly, to the brim.

"Burgmod, son of Burgræd." He stood. "I, Hild, daughter of Hereric Yffing and Breguswith Oiscinga, do swear on my oath, on this mead by this elm under this sky . . ."

Sintiadd put Hild's great folding chair—the lord's chair brought to Mene-wood from Caer Loid by Breguswith, along with the hangings—in the centre of a great grass circle where Coifi's enclosure had once stood. No one had built upon it; no one had ploughed or sowed. But there were no saplings or brush growing, and judging by the goose droppings and tufts of goat hair, it was common grazing land. Almund, the young priest, busied himself setting out his wax slates and stylus. He would be taking many notes.

When the local great and good had assembled, she sat. There was ale for those who wanted it, but no food.

She laid out for them the situation. Eanfrid Iding and the Bryneich. Young Oswine reoccupying York at the end of the month. Cadwallon's numbers. Her belief that he would not be back before next year's harvest, and why. She said again that their job was to work as hard as they had ever worked before to produce from their land.

"And that's all?" Beofer. One of those who came late and skulked about the shadows before joining the feast on the last day. The kind, as Sintiadd might say, who sat on the fence so long he had a dent in his arse. But he had made his oath.

"I will take one-tenth." A light tithe in a time of war.

He tried to hide his glee. She could guess what he was thinking: one-tenth of what he told some absent lord he had reaped need not be much. But he had not reckoned on Gwladus Left Hand, who talked to everyone and saw everything.

"From you, Beofer, son of Athwin, I would expect, in a usual year, five weys of wool from your sheep. But it has been a good summer, with good grass, and will perhaps be a cold winter. Cold winters make for thick wool, and heavy."

"Harsh winters mean lost wethers, which—"

"Your hills are gentle, Beofer. Your folds sheltered. It's good sheep country. I will expect five weys of wool. At the least. And I will know if it is not the best quality." She would not put it past him to try fob off her reeve with sack leavings.

The morning wound on. Every man and woman had to be listened to and answered. But she had their oaths already, and once they had met face-to-face—could go home and say, *Aye, I spoke to the lady herself, I'm that important*—she could leave the rest, the haggling and chivvying and knitting together, to Gwladus.

When the questions began to repeat themselves she held up her hand. "To keep Deira safe we've building to be done. I need hands. When your fields are sown and your grain threshed, when the wool is washed and wood cut, send me your strong young women and men. Send me the ones who are restless, the ones who daydream. Send them at the end of Winter-fylleth, to the new Loidis that will rise where the Yr meets the redcrest road to York. I'll find work for idle hands."

They immediately fell to discussing who would send how many and, as usual with so many who were neighbours, they began to edge towards a quarrel.

"Friends, I'm in need of your counsel." They all sat back looking important: The lady asked their counsel! "While I require the tithes, and very much look forward to the strong young folk you'll send, I am most in need of boats. Do any have news of boats?"

Ruminative silence while they all rummaged their brains, dearly wishing to find a way to curry more Yffing favour.

Eventually one woman—wide-hipped and long-nosed—cleared her throat. "There's a mort of Frisian boats down Brough way. Leastways there was, three days since."

Twelve miles to Brough, and the Frisians had been there at least three days. She would have to hurry.

The Frisians had not moored to the massive timbers of Brough's ancient wharf but beached their broad-beamed, shallow-bottomed boats on the mud flats west of the beck that ran into the Humbre. People with sacks and mules, one with a pony and small cart, dotted the flats and a small group sat by a trestle table before a brightly coloured awning. It was hard to tell from this distance but the way they sat close told Hild they were drinking. She did not see the glint of weapons, but still she nodded to Leofdæg and Cuthred to ride wide on each side while she and Oeric, followed by Sinti-add on the sorrel mare and Almund bouncing behind on Dwmplen, took the direct route down the reedy bank.

When she dismounted onto the hard mud a man with bright eyes and weathered face came to within three paces, nodded at Oeric, then said to Hild, "Bavo the trader at your service, Yffing."

Hild pulled her staff free, and stretched. It was a good road from Good-manham to Brough, but they had not dawdled. "Welcome to Deira, Bavo."

Bavo looked at their unladen mounts and ready weapons. "You'll be here for your tithe, then." He shook his head sadly. "War is bad for busi-ness, as you see."

She spun her staff this way and that, letting the river light gleam on the iron bands top and tail. Frisians never stayed long where there was no trade, and he had been here days already.

"And of course I took your lady mother safe to Lindsey, all the way to Lindum."

She spun the staff the other way.

He glanced again at Oeric. "And, fair enough, I was paid. But I also gave useful news for free."

She waited.

"And now I have more news, only this time not for free. I reckon it might be worth more to you than what you might tithe."

She looked at Oeric. "Take Cuthred and go rummage the boats." Bavo opened his mouth to protest. "But with care, Oeric. Bavo's no enemy. So be careful, but be thorough." She smiled at Bavo. "We will set the value of the tithe first, and then we will consider of the news."

"The news though, lady, is best heard soon, and accounting takes time."

He seemed relaxed and sure: shoulders loose and feet planted easy. The news, he believed, was of real worth. "You understand, Frisian, that I know your name, and my anger could be shoals in your searoad and fire in your hold all through the north."

He shrugged, unworried. Oh, yes, he thought the news worth it.

"Give me this news."

He held out his arm. "News for tithe?"

"News and the tale of how the news came to you." His arm wavered. "I can be generous to my friends, Bavo."

He nodded. They clasped, and spat.

Hild looked at Almund—he already had his tablet and stylus in hand—then back to Bavo.

"Right, then. My cousin Esulf was just in from Bebbanburg with news of the north. The Iding's raised his raven at Din Baer."

"I would speak to Esulf."

"Left for Gole this morning. But he was in the north some time, and he's a sharp-eyed man. Kin, as you know, do like to chat long over good ale, and then of course it always pays to be well-informed about who's doing what and where, and when. Can make all the difference between packing cheese to trade or pig iron or cloth. Which is to say, lady, what Esulf knows, I know. Which is a good boatload. Shall we sit?"

They sat, Almund a pace away, stylus poised, and drank the nutty mellow ale they brewed in the lowlands, and Bavo told her Eanfrid Iding had ridden from Din Eidyn with a double handful of Picts, and the same number of younger exiles' sons. "So young they all sound like Picts."

Northumbrans who had gone into exile with the æthelings but were either so young when they left, or born since they got there, that they spoke like their hosts. Little older than she was.

The Iding had raised his banner at Din Baer and waited for the Bryneich.

"Did the Bryneich seem eager?"

"Esulf reckons it's more that they prefer the Iding to Cadwallon Bradawc."

"And the Bernician thegns?" Many, like Hunric, had followed Edwin to Hæðfeld. But their old fathers or young sons would have been left behind.

"Oh, the old ones are eager for Iding—but they're old, too old to have gone to fight for Edwin Snakebeard. The younger ones . . ." He scratched his beard. "Not eager, not as such, but interested. They like that he's renounced the Christ god. Young fools." He wore no cross but Frankish trade—Christian trade—was rich and it paid to speak to the same gods as your best customers. He drank deeply. "Now, then. Word is, the Iding and Cadwallon are racing for Bebbanburg. There'll be a meeting. Rheged'll be pleased, no doubt."

"Yes?" She poured him more ale.

"After Cadwallon ravaged Arbeia—that dog dung tore out the docks; Esulf didn't even bother stopping at Tinamutha—he fortified Corabrig. And since then he's been preying on Stanegate trade something fierce."

She sat back, thinking. Stanegate, the road that ran along the south side of the redcrest wall, the only trade route east from Rheged. And Rheged had already lost what was in Arbeia. This was good news indeed. Oh, very good. Worth the tithe money and more. "And why is this timely?"

"There's more, Yffing." He grinned. "I've had word from my brother Menger. There's been a to-do in Lindsey."

She sat straight. Her mother. "What kind of to-do?"

"Well, if you wait you can ask for yourself. There's two Lindsey war boats lying off Barton Sand waiting for wind and tide."

War boats had longer keels and deeper draught than trade boats, and tonight was neap tide. In the height of summer even the deeper channels could become tricky to navigate. "And how long will I wait?"

"Oh, I'd say late tomorrow—mayhap early the next day if they're deep laden. And Menger reckons they are."

The sun threw the shadow of her cup long and long to her left and the river was turning red and gold with sunset. She sniffed the wind.

Bavo nodded. "It'll be a good wind tomorrow. Smooth sailing. So, deep laden or not, could be that fleet'll come wafting in on the evening tide."

"Two war boats are not a fleet."

"Ah, but it's not just war boats. They've a gaggle of smaller boats, and three beast barges."

"Beast barges?"

"Three. Menger reckons horses from the smell."

Two war boats, a host of smaller boats, and three floating stables. That was enough for a war band. "Under what banner do they sail?"

"None that Menger saw."

"And why does Menger think they're coming here?"

"No better place before York for a war boat to stop than Brough."

Brough with its deep anchorage and great wharves. War boats. And thanks to Bavo they had warning. "Friend Bavo, this is worthy news indeed. What may this Yffing do for you in return?"

"Since Cadwallon Bradawc, there's been a dearth of good trade cloth. Nothing brings Frankish silver better than Deiran cloth."

"Cloth," she said, and looked at Almund, who nodded even as he cut the letters in the wax.

"Good cloth. They like that hairy thick stuff for cloaks."

She knew what he meant. "I'll see to it."

War boats. And one day to prepare.

"Bavo, York opens for trade next summer. I hope to see you and your cousins and your brother there. Spread the word: The first three boats get the lightest tithes."

Twelve miles on a good road was nothing for Lél and Leofdæg. The next afternoon—still full and rich with sun—when a single long war boat, oars flashing, and a smaller craft, graceful as a gull under one white sail, reefed sail, raised oars, and glided towards the wharf, eight armed riders waited. Despite the heat Hild wore her furs, and she faced the sun so her chestnut hair blazed—the only banner she had.

Now they could hear the slish of prow cutting water, they were slowing, and on the warship a glint of gold, men raising a thick staff, looking at it, waiting for something. Nothing. A banner, she saw, but no wind to lift it, and the boats were within bowshot of the riders on the wharf.

"Sitric." A tok of ash against yew as he nocked an arrow, ready to shoot any enemy bowman.

Shouted orders, two men running to the banner, trying to tug open the heavy cloth, then a puff of wind lifted it from their hands briefly, too briefly. She shielded her eyes against the sun just as another, stronger gust unfurled the banner: purple with the Yffing boar squat and strong in the centre.

She laughed. Only one man could have a banner like that. The man who had escaped to Lindsey with six war boats. "Coelfrith!" she shouted, and when the boat came closer still she saw her mother standing beside him, and she laughed again. But it was when the boat drew even closer and she saw the little burnt man, grinning hideously, and the big bear by him, that she knew her tide had turned. Fate goes ever as it must, and today it flowed her way. She was even glad to see Luftmær, for if ever there was a day for a song of glory, it was today.

Coelfrith walked down the gangboard followed by Wulf and Dudda carrying the Yffing boar for he did not come as a man who had betrayed his king and wanted that to be clear.

Once on solid ground he announced, in a loud voice, that he was there not to bargain but to return what was Yffing to the strongest of Yffings, and to swear his oath to Hild, kingmaker and lord in Deira, and best placed to avenge the killing of Coelgar, his father.

Hild heard her mother in those words. Coelfrith had always been his own thinker yet never fool enough to believe he could lead. That, at least, had not changed. Other things had. Before, the reeve had always seemed harassed as a hen, but this new Coelfrith was still, and set, and grim. He had been a gesith before he was reeve, and now he once again wore a sword.

"Well met, Coelfrith, son of Coelgar. What oath would you swear?"

In reply he pulled free his sword and took a knee, hands resting on the pommel, and right there, one knee in the grass and one foot crushing a dandelion, he swore the oath of a gesith to his king or king-to-be: All that was his was now Hild's; he would protect her with his sword and person; and he was hers to command until death. He held out his sword.

Hild took his sword. She was not a king, but she had seen it done.

She laid the blade on his shoulder with the edge against the side of his neck at the great vein. She could kill him now by sliding forward an inch. She spoke the words: He was now her charge, his honour was her honour. She laid the sword on the other side of his neck. She would trust him as he trusted her; she would rely on his arm and his shield and his loyalty. She lifted the sword a third time and placed its tip in the hollow of his throat. What was his was hers, his life was hers, and she was now his lord and his family; she would feed him, shelter him, and reward him. Just as her feuds were now his, his were now hers. His honour was hers.

Now she was bound to avenge Coelgar, even before she knew who had killed him or why. But whatever the price, it was worth it for what he brought.

Sintiadd somehow found two hard stools and two upturned barrels and set them up in the cool shade of the westmost warehouse to serve as table and chairs for Hild, Breguswith, and Coelfrith. There was cold water dipped from the well and, later, there would be food. In the sun Hild was aware of a din and confusion of horses and men as the other boats moored and began to unload, but between Oeric and whoever Coelfrith had chosen as his deputy—and an overking's reeve would choose well—it would be sorted soon enough.

Sintiadd stayed nearby in case of need and Almund settled cross-legged in the grass, slate in his lap and stylus poised.

A reeve at heart, Coelfrith began with an accounting. Of the six war boats and twelve dozen men he had taken to Lindsey, he was returning with two war boats, fully equipped with sails and oars, threescore fighting men, threescore and ten horses with their transport, four smaller boats, and hold after hold stuffed not only with the implements and necessary tools of war—portable forge, giant whetstones, charcoal, shovels, trestles, barrel after barrel of nails and arrows—but sack after sack from the rich Lindsey granaries.

When he stopped there was only the *tck-tck* of Almund's stylus as he caught up. She looked at the man before her. Two months ago she would have counted it a gift to gain one warhorse; now they had threescore and ten. But better even that that, better than the men, better than the whole grain and the flour, now she had in Coelfrith's head a list of all the tithes of Edwin's land—and the tributes owed by every vill and steading.

"Some might say the boats and their burdens are Yffing by right," she said. Her mother nodded. "Others that it is a great gift you have brought Deira today, Coelfrith, son of Coelgar. I would grant you a gift in return if it's in my power. Tell me of your father."

"Coelgar, son of Coelric, ealdorman of Lindsey, is dead at the hand of Blæcca, self-styled princeps of Lindum."

"Blæcca?" she said.

"Penda's puppet," her mother said, and now it was Coelfrith's turn to nod.

"The lady Breguswith speaks true, though I didn't see it at first."

It took a cunning mind to see others' cunning. Coelfrith was straight as a spear. But, oh, Penda, son of Pybba, was cunning. He was slowly but surely gathering the strings of every people around Northumbre, and when he was ready he would pull them tight.

"When did this happen?"

"Nine days since," he said. "Though my father was beset long before."

He had found out at Blodmonath, at the first feast after the cull, when his father, tired and heavy and in his cups, confided to him that he wished he could get on one of those fine Yffing ships and sail away: find some

land, live in peace, and let Blæcca have it all. After that night Coelfrith began to watch, and saw Blæcca take more and more power into his hands.
He was buying local thegns; Coelfrith saw gold change hands. But Blæcca
seemed in no hurry, steady and patient.

"And then I came with news of Elmet," Breguswith said. "And in two
days Coelgar was dead."

Past the shade of the warehouse, shadows were grown long and the
noise of unloading horses and men had steadied to a workman-like rhythm.

"Sintiadd. Tell Oeric we will eat as soon as may be." She looked at her
mother and Coelfrith. "I'll want the whole tale, but later. Tomorrow we
have to move. We've business in Goodmanham that won't wait, and at the
moon's first quarter Oswine will be in York." Last night had been the dark
of the moon. She had six days. And large groups travelled slowly. Although
now they had boats. Boats! It changed everything. "Coelfrith, are the men
sworn to you?"

"No, lady. Most were sworn to Edwin Overking, then to my father. But
I don't doubt they'll follow an Yffing."

She looked at her mother, who half closed her eyes: Perhaps not all the
men brought from Lindsey were to be trusted. She had to be sure, but
oaths cost precious time.

"Almund. Go to Leofdæg and tell him to bring the ones called Wulf
and Dudda to me. Then go to Sintiadd. Tell her to seek out mead and bring
it. If not mead, then ale. She's to knock heads if she has to." She had not
expected to be away from Goodmanham for more than a night and had
travelled with almost nothing. But where there were men there was always
something to drink.

Dudda's grin was more hideous than ever, with an angry scar along his left
cheek on top of the old burns. He was still bone thin, but when he leaned
to Hild for the arm clasp and back slap, he moved as easily as before. Wulf,
too, had a new scar, on his forehead, but otherwise seemed much the
same: huge, silent, and alert. Leofdæg nodded to Hild: He had told Wulf
and Dudda how things stood in Elmet, Craven, and Deira.

Their gesith's oath had died with the king. They knelt together and
swore to Hild, Wulf in sign.

Then she asked them about the men they had spent more than half a
year with. She asked them both, and if an answer needed more than a yes

or no or holding up of fingers for how many, Dudda checked with Wulf, then spoke for them both. He sometimes checked with Wulf first before he answered for himself alone; that was new.

Sometimes Dudda gave a twisted half-smile to Coelfrith when he was about to say something that might surprise him. Yes, most of the men would follow Hild—after all, the lady Breguswith had already told them what a gold-giver she was, and how she could hold the fate of men in her hand. And they were mostly Deirans; this was their home and they were glad to be back. Not all, though. Wulf had seen one man in close conversation with one of Blæcca's men, and Dudda thought another—a sailor more than a sword man—too ready to agree with anyone about everything; he was eager to be liked, and his eyes too watchful. Could they point them out to Leofdæg? They could.

The pure Lindseymen, though, they were not sure. Most, they thought, could be trusted. They were Coelgar's men through and through, and they knew how much Coelgar had liked her lady mother.

"Though not me."

Wulf made the deep noise that meant Dudda should watch, then gestured too fast for Hild to follow.

"He says most of 'em wouldn't know that, lady. You've not been to Lindsey for an age, and only one of the Lindseymen first came to Lindum with Coelgar and might be expected to remember."

She nodded; he was right. So, three men to watch out of threescore. Good. Very good.

"Stay with us a while," she told her three gesiths. They had many decisions to make and Wulf, particularly, might have insight.

At first light, sixty men knelt and swore to Hild Yffing, and she swore in turn, and at the turn of the tide, two of the smaller boats, one horse boat, and the *Seacat*, one of the war boats, heavy with the tools Grimhun could use to build the new Loidis, took twenty men—including the sailor Dudda did not trust—and Oeric and Aldnoth to Cnotinsleah. She was tempted to send Grimhun so he could begin work but she would need him in York.

In company went the other war boat, the *Seadragon*, led by Coelfrith, with one smaller boat, and one horse boat, but after Gole instead of turning to Yrmyn they were to follow the Use to York. She told him not to dock

Seadragon or off-load the horses until she was there. If she was delayed and Oswine early, if Oswine had more men than she expected, she did not want him tempted to try to take the boat for himself.

The remainder of her people—and Breguswith and Luftmær—mounted and rode for Goodmanham.

At Goodmanham, the thegns, who had been impressed enough by Hild and her band were astonished when thirty armed and gold-gleaming riders thundered into the settlement, and between one day and the next, Goodmanham seemed once again a royal vill, loud and roisterous with gesiths—there was even a scop to sing praise songs of the Yffings and the brave folk of Deira. In the feast hall Hild wore a good dress but instead of a veil band and rich sleeves she wore her furs flung back and gold cuffs on bare arms. The glittering veil bands belonged to the women flanking her: on her right her mother the lady Breguswith with her Centisc-work brooch gleaming, and on her left Gwladus ferch Heddwen, Left Hand of Hild Yffing, Butcherbird, Cath Llew, and light of the world.

Gwladus smiled richly at Hild. While Hild had been gone, Burgmod, every local thegn, husbandman, and land-holding widow, had fought Gwladus hard and given ground as meanly as an enemy shield wall, bargaining over even the smallest tithe as though their holding would be ravaged and land sown with salt if they overpaid a single grain of wheat. But now, in the face of this overwhelming might, every land-holder would fight to be first in the Left Hand's favour that she might take good word to the lady: For her, the price of Goodmanham wheat had just come down. Not only that, there would be gifts, for anyone with eyes could see that fate had just laid a fat thumb on the Yffing side of the scales; to be well placed for the future meant being in well with the Yffing's Left Hand.

In York, the day before the moon's first quarter, Hild had word of the approach of Oswine and his band and watched unseen from the wall as they arrived. She had known Oswine since he was a boy—a boy always happier to follow than to lead; a good-hearted boy, but easily swayed—but men changed. He was now eldest and only male Yffing and ealdorman of Craven, or would have been if there were a king to kneel to. The only recent judgement she had of him was Uinniau's, and Uinniau was his friend. No, she also had Begu's. But her gemæcce did not know much of men's ambition, and like Uinniau and Oswine himself, knew nothing of war.

Where was Begu now? Had she gone north to Colud, to the Bryneich? Had she been caught up in the Iding's arrival less than twenty miles away in Din Baer? It was a worry already worn smooth from use and there was nothing she could do. She set it aside to watch Oswine's entrance.

Twenty men well-mounted, plus Osthryth and her bodywoman: tired, their gold dulled by dust, but sitting proud, expecting to be knelt to as the armed power of Deira. Milling in temporary confusion when they found, instead, the gate guarded by two gesiths—one small, one large, but both with that unmistakable air of having defended their lord against healthy odds many times, and to the death. Oswine was forced to name himself ealdorman of Craven. The big gesith stood silently, and Oswine hunched, perhaps thinking Wulf's silence scornful: *So this is the son of the craven of Craven who hid in his iron hills while we bled and fought.* After a while Oswine's mouth turned down and his chin thrust forward.

She had seen that pout and thrust before, always before he shouted, *It's not fair!* She knew he would feel the need to explain to everyone that it was not his fault he had remained in Craven, not his fault he had not fought at Hæðfeld: He had only followed his father's orders, as a son must.

That, at least, had not changed.

On the parapet she turned and watched as the men of Craven passed through the gate and found that the best byre already stabled nearly twoscore warhorses. Watched as any thought about claiming Deira for himself—put in his head by ambitious men, or his sister—was shaken to dust. And tomorrow, when a fully manned war boat glided to the wharf, tied up, and spilled another score of fighting men all sworn to Hild and bearing the Yffing banner, she knew he would feel that dust crushed under the hooves of their warhorses.

She breathed deep and stretched. Oswine, son of Osric, would make no murmur when she spoke to him of what must be done. He would fall back gratefully to the stance he knew best: doing as his lord Yffing told him.

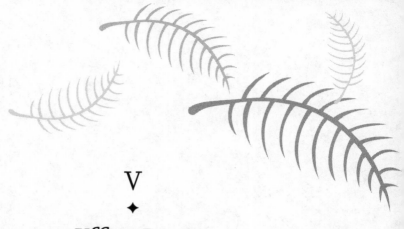

V

◆

Yffing Boar

York—Bay of the Beacon—Loidis—Hillacleg Moor—
Menewood—Urburg

(Harvestmonath 633 to Hrethmonath 634, 25 weeks)

24

✤

EAST OF YORK, over what had been Wilgar's valley, corn buntings gathered in the dusk, roosting in flocks in the damp pastures. One alighted on the low bough of a hornbeam that was beginning to fruit. Against the purpling sky the bunting's outline was still fluffy—barely fledged; there must have been a second brood. It had been a rich summer here.

Hild stopped in what had once been Wilgar's big, busy garth. There should have been rows of just-planted peas; here, where there was full sun, they would have been planting the last carrots. And turnips. She looked at Linnet. "Did you save anything?"

"Not much. Cadwallon's men tore it out before they left. Or most of it. These two worked the garth." She nodded at the stripling twins she had taken in. "They found beets and onions out of the way, so we've that at least."

The twins were still thin enough to be knobby at wrist and elbow, but they would fill out. Their knees no longer showed through ragged clothes, and now that they were clean she saw their hair was the colour of rich loam.

"I could've planted peas, I suppose. But it's too open here to any comers. And we didn't know what to expect."

The twins were listening, and their dogs—thin, like them, a mostly grown pup and a bitch who had the alert eye and sharp ear of a herder. Sheepdog? But there were no more sheep in this valley. Penda and

Cadwallon had eaten them, probably most of the dogs, too. That pup was not sired by a sheepdog. He was gangly still, with growing to do, but wide across the chest and with a square jaw. Sired by a war dog—Penda's. Cadwallon did not use war dogs.

"Plant your peas," she said. "Yffings are back in York, and we're staying. You'll speak to my reeve about seeds and starts for what would be best planted here—it's good land. And there's time for a late planting." It was still warm.

The air hissed and curled as a great cloud of starlings darkened the sky. Hild watched as they flowed back and forth, turning and swinging like a cloak, this way and that, then sank behind a gentle rise.

"What's over there?" After their long journey south the starlings would need food: There was something there, something growing. Fruit?

Linnet shook her head. One twin looked away and the other lifted her shoulders: She didn't know, or she didn't want to say; food kept them safe. "Keep it for now," she said. If people felt safe, they stayed.

As they turned back towards York a sharp shepherd's whistle froze the bitch. Hild brought up her staff and the twins crouched. The pup growled, stiff-legged. Another shepherd's whistle, followed by the caw of a jackdaw, then the axle-squeak of a finch, and Hild lowered her staff.

"The starlings," she said.

They could mimic anything. They had come from somewhere north where there were still shepherds to hear and mimic. And what of the chaffinches that would soon be gathering to follow the warmth? On their journey south would they alight for a day in the land of the North Folk and sing a song of Deira for Hereswith and Fursey?

It seemed to Hild that every day she stayed in York she walked a score of miles, always talking, always trailed by people. Some were her constant shadows: Wulf, alert and so silent men spoke in front of him, forgetting he could hear; Almund with his tablet and stylus; Morud as her runner. When her concern was anything to do with trade or tithes, Coelfrith was at hand, for though the store of tally sticks in the treasure room was burnt, he remembered most of it. And often, for building—and so much of what she intended would need building—she brought Grimhun. Her task until the full moon was to get the boulder rolling, get people moving; if everyone understood what was to be done, and if there were enough to do it, they would keep it moving through the winter while she was on to the next place, the next task.

She took Grimhun, Osthryth, and Coelfrith to the wharf where the *Seadragon* was moored. The graceful small boat *Dolphin* was tied to the war boat. It had rained that morning but now a brisk easterly wind smelling of brine sent clouds scudding away, leaving a blue sky. Raindrops sparkled on a brilliant yellow dandelion, one of many weeds pushing up between the great stones laid by redcrests in the long ago. A year earlier they would have been trampled to nothing by the feet and hooves and wheels of trade as ships from all over the isle, and Frisia, Frankia, Norsk, and even Iberia docked and departed. Just over a year ago she had been here with Æthelburh, admiring white fur and amber, hunting dogs and perfume while the long-abandoned city of great stone buildings on the south bank rang with noise and dust as Edwin's men dismantled it. That was Paulinus's work; he was always eager for redcrest stone. Where had it gone?

Osthryth was explaining to Coelfrith why the tithe of iron and lead must be less this year: Craven had lost many men when her father fell to Cadwallon.

"Miners don't fight," he said.

"But farmers do," she said. "And when farmers fall, someone must plough the field and harvest the wood. We need oats as well as ore."

"We need the lead."

"Hungry men can't mine."

Hild sighed. Neither was wrong. "Who trades for lead?" she asked Coelfrith.

"The Iberians. Sometimes Franks."

With few thegns to bribe and show favour, they had less need for Frankish and Iberian goods—silk, perfume, glass, and fine Iberian steel.

"We can get iron from the Pecsæte, lady," Coelfrith said. "In exchange for salt and wheat."

Salt was easy—anywhere on the coast could make it in summer, or with enough wood; Cadwallon's men could not burn the sea. Bay of the Beacon made salt, but Hornessæ and Kilnessæ were closer to Elmet. Wheat, though—this year Cadwallon had burnt it all. "Would they take barley?"

"Perhaps half wheat, half barley."

"Very well." He could sort that out. Everyone knew him, could trust his word. She turned to Osthryth. "From Craven, then, we will take"—she paused to order the needs—"lead, oats, and charcoal."

Osthryth nodded.

"Meanwhile, Grimhun, we've only one berth for big boats year-round. It's not enough. But how many would be enough? Coelfrith?"

"I could get my shipmaster."

"It's not ships and how they work I need, it's numbers. How many ships will come across from Frankia and Frisia? How many will come down from the north? How many up from the south? And when? Will they come at once? Which will have perishable goods and which can lie out at anchor and wait their turn?"

"You don't want to keep livestock waiting," Osthryth said.

For the first time all three nodded. Well, it was a start.

The sun was past its height when they agreed: They could have three working berths by the beginning of next year's trading season. She looked at Almund. "Remind me to get the word out that we'll be open for trade."

He scribbled.

Grimhun was muttering to himself—baulks, the men to cut them, shape them, raise them; rope, hands to twist them—as they walked the wīc field. Last summer when she pondered hunting dogs with the queen, the open land had been hard and dry underfoot but now it was soft and yielding.

"Trade season's nearly done," she said. There would be smaller coastal boats from now to the end of Winterfylleth, and perhaps beyond, but no big trade ships crossing the northern sea. "We've half a year, more, to repair the wharf. First, we need to clear these." She pointed at the ditches Cadwallon and Penda had used as middens. "Otherwise this whole field will be a mire by the start of trade. How long will that take?"

"Clearing them?" He measured with his hands and thumb, squinting. "Not long. But clearing them's not enough." He toed a loose stone. "Half of them need relining."

She looked at him.

He sighed. He was learning what she wanted. "But yes, it can wait, though not past next summer. Meantime I'll see they're cleared."

And so it went. With Oswine she toured the walls, and had to explain, again, that even if they repaired that wall Cadwallon had half torn down, even with their combined strength, they could not hold a fort this size against an army. The smallest number they would need was three hundred and they had nowhere near that, and those they did have had other tasks.

"We can't stay here?"

"We can. We will—or you will. I'm relying on you to stay here. But we can't hold the fort against an army. My task, therefore, is to stop any army reaching York. Your task"—that was, the task of the people she trusted who she was leaving behind while Oswine played lord—"is to make York what our uncle always intended it to be: the centre of Deiran trade and news."

And she explained, again, about the rivers and roads, and how from York messages could come from anywhere in Deira and from there could reach any corner of the isle. She wondered if she should draw it in the dirt with sticks and stones as she had for Æthelburh's children.

"But only if we have people here to watch over trade, to make sure there's feed for horses—the Craven oats—supplies for boats, hands to gather the harvest. And of course an Yffing, you, bright and strong and splendid, to reassure the folk."

He liked that.

"For that you need to keep your men happy. And what pleases men is ale. And I've already started on that."

Linnet's malting had gone well, the beer was brewing, and they had cleared out a small building just beyond the main byre, where any travel-ler, coming or going, would pass. Just the place for thirsty folk to stop and drink and spread gossip from their local valley. Between them, Linnet and the twins would hear everything. Which Linnet would make sure reached her or Gwladus.

She would need to keep messengers and horses here. Two small, swift boats—she would have to get one back from Elmet.

Nights were when she mixed with the fighting men of Craven and Lindsey. She drank with them, sang with them, listened to their stories, and praised them. She offered rings and hero's portions to those who won the riding races, the wrestling matches, the axe catching, and knife throwing. She played taff and groaned when she lost—carefully, and to the right men—encouraged Luftmær to sing the right songs, and helped lead the cheers in the right places for the right people. Gradually she began to get a feel for the tool in her hand and to shape it.

With those in Elmet, Oswine's from Craven, and her old and newly sworn gesiths, Deira could now field close to a hundred fighting men. A not-so-small army. But she would not use them as an army; she did not want them in shield walls marching bravely to glorious slaughter. She did not want a single, unwieldy whole. She began to group them in her head, testing, recombining . . .

Linnet tracked down, one by one, women and men who had fled York, folk with the skills and knowledge to maintain large groups of people: to bake bread in the huge ovens and keep the dye vats clean and the street gutters sluiced. They needed someone to patch the thatch; Linnet found one. Linnet was already known to Morud and Gwladus and Oeric; but to the others Hild introduced her only as the trustworthy woman who, with her two young ones, would run the alehouse.

In the creamery, Hild, Breguswith, Heiu, and Osthryth took stock. The walls needed repacking with straw against the heat and cold; they found the churns and trays, or most of them, though they would need to turn three new paddles, and one tray had warped with damp. Again, replacing such things was winter work.

The creamery was just the beginning. Hild needed to bring back the cloth trade, and these three women—and Begu, when she returned—were the ones to do it. They met midmorning every day—in the creamery, the garth, the kitchens, the left-hand apartments—discussing what they needed. Aberford had once been the centre of the fibre work but now it might be best to move to Goodmanham.

"They've good sheep in Goodmanham, and a fair few in Elmet—good woollers."

"Bad road, though, from East Farm," Breguswith said.

"But a good river," Osthryth said. "If we've a boat."

Small boats were not a problem. Once the horses were pastured the beast boats could be repurposed. They were slow, but wool did not turn after two days in the sun, and the Weorf was swift, the Use well-charted—

A shout from outside. She stuck her head out of the door. Morud. "Lady, it's Gwladus and Gladmær back from Goodmanham."

"Good. Tell Gwladus I'll see her in the apartments later." Let her get settled. In the creamery she said, "We'll need to find weavers."

Breguswith waved away the problem. Even the poorest Anglisc weaver was a wonder-worker compared to the fools in Frankia. She knew how to make the shaggy cloaks the Franks prized, and she could teach others. "Your gemæcce has a rare eye for colour. With her, we could do dyes at the new Loidis," she said.

"No." And the vision was suddenly sharp. "No. You're going to run Caer Loid when we rebuild. Use the vats there." And they could bring back the orchards and use the pasture to breed horses.

And before she left the creamery she rested her hand on the edge of the chipped cold counter and thought of Hereswith and her buttermilk, and Penda bending his mind to the next king to topple. The East Angles would be next. Had her sister got her letter?

Again, she thought of the boat tied to the *Seadragon*, sleek as a porpoise. If she did not hear from Hereswith soon she could send the *Dolphin*. But she was worried about Begu, too.

The church was made of stone. The treasures were gone—Paulinus's doing—and the vines at the base of the font hacked off. The altar stone had been dragged from its base but not broken. Her men had cleared the worst filth and set the altar stone back on its base; the rest would be improved over the winter. Now it was empty, echoing and forlorn.

She sat on a broken bench to one side of the altar and looked at the chipped marble. Christ, Woden, Eorðe, wood ælfe, and hægtessan, all part of the same pattern. But just as she spoke Irish to Fursey and those priests of Hii, British to Rhin, and Latin to those who followed the Christ of Rome, perhaps different gods heard differently.

A wood ælf or water sprite was not to be addressed directly or asked for favours; a hægtes was only to be minded and not crossed; and Anglisc gods were to be bargained with—but carefully, for they were full of tricks and cunning. But Christ priests spoke plainly to their god, and asked clearly for this gift or that favour. Perhaps blunt words to the Christ god might be heard more easily than sideways wishes to wood ælfe and water sprites.

"Christ god, keep my sister safe among the North Folk and my gemæcce safe wherever she is. Especially if she's been fool enough to go among the Bryneich. If she's thinking of that, send her a dream; tell her to stay with Onnen and Mulstan until—" Until when? Again, she saw the *Dolphin* riding the river, tidy and dry next to the *Seadragon*. "Tell her to say at the bay until I come for her. Tell her I'm coming soon."

She listened. Nothing.

Anglisc gods liked to bargain. Perhaps the Christ was the same.

"If you tell her to stay there—and if she stays, that's important; you have to make her stay—I will make a new and splendid church for you." That was a good offer. She hoped the Christ would take it and not notice she had not said where, or when.

Often before she broke her fast, she exercised with the Fiercesomes: staff and seax against shield and sword. They rode together; they talked. She knew Leofdæg's story, she knew Gladmær's, she knew Bryhtsige's. She needed Wulf's and Dudda's. And they needed to tell it to the other Fiercesomes; they needed to know and trust each other. She was beginning to see the shape ahead and more than any other this core group must be one solid fist, hard and tight, ready at her direction.

At the water trough in the exercise yard, while the men took turns sluicing each other down and she sat eating an egg from her purse, she told her story to Wulf and Dudda. Wulf gestured to Dudda, who asked questions: Who had she seen fall, and when?

She told them of Coelwyn, the brothers Berht. Cian.

More gestures from Wulf, put into words by Dudda: Boldcloak before he fell had killed a score of Penda's men; his deeds should be a song.

"Tell Luftmær," she said. "He's making a song of the Battle of Hæðfeld."

They had seen Cian fight but not go down. They did not see her and her Hounds tear into Penda's flank. She told them nothing of her fight, only of her wounds, though not the long tale of hovering near death; the fever rising again; dead flesh sloughing away; the pain. They were gesiths; they knew. It helped, to talk with those who understood some of what happened, to talk without having to explain and feel the fear, the pain, the rage, the hopelessness, the rage again. Each time she told it, she felt it a little less; telling it while safe and calm built a wall between the thing and the feeling of the thing; sometimes now she could look at what happened, and remember, without wanting to howl like a dog.

And then she heard how Wulf had gone down, blinded and dazed by a spear thrust past his forehead. Dudda told it—clearly he had told it many times: how Dudda dragged the enormous Wulf away, staggering, reeling like a pole-axed bull, "Bellowing the same, too."

Hild had heard that tongueless, formless bellow. It was enough to melt the marrow.

"He sounded like a wight born of a hægtes of the Hel boundary, and they slowed and wavered, and I screamed and went for them—there was no choice; we were going to die anyway—and they ran. And I felt mighty, I can tell you, only then I saw they weren't running from my fearsomeness, they were running towards the falling banner, howling victory. So I grabbed Wulf with two hands and hauled him away. And the only way to go was south. We reckoned Coelfrith would have gone to Lindum, to his fa."

"It's a way to Lindum," Gladmær said. He wiped himself under the arms with his tunic and basked half naked in the sun. Angry scars crossed his ribs.

"We took a cart," Dudda said. "Wulf chose that moment to turn white and go down like a felled oak." She recognised his light tone: There was more to it, much more, but he did not like to remember those parts.

Ermine Street was wide and well-cleared on either side. They could hear and see riders in plenty of time to leave the road. They had to hide often; even so, the forty miles to Lindum took less than three days.

"So we got there, found Coelfrith, and with Edwin king dead, well, we swore to Coelgar. And that's it. Until your lady mother came and we found out how things were. Then we didn't know what to do: Coelgar had our oath but you're Yffing—our Yffing. But then wyrd flicked the dice in our favour and Coelgar died. As soon as Coelfrith spoke of boats, our way was clear."

Wulf gestured.

"He says, did you know it was Blæcca that did it?" Dudda snorted. "Well of course she knows. She's Cath Llew, she knows everything."

She looked from one to another. "And if I didn't. What else should I know?"

Gestures. Frowns from Dudda. "They were?"

An emphatic nod.

"Well, how do you know that? They—"

Rapid gestures.

"Ah. So, lady, there were two East Angles there. Or they said they were East Angles. But Wulf says they weren't, they were East Wixna or maybe South Gwyre. He lived there as a lad—I didn't know that," he said to Wulf.

East Wixna and South Gwyre. The buffer between Mercia and the East Angles. If that buffer were already thinning—

"And Wulf said they talked to Blæcca's men, not Coelgar's."

She needed to talk to Coelfrith, find out if her letter to Coelgar had arrived, if the priest had ever come to Lindum. If he had not, then perhaps her letter to Hereswith had also never arrived. Though even if it had, would she heed it?

Coelfrith nodded. "Priests in Lindum? Aye, lady, plenty. Priests who kissed the ring of Paulinus Crow. Though my father had no love of them, as you know. But a letter from you? No, lady. At least not so as my father chose to tell me—and he would have told me that."

"Perhaps he thought you'd leave for Elmet with those ships if you knew an Yffing was there."

He fiddled with the buckle on his belt.

"Perhaps not?"

"Perhaps not at that time."

She clapped him on the shoulder. "No harm done." At least he told her the truth. But it seemed her letter to Fursey and Hereswith was lost.

She asked Linnet, and Gwladus and Sintiadd, to start nosing about to find out if anyone from Craven or Lindsey had heard anything, no matter how thin and vague, of the East Anglisc.

How long until Penda made his move? How long until her sister was in danger?

She and Coelfrith looked at the empty treasure room. The damage here had been theft and a fire, but the treasure room, like the church, was strong. The massive door was whole. The lock was unbroken but without a key it was useless. With a new lock it could be used tomorrow. It would be used tomorrow. They would begin with the weapons unloaded from Coelfrith's holds; weapons were treasure now.

"The lock will take some time," Coelfrith said. He was looking worried again, which Hild found reassuring: Coelfrith was once more Coelfrith.

"We have time. In this thing at least." But in other ways she needed more time than they had. "How fast is that small boat of yours?"

"*Dolphin*? Fast, lady. At least when there's wind. If the wind fails, you'd want *Seadragon*."

She might want both. "How fast could they get me to the Bay of the Beacon?"

"From here? *Dolphin* a day and a half and *Seadragon* less than two days—if the wind holds fair. Rowing? Three or four days depending on headwinds. You'd need strong men."

She had strong men. Overland it would take four days in good weather and use horses and men hard. "Can *Seadragon* take horses?"

"Not unless that's all you want to take, then you couldn't row to speak of."

Hild nodded, disappointed but not surprised. The *Curlew*, wider than the *Seadragon*, had only managed five horses. "And from here to Caistor, or Cromer?"

"The North Folk?" He was one of the few men she knew who did not have to use his fingers to count. "From here, two days by sail, four by oar—maybe more. And from the bay, three days if the wind's in your sails, less in *Dolphin*. Rowing? Hard work. A week? Maybe less."

Three days if she was lucky, a week if she was not. And Hereswith would not be at Cromer or Caistor, she would be at the North Folk's royal vill: Deorham, or maybe Elmham. That could be another thirty miles overland for which they would need horses.

The moon was past full but still bright. She could be in the bay and gone long before the new moon—if fate smiled upon her in the next days. Hereswith might be in danger soon—but not so soon as Begu with the Iding raising his raven at Din Baer. Begu first.

The weather was beginning to change. Today mist lay over the Use and, in the hedgerows, spiderwebs glistened; for the first time on one of their rides she saw the brilliant red flash of a turning leaf. Their hooves drummed and echoed against fallen stone as they galloped past the ruins of the red-crest city on the south bank. Hild urged Bone faster after Lél, who was dodging sinuous as an eel between the mixed willow and alder. Such a beautiful horse. Bone was not beautiful but his strength was, and her heart lifted as she urged the powerful beast beneath her faster, faster, laughter muffled by the mist as Leofdæg switched back on Lél and past her, and Dudda whooped. It was a good group, a fine group. Bryhtsige should be here, too. Perhaps this rush of speed, the sheer joy of riding a fine horse in company of others, would banish that awful emptiness in his eyes.

They had shared their stories and had begun to adjust to this new place. York, but not the York they had known. They were all different, now, too. With her sleeves on, she had few visible scars, though after a hard day she still limped, and even now her hip would sometimes catch when she lifted her left leg. Leofdæg had not taken any new wounds, but he had changed in other ways—he still drank often, but less when he did, and now sometimes he talked unbidden, usually about Maer; he was eager to get back to her.

That might have to wait, but she said nothing.

Dudda looked the same, and behaved the same—if Wulf was in sight. If he was out of sight Dudda became jumpy and reached for his sword at any small noise. Wulf himself now had that crooked scar on his forehead— like all wounds that were not kept clean it had healed with a pucker where it had swelled and burst open. But the pucker was not just rearranged skin: Some of the bone was missing. He was lucky. He too seemed more alert than he might need to be—but he saw everything.

Of all of them it was Gladmær who seemed the least changed. Like Hild, though he had more scars they were mostly hidden and the only noticeable difference was a proneness to a far-away stare when anyone sang of battle. Since Cuthred had left on the second war boat with Oeric, he seemed quieter. But that could just be that he was growing up.

They slowed their horses, walked them across the bridge, then dis-mounted to lead them through the gate. Bone was steaming, but Lél looked as though she had only trotted to the river and back.

"If she was bigger I'd want her for myself," Hild said.

"Ha," said Dudda. "She's too pretty for war. Just like Leofdæg."

As they cooled the horses down they talked of the beasts brought from Lindum, and the horses of Craven. Then they talked of the men who rode them. The weather was changing and time growing short. She had the outlines now of the first part of her plan, but it needed to be firm and clear, the names or the men for each task decided.

When Bone was brushed down and eating hay, she went to the hall, where, as she had every morning, she broke her fast with between a dozen and a score of her counsellors. Her mother, of course—and Luftmær, who was often with her—and Gwladus. Sintiadd, there as a bodywoman but learning fast; Hild had noticed her lately pouring ale more slowly than she needed, which had always been a favourite trick of Gwladus's when she was listening to the talk at table. Morud, there by default: trusted but not consulted. And Grimhun, Heiu, Coelfrith, Osthryth—and Oswine Reed because he was, after all, Yffing and must be seen to be included.

She sat at the bench, tore a small loaf in half—the smell made her swal-low and wipe her mouth so she did not drool on the board—smeared a glob of luscious dripping onto the heavenly thing, and bit into it. She closed her eyes and felt glad to be alive.

"Have you found God, lady?" Heiu said, with the Irish amusement Hild knew well.

"This bread," she said. "These drippings . . ." She could not remember the last time she ate beef drippings on good bread. There was nothing like a loaf of fine wheat milled well and baked in a big oven by one who knew what she was doing. It was the taste of size and scale, of safety.

"Good bread is a gift and a blessing. If only you could turn this loaf into enough to feed fifty hundred."

"I hope never to have to feed so many! Fifty hundred?"

"The feeding of the multitude, according to the Gospel of Matthew. Though perhaps you would need fish, too. Five loaves and two fishes, according to the Apostle John."

Hild bit and chewed and swallowed again. She had never heard of two gospels compared. "Do you read, Heiu?"

"I do."

The first person to do so who was not a priest, apart from her. "You are Christian?"

"How else would I have learnt my letters?"

Hild nodded. She herself had learnt her letters before she was baptised—though it was a priest who taught her. There was something important here. Something . . . But then Sintiadd brought in a great plate of fried fishes, and Heiu laughed, and in the busy bustle of serving food she turned her mind to other things.

They ate and talked among themselves. When most had finished, she sat back a little and rapped on the board. They quieted.

She began to lay out what they had done, what they had decided to do, who would do it, and when it must be done by. Most of them would be leaving York to work elsewhere.

"Cousin." She looked at Oswine. "York needs an Yffing. And if you agree, your sister will return to Craven while you overwinter here."

Pleased, he raised his cup. He would be the Yffing holding the great fortress of York!

"With you will stay twenty men—though not all men of Craven. We have to start blending our people." She needed trusted men in every important settlement or stronghold. "So, with you, cousin, will be ten men of Craven, eight Lindseymen, and two Elmetsæte."

"The rest of Craven men return with me?" Osthryth said. Her task was to increase lead mining and grow more oats, and, when Begu returned, agree trade amounts between regions.

"Some, yes. But some come with me." She had talked with each about their part, but this was the first time most had seen the whole and Osthryth was looking dubious. "But you'll have other willing hands to work in Craven."

"Who?"

"The folk—they'll come to us. Harvestmonath's turning to Winterfylleth, and as the world turns from the light, young folk, strong folk will come here." She looked at Oswine. "Put them to work, cousin—but treat them kindly, treat them well. There's a lot to do. The well's cleared out and working, take care of it. Leave the church to the priests. Repair the hall as you see fit. The garth's begun but needs more, and we'll send some people to look over the valley farm."

Oswine looked less pleased: He was not a reeve or a steward; he had come here to hold a fort not run a farm.

"Cousin, Cadwallon and the Iding will fight each other, but not til spring. There'll be no army on our doorstep before summer. But we have to be ready. And part of being ready is trade. It's trade that brings silver, and silver brings men, and men carry swords. And we need swords."

He nodded: Swords he understood.

"Your first task is to make York fit for Yffings again—the trade, the travel. The swords will follow."

It was always good to repeat the important things.

"I'll enter and hold Urburg, but not til spring. We'll stay close over winter, share our plans—I'll leave Aldred here with you." Even this otherwise-useless priest could read and write, and written messages were sure. "Meanwhile, cousin, keep your men fit and their blades sharp. For although today the trouble's north of the wall and south of the Humbre, it won't stay that way." Not with Penda's puppet on their doorstep in Lindsey. "I'll leave you one boat for messages. I'll take *Seadragon* and *Dolphin*, and when I am back in Elmet, I'll send the other war boat *Seacat*, to York." Though not the men; he did not need to know that yet.

She looked at the rest.

"We leave tomorrow."

25

✛

THE *SEADRAGON* AND THE *DOLPHIN* LEFT YORK midmorning two days before the moon's first quarter. As they glided past the confluence of the Weorf a flock of whinchat lifted, wheeled, and turned south, and not all the wings and backs were the pale young who usually left first. Not quite Winterfylleth and the older birds were already leaving; autumn would be hard and early. She tapped one of her lesser arm rings and said to Aluin, captain of the *Seadragon*, "This is for you if I'm standing on the banks of the Esc before the rise of the last quarter moon." She jerked her thumb over her shoulder to the barrels of fresh, strong ale tied and netted by the rail. She raised her voice. "And one of those for your crew."

The sail bellied out and the *Seadragon* picked up speed. Hild nodded. Good. She needed Begu to still be there when she arrived.

By afternoon they were in the wide Humbre. The water was less brown than in spring—the rain had been light all summer and good Deira dirt had stayed where it would do most good, in the fields. Not far from Brough the *Dolphin* cut through a huge flock of ducks resting by the sand bank and a hundred or so took flight. The ducks were early, too. They needed to hurry.

The next morning they sailed so close to Hornessæ that she could see a woman by the salt pans lift her hand to shade her eyes against the water's glare as they passed. She must remember to tell Coelfrith that Hornessæ's salt season was a long one this year; more salt to tithe for trade.

The sun was fattening and beginning to tint the grass on the cliffs red-gold. By the time they reached the mouth of the Esc the wind would turn towards the land and waft them easily between the two cliffs.

"Wulf!" He was there. "We'll fly the Elmet banner."

It would be another hour before they came in sight of the redcrest beacon, but in these times Mulstan—or Onnen—would have watchers on the coastline. No harm declaring themselves now. A war boat was always something to beware; she did not want them sending a flock of fire arrows arcing onto their deck when they were between the cliffs.

In her mind's eye she saw the cliffs so clearly with archers ranged on either side, that she was startled when Leofdæg said, "My sister lives just inland there, at Hacanos."

She dragged her mind back to here and now. Leofdæg had a sister. "Leofa," she said, remembering the tiny woman who had married the giant Forthere. "She had . . . a son?"

He nodded.

"Tell me of Hacanos."

"Good sheep country. And where she is, where two becks meet just above the Deorwente, it's sheltered by hills. Good for growing things."

"She's well?"

"I don't know, lady. I haven't seen her in three years. Lady . . ." He went on in a rush. "Hacanos isn't above six leagues from the bay. And there's a hythe not four miles from the steading, a good path. I'd be gone less than a day."

He was asking less than a day to see his only kin. If she was still alive. "If it can be done, it will. But the bay first."

She stood in the bows, furs flung back and sun blazing on her chestnut hair—an Yffing badge to go with the Yffing boar on the banner—as they coasted in on the wind and tide towards the floating dock, where she had her first surprise. The docks were bigger, much bigger since last year, and two ships were already berthed. She was climbing onto the taffrail to jump down, when she had her second surprise: Begu, yellow as a buttercup, waiting quietly.

Begu here. Safe. She closed her eyes and thanked the pattern—ælf, sprite, Christ, she did not care. Her gemæcce was safe; she had got here in time.

As the boat glided in she readied herself to jump, then understood why Begu might be so still. She stepped back down onto the deck—now was not the time for energy and eagerness—straightened her furs, and waited for the *Seadragon* to be moored head and stern. She walked down the gang-board to her gemæcce.

"He's dead," Begu said.

Hild opened her arms and held her. She knew how it was to lose a fa-ther. And she had liked Mulstan. She held her for a long time, then let go. "When?"

"Last Winterfylleth. Not long past the full moon. Almost a whole year." She sounded tired. Grief did that. It might have been a whole year for On-nen since he died but for Begu it was less than two months since she had the news.

"How's Onnen?" She looked about.

"I told her about Cian."

And so Onnen's grief for her son, like Begu's for her father, would be fresh and raw. "Where is she?"

Wulf joined her, moving quietly as he always did.

"Wulf," Begu said, her pleasure at him being alive dulled by her grief. Wulf nodded; he had always liked Begu.

"Where is she?"

Begu turned, beckoned. Bryhtsige stepped forward, nodded at Wulf, who nodded back—neither showed surprise at the other still living and breathing—and said, "Well met, lady. I found the lady Onnen a mile up-stream and told her you were coming into dock. She said, 'I'm done danc-ing attendance on Yffings,' and went back to digging."

As soon as she scented the waft of minty-sage, she knew what roots Onnen was digging for. And sure enough when she turned the bend in the river she saw the lady of Mulstanton kneeling in a patch of tall green stalks, dig-ging with a hand spade. Unlike almost everyone Hild had seen in the last year, she did not look thin.

She shook a root free—a fine one, as long as her hand—laid the plant on the sack spread behind her, and turned back to the mugwort. Without looking up she said in cold Anglisc, "Are you going to help, or like most Yffings just watch as others work?"

Hild left the path and walked through the grass.

"Use that death knife for something useful." She pointed with her spade at the row of pulled stalks with their silvery white undersides.

Hild knelt by Onnen, as close as she dared, and cut the first root from its stalk. She stole glances as they worked; Onnen's face seemed heavier, weighted with grief. But there was no grey in her hair and her skin was smooth. Onnen ignored her.

They moved through the patch, left to right; digging, shaking, and cutting as the tiny clouds low on the horizon turned pale pink, then a deeper rose. When Hild put a root on the top of the pile and it rolled off, Onnen sat back on her heels. "Enough for now." She stood and stretched.

Hild longed to stand and hold out her arms, to hold Onnen, to be held in turn as she had been as a child, folded into Onnen's warm, woman scent; to feel safe; to feel she was home. But Onnen's hazel eyes, dull and hard as stones, warned her away. She waited. The river ran. From a distance she heard a familiar *skrak skrak skrak* and was not surprised to see the grey outline of a wariangle against the reddening sky. Her wyrd was mocking her.

Onnen saw it, too, but said only, "Those roots won't carry themselves." Hild started putting them in the sack. The setting sun made the scars on her arms dark and textured. Onnen's face tightened at the sight, but she made no comment.

"And the leaves?"

"Past their best. Leave them for the sheep. Or, no, bring a few." She set off walking without another word. Hild scooped up a double handful of the aromatic leaves and caught up with her as the path cut through a gap in an old hedge. As they passed through, Onnen nodded to the mouse and two voles impaled on the thorns, and this time she said, "The butcherbirds are back."

After a while the ground began to level out; they were nearing Mulstanton. "Onnen. I am sorry."

"So am I."

When they reached the yard before the hall, Hild smelled meat roasting over crabapple logs and wiped her mouth. She held up the sack. "Where do you want these?"

"They need washing. I'll take the leaves to Guenmon in the kitchen."

Hild washed the roots one by one, aware she was being watched from doorways. They knew who she was. They also knew their lady was angry. They would wait and see. Onnen was gone for some time.

When she returned, Hild could still read nothing on her closed face as she watched Hild rinse a root, then start to work on the next, delicately separating the pale brown tuber from the thin worm-like rootlets with the tip of her seax.

After a while Onnen said, "You're good at that. Better than your mother." She pulled a root from the sack, scrubbed a clod of dirt free with her hand, and dunked it in the bucket. "Your mother was always impatient."

Hild put her seax down. "Onnen—"

"Don't," Onnen said in British. "Just don't. He's gone, and no amount of talk will bring him back. I can't bear it."

Hild looked at her hands.

Onnen threw the root into the trough, hard. "I told you not to. I was clear. You can't have him, I said. I told you."

"Yes."

"But you had him anyway. You had him deliberately." Her voice was bitter as ground acorns. "You're not careless like your mother, not impatient. Don't tell me you had no choice. Perhaps you did, perhaps you didn't. But you wanted him, so you had him. And I forgave you. But only if you kept him safe. I told you to keep him safe. I was clear."

"Yes."

"I even begged you. I begged you! But you didn't. You didn't even do that."

"No."

"You should have saved him."

"Yes." Big hands, strong hands. She should have saved him.

"He shouldn't have been there. What was my son, a lad of Elmet, doing in a fight of kings? He shouldn't have been there."

"No." The black and red cloak torn and trampled. Guenmon was wrong: It had shown the mud; it had shown the blood.

"He shouldn't have been there, but he was. You didn't save him. And now he's—" She made a terrible sound, dark and bloody as torn liver.

Hild wanted to reach out, wanted to hold and be held, but she imagined her scarred arms lifting, reaching, and Onnen taking one look, one look at the crisscross of white and pink and dark, dark red, and in each stroke seeing death, and backing away, and if she did that Hild's heart would crack.

"My boy. My fine and shining boy."

The broken puppet lying in the mud, propped against a dead horse. She did not save him. "I am sorry."

Onnen slapped her, a sharp ringing crack. "Sorry!" Her voice blazed. "Don't you dare feel sorry! What right have you? Did you kill him?" She caught Hild's big-knuckled hand between her two small ones. "This hand. Was this the hand that held the blade that let his blood?"

"No."

"Then don't tell me you're sorry. Don't you dare. You didn't kill him. Tell me who did."

Blood like rain, banner bedraggled in the mud. Other checked cloaks in the men heaving back and forth. "Cadwallon's men."

"Then Cadwallon killed him." She shook Hild's arm, a short hard jerk. "Do you hear me?" Her eyes were hard as beryl. "Cadwallon killed Cian Boldcloak. Cadwallon killed my son. And you will kill him."

Kill a king.

"This you will do for me. You will kill the man who killed my son. I don't care how, I don't care when. But he will die at your hand. Swear it."

The crown of Onnen's head barely reached Hild's collarbone but she held Hild's hand between her own two like a queen with the power of life and death.

"Swear it to me now. He will die and he will know why."

Hild met her gaze. She brought Onnen's hands to her forehead. "He will die," she said in British, the language of kin-killing and clan feud. She brought the hands to her mouth and kissed each as though it wore the seal ring of kings. "He will know why." She raised her other hand and wrapped both around Onnen's, brought them to her heart. "For Cian Boldcloak, your son, my man, I will kill Cadwallon Bradawc. For Little Honey, your son's bairn, my daughter, I will kill Cadwallon Bradawc. I will kill him and he will know why."

Onnen's eyes did not soften but she nodded once, short and hard.

The hall seemed dim after the sun and sea light, and Hild waited by the door for her eyes to adjust. It was much as she remembered it, two-thirds full of the folk of Mulstanton come to eat in the hall with the lord—lady, now—as they had every quarter for time out of mind. They would sing, eat well, drink well, then be listened to as they complained with a full belly, when all complaints were milder. It was a good custom.

The music was different, though. Very different. A harp, and played well, and someone singing in British. There, on the harper's stool, a woman with smooth dark hair held back by gold and tortoiseshell and a dress the blue of summer twilight—a dress that would match her eyes.

Langwredd.

"Shut your mouth, it will fill with flies," Begu said from behind her.

"But how . . . ?"

"Let her finish her song—she's very good; I've no idea what she's singing about but I like it. I didn't know she played the harp so well, did you? But then I doubt you had time for music. I'll tell you the how and why when she's finished. For now, come and sit, and—oh, well, now she's seen you. She can tell you herself."

Langwredd played the sinking chords that meant the song was ended, and stood, smiled at the fists beating on boards, and handed the harp to the next singer. She came towards Hild, hands outstretched, smiling. She wore the same blue-grey stone nestled in the hollow of her finely muscled neck, and gold banding her wrists, but no Pictish brooch—no Pictish brooch given in alliance to the Bryneich by the Iding. She squeezed Hild's hand.

Hild's thoughts exploded in a welter of images like a covey of ducks: Langwredd in her bed, that throaty laugh of satisfaction, but also Langwredd as wife of an ally. Both. But a hunter who shoots at two ducks hits neither. Wife of Coledauc, prince of Bryneich. Yes. Langwredd, wife of an ally and mother of his children. Not for her bed. Not for her. "A pleasure unlooked for," she said in British. "I never thought to see a princess of the Bryneich south of the wall. Are your children with you?"

In the kitchen Sintiadd ignored the boys and young women running about and asked the woman in charge where she might find the wine.

The woman did not look up from the goose she was setting on a great platter. "Over there." She waved a hand at jars leaning by the wall. "Rhenish in the tall ones, Gaulish in the fat ones."

"Different, are they?" Sintiadd looked over her shoulder where the high table could just be seen through the hiss of steam and fat—the lady was still talking, though she did glance up and see Sintiadd in the kitchen before turning back to the talk, and she was still sipping—so their cups weren't empty. Yet.

The woman in charge said, "And you are?"

"Sintiadd. Bodywoman to the lady Hild."

"Well, Sintiadd-the-new-bodywoman, I'm Guenmon, and this is my kitchen, and there's a world of difference between wines, as you should know."

"And how is it that I'm supposed to know? In Elmet we drink ale in winter and fine mead in summer. Not foreign piss and vinegar."

"You're one to talk of piss and vinegar! Ach, don't mind me. It's not your fault the sad folk of Elmet never get to drink wine straight from the trade jar. So. What wine were they drinking?"

"How would I know that?"

Guenmon sighed. "What colour did you just pour?"

"The colour?" Was this like one of Gwladus's questions about dress colours? "Like the juice from crushed raspberries, only deeper. Like rubies."

"Aren't you a poet. Red is what you mean. Wine is red or white. You'll want the Gaulish. But mind how you pour; it's strong stuff."

"Tell that to them," she said, jerking her head back to the doorway and the highfolk. "I've never seen Herself drink like that." She poured carefully from the heavy jar.

"When you're done with that, help me with this."

When the jug was full, Sintiadd held the goose legs while Guenmon cut the twine.

"Drinking heavy, are they?"

"They are—all the ladies. Herself and Begu, Onnen and that fancy piece with the airs and graces. It seems to me they're all ganging up on Herself about something. But mostly Lady Fancy. Who's she to give herself airs and graces when she's as British as you or me?"

"Langwredd. Princess of the Bryneich." Guenmon stepped back from the goose, nudged one leg critically, then nodded approval. "Now. You'd best wipe your hands and get that jug in to them before they run dry and call for your hide. But come back when you can. Most of this lot don't know how to serve a feast. The old lord never really bothered, bless him."

In the hall someone else was singing now, a wide-faced man, too rough for a houseman—his left eye looked like it had been blacked for him a week ago—and though he sang in Anglisc she could tell he was British. Lots of British here; must be because of Lady Onnen. But he was making good music, and that made her job easier: She could wend her way past the boards without folk plucking at her skirt and asking her for this or that.

At the high table the women were ignoring the singer, leaning forward to see each other along the board, Onnen in the middle, Herself to her right, Begu to Herself's right, and Lady Fancy to Onnen's left.

She filled Lady Begu's cup first, pouring slowly and carefully, listening as Gwladus had taught her. "No," Begu said, sounding cross, as though she'd had to say it twice already. "Only if it was dangerous, you said. And it wasn't—though I knew if we waited it would be. I heard the news in the harbour here that the Iding had raised his banner in Din Baer, even before I stepped off *Curlew*. And you said it was important. So I gave Cenhelm no choice. I told Bryhtsige to not even bother unshipping the horses, but just hopped off, gave Onnen a hug, and said we'd be back in a few days, and hopped back on again."

She filled Herself's cup. "Did you speak to Coledauc?"

"No, I—"

"She'd no need," Fancy Piece said, leaning forward to see past Onnen, and toying with that big blue stone at her throat.

Herself lifted her cup and took a hefty swig.

Fancy Piece smiled and switched to throaty British. "Don't blame your friend, my heart. Coledauc prince told me all that was needful. I told that to your friend and claimed the privilege of ally and cousin of the knife. We had to leave."

Herself gripped her cup hard and nodded at Sintiadd: more. Sintiadd refilled it. The lady took another gulp. "Did Bryhtsige at least—"

"I told you, no," Fancy Piece said. "Listen to me now."

No one talked to the lady like that!

"The Iding raised his banner at Din Baer and sent thirty of his men to Calchfynydd to 'bring the prince and princeling and other of the royal clan' along with his best fighters to the stronghold as soon as may be. Thirty men! And half of them were Picts. I had no fancy to be hostage to the whims of a half-Pictish Angle, so left with my woman and the two bairns and made for Colud in the hope of a ship heading south to the land of the Yffing, where we could claim hospitality from the Yffings and refuge for the Bryneich princelings."

She poured for Onnen, who was turning her head back and forth from one to the other as they spoke, like a mother watching her bairns toss a ball.

Herself said, "Cuncar is princeling of Bryneich. He's not here?"

"The princeling reckons himself a man, and proud with it. He went with his da."

Herself drank and muttered, "Stupid boy." She got a grip. "So now he's hostage to the Iding."

"He is, though he'd not thank you to think of him so."

Herself leaned forward. "And did Cuncar ask you to ask me, as cousin of the knife, to come to his aid?"

"He did not."

"So what did he say?"

She was now at Fancy Piece's elbow and pouring for her. The Bryneich's skin was flushed, her eyes bright, and she was holding herself so that her breasts were facing Herself and heaving up and down. Gwladus had shown her how to do that; it took a lot of effort and was not something that happened by chance. "Well, he said nothing to me in so many words. Because I left with Denw and the little ones that very night for Colud, and there was no time."

"Do you now claim to speak for the Bryneich as an ally of Yffings?"

Claim. Ooh.

She'd barely finished pouring when Lady Fancy snatched up the cup, drained it in one swallow, and nodded for more. "I've no token to show, but Coledauc prince is provoked beyond endurance. Was he not the Iding's first ally? The first south of the Pictish wall to offer allegiance? And what is his reward—the first portion and place of honour? No. The right hand? No. He is treated as a houseman while the honours go to old Anglisc thegns who hid these past twenty years and now clamour with their puling sons and shout their loyalty and wave their crooked spears and rusted swords dragged from byres and hay lofts!"

Now she refilled Onnen, and Herself, and Begu, and even though she poured slow it was time to fill the jug again.

The kitchen was a hive as Guenmon snapped orders and housefolk lined up with serving platters. It seemed most of them didn't know which way was up.

"I've to fill the jug—Lady Fancy's cup's going up and down quick as a new wife's nightie—but after I'll come back and help, shall I?"

She did, and when she served food she made sure it was at the high table, trying to follow what was said, while in the kitchen Guenmon, exasperated, berated everyone enough to achieve a kind of order. But then someone dropped one of the platters meant for the lower tables and roasted crabapples went rolling every which way, and she had to help clear up the mess. By which time the highfolk seemed to be talking about horses, which held no interest for her, and some old Anglisc thegn was plonking on the lyre and getting sentimental about hearth and home, so she made sure her table had a spare jug of wine and went back to the kitchen.

The roasted crabapples were particularly fine with the goose; she told Guenmon so.

"It's the mugwort leaves," she said. "Onnen—the lady Onnen as I should say now, though she wasn't when she first came—taught me that. She's a rare hand as a malster, too—you haven't had gruit worth the name til you've had hers, though come to think of it, she said that was an Elmet recipe." She shook her head. "I taught her about spices, though. She only stretched as far as a bit of tansy. And I've lived in a trade port all my life: ginger, mace, cardamom, and pepper as free as salt."

"Truly? As salt?"

"Well, no."

They smiled, understanding each other, and Guenmon helped them both to more wine—Rhenish, seeing as the ladies had made such a dint in the Gaulish. Besides, it went better with fowl, Guenmon said.

"And speaking of tansy, tell me what happened to Gwladus—very fond of tansy that lass. Did the lady finally get sick of her?"

"Sick? Of Gwladus ferch Heddwen? Oh, no. Herself values her highly, though now for things more important than bed games."

"Ach, don't you believe there's anything more important than bed games when a woman's got her mind—and other parts—set for it."

The wine was loosening up the older woman. Sintiadd leaned forward conspiratorially. "Tell me of this Bryneich."

"Ah." Guenmon laid her finger alongside her nose. "Speaking of bed games."

"You think?"

"Oh, I know. Before Herself—ach, now you've got me doing it—before the lady Hild came, Onnen, Begu, and the Bryneich talked up a storm, and it was easy to listen because Onnen was always having to translate for one or the other."

"Tell me." She poured more wine, and Guenmon settled back comfortably.

"Well, it seems when Herself was up north and big with child she had to do with the Bryneich woman—imagine, her host's wife! And now the Bryneich has come here thinking to claim guest right for herself and Coledauc's heirs."

"I thought the heir was a hostage."

"He is, but he won't last a day in a fight, at least according to Denw, Langwredd's bodywoman. So I'd guess the Bryneich's here for two reasons. First, for Coledauc's sake, as a kind of backup: At least one heir will survive, and perhaps the Yffings will come to his aid when the Iding gets slaughtered, which everyone knows he will be. Because why? Because all he has under his banner are a handful of Pictish younger sons—not even from the proper war band according to Denw—some old exiled Bernician lords come back with their ætheling and bringing their sons young enough to sound like Picts themselves. The northern Anglisc aren't going to flock to his banner, why should they if he'll give their land to those who were in exile with him. And any as do'll be poor."

Sintiadd nodded. What she had overheard was beginning to make sense.

Guenmon shrugged. "Well, it's not much to do with us."

"I don't care a dot for hostages and Idings. But if that Bryneich woman's going to cause trouble for Herself it'll be a strew of rocks in my road."

"And that's the second reason, I'd wager." Guenmon nudged the plate of pasties to Sintiadd. "For her own sake. Tell me about Herself. And Gwladus."

So Sintiadd filled Guenmon in on all the juicy tidbits—at least as she understood them, and at least as far as she thought Guenmon needed to know, but not further; Gwladus had been very clear on that.

"Well. I always did like that one. But I had to tell your precious lady to take care of her; she treated her worse than a dog. Of course, the lady had plenty of worries—and she was just a lass herself; it was long before she might have been interested in the little lynx's shall we say talents. Though if what I overheard last year between Herself's mother and Onnen is right, it was the mother who set all that up." She shook her head. "That mother always did expect too much of the lass, and too soon."

Sintiadd sighed. "Everyone expects her to hold up the world. But do they stop and think she's not long past being a bairn herself?"

"Careful. You sound as though you almost like her."

"Well, and what if I do? We all need a bit of kindness. She's lord and king and war leader and godmouth and lady and mother to half Deira, and no one to turn to but her friend the butcher."

Guenmon seemed to be musing on her wine. "Do you find it a strange thing, a land with a lady and no lord?"

"No more than you I expect: Isn't the bay in the same case?"

"So it is. The lord Mulstan died not quite a year since—Winterfylleth. I feel for the lady Onnen. It's a hard thing to have your man die at the same time as your child."

"Aye. As with Herself."

Guenmon looked surprised.

"She lost Boldcloak and the bairn at the same time—and that was Winterfylleth too."

"So it was. A lot of death, and all tangled together. Well, even more reason for Onnen to have me, and Herself to have you looking out for her."

"That's right. And I don't want that Bryneich running about Menewood catching like colewort in everyone's teeth."

"Mark me, though, that's what'll happen: her going back with you. The lady Onnen doesn't want the Bryneich here. She's enough to do to set the bay to rights without making it a target for anyone looking to set themselves up as a power in the north. The Bryneich and her bairns might not be as high as she likes to think, but they aren't nothing. And then, too, the Bryneich's half wild and wholly wanton and not like to do as she's told. Onnen won't want that—and she still has some of the sway of a mam over Herself, so she'll get her way. Oh yes, the Bryneich'll be leaving with you."

The old bird was talking freely now. "So. Well, Herself's butcher friend won't like that one bit." She told Guenmon about Brona.

"A butcher lass." She mused for a bit on her wine. "Does Herself run roughshod over her, too?"

Sintiadd laughed. "Oh, that Brona gives as good as she gets. Gives the lady a run for her honey."

"Good. Someone needs to keep the lass from wildness."

"Wild?" She yawned. The last days had been a whirlwind, and that wine was strange, strong stuff. "The lady's the opposite of wild." She glanced over her shoulder at the high table. They were still there; still not noticing she wasn't dancing attendance. Well, Herself knew where she was and what she was doing. "She weighs every move before she makes it."

"Don't you believe it. That's what she thinks she needs to do but it's not who she is, deep down. She was here as a lass, and I saw how she is. I thought a man and bairn might steady her down but if it's not meant to be . . ." She shook her head. "She's not much more than a lass even now, and though she keeps herself on a tight rein, deep down she's a wild one. One day she'll throw off those traces. You just wait."

As Hild and Onnen walked to the drying hut they left tracks in the dew. The web stretched across the hut door sparkled, and the spider sitting in its centre was fat, and when Onnen pushed open the door it took a moment before running up into the eaves. The year was thinking of turning.

"I saw salt makers out at Hornessæ," Hild said in British as she and Onnen spread the clean roots from yesterday on a board in the sun.

Onnen shook her head. Hild agreed: It was foolish. When the wind turned, and it would soon, there would be rain, and all the work for nothing.

Onnen counted the roots. A goodly number for this time of year. "If we can dry them in the sun just a day or two, we can bring them into the drying hut before the weather turns."

Inside the hut they poured sea coal into the three braziers. Onnen lit two while Hild was still trying with hers. The spark was easy—a strong strike of steel on flint arrowhead caught in a pinch of dried birch shelf, and then the fluff—but then the damp coals smothered the kindling. Hild was not used to making fires with coal.

"Here," said Onnen, and she took two pieces of coal from the unlit brazier, held them over the flame of another, then took them back, rearranged the coals, moved the kindling, and with one sure strike set the whole going.

They moved to the trays of mugwort roots that were already shrivelling, and began to turn them over.

"So," Onnen said. "You'll be taking that woman with you when you go."

Hild sighed and rubbed the scar on her hand. "I can't change your mind about keeping her here?"

"No."

Sintiadd had warned her it might be so last night. "Then, yes. I suppose I must."

Onnen bent a root; it did not snap. She put it back on the tray. "Better than Coledauc going over to Cadwallon."

"He wouldn't."

"Wouldn't he? Pride makes men fools. Langwredd spoke of his rage at the way the Iding treated him." She bent another root; this time it was brittle enough to snap. She dropped it in her belt sack. "I met Coledauc, remember."

"It was years ago."

"And still. He's cunning in his way." Onnen looked past the roots, remembering. "Does he still have the same bard?"

"He does." There was a look on Onnen's face she had not seen since Onnen first met Mulstan. "You and Moryn?" She had had no idea; then again, she'd been a child.

Onnen just smiled, then nodded at the seax in Hild's belt. "I was younger then, and he was a canny giver of gifts that one."

Hild smiled back—better gifts, clearly, than she knew. "Do you remember the buckler he told Coledauc to give Cian, the buckler he became so proud of?"

"I do, too. Proud as stag. He was so happy."

Their smiles faded at the same time.

They sorted the roots in silence. After a moment, Onnen said softly, "Was he happy?"

Hild turned a root she had already turned once. Turned it again. "Not always. Though he began happy, and I believe he ended so."

Onnen said nothing for a while. "We'll finish here but then let's to the cliffs. I'd hear of all of it—all of him, happy and not."

On the cliff, the blackthorn sloes were the size of Hild's thumb joint and greenish black against leafless wood the same bright chestnut as Yffing hair. Her hair, and his. A strange and bitter fruit, but worth the trouble for some uses.

Hild held a branch back so Onnen could get to a ripe sloe deep in the tangle—and Onnen, usually skilled in such things, hissed and jerked back her hand and began to curse, only stopping when she sucked at the heel of her hand.

"I hate thorns," Onnen said in a thick voice. "I hate them. Such hateful things to grow from such bright wood."

She turned blindly to Hild, and Hild held her, held the body that had been more of a mother to her than Breguswith, that had birthed Cian, father of her own dead Honey. And they both wept.

After a while they sat among the daisies with the sun warm on their backs and their faces tightening as their cheeks dried. The sea was dark blue, deep blue, heaving and huge. She had never been up here in autumn; it was beautiful.

Looking out over the sea, with the old redcrest beacon's shadow shrinking as the sun climbed higher, they talked. Of how Cian had felt the weight, and how hard he found it to stay in Elmet while Hild rode and ranged. "It hurt his pride." Men and their pride. "But I had no choice. I did it to keep us safe."

Onnen said nothing, but it was the kind of nothing Hild knew.

"You think there was a choice. Perhaps there was. I don't know. Truly, Onnen, I don't know. I wanted, I needed to move in the world, through the world, to get out, and I thought it was for the best."

"Also you like being the light of the world, Butcherbird and Cath Llew. You like people to tremble at your regard. That's your pride."

Did she? She had come to expect it, backed by Edwin's power, and then by her reputation as hægtes who walked with the wights. She no longer wanted to be feared for what she was not. But did she want to be feared for who and what she was?

A black-headed gull wheeled, turning around something below on the beach, then tilting away with a lonely cry—the cry that was a lie, for gulls were never alone.

"Perhaps we should have run, just packed up and taken ship for the North Folk, and Hereswith." And abandoned all her people? Broken her word to so many?

"Take ship—you mean run? My Cian would never have run."

Boldcloak, who spoke Anglisc, Boldcloak the gesith, lord of Elmet, oathed to the king, would not have run. But could she have persuaded her Cian, the Cian who carved in wood and sang to her in British, the Cian she had frightened with tales of the hægtes frog, to leave the Anglisc to their Anglisc fight? She didn't know.

"And did he—" Onnen turned to face her, though Hild kept her gaze on the horizon, for she knew what was coming. "Did he know who his father was?"

"For a long time I thought not. And I tried to protect him from it." She swallowed. Or to protect herself—not just her body, but her pride: protect herself from sneers and laughter. "But he knew. At the end, he knew."

Waves rolled in, one after the other.

"And the child."

Hild looked at her feet. She felt that shiver in her marrow, only this time it did not stop. "A girl. So small. So very small. She weighed no more than a baby bird, and she was so still. She was, she was . . ." Her legs were shaking. And all Hild could see was that tiny scalp coming off in her hands, the seethe of maggots over the little bones, and she shuddered.

"Oh, little prickle," Onnen said, and took Hild in her arms, and Hild howled. She howled like a dog whose master had beaten it, howled like a child left on a black stone beach on a moonless night with the water rising dark and fathomless and the knowledge no one would come.

Onnen murmured nothings and stroked her hair, and after a while the howls were sobs, and then the sobs slowed and quieted to the last tired hitch of breath of a cried-out child who no longer cared for anything but to fall into the pit of sleep and hope that when she woke it would all be better.

"It wasn't meant to be, little prickle. No matter how you tried, how I tried, it wasn't meant to be. The sword was his path. Since the day Ceredig king gave him that wooden sword and wicker buckler, it was his path and his wyrd. He was a man of the sword."

He was a gesith; death was his wyrd. If it had not come that day by Caer Daun, it would have been another. Like kings, it was what gesiths did: They fought, and they died. She did not know if he had seen her coming for him, she had not seen his face, could not know his heart as he went down. All she remembered was mud and blood and the noise, the terrible noise, and then the blank mere where she had left him. Gone. All gone.

Sea breeze riffled through the grass; below, the waves rolled, endless, soothing. A good harbour: From here anyone with a ship could reach anywhere on the east coast in a day. Halfway between York and Bebbanburg. Good trade. Good farmland. And from here you could see trouble coming from miles away.

"This is a good place," she said.

Onnen gave her a look she could not read, and said in Anglisc, "A fine place, yes. And my home."

The Anglisc was like a naked blade between them and Hild realised she was the one who had unsheathed it. "Always your home," she agreed.

"But?"

"But how will you hold it when kings come taking?"

Onnen rearranged her skirts and leaned back on her hands. "I will make a bargain with them, for trade."

"I could protect you."

Like you protected him? But no one said it.

"I could keep a war boat based here in the harbour."

"And swaggering men at Mulstanton? And how long do you think it would remain Mulstanton?"

It was already no longer Mulstanton. Mulstan was gone. "I could help you keep trade open."

"At what price? No."

"But I can keep you safe."

"I'm safe now."

"Not for long. If nothing changes either Cadwallon wins and comes slaughtering, or the Iding wins and takes your twins as surety, or just pushes you aside and puts one of his men in your place."

"Mulstan might have been old, and his heart weak at the end, but his mind was not weak. He knew he was not long for this earth. He reminded me that Edwin king didn't throw him, Mulstan, Æthelfrith Iding's thegn, into the sea. And he didn't take hostages. Because he knew Mulstan, knew he knew trade, knew he could keep the trade flowing and keep Edwin's coffers full."

"The Iding will need to reward his followers."

"And I'm the best person to make the gold flow to help him do that."

"It won't matter, not to the Iding. The bay is a plum, he'll want to give it to a man with a sword who's killed for him, killed the Iding's enemies—to the same man who, if he's not rewarded, will start killing the Iding's friends." When war ended, gesiths had to be kept busy. It was the age-old problem of kings.

Onnen folded her arms. When Cian was about to dig his heels in, he had jerked up his chin. But both had the same set, stubborn jaw.

"Onnen, if you're willing to bargain and pay tithe to the next king, why not tithe to me meanwhile? It's not for my coffers—or it is, but only to make Deira strong so we have a strong hand to bargain with the king to come."

"The king to come." Onnen turned to her. "You know the Iding can't win. And you're going to kill Cadwallon. So what king are we talking about?"

"The dice are still rattling in that cup," she said. Though Mallo may well have run off with the cup or thrown it in a ditch. Or perhaps Aidan had ground the dice into the mud beneath his sandalled heel and not passed them on. Fate goes ever as it must. There was no arguing with wyrd but, just in case Onnen might try, she said, in British, "Tell me of Hacanos. Does it tithe to the bay?"

"No. Though Mulstan meant it to, one day."

"Perhaps that day's come. Leofdæg has a sister there. He tells me it's a well-sheltered place—a good place for a woman and her children to bide, hidden. He'll be going there tomorrow. If you've a message, you could have it delivered by the Fiercesomes. Let me deliver your message."

Let me give you Hacanos. Any message delivered by five Fiercesomes glittering with gold and hard-edged iron would be listened to very carefully.

Hild walked the grass on the cliff with Cædmon and his cows. They found a patch of the little mushrooms he called fodder savers.

"Bote uses them in the goat byre—if you mix them with the bedding the goats won't eat it. I tried it with the cows, and it worked. And Bote says the mucked-out bedding works wonders in the garth."

Hild put one in her pocket. She would try it. "How is Bote?" She had not seen his sister this time.

"She's taken a fancy to that unearthly one who came with the little maid."

Bryhtsige. "He's shown interest?"

He snorted. "She might as well be a thorn hedge for all he wants to get close."

"Well, if he does pay attention, you've no worries. He can't sire a child."

"Oh, she knows right enough he's gelded—that's what makes her greedy as a bairn for a honeycomb: something new. And when she sets her mind to a thing." He shrugged. "I'd not wager against it."

They needed more folk like that, folk who knew their own mind and could get things done. "Something new. Does your sister want to explore somewhere new?"

"Well, there's new and then there's new. You'd have to ask her. But I don't know if she knows what she wants."

Hild listened to the dull music of the cowbells; music only Cædmon's cows made. "And what of you? I heard your harping last night. You sang well, though I didn't know the song."

He looked at his feet—bare and bony against the grass—and muttered something.

"You made the song? You should make more. I'll ask Onnen to let you use the lyre."

"Harps are better."

"Use the harp, then."

"It's not our harp," he said. "The Bryneich woman brought it. Besides, I've the cows to see to. Goats, too." He looked around the clifftop pasture-land as though seeing it for the first time. "The little maid always helped with the goats, jabbering away all the while, like birdsong. I always thought she'd be lady here one day. She's the only one who ever comes up here now. Except you."

And Cian, when he was there.

The same thought occurred to him. "I'm sorry about your man."

"You teased him hard."

"I did. Sorry about that, too."

"He needed it."

"Oh, aye. Waving that silly wooden sword about! I thought he'd burst into tears when the stone fell out." They both smiled, remembering. "Still, he seemed like a good 'un, even if he could never make up his mind whether he was British or Anglisc."

"We can't be both?" His Anglisc was so much better than it had been.

"Eh, maybe some, but not me. I belong up here, with the wind and the sea and the scent of cow shit. It's who I am. Why should I want to change?"

A question for the ages: Why can't everything just stay the same?

A flock of throstles and a handful of chaffinches gathered on the west clifftop on the other side of the harbour. They would wait for the wind to change to the northwest and aid them in their flight south. She wanted a northwest wind, too; the throstles were a good sign.

Below, four wide-beamed Frisian ships were nosing into the river mouth between cliffs. One had the striped sails of one of their important men.

"Come to the hall again tonight," she said. "There'll be guests. They'd like your harping."

The hall was busy: The Frisian merchant was well-known to Onnen, and Mulstan before her, and he and his family and chief men were invited to the table. Hild greeted him and exchanged names—no, Dieuwke was no relative of Bavo, though he knew the man, a shrewd trader—and left him to talk with Onnen. Clearly they had business, and she wanted to hear from Leofdæg about how it went at Hacanos.

The Fiercesomes took it in turns to tell her about Hacanos—Wulf's only comment was to circle his pointing finger like a spindle then bring the finger and thumb close together with a dismissive frown: small place— and Begu wanted to describe in great detail Leofe's baby, Fortheric. At which point Wulf pointed to the future and moved one hand far up from the other with raised eyebrows: He would be tall! Hild nodded: He was the son of the giant Forthere after all.

Cædmon started playing Langwredd's harp, and people quieted to listen—enough that Hild overheard Onnen use her name.

". . . Hild will want to hear that."

"Hear what?" she called.

"News of the Iding," Onnen said, and beckoned her over.

She sat opposite them both and listened.

The Iding had raced Cadwallon to Bebbanburg and won, Dieuwke said, but it was a close-run thing. "He abandoned some of his grain wagons, and now he's inside the walls and Cadwallon's outside."

He was trapped. "A siege?"

Dieuwke shook his head. "Cadwallon burnt the grain barns, burnt the fields, slaughtered the cattle, and rode for Yeavering."

"Any word of the Iding's hostages?"

"No." He assessed her gold, her seax, the jewels winking from fingers and breast. "No word, and no word of fights or flights."

Likely, then, that the Bryneich hostages were with him inside Bebban- burg. "Thank you, friend Dieuwke. How may I repay you?"

Another pause, another assessment, then a crooked grin and a sigh. "Nothing. You owe me nothing. The lady of the bay already paid for news." He shrugged elaborately: It pained him to admit it, but, as an honest man, what else could he do? But his eyes were bright and watchful.

She took off her wrist cuff—it was a good one, thick gold with intricate coil work—and tapped it. "For this I would know what other Anglisc pay for your news. And also your word that if another asks you the same ques- tion, you keep my name hidden." The cuff was worth more than that, but it was often useful to be generous.

"Ah, but how can you know I've not already made the same bargain?"

"What would you pay me for the answer?"

He laughed, and she laughed, but neither looked away from the other for an instant.

"You're a wise man, Dieuwke. You know my name and no doubt my reputation: a good friend and a bitter enemy. But I understand that a trader must be seen to be friends equally with all those he trades with. So you should know that I also deal well with those who are neither friend nor enemy—if they deal well with me." She tapped the cuff. "So?"

He looked at the gold. "For that cuff I'll answer you true now, and not utter your name to another. But I won't lie to you or any other for gold."

A false impression was not a lie, nor not telling all the truth. "Say, then, to neither use nor hint at my name."

He nodded and she pushed the cuff to him.

"So, Yffing. Your answer: You are the only—" He glanced at Onnen. "Or perhaps the only other Anglisc who pays me for news." He raised his eyebrows: Did she understand he was well-informed enough to know Onnen was not Anglisc? She nodded. "Then know this, and for nothing: The Oiscingas are always eager for news from Frankia and Iberia, and pay well."

She said nothing. Why should she care about Centisc concerns with other lands?

He saw that this news had no value for her. He hefted the cuff and clearly liked its weight. "Then how is this: Now and again the men of Rheged pay for news when they trade from Tinamutha. Though now they won't be trading for some time. A pity."

"Yes. Bavo spoke of Cadwallon's ravages." And this news was no favour: It was in Dieuwke's best interests for the king of chaos to be gone so that trade could resume.

"He's gathering supplies to overwinter at Corabrig."

Not a surprise. At Corabrig he could move east or west, north or south. And with the Iding—with his Picts, and hostages such as Coledauc and Cuncar—bottled up in Bebbanburg for the winter, Cadwallon would be free to ravage. "Would you risk lying in at Bebbanburg hythe for gold?" A single ship could bring away a handful of men. Free, the Bryneich princes could be a nuisance to Cadwallon.

"Now? No."

"Your kin?"

"Not unless they're fools: When Cadwallon's done with Yeavering, he'll have enough men to block Bebbanburg and harry Stanegate both."

The Iding was in for a hard cold winter, and, as Gwladus might say, north of the wall the price of wheat just went up.

The Bay of the Beacon was safe for some time—Cadwallon was occupied with the siege, perhaps for as much as another year if Edwin had left supplies at Bebbanburg; Coelfrith would know. But what of Penda? He already had Lindsey, and perhaps East Wixna and the South Gwyre. And now that Blæcca knew there were Yffings in Deira soon Penda would, too. While Cadwallon weakened the north for him, Penda would be looking elsewhere. Cent was too strong, which left the East Angles.

They talked more, but now of trade: who was buying what, where, for how many, and how much. They talked more of wind and weather. He was away tomorrow, heading south. They agreed the wind was about to turn northwesterly, though Dieuwke thought it would not last more than two days. Even if she left tomorrow that was not long enough for the heavy *Seadragon* to reach Cromer before it changed.

"Though Caistor may better suit your purpose," he said. "The prince of the North Folk—and his lady wife—will be there for the building of a great church." He spread his hands as if to say *It pays for a trader to know who he deals with.*

His boat was lighter, of course. He spoke of sailing on the turn of the tide for Gipeswīc, the trading wīc of the East Anglisc—they could row well enough after Caistor—but she was barely listening.

If a Frisian trader knew of her sister and where she was, no doubt Penda would, too. She had to warn Hereswith. Though warn her of what in a way she would listen? And Penda was not like Cadwallon, he did not kill Yffings because they were Yffings, so perhaps—

". . . rare trade at Gipeswīc for those who get there before trade closes for winter. There's talk of the king not being the king for so very much longer. There'll be rich pickings—new kings being so greedy for fine gifts to bribe followers."

A new king.

Dieuwke tilted his head at her expression but said nothing. He knew full well what he was telling her.

There was no time for her to travel to Hereswith, and there was no time to write a letter before the turn of the tide. "How much would it cost to stop at Caistor? To take a message? And wait for a reply?"

He rubbed his chin. "An extra stop—being late to the trade at Gipeswīc. Worth more than you'd like to pay, I should think. And waiting for a reply? Perhaps for days? Not worth it at any price."

They began to bargain in earnest.

Hild left the bay a day after Dieuwke. The Frisian knew his weather. The *Seadragon* had barely reached the Humbre when the wind faltered. They began to row. Aluin drove the men hard, glancing at the sky.

As they passed the mouth of the Treonte the weather turned. The sky swelled with cloud dark as wet ash, and between one breath and the next they were rowing into the teeth of the wind. Icy rain sheeted flat across the boat making it hard to breathe. Begu and the other women took the children to huddle under the tent, but the wind whirled it away. Hild wrapped the children about with her furs, and the other women circled the children in a tight knot. Midships, one man's oar was wrenched from his hand by a massive log shooting by, and he screamed as it stove in his ribs. Hild leapt to save the oar, and took his place. The injured man moaned as Begu and Langwredd bound his ribs. The Humbre, thick with mud, made rowing feel like wading uphill through a bog. Soon all she knew was cold and wet and the pull-bend-pull of effort.

On and on it went, the day turned to night by cloud and rain and flying river water. On and on. Water ran back and forth across the deck and pooled around Hild's feet. Sodden, they rowed on.

The grunts of the rowers, the smell of rain and sweat took Hild back to Hæðfeld. Her hip hurt and her womb ached and her scars glistened in the wet.

And then the wind stopped, but not the rain, though now there was ice in the rain. And they floated in the dark and the grey and the cold. It was almost one year since Cian had died and Honey came into the world wet, and was now cold when she should have been warm. She stared into the flat grey world. Nothing but cold.

26

✦

ON THE FOURTH DAY OF BLODMONATH, her birthday, Hild rose from
Brona's bed with the morning star. As she had on this day every year
since Hereswith had left the north, she stood alone in the cold and faced
the dawn—not because it was the dawn but because that was the direction
Hereswith lay at Deorham, and, with her, Fursey. Every year, too, she had
then turned to face Cian wherever he might be: the Bay of the Beacon;
Gwynedd; York. But now she had nowhere to turn because that was where
he was: nowhere. Not just dead but gone, bones sunk into the thick mud
south and east of Caer Daun and flesh dissolved into the peaty, pathless
mire that rose and fell with the brackish tide. But the place she had left
him, not far from Ynys Bwyell, lay in a direct line between her valley and
Deorham. So she breathed in deep, and breathed out a cloud of breath-
frost, imagining her love curling ahead of her like a windblown pennant,
streaming south and east to settle and fold down like a loving hand on the
head of Cian, asleep under the waters, on the tiny skull of Little Honey,
asleep in her green and gold tunic under the roots of a tree, and on the
tight, tidy braids of Hereswith, sleeping safe in her bed at Deorham.

It was three weeks since she had returned from the Bay but she had rarely
spent more than a single night in one place—barely a day in Menewood
itself before she had left again for Urburg—then York; Caer Loid, then
Aberford; East Farm, then Loidis, and back to York—making sure her people
would be safe for winter. Now she was back to stay, at least for a while.

As Blodmonath deepened, mist twined through the trees, and hoarfrost lasted until noon. Mastfall was gathered, the pigs ate their fill, and the ones to be slaughtered were penned in single enclosures without food. Brona sharpened her knives and saws, everyone who could be spared from other work collected firewood, ovens were fired to a low, continuous heat, and old and stale bread was gathered, chopped, and dried. Hild made sure the beams of the new cool-cellar would support the weight. Word went through Menewood that for two days there would be no dye-making and root-washing, for all the tubs and cauldrons were needed for making sausage, and those tubs and cauldrons were gathered and cleaned.

At the north end of the valley, cull day dawned quiet and cold. The air stung their lungs like salt as they walked to the long house where Bregus-with and Begu had made sure there was enough food to satisfy the whole of Menewood. Though there were fewer than there had been—half the folk were now in the new Loidis, or rebuilding Caer Loid, and some already at Urburg—slaughtering, butchering, and sausage-making were heavy work. So there was enough for a war band, and good strong winter ale, for some had never worked a slaughter before.

The south end of the beck stank: blood and guts and smoke and scalded hair. Children carried buckets of blood from the hanging scaffold up to the mixing huts. Giant pans boiled over the fires. Bled-out carcasses were dipped and scalded, carried to Brona's board, where she opened them while two other sets of hands rolled the guts gently into tubs, careful not to damage them.

Closer to the stream, old Llweriadd was working to carefully separate the skein of white that wrapped and tangled together the guts from one of the young pigs. It was delicate work; if she nicked the glistening snakes of gut they would be useless for sausage skins.

"Not ready for you yet, young giant," she said to Hild, and nodded at the knife on the stump. "Meanwhile that knife needs sharpening."

At her board Brona was now separating heads and feet and cleaving scalded carcasses in two. Older children carried the heads and feet away, while men in pairs took the carcasses for another rinse, then up the hill to the cooling cellar. She stood wide-legged, working fast, small muscles in her forearms flexing and stretching, blood and bristles smeared over her leather apron. The only part of her not covered in gore was a spot on the back of her neck, but Hild did not kiss it: That knife was too sharp and working too fast for distraction. They nodded and smiled, but Brona's rhythm did not pause as Hild reached past her for the sharpening stone.

When she had whetted the knife, she rinsed a pail in the beck and brought both back to Llweriadd.

The guts were now a long, thick rope. Hild gave the old woman the knife, took one end of the rope, and lifted it high—higher than anyone else could. Llweriadd grasped it firmly and with a gleam in her eye cut it a forearm's length above the grass. "And haven't I wished to do that to a man or two in my time."

She passed Hild the jug of water. Hild poured the water into the tube and Lweriadd massaged it down with her knobby hands.

"And I did do that a time or two!" She winked. "And not so long ago, neither." Hild poured again. As Llweriadd massaged she jerked her head back towards Brona. "Yon butcher's happy to have you back, lass. Mind, so am I. A vill needs a loaf giver; doesn't work right without."

A vill. "In times like these, yes." In usual times Menewood worked very well without her. But then in usual times it had not been a vill but a small, sleepy hideaway to visit without a care.

"Bairns are happy you're back?"

Hild nodded as she poured. "They are now." It had taken Wilfrid a day of sidelong looks before he had let her pick him up.

Llweriadd massaged. "One more." This time the water ran clear. "Sintiadd—you're happy with the little featherbrain?"

"She's working out very well."

Llweriadd turned up the lower end of the gut like a cuff. "Don't 'ee fill her head with nonsense." Her knobbed hands were steady as Hild poured water into the turned-up cuff. "Don't give her ideas. She's wealh, and she knows she's wealh, not like others I could mention."

"Sintiadd is Elmetsæte, like you, like me," Hild said. "Like Gwladus." She had said it a hundred times.

Llweriadd shook her head and muttered something. Hild wondered what that was about. But then the old woman was nodding to her, and Hild lowered the gut slowly, carefully as Llweriadd pulled up, slowly, steadily, and the gut turned itself inside out as neatly as hose.

They rinsed that, then put it in the pail. Then started again on another piece.

Under the rough shelter Rulf had put up on the other side of the beck, open to the air and light, Hild paused with a knife over the woody onions and stared at Brona. "She said what?" But she had heard plainly enough. "So what did you say?"

A flock of young crows wheeled and cawed over the trees. Brona scrubbed at the cut lengths of gut with a handful of coarse salt. "I told her to talk to you, that I wasn't your keeper, or Sintiadd's." She rinsed the gut skin, then dropped it in the pail of water and onion. She picked up another, looked it over. "Also that if Sintiadd wanted bed games with her lady that was nothing to do with me."

Hild rubbed at her cheek—where was Llweriadd getting these ideas?—then hissed as her eyes streamed at the onion. "Love—"

"I know," Brona said. She ran the next skin through her fistful of salt. "Then she said, 'Well, just see you keep her happy. The last we all need is bad blood over bed fights.'"

"'Bad blood over bed fights' . . ." They both shook their heads. Hild wiped her face against her shoulder, decided there were enough onions, and swept them into the pail. "Done here."

"Then help me with these."

The wind began to pick up and both stopped every now and again to shake feeling back into their cold fingers, but by the time the afternoon was darkening all the gut was cleaned and soaking in the pails. They covered them, and weighted the covers with stones. With the onion, Ceadwin's cat would not come close, but goats would eat anything, as would crows. They would leave them overnight and tomorrow they would be ready to make sausage.

Hild carried the tub of salt, and Brona the knives and boards to the long house. Again, there were boards of food set up, with Breguswith and Begu and Langwredd and other women serving, and children running up and down, shooed away from the boiling cans and kettles and cauldrons where necks and heads and chopped tripe seethed over the coals.

Sintiadd and Langwredd, at different ends of the board, saw them at the same time and bustled over: Langwredd with a small kettle and ladle and Sintiadd with a platter of bread and cheese. "No need!" Sintiadd sang out. "I've their food here!"

"Ah, but a bit of hot soup on a cold day will put the fire in their bellies. Don't you think, Hild?"

Sintiadd bristled at the familiarity.

"Well, I'm hungry enough for both," Brona said.

Hild smiled vague, general thanks, then nodded over to where Begu was crouching to talk to Langwredd's toddler son on the other side of the room. She said to Langwredd, "I think you're needed."

"And not by us," Sintiadd muttered to her back. No love lost there. "Well, if you've everything you need?" Hild nodded and she went back to the hearth.

Hild and Brona sat shoulder to shoulder to eat, but there was no chance to talk. As people came and went they bobbed their heads to Hild or smiled shyly, and some spoke a word or two to Brona while Hild ate and pretended not to listen.

"Nanny's coming on nice since you dosed her, lass. A right clear out!" And "We'll know by tomorrow, then?" Or just exchanged a significant look.

When they were alone again, Hild said, "The nanny?"

"Ate one of Maer's shoes. I dosed her with flaxseed oil." She smiled at Hild's look. "They think that if I kill the beasts I should be able to cure them."

A boy no older than three ran over and offered Brona a hazelnut. Brona ruffled his hair and thanked him for the nut. When Hild smiled at him he burst into tears and ran away.

"He's afraid of blades," Brona said, nodding at her seax.

Hild had not known that, and she found she did not remember his name or who his mother was. But Brona did. Brona had been here every day for months while Hild came and went, and Rhin and Breguswith and Begu ran Menewood between them. The butcher leaned back against the wall, cup in hand, at home in her world. "And tomorrow," Hild said. "What will be decided by tomorrow?"

"Ah. Well, three families have represented to me that they would like to be part of the group that moves back to old Caer Loid when your mother goes. And I told them I'd mention it to you and get an answer soon."

"That's up to my mother. Caer Loid's hers."

"Lady Breguswith's fine with it, as long as you are. Are you?" Brona sat with her knees apart, tired but easy.

Hild considered. "Should I be?"

"That's not for me to say."

"But I'm asking you."

Brona shrugged. "If I understand right, you want Caer Loid for pasture, orchard, and cloth finishing. One family grew fruit past Kaelcacaestir way. She told me they had dogsarse there"—what some British called medlar; it grew only where redcrests had lived in the long ago—"said she'll bring me some one day, and would be good in the orchard, and the others seem more the sort to work quietly as they're told than the kind you want for Menewood."

The kind she wanted for Menewood. "What kind do I want for Menewood?"

"Your words, not mine. You said you wanted curious people, clever people. People who listen, people who learn. People who have to be told only once. And people who aren't afraid to try a better way."

Hild looked at Rhin, at Begu, Oeric, Fllur, Sintiadd. Leofdæg with Maer at his knee, Gladmær playing knucklebones with Dudda. Breguswith with folded arms watching Langwredd, who was listening and smiling at whatever Ceadwin was saying—it involved him spreading his arms wide, which was very wide indeed—and Wulf, who was listening to Dudda while holding bread in one hand and with the other absent-mindedly catching Wilfrid everytime he slipped and nearly fell off the table he was climbing.

Every single one of those people were those who had not suffered their lot quietly, and who had survived.

"What else do people bring you?"

"Things they're too shy to bring to your mother, or to Rhin while you were gone. And now things they think you should know but don't want to bother you with."

Brona was watching her steadily. Hild sighed. "So tell me what is it I need to know but no one else will tell me."

"Langwredd. People see trouble there."

So did Hild, but perhaps not for the same reasons. "What do they see?"

"She's wealh—"

"Elmetsæte."

"—but she wears gold."

"So does Gwladus."

"No, she doesn't. Not here in Menewood. Just as you don't."

She did—her cross, and a ring or two—but not much. Gwladus, too, stripped the sparkling finery in the valley. Even the Fiercesomes wore less of their wealth at home. But Langwredd wore her gold. "She's a guest," Hild said. "She's not sure of her place."

"She's careful when you're here but you've not been here more than two days at a time the last months. A guest, you say, but guests don't tell people what to do as though they're in charge. Sintiadd hates her. And if I offered a pound of silver as wager I'd get no takers against your mother coring her like an apple before Yule."

"Just because she thinks she's better than everyone else?"

"I don't think she does."

"But you—"

"As you say, she's not sure of her place, not secure. But she has notions of what her place should be." She sipped her ale. "Only I'm in it. Or she thinks I am." She smiled. "No, no. I've no worries. But it's a mystery why you ever . . ." She shook her head.

It seemed another lifetime. "She was different with her own people. And it was spring in the north with the air fresh as morning and a sky that went on forever. And she had a lovely voice, and a better laugh."

"She still does."

"Does she?" She had not heard Langwredd laugh lately. But as Brona said, she had not been there much. "Perhaps I should spend more time with her, reassure her of her place."

"She's twisty. She's always hinting at this and that, and setting people against each other. She tried to pit Sintiadd and Gwladus against each other, and when that didn't work she whispered in Llweriadd's ear about how you would use your bodywoman."

So that was what that had been about. "Llweriadd doesn't believe it."

"Not yet. But repeat a whisper often enough and it becomes true."

"What's she said to my mother?"

"That I don't know, but they step around each other like cats."

They watched Breguswith and Langwredd for a moment. Now that Hild was paying attention she could see that Langwredd was smiling too deliberately, too consciously, pretending she did not have a care in the world.

"So you think I should make her leave?"

"Not for me to say. That's your weight to carry."

Langwredd was the mother of the younger Bryneich princelings. They could be useful, depending on what happened in the north. "I won't know what's best until spring." Until Uinniau and Mallo brought back answers to her questions. Though perhaps before spring, if both made good time in their separate travels. Where was Mallo? How far north was he with her careful letters? And Uinniau? What news would he bring her of Rheged and Alt Clut? And James—if he did not make the journey soon, the weather might keep him in Craven.

Prince Uinniau had warned James but her voice shocked him, rough and torn about the edges, but it was nothing to the sight of her: tall and smiling but, as she came closer, hands out for his, the loss behind her eyes seemed older and deeper than the catacombs of the Eternal City.

"My dear! Hild, my dear." He was in danger of babbling. "You're alive! For a time we thought— Oh, you are a blessing on my eyes!" He took her hands, and tried not to flinch at the terrible marks on her forearms, and they squeezed, then laughed, then hugged—and oh, dear sweet Christ, she was like a shard of marble, so thin but so hard.

She hugged him hard, then stepped back and assessed him like a farrier looking at a lame horse before choosing the right tool.

"I brought the parchment," he said, flustered. "And ink."

She smiled and said, "Thank you," in the kindly tone young people reserved for foolish old uncles who brought the kind of gift suitable for a much younger child. It seemed she no longer needed the parchment.

The look she gave the prince was equally swift and penetrating. "Well met, Uinniau. You had no difficulty on the journey? Good. Then you should go find Begu and I will walk with James to the paddock, where we'll see to his ass."

And, like a king, this lass who had only a score of years if that on this earth, did not look to see if she was obeyed by a prince of Rheged and a deacon of the Holy Roman Church, but simply took the ass's halter from him and turned to walk down the valley—no *How have you been?* or *I am so glad you have come at last!*—yet, as he knew he always would from now on, he hurried to catch up.

But then she turned and threw him that quick, arrow-to-the-heart smile and said, "I am eager for a long talk, and we will have it, but not today. Today I would hear news of the Church of Rome, and your thoughts on the priests of Ireland so I may understand and weigh them before I hear from Uinniau."

Hild and Uinniau went riding, Hild on Bone and Uinniau on Wolcen. They rode gently, for though Wolcen's belly was once more tight, her muscles were not yet hardened. As it was, all the way down the valley she kept trying to turn her head to find her foals. Uinniau patted her shoulder, reassuring her in British that her baby horselings were fine, just playing with each other as young ones do under the keen eye of old Dumpling—she knew Dumpling, didn't she?—and she should stop fussing. And finally, once they passed young Aldnoth standing guard by the old pollard at the mouth of the valley, Wolcen did.

They rode south, at a trot, then a walk, then a trot, for the new Loidis.

This was known country, full of her people, yet Uinniau was watchful. He was leaner than he had been, and harder.

They began with news of the Idings with the Dál Riata. Æbbe had still not married Domnall Brecc, and Uinniau did not think she ever would. He had no news of Oswald, other than that he was with Domnall Brecc—as was Æbbe's twin, Oswiu.

"He's no longer with the woman of the northern Ui Neill?"

"Fína gave birth to a son and died. And the son now passes, in the Irish way, to the care of his mother's kin, the Cenél nEógain. To be raised as a priest, they say."

If it was the father who died in childbed, perhaps men would father fewer children.

They trotted for a while. "So now he's back with his brother. Are they gathering men?"

"No. Or not yet. But they are sending messengers. One came to Alt Clut—which is how I know all I do."

"Ah."

"The messenger was not well-treated. Nor was I."

Which might explain why he was early.

Wolcen seemed to be slowing. They decided to dismount and walk.

"You remember Eugein." The sullen prince who was friendly with Honeytongue. "He is now king in all but name—Beli is not long for the world. And he believes he can do better than his father." He kicked a stone viciously enough to make stolid Wolcen startle. "He wants Rhianmelldt."

Hild stopped so suddenly Bone bumped into her. Rhianmelldt, and the news of Oswiu . . . She grinned fiercely. For now one shape was rising from the mist, and sharpening: Rhianmelldt could be the key to everything.

She took her seat at the head of the board and looked at her people—her counsellors, as Brona would say. Her mother, Gwladus, Rhin, Oeric, Coelfrith, Begu, Uinniau, Leofdæg, Bryhtsige, Wulf—and with him Dudda—and, for now, Langwredd and James, with Almund—who was blushing and flustered at the greeting he had from James, who had stopped and stared, then beamed and called, "Dear boy! Dear boy! How is your lovely voice?"—to take notes and Sintiadd to pour and listen.

"Uinniau brought me news," she said. Most of them had heard much of it, but now she laid it out in order. "And I have a thought that might suit many of us, here and elsewhere—though not, I think, Alt Clut."

They were watching her attentively.

"Eugein mac Beli intends to offer for Rhianmelldt of Rheged. But we don't want this to happen."

Begu looked at Uinniau. "We don't?" It would solve all their problems.

"Rhoedd doesn't," he said.

"Nor do we," Hild said. "Alt Clut's not a friend of Deira or Bernicia. What Rhoedd wants most of all for Rheged is to be allied to a strong neighbour. Alt Clut isn't strong. Under Beli, it was forever quarrelling with its neighbours, and Uinniau tells me Eugein will be even worse."

He nodded. "They're singing the old songs again, yearning for Yr Hen Ogledd."

"They would side with Cadwallon. So we have a better idea. The safest ally for Rheged would be an Yffing king."

"An Yffing?" James said. "Oswine? You want Rhianmelldt for Oswine?"

"Rhoedd's already decided against Oswine."

James looked at Hild, surprised.

"Not Oswine," she said.

They all looked at each other, and one by one their confusion turned to dawning horror.

Hild laughed. "No, not me. I don't want to be king."

Kings died young. Kings never had any peace—when could a king roam the moor alone? Kings were as trapped by their wyrd as any ceorl.

What she wanted was for whoever was king to stay away and leave her to build her own corner of the kingdom.

"Let me tell you a story." She nodded for Sintiadd to fill cups. "It is a story of kings."

They already knew the various parts of it, but she needed to lay it out clean and plain.

"Thirty years ago, my elderfather, Æthelric Yffing, Æthelric Spear, was king of Deira. He had a much younger brother, Edwin, by a different mother, who had a sister, Acha. My elderfather took to wife a daughter of the East Anglisc, who gave birth to my father, the ætheling Hereric."

Everyone nodded.

"Farther north, Æthelfrith Iding—Æthelfrith Flesaur, the Twister—married Bebba of the Bryneich and became king of Bernicia. Bebba died birthing their son, Eanfrid. Æthelfrith Iding then invaded Deira, killed my elderfather, and drove my father, Hereric, into exile. He also drove Acha's brother, Edwin, into exile, but not Acha. Acha he took to wife—Acha my uncle Edwin's sister, my elderfather's half sister—and claimed kingship over all Angles north of the Humbre."

Uinniau cleared his throat. Hild gestured for him to speak. "In Rheged, Æthelfrith Iding is named Fflamddwyr, Flame Bearer, for he tore out the heart of Rheged when he torched our stronghold in the hills north of the firth, fired it with a flame so fierce it burnt for a week and could be seen across the water. It's because of Fflamddwyr that the Franks and Frisians no longer send their ships to the west coast. Because of Fflamddwyr we must move goods along the wall road—all so he could tithe every sack and tun through his own wīcs. It is because of Fflamddwyr that Cadwallon can now bring us to our knees without even a battle by blocking trade along the Stanegate." He caught and held Hild's gaze. "I tell you now, Rheged has no love for Idings."

That was a story she did not know. Her thoughts darted about, formed another pattern. She nodded and went on with her story. "Acha bore Æthelfrith Iding many children, and in time died birthing twins. Some time later, her brother, my uncle Edwin, returned, killed Æthelfrith Iding, and drove his children into exile—Bebba's son Eanfrid to the Picts, and Acha's children to Dál Riata."

Her uncle had also probably killed her own father, the ætheling, so he could claim kingship. But she had never been sure.

"So. Edwin Yffing in his turn is now dead, and Eanfrid Iding, Bebba's son, has returned from Pictland to claim kingship." She looked at them one by one. "Eanfrid Iding is not our worry. Cadwallon will kill him."

Again, everyone nodded: His odds were poor.

"But three of Æthelfrith's other children, by Acha, an Yffing, are yet living."

Silence.

"Oswald?" Coelfrith said at last. "You want to give Rheged to Oswald Iding?"

"Say Oswald Yffing, for he has as much right to the Yffing boar on his standard as I do."

Uinniau stared at her. The sound of ale pouring from Sintiadd's jug to Breguswith's cup was loud.

She smiled. "But no, not Oswald. I speak of his younger brother, Oswiu, Acha Yffing's last son, who is newly in need of a wife. For there's no more natural an underking to a powerful neighbour than a younger brother."

The meaning of what she had said began to dawn on them, but it was Oeric who said, carefully, "You want Oswald Iding to be our king?"

Hild leaned forward, put both fists on the board, and stood. She caught their gazes one by one. "I would have Oswald called Iding claim Bernicia, and Oswald called Yffing Deira."

Silence. Then James threw back his head and his tight curls shook with laughter. "Oh," he said. "Oh, my dear. A stroke worthy of Solomon!"

And then everyone was talking at once.

It was a windy day and what leaves were left were lonely, forlorn things clinging to black branches. In the north pastures Hild watched Bryhtsige lead the mare he thought most likely to suit her.

"Big, as you see," he said. "But she's not easy—she'll take to you or not."

The mare was tall, and made taller with a high-standing mane—black, like her tail and legs, made blacker still by the creamy-yellow of her body. Close up her coat was the colour of untanned deer hide; a step back, and against those black legs and mane, more like creamy curds.

"Flýte," she said. Cream.

She was big-barrelled: deep lungs and a big heart. Wide back. Big withers—always useful. She ran her hand over the mare's hide and it barely wrinkled: not too sensitive. Thick-skinned, in all ways. Her winter coat was shaggy and thick, an inch long or more. Big hooves, sturdy fetlocks, and standing four-square, watching Hild with attention. She had deep brown eyes with long, thick eyelashes Gwladus would have killed for.

"I like the look of you, Flýte. Let's see how we get on." To Bryhtsige, "We'll take the same track as before." Yesterday they had tried a beautifully mannered black—a true black, unlike Bryhtsige's brown-nosed Shadow—with a sharp blaze on her forehead that someone had already named, unsurprisingly, Steorra, but Hild had not been satisfied: pretty but not brave.

She boosted herself onto Flýte's back, belly first, then swung herself upright. Flýte did not move, but Hild could tell by the tilt of her ears she was paying attention. She kneed her and lifted the reins, and Flýte moved into an easy walk, north, up towards the moor.

Bone was a good horse. He had regained his conditioning and could take her weight, and was now steady enough to recall his war training, but if the months ahead were to go as she hoped, she and every mounted fighter in Deira would need two strong mounts for a long, hard campaign always on the move. Many gesiths preferred stallions, but she was trading away as many of those as she could for geldings and mares: mounts that would not lose their heads if the enemy paraded a mare in heat across their path. Geldings were steady but in a close fight mares kicked better, they had more stamina, and they were used to leading.

Once up the first rise, they moved to a trot. Flýte's big hooves absorbed some of the jar and jolt but not much, and Hild was happy when Bryhtsige nudged Shadow to a canter. She followed suit, and Flýte fell into a smooth, three-beat gait. Shadow was four lengths ahead, and Hild could feel a hint of tension on the reins as Flýte itched to be first, but she did not pull, did not insist.

Hild guided the mare into some smooth, easy curves. Then she curbed her a little to collect the canter to a more deliberate pace, one every warhorse needed. Again, Flýte answered quickly, smoothly, and willingly.

The low dyke was ahead, where Steorra had been reluctant, but had not actually refused. Hild set Flýte at it and, even as crows flew over them, jeering, she took it without changing stride or slowing a hair.

"Good girl." Flýte flicked her ear as if to say, *Ask me something hard.* She was bursting with energy, ready to run, wanting to be asked.

Grey clouds were scudding from the south and west, low and heavy with rain, and in the wind the crows that had flown overhead blew this way and that like leaves—cawing, laughing, slipping and falling like mummers tumbling for an audience in a warm winter hall. Ahead was a good stretch of tussocky ridge.

"Let's run."

She kicked, and Flýte's level-backed canter exploded into the lunge-necked rock of a gallop. Hild crouched and balanced and was amazed at the long, long moment between each thrumming four-beat when they seemed to float forever without touching the ground. Drum. Float. Drum. Float.

They led their mounts—talking about fodder and grain for a long campaign; did they have enough if they had to move before the spring grass was in?—back down to the pasture. Their herd was made up of sturdy beasts for the most part, and in the sheltered valley they would not need to be byred over winter, but not all of them could stay in the valley; they would need to start dividing them for their winter pasture.

They untacked their mounts—Shadow still used no bit, and he was still uncut, which worried Hild a little, though, after watching the way he and Bryhtsige worked together, not too much—and rubbed them down with handfuls of straw. She half listened to Bryhtsige talking about fodder weight, and pack animals, and half listened to Flýte's breath: steady, strong, clear. Yes. This was the one for her; Flýte and Bone would make a good team.

She sent her back to the herd with a slap on the hard muscle of her shoulder, waited for Bryhtsige to be done, and they walked down towards the long house together, talking about modifying the magnificent jewelled tack Bryhtsige had stolen from his captors. Flo, the valley's leather-worker, was good with shoes and belts, but—

For a moment she thought the beast being walked around the trough by the long house was Lél, but in a blink she saw it was another messenger horse—a gelding, one of the mounts they kept at Cnotinsleah and Aberford for quick relays—and still steaming.

The messenger was being fed by Langwredd, who was questioning him closely. But when he saw Hild he put down his bowl and straightened.

"Lady," he said. One of the Lindseymen, slighter, as messengers tended to be.

"Betlic," she said. "What news?"

"From Bavo the Frisian, lady. He sends best wishes for your health and hopes—"

"The meat of the message, Betlic."

"Cadwallon Bradawc has burnt Yeavering to ash and killed any Bryneich he came across." He glanced at Langwredd, who had folded her arms and was fuming with impatience. "Now he ravages Stanegate, hoarding food and weapons at Corabrig."

He slid his eyes sideways to his bowl.

"Sintiadd," she called. "Bring food." Others would start to arrive to hear the news. And to Betlic: "Come sit. And talk while you eat."

From Din Baer to Calchfynydd, and all parts between, Cadwallon roamed and burnt and slaughtered. He was savaging all the Bryneich, Bavo's man said.

Others began to arrive and help themselves to food as they listened.

"All, he says," Langwredd said, her Anglisc lighter and more lickering with British than usual. "But how many, man? We're good at hiding from reavers."

"The Frisian said all, woman," the messenger said dismissively. "Women and children, young and old, not only fighting men." He said to Hild, "He has their cattle. And their winter stores."

Langwredd's taloned fingers curved, but Hild silenced her with a look. "Betlic," she said, "this is Langwredd, lady of the Bryneich. Address her as such."

"Yes, lady."

"Now. Cadwallon took food, you say?"

"Cattle from the Bryneich."

"Did he drive them or kill them?"

"Drove them. To Corabrig. Along with wagons of feed."

He was settling in for winter, just as Dieuwke had said.

Betlic ate another spoonful of stew. "From Corabrig he's sending out small raiding parties to pluck rich trade."

"The only rich trade is Rheged's," said Uinniau.

Bad for Rhoedd, good for her. She nodded. "He's saving his horses and men, keeping them fit over winter. Any news of raids north and west, on Alt Clut?"

"Bavo's man made no mention, lady."

"Well enough. Finish your food. You'll stay here tonight. We might have messages for you to carry in the morning."

Langwredd followed her to the hearth. "The Reaver is killing my people. What will you do?"

"There's nothing I can do."

She folded her arms. "You swore friendship to Coledauc and the Bryneich. I took you to my bed and I spoke for you to Coledauc."

Hild was still not sure how much one had to do with the other. "You did. And I thank you."

"You thank me?" Her voice rose dangerously, and again her hands curved, ready. "You *thank* me?"

Others were carefully not looking at them. "Would you rather I didn't?"

"I want no thanks from an oath-breaker!"

Hild breathed, and again, and took her hand from her seax. Her jaw was tight and each word distinct. "To Coledauc and the people of Bryneich I swore friendship on behalf of Edwin king. The king is dead and the oath with it. Coledauc himself declared it so, and declared for the Iding."

Langwredd seized Hild's left hand, turned it so the scar on her palm showed pink and twisted in the firelight. "And this. Your personal oath to Cuncar ab Coledauc. Is this oath dead? Cuncar is your cousin of the knife. He is *hostage*."

For the first time in a while Hild saw the Langwredd she had known in Calchfynydd: straight as a spear, fierce and flush-cheeked, with blood thumping at her throat—a woman people would follow.

"Cuncar is hostage to the Iding. The Iding is not the one killing your people." Hild took her hand back, but gently. "You'd have me fight the Iding who will be fighting Cadwallon—who is killing your people?"

Langwredd sneered. "And so, like Solomon, you'll split hairs and let Bradawc split babies?"

She was magnificent, a woman of hero songs. Hild's mind leapt to spring. "Without Coledauc, would the Bryneich follow you?"

Langwredd jerked her chin up, a sharp lift that if she had had a knife in her hand would have been a fight challenge. "What is that to do with your oath?" But Hild could see she was listening.

"Would they?"

"Would I want them to?"

Hild nodded slowly. "You might. There might be a way for us to help each other, to help your people."

27

✤

THE FIRST FROST WAS SHORT and soon gone, unnoticed except by those who lived through their bellies, for the cold had made the parsnips still in the earth taste their best; slow roasted in the embers overnight, and eaten with butter and dried sage the next morning, they were, in James's opinion, the very taste of heaven.

"At least, heaven as I see it in the winter months," James said, sighing with pleasure and wiping his hands on the cloth. "And now I am fortified for our walk." He stood, but Hild did not move. She had known James ten years, and when he said he was ready what he meant was, he would now begin to get ready. And in the cold months that meant finding boots and extra hose, digging out his woolly muffler and wrapping it three times around his neck from chin to collarbone, and finally finding his cloak, the one with the marten-trimmed hood.

This lovely hood was all that lay between him and madness. The cold could do that to those of a sensitive disposition. He had lived on this god-forsaken isle at the far northwest edge of the world for three dozen years, and the only time he truly felt warm to his bones was when he dreamt of sleeping in the August sun under the vines of his youth. And here was this young bare-armed giant, simply picking up her great staff and declaring herself ready, and dragging him off willy nilly into the howling wilderness to see some heathen stone or other.

So now he was on the back of some vicious beast—well, no, not vicious if truth be told, but one of the boniest of God's creatures, dreadfully bony. If he were not so fond of her he would protest.

"We could walk," he said. Because the stone, of course, was a disguise, a cloak for her real purpose, which he had very little doubt would be to talk about something without being overheard. But surely they could do that somewhere in the valley where there was at least a suggestion of shelter.

She looked down at him from her gigantic mare with the terrifying stiff crest. "It's ten miles, high on the moor, to the stones. Besides, the horses need exercise."

"My mount appears an entirely admirable beast," he said. "Hardly portly at all."

"His name is Bone. And that's because he gets a lot of exercise."

Perhaps he looked glum because she laughed—the heartless wretch—and said, "Any other winter and I might agree, but we need them fighting fit, so that when we get word we can leave within the week."

He did not ask, *What word?* He had heard already about the struggle with the parchment, and the ink, and getting the seal just so. He had learnt how important the message north and its reply were.

They moved to a trot, then an easy canter, then back to a walk. She was watching him as they rode in that way of hers that, when she chose, made you feel as though nothing on God's green earth was as interesting as you.

"Have I sprouted horns?"

"I had forgotten how you've changed in your years in Craven."

She had changed more. Her voice of course, though now he was more used to it, it was not unpleasant. And strangely she seemed more inclined to laugh—as a child she had been a solemn little thing—though perhaps it was that she was now a bowl turned and hollowed by sadness in order to hold more joy. And of course it was true, he had changed, too. There had been a time when he rarely ventured outside the walls of York—rarely even left the great basilica, now hall, then the small church that could become great. In those days his skin would turn pale and ashy in winter—more like the top of a mushroom than its rich dark gills. (Did they still make those potted mushrooms he had liked so much at Caer Loid?) Now it stayed glossy as good ink even in winter because now he spent his days outdoors. He had less hair than he once did, too, though what he had was longer and the curl a little looser, and Druyen, the dear man, had told him his eyes were no longer quite black but warm brown.

"You've lost some . . ." She gestured at his belly.

"Padding," he said comfortably. He would never be what one might call slender, but walking the hills of Craven day in, day out had thickened his legs and hardened the muscle in his torso.

"How old are you?" she said.

"Just the age I should be. Which is to say, this is my fifty-third winter in this world."

"You must have been just a boy when you came to the isle."

"A youth, younger even than you."

They rode in silence for a while, and he remembered all those who had crossed the seas with him—Justus, Mellitus, blessed Augustine—all dead now, except of course that ambitious brickle of bitterness, Paulinus. Bishop of Rochester—or overbishop, as he still called himself, mantling over his sapphire ring like a moulting old hawk—while in Cantwaraburg Arch-bishop Honorius, himself annointed so in Lindum some years before by Paulinus, refused to send more bishops north until the unseemly confu-sion of bishops in the south could be resolved. Or so what little gossip he had been able to pick up would have it. Gossip or no, it was news Hild had found pleasing, which of course pleased him, seeing his parchment had come so late.

By the time they reached the old Roman fort and its lookout, he had warmed up, and he got down from the bony beast to dress in reverse—the cloak and hood, the muffler—and stuff them in the saddlebag.

Hild exchanged a few words with the lookout, who, when he had seen them coming up the rise, had jumped up from the stone lean-to and stood at the northwest corner, scanning vigilantly for invaders. Her people did so like to please her.

After some exchange of pleasantries to do with a badger in the spinney, they were off again.

"He seems a pleasant young man," James said.

"Cuthred?" She looked surprised. "I suppose he is."

No doubt the young man was older than she was, but even so not a day past twenty. Far too young to be killing people. Though of course she had been younger.

Heavy cloud was moving in from the north. The ground began to slope; they slowed to a walk. Some horrendous-looking stony outcrop, more like a cliff, lay ahead. He was relieved when she led them around its foot and then on again.

Farther west on the north slope looking towards the Weorf valley, and just by a spring, they swung down and hooked their reins loosely around their saddle horns to let the beasts drink and browse at their leisure.

She lifted down her saddlebags, which looked intriguingly heavy, and led him to a line of rock jutting knee-high from the tussocky grass. In the thin, patched cloudlight—oh for some blue sky!—he at first saw nothing but a grey, lichened rock, but, no, they were carved with curious patterns. He traced one carving with his finger, as best he could given the profusion of moss and lichen growing in the crevices. Now that was something one never saw in the Blessed City. Here on this damp island moss grew on anything that did not breathe; it was as common as air.

But this, evidently, was what he had been brought to see. He knelt and looked more closely. It did not help. "What is it?"

"I don't know. Something from the long ago." She knelt next to him and traced the carvings. "They look like giant tadpoles."

"No, no," he said. "Look. It's a cup."

"A cup with legs?"

"Or maybe . . ." He tilted his head. "People? These are the heads, these the legs, the arms . . . Dancing?"

They both shook their heads. Good. Perhaps now that they had agreed they did not know, they could come to what she really wanted to talk about—but no, she was taking out her great knife and digging grass away from the base of the stone and scraping at it. After some time and effort she sat back. "Look."

A thin line. Barely a scratch.

"This is a good blade." He did not doubt it. "But these." She gestured at the dancing four-legged starfish or crooked cross, cut deep, deep into the rock, and their edges rounded and worn. "These would have taken a long time to cut. They've been here a long time, too. Before the redcrests."

"Romans, my dear. Romans. You're forgetting everything we learnt together."

She pulled her saddlebag to her. "I didn't forget this." She pulled out a wineskin.

"Wine! O blessed child! Wherever did you get it in these troubled times?"

"Why, from God's glorious grape," she said in slow but serviceable Latin. "Grown in the blessed heat of the southern sun." She switched back to Anglisc. "Though this in particular I brought from the Bay of the Beacon just for you. It's Gaulish. There's more back in the valley, so drink up, but don't forget we've to ride back."

He drank. A very acceptable red. He savoured it, thinking once again of the warm dry dirt under the vines . . .

They shared the cheese—goat cheese, with some pleasant herb in. He asked her which, and they spoke of herbs. He told her of Druyen, the farrier, and how he did; she told him the story of how she had met Brona over the body of a horse.

"It seems there are few important parts of your life not begun in blood."

She could not have failed to hear him, but she said nothing, only looked west, out over the great moors. "Cuthred, that lookout—the young lookout—learnt of blood and the spilling of it not far from here, when Osric sent men to raid."

So they were to talk of Craven?

"There are more stones there, like this, only bigger. And each is in sight of the next."

Stones again. He sighed internally. She was looking at him expectantly. So he considered their earlier conversations. "Beacons?"

"No, they're not tall enough. But they must be important, or why would someone do so much work?"

He took a drink. Wine was a wonderful lubricant for one's thoughts. "Those other stones. How close together are they? Close enough to walk from one to another, in turn?" He drank another mouthful. "Like the stations of the cross—you recall the stations of the cross?"

"I do."

The wine was growing on him. Really not bad at all. He smiled.

"What?"

"Do you remember when I told you that each station represented the Christ's sacrifice? You said that sounded silly, like celebrating the sacrifice of a bullock: Here he fell down; here he lifted his tail and squirted the priest with shit; here the mother cow lowed to soothe him."

"That was in Derventio, when you were explaining the paintings in the church." She beckoned for the wineskin. He passed it over. They talked of Derventio for a while, passing the wine back and forth. "Cadwallon destroyed the paintings," she said.

He crossed himself. "A Christian to desecrate a house of God. Unfor-givable."

"Even after confession?"

Ah, confession was it? He breathed deep of the fresh air to clear the fumes from his head.

"Fursey called confession the ritual cleaning of sin from the soul."

He felt his way cautiously. "And you told me you were not sure you understood sin. Do you now?"

"It is anything against the ten commandments. And you told me there is no commandment against love. That Christ is the god of love."

He nodded, waiting. Sin and loving was an old conversation. But she was staring off into the sky again.

Over the moor now the clouds were almost black, and a hawk of some kind, lit by the slanting sun, gleamed in sudden gold. As they watched, it stooped and fell like a stone to kill something below their horizon.

"Can falcons kill without sin?"

"Animals don't sin. They act from God-given instinct."

"I know a cat called Clut that plays cruelly with her prey."

"Animals have no souls." He took another sip, rolled it around in his mouth, swallowed bit by bit, letting those blessed fumes curl delightfully around his tongue. "But for the sake of argument, it is an interesting ques-tion: Does pleasure make a killing murder? In this particular case . . ." She was not listening. No matter; she would find her subject when she was ready. He sat quietly, enjoying the wine, deciding that, on the whole, no, not murder if the death does not go to waste.

"Can deacons take confession?"

"No, and yes. Properly, the taking of confession is for a priest."

"Why have you never become a priest?"

"I meant to, when I was young." But then he had found his calling to be more that of church business, and of course music, than the health of souls.

"Must it be a bishop who makes you a priest?"

"It must."

"A Roman bishop?"

"Hild, my dear, what are you asking?"

"I need a priest to confess to, a priest I trust."

"Rhin is a priest, not a priest of Rome but a good priest nonetheless. And if for some reason you don't trust him, you've other young priests." Almund might make a good confessor. A fine young man, lovely voice.

"I trust Rhin—but he came to me. I hid him. I need someone who doesn't depend on my gift and favour."

"You wish a priest with the spine to disagree."

"If you became a priest you could be my confessor."

"I have no wish to become a priest."

He saw the look on her face and recognised it, and waited. "Earlier, when I asked if deacons could take confession you said no—and yes. Tell me of the yes."

She was trying to bargain with God through him. After so many years among the Anglisc he had grown used to it. "Long ago, my dear, in kinder days, we spoke of sin, venial and mortal. You will remember: They are not equally grave."

She nodded.

"The small sins, petty sins—those sins you can confess to anyone. Why? Because those small and petty sins may be forgiven through humiliation before your lay confessor."

She stared at him. "The Christ will forgive you if you're embarrassed enough?"

Put that way it did seem a small-minded, narrow-hearted thing for a loving God. He leaned back on his hands. The grass was cold. "Augustine could no doubt say it more eloquently but yes. Your humiliation is proof that you wish to repent, and wish it enough to suffer for it."

"But mortal sin can only be forgiven by a priest?"

"By God through a priest. Yes, ordinarily. But Augustine believed that if you needed to confess, and wished to confess, and would so confess if a priest were present, you could confess to someone else—to anyone— and it would have the same force as though you had confessed to a priest."

"So if I needed to confess right now, this hour, I could confess to you?"

"If you were in immediate fear for your life, yes. Please pass me back that wine now, my dear."

"So I would have to think that there was someone hiding behind that rock with a sword about to try to kill me?"

"Not only that, but both you and your confessor would have to believe that you might, unaccountably, not be able to kill the attacker first."

"How about—"

"And if you believed there were ten men with swords, axes, and bows intent on killing you, I would ask"—he took a healthy mouthful—"I would ask, because I know you, why are you sitting here confessing instead of leaping on your big strong fast horse and riding away?"

Silence. The wind hissing now over the grass.

"Hild?" She looked at him, and for a breath, so brief he might have imagined it, she seemed forlorn. "I will never be your confessor, but I am your friend. Perhaps if you tell me what the trouble is, I can help."

She sighed. "I have to kill a man. And the Christ says I can't, not if I don't need to, but I must. So I need to understand."

"Why, if you will kill him anyway?"

She took the wineskin from him and took a hard, angry gulp. "You remember Stephanus, and his boc."

"I do."

"Once you have used a boc, kept the tallies in writing rather than sticks, you never want to go back. But writing is a Christian tool, a Christian habit. If we follow Christian habits, does the Christ god now set our wyrd? Only a fool does not try to understand her wyrd."

A gust of wind blew a curl of hair in his mouth and he shivered.

She stood. "I'll get your cloak." Above the shelter of the stone the wind cut at her, and she looked at the sky. "It's going to rain. We should ride back."

"I'm not doddering," he said. "I won't melt."

"No. But the horses'll get cold, and it'll be dark early."

"I've come all this way onto this godforsaken heath and if I'm going to be rained on then I may as well hear what it is, exactly, that's gnawing at you."

She stared at the dark cloud where the bird, the falcon, had dived and killed, then sighed, and sat again, hugging her knees to her chin. "Kings," she said slowly. "What are kings for?"

"A king is annointed by God to lead his people and keep them from harm."

"No," she said. "A king's place, his reason for being king, is killing."

Not a perspective he had considered before.

"A king's task is to collect gold and food and weapons so that he can feed and arm and reward men to kill those who try to take them away. It's what they do."

"Surely not all—"

"All of them. I'm not old, but even in my time Deira's had many kings. My elderfather. Then Æthelfrith Iding. Edwin. Osric. Now the Iding in

Bebbanburg calls himself king, though he won't—" She shook her head. "All kings. All killed by another man who was or wanted to be king. But if, as you say, kings are made and appointed by god, is killing a king's god-given instinct?"

"A king is a man. A man has free will."

"How, then, do you confess a king? Because a king can't truly repent unless he takes off his crown and stops being a— Oh. Sigeberht. So that's why."

"The East Anglisc—"

But she was shaking her head. "What matters is that the whole purpose of a king is to break the fifth commandment. His life as king will be breaking that commandment over and over."

He was back learning rhetoric as a young man, disputing with his elders and peers over wine warmed in southern sun. "Ah," he said, "but if the war is a just war, and if the king holds no malice in his heart, then the heavenly host—"

"Stop!" She jumped up so fast his heart stuttered in his chest. "Just stop. When you say a thing in Latin I know you don't believe it; it's a game. You sound like I did when I was a child—speaking as a godmouth. Don't you get tired of it? You don't have to do that with me. I want to know what you think—you, James the Deacon. What does James my friend believe?"

He was not sure how he had found himself so suddenly in treacherous waters with no paddle. "But, Hild, you're not a king. Why does it matter?"

"I have to understand. If you don't understand the rules you're a fool to make a wager."

"A wager?"

"Following a god is a wager, a wager of wyrd. If I wager on the Christ and I'm right then I win. But if you're right about sin then even though I win I also lose. Because I am going to kill Cadwallon. Even though I'm not a king I'm going to kill him. He killed Cian. And Little Honey. He killed my people and burnt the heart out of Deira; and if he lives he'll do it again. So he must die. Even if I'm not a king and won't be forgiven, I must kill him. I've sworn it."

He could weave a pretty web of half truths about a just cause and the greater good, but she would dismiss it all as trickery and, now that he thought of it, he was tired of speaking as he should, not as he wanted. And he sensed that this answer might be one of the most important he ever gave.

He stood, held out both hands. After a moment she took them. "Listen to me. I am not your confessor. But if I were I would want you to understand that the Church and its law are not perfect. God is perfect, His word is perfect, but His word is written down by men, and men are imperfect. And so I say to you—I, James the man, James your friend—I say Church law is imperfect and fallible. The core of God is not law. The core of God, His essence, is love. And no matter what our faulty, fallible, imperfect laws may say, I believe—I know in my heart—that a loving God will forgive any sin." Well, any but the eternal, unforgivable sin, which not even the Christ could forgive, but that was not this. "I know, deep in my heart, that any sin—any!—committed from a place of love—love, not fear or hatred or greed—sin committed from love or in defence of love, that sin will be forgiven."

Her big hands—so much less scarred than her arms—lay lightly in his; she had learnt to not lean on others or the weight of their word.

28

✦

ON A QUIET DAY OF FREEZING MIST when the Blodmonath moon had passed its last quarter, Mallo rode from under the dripping, bare branches of the elm wood on a lean black and white horse. Mallo, too, was lean, and as he warmed his hams at the long-house hearth Hild saw he was no longer bothering to assume the air of a diffident, faceless priest. His hands and face were weathered and his muscles whippy. Like his horse he had travelled scores of miles in hard weather and come through less worn and thin than hard and honed. This was the true Mallo.

Sintiadd put some more wood on the fire, and at a nod left the long house to Hild, Mallo, and Clut, Ceadwin's cat, who sniffed the priest's saddlebag and then went back to cleaning herself by the hearth.

"Come sit," she said. He did. She poured them both good winter ale, sharp and aromatic with bog myrtle. She nodded at his bag. "You bring a reply to my letter?" All that work and planning, for this moment.

"I do." He reached into his bag and drew out a sealed packet. He held it in his lap, covered by his hand. He looked at her, solemn. "The first reply is from Oswald Lamnguin, given direct from his mouth to my ear and now from my mouth to your ear."

Oswald Lamnguin: Oswald Brightblade—or perhaps Whiteblade, or Rightblade—choosing neither Oswald Iding nor Oswald Yffing. She nodded, braced.

"Oswald Lamnguin to Hild Yffing says, yes."

Yes. She sat back.

"Yes, in principle."

Yes. Yes! All those hours for parchment and ink, pens and wax. Yes. If they could agree terms, yes. And now her wyrd was set.

Mallo was watching her.

From his mouth to his ear. He had spoken directly to Oswald. No wandering priest could do that, especially not a British priest. "Your name isn't Mallo, is it?"

He smiled, inclined his head, and said in flawless, fluent Irish, native Irish, "It is not. I am Laisrén mac Ciar."

And she had scorned his Irish as less than her own. Pride—he had played hers like a lyre. "And you didn't just wander here by chance."

"I was sent by Brightblade, at the suggestion of Aidan mac Ailbe, to find and learn of Hild, Cath Llew, in the Anglisc land of Deira, that he might know if Lamnguin should call her cousin."

Cousin. "Thou shalt not lie."

He spread his hands.

"Are you even a priest?"

"I am." He switched back to Anglisc with the northeast British accent. "And my mother, who is from Ad Tuifyrdi, had a brother named Mallo." And back to Irish. "So I walked at least in the company of truth."

Ad Tuifyrdi, between Tinamutha and Bebbanburg. She marked it in her mind, then set it aside. "And the other answer?"

He picked up the packet, tapped it twice on the table, and handed it to her. "From Aidan."

She turned it over in her hands. Sealed with blue wax. She turned it this way and that in the dim light, trying to make it out. Some sort of beast. "What is it?" she said.

He looked amused. "A seal."

"I can see that. I meant—oh." Aidan's jest. A seal of a seal. "Well, he could do with a better carver. It looks like a slug." She felt, as she never had before, the rudeness of the building and low roof, the beer served in simple cups. At least Sintiadd had brought rings and cuffs for her to wear before she brought him in. She put the packet on the table in front of her. "Do you know what it says?"

"I do."

"Then Sintiadd, when she comes back, will take you to the priests' house, where you may find a hot bath while I read."

Sintiadd, who had been listening from the bower, came back.

"Make sure the good priest sees that his horse is well content. Then take him to James and Rhin and a hot tub so that he may refresh himself. If they have food for him, even better." *Keep him out of here for a while.* Sintiadd nodded her understanding. To Laisrén she said, "You've had a long journey. We'll talk later."

She wanted James's opinion of their guest, and a second opinion from Rhin, and she did not want Laisrén listening and watching while she read.

Hild banged her cup on the table. They quieted. "Bryhtsige and Leofdæg are keeping our Irish friend talking about his journey, and his horse, but they will be here soon. We've talked enough. Time to decide."

None of what they needed was possible until Cadwallon left Corabrig again—but when would that be? By Hrethmonath the Iding, mewed up in Bebbanburg, would be starving and desperate; Cadwallon would go there and finish him. But what if he did not? She would have to make him. But for that she needed Langwredd; she needed Rhoedd; she needed Mallo—Laisrén. She would need the Frisians and their messages and, further, for them to agree to her request. And that was only for the first step, to attack Cadwallon. To protect Menewood from any sideways move by Penda while she was gone she needed to send to Afanc and Eirlys and Pabo to persuade the people of Ynys Bwyell—and Thorne—to block the Treonte against any ship from Lindsey. And hope Penda was forward-thinking enough to not try another straightforward attack on the north. No matter what she did, Elmet—all of Deira—would be vulnerable to attacks from the south while she was gone. She must see that word of their movement did not reach Penda, and she must guard that secret for months.

"If we do this, we'll be gone—I'll be gone—from Menewood for half a year."

"Again," said Begu.

"Again," Hild said. She looked at Breguswith and Rhin and Oeric and Begu and James. "Last time I had no choice," she said. "And none of you had a choice, or warning."

"We might have warning this time but we don't have a choice," Breguswith said.

"You have to go," Begu said. "It's the only way."

"No, it's not," said Gwladus. "This must be said: She could flee."

She could not—there was nowhere on the isle to run that would be safe from Penda for long. Gwladus knew that. She also knew that before long-lasting decisions all things must be aired. But Gwladus may as well have spoken in Greek. Hild's people looked at one another, puzzled: Hild protected her people, and she could not protect them by running.

"Hrethmonath will be here sooner than we know," Breguswith said briskly. "And either way, running to or from, you'll still be leaving us. So it seems to me what we have to decide is not whether we agree, but who should be in charge of what, exactly, when you're gone."

The next day was another of dripping mist, colder than before, and to those around the long trestle—Hild and Laisrén, with Coelfrith, Leofdæg, Wulf, and Grimhun (just back from Loidis, where he had left Oeric), Bryhtsige, and Gwladus, served by Sintiadd and Morud—the air felt hot and thick and overused.

"I worry about the Bryneich," Bryhtsige said. Leofdæg nodded.

"We need them." Hild went through the numbers again: Oswald could bring only half a hundred men. Good men, Laisrén had told them. Experienced from battles in Ireland, and well-equipped—but only half a hundred. Rhoedd would field the same. All of Deira together, for they would be far from home and supplies, and must take only well-mounted and well-provisioned men, threescore. Eightscore fighting men in all. Against them Cadwallon had at least as many, plus a handful of Bernician thegns and their followers. In addition he was entrenched at Corabrig with supplies and rested mounts, and his men had fought together for over a year with nothing but victory. "We need the Bryneich."

"But can we trust them?"

"That will be Langwredd's task."

No one said, *And can we trust Langwredd?* But the worry was plain on their faces. "We'll get the Bryneich," Hild said.

"And there are ordinary folk of Rheged who will help," Uinniau said. "All those who have lost trade and can't stand to lose more."

Gwladus said, "We'll recruit help at every turn. Laisrén's mother's people are from the coast north of the wall, and he tells me there are many who would aid an Yffing."

"But are they mounted and armed?" Coelfrith said.

"They don't need to fight," Hild said. "Only to not fight us, and to offer aid and shelter as we need it—if we need it." She looked around the table. "So. A final word: yes or no."

Wulf gave a nod of his fist and a short grunt of affirmation.

Leofdæg said, "The path you would have us take is out of the way of prying eyes and ears. But it's not an easy way. We'll need supplies. If we're supplied, and only if, then yes."

They all looked at Coelfrith. "I'll need further accounting from Goodmanham and the east," he said. "But yes. We'll have the mounts and packhorses."

"Grimhun?"

"Urburg has water, and shelter enough for a small group today, and by Hrethmonath for more. Yes."

"And when we get to Pennrid?" she said to Uinniau.

"Rhoedd will accept the terms outlined. Yes."

And she hoped to sweeten those terms further. She looked at Laisrén, who said, "To reach Oswald in time will require the supplies we discussed."

Hild looked at Coelfrith, who said, "You'll have them."

He nodded. "Then, yes, I undertake to reach Oswald Lamnguin over Christmastide. He will make his decision with haste, and I believe he will agree to the terms."

"And his brother?"

"Oswiu doesn't care who his woman is as long as she catches his eye."

"Rhianmelldt will," Hild said.

"The timing of Oswald's arrival south of the wall, however, will depend on the agreement and movement of others, the men with boats." Laisrén put both hands on the table. "So while I will undertake for him to move with all speed I cannot speak to when."

"If it comes to a choice I'd rather it be sooner and with fewer men," she said.

He pondered, then nodded. "Then I believe yes, you will have your answer by Hrethmonath."

Hild looked at Bryhtsige. His smile was otherwordly. "Yes." And she knew that if she did not kill Cadwallon, he would.

She turned to Gwladus, who talked to the high and low all over Deira, all the time.

"Deira and its people will accept the terms," Gwladus said. "They will accept Oswald Lamnguin as king. But only if we begin telling that story now."

"Luftmær has some thoughts on that," Hild said.

"Then yes."

So now the die had stopped rattling in the cup. Time to throw. "We will begin."

She worked on the wording of the letters at Brona's house, one for Rhoedd and one for Oswald, running over the terms and the phrases out loud while the boiled fat separated, Brona sharpened her blades, and Wilfrid slept hunched up with his bottom in the air like a caterpillar.

Brona tested her skinning knife, nodded, set it aside, and listened to Hild rehearse. "You've been saying the same things to the king of Rheged, over and over. Will you be done soon?"

"I need him to understand: This is the only way he'll stay king. And if he doesn't, he'll be dead and Rheged destroyed within a year."

Brona came and stood at her shoulder. "Which shape is his daughter's name?"

Hild pointed.

Brona touched the wax gently. "And is she truly beautiful?"

"She's . . ." She had been a child banging her head on the wall when Hild met her, but even so the woman-to-come had been apparent. "Rhianmelldt's beautiful the way Bryhtsige is beautiful. Her eyes are very strange, the colour of violets, so lovely and perfect they seem like they should smell of the flower." She put her stylus down and wrapped her arm around Brona's waist, pressed her face to the arch of her ribs. "You are strong and solid and real. Rhianmelldt seems an impossible thing, a flower growing from ice or air. But yes, at first glance she's beautiful, and Laisrén believes that with women Oswiu Iding rarely goes deeper than his first urge, before wanting to get back on his horse and go kill something."

"So this priest turns out to be Irish. He's already lied to you. But you believe him?"

Hild nodded. It sounded rash when said aloud but she did.

"Why are you putting such stock in one Irishman's opinion?"

"Not just one. Another I met, Aidan, said much the same thing. He told me Oswald's the brother who thinks, Oswiu's the one who fights." And neither of them said anything about the sister. Then again, they were both priests. She stood. "I'll check the fat."

Outside the cold had chilled the water and the boiled fat had risen to the top and turned hard. The iron handle stung with cold.

She brought it in and skimmed the fat into a shallow pan. Brona was splitting reeds.

She stared at her wax tablet, unsatisfied. "But Oswiu. Will he be content to be prince of Rheged?"

Brona shrugged. "Oswiu. Oswald. Oswine. Osric. I don't know how you keep them all straight." *Or why you bother*, her tone suggested, and clearly she wanted this writing nonsense done with for the night.

But it could not be done until it was done. She set the pan on the embers, added twigs. Oswiu would have to be content. Or none of it would work. Perhaps none of it would work anyway. She felt like a mummer at a fair, keeping hoops spinning on each leg and arm, around her waist and neck, some going this way, some going that, all while juggling, and singing out jokes. "Oswiu has to be content with Rheged, because Oswine of Craven needs to believe that he himself will be underking of Deira. If he believes that then he'll stay here, thinking he's holding York against our return."

"Sounds like you just want Os-of-Craven out of your hair."

It was more than that, but Brona did not want to hear it. The fat began to bubble. "Are those reeds cut?"

Brona held up a fistful of split and half-peeled reeds. "What about you? You're doing all the work"—she gestured at the tablet and stylus cluttering her house—"so what do you get?"

"We get Elmet."

Brona huffed dubiously, whether at the *we* or the notion of getting Elmet, or of Elmet being enough.

"We will. And I'll be satisfied with that. Well, if it's the whole of Old Elmet: Gole to Caer Daun to the Gap to Urburg—or, no, past Urburg to Hrypum."

Brona laughed. "Now I believe you: more, more, and more again. And you said you didn't want to be king!"

"Oh, just give me one of those!"

Brona handed her a reed.

She dipped the reed in the bubbling fat and watched the pith wick it up. She laid it on the mat. "I just want to keep my people safe and live life from season to season."

This time the huff was an outright snort. "To collect dung and make tallow dips?"

It was true, she hated tallow dips. Hated the smell, hated the dim yellow light. "Say rather to have enough time and people, and land and silver, for other people to collect the honeycomb and make beeswax candles for me."

"As long you get them to write the letters so you don't have to bother." So I don't have the clutter.

"Just so."

They peeled and dipped, then sat by the fire hand in hand watching Wilfrid sleep while Hild hoped she could keep the hoops spinning, and not get killed, and come home safe.

Two days before the new moon of Ærra Geola the wind moved to the south and west bringing warmer, wetter weather, and Laisrén, Uinniau, and Bryhtsige left without fanfare, riding north to the redcrest road over the moor before winter's bitter cold bit too hard for man or beast. Uinniau would return from Pennrid with Rhoedd's reply, but Laisrén and Bryhtsige would go much farther, by the long but more sheltered coast paths up to Dunadd where Oswald would spend Christmastide among the Dál Riata and with their king, Domnall Brecc.

The first day of Ærra Geola dawned cold and clear; grass glittered like tiny spearpoints under Hild's bare feet and the guttural *cra cra* of a raven sounded like the only living thing in the valley, though she knew it was not: She could smell the warming bread ovens. They were still new enough to please her every morning. She brought in the basket of wood she had meant to bring in last night, stirred the embers, and added sticks.

Brona leaned on her elbow and watched. "It's not a limp exactly, is it?"

Hild shook her head. When the flames were strong enough she added a thick chunk of wood and went back to bed. Brona, used to her ways, tucked her legs out of reach of Hild's until they warmed up. She put her palm on Hild's belly and touched here and there, eyes closed, then she put her other hand on her haunch, and pushed again. "Does that hurt?"

"It pulls."

"Hmmm." She sat up, pulled the covers over her shoulders to keep warm. "Did you know that the best cut of a cow is the big muscle that runs from the ribs, about here"—she touched Hild's second-to-last rib—"to here." She ran her hand down her belly, over the crease of her thigh and belly and into her groin. Hild smiled and reached for her. "Stop it. I'm thinking. Lie on your side, no, the other way, facing the wall. Good." Brona put a hand on her ribs and another on her hip bone. "It's a long muscle, heavy and thick, and the threads of it, the cords, are long. It's like a snake, only a snake with fingers that cling to every backbone and rib. If you put a calf on the slab and pull that muscle, its leg moves. I've seen cows with damaged legs whose snake muscle is thick and short from doing the work of other muscles." She began to ease her hands apart. "Let me know when it hurts."

"I told you, it doesn't—" She hissed.

"I thought so. How about this?" She dug her hands under the bone of her bottom.

"Nothing."

"Hmmm." She moved her hand slightly, probed deeper with strong fingers.

"There. I felt that."

She pushed Hild's nightshirt up and followed the line of the scar. The bed moved slightly as she nodded. "That's your problem. Your snake muscle has shortened."

"I've stretched."

"Show me."

Hild did, reaching up and over.

"You're only getting part of it. I could help you."

"It doesn't hurt, though." She sat up and faced the butcher.

"Not yet. But I've seen that moment, that hitch, that shouldn't be there. It could become a limp. I don't want you in a shield wall with a limp."

"There won't be a shield wall." If there was a shield wall they had already lost.

"You know what I mean. You're exercising your horses to make them hard and fast and supple and fit. You're exercising your gesiths. You need to be fit, too, fit in all ways. So we're going to stretch that muscle. We're going to stretch it every day."

Hild lay down and held out her arms. "Let's start now."

"I'm serious. And you won't like it. It'll hurt."

"Then come lie down with me first. You can begin by explaining every muscle in my back."

Brona was naked on her belly with Hild on top of her, kissing the muscle at the top of her shoulder blade when someone opened the wicker gate. A rap at the door, brisk and confident, and Sintiadd called, "Lady. A messenger. I left—"

Hild, naked, opened the door. "Come in, get warm. Help Brona with Wilfrid while I dress."

Llweriadd brought in the fresh bread just as Hild came into the long house. The messenger was Oeric.

"How's Loidis?"

"Good, lady. The hall timbers are marked, the trenches dug. You'll have a proper hall for Œstre Mass, or the shell of it anyway."

"You've a message for me." He handed her a palm-sized packet, waxed and waterproofed. "From the Frisians?"

"They left it with Grimhun at Cnotinsleah. They left no name, said only that they were lately come from Anglia."

Fursey, or Hereswith.

Brona came in with Wilfrid.

"Break your fast with us," Hild said to Oeric. "Tell us how things proceed while I read this." Until Rhin arrived there was no one in the long house who could understand Latin. So while the table filled—Breguswith and Begu and Langwredd, and Denw with the Bryneich princes; Luftmær eager for news, always eager for news—she opened the outer packet. Two letters. One from Fursey, sealed with the simple cross he had used for years. The other . . . She turned it over and shock speared her under the ribs.

"Mum-mor?" Wilfrid, plucking at her sleeve, peering at her. She picked him up and let him stand on her thighs, keeping him balanced with one hand.

Two seals side by side: Hereswith's boar, and the blue three-headed bird with feathers like crowns, the seal of Wuffing kings.

Brona put a hand on her arm. Hild looked up. Begu said, "You're white as chalk."

She broke the seal, spelled out the first two lines, and put the letter down. She had dreaded this news, but had hoped it would be a year, perhaps two.

She looked up. Everyone was waiting.

"Sigeberht took the tonsure. Æthelric Wuffing is now lord of the North and South Folk, king of the East Anglisc, and Hereswith his queen."

29

✦

IT WAS A MORNING OF CEASELESS, WIND-WHIPPED RAIN and the long house, though oddly sparse—newly whitewashed, with all the hangings waiting to be restored, and fresh-swept floor waiting for its own coat of colour—was warm and snug and smelt of the dried heather Llweriadd had tossed on the crackling fire.

Hild and James sat at a bench, reading: James his psalter and Hild re-reading the letters from Hereswith and Fursey. It was difficult. As far as she could see, her last message had arrived but the letter before it had not. And it seemed at least one letter sent by Fursey had not made it to Menewood. Both he and Hereswith were talking about plans she knew nothing of and people she had not heard of.

As she read, people came and went: Gwladus conferring with Sintiadd about Hild's clothes, and occasionally popping out of the bower with a question for Hild about timing or weather; Brona talking to Rhin about the stomachs she had salted for the cheese—nettle rennet was no good for the aging of good hard cheese, and they would need hard cheese for the war band's travels . . .

War band. She had a war band.

. . . But the stomachs weren't ready, they wouldn't be ready, and did they have enough rennet from last year? Breguswith and Begu tugging their chins over the hangings, which needed perhaps a bit more gold thread, while wondering when Heiu would be back; they hoped it would be soon because the weather was getting chancy. The comings and goings comforted Hild; the hall felt a haven; it felt like home.

"We really must have music for Christ Mass," James said in Latin; it was easier to stay in one language for reading and talking. "Listen: *For it is good to sing praises unto our God; for it is pleasant; and praise is comely.* And then, later, *Sing unto the Lord with thanksgiving; sing praise upon the harp unto our God.*"

She put her finger on the line she was reading, about someone called Foillan who had news from Frankia. "The only harp we have is Langwredd's."

"Well, perhaps not the harp then. But singing certainly."

She remembered the unearthly music of men singing together in the bare basilica at York, the music of stars. "Can Rhin sing?"

"Rhin? I have no idea."

"I don't know who else would know god music. Except of course Aldred and Almund."

He beamed as he always did at the thought of his former young singers. "And when will Aldred be here in the valley?"

"He's in York. But all my people who can are coming. Shall I send for him particularly?"

"Yes, by all means. Aldred had a lovely voice as a youth—dull as a lump of lead in most regards but he had that voice, at least, to recommend him." He shook his head. "One mustn't be uncharitable. Almund and Aldred, a gift unlooked for to see them again—Almund's voice is celestial."

She looked up. "*Caelestis.* You used that word before, on the moor." She switched to Anglisc. "His voice is . . . the sky?"

"Heaven. Heavenly. But even such beauty needs a chorus to lift it to great heights. And we have only two singers. Well. I shall think of something. The point of singing praise is to make a joyful noise."

She let him muse while she went back to Fursey's letter.

. . . the way of Sigeberht's piety, and your second message, by way of the Frisian, came too late. And, my heart, though you have the mind of the world, there is no mortal message that could have turned this tide. Sigeberht's path was set long ago, before he even left Frankia. I may not tell all of what I know, nor exactly how I know it.

Confession.

> Before even he left Frankia, Sigeberht, being a pious man, would rather be monk than king. But he was persuaded otherwise by Dagoberht, king of the Franks. As a king beset by intrigue, Dagoberht wished allies beyond the Oiscingas of Cent.

She understood the words but the whole made no sense. If Sigeberht was no longer king how could he be of use to Dagoberht?

> Once Sigeberht landed on these shores and took up the crown, Æthelric was always one day going to be king and Hereswith his queen.

She wished Fursey were sitting there beside her, sipping his wine, scratching his wine-stain birthmark, and giving her an amused look as she tried to set the thing in an order that made sense. She would make guesses, and by the way he lowered his eyelids, or gave her a half smile she would know if she was getting hotter or colder on the trail of the truth.

But he was not. Instead on the next page he was talking about some special kind of floor, a very Roman floor, for his splendid new church at Cnobheresburg; the admirers of the magnificent edifice-to-be.

> . . . my horror when faced with a man lately king kissing my ring and threatening to kneel!

His ring. Fursey's ring.

"I think Fursey is a bishop. Truly a bishop now."

James looked up. "A bishop? Are you sure?"

"Unless new-made monks kiss the rings of priests who are building great new churches."

He looked doubtful. "Would Honorius make two bishops for the East Anglisc? But Felix is from Burgundy. Perhaps that's permissible in Frankia."

Frankia again. She remembered talking to someone in the Bay of the Beacon . . . Dieuwke. She laughed ruefully. "Fursey, next time a Frisian offers you something for free, ask the next question."

"Yes? Well, no doubt you'll explain that in good time."

"James, what do you know of Franks?"

He put a finger in his reading again. "I was there a year with Bishop Augustine and Paulinus—still mere Father Paulinus—but I was very young, not much older than young Ceadwin there. I did meet one Frank in particular, whose sister Ymma is now the Centish queen. He was an ambitious man, even then. Oh, yes." And his lips pursed.

"You didn't like him?"

"I didn't like any of them. Franks are an unctuous, untrustworthy, slippery tribe of eels. They smile and swear friendship, then poison your wine."

It was rare for James to take against anyone. She wondered what the ambitious Frank had done, then shrugged. None of this made her any the wiser. She set aside Fursey's letter and its problems for another time, and picked up Hereswith's instead. It was much better written and better spelled than any she had sent so far: the work of a scribe.

A queen of course doesn't write her own letters.

She tried to imagine how Hereswith had said that to her scribe: with a smile, a bitter laugh, smug satisfaction?

My husband has brought his wildflowers with us to Rendlesham, and I watch them, and wait.

Wildflowers she understood: Æthelric's children by his other woman, of the South Gwyre—one of whom, Balthild, Fursey had told her in another letter, was becoming a beauty. But *I watch them, and wait* was more difficult.

She had liked it better when Hereswith had written her own letters, when she could tell from an ink blot, or a word blurred by a tear, or a word scored viciously deep in the page how she felt when she wrote it. She would know whether her sister meant she was waiting until they were grown to make friends, or waiting for Æthelric to be distracted so she could smother them in their sleep, or preparing to banish their mother. Hereswith could be ruthless. But how ruthless? If her sister were here she would know by her secret smile as she brushed the nap of her new dress this way or that, or how fast she kicked her foot back and forth as she thought, or by the energy with which her words fell out, dropping in a tumble and thump like horse dung.

She missed her so much. She set that letter with Fursey's, and sighed. "Writing is a miracle," she said. "But a dead one."

"Ah," said James. "You should read poetry. You should read the psalms."

She looked at his book, *The Lord lifts up the meek and casts down the wicked,* shook her head, and handed it back.

Sintiadd, who had been waiting, said, "Lady, when you've a moment Gwladus has a question about thread."

Hild looked over to where Gwladus and Breguswith and Begu were talking. She could tell by their shoulders they were not agreeing.

James grinned. "Shall I get to see you being Solomonic again?"

She ignored him. "Sintiadd, tell Gwladus that I don't need gold thread for more than one set of cuffs when I ride with the war band—but that I will need a lot of gold jewellery. So no one will be beating it and snipping it into gold thread for anything for a while." She turned back to James and pointed at his book. "I don't understand why a king would lift up the meek and set people free. Kings always have slaves."

"Do they? I don't see slaves here."

"I'm not a king. But no, there are no slaves in Menewood."

"Oh, yes there are." Gwladus, with Sintiadd at her elbow.

Hild frowned. "Who?"

"Denw, Langwredd's bodywoman."

Hild tried to remember if she had ever seen Denw wear a collar. It did not matter. "If she's in Menewood, she's no longer a slave."

"You'd better tell Langwredd that."

Hild nodded.

"And you're wrong about the cuffs and the thread. We're looking to after the fighting, when the king comes. He has to see glory in Elmet. And like supplies for the war band, glory isn't something you can make in a week. We need to start now. We can melt some scrap gold; you have a lot. There's a smith come in at York who can do that kind of work. I'll see to it, shall I?"

"Yes. And thank you."

"Just don't forget to talk to Langwredd."

James grinned again. *"Blessed are the meek, for they shall inherit the earth."*

She shook her head, trying to imagine inheriting the whole earth. All the decisions that would mean.

"Tell me why you have no slaves here. There are plenty of wealh."

"No, there aren't. In Menewood there are no wealh, no Anglisc, and no slaves. Just Elmetsæte."

"But there are rich and poor."

She frowned.

"Never mind, perhaps a conversation for another time. One day you really should read the Gospels. We could have fruitful conversations about the Beatitudes. Meanwhile, I believe Father Rhin wishes your attention."

They built the small church as they had built everything else in Mene-wood: wooden sills laid on dry stone, larger corner posts and smaller staves inserted at intervals, with hazel rods woven in and out between them to form the walls, which were then covered in a mix of lime and dung. The difference was the care with which Rulf had chosen the upright posts—tall enough that even Hild could stand without difficulty and not be able to touch the roof—and the beauty of their upper branches on which were laid the roof joists.

Hild had not had time to spend there in the last month, but now, with Rhin, she saw that the floor, too, was finely made: smooth, polished wood laid in wide planks that did not creak. The door posts were carved as finely as those of any great hall—though Rulf had taken so long with them that the masterpiece of a door he had promised was still not done. For now there was a rude, temporary door. The daub inside and out had long since dried and been smoothed, and now the whitewash was drying. In what would be the nave, Rulf and Rhin between them had worked out how to inset a triple window high in the wall behind the altar. They did not have glass but they did have, laid between wooden window frames, parchment pumiced so thin it was translucent.

Inside the small building the corners were sharp and clean, and led the eye up to the spreading roof trees arched over congregants like living trees of the forest, only a forest on a clear day, the air white and bright enough to lift the heart.

She clapped her hands and there was a faint echo—not the hard bounce of sound you could get from stone but more than from the usual wooden buildings. Perhaps it was the height, or the fact that there were no hangings, no cross yet on the altar, no cloth, and no benches to sit on.

"James'll like this." His music would sound fine here.

Rhin nodded. "He does."

The altar stone was the old one from Rhin's first church—very old, carved in the time of the redcrests, not with flowers and vines and grapes but a strange cross that seemed not only upside down but had too many crossbars. For Saint Peter, he said.

"What's that?" She pointed at something that seemed to be hanging off the cross.

"His keys."

They were so blurred by time that they could have been anything. "Can Rulf carve stone?" Perhaps he could make it more clear. "No, never mind. He's too far behind on everything else." He would insist on making things beautiful when sometimes all they needed was plain and sturdy. She looked around again, admiring the light and clarity of the church. "It's lovely. You've done a fine job."

"It needs more."

"More?"

"Beauty to echo the glory of God and the rock of His church, Saint Peter."

"I've just had this talk with my mother and Gwladus: We can't spare any gold; we need it for other things." He did not move but his spirit seemed to droop. She sighed. "What did you have in mind?"

"An altar cloth. In silk. With embroidery."

She nodded. "But it'll be summer before we can get the silk." When the Frisians were back. "I'll see about fine linen meanwhile." Begu would have some ideas, she might still have some of that silk thread she had hoarded—unless Gwladus had wheedled it from her for Hild's clothes.

"And Ceadwin would like to paint the walls. He has in mind two stories of Saint Peter."

"If he can make the pigment, fine." Too late it occurred to her that some of the pigment would come from grinding up jewels, like lapis, but Rhin had brightened so much she did not have the heart to say anything.

"And when there is gold, lady—and silver, and ivory, and perhaps a few jewels—we need plate. And a cross."

"By next Christmastide you will have beautiful plate for your church, a cross as tall as you are, and the best altar cloth in the north." Because by then either she would have riches greater than anything she had known, or she would be dead and Menewood destroyed.

At Brona's house, Hild and Leofdæg and Coelfrith and Oeric were in the habit of eating together in the middle of the day and talking late into the afternoon, often until dusk. It was the only place Hild would not be constantly interrupted. Sometimes they invited Gwladus, or Rhin, or Grimhun, or Langwredd but most of the time it was just the four of them and Brona, with Sintiadd attending to their needs.

Brona had not wanted that at first. "I don't need to be there for your council."

"But it's your house."

"Well, if it's my house I should play host."

"But I need you listening. I need your advice."

Brona shook her head. "That's not my—"

"And you're not my servant—and I won't have you treated as such."

So Sintiadd was usually present, quietly bringing them food and ale, keeping the fire burning and, if they talked late, the tallow dips trimmed. And sometimes Brona was there, and sometimes she even listened, but most often she found a way to not stay. She was a woman who liked to do, not talk.

"Oats," Coelfrith said. "I've already sent on what we have to Urburg, but we're still expecting weys from Craven."

"I thought they'd sent that."

"They sent some, with the salt."

Which led to discussion of the salted meat, and what proportions they would need for how many.

She was glad they had Coelfrith, who had done this many times before. He knew how many oats and how much barley a warhorse ate, and how much a packhorse, and how much a mule. He understood how much fodder of what quality they would need, how much of that could be from grazing, and how much time it took to feed and water 170 beasts. He explained to them how much each beast could carry, and for how long. How far they could travel, and how that would affect what they needed to eat.

"The grazing won't be good in Hrethmonath; we'll need more fodder." But that was fine, because getting fodder to Urburg was not hard—they could send it in relays from York, which would get it from Goodmanham.

After Œstremonath, as they moved north from Urburg—if they moved; if she got the answers she wanted—they could rely on high-quality pasture when the grass was young and fresh and full of strength-giving life.

"But grazing takes time."

"For every hour's grazing we need a pound less fodder," Coelfrith said. And this was where Leofdæg and Hild had to combine their understanding: which part of the route might be travelled when—speed versus secrecy, ease versus difficulty, fewer supplies versus more. Where they could cache supplies safely, where they could camp—not only where 70 men might sleep safely but where 170 horses could water swiftly in large groups. And if they had good pasture, even better.

Once past Pennrid in Rheged it would become more complicated because they would split into different bands with different tasks travelling different routes.

"And we'll have Rheged with us."

"We might have Rheged with us," Hild said. Though they still did not know how many.

"We've the barley, at least," Oeric said. "That's already at Cnotinsleah. And the whetstones came in from the Pecsæte."

"Horseshoes," Leofdæg said. "Have we enough?"

Coelfrith looked blank, and Hild clenched her jaw and nodded at Sintiadd: Go get more wine, and tell Almund to write down *horseshoes* and remind her tomorrow.

And on they talked into the evening.

At night, she lay in Brona's arms and told over lists in her head: They had to guess so many things. It would be a long campaign and she could not think of everything. And at any point plans could change—would change; they always did. At some point, she would weep, she knew, for the lack of something simple, something she had not thought of.

"I understand now why Coelfrith always looks worried," she said, and Brona held her tight and told her, again, that she could not hold the reins on everything, that she was wise, her people were cunning, and this was her wyrd. And to please go to sleep. And eventually she would sleep.

Hild stared at the beast surrounded by children. "Why is there an ass in the church?"

"Because Joseph put Mary on it to escape," Maer piped up.

For the first time in Hild's memory Fllur was beaming. "And my Geren is baby Jesus!"

"He is?" Hild saw a rough wooden crate. She frowned. "Is that hay? What's it doing here?"

"It's a manger," Maer said.

Hild turned to James. "You said to come listen to singing."

"And there will be singing! Just as soon as the three wise men have found their drums."

"Their . . . ?" Three children, one of whom she did not know, seemed to be squabbling over something in the corner. Just then Clut sauntered in, tail up, and Hild decided there were many other things that needed her attention.

The rain turned to sleet, then back to rain, with a wind that could not make up its mind. Thick cloud, dark as filthy fleece, smothered the valley. Hild fretted, wanting to do something, but all that could be done was being done. She found warmth and comfort in Brona's bed, covered now in a bright and beautiful coverlid presented to her by Begu, who said, "Don't tell your mother. She wanted that red cloth for a cloak. It was meant to be your Christmastide present, but I'm tired of seeing you look grey and haunted; you should at least have something pretty to look at in that love nest of yours. Something besides your butcher, that is. And anyway, it's only a few days early."

There was comfort, too, in the long house, where every day people bustled with wreaths and sprays of greenery and bright holly berries, and the new kitchen smelled of spices more usual in York or the Bay of the Beacon. Breguswith had chased her out of the malthouse twice, saying only she was trying something new.

And then, like a gift, four days before Christ Mass, midwinter day dawned sharp and cold and clear. She felt it as soon as she woke: the change, the different birdsong, the cut in the air and the lightness in her heart. She tucked up behind Brona and smiled.

"Are you humming?" Brona asked sleepily.

Hild put her mouth to Brona's spine and hummed deep and wordlessly so Brona's body vibrated with the sound and she shivered, but not with cold.

"Let's go for a ride," she said. "No, let's go hunting!"

"I kill things every day," Brona said.

"You wouldn't have to do the butchering."

"No, because I'm going to stay close to the fire. But you should take your Fiercesomes. Go galloping about in the woods. Bring me something interesting, I'll make you some doe sausage."

"I love watching you make sausage."

The doe hanging in the cold cellar was about ready to butcher, and if she ignored what went into the filling she would never tire of watching Brona fill and twist and loop and hang sausages. Unerring, over and over, faster than she could follow. She had tried it, but even working slowly she could only manage five or six links before she started pulling up when it should be under and the orderly chain of sausages turned into something that looked more like one of Sintiadd's strange notions of a hairstyle.

"I'll get the knack of it one day," she said. But Brona was already falling back to sleep. Brona was right, she realised: she wanted to gallop about, run around the woods. And she didn't want to hunt so much as to teach others to hunt—but hunt her way.

The air was bright as a knife. As they thundered along the north bank of the river, sharp black shadows racing before them in the early sun, Hild laughed aloud. Behind her, Gladmær whooped and Dudda shouted. A glance to either side showed Leofdæg grinning fiercely and Wulf seeming to float on top of his big gelding like a cloud over a mountain. She felt a fierce love for them, for Flýte, for the Yr valley and Elmet, for life.

Two miles west of old Caer Loid she saw the dainty slots of roe deer tracks but she did not turn aside. Today she was after other prey.

She slowed them to a walk at the next curve and pointed. High above, a brilliantly underlit falcon rose slowly over the clearing half a mile away. Ahead of it, as it rose and turned, a cloud of finches lifted in a puff of panic, gleaming in the sun like thrown flaxseed.

They watched as the hawk turned, hung motionless, then fell, stooping in a heart-stopping dive, right through the cloud of finches and out of sight behind the trees. After a moment it rose above the trees again, empty-fisted. Again it turned and rose, turning and turning until it tilted and slid sideways, smooth and clean as Brona's knife gliding between fat and meat, and away, out of sight.

"Follow me."

They rode on to the clearing. After a moment she saw what she was looking for and pointed. A headless wood pigeon, breast torn out and bloody feathers piled neatly to one side. A show of waste and power and blood: The falcon had already eaten; she had not needed to dive for the little finches.

"Hawks are like amber," she said. "If you rub amber on your tunic, then run it a fingerwidth above your arm, the hair rises up to meet it. You can't stop it; it just does. The finches can't stop it, either: Fear of the hawk's shadow drives all thought from their heads and draws them up, up from the safety of the trees towards the hawk as surely as the amber draws hair."

Gladmær scratched the thin skin over his nose; the cold often made it itch.

"Cadwallon's like a hawk," she said. "His attacks are showy and terrifying. His mere shadow now will drive thought from people's heads and they do foolish things, and then he's among them, a hawk among the pigeons, killing wastefully and leaving his kills in bloody display to make his fear-shadow even bigger. But it means he can be goaded to attack even the small and helpless, too small to make much of a morsel—even when he'll miss and waste his strength. Remember that."

Three miles past the clearing the hills began to rise as they approached the wildwood. Here freezing mist still hung about the trees, and behind them what should have been the low dazzle of the sun was spread to a ghostly silver shine. They slowed to a walk as they moved under the trees. Leaves laced with frost crackled underfoot, small twigs crunched. She nodded to Leofdæg, and he and Dudda and Wulf turned a little north while she and Gladmær moved deeper into the trees. It was Gladmær who was the youngest and most hotheaded; this lesson was for him.

She watched the bare branches carefully; Gladmær watched, too, though he had no idea what he was looking for, or perhaps the quiet was making him uneasy.

She raised her hand: Here.

Under the young oak their breath plumed and hung for a moment before slowly dissolving into the ground mist seeping among the bare trunks. Their mounts, well-trained, were still and silent. Two siffsaffs hopped about busily in the tangle of bramble.

She put her finger to her lips and pointed up and to her left at an old wych elm. Gladmær craned his neck, frowned, looked at Hild. She raised her eyebrows: Just wait.

Slowly, the siffsaffs hopped closer to the wych elm.

The sparrowhawk hidden among the lace of bare black twigs opened her eyes: From the gloom they glowed a gold so deep it was almost red. She was an old hawk, a big one, and patient. Gladmær saw her now.

Still the hawk did nothing, just watched the birds hopping busily about. Then, like the falcon, she tipped and fell, only it was from just over Hild's mounted height, and the little bird had no idea it should even be afraid before it was gone, caught in the sparrowhawk's fist, and with two quick flaps she glided to the next tree, raised her foot, and tore out its heart with her beak.

"And that is how we'll hunt Cadwallon," she said. "No show, no waste, and never striking until we're sure."

They made a small fire under a group of alders standing stark and bare on the riverbank. They did not need it, but a fire made people feel human, a fire was something to gather around.

The sun was high now and the river glittered a deep blue. They talked of roads and watering places in Bryneich country if they had to go back there; the path they had ridden down from Colud, blades gleaming, and gold lit to fire by the sun: gods descending from the hills.

"I bet that's how the falcon felt," Dudda said.

"Maybe so," she said. "And it's good to feel mighty and magnificent. But now we hunt a different animal and we'll have to hunt him another way. Many different ways." She turned and nodded downriver. "Look at the heron."

They looked at the heron standing farther down the bank on an over-hanging root, as still and spare against the bright sky as the alders.

"The siffsaffs couldn't see the hawk even if they looked up, not until it opened its eyes. The heron's not like that. When the fish look up they can see it. But like the sparrowhawk it wastes no energy. It'll stand there until the fish decide they're mistaken, that it's not a heron after all, it's a tree, an old dead branch. And they'll rise to feed, and it will strike. Even if there are twelve fish it will know which fish it means to take; it'll ignore the others."

Gladmær nodded, eager to prove he had been listening and learning, for she had said this before. "If you chase two deer at the same time you won't catch either."

The stab under her heart at Cian's words coming back to her was quieter every time. "Yes. Always choose your kill before you begin and watch only that one."

Wulf made a gesture, then another. She was getting good at understanding his signs but now he was speaking with his hands and his face so fast she could not follow. She turned to Dudda.

"He says you're talking about hunting, not fighting. We're gesiths, not bandits."

She nodded, and said to Wulf, "We are gesiths, but we're outnumbered. We'll make no shield walls, no glorious stands worthy of song. When and if we fight, we kill. And sometimes we'll kill from hiding, without fighting. But we'll only kill armed men, and we'll kill clean."

He regarded her for a moment, then nodded.

On the way back they took turns racing each other. Gladmær's horse seemed less willing to exert herself than the others, or perhaps she was not yet fit enough. In the open along the bank, nothing could touch Hild and Flýte. Among the trees, Leofdæg on Lél was king.

"She moves like a snake," Dudda said. "But how is she in a fight?"

So then they charged at one another, shields on their arms and taking it in turns to throw Hild's staff like a spear. All the horses moved well and stopped shying after the first cast.

They tried four horses on one, and found of all of them Lél liked that least. The second time, it was all Leofdæg could do to stop her bolting.

"I'll take her in hand after Yuletide," he said.

"Good. No, wait." She thought for a moment. "What's your other mount?"

He shrugged that lopsided shrug.

"Then choose one that's steady in a scrum. We don't need all our men or all our mounts to be able to do everything. We just need to know for sure what each can and can't do."

Wulf nodded.

"After Christmastide we'll find out what we have. And we'll lean them down. Gladmær, let's run some more. Your mare's getting lazy."

And running on a fine sharp day made the blood sing in her veins.

That night she told Brona about the hunting lessons. "Are you sure you don't want to learn?"

"I kill enough things. I just like the way you tell the stories."

And Hild realised how much she wanted to show Brona more things, to watch that moment when understanding lit like a candle behind her eyes. Like teaching Maer about broom and birch twigs, or Wilfrid how to count—though that was not going well. "Well, I won't be taking anyone hunting until after Christ Mass. Tomorrow night before the feast James is very eager for me to admire his story and music."

Brona laughed: Hild had told her about the ass in the church and the three wise men fighting.

She grinned. "Don't laugh too soon. They have persuaded me to let them perform in the long house before the feast—so you'll be watching, too. We all will."

When all the blood and manure had been cleaned up, the ass led away in disgrace, and the children consoled with honeycomb, the appreciative crowd wiped their eyes and found places on the crowded benches. Luftmær struck up a merry tune, and while Aldred, Almund, and Aldnoth sang—their voices fit beautifully together—the food began to arrive.

James joined them on the bench. "Well, that could have gone better."

"No, no," Oeric said, grinning. "It was just what we needed."

"Better than a mummers' show!" Grimhun agreed.

"I howled when Joseph walloped the wise man for saying Jesus had widdled in the manger," Begu said.

"And when the ass started eating the hay and tumbled poor old Geren, I mean Jesus, out of the manger—"

"And Mary tried to pull it away—"

"And then the ass dropped dung all down her dress!"

And they were all laughing helplessly again.

"With hindsight," James said, "my mistake was not feeding the children earlier—"

"Or making them all use the pot first," Gwladus said, and speared a sausage before passing the platter on.

"That, too. The song they were to sing really could have been lovely."

"Were they supposed to bang their drums and shout at the beginning? When the angel—"

"I liked the angel's halo," Begu said.

"One of Rulf's hoops painted yellow," Hild said. She passed on the sausage; she would wait for the thick roll of doe haunch just coming off the spit.

"No," James said. "The banging and shouting and jubilation was supposed to be during the second song, the song of triumph—when the angel declares that the baby will be Christ the Saviour. The children got excited."

"Maer does get a bit previous when she's excited," Sintiadd said as she filled cups.

"So when was the song supposed to be?"

"Right after they named the child," Hild said.

Brona laughed, and imitated Joseph's high-pitched voice. "What shall we call him?"

"I know!" said Gladmær in a surprisingly good imitation of Maer's sturdy Elmet accent. "We'll call him Berht!"

"Or Du!"

"Or Ulf!

"Wait, I know!" Brona gave them a significant look and they all joined in: "Let's call him Jesus!" Then they all howled again.

"You should do that every year," Hild said to James. "Imagine how splendid it could be when we have a proper hall." And when they would not have to risk their precious horse blankets, worn by the wise men, being trampled in a fight.

"I fear no bishop would approve of such levity," he said.

And Hild realised that if her plan worked, there would once again be bishops in the north. The question was, whose bishops?

Two days after Christ Mass Hild was feeding Whisk a sliver of wrinkled carrot as high clouds began to appear in the sky from the north and northwest. When he was done Whisk kicked and ran round and round his pasture, watched benignly by Flýte and Bone and chased by his sister. They did not seem to be missing their dam. Hild wondered where she and Uinniau were: still with Rhoedd or on their way back?

When she got back down onto the valley path the clouds were coating the sky like eggwash, whiting it out, veiling the sun. By the time she entered Brona's house, a cold wind was rising from the north.

It began to snow just before dawn, thick feathers falling silently and settling like swan's down over the paths and in the ruts, sinking into the pond and then beginning to rest on its surface.

The valley woke to a bone and ivory carving of Menewood, and still the snow fell. Hild watched it from the doorway of Brona's house, then, like everyone else, acknowledged that the world had folded down for winter and there was no more to be done. She went back to bed, warm with Brona and smelling of applewood and welcoming woman.

30

✧

WULFMONATH, SHARP-TOOTHED AND STILL. The waxing crescent moon rose in a black glass sky, brilliant as a silver sickle, throwing shards of light from the snow beside the beck. Shadows were savage and steep-sided, and as the moon passed its height the world of black, grey, and white slid into an otherworld of bone and ivory, alders stark as streaks of charcoal by the water, and stones shimmering and unreal beneath the surface.

Hild crunched through the snow on the far side of the beck where there were no footprints; no one walked here. In Wulfmonath, this path, where the beck bent north around the hill, undercutting the hillside, was the hissing heart of cold.

She loved the night, loved the quick rustle and thump of a clump of snow falling away as a stoat crept headfirst down the birch trunk, lifting its white face, black eyes glittering, teeth small and sharp. When the valley slept she could listen. She listened now as she walked, alert to the beck— only the deepest part in the middle still moving—alert to the snow: still crisp, no sign or scent of melt. The world was wrapped deep in cold.

Even in the day colour was muted. The sun, when it was visible, managed only a pale squeezing of light, colourless as whey. The deep green of holly leaves was dulled, and its red berries seemed less like drops of fresh blood than an old, tired memory of a battle in the long ago.

Under the snow, she felt the earth's light and life dimming; not dead but banked deep against the cold. It would get colder. In the hills streams and springs were slowing and thickening. Soon they would stop and the beck would fall silent.

The moonlight dimmed. She caught the flicker of movement from the corner of her eye and something cold touched her nose: more snow.

Hild stared at the flames in the small bower without really seeing them, wholly focused on the mead in her mouth: First the rich, warm glow of fine Menewood honey, then flavour bursting tart and brilliant as a drop of light on the tip of her tongue, followed by a sharp complication, catching and confusing her taste the way a spin-weave caught the eye.

"Crabapple?" She knew as she said it she was wrong. It was too interesting for that.

Breguswith smiled smugly and shook her head.

Hild looked at Brona, who grinned: She wasn't telling.

She had another sip. She had never tasted anything like it. Except . . . She found herself thinking of Stephanus and Paulinus picking their way through the ruined redcrest villa in Derventio. She took another sip and rolled the mead around her mouth, swallowed, tonguing the taste up, up to the back of her throat and nose.

"Derventio," she said.

"Oh, ho ho," said Begu.

"Getting warmer," Gwladus said.

Derventio. Autumn sun. A corner of a redcrest courtyard with a gnarled tree with tiny fruit like pear-coloured rosehips. "Openeye!"

Openeye was the polite name for dogsarse, the fruit that looked like nothing but an open arsehole between two cheeks. In hot foreign lands they said you could eat it straight from the tree, but not here in the north; it was too sharp to eat fresh. Hild had tasted it only once, in Rendlesham, where it had been aged in its skin, then served mixed with eggs and butter and spread on bread like a kind of fruity cheese.

"How?" she said.

"Luck," Gwladus said. "The late warmth, picking them at the right time, then bletted to the full just as your mother was making the mead."

"Luck!" said Begu to Hild. "Is it luck that she remembered how much you'd liked that eyecheese in Rendlesham? Luck that when she found out that they were still growing in Derventio she offered a reward to a woman near York to check every two days and make sure to pick them before they were ripe for the wasps? Then brought them to your mother? And your mother then timed the mead for when they were bletted? Luck, ha!"

"Luck," Hild said. "Yes." Lucky to have found Gwladus when she did and have the money to buy. Lucky, now, to have such a Left Hand. Lucky to have such a mother, such a gemæcce. "Yes, I'm lucky."

Brona rested a warm hand on her shoulder and Hild leaned back, glad to have the rise and fall of this woman's breath to distract her from the strange rising and swelling under her breastbone and the urge to weep.

In the tiny church Ceadwin and Rhin had set braziers burning against the bitter cold. Hild watched Ceadwin mark the whitewash with a stub of charcoal. The two long walls were covered in figures to their full height; she saw a boat with a large figure next to it, arms wide open.

"Is that one getting out because the boat is sinking?"

Ceadwin was at her shoulder. "It's not sinking! It's going up and down with the waves."

She peered at it dubiously. "These are waves?"

"Those are fish. These are waves."

"You'll be able to tell when it's painted," James said hastily. "I believe it will be as good as the art in the houses of God in the Blessed City."

"I long to see them," Ceadwin said.

"Perhaps one day I shall return there. And then, young man, should you still wish it, we could travel together." But Hild understood that although James might think about going back to Rome, he never would: This isle and the people in it were his home.

She took Cuthred and Aldnoth out to learn together. They set off on foot as dawn was lightening the southeast and the full moon was setting in the southwest—though you had to know where to look to see the glow in the pale grey sky. By the time the sun was up they were at what had been a tumble of water where the beck fell down the rock steps south of the redcrest fort, not far from where Hild had watched the vixen with her cubs. Now it was frozen, and ice ringed the rocks in ripples of yellow and grey, like overlapping bacon rinds. The sun was smoothed to a glow by a soft white rug of cloud.

She pointed at the wood, dark on the horizon. "We'll look for boar in there."

"Under the trees?" Aldnoth licked his lips.

She looked at him. "Of course under the trees."

They squared their shoulders and trudged forward. Hild shook her head at the effort they made pushing through the snow. Aldnoth had already forgotten what she had shown him about lifting his feet.

They were scared. Last night she had heard Gladmær filling their heads with stories of how she would take them alone, one at a time, into the deep dark wood and leave them under a tree with a red-eyed hægtes disguised as a hawk that they wouldn't see until she was about to rip their hearts out. A hægtes that only she could see. And if they displeased the lady in any way she would let the hægtes have them. She supposed it was better than being the hægtes, at least. Perhaps by the time she was stooped and grey they would fear her only for herself rather than rumours of the uncanny.

Cuthred and Aldnoth were close to the trees, and Aldnoth was looking back to her, then forward to the trees, back and forth so fast she thought he might twist his head off. Cuthred was not helping. Why did men do this to each other?

"Follow me," she said. "Stay together." She pretended not to see the relief on the stripling's face, and led them under the dark tracery of branches. The wood was quiet; their blundering had scared away the birds. "Boars are set in their ways. They follow the same paths over and over; they're easy to find."

"Like this?" Aldnoth pointed to a thin line in the snow.

"No. See the paw prints?" Dimpled with blunt claw points, nothing like a boar. "They're small. And see where they go around that bramble? Tell me why something would go around."

"Too big to go under," Cuthred said.

Hild nodded.

"Too small to jump?" Aldnoth.

"Not necessarily."

Neither seemed to have any more ideas.

"It could be saving its strength. For example, foxes jump."

"So it's a fox?"

"It is. But jumping's a lot of work. Why waste its strength when it can go around?"

"So what does a boar run look like?"

"What do you think?"

"Well, they're big . . ."

Hild nodded. "Boars wouldn't bother going around something like that, they'd just crash through. And they travel in groups. The sows and their litters close together, and the boar a little behind. Other boars follow their scent. The runs are always wide and rutted and churned."

"Is that good or bad?" Aldnoth asked.

"What do you think?"

"Makes them easy to find."

"Easy to creep up on, too," Cuthred said. "Noise doesn't scare a big tusker."

"That's right," Hild said. "They can hear you but unless they smell dogs they don't scare easily. They don't see well, either. If you crouch in the run with a boar spear they'll see you, but they can't tell how far away you are, and when you lower the spearpoint they get confused about how far in front of you it is. They charge."

"You'd have to be quick, then," Cuthred said, imagining it. "And your spear'd have to be long enough—"

"And thick and strong enough." Aldnoth, half crouching as though with a spear in his hands.

"And with a really good cross piece to stop the boar running right up to you." Cuthred.

"Yes," Hild said. "If you're very strong, if your spear is strong and well-set, if you're ready and your foot is braced, if you drop it fast enough to catch the beast in the chest as it charges, if your cross piece holds as it gores itself trying to get to you . . ."

The young men looked expectant.

". . . you will be bright with joy just as the boar rips open the back of your knee from behind, your blood gushes into the snow, and you fall screaming, and die seeing that the beast you tried to spear was a sow, and you missed anyway."

Aldnoth looked shocked, his vision of the glorious face-to-face challenge, the taunts and the triumph, the glory of conquest left torn and destroyed.

"It's not a fight. It's a hunt." She looked at Cuthred, then Aldnoth, so young he still believed in hægtessan in the wood. "I want you to think like hunters, not gesiths. Forget the songs. The best way to kill a pig is cunning, a plan, the right tools, and strength in numbers. Killing for food is not about winning, it's not about glory. Nor is killing Cadwallon. Would you cry challenge to a pig that has gored your child? To a wild dog that has savaged your flock in blood glee? No. When we go north we won't cry challenge. We won't pit our strength against theirs. We'll pit our strength, our cunning, against their weakness, against their vainglory. They're invaders and destroyers, nithings and thieves. They're bandits wearing gold and fish-scale armour. And they outnumber us. So we hunt them, we kill them quietly, then we hunt some more. We hunt to rid our land of vermin."

They stayed under the trees for a long time. Hild showed them signs of deer: the nibbled ferns. Deer were harder to catch than boar.

"They can smell you for half a league. They can hear you, too. And they see movement. You have to guess their path and wait alongside, hidden."

"What does a deer path look like?"

"It's not something you see; you feel it on your cheek. Deer walk with their noses into the wind to smell their hunters; their path is the wind's path. Find which way the wind usually blows and wait many paces to one side of the best route between the trees."

Cuthred turned this way and that trying to feel a breeze but the air was still. The sun was coming out, slicing down between the bare branches, catching in his hair, calling a gleam from his one silver cuff.

"It's easier in the first frost, or on a dewy morning, or even after mist," Hild said. "Harder when it's cold. Today spiders are hidden under the snow, keeping warm; they're not making webs. Webs are the fishing nets of the air, strung across the current to catch the things that flow along it."

Aldnoth and Cuthred looked blank. She sighed. Brona would have understood.

"You can tell which side the wind blows from by which side the flies are on."

Aldnoth looked amazed, then realised that, as a spearman-in-training, he should not be amazed by anything, and nodded soberly, like Cuthred. At least they were listening.

"With Cadwallon it'll be easier. He won't be able to smell us so if we hide well enough we can wait right in his path." And much of his path would be trade routes.

They left the shelter of the trees and walked into a bright world of cold glittering sun and snow. Behind her Aldnoth complained he had not broken his fast, and Cuthred laughed and told him he should be carrying food. On the war trail some men found cheese good, but in his experience an egg or two was best, fresh and clean in its own wrappings, easy to eat with one hand . . .

Perhaps she had talked about eggs a time or two too often.

The branches at the edges of the wood began to glisten and a clump of snow dropped with a soft thump. She stared at a drop of water at the end of a twig—a whole world in a drop of water—thinking. That stoat, creeping down the tree in moonlight, its coat perfectly matched to the snow until it lifted its black muzzle. Stanegate. They could travel Stanegate as traders.

Drip. The glisten at the end of the branch fell. Drip. Drip-drip. Falling everywhere. The snow began to look worm-riddled. Worms. They would think it was raining and come up, thinking it was safe, and then the birds would swoop, and hop and stab with their sharp beaks. If she could make Cadwallon think it was raining . . .

The thaw was brief. By the time the full moon rose, tight and hard and brilliant, it shone again on a hard glittering world of ice. Hild woke to Brona stroking her hair.

"Burning," she said. "The hall's burning."

"You were dreaming, love."

"No," she said. "I mean yes. I dreamt of a hall burning but without the burning. Because, do you see, you don't need fire, just smoke. Heap the leaves against the sill and set them alight and smoke seeps through the gap and men run out to put out the flames and you slaughter them, slaughter them all. And you still have the hall, unburnt."

The stoat in disguise. The traders. Cadwallon safe behind walls—then running on the trade route. The plan began to thicken, like soup over the flame.

They filled the long house with beeswax candles, and women gathered with their cloth and shears and needles; Breguswith stood over their precious metal thread.

"War banners," Hild said briskly when the Fiercesomes came at her summons. "Many banners."

Wulf grunted: Why? They already had banners for the Yffing boar of

Deira and the hazel-tree-and-boar of Elmet. Oswald and Rheged would, surely, bring their own.

"I want banners for Craven, for Lindsey, for the North Folk and South Folk. Banners for the Bryneich." They looked at one another. "Banners that lie," she said patiently. "Leofdæg, when you see a mass of men riding right at you with banners, do you stop and wait to see if, perhaps, they're only scared farmers with bits of metal tied to poles to glint in the sun like spears?"

"Not until I'm far enough out of sight to back away without being seen once I've looked."

"That's right. You think, 'There's a warband come to eat my tripes' and you get out of sight." She grinned. "And that's the point." She slapped him on his crooked back hard enough to rattle his teeth.

The priests were coming in now, kicking snow from their boots and puzzled by all the company. She nodded at them to wait and spoke to the four Fiercesomes. "Talk to my mother and Begu about how many big banners, how many standards, how many horse pennants we need for how big a war band. Wulf, if you know the banners for the South Gwyre and East Wixna, try those, too."

"What about the Pecsæte?" Gladmær said.

"Every banner you can think of," she said. "But only if you're sure of its shape and colour. We want the north, the east, and much of the middle. Gwladus could draw us the green dragon of Dyfneint—but why might the Dyfneint be north of the wall with the Yffings? They would not. We need the banners to be believed, if only for a while."

After the Fiercesomes had gone to their next task, the women laid out their cloths and needles on the wide boards and talked, and pointed, and disagreed, then agreed, then pricked out patterns. Luftmær settled nearby, playing softly on his lyre, sometimes repeating a set of sounds with a dreamy look.

She half listened to the priests, half watched Langwredd and Begu, heads close together, as they compared two sets of yellow thread. She had not heard Langwredd play her harp in Menewood; she had not even seen it.

". . . it was the cross." Rising loud and sharp from the general hum.

"It was not!"

Hild turned, surprised, at the heat in James's voice. He and Aldred were glaring at each other. She looked at Rhin.

"Lady, the deacon and the good Father do not see eye to eye on the matter of what, precisely, the redcrest Emperor Constantine put on his banner."

"A great cross," Aldred said. "Bishop Paulinus taught us so. And a mere deacon must bow to the word of a bishop."

"It was not the bishop who taught you so, it was Father Stephanus, before your voice ever broke," James said. "And as this mere deacon had the teaching of Stephanus I can assure you he did not say Constantine put a cross on his banner. His vision may have been of a cross, yes. But the sign he used to bless his cause was the Chi-Rho."

Hild said to James, "Draw me this sign."

He dipped his finger in the dregs of his spiced ale. "Greek, of course," he said. He drew on the elm board. "The Chi." An X. He dipped and drew again. "And the Rho." A P with a very long tail bisecting the X. "These are the first two letters of our Christ's name in Greek, Christos."

She looked at Rhin and tapped the table next to the sign. "I don't know this sign. Do you?"

He nodded. "All men of God do. But everyone knows the cross. And it is simpler to paint."

The cross was a strong sign; you could see it from a distance. "And what would be a good colour?"

"Red," all three men said at once.

The night was clear and black, the new moon of Solmonath dark. Near old Caer Loid Hild lay on her back at the top of the ridge, trees rising like a wall of nothing to her right, snow falling away to her left down to the icy river glimmering in starlight. She imagined her spine lying on the divide between bright and dark. Her left-hand path was light and life and lifting up; her right, the dark and death and destruction. Staff and seax. Skirt and sword. Book and blade. She was the sow Cadwallon would see; she was the boar he would feel, the Yffing boar who would rip him open and spill him out.

She looked up, up, and up, to the great twist of stars. Heaven, James said. It was up there. Heaven, where God sat enthroned in heavenly glory, Christ at His right hand. *And where is the Holy Ghost?* she had asked. *His breath is in everything,* James said. Perhaps that glow around the sharp stars was his breath, like a freezing mist. Heaven must be a sharp, stinging, spangled place, at least at night. In the daylight it would be blue.

Blue is better, she had told Edwin that night long ago. Better than red. But when she moved north, her colour must be red.

Red. Would marching behind the cross, killing below the cross, make it any better? She tried to remember what James had said about righteous war but even as he had talked it seemed to her he was a man skating around on thin ice and calling out that everything was fine, come and see.

She would think about it another time. For now, everything depended on her making the right choices, being in the right places at the right time. Rhoedd must say yes, Oswald must say yes to her terms. Rhoedd's yes would be enough to defeat Cadwallon. But Oswald's yes would secure the kingdom. If she had everyone in place and ready.

She breathed and watched the stars and felt the world turn about her. Fate goes ever as it must.

31

✦

JAMES SAT ON THE BENCH outside the long house, face tilted to the early Solmonath sun, eyes closed, soaking up the warmth like a piece of felt. Hild was listening to the birdsong—only robins were singing in the hedgerow—and thinking of water and mud and mist.

"The deep thaw's coming," she said. "We'll harvest the last of the parsnips today."

"Toasted parsnips and sunshine," he said dreamily with his eyes still closed. "I'm in heaven."

"We'll still have some days of cold mist and snow."

"Snow like wool and mist like ashes."

That was from the psalm he had read her the other day. "It's not the mist and snow that worries me, it's the rain and mud when everything melts."

"*He shall send out his word, and shall melt them: his wind shall blow, and the waters run.*" He smiled and behind his lids his eyes moved back and forth as they do when a person is remembering something pleasant. "Then the sun slips the water's chain and the frozen fall thunders again."

She was not feeling poetical, she was worrying about timing, and travel. She needed Rhoedd's answer. Mudmonth. How would it affect Uinniau's journey? "The real thaw will take some time." She hoped. "Before that I have to go to Loidis, to the forge there, and to York." So many pieces great and small to set moving. "But I'll be back, and when I leave here finally for Urburg, travel with me. From there it's not far to Cetreht. And if you want to get home it'll be easier to travel after the ice melts but before the snow turns to mud."

He opened his eyes. "It'll be good to be home."

Home was Druyen, the farrier. She had business with him, too—with every smith within forty miles—but hoped James would see to that for her.

Most men and many women used bows for hunting; gesiths rarely used them once they had their sword. She summoned Sitric from East Farm and showed him twenty bow staves.

"I need a man trained to each bow."

"It's lambing season," he said.

"Not for you." She doubted he knew much about lambs. Grina would be fine with Duv and his daughter—the ewes did most of the work. "You won't be working with sheep again until shearing." And perhaps not even then.

He took a breath, saw the look on her face, and swallowed his sigh. "What arrows have we?"

"Two barrels of war points coming from York; more from Cetreht. We've sheafs of shafts, though not enough yet—more are a-making—and feathers for fletching." The glue would come from Loidis. She hoped. "See to—"

"Lady!" Morud. "The lord Uinniau is back."

In York the church was colder than she had ever felt it, far colder than outside. Just as the stones at Harvestmonath seemed to hold on to the warmth of high summer, now, in Solmonath, they clung to the bitter cold of Wulfmonath. The walls deadened sound from outside, too, while amplifying the low voice of James, near the altar with Almund, pointing to something.

On the south side of the nave, Oswine stood with Uinniau and Hild. He was taller than Uinniau, but next to the prince of Rheged he seemed pale and soft and young, and so clean as to be unfinished.

"But I must stay in York?"

"As we agreed," Hild said. Now that Rhoedd had said yes, she was on fire to begin.

Oswine bit his smooth, unchapped lips with the same sharp white teeth as his sister, looked at Sintiadd as though he had already forgotten who she was, and frowned.

Hild nodded at Uinniau: *Stroke his pride!*

"You're the Yffing of Deira, man," Uinniau said, and though his face was still drawn with fatigue, none of it showed in his voice. "If you came with us to Rheged, Rhoedd king would feel your presence a threat. Best you stay here in York, the stronghold of Deira. So when he comes you can negotiate from a position of strength."

Oswine nodded: Strength, he understood that. She was glad Uinniau was there; her patience was worn thin. Oswine had forgotten, again, all her careful explanations of why he did not have enough men to hold York; even with five times the number it would not be enough. Yet here he was thinking he could hold Deira by holding York. She was tired of having to guide foolish men gently, from the side, instead of ordering them.

"You'll keep your chosen men about you," she said. She would find a way to make sure he chose ones she did not need. "You'll have no worries about our southern borders. I've sent my Left Hand to our allies in the fen, as we agreed."

He looked confused but she pretended not to notice. It did not matter that he had no idea who Gwladus was. It did not matter that he did not remember her explanations of Ynys Bwyell and Afanc's folk at High Brune; the redcrest canal between Lindsey's River Withma and the Treonte, and the Treonte and the Daun, still deep enough in winter to bring boats deep into their heartland—Lindsey ships dancing to Penda's tune. What mattered was that the boat road would be closed because she had entrusted Gwladus to make that happen. The silver she had sent, and the tuns of honey, would not hurt. And travel by boat was fast, which meant there should be time—there must be time—for Gwladus to make it back to Urburg before Hild moved north.

"I've sent out the call," she said. "Men will begin to arrive by the full moon. I'll lead them from here to Urburg, then on to Cetreht. I'll be here only two days. But I'll leave men to organise the muster. Coelfrith—you remember Coelfrith?"

He did.

"He'll see to things." She had always admired how efficiently the reeve could organise people and baggage for orderly, timely travel. She smiled. "Meanwhile, I'm well pleased with your work on the berths and supplies."

He had not had much to do with it, but at least he had not got in the way. The docks were almost finished, the water supply clear and clean, the river dredged. The hay and beans, the flour and the vinegar they would need for the work in the north had arrived and were properly stored. "The supplies are ready to go out. My men will begin that tomorrow." She caught Sintiadd's eye. "Meanwhile—" Sintiadd put the heavy, smooth bundle in her hands and stepped back.

Hild held it out to Oswine. "Here, cousin, into your charge, is the Yffing standard, the royal boar of Deira, to fly from York's walls so all can see an Yffing is again at home in his fort to defend the land while people go, at his bidding, to strengthen the northern borders."

He nodded solemnly and accepted the standard.

Good. That was done. If and when she returned she would never have to speak to him sweetly and make suggestions again.

By the end of Solmonath everything in the long house but the banners was the colour of mud. Everyone was busy with mud: brushing off horses' legs—the grey-brown of war street mud, or the black of riverbanks; knocking out the thick clods from wagon wheels—the red-brown of the well-drained fields of Goodmanham, the redder mud of the heavy carts bringing ore from Craven; washing and rewashing the brown-caked clothes of those travelling forest paths, unless they were slimed yellow-grey from the deep mossy springs dug for their iron. All who left Menewood—or Urburg when she was there—took with them stories of the uncanny wit of the lady who could look at a man and greet him by asking, *What news from the mines of Craven?* before he even opened his mouth. And she was surrounded always by Fiercesomes, killers who would slaughter a person at a look, and women with tongues sharper and faster than the best sword, women whom everyone obeyed, sometimes even the lady.

Sintiadd became tyrannical, making Hild take off her clothes—breeches if she wore them, dress if not, hose, boots—in a lean-to she had built especially outside the bower so that Hild did not track mud into the long house. The long house was the only place bright with colour, the long house where women sowed the banners, standards, and pennants as soon as the dyes were set. They hung about the place, drying and setting, settling and smoothing, until they were carefully folded and sent with the next batch of arrows or sacks of beans by cart to Urburg.

From Urburg, Leofdæg and his men scouted north for camping and grazing stops, and then Coelfrith determined what went where, and the carters and baggage drovers took them there.

It was not far from Urburg where she said farewell to James.

He was driving a cart near the front of a column heading from Urburg to Cetreht. For the start of the journey she rode alongside wearing her new warrior jacket, still stiff with tow stuffing, and tightly cinched; it was uncomfortable but she would get used to it. After two miles she held up her hand and the baggage train slowed to a halt for drivers and riders to make their check of girths and harness.

She and James looked at one another. "Tell Druyen we'll need everything by the full moon—"

"Or the last quarter at the latest. Yes."

"Tell him if for some reason he can't—"

"He will. He's a good farrier. A man of his word."

"He's a good man," she said.

"He is." He smiled.

"Are you happy? With Druyen?"

"We're comfortable together."

"You're lucky to have him."

James tilted his head. "Are you not lucky in Brona?"

"I am." But even she heard that faint undecided note in her voice.

"And?" he said.

"She's a fine woman. And kind. And handsome. And with a good clear mind."

"And?"

"And I trust her with the children. And yes, we're comfortable, too."

"Comfortable," he said, musing. "Comfort can be a good thing. Certainly it is for me. But I'm old. Our animal spirits sink a little with each year we walk this earth. Perhaps yours are banked now but they're fierce, they'll roar again. It might be that Brona is the right one for you, banked or roaring; only you can know. I do like her; she has made you smile again—I could love her for that alone. But mine is not the heart that matters here."

She looked at the sky. Low and grey, charcoal and ash, with the tinge of yellow that meant sleet or snow later. James might make it to Cetreht before it fell, but it would be a near thing. She had no worries for his safety. Her men were up and down this stretch all day; he could ride naked and covered in gold and arrive untouched by any hand. But, as he had said, he was old. She did not want to risk him when soon she would be risking almost everything.

All around them men and women were climbing back into the saddle or cart seat.

"Well, I can see that it's time for you to leave me," he said. "I will say one thing. You could do worse than take Father Almund as your confessor. He has a good heart and—something not to be taken lightly—he likes you, when he's not being terrified."

She nodded: She would think about it.

"Then fare well, Hild Yffing. Remember there are many who love you for you, not your Yffing blood, and we would wish you to take care."

She rested her hand on his shoulder briefly, then nodded to the driver at the head of the column, turned Flýte, and cantered back towards Urburg, her thoughts already bending to the next thing on her list.

The last of the men—and one woman, who had come to Menewood from the steading near Ceasterforda—shot their arrows and unstrung their bows. All had hit the target with all three arrows.

"Good." She clapped Sitric on the shoulder and barely noticed him stagger or the way the archers threw their shoulders back and puffed out their chests—though Sintiadd did, and would point it out later when she was brushing her lady's hair. "You're ready. You leave for Urburg . . ." She thought for a moment. "The day after tomorrow." They could escort the shipment expected from Cnotinsleah.

She strode back along the beck; the path squelched beneath her boots. "Is Leofdæg back yet?"

"No," Sintiadd said, a bit breathlessly. She had learnt to hitch her skirts and trot at times like this. "But Wulf and the other one are."

She never used Dudda's name, though Hild did not know why and there was never time to think about it.

"The horses?"

"Lady Begu thinks they're all well-hardened in the legs now. Also that Flo has finished the extra straps, that your lady mother wishes a word, and that you need to have a word with Langwredd."

She pretended not to notice the lack of honorific. "That Begu needs me to, that I need to, or that Langwredd needs me to?"

"I'd say a bit of all three. A lot of all three."

Too much to sort through on the move and there was no time to stop. "We'll talk to my mother first."

"Lady—" Sintiadd slipped and recovered.

Hild turned, eager to be moving.

Sintiadd hesitated, then spoke in a rush. "Lady, the lady Begu didn't mention her own needs. But to me she looks in need of your word." Sintiadd stuck her chin out, determined now. "The butcher thinks so, too."

Begu was her gemæcce—she would know if there was something wrong. Or Begu herself would tell her. Yet here was Sintiadd bringing Brona to bear like a shield. Had she become so impatient? Brona. Begu. Her mother. And Wilfrid, Maer, Ceadwin. When was the last time she just . . . listened? But there was no time. All her people, all her tasks, buzzed in her head like angry bees. She breathed deep. Think.

"Wulf and Dudda first." Wulf would have news of their scouting, which would help her understand some of what lay ahead. "Then my mother, then Begu."

And Begu and her mother between them would tell her what the problem was with Langwredd. And she would see for herself how Begu was.

"And tell Flo I'm very pleased." She wished again for Gwladus to be here instead of this girl. But Gwladus had chosen Sintiadd, and trained her; she would have to trust she knew what to do. "If you think I'll have time later, please bring her to me so I can thank her myself. If not, choose something suitable for a gift."

With Hild gone so much, Breguswith had become once again the lady of the valley. She sat on her bench like a queen on her throne, and all around her folk moved quietly and quickly. Mindful of the banners and cloths on the benches, Hild took off her boots and Sintiadd handed her a rag and waited while she wiped her hands. Hild nodded for her to go get herself something to eat, then sat to wait while her mother finished giving Morud some instruction or other. She was reminded again of the summer in Goodmanham when her mother had ruled with a weft beater as her rod of iron and steered the river of work smoothly, effortlessly.

"You're filthy."

Morud was gone; her mother was waiting. "You wished a word."

"I did. But I see you're already impatient to leave. Most of it will wait."

"But not all."

"No. You spoke to Wulf. When can we expect you to leave?"

She had planned to discuss her plans in a day or two. "The report was good. We leave in ten days."

"Ten days." Hild could not read her voice. "I see. Perhaps you would be so good as to tell me what I should expect."

"There's plenty of food . . ."

"I'm not speaking of food."

"Then be plain."

"Plain?" Her laugh was short. "Let us both be plain. Tell me who stays and who goes—where, when, and with whom? Who rules in your absence? Will I have men to back me?"

Could this not wait until she could tell everyone at once? "You'll have men. Three, perhaps. Mounted. Based here. And Oswine has men in York. I sent a message to Osthryth, by James, that she's to back you with Oswine if needed."

"I need no help with that fool."

She did not doubt it. "Rhin'll stay here. You stay here with Begu and Heiu until the halls at Caer Loid and Loidis are ready. How soon they're ready will depend in part on you. When and if those halls are ready, you may move or stay as you choose. While you're at Menewood, everyone but Rhin lives at your word. If you leave Menewood, then Begu—who I think will stay—and Rhin will once again run the valley where your word will have no sway. Though you will run Caer Loid and Loidis. In all cases, if I send written instructions to Rhin, you're to follow them."

Breguswith said nothing.

"You wanted plain."

Was that look pity? "Have you been to the garth lately?"

The garth?

"Perhaps you haven't noticed how the pennyroyal has been disappearing. And parsley from the dry store."

"Is that surprising?" Men—young strong men—were moving through all the time. The young women were hungry, but they knew now was not the time for babies. What was this to her? Unless— "Is anyone being mistreated?"

"Would I need your help with that? No."

"It's Langwredd, isn't it?"

Her mother opened her mouth to say something then turned it into a shrug. "I'll just say I'm glad she's going with you." She rolled her shoulders and crooked her finger at the houseman. "You've time for mead."

It was not a question. As he poured for them Hild wondered if her mother had had occasion to use the pennyroyal herself; the houseman was just the kind of young man her mother liked.

"Now. While there are no open ears but mine, talk to your mother. You're going to war against a king-killer, a man who would slaughter you most horribly and laugh while he does it. He outnumbers you—two to one?"

"More." Three to one. "But, Mor, I have to face him."

"I know." She waved that away. "You must, and you'll go whether I will it or not. I'm not trying to stop you. I'm just asking . . ." She sighed. "Hild, you're not speaking to swell the hearts of your men now, but to your mother. Tell me true: Will you come home to me?"

There was a small smear of mud still on her thumb knuckle. She pulled off the ring, licked her knuckle, rubbed it on her hose. Put the ring back on—one of her favourites with the great green stone like glass. Her mother was watching her, waiting. "Yes."

"Even without Oswald Brightblade?"

She nodded. "Even without Brightblade it's a wager I'd take. That I am taking. I'll win."

"If it's your wyrd."

She sat back and crossed an ankle over her knee. "Then we must help my wyrd."

"How?"

"With Rheged and the Bryneich I can beat Cadwallon even—"

"The Bryneich—that's why you're taking that woman."

She nodded. Langwredd had brought Coledauc to heel; perhaps she could do the same with his folk. "But first I have to show them that Cadwallon's weak. I have to show them our high hearts, and eat the heart from Cadwallon's men. For that I need Luftmær."

Mist was rising, and down by the beck a row of jackdaws huddled in the bare elm like hanging loom weights. Hild whistled Luftmær's tune as she hiked up to the foals' pasture, and from the leafless blackthorn hedgerow a robin sang back. It was cold but a good cold; buds on the thorn showed a frill of white and pink.

She felt better after talking to her mother; clearer. The lists had fallen from her head and now she was focused on her people—not people as numbers moving like counters on a taff board but people who sighed, poured mead, and wanted to know if their daughter might come home alive.

She studied Begu from a distance. Small, bundled against the cold, with a heavy brown overcloak wrapped about her own yellow. Hair tucked beneath her hood. Resting her head against the shoulder of Flicker, one hand on Whisk's mane, all three wreathed in mist.

Flicker heard her first and lifted her head. Begu straightened. The top of her head was the same height as Flicker's withers. In the heartbeat before Begu recognised her, her face was pale and hollow, almost gaunt. But then she smiled and waved and Hild wondered if she had imagined it.

No. As she got closer she saw that despite the cold-pinked cheeks Begu was pale, and much thinner than she had been.

"Hild! I hadn't expected—"

Hild wrapped her in her arms. The two foals galloped away. She held Begu close for a moment, then let go. "I wish you'd told me. When?"

The foals trotted close, then stopped, uncertain.

"Wulfmonath. I guessed before then but by the first quarter I knew."

"Nearly two months!" Her own gemæcce and she had not even noticed.

Begu misunderstood her. "I know it's dangerous to wait—but I could've been wrong. And I couldn't believe it. Not now, not when we're so close to . . . And it's so hard. All this time I've had to fight to not kindle, all while I've longed to kindle. So I didn't want to get rid of it. I didn't want to! What if there can't be another? If—" If Uinniau died in mud and blood by the wall. But she could not say it. Naming calls.

Hild reached and tucked a stray strand of Begu's hair back under her hood, patted it into place. "I know." And she did.

"But I had to. Do you see? I had to."

"Yes." War was no time to be big with child.

"And then I thought how hard it must have been for you. Your man was already dead. And your Little Honey had already breathed in your arms, had already suckled at your breast. And you had so much pain—so much. So what right did I have to weep when I was warm and safe and my man was alive and if we're lucky—if you're lucky, gemæcce—we'll try again one day?"

Hild ached: for Begu, for herself.

"But, oh, love. It hurt so much; so very much. Those dark clots lying in the bucket like red turds—our baby. It hurt my heart. I should've come to you, I know, but you need to be strong, you need to be clear, or we'll all be hurting so much more. So I said nothing. Do you understand?"

This small woman, small enough to break with one hand, was trying to protect her. "Yes," she said. She would make it up to her. She would make it right. "Does Winny know?"

"No."

Hild nodded. She would make sure no one told him. But she would do more than that. She took Begu's hands in hers; they were cold.

"You will marry Uinniau of Rheged. It's your wyrd. I swear it to you." Even if Oswiu did not marry Rhianmelldt she would find a way to make this happen. "I'll keep your man safe. But for now, it's you I want to keep safe." She rubbed those small hands. "Let's get you to a fire, and something hot to eat."

"Oh, don't worry about me." She smiled with a semblance of good cheer. "I'm fine. But while I've got you to myself for a bit, let me tell you about these two." She lifted her voice. "Whisk! Flicker!"

They came trotting up, Flicker first. And now Begu's smile was real.

"Look how big they are!"

They would never be big—not compared to their dam—but they would be bigger than Begu's pony, bigger than anyone thought they could be when they were born so unfinished. And they were beautiful; perfectly proportioned.

"Winny says they're mine, because I saved them. Well, I couldn't have saved them without Bryhtsige. But I did do all the work while he wasn't here. Well, Brona did some of the work when I wasn't here, when I was off collecting Langwredd. Have you talked to her lately—Langwredd? You should. I'm not the only one who's been eating pennyroyal."

Whisk allowed Hild to run her hand along his back. His coat was soft. She was tempted to dig her hands in and, like Begu earlier, just lean her forehead on his warm, living flank. She patted him instead, and he pranced away. "She's a grown woman."

"A grown woman who's plotting something."

"Bed games aren't plots."

"They are when she plays them with all your fighting men."

Hild blinked. "All?"

"Well, half a dozen. Including Sitric, Cuthred, and Gladmær. I think she tried with Oeric, too, and that other young one who trails Cuthred about."

Aldnoth. Aldnoth, Cuthred, Sitric, and Gladmær. All fighting men. "I'll talk to her. What else do I need to know?"

"Nothing important. But." Begu grinned, almost her old self. "Did you know that before Gwladus got on the boat to go back to that vile swamp she was making herself riding breeches?"

Hild stared. "Breeches?" Gwladus in breeches. "What for?"

"Why do you wear them sometimes, why does Brona? They're very practical. She's going to be very busy when you're all north of the wall; it's easier to keep clean in breeches, she says. Anyway, she was making two pairs. But she'd got no further than cutting the cloth—dark cloth, very sensible. So I finished them for her. I hope she's back in time for them. I made two pairs, and I made one of them pretty because practical doesn't have to mean ugly. When you leave you should take a pair of them with you just in case there's no time for her to come back here first. You're going soon, aren't you? Winny guessed a fortnight, but I know that restless look. It's going to be sooner, isn't it?"

"Ten days."

"So will she be back by then? If she's not, maybe I could ride with her up to Urburg—"

"No."

"—just to wait with you until you get word. Though what if you don't get word—will you go anyway? Oh, I am so tired of being left behind!"

"Gwladus was the one left behind when we went north the first time."

"That was a safe trip. This is war. You nearly didn't come back from the last one. What if you don't come back this time?"

"I'll come back."

"But what if—"

"I'll come back. I'll bring Uinniau back. I'll bring Gwladus back." And leave Langwredd behind to be queen of somewhere or lady of something. "I'll bring back more gold than these two fine strong beasts—" She smiled at the two foals, and Begu smiled reflexively, as Hild had known she would, and it was hard for a person to keep worrying when they were smiling. "More gold than they could carry between them."

"Make it more gold than they'll be able to carry when you get back."

"Done."

"Ha! They'll be yearlings by then. That's a lot of gold."

"A wager then. If I don't bring back more gold than they can carry, I'll give you a jewelled harness for both. I'll even find you some yellow jewels for them. But I warn you: I know in my heart this will happen; my wyrd is strong!"

Begu snorted. "You're boasting like a gesith who fell into a mead barrel. And if you win? Hmm. Then I'll make you two pair of breeches, too. It's a very sensible idea." Then she looked cross. "Except that won't work because I've already made them for you, to match your warrior jacket, and it'd be a waste for you not to have them before you go. And, oh!" Her eyes sparkled with greed. "If you bring back that much gold you can easily afford to give me the harness even if I don't win."

It was good to see her gemæcce being herself. "Then you shall have the harness no matter what, just as I shall have the breeches to match my jacket. But mark me, I will bring back enough gold to make your foals stagger." That or she would be dead.

Ceadwin's long, spidery fingers felt the cold, so though Hild found it mild for Hrethmonath, she had again set up braziers in the church for him to paint by. It was here she found Langwredd with Luftmær, taking advantage of the warmth to play the harp and lyre and benefit from the round, ringing sound.

She half listened to their music—the bright metal shimmer of the harp and the warmer pluck of sinew—as she walked around the walls with Ceadwin, admiring the colours of his waves and boat and fish. She stopped for a closer look at the spots on one particular fish.

"I don't know if they had salmon in the Sea of Galilee," he said. "But Father Rhin said it wouldn't matter, just so long as the people know the fish."

"Cian Boldcloak told me a story once of the salmon that ate the hazelnut of knowledge. The more spots the fish gained, the more knowledge it held, and the more knowledge gained by those who ate it."

Ceadwin reached out as though to touch the fish but did not. "Should I add more spots, then, do you think? For the Christ was very wise."

"More spots, certainly."

Now Langwredd was playing a tune Hild knew, her Butcherbird song. She sent Ceadwin back to his paints and brushes and sat cross-legged by the players' stools.

"Stop." Luftmær leaned forward, a furrow between his brows. "That's not how it goes."

"No," Langwredd said. "But this is better." It did indeed sound better that way to Hild, and the Bryneich's Anglisc, too, was better than it had been, though the British accent—or not the accent but the up-and-down lilt—was still strong. "Don't you think? Hild?"

It would not do to take sides between two singers. "Better in what way?"

Whatever else she might be, the Bryneich was quick-witted, and she saw the way out. "Why, better for the harp, of course, and for the hearts of the men of the north. For lyre, and here in Deira, it could not be bettered."

Luftmær leaned back, mollified. "If you can play it with another who does the drone underneath it would sound more uncanny."

And less sad.

"A drone underneath and an unearthly cry above. You drone at the chorus." She nodded at Luftmær, and they played together, and where before on the lyre it had been a simple tune, and on the harp a sad and beautiful one, playing together Langwredd added a ripple on the harp and loosed a high, mournful cry like the ghost of a gull while Luftmær plucked an eerie drone over and over. The strange contrast, the clash, caught at the edge of Hild's heart, like a blade under a limpet, and levered something loose.

When they saw her shiver both players said, "Ha!" in the same way, and stamped in satisfaction.

"Both sound very well," Hild said. And they did. The "Song of the Butcherbird" had a tune not unlike the darker parts of the "Song of Branwen," and the double-handed version turned it otherworldly. "Have you the 'Song of Cath Llew' yet?"

Luftmær plucked a few idle notes. "It's coming along."

"Now that is a song I could sing with some knowledge," Langwredd said. "It needs the drift of the mist in the damp green hills, the empty socket of a dead sheep, and Cath Llew knowing what lies beyond the hill when she speaks to the birds."

Hild had told her that story as they lay in bed in Coledauc's tent one afternoon. "And the blood oath on the fairy hill after the death of the Picts."

"Yes! Yes!" said Luftmær. "I have just the . . ." His mouth made soundless shapes. "I must . . ." He stood. "Forgive me, lady." He bent his head briefly, picked up his lyre, and left, eyes tracking a scene only he could see—he would have fallen over Ceadwin's pot if the boy had not snatched it away in time.

"You're a sly one," Langwredd said in British, and there was a teasing laugh, a lilt in her voice. Ceadwin glanced over, clearly understanding the tone if not the words.

Hild sat on the empty stool. "Sly is for when you don't want others to know your purpose. I wish all to have no doubt as to my purpose: to bend my will, and the will of all sworn to me, to the death and defeat of Cadwallon Bradawc."

"But I am not sworn to you, Hild Yffing." She gave her a look from under her lashes. "Would you have me if I wished it?"

It came back to her—sudden as a hand thrust in her drawers—the game they had played in Calchfynydd: Langwredd leaning in, bending to her, bending her words, the meaning running through her hands like water, flowing back unexpected from another direction, cool, lively, quick.

Langwredd leaned in now, put a hand on her thigh. "Would you have me?"

She did not know how it might have gone if Ceadwin had not taken that moment to stir his paint, which made Hild think of Langwredd's hand on Gladmær's knee, the smug look on Sitric's face when he came out of the woods after Grina, and she would not be played with that way. "I would have your help with the Bryneich."

That lovely hand slid up Hild's thigh as she leaned farther forward. "And what would I have from you?"

Hild took the hand in her own. "What you have already: my roof over your head, my food on the table, and a place for you and your children." She put the hand firmly back on Langwredd's own thigh. "Meanwhile you must keep to your own bed."

"Must?" Those deep blue eyes sparked. "You would say must to a woman of the Bryneich? My body is my own to do with as I wish, and to twine with any other body who wishes to."

"If it were only needs of the body, the joy of the bed, yes. But with you, now, it's not." She wondered if it ever had been, even in Calchfynydd. "You're bedding my fighting men, the ones closest to me who are young enough or foolish enough to be led around by their sticks. What do you whisper to them in their throes? What do you bid them do? And whatever you're asking them for, why not just ask me?"

"I'm tired of asking Anglisc favours."

"In Menewood there are no Angli—"

"Oh, spare me your cant!"

Hild looked at her, really looked. She was older than Hild but nonetheless young, and beautiful—in the flower of her beauty. She wore gold—but it was the same gold she wore every day. And her dress was fine—but it was the same dress. In this strange land she had only her wits and what she stood up in, and her children and her harp. North of the wall she could be reckoned a princess but here in Deira when she opened her mouth she sounded wealh—she was wealh.

"Don't you dare pity me!"

And Hild heard how empty that threat was—Don't pity me or . . . what? What could Langwredd do? Nothing. And she knew it.

Hild held all pity from her voice. "You are Langwredd, lady of the Bryneich. Player of the harp, beauty of the north, mother to Coledauc's heirs. You're key to my plans for the north. I don't pity you, Langwredd, I need you. You can help me, and I can help you. We were easy with one another once. Won't you speak to me plainly?"

Langwredd turned away but not before Hild saw the brightness in her eye. Hild wished she had thought to carry a kerchief, but in the company of highfolk that was always the task of her bodywoman. She looked about, saw Ceadwin wiping one of his brushes, pointed, and crooked a finger. He brought his pile of rags and she nodded him back to his pots.

She touched Langwredd's arm and handed her a clean rag. "Tell me how I can help."

Langwredd mopped her eyes, turned back. "Why should I trust you? I'm not an ten-year-old boy to be dazzled by your Anglisc blade, then abandoned."

"A ten . . ." This was about Cuncar? Langwredd did not even like the boy. "You said Cuncar didn't ask for my help."

She pulled the rag through the ring of her finger and thumb, over and over. "Should he need to ask? You are his cousin of the knife." The tendons in her neck were taut. "If you won't help him, then how can I trust you to keep your word to anyone else?"

At the other end of the church Ceadwin was humming under his breath the "Song of the Butcherbird," but with the sadder rise and fall that Langwredd had first played rather than the marching beat of Luftmær's lyre.

"I mothered that boy for a while—I was more of a mother to him than his own had been. He's a rival to my son, yes, but even so I'd not see him left to be slaughtered like a faun by the Iding, or if not, then by Cadwallon Bradawc."

And even though Hild finally understood that this was not about the piglet prince but about Langwredd being able to trust an Yffing's word, Hild thought of the boy clutching her knife, his fear, his hurried slash, the blood. The pride on his face as she bound him up. She remembered the feel of his small hand in hers.

"You could help him. You're the Butcherbird. You're Cath Llew. Yffing of Deira."

"Even Cath Llew couldn't steal Cuncar from the Iding in Bebbanburg, a fortress that's never fallen, then carry him, unseen, across land held by maruaders of a madman who hates all Yffings unto death and outnumbers me three to one." But oh, what a song that would make! Visions flamed in her heart of scaling the walls of Bebbanburg at night, smuggling the boy out, a hero's ride across wild country . . .

No. It could not be done.

"Surely—"

"Langwredd, I swear by breath and bone that the thing cannot be done. Even if I left now, today, I would not be in time. Inside Bebbanburg they'll already be eating their weakest horses, for those horses must by now be skin and bone and the men as bad. And when they've chewed the bones they'll choose either to come out and bend the knee to Cadwallon, or come out and fight." Either way, they would die before she passed the wall. It would not surprise her to hear they were already dead. People and the news they carried travelled slowly in the cold and mud and rain. "If by some stroke of chance I were in time, all I could do is witness his death, and the death of his father."

Silence. "Even if we rally the Bryneich?"

"You know the Bryneich better than I do. How long would that take?"
Her face was her answer. "Truly? There's nothing to be done?"
"Nothing."
Langwredd stared at the cloth in her hand.
"But though I can do nothing it doesn't mean there's no hope. No one knows Cuncar's wyrd. It might be that on a whim Cadwallon spares him. It might be that he'll escape. And I swear to you that if, when we get there, there's anything to be done, anything, we'll do it. We'll rally the Bryneich—with your help—and we'll save or avenge your princeling, my sworn cousin of the knife." Yet another promise. How many promises could one person keep? "But I need your help. Will you give it? I need that harp of yours. I need your fierce heart, I need your silver tongue."
Langwredd looked up.
"You have that power, Langwredd. You have presence."
She liked that.
"I need to uplift the hearts of the Bryneich, of Rheged—all the men of the north. Write me the 'Song of Cath Llew and the Fiercesomes.' But also write me a song to put fear in the heart of those Gwynedd men, those murdering marauders from the wild hills of Gwynedd. They've made sport of killing Deirans. Now I want them to tremble at the thought of our revenge."
"And you'll uphold my position? You won't abandon your promise to me?"
"If it can be done, I will do it."
"No." Her eyes sparked like steel on flint. "No. Say you will do it, not that you might but that you will."
"Langwredd of the Bryneich, I will uphold your claim and that of your sons."
She nodded, mollified. "Then I will write your song."

She sat on the great bough of the pollard, looking through the thin morning veil—part mist, part drifting rain—at her valley, at the beck and ponds, the roofs. The last smoke from the bread ovens—the coals had been raked out to bake the first of the day's bread—was slowly beaten down as the rain thickened. Somewhere out of sight a goat bleated, unhappy in the wet. So much busier and burlier, but smaller, too, somehow, than when she had sat here two years ago, with Little Honey an unanswered question in her belly. She cupped her belly but it was flat and hard; everything had changed. The valley smelled different, too: a place no longer afraid to be seen and known. Even the tree felt different between her legs and at her back. It was not just that there was a hint of green in the folds of the grey bud scales where before they had been tight and black, the tree itself seemed a different shape, which made no sense. She shifted a little to get more comfortable but could not. The knot in her back—

That knot, which two years ago had rested comfortably in the small of her back, now pressed on a bone farther down. She looked at her hand, laid it next to the carved hedgepig. It was not the hedgepig that seemed smaller, she was bigger. She had grown, and because of all the other changes—her swelling belly, her injury and illness, half starving, then filling out again—she had not noticed. But it was not just her height. Her wrists were thicker; it was no wonder that the dense bog oak of her staff felt as light as living oak once had.

She stroked the hedgepig, imagined—though it felt more like remembering now—Cian carving it in the heat of summer.

"I'm leaving tomorrow," she said to the Cian in her mind's eye. "I know you always thought this place a bog, but watch over this valley, wherever you are. And if you're up in the sky, with the stars in heaven, and if you see Honey there, sing her a song for me. Sing to her of Branwen; she'll know that song. I sang it to her when she suckled." She felt a ghostly tug on her nipple and the drop in her belly she had not felt for over a year and even then it had been for Wilfrid. "Tell her, tell her to watch over Wilfrid, who has thrived on the milk I made for her." She had never sung of Branwen to Wilfrid. That was her song, and Cian's, and Honey's. "Watch over this valley. Watch over my mother, and Begu. And—" Was it right to ask him to watch over Brona? "And all those I love. And if you can watch so far afield, watch over your mother in the bay, for if—if I fail, she'll need a shield."

A jackdaw landed on the bough above her, stropped its beak back and forth on the bark, and fixed her with one black eye, then the other, as if to say: *Time's wasting.*

"Cian Boldcloak, I swear to you now, by this tree in this valley, by the love you bore for me and Little Honey, that I will throttle the forces of Gwynedd, tear the heart from them, and crush their will. I will drive them from this land. I will find Cadwallon Bradawc and he will fall at my feet. He will see in my face the payment due for your death, and the death of our Honey—he will know, and then I will kill him. And you and our Little Hedgepig can sit among the stars—I hope they are warm as well as bright; I hope the clouds are like blankets made of lambswool and duck down; I hope the fruit tastes like a summer afternoon and the mead and milk like the dream of evening—and listen to your enemy scream his torment from the cold and endless mud of Hel."

The drizzle was turning to rain, fat drops falling between the branches. The hedgepig glistened, alive once again.

"And, love, I wish I'd done better. If ever you can spare me a thought, help me be strong. There are so many people. So very many. And sometimes . . ."

The rain was coming fast now and, though many of the men and supplies had gone ahead, there was still much to be done before nightfall.

"I have to go. Hold me in your heart."

She threw down her staff and held Brona to her, belly to belly, hip bone to hip bone, not caring that she was soaked and Brona dry. She kissed her hard, hungrily, and after a startled pause Brona kissed back, pulling Hild onto her thigh, moving between her legs. Still standing they reached inside each other's clothes. Hild drove them both back, and back, until Brona was against the wall, then Brona was turning in her arms, panting, tearing down her own breeches, leaning her hands against the wall, looking back, eyes black and wild, while Hild kilted up her skirts and pushed herself against Brona's soft, plump cheek, and reached down and around to the hot slippery slick between Brona's legs. For a heartbeat both stayed still, then they began to move, slowly, focused like a hunter over her arrow following every move of her prey; hunter and hunted bound on the same path, moving together, hearts beating in time, breath coming faster, deeper, blood coursing through their veins and tendons taut, the heat between them tightening down to a hard, tight star, pulsing with light, brighter and brighter, until they both stretched up, heads back, and cried out.

After, they kissed for a long time. They ate. They lay in each other's arms—naked now. As the fire dulled to a glow they became warm shapes, shadows that smelled of themselves and each other. They talked.

"Fllur will sleep here, with the children," Brona said.

"Good. And Rulf has—"

"Yes." She kissed Hild on the cheekbone, then nuzzled close to her nose. "I love the way you smell, just here." She breathed deep. "There's no smell like it, like a bilberry fried in bacon fat. Sharp, sweet, salty, rich."

"But Rulf—"

"Yes! He will build it as we said." Her voice roughened. "Love, you leave in the morning. I won't see you for months, even half a year." And maybe never again, but neither of them said that. "So hush now. Hush about the things I'll do while you're gone. Be here now."

And so they talked quietly of bones and birds, the small boys and Maer, the taste of fine bread with good butter, and the wanton joy of sprawling unclothed on a sunlit hillside, and Hild fell asleep with Brona a dark shape propped up on her elbow, stroking her forehead.

The morning rain was light but steady. The main body of men were mounted and waiting near the mouth of the valley, along with Sintiadd, Langwredd, and Luftmær, but the Fiercesomes stood with their two mounts each—Dudda also held Flýte's headstall—just beyond the long house while Hild said her last goodbyes. She had said most already, and now she stood by Bone's shoulder. Her closest people crowded the long house's doorway, out of the wet, and now, second to last, her mother came to her, and they embraced. She held her a long time. They stepped apart. Hild followed the line of her mother's face, the curve of her shoulders, the folding of her fingers together before her. *Be here when I come back. Be here.*

"Don't let that fool scop be more foolish than usual."

"No." Forget-me-not-blue gaze met blue moss agate. There was no more to be said. "Fare well."

Breguswith nodded. "And you, do what must be done. Come home safe." She stepped back under the shelter of the doorway, and now Begu ran to her.

She clung to Hild fiercely. "Oh, I hate this! I've said goodbye too many times. And I did this just three days ago with Winny."

"I'll keep him safe."

"Yes, yes, you already promised. But do look after yourself, too. I don't want you coming home a bag of bones like last time. I'm tired of sewing you new things! And speaking of that, those breeches suit you. And they're so much easier to make than dresses—we should all wear them. You packed the ones for Gwladus, didn't you?"

"I did."

"You should wear your jacket."

"It's too uncomfortable for everyday."

"But it'll keep you—"

"And you should go back inside now. You're getting wet."

"I'm not going back inside until you're out of sight!"

"Then I'd better begin."

She turned to the Fiercesomes and nodded. They mounted.

"Well, go on then. Go on."

Hild smiled. "You'd whist at your gemæcce like your ducks and chickens?"

"Someone has to. Look at you, no more sense than a goat standing out here in the rain. Go on with you."

So Hild swung into the saddle and took up her reins. She looked down the trail, where everyone stood in their doorways, and felt her heart lift as it always did when she was setting out on a journey.

"I'll be back," she shouted in a voice that could be heard in Aberford. "Work well, fare well!"

She was about to urge Bone forward when she looked down, and laughed.

"And someone get that cat out of the way!"

Three

✦

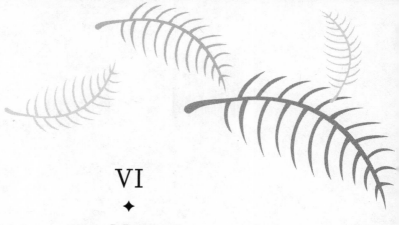

VI

✦

Baedd Coch

32

⊕

THE RIVER UR ROARED, thick and wild and swollen with rain, and the wind was raw as a washerwoman's knuckle, but inside the fort they were snug and warm, if somewhat cramped. Grimhun had done well—as had Coelfrith. The horses were well-provided with feed and water, with a cunning water supply run from the well, and for the nearly threescore people there were even straw pallets to lay their travel cloaks on, and giant trestles and boards that doubled for eating at during the day and sleeping on at night. There would be time for their tents and bedrolls on hard ground when they were on the road; for now, they could be warm. Some had been here a fortnight, some a week, others three days, with Hild and the last of the men arrived only yesterday.

She sat with the Fiercesomes; and Uinniau, Grimhun, and Coelfrith; and Langwredd and Sintiadd. They had to raise their voices over the noise of men eating, boasting, singing, laughing. They were marching to battle soon; they were young and strong, trained and ready. Everything was already mended or cleaned or sharpened. They loved each other, they loved their weapons and horses, and they loved life. They were loud.

"Their hearts are high!" Gladmær said to Luftmær. "It's a good song!"

Langwredd smiled and patted Gladmær's hand. "You told us a good story."

"Not a story," he said, looking around at the other Fiercesomes for support.

Dudda grinned. He was just in from a patrol and his burns were hideously red from the cold and wind. "The red-eyed hægtes of the wood. Oh, yes. We were all there!"

Luftmær said, "So now we have the 'Song of Cath Llew,' the 'Song of the Butcherbird,' and 'Hægtes of the Wood.' The first's to uplift our hearts, the second's a warning, and the third's to strike fear in the hearts of our enemies."

"We can strike fear with all of them, depending on the notes," Langwredd said. She drew a haunting, uncanny ripple from her harp. "And we can uplift with all of them." A chord: brighter, bolder.

"We need to start singing them soon," Oeric said.

"When we're close to the wall," Hild said.

"And when will that be?"

"Soon."

"I'll need the final route two days before the main body set out," Coelfrith said.

The crowd near the door roared with sudden laughter. Hild waited for it to die down. "You'll have it." The first part of her route was already decided—north to Cetreht, then a day's pause, then to Getlingum—but there she must decide between Dere Street directly north to the wall, or the road over the Spine and the twenty hard leagues to Pennrid. It would depend on the answer she was waiting for. "We'll know by the full moon."

The full moon of Hrethmonath, when Laisrén and Bryhtsige would be there, or not.

"Six days," Luftmær said. "We'll have time to make another song."

Gwladus arrived two days later. She wore a short dress with breeches, and with her gold and jewels and corn-coloured hair braided back she rode from the mist with Oeric at her back like a queen of the north before the redcrests came.

Hild watched the men watch her as she walked past the benches to Hild's table, Oeric at her left shoulder as he had always been at Hild's right. Desire in the men's faces, yes—Gwladus had always provoked desire—but now her walk was different, less a promise to please and more a demand to be pleased and, beyond that, the certainty that she could open paths for those who pleased her; she shone with worth. It was a quality Langwredd did not have, and Hild found herself revising plans. Langwredd could not bring the Bryneich to the right place at the right time alone.

"Welcome." Hild stood and greeted Gwladus as she would an equal, and watched the men take note. She seated her at her right, and Sintiadd was pouring for her before she had even settled and unpinned her cloak. Then Hild listened.

Eirlys and Pabo had undertaken to persuade the folk of Thorne, Wroot, and Balltreow to hold the water roads against the boats of Lindsey. If that were not possible, they themselves, on behalf of the people of Ynys Bwyell, undertook to send news of movement. It had cost a chest of hacksilver—

"That's all?"

—a chest of hacksilver and the promise to demand of the new ruler north of the Humbre that he not tithe the fenland for three years—

Here Gwladus smiled. "They don't know the new king barely knows the fenland exists, and won't have time or men to even think about demanding tithe for some time."

A good bargain. Gwladus was a jewel.

—but she had had to vow one other payment: that once the lady of Elmet was returned from the north, she would visit and thank the people of High Brune in person.

Hild looked at her.

"That was Afanc's price. She said she knows the waters best, and that you swore you would come when called, and so she is calling."

The weather turned. The wind calmed and the cloud thinned, and for two days it did not rain. The mud began to dry and the days were brighter, lighter, and longer. Perhaps tomorrow the full moon would rise in a clear sky. But then, as the afternoon closed in, the wind started to rise again and rain to drum on the sturdy timber walls. Somebody moved a bucket back under the drip in the northwest corner near to the partition behind which Hild slept.

Langwredd and Luftmær were moving from board to board, teaching the men a song. Hild had already broken them into small groups: some who would stay near the wall, dealing with Anglisc and British, and some who would move north. The groups went out on patrol, to explore, to practise riding together, to keep the horses fit. She rode out with each more than once, listened to them sing as they rode. All groups learnt all three songs both ways—the British harp and the Anglisc lyre—but few liked the British version of the hægtes song. And now, as she walked down the hall, she was hearing the same for the new song, the fourth song the players had made. No one liked it, whether played with harp or lyre; it had no bite.

She stopped halfway down the boards, opposite the south door, and listened—partly for the return of the patrol that was still out, but mostly to the song. The tune was wrong, and the words seemed to slide off the mind like water from waxed leather.

"It's not working," Gwladus said at her shoulder.

"No. Songs of rolling hills and golden grain are not songs for war."

"But we need a song of Deira."

Hild nodded. "Come," she said to Langwredd. "Come," to Luftmær, and moved some men aside so she could sit. "We'll start again. You," she said to one come from Goodmanham via York. He blushed the red of the cross on some of their banners hung on the wall. She had seen his sword work and his riding, he was more than able, but he seemed barely old enough to grow whiskers. "Deira. What do you think of?"

He pointed behind her. She turned. The banner of Deira: the boar of the Yffings. She looked at the next man down. "You?"

He pointed to the banner.

She looked at Luftmær. "Write me a song about the boar of Deira."

"Aye!" shouted Cuthred from the other side of the hall. "The boar of the Yffings, the red boar that will rip you open from behind when you're not expecting it!"

The door opened—the patrol returning—and half a dozen men shouted at once to close it, close it!

"A boar!" she called, loud enough to quiet the room. "I need a song of a boar that will put heart into those who fight with us and freeze the blood of our enemies!"

"Then," said a voice behind her, "you must surely hear the 'Song of Muc Dubh.'"

She turned. Laisrén, and next to him Bryhtsige, both honed to an edge that would cut the wind.

She stood very still. She could read nothing on either man's face. "Come. Sit." To Langwredd and Luftmær she said, "Stay with the men. Work on the boar song."

"But—"

She cut off Luftmær with a slice of her hand. "Mallo will sing the 'Song of Muc Dubh' later."

Coelfrith, appalled, said, "All?"

"All." Bryhtsige was calm.

"Under the green branch of truce? Even the child?"

Bryhtsige nodded.

"I understand killing the Iding," Coelfrith said. "It's war. But a child?" He sounded bewildered. He had not witnessed Cadwallon's vile work in Deira.

"He wasn't a child," Bryhtsige said. "He was Cuncar ab Coledauc, prince-in-waiting of the Bryneich. A rival."

Poor little Cuncar. Had he believed to the end that Cath Llew would swoop from the hills above Bebbanburg and rescue him? Was he still hoping when he rode out with his father and the Iding under a green branch to talk terms with Cadwallon Bradawc? When Cadwallon grinned and broke the branch and drew his sword? But now the Iding was dead, and Coledauc, and Cuncar, too.

"He's mad," Coelfrith said.

"He's not mad," she said. "He wants what he wants and doesn't care what it takes. Now he believes he has no rivals for Bernicia and Deira other than Oswine, and he knows Oswine's no threat." She felt a dreadful, hot eagerness, for now Cadwallon's guard would be down.

"But they were under truce!"

"Even so."

"He's the devil," said Laisrén. "And his men have given themselves to demons."

"How can we fight that?" Coelfrith said. "We can't fight that."

"We can," she said. She looked around at her close people: Gwladus; her Fiercesomes; Uinniau, Grimhun, and Oeric; Coelfrith; Morud and Sintiadd. "Cadwallon is a man. He breathes, he bleeds. As do his men. They haven't given themselves to demons but only to the wants of men: gold glee and blood joy. His men fight for Cadwallon because he wins. That will change. For now, for the first time, he faces the boar of Deira—"

"Cath Llew and her Fiercesomes," said Leofdæg.

"The Butcherbird and her Hounds." Grimhun.

"He faces the will of the north. And we'll crush him."

"And now the north has a new champion." Laisrén turned to Hild, straight and formal. "Oswald Lamnguin accepts the terms offered and will bring men to Hild of Deira, and Rhoedd of Rheged, at Caer Luel, to defeat Cadwallon Bradawc and take the oath of all folk north of the Humbre."

Take, not accept. Defeat, not help to defeat. Oswald as champion—not Hild Yffing. She said nothing. Pride. It was pride that got men killed.

She took a long, slow breath, then turned on the bench a little, and gestured Laisrén and Bryhtsige closer to talk for her ears only. "Caer Luel when?"

"Not before Saint Brendan's Day, perhaps by the Blessed Columba's Day, but most certainly before the Feast of Saint John the Baptist."

Hild looked at Bryhtsige.

"Not before the full moon of Thromilchi, possibly the first quarter of Litha but no later than the last quarter."

"Indeed," Laisrén said. "Samhradh, as agreed." Midsummer. "It will take that time to gather the boats to carry men and some horses. For as Prince Uinniau"—slight bow—"will attest, Rhoedd could not undertake to provide all the mounts for Oswald's war band."

"How many—the war band?"

"Oswald has perhaps two dozen and Oswiu a dozen or more."

Two war bands. "They'll fight as one?"

"Oswiu will follow his brother in this."

In this. Not in everything? "And the matter of Rhianmelldt?"

"They will handfast at Caer Luel."

She nodded, aware of Uinniau holding himself still—so close to the moment of his dreams!—thinking. If she reckoned twoscore from Oswald, then with Rhoedd's men they could field sevenscore against Cadwallon. More if those songs worked on the men of the north. "And the rest of the terms?"

"You may keep Elmet to run as you see fit, tithes to be reckoned directly to Oswald. Oswine may continue as underking of Deira, but may not tithe Elmet."

Better than she had hoped though she was careful not to show it. "And Oswine's tithe?"

"To be negotiated in person. Though not to exceed the customary duty."

Bryhtsige gave her a bland look.

"And is customary duty for Oswald what we in Deira might consider customary duty?" she said. "One-tenth part?"

Laisrén smiled. "It is not."

"It's half as much again," Bryhtsige said.

She considered. "And for Elmet?"

"Elmet we consider a separate case. One-tenth for Elmet."

"Laisrén, what power do you have to speak on Oswald's behalf, here and now?"

"Some little room, but not much."

"Then consider that this point of Deira's tithe makes me unhappy but I'd hear the rest before we agree." Deira's tithe was more Oswine's battle than hers and there was much still to sort. "Let's speak now of spoils."

"Ah. Here I'm afraid that my lord Oswald was most definite."

Bryhtsige leaned forward. "He would agree to nothing less than three-fifths of the battlefield spoils."

"He will, you see, have many followers to reward, beyond those in his war band," Laisrén said.

"I do see." She had also heard Bryhtsige's faint emphasis on *battlefield*. "But most of that spoil was stolen from Deira, where it properly belongs."

Laisrén spread his hands. "And no doubt if you were able to defeat Cadwallon on your own, you would deserve all the spoils."

"Oh, with Rheged I could defeat him without your lord. I just can't hold the country long in peace, which is what I most want. And I have done much, taken many risks, expended time and men in getting so far."

"Risks you undertook before our agreement."

That she could not argue. But it was also true that the two-fifths would go directly to her, and not be shared with Oswine unless she chose other-wise. She turned. "Morud? Find Almund. Tell him to bring his pen—not stylus but pen." She leaned back, rolled her shoulders as though she had been tense but was now resigned, then leaned in again. "We'll come to agreement here and now. Almund will write it down. We'll both sign it." Almund came in and busied himself with his folding table and roll of parchment. "It will take some time but I find it best to sort things clearly from the first. Agreed?"

Laisrén nodded.

"Very well. Here, then, is what we'll agree." She listed her tithe, one-tenth part; Elmet; Oswine as underking of Deira but not tithing Elmet. After each part she paused for Laisrén to agree and for Almund's pen to *scratch-scratch-dip-scratch* and then for him to shake his pot, wait, brush aside the sand, lift and tap the parchment, and redip his pen. She varied the timing, watching the rhythm of Laisrén's attention, when it sharpened, when it moved ahead, when it fixed on something already said. "And lastly we agree that of the spoils taken"—*scratch-scratch-dip-scratch*—"together on the field of battle, Lord Oswald will take—" *Scratch-scratch-dip-scratch. Shake-brush-tap-dip.* Laisrén tried hard to appear easy but she saw the thump in his neck and the slope of his shoulder as he focused now only on what Oswald would take at the expense of what was already said. She sighed. "Lord Oswald will take three-fifths." Laisrén breathed out. *Scratch-scratch-dip-scratch.* "And the lady Hild two-fifths, each to apportion their own share as they see fit." *Scratch-scratch-dip. Shake. Brush. Tap.* Laisrén was smiling. "Agreed?"

He nodded and held out his arm, eager to seal the agreement. They clasped.

"Then let us sign."

They did. His signature was neat, hers bold.

"Almund will write another copy for us to compare and sign. Then we will seal both and each keep one."

Laisrén nodded.

"Good. Now, rest," she said. "You've a song to sing for us as we feast tonight."

For, oh, they would feast! For Oswald was coming, and she had done better than she had hoped with regard to the spoils. Now her path lay open before her.

"We'll talk more at meat. Coelfrith." Like every man at the board he was quivering, eager to begin. "We leave the day after tomorrow, over the Spine. See to it." For now she had a time to aim for, and numbers to assign, and her plan was ready.

On her orders, Oeric broached two casks of ale and a small one of mead, they built up the fires, and they served generously from their stores, for they might not feast again for a season. And Laisrén—for now he was truly Laisrén, the speaker for Oswald Brightblade, the next king of the north, with no need to hide his Irishness—sang the "Song of Muc Dubh," the black boar of Connacht. A boar so fearsome, so huge, that the great earthwork, the Doon of Drumsna, was ploughed by his tusks, the Lough of Mask was his mud wallow, and his black bristles were so deadly they would kill at a touch even after he had rubbed them off against the great yew of Eó Mugna—the yew whose own poison was no match for Muc Dubh's, and in the great boar's presence shivered and broke into kindling too small even for bow staves.

It had a rousing, thundering chorus that the hall was soon singing while banging their travel cups on the board. *Muc Dubh, Muc Dubh!*

"Sing instead Baedd Du! For the men of the north speak British!" Uinniau shouted. He was drunk: Soon, now that all things were agreed, he would marry his love, Begu, he would win spoil in a great battle—for his spoil was his own; he was sworn to no man but Rhoedd—and all his hopes would be realised.

"No!" Grimhun, cheeks hectic. "Instead of the black boar, say the red boar! The red boar of the Yffings!" And he raised his cup to the banner, and then to Hild, and drained the whole thing. Men pounded the boards. *Red boar! Red boar!*

Uinniau turned dull red—a prince of the old blood to be told no! to be told to sing in Anglisc in his own country!—and his hand dropped to his knife.

Langwredd stood, put her fingers to her mouth, and whistled high and clear. She raised her cup. "For the men of the north, Baedd Coch—red boar—does not sound so ill!"

Everyone roared. Grimhun beamed and raised his cup to Uinniau, who laughed and raised his own.

"Red boar! Red boar!" bellowed the men who would stay by the wall.

"Baedd Coch! Baedd Coch!" thundered those who would go north, their veins sticking out on each side of their necks in an effort to out-shout their rivals. Only now there was no danger of knives and blood. Now they were shouting the same thing.

"The red boar eats nails, not acorns!"

"Baedd Coch's piss melts stone!"

"Red boar! Red boar!"

"Baedd Coch! Baedd Coch!"

She looked at Laisrén, Bryhtsige, Coelfrith, Gwladus, Wulf, and Leofdæg, and nodded to the door to what passed for her chamber. Time to sign the second copy, and to plan, for even as her groups sang, she was rethinking her ideas. She knew every plan must be ready to change at the least flutter of wyrd—in war, the winner was the one who could turn on a wingtip and snatch the enemy from the air. Cadwallon had killed the princes the Bryneich looked to; the time to rally them was now.

33

✦

IMPATIENCE SEETHED IN HILD'S BONES, and she did not stop at Cetreht but moved directly to Getlingum, where they pitched their tents before the great dyke athwart the redcrest road over the Spine. The road ran from Getlingum to Broac to Pennrid to Caer Luel at the west end of the wall; it was as wide as Dere Street, but unlike the war street she knew so well, this road climbed steadily as it cut west, then northwest. Over time the height and harsh winters of the mountains had heaved some of the heavy cobbles from their beds, and what had once been covered stone gutters were now broken and twisted. But it was still a good road, a wide and fast road for those with heart and hardened mounts.

The next day they rode fast. From Getlingum to Rhoedd's spring seat in Pennrid was fifty miles, and Hild wanted to spend only one night in the open. She did not know this road but she knew mountains, knew what it meant when the only birds she saw were close to the ground or high and hunting: What was bleak could become deadly if the wind veered to the north bringing snow and cold that would slice through the leather of their tents.

They stopped at a broken fort where many burns and streams came together in a rushing brown torrent that became the Edene. In Urburg it had been spring, but on these heights the grass was pale and new and not yet strong enough to feed their mounts. The crease between Coelfrith's brows deepened but Hild did not worry; they had planned for this. There were two caches of fodder—more than they needed in case a turn in the weather kept them pinned down for a while—though the redcrests had chosen well: This fort, or what was left of it, was sheltered from the north wind by some of the highest peaks of the Spine.

The next day they made good time, and their unsaddling rest—that they took halfway through every day—was at a big fort, with many courses of stone still standing, and what looked like a track moving at a steep slope north and east over those same high peaks that had sheltered them last night.

She was too restless to keep still, and at some distance from the bustle of men and horses she paced back and forth near the track up into the high hills, trailed by Gwladus, and Leofdæg and Uinniau, who all had questions that only she, it seemed, could answer. She answered them shortly, but there seemed always to be more, and eventually she chopped off Uinniau's question about shields, pointed at the track, and said, "Where does that go?" Unknowns worried her.

Leofdæg said he had ridden the track some way in Solmonath but had not gone far because of ice and wind. Uinniau said it went to the old fort that few visited now, White Fort, they called it, a place argued and fought over in days past, but the land was useless and so not worth a fight. He could not remember anyone mentioning it since he was a boy.

"It has a redcrest look," she said of the track. At least five paces wide.

"It does," Uinniau said. "But narrow."

"How narrow?"

"Enough for two laden packhorses abreast."

Packhorses. Laden packhorses. She remembered Coelfrith's father leading packhorses of spoil down a steep track to York, long ago. "How far is this fort?"

"A score of miles. But the way's very steep."

She looked at Leofdæg, who nodded: That was his experience, too.

"From White Fort there's a road directly north, to one of the forts on the more easterly end of Stanegate," Uinniau said. "Or was a road. My father's father, Rhun, broke it to leave no easy path for invading Idings from the wall deep into our heartland."

Instead, Æthelfrith Fflamddwyr had gone north and west and burnt the great hill fort on the other side of the Solwade.

"So now White Fort's the road's end." She would like to see that. Gwladus, who knew her well, gave her a look: *Your place is here.*

Leofdæg cleared his throat. "When I was a stripling, I rode a track from near Corabrig that ran south and east. I didn't ride far—it was the white winter—but it ran the way a road to this White Fort might run. Under the snow it seemed a good track, too straight for a drover's road. As a stripling I wasn't much given to thinking, but thinking back now that track, too, had a redcrest look."

"And how steep was that rise from Corabrig?"

Leofdæg looked around, thinking, squinting against a remembered snow-dazzle. "It started higher than we are now, and the rise . . . not gentle but no more than today's road."

She turned slowly, looking at the sky, smelling the air. This track was important. It licked at the back of her mind like the rasp of a cat's tongue. "How's Lél?"

"Fit."

"Then take one man—young and quick and British-speaking; let him talk to anyone you meet—and ride this track. First to White Fort, and then on towards Corabrig. But don't be seen from Stanegate." It was unlikely Cadwallon would be back so soon from near Bebbanburg, but he would have outriders.

"What are you thinking?" The top of Uinniau's black-haired head came only to her collarbone but his quick hazel eyes were sharp, and he was Uinniau ab Rhun, Rhoedd's sister-son, prince of Rheged.

"Cadwallon has killed and picked clean almost every stronghold and war band in the north," she said slowly. Packhorses . . . "His treasure chests will be groaning with gold; the lowest among his followers can return home and be the richest man in his valley." Yes. Her words came faster. "Yet he's made no effort to hold the land he's plundered and burnt; he's not built herds, or rewarded his men with land. What does that tell you?"

"He won't stay."

She nodded. "He was never going to stay. He hates the north, and doesn't care if the north hates him." She was sure now. "When everything he can kill is killed, when everything he can steal is stolen, he'll return to Gwynedd to buy back the kingship."

Leofdæg was listening but asked no questions: His lady would tell him what he needed to know. But Uinniau had been raised to kingship and Hild was not his sworn lord. "So what are your thoughts on this track?"

Gwladus was narrowing her eyes; she was already seeing the path of Hild's thoughts. Hild wished she had a hundred of Gwladus. "Cadwallon will leave before winter. Which way do you think he'll return to Gwynedd?"

"You think this way? Surely not. Dere Street's the better road, and faster. He's beaten every war band along its path, or so he thinks. It's the best and surest route to win his way home with his gold."

"You would choose that way. I might choose that way. But there is still one country in the north unruined, unravaged, and unplucked."

He stared. "Rheged? He would not! From time out of mind Rheged and Gwynedd have been the twin pillars of Yr Hen Ogledd! He wouldn't dare."

She just waited.

He sighed. "And yet he's raided our trade."

And allied with Anglisc Penda. "And we know he's greedy. So, yes, he'll come down the west road. Most likely along Stanegate to Caer Luel and down the West Way—it's a wide way, and easy. But if he has to . . ."

"He'd come across the top of the Spine."

"Yes—but only if the uphill way from Corabrig is not too steep for beasts burdened with treasure." She looked at Leofdæg. "Which is what you'll find out."

Uinniau was now half turned back the way they had walked, where Wolcen waited. "If Cadwallon might come . . . I must warn my uncle. What if—"

"Cadwallon Bradawc's in no hurry. He won't leave the wall until he's sure he's picked the spring and summer trade clean. As before, he'll dig himself in at Corabrig, where his hoard's safe, with all the supplies he needs. He's no reason to believe he should leave before Harvestmonath."

"How can you be sure?"

"Think, man. He's been fighting for a year and a half and hasn't lost. Not once. By now he believes he paves his own path and weaves his own wyrd, that nothing of this earth can stop him. In Deira I watched how he works. I know how he thinks." And she was done with doubts and questions. "Trust me, Winny. And go see to your mare."

When he was out of earshot, she said to Leofdæg, "Once past White Fort, pay particular attention to sign that Cadwallon's men have ridden the track." If it was passable to their treasure train she needed to know if they knew that. She had the glimmerings of an idea.

"And also to places where their men might be surprised?"

She smiled. "Good man! And also places they might watch from to avoid being surprised." She slapped him on the shoulder. "We'll stay in

Pennrid no more than three days." Less if she could help it. "After Pennrid we'll be near Caer Luel. Take what time you need. If you're delayed enough to miss us at Caer Luel you'll be able to follow our trail and find us before we move north of the wall."

After that, they would be ghosts on the wind.

They reached Broac, just half a dozen miles from Pennrid, well before gelotendæg.

She was on fire to move on, but Gwladus raised her eyebrows—was that wise?—and Hild sighed and signalled a halt. Here they unpacked and shook out the wrinkles from their pennants and banners—Craven, Deira, Elmet; Baedd Coch, Cath Llew, Butcherbird; red crosses—and tied them to their spears and the fitted-together standard poles. They combed their hair and curried their mounts, put on their heaviest gold and wiped the mud from their boots. They ate and rested and began to believe their own magnificence.

Hild let Sintiadd fuss with her hair, then squatted on her hams and wiped her blade with flax oil until it shone. She passed her oiled rag to Uinniau, slid her seax sweetly back in its sheath, and watched Uinniau wipe his own sword. "A fine blade," she said in British. "And a long way from the stick you fought Cian with, just over there, all those years since." Barely ten years ago yet more than half her lifetime; it seemed another world.

"You remember that?" He grinned at the memory. "We were just striplings." Hild had not even been that. "He was jealous of my horse, I think."

"It hurt his pride that you had that great mare and he only a pony." She nodded to the bare-branched alders by the river. "And I climbed those trees. I was bored of boys fighting." They both shook their heads: Now fighting was the whole of their days. "The branches were leafy then. I sat up among them and dreamed of the redcrest horses galloping, galloping away, while you and Cian walloped and wailed verse from 'Y Gododdin.'" It had been a fort for horse soldiers. This was cavalry country; it always had been. She turned the carnelians on her wrist, and the different stones glowed: sun, then flame, then ember. Hot stones from a hot, sun-beaten land. According to Uinniau they had been dug from the ground not far from here, buried with the bones of a horse and its rider.

Laisrén and Langwredd came to join them. "We'll be leaving soon?"

Langwredd shivered and pulled her shawl tighter. "I don't even know why we stopped, why we're wasting time here when we could be having a hot bath and sitting in a real hall."

Hild forgot, sometimes, that others did not know the war trail. "My uncle Edwin king explained to me that when a stronger force demands tribute from a weaker, it soothes the humbled man's pride to bend the knee to an overwhelmingly strong, proud foe arrayed in battle-won magnificence. The more unbeatable a foe looks, the less likely the other is to second-guess yielding."

She shook her beads down into a more comfortable position. They were a little tight on her bigger wrists.

"And so I wear my marks of rank—and gifts shared in friendship—when I come to speak to Rhoedd of Rheged."

Langwredd frowned. "But—"

"He's a king, Langwredd. Coledauc called himself prince of the Bryneich but Rhoedd is a king of a long line of much-sung heroes. He's proud. And though we come here smiling, saying we ask for his grace and good word, we all know we're not asking—he has no real choice. Refusal is the path to ravagement and ruin, the ripping of Rheged from all remembrance, and the weeping and wailing of her people. Yet accepting our path leads to the fading of Rheged, to it sinking slowly into the west and becoming, at last, one with the Anglisc Northumbrans. Our path is a chance for his people to live out their lives on their own land; a chance for Rheged-that-was, its hero songs and kinglists, to be remembered kindly, for a time." She caught and held Langwredd's deep blue gaze. "Rhoedd is a good king with a bitter choice. We do him what kindness we can."

Rhoedd made his bitter choice and Hild left him in Pennrid with Laisrén, Morud, and Sintiadd, and rode for Stanegate. They would all meet up again in Caer Luel when Oswald came, between the full moon and the last quarter of Litha. She had planned to leave Gwladus in Pennrid also, to befriend Rhianmelldt, but Rhianmelldt remained in Caer Luel. And she might need Gwladus with them to hold Langwredd in line, keep her from getting them all killed.

The burns and streams and rivers already began to grow less thick and dark with runoff from the hills; by Thromilchi they would run clear. But Œstremonath in the high hills on either side of the wall could be treacherous: One day the sun shone, birds sang, and white stitchwort dotted the ground as a invitation to stop and sit a while; the next, lead-grey cloud slid over the brow of a hill in advance of a hard, cold north wind that turned the friendly pasture to bleak moorland.

When they could, they rode along the valley on the ancient track that the redcrests had widened and straightened and laid with stone. Stanegate was now the trading route and link between coasts. From the west coast of Rheged it ran up to Caer Luel, and from there east as far as Corabrig, the old redcrest fort that guarded the Dere Street crossing of the Tine and passage to the wall. From there, traders could sail down the Tine to Tinamutha and the sea. But until Corabrig, the only route for trade from the west was Stanegate.

Here at its lowland western end, the road seemed wider and less forbidding than when she had last ridden this way as a child—but when she had last ridden it, the days had been shrinking and the winter drawing in. Now the days were lengthening, the grass darkening and strengthening; and now when they rode they could carry less fodder, for these lowlands and foothills were lush. Coelfrith began to look less worried, and sometimes even smiled. Also, growing season last year had ended late and this year was come early, and farms—those in the west that had so far evaded Cadwallon—could be persuaded to part with fodder for silver and a promise of protection. When they could, the farmers shared their news, and Langwredd or Luftmær would share a song—and Hild's gesiths would share rougher songs when the folk believed she was not listening. Her Fiercesomes—and her Hounds, and now her boars—knew she was always listening, was always aware of what folk said, even when they whispered in dark corners; they knew she could read the air and understand the birds who brought news from afar. They told the folk of her power, her cunning wit, her uncanny luck.

"See this?" Dudda, who had been idly shaking his cup and dice, pointed to the thick gold band pushed high up on his scarred arm. "I got that in Cath Llew's service. Because why? Because those who fight for her always win. She's powerful luck and it rubs off on those around her."

The rough farmer—young and strong with muscles like a bull calf—snorted, swallowed his ale, and flexed those plump muscles. "These are my luck, mate."

"Want to try your luck against mine?" Dudda shook the dice enticingly. "Tell you what, I'm so sure I can beat you three of five, I'll add this to the pot." He took off the ring and laid it on the board so that the rushlight shone luscious and rich on its fat curve. The farmer licked his lips. "And if you lose you tell me what I want to know. Yes?"

"Yes."

And Dudda would win—he always did, because when he played dice it had nothing to do with luck—and the farmer, or farrier, or herder would tell him everything he knew of Cadwallon.

This far west much of what they knew was rumour but Hild listened to everything Dudda—and Wulf, who people forgot could hear even though he could not speak, and Gwladus among the women, and Almund gossiping with the priests and old men—brought her, and pieced together the story. Over the winter Cadwallon had ravaged the countryside from Corabrig. Now he was far north of the wall, moving slowly back south down the Devil's Causeway, carrying the Iding treasure, stopping here and there to send men down unexplored tracks and take whatever they could from steadings they had missed the first time. His men—both those he had left at Corabrig and those with him on the Causeway—had begun to torture farmers as a matter of course: seeking every hoard from every hearth, no matter how small.

It was the same pattern Cadwallon had followed in York: Dig in to a large, fortified base, then send out foraging bands of a dozen or a score, set them loose to use the countryside as they would for a week or as much as ten days, then, when they returned with their spoils, divide some among his followers and keep the rest.

These bands terrorised the land, for no one knew where or when they would strike. The farmers and shepherds and cattle herders could not hide and hope the invaders would go away, for as one swollen-knuckled farmer said: We have to sow, we have to plant; and calves come when they're ready. And his thin-lipped wife said: Aye, and where would we go?

She asked them: How do Cadwallon's men ride? As they pleased, and out in the open, uncaring who saw them, for no one could beat them; they thought northerners mere sheep. How do they fight? On horseback with sword and spear for the most part, small shields, more like bucklers. Bucklers were good to bat aside a slung stone or hurled hammer, for they'd not faced a shield wall since Caer Daun and no chieftain here could field such a thing. Did folk ever resist? Sometimes, in ones and twos, foolish folk, or folk when they knew they would be killed anyway so why not? But, no, mostly folk ran. Though as the thin-lipped woman said: And then they're run down and killed anygate.

Did Cadwallon ever ride with them? No one knew—unless he was the giant brute with the great bronze war hat? No, no, he was the mean black-haired one with the high-pitched laugh. Or red-headed. Or blind in one eye.

And then Hild would tell the headman or headwoman to bring together their people, and she would show them the great banner, the boar of the Yffings, and tell them that before harvest their land would be free again, safe under a strong king. And meanwhile she was here, and neither she nor her men would take, but would buy, and with good heavy silver. And any who brought her information about Cadwallon and his men—to her personally or to any man who rode under the lynx, the boar, or the butcherbird—would be well-rewarded. For good times, steady times, safe times, were coming when folk could once again sow and reap, herd and fatten in peace. There would be glee and gold, law and laughter, and no man, woman, or child need fear for their life or livelihood—save those who crossed her will. And then Luftmær or Langwredd, or Cuthred or Almund or some other would lift up their voice, and the frightened farmers would become a little braver, a little more hopeful, just for a while—though often, after Hild left, they would find themselves singing one of those songs in the fold or on the hill, and remember their bravery, and hope.

She began to remix and re-split her groups, looking for those that worked well together, that could speak British and Anglisc, who were a balance of daring and cautious, impetuous and patient in ways that suited the tasks she had in mind, with at least two trackers or scouts with fine mounts, at least one singer, and at least three good bowmen, until she had three bands, led by Oeric, Grimhun, and Coelfrith; men she trusted, steady men, well-blooded, who understood her goals and her thinking and could bend others to follow even when those followers did not understand. She gave them clear instructions, which she had them repeat back to her, and then questioned them until she was satisfied they understood the thinking behind them, and that if they had to change the plan—and they would, for no plan ever survived the first drawn sword—it would be towards the same purpose. Outside those groups she reserved her own, personal band who would travel north to the Bryneich: her Fiercesomes, Langwredd, and Gwladus. With the exception of Langwredd she trusted each of them with her life.

As Œstre Mass approached, they were at the place where the road and wall, marching side by side, were separated by the rush of the river Irthin. They began to climb, and climb again, higher into the hills every day, and came to a redcrest fort that was a mix of stone courses and wooden palisades. The chieftain, a proud man, called himself Artorius, count of the Wall, like his father before him and his father before that. Here they celebrated Œstre Mass. Mass was said by a British bishop, assisted by Almund, in a church that seemed like a cowshed from the outside but inside was dense with paintings. She wished there was more light; she wished Ceadwin could be there to see it.

At what passed for a feast afterwards, Artorius poured mead from a milky glass Roman jug—mead brought out specially for Hild Yffing; old mead, by the taste—and agreed that Hild Yffing, boar of Deira, could make free of his land to pass and repass, and that they each would aid the other against the godless fiend Cadwallon. He would allow two of his sons to ride with Hild's men as scouts, and if required they could introduce Hild—or, yes, to be sure, Hild's men riding with Oeric and Grimhun and Coelfrith—to other chieftains and head men and women along the way. And should she come back this way again in summer with a greater host, he might be willing to consider joining her with his hearthmen.

Artorius raised his glass. His lean, clean-shaven face—a Roman affectation, like that of Christ priests—flexed in an attempt at a smile but his black brows were canted up at the centre, and Hild knew he did not expect to ever have to make good his promise. He did not believe any new king in the north would sail into Caer Luel to rule them all. And, if he did, if he and the Yffing had the temerity to believe they could take on Cadwallon Bradawc, they would both be slaughtered out of hand; all their brave talk would end strangled in the mud and their fine gold around the brutish necks of the Gwynedd men. But meanwhile he would send his sons with her men because they could keep an eye on any dangerousness and slip away to report back to him when needed.

That night, Hild walked under a waning three-quarter moon, tired of being in a hall with men, where the very air was too thick as though too much of it had been squeezed into too small a space. She had a headache, and wanted a dip of cold, clear water to wash the foul taste of that ancient mead from her mouth. The farther she walked from the hall the quieter it grew; she began to breathe more deeply. Her headache faded. The scent of animals drew her; there would be a trough nearby. And as always when she walked on her own in the night air, she yearned to run, to ride, to get high up, high on a hill and feel air unbreathed by other lungs blow fresh and cold on her cheek.

She found herself humming the "Song of Baedd Coch" as she approached the byre, swinging her staff in time to the chorus: How she *ripped* up the ditch, how she *tore* down the wall, how she *beat* flat—

A woman cried out. Not a cry of pleasure.

Hild ran into the byre. A man had a woman pinned against a stall, three fingers hooked under her torn dress. He turned, mouth slack and eyes glazed.

"Off," she said. He blinked, licked his lips. One of her men. One of the Lindseymen. She tried to remember his name. A bowman . . . "Eadig."

She took a step forward, filled with the urge to rend this man with her bare hands, tear his muscles out by the root, one by one. He dropped his hand and put it behind his back.

She looked at the girl—a woman. Not old, not young. The soft cheeks of a cheese-maker. With the hunted look now of a hare trapped between two dogs. She took a breath, lowered her staff. "Are you hurt?"

The woman just held up her dress and swallowed and tried to see if anyone was behind Hild, anyone else to fear.

"I didn't hurt her, lady," Eadig said. "She's only—"

"Quiet." She stepped slowly to one side so the woman could see the door. "You may leave. No one will stop you. Or I can walk you to where you want to go." She was not sure the woman even heard her. "Eadig, step away from the woman. Another step. Take off your arm ring—now, Eadig." He did. "Throw it to me."

She caught it, stooped, laid it on the path to the door, then stepped farther out of the way.

"That's for you," she said to the woman in British. "For you," in Anglisc. "Later, we will make more reparation if you wish it."

The woman gave her an agonised look, then bolted, snatching the gilded bronze as she ran.

"Now," Hild said to Eadig. "What shall I do with you?"

He held out both hands. "Lady, I didn't mean to—"

"You just tripped over her in the byre with no one else about and tore her dress as she tried to stop you falling?"

"No. No. I just . . ." He trailed away to nothing.

Her head was hurting again and the taste of mead in her mouth was foul. She hawked and spat. "Draw your seax."

"Lady?"

"Draw your seax." She hefted her staff, swung it this way and that, humming the "Song of Baedd Coch." How she *ripped* up the dyke, how she *tore* down the wall . . .

"No, lady, please. I beg you. I beg your pardon. I don't know what—I didn't—"

"Draw your seax or I'll beat you to half to death and throw you to the pigs."

His shoulders bowed, then he straightened slowly. She was Baedd Coch. He had crossed her, broken her rule, and now she would punish him. He drew his knife with the calm of the hopeless.

"Lady!"

She turned: Coelfrith, and behind him Gwladus. "He needs a beating," she said.

"No doubt, lady. But kings don't do their own beating."

"But he *needs* beating."

Coelfrith said to Eadig, "Throw down your blade and kneel. Don't move, don't speak while your betters talk."

Everything seemed a long way off. Eadig obeyed and she watched as Gwladus stepped past her—perhaps the only one who would be brave enough, she thought distantly—and picked up the seax. She became aware of noise outside: men gathering. She blinked and the world snapped back into place.

"Lady—"

She held up her hand and Coelfrith stopped. "You're right. He's one of yours?"

"Mine, lady," Grimhun said. Next to him Wulf and Dudda. And Oeric. Were they all here?

"Assemble the men by the hall." Oeric left. "Gwladus, my respects to Artorius and we'll be punishing this man immediately. We'll make reparation to both the woman and to Artorius as her lord as he sees fit. We'd welcome him as witness but this is a matter for me and my men. Give Grimhun the blade."

She nodded for Wulf and Dudda to watch the man—to protect him if necessary from any of the woman's kin—then said to Grimhun and Coel-frith, "With me."

Outside the men were already leaving to assemble by the hall. "Coelfrith, I thank you. Grimhun, you'll punish him."

"Do you have a suggestion, lady?"

"He's your man."

Coelfrith said, "In Lindum, my father once struck off the right hand of a man who hurt a woman."

"We're not in Lindum," she said. "We're on the war trail. Eadig's a bowman?"

Grimhun nodded. "My best. Was the woman much hurt?"

"No. Shocked, frightened, a torn dress."

"Bowmen need two hands," Coelfrith said.

"But not all their fingers," Grimhun said slowly, and nocked an invisible arrow on an invisible bow, and pulled. He held out both hands, palm down and fingers spread, undecided.

"This one." Hild tapped the finger next to the little finger on his right hand. "About here." Just above the second knuckle. "He can still draw a bow, still hold a sword, but every time he strokes himself he'll be reminded not to touch an unwilling woman. Before you cut, wash the hand in vinegar, and heat the knife in a flame. I'll give you bee glue for the wound. Wrap it well and tell him to keep it clean and he'll be shooting again in a week."

Afterwards, Coelfrith came to find her. "Lady, a king's burdens are heavy."

"I'm not a king."

"Lady, your pardon, but until Oswald Brightblade comes, who else is there?"

"I'm not a king!"

Coelfrith said nothing, in the way people said nothing to their king when everyone knew the king was wrong.

She sighed. "Speak."

"Kings need a way to release their burden. Some kings fight, some kings fuck, some kings drink. Every king needs something."

"Even my uncle?" She never saw him fuck and only once drunk.

"Edwin king liked a wager."

"He did?" She had had no idea.

"Vast sums. To make it matter, he said. And afterwards, for a while, his heart was eased and his thoughts clear."

Gambling. She did not care for gambling.

"Find something, lady. Find it soon."

She walked to her tent in a bad temper. It was the largest tent, and in the centre of the camp, surrounded by iron cressets and burning torches that were not put out until she nodded to whoever was guarding her that night. Gwladus had her own tent, but often did not bother to set it up, and instead shared with Hild. She was there tonight, humming and combing her hair.

Hild stripped her weapons and gold, unbraided her hair, pulled her fingers through it, and started to loosely braid it again. Gwladus watched her.

"What?"

"You're not going to comb it?"

"It takes too long."

"If you don't comb it every day you'll have to wash it—which takes even longer. You should have kept Sintiadd; a king doesn't comb her own hair."

If Hild had been holding a comb she would have thrown it. "I'm not a fucking king! I don't want to be a fucking king! Kings die. With a sword in their hand if they're lucky and a sword at their neck if they're not."

"Ah."

"Ah? What do you mean, ah?"

"Is that what you're afraid of, dying?"

"I'm not going to die!"

"Then what is it you're afraid of?"

Hild stared at her. "I'm not afraid." Was she?

Gwladus stood and came to Hild's pallet. "Move over. I'm going to comb your hair for you—just this once." She settled behind Hild and began the familiar, soothing rhythm.

"I'm not afraid," Hild said. It was easier to talk when Gwladus could not see her face. "Or not of dying."

"Of losing?"

"Not—no. Or not exactly. I worry I'll do it all wrong. Make the wrong choice—the wrong guess, the wrong decision at the wrong time."

"You have counsellors."

"You sound like Brona."

"Then Brona's right."

"Counsellors help." She had wanted Brona's counsel, but she'd just shrugged and said, *That's not for me to say.* For a woman so curious about how bodies worked she had no interest in other patterns or how things worked together. "But after everyone's finished talking they all look at me, trusting as kittens at their mother's teat, and they wait."

"Why shouldn't they trust you?"

"It's the way they look at me, all easy, thinking, Oh, the lady knows, the lady'll get it right. And I'm so tired of always having to be right."

"You can't always be right."

"You think I don't know that?"

"Then stop having to always be right." She worked on a knot for a while.

Hild turned that in her mind, this way and that. She was no longer a child with the weight of the world on her shoulders, pretending to see the future and read wyrd just so she could stay alive. "But men follow me because they believe I'm more than I seem."

"Once, perhaps. Now they follow you because you are exactly what you seem: a woman who wins. They follow you because you take care of them, because they get fed and their horses are fed—because they *have* horses."

"That's more Coelfrith's do—ow."

"Sorry. Keep still." She worked the teeth of the comb gently in the lower edge of the knot, tugged the strands free, moved up a little, did it again. "And yes, Coelfrith's a good reeve; the best. He served the overking. Then he fled. But he came back to serve you, Hild Yffing. Why? He knows what a king's for and what a king does. And he thinks that's you. No one expected Edwin king to know what others couldn't—they expected him to be the best king, to find the best people, get the best counsel, and make the best guesses."

Hild thought about it. Edwin didn't need to be uncanny and other-worldly, just the best king. So that's what she should do. But how?

The knot was gone and the endless rhythm of comb-and-lift returned.

"Lady, Hild, you should just lead and stop worrying about being so seamless. You can afford to lose your temper a little, get drunk a little, boast, or laugh at a pretty girl's joke. Be a person. Behave as a person would. You're not a god. You don't have to pretend anymore that you're a seer and godmouth because that's the only way to make them listen. These men and women know who you are: Hild Yffing, Butcherbird, Cath Llew, red boar of Deira. They know you eat and fuck and shit and sneeze, just like them. And they love you for it."

She thought about it for a while. Gwladus was right—maybe she was right.

"There." Gwladus lifted her hair in one heavy mass, smoothed it down her back. "I'll braid it for you."

She half drowsed as Gwladus separated the hair and deftly wove the hanks, tied the thong.

Gwladus tugged her braid gently. "Don't go to sleep. It's your turn to braid mine. And if you don't want to take turns, next time we stop you should find a girl and pay her to do it for you."

She turned around and Hild turned to face Gwladus's back.

"You should find some escape," Gwladus said.

"That's what Coelfrith said. He told me my uncle wagered. I hate wagers."

"What do you like?"

"I want to be on my own. I want not to think about another man, woman, or beast." And as she combed the heavy golden hair she talked of riding in the hills, of watching eagles, of the furze in bloom and the wind in her face. She talked and talked, combed and combed, long after all the knots were gone.

Two days later they moved north of the wall.

The first thin moon of Thromilchi was just risen in a black sky scudding with silvery clouds. Hild stood on the hillside listening to the rushing burn, Flýte like a shadow beside her. When the faint moonlight caught an eddy it gleamed like fresh-cut lead; in the daylight Hild thought it might be thick and brown with a dirty cream froth; it had rained in the hills a day ago. It was not a wide stream but it was fierce—easy enough to jump over for a horse; easy enough, too, to lose footing in and drown; she could tell by the sound it was deep.

Some way behind her, a bit chinked—the only sound to give away the presence of men and women, mounted and ready.

And still Hild waited, listening, scenting the wind. The clouds were thickening. Soon even that sliver of moon might be hidden, and it might rain. She wanted it to rain. Rain hid the tiny sounds of men creeping through the furze and the twang of bowstring and thump of arrow.

She had two dozen—Grimhun's men and her Fiercesomes. The band they hunted numbered half that, but she wanted her people to come through not just victorious but unscathed.

Laughter drifted on the wind from the large farmstead over the brow of the next hill, followed by a drawn-out cheer. She turned, pointed east, waited for the glimmer that was Grimhun's nod, pointed north, heard the churr of a nightjar that was Leofdæg, and Gwladus took Flýte's reins and patted Hild's shoulder. Hild bent low and began to run up the hillside.

Cadwallon's man, staggering outside for a piss with his stick in hand, grunted and stared at the arrow sprouting from his belly. He opened his mouth but before he could find out whether he would have bellowed defiance or cried for his mother, Bryhtsige thrust a blade up under his chin and through his tongue and the roof of his mouth and eased him to the ground.

On the other side of the steading she heard the *twang-thump* of another bow—Tole, the woman from the south steading—then another. Then the sound she had been waiting for, the shattering neigh of a stallion as Gladmær cut the picket line and whipped a row of rumps. Men came tumbling and roaring from the farmstead, right into a hail of arrows. Half went down just as the rain began. No more bow work; now it was the turn of Hild and her men.

Their eyes were adjusted to the dark; they were ready. They were not lust drunk, ale drunk, or blood drunk. They had trained for this. It was fast and brutal, then Hild was inside with her Fiercesomes shouting for everyone to kneel, kneel, killing one man, two, who did not hear or had no time to obey. And then there was just Hild, her men, and what remained of Cadwallon's band—just one man, tangled in bedclothes, lying on the floor, a smear of blood on his cheek.

It was not his blood. She had only to look past him to the bed nook to see that.

Torches flared everywhere as Dudda moved from wall to wall, flame in one hand, bloody seax in the other—they had not even needed their swords.

Hild moved to the centre of the long low room, huge in her furs, head brushing the roof.

She looked around. Said to Wulf, "Gag him. Tie him. Don't hurt him too much to talk."

She said to a youngster—just a boy, really—cringing against the bench along the far wall. "Whose steading is this?"

"My—my da's."

"Where is he?"

He shook his head, started to tremble.

"Your mother?"

He was shuddering now, looking at her, at the hideous men surrounding him. She looked around. "Someone go find Gwladus. Tell her to get here as she can. Bryhtsige."

Oddly, in this reeking hell place Bryhtsige seemed quite ordinary, and he looked like the very image of the perfect warrior: tall, beautiful, tidy. "Give that boy a hot drink. Some bread and honey if you can find it. Stoke the fire, sit with him until Gwladus comes. If we can't find anyone else he'll have to tell us what we need to know."

The dead men, stripped of gold and weapons, were lying in a heap in the rain. Nine of them. With the leader tied up inside there was one missing.

Grimhun rode into the enclosure, dismounted, rain streaming down his face. "We found the trail."

Hild went with him to the trail: dark and smeared. She knelt, touched it, sniffed at her fingers: garlic. "His guts opened. He'll die before dawn."

No one to take word back to Cadwallon: this scavenging party would just disappear; rumours would start to spread.

"Horses?"

"Ten—one broke its leg falling in the burn."

"Can you save some of it?" She wiped her face with a forearm. Meat from one horse would feed the surrounding farms for a week.

"Some."

"See to it."

Inside, Dudda had wrapped the thing that had been the boy's mother in the bed furs and laid her out straight. The boy had Gwladus's cloak around his shoulders and was sipping something that steamed. She raised her eyebrows at Gwladus, who shrugged: She'd got what little she could. Hild tilted her head to the byre: *Go tuck him up, keep him out of the way for what comes next.*

She sat on a stool by the hearth, drinking her own mead from her own cup, a small boar banner hung from the wall behind her. She would not touch anything Cadwallon's men had fouled.

Grimhun gave her a report of his men: one with a broken foot—stepped in a badger sett; he could still ride—otherwise no injuries. He listed the horses, weapons, weight of gold. She whistled soundlessly. It was an enormous spoil to take from just eleven men: what one might expect from eleven petty kings—and none of it had to be shared with anyone but her people. The amount Cadwallon held in his treasure rooms must be staggering.

Gwladus came in, warmed herself at the fire. "The boy's asleep. I found a dairymaid and her son hiding out there, so she'll look after him. She tells me half the folk ran off. Cadwallon's men were planning to hunt them down tomorrow. She thinks she could lead us to most of them, but she's not sure she could persuade them to come back."

"We'll get them back: Promise them a tithe of the spoil and a good roast of horse. And Cadwallon's men won't be troubling them anymore."

"I'll see to it."

She nodded her thanks. Her own task was less pleasant.

Cadwallon's man was going to die, he knew that, but she told him it would be fast and clean if he answered her questions fully and truthfully—truthfully, mind: She would check his answers with the boy, and of course he knew her reputation.

It might keep him honest after a fashion, after she discounted the boasting.

Were there any other bands nearby?

"We're the most westerly," he said. "For we're Cadwallon's most trusted—"

Least important, more like.

Two other bands were farther east, and three in Corabrig with the treasure. Of course any fool could guard treasure in a fort.

Cadwallon himself?

He'd be back in Corabrig before the moon's first quarter.

How often did he send men out once the fort was fully occupied? And how many, usually, in a band?

All the time: They always needed food, and men got bored if they had nothing to do. Boys would be boys, eh? Numbers in a band varied—he had a bigger group than most because he was the best, and his men brought back the most gold.

She discounted that, and guessed ten to a dozen was usual.

How long did the bands stay out?

Three days, a week, more. It was not unusual for a band to be gone ten days.

And how long had he been out?

Four days. He had good men, good horses; they rode like the wind.

She had time, then, before they would be missed.

Then she started asking questions about lookouts and scouts, horse numbers and men. Even accounting for boasting, his answers made her thoughtful: bigger numbers than she had planned for. Last Christmastide Cadwallon had invited Bernician thegns to join him; of those who refused, he tortured and murdered two—children and wives first—and others had then found it sensible to throw in their lot with him, and hope. She wondered how loyal those men would be when Cadwallon began to lose, but did not ask: A man like this could know nothing of an honourable man's loyalty, despair, and terrible choices.

She questioned him about their armour and weapons, the number of bows, bundles of arrows, throwing spears, and thrusting spears. Horses and horseshoes. Fodder. How much food did they have in the event of a siege? He answered readily enough—he was not sure why she asked and so did not know which way to bend the truth.

Would Cadwallon be sending men south of the wall for raids?

Only on Stanegate trade—there was nothing left worth picking south of that—and even so not till Litha when the trickle of spring trade swelled to a summer flood and the takings would be worth the work.

At which point she smiled—that terrible hard dry flex of the jaw the men who had fought with her would recognise—stood, and punched him in the forehead, hard, with the iron-shod heel of her staff. He would never feel anything again; more than he deserved.

"If he's still alive, cut his throat." She stretched and yawned; she could feel morning in her bones. "I'm going to get some air, then sleep. Wake me when the steaders are back—make sure the boar flies in the yard where frightened folk can see it. We'll stay here one more night and be on our way tomorrow." She wanted the locals to know who was saving them.

Her Fiercesomes had seen her fight before, but the men who had now seen her fight for the first time fell silent when she passed, and assumed the worshipful look she hated, but it would pass, and at least they were leaving her alone.

She was standing near the main door, leaning on her staff, looking north, when two men came the long way around from the long house, nodded respectfully, and flung the leader's body on top of the heap; his throat gaped widely at the sky. It was a beautiful pink and blue dawn, a perfect Thromilchi morning. Everything was beginning to fall into place.

And the whisper went around her men: Baedd Coch had smiled at the coming dawn. Good luck lay ahead.

It took them a day and a half to track the first of the easterly bands, and she watched as her Fiercesomes and Oeric's men took them neatly, the only cost being one torn ear and a gashed horse flank. The horse would have plenty of time to heal, for they had many spare horses now. And the man with the bloody ear stood to reap so much gold from his part of the fight that he would willingly give up another ear, and cheap at the price. And now Cadwallon was down nearly two dozen men, and she had lost none, and soon the men in the fort would begin to wonder what ill luck had befallen their friends who had disappeared unseen and unheard.

The third enemy band was the biggest, just north of where the Alen, the lowest western tributary of the South Tine, was joined by its own tributary. It was closer to Corabrig than she had ventured so far, even as Cadwallon was moving nearer to the wall. And time was getting short: She had to move north. Yet Coelfrith's band was unblooded and she needed to know all three bands could work well while she was gone.

She called Coelfrith to her tent. "It's a big band." Fifteen riding together and two ranging wide. Difficult to contain. "Your thoughts?" They did not want Cadwallon getting clear news of an enemy yet. Unease, yes; rumour, definitely. Uncertainty was their friend.

"Big but heavily laden," he said. "With baggage horses moving slowly.

Also, they're overconfident. We—one of Artorius's boys—watched one of their outriders for half a morning and the man showed little caution. But they can move fast."

Leofdæg had given her the same report. He also told her Artorius's two sons were skilled and he would trust their reports.

"I want that gold and I want those men taken off Cadwallon's side of the scale. But more than that I need no firm word of us to reach Corabrig. They're many, and it's difficult country. But you know your men; it's your choice."

"The men believe luck's on our side, lady."

"And you?"

"We don't need luck. We're the men of Baedd Coch." But he looked worried.

Leading all his men and half of Grimhun's, plus all their bowmen, Coelfrith took Cadwallon's men and baggage train. Not one enemy escaped, but one of her men died, another would never fight again, and one was only saved by the quick thinking of Tole, who whipped her bowstring around his leg in time to stop him bleeding white.

She told Coelfrith he had done well. He had: It was open country, impossible to conceal horses, and on foot men were at a disadvantage against mounted fighters. If Cadwallon's men had included bowmen it would have been much worse. But Cadwallon seemed to be keeping his bowmen to defend the fort.

"We need more bows." Ambushing men was less dangerous from a distance.

The heavy baggage was mostly food but the weight of the dead men's weapons and jewels and decorated horse harness was, if anything, greater than before.

By the full moon, when it became clear that one-fifth of his war band had vanished, Cadwallon would become very worried indeed. And the food would be a sore loss; it meant he would have to send another party out soon. And that party would already be uncertain, nervous—

Hild set up the great standard among her tents in a local worthy's pasture. She divided half the food among those who came: She was their loaf giver. She gave them small shiny geegaws and she gave them a feast, with much singing. And among the folk she sent her people, asking for bow-men and bowwomen, and for news of traders.

They gained two more bowmen—though one was barely more than a boy—and Hild took Tole into her small band and spent half a day selecting for Tole's use the two best horses from those they had taken. The archer would have to keep a brutal pace through some of the harshest country in the north.

All her people were blooded now; all knew her plan and her timing. They were ready for her to leave them.

The next day, she took her Fiercesomes, young Cuthred, and three women north.

34

✛

WHERE THE IRTHIN ROSE THEY CAMPED among broken stone walls outside a steading that, in Deira, she might have thought a ruined shieling. Here, on this poor land, it was the dwelling place of a headman of standing. Everything was small—the people, the huts, the hill ponies and little wild cattle—and their tongue, too, was wild, an ancient thorny branch of British that even Hild and Gwladus had to listen carefully to understand, and Langwredd only understood as easily as she did by virtue of her people of Calchfynydd having a long association with those who once called themselves Arfderydd. As for Tole, Cuthred, and the Fiercesomes, they caught no more than one word in ten. The headman's son spoke what he thought of as Anglisc but his accent was so thick it took some time to hear it as such. Once they did, though—partway through comparing one man's rough iron knife to Hild's fine seax—they understood readily enough.

These wild folk had heard there was a mad marauding king about, north of the wall, but no, they'd neither seen nor heard hide nor hair of the creature, though they heard tell of a travelling smith who had heard, up Luseburna way, of terrible trouble. And, aye, they could show them the way. But did they know that was the edge of Bryneich land, and did they truly want to mess with those cursed fiends?

Langwredd assured them she was well with those fiends, and would they like to hear a song, at all, of Cath Llew? And, oh yes, they said. For they had heard of Cath Llew and her Fiercesomes, Cath Llew who frightened even the Bryneich beasts, and who had sworn their princeling to a blood oath on a fairy hill . . .

And as the dark drew in and the firelight flickered, Hild, huge in her furs, loomed larger, her gold gleamed brighter, and the hideous scars on the faces of her men grew deep as the seams of Annwn. But Langwredd began to sing, using some of the wild thorny sounds almost forgotten since her youth, and Hild brought out a precious jar of Menewood mead, and soon the wild hillmen began to think themselves living in a tale of the other world, where fairies once again came up out of the hill only this time to bless them and their line unto the seventh generation, and fairy luck would rain fat calves and fine oats season after season, their sons would grow strong and their daughters sleek as seals. And to Cath Llew they added the name of Baedd Coch, friend to the people of the north.

Valley by valley, riding and sometimes leading their mounts over the high hills, sometimes escorted by the people of the hills and introduced to their neighbours, sometimes not, they moved deeper into Bryneich territory, always north, avoiding the war street and other travelled roads farther east. In this sparsely peopled land, and as part of a band of ten, and all moving to the same purpose, Hild was easy, happy; not badgered from every side. But as they moved north, the war street began to draw closer, and then it was only twenty miles away.

That night, the nightingales did not sing; bad weather was coming. The next day, near the head of the Lidel Water, not far from the very tip of the North Tine, where the valley was high and turned in a great curve against a wall of rock, Hild called an early halt. Today, rather than secure their tents with short iron pegs, they would dig into the hillside a little to shelter from the wind, weight their tent edges with stones, and use leather cords to tie down to this bush—pointing to the stunted elderberry straggling over the slope—and to this one. Langwredd grumbled, but everyone else set to with a will; the lady had a reason for everything she did.

Mid-dig, Gladmær hissed and stepped back: a skull, an old skull with an arrow point buried in it. Hild took it and set it on top of the rise: Let the fallen man see the sunset one more time. Then Hild found a tangle of bones—at least two people, still with a belt buckle here, a broken blade there—and Tole found half a skeleton, whose backbone had been half cut and half bludgeoned.

Battle, Wulf signed. *Big one.* He looked around. *Move?*

"No. The north wind's coming. If you find bones, lay them out with kindness, and tomorrow we'll decide what to do."

Even as they laid the bones in rows the wind began to turn to the north, and before sunset Hild smelt snow. In her tent she turned a blackened bit of silver in one hand and spooned up her pottage with the other.

"What's that?" Gwladus said.

Hild tossed it. Gwladus caught it. "A belt buckle?"

"A belt plate, I think. But look at the engraving."

Gwladus peered at it. "A cricket?" She turned it the other way. "A bird?"

Hild nodded. "A raven. The Iding's totem is a raven."

An Iding battle, many years ago, but she did not know who with, or who had won, or what omen this portended.

She woke a little after moonrise to slanting sleet. She listened for a while, half dreaming of the battle, the ripple of the purple raven banner, and became aware just before she fell asleep again that the sleet had become rain to wash the bones clean.

From then on, the weather steadied, and as they began to descend towards the Tefeged valley nightingales once again sang every night. Now, too, they were moving into Bryneich heartland, and the people they encountered were taller, more brightly dressed, and proud. Now Langwredd announced herself at every stop—she was looking well, Hild thought; she had gained muscle weight, and seemed happy—and introduced Hild, the Yffing who had sworn kinship with the foully murdered Prince Cuncar. She declared that Bryneich's enemies were Hild Yffing's enemies, and it was time to rise, rise once again to greatness!

Now they encountered young bloods with reason to hate Anglisc—all Anglisc—and who resented their gold and their huge horses, their fine blades and bright banners.

The first time it was just muttering, a hot-eyed fingering of blades once the heather beer was drunk. Hild gave no sign she had heard them, even as their comments grew louder and more pointed, but later—in her tent, now raised to its splendid height and flying the boar from its top pole—she ground her teeth and found herself longing to crack skulls. She turned restlessly. There was no time for this. They had less than a month before she was back in Caer Luel and she did not want to be wasting it on these fools. Perhaps a few cracked skulls was what they needed. But kings do not crack their own heads.

"For pity's sake," Gwladus said. "Keep still and let me sleep."

"I can't."

"Then go for a walk up a hill!"

"Not that." Because by now the young bloods would be drunk and would not be turned aside by soft words or pretended deafness. And it would not do to kill the local chieftain's kin.

Eventually she slept but the next day she was bad-tempered, and suffered a particularly tedious meeting with the headman and his counsellors. Why, yes, they said; they understood that Cadwallon needed killing, but didn't see why they should help. Yes, yes, of course they understood that once Oswald was king he could crush them with tithes if he was displeased, but, well, he wasn't king yet, was he? And then, why should they help her help him win so he could become king and crush them with tithes?

So she had to explain, again, allowing no hint of impatience, that if they did help her to help him to win, she could assure them their tithe would be reasonable—perhaps they might even gain some reparation. After all, the dead Iding was Oswald's half brother, and the Iding's foolhardiness had got their fine Bryneich prince and princeling murdered; Oswald Lamnguin owed them blood price. And, too, would they not prefer to be ruled by their own princely heir than lorded over by some Irish-speaking Anglisc thegn?

But the prince and princeling are dead, they said. So she had to explain, again, that the woman who had spoken yesterday, Langwredd—they remembered Langwredd?—was a proud woman of the Calchfynydd, chief wife to Coledauc, and mother of two young, strong sons in whom the blood of Coledauc and the heroes of the Bryneich ran rich and red. Those sons were safe in Deira under her personal protection. At which point they wiped their moustaches and murmured among themselves and said they might, just might, let Langwredd address them again about this, but that they would not be hurried.

Hild gritted her teeth, found Langwredd, hissed at her to make it happen, and make it happen now, shoved her in the chief's tent, and flung herself on Flýte's back, without waiting for a saddle, and went flying into the hills for hours at a pace that might have made the Wild Hunt stare.

This happened over and again. On these nights Gwladus slept in her own tent, or shared with Tole and Langwredd, for Langwredd was often not there, and Hild would come back when the torches were flaring, stride to the Fiercesomes' fire—drink a cup, make sure all was well, and take a report—and go to bed with orders to not be disturbed.

Gradually, as they moved closer to Calchfynydd, Hild could feel the tide turning. More often now they rode into a camp and the young men were wearing their war gold, and waiting, and the older men began to hear her argument more quickly. But now she began to be badgered again—questions from women worried about their sons, fathers wanting to tell her their thoughts on battles past, grandmothers wondering if this Cadwallon was really as bad as people said, headmen wishing assurances and guarantees—and her men could see impatience burning like wildfire in their lady's bones. She rode more often; she rode most nights. And the Fiercesomes and Tole and Gwladus took it in turns to see to it that Bone or Flýte was ready, and well-tended when she returned.

At one great camp near the Ettric Water, where two groups had come together with their cattle, and the young men and women were wild with spring and fresh company after a long winter in the hills, the talk was all of war, of who would join Baedd Coch and who would not. Some were talking rashly of turning their own tide: With the Anglisc occupied farther south, now would be the time to take Bryneich back, break the Anglisc yoke forever!

Wulf, Gladmær, and Bryhtsige were some distance from the lady's tent, telling the young bloods, and some not so young, of the lady's prowess. There was laughter, sometimes boasting. *Baedd Coch doesn't sleep, she waits!* Groans. Shushing for attention, then, *Cath Llew's not afraid of the dark, the dark is afraid of Cath Llew!* Appreciative hoots. Then, *Ha, I've got one: Wights tell Cath Llew stories around the fire!*

Dudda sat at another fire with Leofdæg, who sat quietly, whetting his blade, looking up every now and again for signs the lady might be returning from her ride, while Dudda threw dice, challenging all to try their luck—which he did now mostly when the lady was away; she did not like him to win too much. Eventually the sound of dice lured the son of the top chief to Dudda's fire, and Dudda, seeing his distinctive, oiled-brass hair, offered him a taste of mead. They played without hurry, talking as much as throwing, Dudda letting the young man win just enough to stay interested.

The son had fought his first skirmish in some cattle raid or other last autumn—before Cadwallon had burnt Yeavering; before any of them knew the men of Gwynedd had crossed the wall, when Coledauc was still their prince, and still playing one alliance off another. He was very interested in the lady. Who was she?

Why, she's the niece of Edwin Overking, lord-as-was of all the north. She was his seer: She could see around corners and hear the dead.

"And you," the boy said. "Why do you follow her?"

Dudda tapped the thick armband around his biceps. "For this."

"Gold," the boy said dismissively. He was Adair ab Beatan, son of Beatan the Mighty. He would have gold soon enough.

"And this." Dudda drew his sword and handed it to the boy hilt first.

Adair tilted it this way and that so that hot firelight ran back and forth on the patterned blade, pouring up and down the blood runnel like molten gold.

"It's a fine blade," Dudda said. "But finer still is the chance to match it with a worthy foe." He sheathed it again. "I fight for the lady because she will never lie to you, and she never loses. I fight for her because she weaves wyrd like other women weave cloth."

Adair rattled the dice in the cup and threw. Fours. "A woman, you say. I've heard otherwise."

Dudda scooped the dice into the cup. "She's a woman like none you've known. A woman who gave birth in a battle and still had enough milk not only for her own bairn but another, and she took that bairn to foster." He shook the cup. "She's a woman who can ride any horse, climb any tree"—he threw—"and persuade any man she is right." The boy was rapt—which made it easier to flick over the second die to a three. "Oh," he said. "You win again."

The boy's eyes gleamed in the firelight. "I thought you said the lady's luck was unbeatable?"

"It is. It always is, in the end." He held out the cup, but before the boy could take it they heard the drum of hooves, and with a swirl and sway of flame in the wind of her passing, Hild Yffing thundered into the camp.

The boy watched, slack-jawed, as the lady, wild and sweaty, big and brilliant, and so shiningly alive her laugh might raise the dead, threw Flýte's reins to Leofdæg, exchanged a joke with Gladmær, slapped Bryhtsige on the shoulder, called to Dudda, "Don't ruin the boy!," and strode into her tent.

Dudda hoped the boy would breathe soon but he understood the feeling well enough. He still remembered his first sight of her on the dock at York, big with child and huge in her furs.

"That's a fine horse," the boy managed eventually, lips parted and wet. "Such power to ride."

"The lady rides only mares," Dudda said, straight-faced.

The boy looked at him. "Truly, she doesn't . . . ? Only mares?"

Dudda nodded regretfully. Clearly the heart had gone out of the boy for more dice, but by now he needed no more convincing of the lady's luck; he would follow her anywhere. "So, Adair, son of Beatan, you'll fight with us against Cadwallon Bradawc?"

"I will."

"The lady will want only the best."

"I will kill the Twisting Treacher myself! What does he look like?"

"No one knows," Dudda said. "Except Bryhtsige over there. Hoi!" He waved Bryhtsige over. "I warn you, though, he won't talk about it."

Later, he saw the boy talking to a young woman who was his very spit, even to the colour of the hair, and the eyes of the woman—his sister?—kindled as she glanced at the lady's tent. He thought no more of it until dawn the next day when he stumbled outside to piss. The same young woman was creeping from the lady's tent holding her shoes, and looking thrilled and dazed as a stripling who had challenged a hero to a game of knife throwing and won. And for the next two days the lady smiled often, listened more, and was sometimes heard to sing.

A dozen well-mounted Bryneich rode with them to the Twid valley, where they raised the red boar and progressed down the Devil's Causeway, sending outriders to every Anglisc vill to tell them that the Yffing called them to arms—not to fight Oswald Brightblade, but to join him. They would meet on the site of the shameful slaughter of Brightblade's brother, the Iding, and Coledauc ab Morcant. And, further, she did not care who wore a cross and who a hammer, for this was a matter of honour, not god. And she wanted not just fighting men, but older men, sturdy women, even some strong youth. They did not need weapons—they would be in no danger, for she needed Bradawc to see only the mass of their support from afar—and if they could but get to the place she would name, they would ride fine horses—some of which they might keep.

It was late morning of the new moon of Litha, not yet risen, when Hild rode into the great camp north of Artorius's hall at the head of eleven others—most of her own band, and two more, one Anglisc and one Bryneich, younger sons who had refused, on their honour, to leave her side. She had been of two minds, particularly with Yrre, son of Hunric of Melmin, whom she had never liked, but then she realised that if she could learn the ways of this young man—her own age—then she would have a window into those she needed to persuade. And Adair she took for his sister's sake.

Adair ab Beatan looked about, bewildered. "Is it a horse fair?"

"Look at those beasts!" Yrre, son of Hunric, said. The Deiran horses—even with one band out, there were over a hundred—and the captured beasts, now doubled in number, were picketed in row after row of strong, well-fed backs. "It's like a royal herd."

Hild half listened but she was looking in many places at once. Carts, good. Two women sorting what looked like brightly coloured clothes—oh, very good. Captured weapons—not as many as she would have liked but enough; just one gleaming point per rider would be enough.

She sat with Coelfrith, Oeric, and Grimhun on a stool around the battered camp table set up to one side of her tent, and took reports. They had riders and lookouts at every point north and south of Stanegate from Caer Luel to here, and, east from here, hidden watchers at every high point with a view of Dere Street, north and south, and Corabrig.

Cadwallon was in the fort; he was likely nervous. He had lost men; his supplies were running low. There was no trade on the road.

In one bloody clash—and they were getting bloodier, Grimhun said, for now Cadwallon and his men were wary; they knew there was another, unseen force shadowing them—two of Cadwallon's men had escaped. Either that or someone had miscounted.

"I don't miscount," Coelfrith said. "Nor my men."

She clapped him on the shoulder. "It would be a sad thing for a reeve to miscount!" They were getting tense. She felt it herself: soon now, very soon. "So. Cadwallon knows someone is here—which is no more than he guessed a fortnight ago. They would've seen no tokens?"

Both shook their heads. They did not ride against Cadwallon with banners. It was the second-most important command: No solid word of who or how many was to reach Cadwallon until she was ready. Whispers, yes: Uncertainty bred fear; fear bred a weakening of the strong bonds formed from a year of fighting together. And they needed those certainties loosened.

"And now he knows he has an enemy, a real one of breath and blood and blade. Well enough."

"But we've made sure to stay off the track," Oeric said, breathing its name as though it were holy. And in a way it was; much of their hope hinged upon it. "Except as you directed."

"Good." British-speakers only, arms and gold hidden, and riding hill ponies—nothing taller than a dozen hands. It was her first and strictest command. She needed Cadwallon to think that track unknown and untouched by his enemy.

"We've chosen the ones to play trader?" she asked Grimhun.

He nodded. She could rely on his judgement.

"The Bernician Anglisc and Bryneich know their role," she said. Or as much as they needed to. It was not safe for them to understand the whole of the plan, only that some must appear to be herders and traders—and indeed some were—while others from a distance would glitter with bits of metal to resemble an approaching war band. "They're waiting on the connecting road one mile east of Dere Street."

The pieces were moving to their places.

She looked at them one by one. "It will work. Langwredd's with them; she'll keep them steady." And Gwladus would keep Langwredd steady, with Cuthred to help. He had shown an unexpected knack for soothing Langwredd. "They may still need reminding to gather north of Portgate but not to enter until it's time. And even with good horses they'll take at least two days to get to the Portgate. Don't shave it too close getting the horses to them."

"We won't, lady," Oeric said.

"And you understand—"

"We understand, lady."

She had been about to remind them of which groups would block Dere

Street south and north of Corabrig, and when, but they knew. Everyone knew their role but Oswald, and he would know soon.

She leaned back. "It will work," she said again. It would work if Cadwallon had not hidden more men than she knew in Corabrig. It would work if everyone moved to and from their appointed places at the appointed hour without being seen. If Cadwallon didn't double back. If he believed the rumours she was seeding—if people told the right stories at the right time. If she was right and his greed would drive him. If she could find the right place on the cavalry track . . .

But they were nodding. They had no doubts: Their lady had planned it; it would work.

Grimhun spoke now of the horses, then Coelfrith of their food caches, which were running low.

"How low?"

"Two months."

Hild nearly laughed; it was more than enough. In two months they would have won or died. Tomorrow, people would move once again along different paths. But today, they would feast.

It was an odd feast. A mix of ale and wine and mead, bought, brought, borrowed, stolen—and stolen back—along with good lamb and mutton, and hard bread to dip in hot, oniony pottage. But the sense of what was to come added more savour than any king's board. Not all gathered would live but perhaps most would, and those who did would tell the story for the rest of their days. All knew their part; many had a sense of the overall plan, but few had the whole; and none but the most trusted held the key. Every single one understood this was a turning point in all their lives.

It was early afternoon when Hild stood and Wulf banged the board three times for silence. The sky was scudding grey and wind whipped at Hild's furs as she looked around the mix of folk sitting at the boards and stumps and upturned barrels on the springy turf.

"Well-met," she said. "Well-joined. Well-come. For here today we are the heart of hope for our land. Look around you. Look at your neighbours. Remember their faces. For in years to come, when you sit by the fire with the little ones around you, they will be keen for every detail, untiring in their eagerness. They'll want to know about Yrre's bright pimples." Yrre's face flamed and people threw back their heads and shouted with laughter. "They will delight in the tale of Tole's endless farts." Now Yrre howled and clapped Tole on the back—everyone knew how she farted like a horse when she ate beans.

She picked this person out, and that, made them plain folk to each other, whether British or Anglisc, man or woman, bread baker or blade bearer. They were her people. They held common cause. Each held the others' lives in their hands.

She told them they would crush Cadwallon, crush him, bring a king back to the land, and the north would rise again to shine bright, brighter than the sun at noon, clearer than the moon and stars at night. "We will be the jewel in the crown of the whole isle," she said.

She filled her cup, lifted it. All around her women and men stood. The day seemed to dim.

"We are the people of the north. We will wrap like light around the darkness that is Cadwallon Bradawc and we will burn it from the land." Her shadow seemed to be fading. "To the north!"

"To the north!"

As they shouted the light dimmed now unmistakably: the cloud was not thickening but the day was dimming to dark, then darker still, and what light there was was ill and wrong. The shouts died into uneasy silence as the light thinned and faded and day turned to night.

Wind whipped at their feet, and grey cloud scudded away from where the moon, had it not been new and invisible, would have hung low in the sky. But where the moon should have been, where the sun should have been, was a black hole ringed in pale fire.

Hild's heart swelled and her mind roared. All around her people gasped. A man wailed—even as she tried to fit what she saw into her known world she realised she had never heard a man wail before.

"Hold!" she called in a voice to stop the heart. She held up both arms: bone, scar, muscle, gold, beads. "A sign! Even the sky sees you, Cadwallon Bradawc! The moon sees you, the sun sees you. They have come together as we have come together; and we have come together to come for you! We come to burn out your heart!"

And as she spoke the light began to return. They watched in silence as the sun overpowered the moon. As the light waxed, the moon once again faded. A child laughed, then a man, then they were all laughing as the sun blazed briefly, then was veiled once again in cloud.

They began: Trade returned to Stanegate; all along the great way farriers once again set up their forges and laid out their rasps and nails to shoe the heavily laden beasts walking the road. Malthouses smoked and alehouses opened; the booth shutters swung down and travel wares were set on the counter for sale or barter. To any but those with a very sharp eye all seemed usual enough, and any who stopped by the counter or the forge or fireside heard songs of Cath Llew and Baedd Coch, of slaughter in the hills. After the stories and songs, any strangers who queried the traders further, and even those who did not—for these part-time traders were a garrulous lot, having been mewed up in snow-fast farms all the winter and working like dogs to plant in the spring—heard that their wagons were empty but for bulk goods: Turnips, would your honour be interested in any turnips, very fine this year, though sadly the carrots were a mite wizened. The colewort, now, the colewort would have been good but, well, they old worms munched 'em right up. They'd hoped to trade this sad stuff for more pre-cious items at Walls End, or, aye, or even past it. Past it? Why, yes, your honour, all the way to Tinamutha itself if they had to; yes, they were that desperate for trade since that wicked Cadwallon had been preying upon them.

At Ridge Mill, by the ford east of where Dere Street crossed the Tine; at Hagustaldesham, south of the river just before it forked, just four miles west of Corabrig; and at Four Stones, just past where the mighty Tine forked north and south, Cadwallon's watchers began to hear, from those men driv-ing the almost empty wagons, stories of a great Yffing riding the wall, boasting that the men of Gwynedd were afraid to come face the boar of Deira. And Cadwallon's men would wonder about those bands of their own, disappeared without trace.

Cadwallon's men might perhaps have noticed that some of these traders were uncommonly strong with watchful eyes, their mounts strangely large and muscled for beasts of burden, but they were distracted, for this year the ale was better, and less grudgingly shared. And so the news Cad-wallon's men passed along was that perhaps attacks on trade should wait a month until the wagons began to roll back west, filled with Frisian trade—for everyone, even Cadwallon, knew it was not wise to attack the Frisians (or Franks or Norse) directly. Word had a way of spreading, and making enemies of those with boats never ended well. A man could have all the gold in the world, but you could not eat gold—nor sow it, spin it, or sharpen it into blades.

So those watchers sat happily listening to the stories and drinking the fine summer ale. They did not see the unusual numbers of riders criss-crossing the hills, or pay attention to those stopping to look about and admire a field here or a hill there, nor did they see them drift back at dusk, followed by the soft slump and fall of the Gwynedd watcher on the hill, and then the watcher's reappearance with the same tunic and shield, the same horse, but hair and moustaches of a slightly different colour or standing perhaps an inch or two taller. And in the dark, when all honest men slept, only a sheepdog might have heard the soft muffled hooves as a band of men slipped past other watchers who had been distracted by a song or the offer of ale.

At the White Hill just north of Portgate—where traders had gathered in early summer every year, time out of mind, to pasture their kine and exchange news and gossip while those kine fattened for market—Cadwallon's men watched from the redcrest fort and laughed and shook their heads. Those farmer fools gathered, waiting to become a large group with a larger herd, which they would then drive through the gate in the great wall to be counted, then on the two miles to Corabrig, where in usual times the great market was held and the king's reeve would take his tithe. Let them. If those dull-witted northerners thought Cadwallon would treat them as their old king might have, if they wanted to walk the meat right onto his plate without so much as a thank-you in return, let them! Roast meat would be most welcome after the last fortnight of short rations.

The farmers and their herds kept gathering, and Cadwallon's men grew used to seeing folk sitting idly here or there and passing the time of day with their neighbours with songs and jokes, and it did not cross their minds that almost always these folk rested at a point with a view of another high point and that their eyes were watchful.

The moon was nearly full and the night hot. A nightjar churred. Hild stood in the grove of oaks wrapping the hill that hid her from Cadwallon's men in Portgate to the east and Corabrig to the southeast. To the west the North Tine poured dark and steady under the wall bridge. It was not wide enough to carry mounted men but a mile north was a ford, and half a mile from that another ford across a burn where a track ran north to join Dere Street. With no rain, the fords were passable.

This was the place to begin the final assault. Here. If they were willing to crowd a little, the wall and hill were big enough to hide tenscore men and their horses, and then it was less than five miles to Corabrig.

But not yet. For now there was the ruin of a redcrest fortlet, with just enough low broken wall and giant baulks left to make a shelter for a man and a woman to keep watch in comfort. She would leave Sitric and Tole: good riders, good archers, sharp-eyed and quiet. Reliable—when there were no women for Sitric to chase.

The moon had set; dawn was not soon. Even so, halfway over the ford across the South Tine, the starlight reflected by the river made Bone's coat gleam. Last night her people had seen no watchers but that did not mean there were none. She stopped and listened: nothing but the river and the *slither-plop* of something gliding into the water and swimming away. The wind was from the south; it brought nothing but the scent of sun-warmed grass and river-wet banks. There had been no rain for two weeks and the water was low; even so, it was a wide ford not crossed in a hurry. It would be deadly under the moon on a clear night, or with more than a score riders. Even half a dozen on a dark night was less than safe.

She turned slowly in her saddle. Behind her, the Fiercesomes waited on the bank. Like Hild, their gold and jewels were hidden and their weapons wrapped. Though she knew they were there, away from the water they were barely visible. Ahead, south and east, rose hills that, again, hid the ford from Corabrig—but not from Hagustaldesham.

She signalled for Leofdæg to join her but the others to stay back, then slid down from Bone to lead him across. Behind her, Leofdæg did the same. She needed to know the lay of the land exactly before Oswald arrived.

35

✦

Even high up in the hills, half a mile north of Artorius's fort, the air was hot and still. Oswald Lamnguin stood with two other men, both with shaved foreheads, looking down into the sandstone gorge and its waterfall. He seemed to be watching something—perhaps the same kingfisher Hild had seen a fortnight ago. She could not tell; he had his back turned to her. From this angle, he did not look much like an Yffing. He was not particularly tall, he was not particularly broad, and his hair was short and dull-dark, like drying peat, with a slight wave. His chain mail and belt, even the sheath of his seax, too, was subtly different, with sinuous Irish chasing.

She did not know if she could trust him. So far he had been a man of his word, and he treated her as he treated everyone else: well-mannered enough, but with the air of not quite believing she was real in any way that mattered. Then again, he himself seemed a thing made of wood, lifelike but not alive. He had no laugh lines and no frown lines, nor any nervous habits.

Hild wiped her eyes—she hated the stinging burnt-and-rotten-egg stink of the nearby spring—and cleared her throat. When Oswald turned, he was all Yffing: the blue-green eyes, the broad brow, and the same pent energy she had seen in Cian and Edwin. Once again she was shocked by his smooth, clean-shaven face with the cleft chin: Like a priest's it showed little use. He was ten years older than her—thirty to her not-yet-twenty—but the only mark on him was a chipped, blue-grey front tooth, broken and dead from some long-ago clash. She had yet to see him sneer or smile, and his voice was always even. This was what an Yffing priest would look like. When she had first heard him speak, his Anglisc, too, was familiar: the Anglisc of Edwin—of Acha, his mother, Edwin's sister—and slightly old-fashioned like that of older northern thegns too long away from royal vills.

But now he spoke Irish. "Later," he said to the long-faced bishop, Cormán. "Your turn is later, for now we speak of war."

Cormán left, and she was glad; she did not like or trust him. He seemed a man made for judgement, and always harsh. The other monk-priest, Laisrén, now openly wore a sword and made no move to leave. From talking to Aidan she had learnt that Laisrén had been Domnall Brecc's man before Oswald's, and perhaps still was; Aidan did not wholly trust him. But she was still not sure how far she could lean on Aidan's reporting—not that he tried to fool her, but that perhaps he fooled himself. He was not always clear-eyed when it came to Oswald. Oswald, on the other hand, treated Aidan as he did his horse: kindly, in order to get the most from the tool.

"Welcome, cousin." Then he nodded past her to the silent Wulf. "Do we need my brother also?"

"No." After four days she knew Oswiu was happy to leave the thinking to Oswald, and meanwhile preferred to drink and match knife throws with his men. He was the kind of gesith she understood. He might sound more Irish than his brother, but with his gesith-broad face and gesith-long hair, his eyes Edwin's blue-green and his moustaches and hair like oiled brass, he looked more Yffing. She knew how to work with his kind: He had responded to the beautiful but fey Rhianmelldt as she might have guessed, and certainly as she had hoped. He—like his twin sister, Æbbe, still in Dunadd, with Domnall Brecc—was perhaps two years older than Hild, but seemed in some ways younger . . .

She realised she had been thinking and not speaking. "No," she said again. "I come only to say Uinniau agrees: He believes his uncle Rhoedd will be willing, and so has sent word."

She relied on Uinniau's judgement regarding Rhoedd—but had her own certainty about Mot Oer, Rhoedd's war chief. He would come—she had dazzled him in Pennrid. She had ridden in on Flýte, seen the great stallion that was the exact colour of Whisk and Flicker, and said to him, *So you are the one who is man enough to ride the stallion who sired living twin foals, a wonder beyond living memory.* And she had heard him, after, asking how she had known who he was, and heard Gladmær saying, *Oh, the lady knows everything, and she is never wrong,* after which Dudda offered to play dice.

Laisrén's eyes tightened a little as he calculated whether this lack of consultation was an insult or simple efficiency but his master's face stayed as smooth as ever. Even the hand resting on his sword pommel did not tighten. If she had not known Oswald's reputation—a leader with few equals in skill or courage on the field—she would have said the hand, too, was that of a priest: Though strong and well-veined it was also unscarred, delicate, and deft, a hand for a pen as much as a blade.

"Let's walk," she said. "Away from the stink."

Oswald nodded, but after a pause, and she wondered if he had even noticed the smell.

They walked together along the lip of the gorge, through the ferns and primroses, though a prudent distance from the edge, and from each other. Both walked without sound: soft footfalls, no jingle of metal. She found herself wondering if she could beat him in a fight; she was taller, and very fast, but she could tell from the rope of his muscles that he, too, would be whip-quick, and strong. And she already knew that when he decided something he gave away nothing until he committed, which he did fully, and fast. Watching him walk she thought perhaps he could fight with both hands, as she did. She set the thought aside: They were cousins, on the same side; they would not fight.

The sky was a bright wide blue. Below, flycatchers flew over the water, in and out of the beams of sunlight slanting through the overhanging trees, snipping up midges. The water's flow was stately rather than rushing. It had not rained for a month.

"We should ride another three leagues today," she said.

"We've already come five leagues. More." He was not disagreeing, just stating truth. She had seen him do this with others—a way to draw them out. He knew as well as she that their leagues today, until the last mile, had been easy: Along Stanegate, broad and even, but, now that they had crossed north of the wall, the going would be rougher, and it would be much harder to travel unseen.

"While the weather holds it's best to do what we can when we can." Three leagues today meant a short ride tomorrow, and a long rest and time to prepare. And they would need time; they had many different bands of men to forge into a single weapon.

"So. The prince Uinniau believes Rhoedd will ride from Caer Luel. You, too, so believe?"

"I do. But what matters is that Cadwallon believe it—and he will. I've already spread word where Cadwallon will hear it that the Rheged war band will be travelling Stanegate in force to meet and protect the trade wagons coming west from Tinamutha. In two days he will see those trade wagons approaching Corabrig from the east." And herds coming through Portgate. All while her taunt—*An Yffing still lives!*—would be ringing in his ears. Cadwallon was not rational when it came to Yffings. "He will believe it. And we will draw him out."

And she needed him to come out. He still outnumbered her, and if he chose to stay behind the strong walls of Corabrig he could outlast her—as long as he had food enough, which was why she had choked off his supply. If his supplies were dwindling, and if he thought there were not only rich pickings to be had along Stanegate—Rhoedd and his wealth-wearing men—but also laden food wagons to carry away the spoils, and feed his men on their way, then he might come out. And if he came out, and if she was right about the path he would take home to Gwynedd—the path through Pennrid, rich and untouched and now undefended by Rhoedd's men—she would be ready. If it was her wyrd.

They rode on, and as she rode she tolled off her beads, darker to paler: Artorius's settlement was the large ember-coloured bead; next—three leagues east—there was the ruined settlement south of the wall but they would stay north of the wall, and camp some way past, in the foothills of the climb they would face the next day. Then the small bead—where they would unsaddle and eat; the off-centre bead where once again some would want to stop and she would say, no, on, push on; and then, when she prevailed, the rich flame-coloured bead, that night's camp. At that camp the wall was two leagues north of the road and in a dip between hills, invisible to watchers from the south—their second-last camp before battle was joined.

The tension knotted under her breastbone would not let her rest. She climbed the wall west of their camp, far enough along to see for miles. The sun had set and high overhead the sky was a clear blue-black. The evening star shone soft and white a handspan over the horizon; in its light the hills before her rose and fell like the backs of a great school of whales swimming towards Caer Luel, and the wall and Stanegate came together and ran side by side into the distance like the cart tracks of a giant. Behind her, the sound of sixscore men and their horses settling for the night should have been soothing, but she felt an itch deep in her bones and winding tight around her muscles.

The last of the moon was a mere sliver, and the broken remains of the redcrest fort were shadowed and ghostly. She wandered it alone, following the scent of late-blooming garlic. She found it growing tucked against a wall that sprouted a stunted hawthorn and a rowan. She wondered how the garlic at Menewood was doing; were they harvesting it yet? Perhaps Brona was roasting it in the embers and smearing it on bread while Wilfrid screamed Nuh, nuh! and Maer offered it to Clut the cat.

Moonlight glimmered on smooth stone: a trough of some kind. She followed it to a wall, and a carved face—an open-mouthed bull—loomed. She peered into the mouth: a lead pipe. A water pipe. Water piped into the trough . . . She followed it back to the other end, and found a fallen stone carved with a figure of a man in a strange helm, and another bull. It reminded her of something: the undercroft at York before Yuletide, she and her mother stacking truckles of cheese in what had once been a temple to some redcrest god.

She touched the worn helmet. What name had this god used? It did not matter. All gods were the same, all part of the pattern, part of the life behind the rock, the rowan, the garlic, even the nightjar churring again.

She roamed the turf, starred with speedwell like ghostflowers, and startled a hedgehog nosing under dandelions for beetles; it curled into a spiky ball. She watched it for a while. Eventually it uncurled and sat up on its hind legs. It could be Cian's carving come to life, and the thought brought his presence to her so strongly she thought she felt his hand in the small of her back and Honey in her belly still.

The hedgepig regarded her for a while, then dropped to all fours again and huffed. It turned and trundled under the cluster of dandelions and she heard it moving through the undergrowth. She followed it to a narrow burn, deep-channeled, but running shallow now, water lying along the bottom of its twisted length like a bent and burnished blade. So deep for so little water. The storm runoff in these hills must be terrifying. She remembered the thick brown gush of the river in the Rheged valley hours after an upland storm.

She stared at the burn for a long time, then at the hills.

She was not sure if she slept or floated in a waking dream, but gradually she realised that though the world was still stained in shades of grey, the shadows were no longer the sharp, steep-sided black of night but softer and more subtle; dawn was coming. She sat up. The knot under her breastbone was loosening—because now she felt the gathering tension in the air itself, drawing tight, thickening and curdling: The weather was changing. A storm.

She thought of the hedgepig and the burn glinting thinly from the deep, steep-sided channel, and saw, sudden and clear as the light in Honey's eyes when she first opened them, the path she must take—take now, without pause, without stopping to think, like catching a bird from the air or a blow on her staff and sliding and turning that strength against her foe. She would have to race the storm.

By the time colour began to seep back into the world, turning the ghost grass green, she and the Fiercesomes were thundering east: six people and twelve horses. Behind them, cookfires were being stirred to life, but Cath Llew and her Fiercesomes would eat in the saddle if they ate at all.

Hild whistled and Tole stepped out from behind the tumbled stone corner, lowering her bow. Nearby Steorra, her mare, whickered to Flýte.

Sitric popped his head from the ruined doorway. "Lady! We didn't look for you til the end of the day. We have—"

Hild cut him off with a flick her hand. "We're not staying. But get ready for people to come soon. They'll know the whistle. Have you seen or been seen?"

"An old goatherd up past Barra's Ford. He asked us if we were thinking on taking over old Caelestis's fields and farm. We said no, and who was Caelestis? And he said, Why him who lived here, in course, but he won't be bothering you, oh no, being nothing but bones and dust since before the redcrests left—"

Her thoughts roamed. Caelestis's fields. Heavenly field . . .

"—and he said, Good thing, because they murderous devils at Corabrig would have our tripes for dinner. He gave us some cheese. We gave him ale."

She had forgotten how well he could mimic the speech of others.

"Also Portgate," Tole said. "We were practically in the gate last night, lady. Right by the wall and the gate was wide open. The northers"—what she called the Bryneich—"were singing, and juggling with torches, and sending heather beer up to Cadwallon's folk in the fort. A gift, they said, from the Lord of Calchfynydd."

The Lord of Calchfynydd was Coledauc, and Coledauc was dead. Heather beer. "A lot of beer?"

"I don't know. But two men took it. And the men in the fort cheered."

What was Langwredd up to? At least Gwladus was with her, for a little while longer. "Keep watch, and rest as you can. We're going north a way on the track, then coming back, but perhaps not this way. You know our mounts? Good. We may not wish to whistle. Don't shelter under the oaks; stay away from the hilltops. There's a storm coming. Be ready!"

She rode the track north that cut across Rede Water—and eventually curved north and west towards Dere Street—but once on the other side of the Rede she reined in. Only Leofdæg was to go on towards the war street. He could sneak past anyone and blend into any crowd, and after so long on the road Lél looked shaggy and rough as any hill pony, if bigger. He carried her token and instructions for Langwredd and Gwladus: Ride into Portgate now; take it—quietly. Hild's men and Bryneich fighters disguised as herders and traders were to go on to the traditional cattle market ground by the ford east of Corabrig—but stay north of the Tine as long as they could, colourfully clothed, weapons hidden, so as not to arouse suspicion. But watch the river, watch it carefully. The real traders were to pour through Portgate at dawn: banners waving, weapons glinting—at which point the fighters, too, could ride up Dere Street from the south—weapons out now, banners flying. They were to sit athwart Dere Street on either side of Corabrig, blocking easy escape north or south. There were a lot of people—horses and men and women and cattle and carts. And enough weaponry to look convincing. She hoped.

In a storm Dere Street itself would remain passable; the redcrests had built well, and king after king had repaired as they could. The cavalry track, too, would do well enough. The ditches were blocked, but enough camber remained to keep it passable.

With her other Fiercesomes she rode north and west, to Barra's Ford over the North Tine; the others stayed mounted but she slid off Flýte and watched the sky. Still blue in all directions, heavenly blue. Which way would the storm come? At this time of year, usually from the north. She needed it to be from the north. She needed Cadwallon to not understand until it was too late. She knelt among the loosestrife and cow parsley, watched a ladybird on a leaf, crouching on the south side. Yes, from the north—but butterflies still fluttered over the cow parsley, so not yet.

A lot of heather beer, Tole said.

From here, as her band moved south they could not be seen from Portgate until they reached Fourstones; after that she would have to hope the weather had begun to change or Cadwallon's mens' heads ached enough they would not want to stare south and west into the full summer sun.

By midafternoon black cloud was gathering on the brow of the hills to the north. She had done her best to spare the horses overwork, but when she saw that was no longer possible, the Fiercesomes switched to their secondary mounts and would stay with them to save their best for tomorrow.

Then she rode herself and poor Bone half to death, checking the fords, burns, rivulets, and streams between Dere Street just south of the wall and the great curve of Alen Water that fed into the South Tine between two ranges of hills. Bone was strong, he would be fine with a few days' rest, but she had to drive him, drive herself, drive them all now, drive them to their utmost, for unless she could be sure of her ground, none of them would ever rest again except as bones.

Bone's tail swayed in a sudden gust of wind and he shook his head. She patted his shoulder. "Not long."

Were there enough men? What if Uinniau had been right a month ago, and instead of being greedy for Rhoedd's gold Cadwallon staked it all on fleeing south down Dere Street? Then she had lost—the die was cast. Everyone was in motion. From the west, Oswald and half her men would be arriving at Caelestis's pasture; Gwladus and Bernician thegns and their men arriving there from the east. A quarter of her men would be moving among the cattle—by the ford now, she hoped, and soon to cross the Tine and wait by the curve—

A drop of water burst on her forehead, soft and warm as ripe summer fruit, with the promise of more to come. The wind gusted again. The air rumbled.

It was here. She climbed onto Bone. He was a strong horse. He would need to be. At least from here they could ride direct. No one would be watching now, and if they were, they would see only rain.

Lightning cracked and wind howled. Rain came sideways in a great sheeting blade. Bone's hooves slipped and he heaved himself up the last slope.

Rows and rows of horses turned their rumps to the wind. Hild slid off his back and led him, striding and splashing through mud to the deafening drum and thunder of rain on the leather tents. It was not even sunset but the black cloud made it dark, and the camp had the air of a place closed down for the night. She found Oeric, handed him the reins, and shouting over the wind's howl, told him to see that Bone got under cover, and warmed, and dried; he had done a hero's work.

She pointed at a plump dappled gelding in a warm horse blanket eating from a manger under a rough roof. "This shelter will do! Move that horse."

"It's the bishop's beast," Oeric shouted, his hair already plastered to his head.

"I don't care." She was unfastening Bone's girth, setting her feet to lift the saddle off.

Two monks appeared, splashing and slipping in the mud, their hoods getting so wet they hung down over their eyes, half blinding them so they blundered about, bleating and flapping their hands. Another great crack of lightning and an explosion from among the oaks, followed by a creaking crash.

One of the monks jumped and bumped into Bone, who shied.

She picked the monk up, and, though she did not throw him, she set him down more forcefully than she might have, then rounded on the other. He froze and backed away. They scampered off.

She lifted the saddle off Bone to drape over Oeric's arms. She picked up her staff. "I'll leave the rest to you. I must—"

A harsh torrent of Irish overrode her words.

Cormán, big chin working in rage, pointing at her, spewing Irish like a burn in spate, with two armed men behind him. "—man of God! That a mere woman would think—"

"Shut up," she said in Irish. She spoke past the bishop to the men. "This horse has just saved our lives. I don't care if that fat gelding belongs to Christ himself, I'll not see him warm and dry while my horse stiffens with cramp. And I've not the time to argue."

Now her men were beginning to gather.

"Take care of Bone," she said to them. "If you have to, put him in the bishop's own tent."

"I'll speak to Lord Oswald of this! He—"

"Lead the way. He's who I need to talk to." Coelfrith appeared at her elbow. "Which is Oswald's tent?"

He pointed to the big, plain tent standing on its own with two men standing guard under the awning. "But watch for the hole."

Hole? "Get our people up, get them fed. Pack for fighting needs; no extra weight."

There was, indeed, a great hole dug beside Oswald's tent, filling with muddy water, and a great baulk of ancient timber lying beside it. She could not imagine its purpose.

Cormán had vanished. She towered over the men guarding the tent, huge in her furs. Dark, no gold showing, a black shape lit from behind by silent lightning as the storm moved south. She slid her seax free, reversed it, held it out haft first. "I'm Yffing," she said in Anglisc, then again in Irish just in case. "Let me pass."

Thunder rumbled across the sky like a giant boulder. She stepped at them and they moved aside.

She ducked through the flap in a gust of wind and spatter of drops. The tent was dark with rainlight. Oswald was lying on his back on a camp bed, drowsing. She loomed over him.

His eyes glimmered as he opened them and looked up at her head brushing the roof of his tent. "Are you an angel?" He sounded calm, curious.

"Get up."

"You don't sound like an angel." He wiped his cheek. "You're dripping." And then his face sharpened and the man himself flowed back from the land of dreams to behind his eyes. He sat up. "Hild Yffing. You're wet."

"Get up."

He swung his legs and put his feet on the floor. "What's happened?"

"You have to get up now."

He reached for his boots and was pulling on the second as his brother Oswiu ran in, knife drawn.

"You!" he said in Irish. Then to his brother. "Is all well? They said—"

Lightning cracked and lit the inside of the tent in a silent flash.

She said to Oswiu, also in Irish, "We have to change the plan, and move much sooner."

"You can't just—"

Thunder crashed and rolled so loudly it felt like a landslide coming to sweep them away. "Be still and listen."

Oswald held up his hand. Oswiu quieted. Oswald gestured at Hild's dripping furs. "The weather is foul."

"Yes. It will serve us, if we're ready."

"Is it day or night?"

"Æfen. The sun isn't yet set but it's storm-dark. You and your men must be ready to leave before úht. Are you awake now? I haven't much time."

"I'm awake."

"You must be in place by dawn on Stanegate, just before the river fork. One of my men will lead you. Cadwallon must wake at dawn to find you there. He'll also find—" She broke off. "I have to leave within the hour. If you send for food I can eat as I explain."

Oswald nodded to Oswiu, "See to it, brother. Then start waking the camp." Then he lit two tapers, sat down again, and focused on Hild. "Go on."

"It's the dark of the moon. The rain is thick as a curtain. If we move now Cadwallon won't see us approach—"

He nodded. Surprise had always been the difficulty.

"—but will wake at dawn to find himself almost trapped. He will look north and see his way closed by Bryneich athwart Dere Street between Corabrig and Portgate. His way south to the river will be closed by traders—armed like gesiths, looking like gesiths; and some of my men athwart Dere Street just south of the river. East is wet ground and no road even in fine weather. And west—he will look west and see the Iding raven and the Yffing boar flying together, halfway between the wall and Hagustaldesham, lit by the dawn. And it'll be a bright, fresh dawn, for by then the storms will be gone." She hoped. They almost always were at this time of year.

Oswiu came in with a crowd of others: Wulf, and three men bearing food, a table, stools.

While the men laid out the food and table, Hild tore a mouthful of meat from a leg bone, chewed, and swallowed.

Oswald poured them both small beer. "Why must you leave so soon? To reach any of the places you name won't take more than three hours."

He had a good grasp of the lay of the land for a man who had not ridden it. She gulped, chewed some more. Swallowed, bit, chewed.

"And *almost trapped*, you said." His face was as smooth as butter, but his eyes moved with his racing thoughts. "And you want us only—halfway?—halfway between here and Hagustaldesham."

"That's not trapped," Oswiu said in his heavily accented Anglisc. "If you want him trapped, if you want us to hold the animal in our very jaws, he should wake to find us on Stanegate hard by his walls." Oswiu, too, understood the shape of things. This was good; very good.

"I don't want him trapped," she said. "If he believes himself trapped he won't come out. And we want him to come out."

"Rhoedd's not yet come—and without him Cadwallon outnumbers us," Oswald said.

"Yes. He'll look and see our numbers and feel we're fools. We want him to laugh at our mistake and set out to slip with his treasure past our trap."

He spoke slowly, deliberately: "But he outnumbers us."

"And as he leaves Corabrig he knows we can't help but see that. He wants us to quail and falter. He'll run west on Stanegate as though to overwhelm you just north of Hagustaldesham, to drive through you and along Stanegate to Caer Luel, and then down the western war street to Gwynedd. But he knows Rhoedd will be on Stanegate, heading his way—I made sure he knows—but he doesn't know we know he knows that."

Even as she spoke she was struck by what a fragile daisychain of who knew what, or thought they did, she had built their plans on, and for one gaping moment her certainty teetered. She closed her eyes, remembered the hedgepig, how it had led her to the answer, and shook off the doubt.

"But he does know that, and he won't want to charge through you and be trapped between two forces. And you'll make sure he won't charge through you, for you'll be marching with big shields, as though to make a shield wall, and he doesn't want to fight long and hard with more enemies coming up behind him on Dere Street, and Rhoedd on the way. No. He'll charge only enough for you to dismount, form a shield wall, and brace, then he'll veer south and west along the old cavalry track, escaping our trap. He'll aim to take that track through the hills. Across the Alen. South and west to Pennrid. To add Rheged's treasure to that of Deira and Bernicia, and a coffle or two of slaves. Then home to Gwynedd, laughing all the way, while we cower behind our shield walls and quake in our boots."

Oswiu leaned forward, eyes gleaming enamel blue in the half-light. "And you *want* him to do this?"

"I want him running on that track, yes. Running full out, committed, leading his burdened packbeasts, unable to turn around and run back to Corabrig—because by then there will be Bryneich in Corabrig, your men back on their horses and coming for him along Stanegate, and men to his southeast on Dere—"

The leather flap slapped back and Cormán strode in. He stood there, surveying them, rain running down the seams in his long face and dripping off his shovel jaw. "My lord Oswald," he said in his harsh Irish. "If it is true we are now to leave before daybreak, as I have heard, then the blessing we had planned for the morning must begin now, before the last light of day is truly gone."

"Must?" said Oswiu, also in Irish, but in the same *I-will-peel-your-muscles-from-your-bones-and-make-you-eat-them* tone Edwin had used when angry and uncertain. "Priest, do not address my brother, soon to be king, with musts."

Aidan came in, took in the situation at a glance, and bowed apologetically, torn between his bishop and his prince.

Hild said, "We've no time for prayers."

"There is always time for God!"

"The bishop is right," Oswald said in Anglisc, and again in Irish. Oswiu scowled; Cormán looked triumphant. "Go make ready," he said to the priests. And to Oswiu, "Chivvy the men, brother. And if you have to, help the priests."

He looked at Wulf, then Hild. Hild said to Wulf, "Go check on everything."

Then it was just Oswald and Hild. "We were speaking of Cadwallon running—escaping."

"He won't escape. Once he's committed it'll be too late, for that's when he'll see me and my men riding on that very track towards him."

"How will he not see a troop of horse coming towards him?"

"There is a—" She looked about, reached for bread, pushed things aside. She drew a thick line of small beer across the table near the top. "The Tine." And above and parallel to it a thick smear of butter. "Stanegate." From Stanegate, slanting down to the bottom left of the table a wavy line of beer with a loop bulging out about halfway down. "The track."

He looked at it and nodded.

"Now." She tore off half the round of bread and set it on its base to the right of the track, in the loop. "A hill. Anything standing here, behind this hill"—she crumbled some bread bits to the lower left of the loaf—"can't be seen by anyone from here"—she gestured to the whole board above the bread—"or here." Everything in the upper right. "But to get to that hidden point unseen I have a long ride in the dark on difficult paths."

He squatted so the board was eye level. Moved, squatted again. Looked throughtfully at the board. "And here is Corabrig?" He pointed just above both Stanegate and the Tine near the right-hand edge of the board.

She nodded.

"And you're sure he won't see?"

"I have ridden the ground. And I will be there, waiting."

His eyebrows rose, and she thought he might be about to smile, but then he frowned. "But he will outnumber you—why should he not just ride through you?"

"It's hard to move fast with laden packbeasts. But more, he knows the track. He will see me come from behind the hill here, while he's still here—" She pointed to a spot not far south of the Tine. "And he'll think, fool! And leave the track thinking he can neatly cut the neck of the loop, regain the track behind me, and escape."

"But he won't?"

"No." And she smiled. "Because of the rain." The lovely, wyrd-given rain.

"You said it would no longer be raining."

"It won't." She smiled again. "It will be a gentle summer day."

The rain was slowing and the sky had lightened from wet ash to sea grey as the storm swept south and east; to the west the sky was bloody; it would not be long before sunset and real dark. Far to the north and west the clouds were as dark and dense as black wool: more storms coming, but moving slowly. Hild's men had stowed their tents, loaded light packs, and were eating their last meal before mounting; she had patted Bone and made sure he had taken no harm from his ride. He would stay here with the camp and baggage animals, along with the other secondary mounts. She had reluctantly agreed to leave three good men to guard them and the spoil they must leave behind.

"We ride like kings, every one, to strike fear in the heart of our foes. So wear your best and brightest, but not too much. Speed is our friend and weight our enemy. You'll need to be able to jump a man's length over water, waist-height over walls—and that after a hard ride uphill. So leave the spoil here safe under guard." With Gwladus to watch the guards. "When we win, there'll be more, very much more!" She did not bother talking about if they lost. Dead men had no need of gold.

Flýte was saddled but her girth not yet tightened, their banners were unshrouded but not unfurled. Hild and the Fiercesomes were glorious in gold and gleaming weapons. She took another hard-boiled egg from her belt pouch, tapped it on the pommel of her seax, and rolled it between her palms with a satisfying crunch.

Gathered in a knot were the men made thegn by Edwin, together with their sons, eyeing warily the older thegns of the Iding Edwin had slaughtered and driven into exile but were now returned, and whose own sons, like Oswiu, sounded more Irish than Anglisc. Laisrén stood with two of Domnall Brecc's men—there to witness, they said, not to fight—but their hands were as white on their hilts as those of the other men, and Hild had no doubt that when it came to it, they would draw those blades. Uinniau and six men of Rheged stood with Hild's people, another score of Rheged with Oswald: If he won, he would be their overking. She nodded at Mot Oer, and slipped the egg free of its shell.

Yrre whispered to Adair, "Why are we waiting in the cold?"

They were waiting for Oswald. But he was not at his tent—only two priests doing something with the great oak beam by the pit.

"Where is he?" she asked Gwladus, and took a bite of egg. She marvelled at the intense rich of the yolk. Begu would kill for a dress that colour.

"A priest came to get him. He seemed upset—the priest. Why are you smiling?"

"I was just thinking of Begu. Which way did they go?"

Gwladus pointed down the hill to the remains of the fortlet on the wall.

Hild popped the rest of the egg in her mouth, brushed the last bits of shell off her hands, and walked down to a knot of priests standing around a heap of mud and uprooted saplings by a ruined corner of some old stone building.

Oswald stood by a pile of rope, an axe over one shoulder and his fist on his hip. It was the first time she had seen him unsettled.

He looked up. "It's stuck." A great baulk of timber, bigger even than the one by his tent, buried in mud and rubble. "It was to form the upright of our standing cross but now it's buried."

A cross. Ah: The hole by his tent to slide the cross foot in, a cross to tower over the camp. They had talked in Caer Luel of raising a cross, a symbol for them all to march under, but she had imagined a standard perhaps the length of her staff. Not a giant totem. "That's not coming free anytime soon."

"It must. We can't make a cross from one piece of wood. And I swore to God and the abbot of Hii that I would come to the throne of the northern Anglisc under the word and power of Our Lord, the Christ."

"You might not come to the throne at all if I don't move soon. We have crosses on banners."

"We need this cross," he said. "We need a mighty symbol of our hope. We're Anglisc and British, men of Rheged and Bernicia, of Hii and Dál Riata. We're Yffing and Iding. We must kneel before the cross as one, a cross bigger than anything around us. Aidan is carving a psalm on the cross piece even now—"

He meant it. He was not moving until he had a giant totem of a cross—though she was not sure how he might expect Bernician thegns who had lately thrown away their crosses and resumed their hammers to kneel for a god they had shunned once.

"—can we find wood?"

Wood. Woden . . . Oak trees. The crack of lightning and a great, creaking crash. "Come with me. Bring your axe."

Wyrd was with her still. The oak had lost one of its great lower boughs, thick around as a big man's chest and the length of two horses. It hung from the trunk, connected by a splintered twist of wood and a complication of leafy branches dotted with small green acorns and the white berries of mistletoe. Every sign she could wish.

"Here's your upright. Give me that axe. Go get the priests and the rope."

The cross slid into the hole with a splash and priests heaved on ropes, but the great baulk cross-piece, thicker than the upright, overbalanced it; every time it began to rise it slid in the mud. The hole was too big, and the socket stones they had placed at the bottom were toppled by the water.

Behind her, her men were getting increasingly restless. The rain was thinning, and the cloud, but the light was fading from the sky. She fished in her pouch for another egg, tapped it.

"Are we truly to kneel to this milksop of a god?" Yrre whispered to Adair. "My da died with Edwin king and my uncle threw away his cross, said we lost to Penda because Penda still wore the hammer. The Christ god is weak!" Around him, Bernicians—and not a few Deirans—murmured agreement.

The priests were bedraggled, mud-spattered, and despondent. Cormán exhorted them in Latin.

"Yrre!" He looked up, saw it was her who called, and straightened. "You'll kneel if the king-to-be says kneel." She rolled the egg free of its shell. "Christ, Woden, it's all one." All gods were part of the pattern. "We fight together, and we fight for the one god."

"Yes, lady."

"You sound doubtful."

"No. No, it's just . . . how can two different things be one?"

Now the priests were praying, all except Aidan, who was paying attention to Hild while trying not to be noticed. Everyone else watched Hild.

They needed to believe. They needed to believe they were on the winning side, that they knelt to the winning god. Hild weighed the egg, thinking. Then she laughed. "Catch." She threw the egg and he caught it. "Take a bite."

He hesitated.

She laughed again. "It won't bite back." All around her, men grinned.

He bit.

"Look at it. What do you see?"

"An . . . egg?"

"White wrapped around yellow. Different. Unmixed. The white is the white and the yellow is the yellow, but together they are one. Together they are the egg."

He looked at it, blinked.

"As with the egg, god. Woden, Christ, it's all one."

He held the egg out to her with reverence.

She grinned. "Oh, no. I don't want that back. Eat it up. Don't you know before a battle you should eat whenever you can?"

Men laughed. A few reached into their own pouches for a lump of cheese or strip of fruit leather.

Now the priests were taking hold of the rope once again. The bishop raised his hands to the sky and his sleeves fell back from his bony arms. "We pray for your strength, Dear Lord, Holy God, Almighty Ruler of Heaven! Aid us now!"

Once again the cross began to rise. The rain stopped. Everyone held their breath. Up. Up some more. Oswald's men began to smile. But then a priest cried out and the cross began to slip.

With a shout Oswald leapt into the pit and set his foot against the base of the oak, wrapped his arms around the bark, and cried, "Christ aid me!"

It might just work. "Wulf!" she shouted. "Those planks. And those." Dudda and Wulf saw what she meant and threw them into the pit on the side opposite Oswald. Then others caught on and wood and stone began to rain down. Dudda jumped in and started jamming them between the oak and the sides of the pit to brace it. One man shouted encouragement, then another.

"Pull!" she bellowed to the priests, the only one who could make herself heard. "Heave!" And up it went. "Hold! Hold there!"

And over the cross, behind it like a great gateway in the sky, sprang a rainbow.

The priests knelt. The thegns held their hammers. They all forgot that Oswald was still down in the pit at the base of the cross while Dudda cursed and jammed and braced.

And as the sun sank the rainbow began to change. All the colours faded except red, from salmon pink along the inside to a faint ember-grey outside.

"Behold!" Hild called in a great voice, turning into the path of the sunset so that the pearls in her cross burned like drops of blood. "Christ shed his blood for us. God His Father made the oak, and Woden struck off its limb today, for us, to form the symbol of Christ. For while He has many names, there is only one God, and now the Holy Spirit breathes upon the world in His sign. Kneel to Him, for see! Even the symbols of Woden pay tribute to Him." Now even the mistletoe glowed milky red. And one by one every man knelt, even the thegns.

Oswald scrambled out of the pit, covered head to toe in wet mud that glistened red in the light, like blood.

"And behold! Rising from this field, at the foot of His cross, slippery as a newborn, the man who will rule here, beneath the heavens in the north of this middle earth, Oswald Brightblade, boar and raven, Yffing and Iding, Deira and Bernicia, all in one."

The sun sank but the red rainbow lingered.

Aidan, quicker-witted than his bishop, or perhaps able to understand the Anglisc where Cormán had not, launched into a song of praise in Latin, and after a moment, all the priests joined in, followed by the cross-wearing exiles returned with their prince.

She could see Cormán drawing breath for some long sermon or other that no one would be able to understand and fewer cared about, so she nodded at her men, and shouted in a voice that could be heard for half a mile, "Oswald Lamnguin, the boar rides now. Boar and raven will meet again on the field over the bodies of our enemies!"

Hild and nearly twoscore riders raced the second storm west along the wall and over the North Tine—now beginning to swell—then south and west again as the light faded, through the hills, west on Stanegate, then, in the pitch-black, off the road. The rain caught them as they moved slowly south to the ford over the South Tine. Leofdæg could find his way over any ground, and Hild had now ridden this path three times; they were slow and careful but sure. The ground was already soft. Leofdæg went ahead, found his marker on the bank. They peered into the moving dark. The water seemed only a finger or two higher. Dudda took Leofdæg's place, holding a coil of rope, and Leofdæg, holding one end, moved surefooted on Lél, one step at a time to the centre. The marker on the far bank was a cairn of white stones; even so, they could not see it.

Wulf, one hand against the rope, and another coil around his arm, moved out to the centre, massive on his great grey, barely visible against the moving dark. He took the end of the rope from Leofdæg, tied it to his waist, gripped one end of the second coil, and handed the other end to Leofdæg. Leofdæg moved ahead, swallowed by the dark. All they could hear was the river and the hiss of rain. They could see nothing beyond the ears of their own horses. Time passed. Finally a whistle: He was across.

They crossed one by one, with the rope as guide, and Hild, last, took up the marker and rope on the north bank. By midniht she doubted anyone would be able to cross but she wanted to be sure.

Thunder rumbled in the distance. Behind them the river continued to rise.

It should have been a nightmare ride two leagues uphill into the wild dark and slashing rain, with lightning cracking around them, but Hild's bones fizzed and her heart sang. She laughed and shouted and her exhilaration spread to the riders and they rode like Hægtessan of the Hel Boundary. Flýte moved like a hero beneath her.

Slowly she came partly back to herself, and somewhere between mid-niht and úht they were moving east past the Dardenburna. Some time later they hit the cavalry track.

She called a halt and sent Leofdæg to find the place they had chosen what seemed like a year ago, but was little more than a day. How long had it been since she had slept fully? It didn't matter. She would sleep soon enough, one way or another.

They camped against the western slope of the hill that would shield them from view of both Corabrig and Hagustaldesham. They left their bedrolls buckled behind their saddles and sat with their backs to the hill, facing the cavalry track. Twenty paces to their left was an unnamed fork of the Diptonburna, which, when they had checked two days ago, was dry. Still nothing ran in its bed, though the dirt was soft and damp.

The storm had passed south and now hung over the high hills beyond Alendale, pouring torrents onto the heights where the dirt was a thin skin over rock. But here, now, the air was dark and thick, soft with the torn, fecund scent of dirt after long-awaited rain. A moth fluttered by and she felt the sudden tilt of air that meant a bat had taken it. On such quick flicks of fate are battles turned and lives lost.

All around her figures sat in groups. Some dozed, or pretended to, but most, like Hild, knew they would get no sleep.

She was in the world but not wholly of it, as though someone had thinned the skin between this earth and the next. She listened: a ruffle of wind on the grass, a horse huffing down its nose as it shifted, a man's quiet laugh.

By now Oswald's men would be over the wall and on Stanegate. The fighting men would be drifting away from the traders blocking Dere Street just south of the river—*Soft and quiet*, she thought to them. *Steady, be steady*—and in Portgate, if she guessed right about Langwredd's heather beer, poisoned men would be having their throats cut, then the great north gates would be barred behind the creeping Bryneich so none might pass the wall and surprise them from behind on the stretch of Dere Street between Portgate and Corabrig.

Between one blink and the next she saw a line between sky and hill so faint she could be dreaming it. She lifted her head. Equally faint, a new sound of trickling water.

She stood and wandered over to the closest group, Aldnoth and Sitric, and exchanged a few words. Did they remember how it had been at Adlingfleot, the wonder of sausage and onions and ale after so long? Then to Uinniau and the men of Rheged: That fountain in Caer Luel was the wonder of the world. Then on to the knot of archers, including Tole, to laugh about their terrible aim when they first came to Menewood. Coelfrith and Oeric and Grimhun: Some good Menewood bread made with Goodmanham wheat hot from the oven would go well with cheese about now. And on and on. Ordinary conversation, relaxed, cheerful, quiet. And all the time the trickle in the stream bed grew.

By the time she said to the Fiercesomes, "Soon now," she could see the look Dudda shot Wulf, though only in shades of grey, and the trickle was a rush, and through her feet she felt rather than heard the tearing roar where the rivulet met and joined Diptonburna. And then it was time to see to their horses.

Now the world was sharp and clear. She felt everything: saw it, smelt it, heard it, every blackbird startled from its song by the unexpected riders; the creak of the leather hard under her thighs, Flýte's muscles sliding under her cream coat, the charcoal mane standing stiff, and dawn rising behind the hill to her right. Now colour tinted the world, faint at first, but firming and steadying, like her place in it. She sat tall in the saddle, chestnut hair, gold thick around her bare neck, wide as a breast plate and studded with agate, gold around her arms and wrists, gold at her belt, though nothing dangling at her ears, and her cross was tucked beneath her jacket. Black and grey furs thrown back over her bare shoulders, black boots. A tall woman on a tall cream horse also pointed in black, with tack heavy and bright in agate-studded gold.

She rode in the middle of the fifth row of three riders, Wulf on one side and Dudda on the other. The first three rows were archers; the next row was Leofdæg, Bryhtsige, and Gladmær. Behind her, Oeric and Grimhun flanked Aldnoth who carried the great boar standard; even with two horse-lengths between them she could feel his heart throbbing with pride.

They walked steadily, deliberately, letting their mounts' muscles warm and their rhythms match.

Now the summit of the hill was behind them and the height of the rise alongside them began to lessen.

"Ready," she said. "Steady."

They kept walking but now hands rested near blades, and the archers brought their quivers closer to their bodies, for in half a mile they might be seen, dark on the skyline, by watchers on Stanegate.

On a little more, feeling the steady lift and placement of Flýte's hooves, the shift of her shoulders and haunches. She whistled softly. They halted.

"Leofdæg."

He turned, nodded, and with no fuss edged Lél off the trackway to skirt the hill closer to its base: to see without being seen. Lél was not a heavy horse, and her rider was light; even so the turf was wet enough to spring back only slowly in places and not at all in others. After some time she heard a horse cantering away.

The sky slowly brightened. It was a beautiful day.

She drank from her water bottle, wiped her mouth. Drank some more. All the Fiercesomes were doing the same, and behind her she heard Grimhun reaching for his.

She slid off Flýte and led her down the line, reminding those new to war to drink water, then drink more, drink until they thought they might burst. Eat if they could—they had their eggs? fruit leather?—piss if there was time, but first and always, drink water.

She set Flýte to drink upstream from her, then squatted beside the roadside ditch and pissed like a horse, watched her piss join the flow of rainwater, deep enough to float twigs, rippling every now and again as more rainwater seeped from the hillside. A sudden surge dislodged a small stone from the ditch's bank, and it tumbled along until lost from sight. By the time she pulled up her breeches the water was already a fingerwidth higher than when she had pulled them down. Near Corabrig the Dubhglas would still be serene, but everything else was beginning to move fast. Her bones felt filled with air and her head began to hum.

They were leaning against their horses, talking of this and that, when seemingly out of thin air Leofdæg was walking towards them leading Lél.

The hum in Hild's head rose a note.

"Cadwallon's out."

Yes! She thumped her thigh. "The Bryneich?"

He nodded. "Out of Portgate and making a noise like a drunk fair. Rolling straw-filled carts and holding torches."

Blessings upon Langwredd's head, blessings three times three. Fire carts. Why hadn't she thought of that? Cadwallon would not want to be anywhere near that fire; he had taken one look and it had made up his mind. Now anything was possible. "How many men has he?"

"Many."

Leofdæg had the best farsight of anyone she knew and he had been counting the enemy all his fighting life. From that distance it would be a guess, but it would be a good guess.

"Twelvescore."

Her heart jolted like a cartwheel hitting a rock; the sudden stink of a man's bowels letting go greased the air. Twelvescore. Twelvescore and, if she was right, all heading her way. "Where are they now?"

"Stanegate, but not far. And he's hardly moving."

She nodded. "Oswald's in place?"

"Mostly."

She knew exactly where Cadwallon would be: at the branch of Stanegate and the fork that ran to the small bridge over the Tine near Hagustaldesham and on to the cavalry track. He was seeing the Bryneich, seeing Oswald but uncertain of his numbers; knowing Rhoedd was coming, that Baedd Coch was out there, somewhere. Deciding which way to run. "What else?"

"Traders aren't close enough."

The ones on the south side of the Tine. "How far south?"

"Two miles."

Two miles. "Will he see them?" She needed him to see them, but she could not remember exactly where the hill was, whether it would block Cadwallon's view. It depended on where he was on Stanegate.

"Might see some. There's a small band ahead of the rest."

"Enough?"

Leofdæg gave his lopsided shrug.

There were fifteen of her men with the traders; half were archers. Now she wished she had sent more archers. A dozen or more men with bows at the end of a bridge could be a powerful argument against trying to cross. "Tell me the others have begun to move, at least."

"Some. They're past Ridingburna."

Even with weapons in hand they were, at heart, farmers and traders.

They had always been a risk. Cadwallon would either stay on Stanegate and run for the track when he saw Oswald, or he would turn and run for Dere Street. There was no way to tell. And now she would have to choose without knowing which.

Fate goes ever as it must.

"Mount."

She turned, grinned at Aldnoth with the reckless joy of someone who has cast the last die. "Wipe your hands now, man. You're going to need a good dry grip on that banner for this ride. Stick to me like honey."

They were all looking at her. Some were white around the mouth.

"I chose you all. You're mine. You're the riders of Baedd Coch. Who are you?"

"Baedd Coch!"

"Today is a beautiful day. Today we ride into a hero song! For we are heroes, every one. And we will win. Because who are we?"

"Baedd Coch! Baedd Coch!"

"We will thunder down from the hill, trample our enemies under our hooves, and laugh at their screams!" They laughed, banged the hilts of their swords on their shields. "Archers, you know my signal; follow Sitric, follow Tole." She slid her seax in and out of its sheath; smooth as cream. "The rest of you, follow the banner. Match its pace—no one get ahead, no one fall behind." She reached behind her, took up her staff. "Spears." Everyone but Hild and the archers brought their throwing spears forward, with one in the hand. She settled firmly in the saddle. The hum in her head rose to a whine. "Slow and steady to start. On me."

The sun was bright on their cheeks as they moved from the shadow of the hill. Above them, a hawk caught the golden light as it rose on a column of air.

"Hup," she said, and their walk became a trot, and "Hup!" and it was a canter, and the beat of Flýte's hooves merged with the beat of Hild's blood, and the whine in her head rose and merged with the tumult of water hurtling now in a great rush down from the hills.

Down they plunged, down the track, and she saw everything at once, as though merged with the hawk high, high above: Cadwallon running— but not fast, because he was heavy with gold, the gold of all Deira and Bernicia stripped from the split necks and severed fingers of her people— running towards the bridge by Hagustaldesham, the bridge that would lead to the cavalry track.

And Oswald—so far behind!—just now leaving Stanegate and marching . . . to the old bridge. Too small, too narrow—wide enough only for two men on foot or one mounted. Oswald would not turn him.

On such a flick and turn are battles decided.

"Banner!" She kicked Flýte to a gallop, that gliding run that cut like a polished plough through her own column and folded them in behind her. And she sang, and they sang with her: They needed to be noticed.

And now Flýte stretched out, her heart pumping like bellows, and Cadwallon's men looked up in shock at a vision of death falling upon their heads: a giant, on a giant horse, gleaming with gold and wrapped in a black cloud of fur like some hell beast, and behind her the hated banner, the banner they thought they would never see again, the banner they had killed twice—at Hæðfeld, at Urburg—the great red boar that would not die, Baedd Coch, death to all to who touched it, bright and blood-eyed and bristling. And with the banner, bright blades borne by men fearsomely ugly and inhumanly beautiful, singing like devils and laughing like fiends. And from behind these fiends a hail of arrows plunging into the track before them as they left the bridge.

One horse reared, another swerved, and in a mill of confusion some of Cadwallon's men broke from the track and ran south, hoping to leap Diptonburna and run again west and behind them to regain the cavalry track.

She whistled, pointed Sitric and Tole and the archers south and east to head them off, then leaned along Flýte's neck and whispered in her ear to run, run like a deer. Flýte's stride now seemed barely to touch the earth; they were floating.

She floated in a silent world, her thoughts slowing until around her men and horses, golden in the morning light, moved like flies caught in honey. Men from just south of Corabrig—her fifteen men—were moving off Dere Street riding to the Dubhglas to cross, but there was no crossing it there, not now. It was in spate, the blackwater of its name foaming brown and grey, and strong enough to sweep any horse off its feet. They began to run south along the east bank of the burn, seeking a ford. It was a race, for those of Cadwallon's men who crossed Diptonburna and reached the Dubhglas ford first could cross and run for Dere Street, down again into the heart of Deira, and there would be none to stop them.

Oswald had made the bridge, and his mounted men were crossing it fast, forming bands of five or six, and now Cadwallon's men saw them, and one small figure—in a golden breastplate, with a band of men with white banners flying the red dragon about him—moved parallel to the track, aiming for where Diptonburna in summer was a dry watercourse, to cross and cut the angle back to the track. Cadwallon. And with him the bulk of his men and the baggage horses.

Laughter swelled in a lazy bubble deep in her throat. The watercourse was no longer dry, and no horse carrying three hundred pounds of gold could leap it. The ground around it was now turning into a mire, and unless those horses had wings, they would be labouring upslope and slipping and skating in mud; they could not outrun her.

But he outnumbered her. He had only to stop, and turn, and dismount and wait. So she would not give him time to think or time to stop.

The bubble of laughter rose from her and burst, and the world splashed over her in a fury of sound and speed, and she scythed into Cadwallon's men, her staff sweeping this way and that, Flýte swerving, Hild ducking. A flight of spears from behind her took a row of Cadwallon's horses down, smashing and stumbling into one another, men tumbling into the grass.

She was wheeling, running, coming back around. "More! Don't let them think."

More spears. Now things were moving too fast and hard to follow what was happening around her. A cry to the north meant Oswald had come up to Cadwallon's rearguard. She looked for the gold and the dragon. There: the Reaver, unhelmed to be heard in battle—grey-flecked golden hair flying loose—and eighty armed men with ten others leading baggage horses, moving steadily and with discipline.

"Archers!" But they were too far away.

Without turning—she could not afford to turn—she called "Fiercesomes!" leaned along Flýte's neck, and kicked her after Cadwallon.

Flýte's stride ate the distance, climbing the hill as though it were a gentle meadow. Just over the rise she almost ran into ten dismounted men, shields dug into the turf and spears pointing forward. Flýte swerved and she swept her staff across three spears, breaking two. One brave fool moved his shield aside to thrust with his spear, but he moved so slowly, and it was the work of a moment to jam the staff back and smash his jaw shut with a *clop* and he fell. She ran in a great curve, laughing, singing, charging back, charging straight at a ragged line, only now she was flanked by the Fiercesomes and Grimhun, king's gesiths, with a handful of others coming up, and they thundered at the gap in the shield wall and tore it to pieces.

But ahead was the sudden crumpled green cloth, the dips and folds, of hill country, the ups and downs filled sometimes with a steep drop to water, sometimes with trees, sometimes nothing but grassy slopes. And across the one clear path downhill another line of ten men behind braced shields, and behind them ten more, and behind them the rest of Cadwallon's horses milling and men tugging on loads, feverishly trying to share out the weight to get across the foaming Diptonburna.

"Horse!" she shouted. "Stay ahorse as long as you can! Aldnoth, furl that banner!" She swerved right, into the woods that ran along the burn, moving uphill, upstream. She spread herself low on Flýte's back, moving under the branches of crack willow and alder. She wished Leofdæg were by her. Somewhere along here the furrow between hills widened and the water slowed enough to ford. She slowed from a canter to a walk.

There.

There was no bank, just water suddenly snaking between tree roots. She guided Flýte into the current. Barely past her pastern. She would not even have to dismount. She whistled.

They crossed, nine of them now. Nine against Cadwallon's twoscore— more if his other men had rejoined them.

She led them back downstream at a trot that became a canter as they heard the scream of a terrified beast swept off its feet. Then they were running, throwing spears, driving thirty men and five panicked packhorses east and south, downhill. And then, ahead, there was a battle: Her men had crossed the Dubhglas ford and caught the first run of Cadwallon's men between them and the archers.

Cadwallon and his guard broke hard west, running along the base of a hill, parallel to another rushing burn. She did not know its name.

They were slowing. Now they were moving uphill again. The sun was hot. They had been riding for what felt like a year; her arms ached, and her thighs, and her throat. She was too tired to sing. And she had no idea what came behind her: Scores of Cadwallon's men? Wild Bryneich? Oswald? She only knew Cadwallon lay ahead, and Cadwallon was why she was here.

The burn shrank to nothing, no longer a barrier, but the slope ahead was too steep and too wet for burdened horses, and Cadwallon and his men were running south, and now they were trapped between a great sheer slope to the west and the burn to the east—deep and narrow, like the one the hedgepig had shown her.

She slowed, fumbled for her water bottle, drank while Flýte plodded on. She nearly dropped the bottle; her hand was slippery. She stared at it. Blood. Trickling down from a cut above her elbow. She had not even felt it. She was so hot.

Cadwallon was trapped. But he outnumbered her three to one. She would kill for a handful of archers.

She stopped, drank some more. Stoppered the bottle carefully, hung it back on the saddle. Think.

She turned in her saddle. Eight men behind her; most, like her, a little bloodied, their horses tired. Only Bryhtsige still with his throwing spears. Thirty men ahead. None injured that she had seen; their horses tired, too, but fresher than hers.

Two advantages: Each of her horses carried less of a burden, and she was chasing, not being chased. Not much to set against three-to-one.

"This is a good place," she said to Aldnoth. "Hide the banner, and mark the spot." Cadwallon knew who was chasing him, and the less weight the better.

She set Flýte to a slow walk again. A bright sky, green grass, birds flicking this way and that, gorging on the worms up from the wet dirt. Water pouring like music. A beautiful day but for the distant screams and roars of battle, and the bone-deep weariness.

She kneed Flýte over to Lél until they were pacing side by side. Leofdæg's face was shrunken with exhaustion. "Tell me of this burn."

"Deniseburna." His voice was tired, as though he had not the breath. "Steep, deep, rocky. Weirs, waterfalls, hidden traps."

"Can he get through a gap in the hills and back to the causeway?"

"No." He made an effort. "Or not with gold."

Gold. Cadwallon could escape if only he would leave the gold. Would he? Would he know he had to make that choice? "We have to get above him."

They needed archers, or at least more throwing spears.

They stayed high and mostly hidden in the trees or the folds of hills, used their voices to seem like a greater number, calling from here and there, driving Cadwallon farther and farther south and west where the ground grew steeper and steeper and the burn deeper and more narrow. He lost men: two who tried to cross a deceptively smooth-looking stretch of water on horse, one whose tired mount slipped on a steep bank and plunged into the water, and another on foot who attempted to leap from stone to stone across a jagged weir.

At the top of one steep wooded slope they found a tumbled ruin of squared redcrest stone and brick.

Hild shouted. "Gladmær!" She pointed. After a moment he understood and scrambled down, followed by Bryhtsige, and they passed stones up to the others, who filled saddlebags, pockets, even took off tunics and bundled them up.

Redcrests built such towers to protect something. A mill? A ford? Most likely both. But where?

They moved forward in the mouth of the gorge between the hills where Deniseburna ran and the sound of battle vanished; they were in a sound shadow where all they heard was a light breeze in the trees, water running merrily, and the rapid, falling call of a kingfisher.

She lifted her face to the breeze coming from the high moor and crag south and west. She turned slowly in the saddle following the dips and splits in the hills. Ahead was where the burn began, spreading into a fan of sykes and cleughs springing from the surrounding horseshoe of high rocky crags. She had him now.

"Gladmær, Oeric. You have water? Drink it. Stay high. Don't let them rest."

Now was the time to be patient.

"Eat," she said to the others. "Rest. Tend yourselves and your horses."

Coelfrith, ever the reeve, collected the water bottles and went to fill them.

She slid from the saddle, ran her hands over Flýte. A small cut on her left foreleg—not unlike the cut on her own arm.

She dug out her wound roll, smeared bee glue on her arm, then on Flýte who snorted at the smell. At least she still had the energy to complain.

She sat in the grass, chewed fruit leather, mindless as a cow with its cud. Sipped water. Chewed. Her mind was blank, a piece of wood floating on a great dark lake of exhaustion. She must float a little longer.

When her fruit leather was gone she said to Aldnoth, "You and Grimhun, up. Relieve Oeric and Gladmær." She needed to sit a while longer. Just a little longer.

They hauled themselves to their feet.

"No. Wait." She stood, took deep breaths, sending her blood pumping. "We all go."

Perhaps it was the food, perhaps the water, perhaps just a sudden flick and flirt of wind but now she felt the need to hurry. "Up. Everyone up. Now. We go now."

And when they were all mounted she looked at them. They all had thrusting spears except her; she had her staff, and Bryhtsige two throwing spears. They had swords, seaxes, riding shields, and stones, many stones. Not the stuff of songs, but it would have to do.

She broke them into three groups of three, and sent them to different parts of the hill. Then she took her staff in both hands and with her knees steered Flýte along the ridge and looked down.

Twenty-six mounted men. Six baggage horses. Straggling in a line along the inside of the curve in the burn where the slope before them was gentle and the water behind them deep, but the opposite bank rose sheer as a cliff. At the centre, beside his banner bearer beneath the great dragon, Cadwallon, still golden in his mail.

He was a fool not to take that off.

"He's vain," said Bryhtsige, and his voice was shivery with something between hate and joy.

She had spoken aloud. Or perhaps Bryhtsige had plucked her thoughts from her mind. He seemed otherworldly, his eyes black.

Then stones began to rain down from the hill, and the horses below bucked and kicked, one fell on a ruined leg, screaming, taking its rider. The line bunched up, edged closer to the water, men with their hands on swords, and heads swivelling.

Stones rained down from the other direction, and she could tell Wulf was throwing, for the stones were huge and thrown, always, for the horses' legs.

Stones again from the first direction.

Below, men and horses were getting in each other's way. Horses were down and the terrible high screaming of that first horse scraped her mind.

Two broke desperately for the hill. "Now," she said. Bryhtsige moved with all the time in the world and cast one spear, then the other. The first took one horse cleanly through the neck, and horse and rider went down in red ruin; the second scored along a beast's shoulder and into its rider's thigh. Leofdæg galloped from the trees, swung at the rider's head. There was a great shower of blood and Leofdæg was galloping back to them in a great arc, the fallen man's throwing spears in hand. One spear for himself and two for Bryhtsige.

Another rain of stones, from different places, and now Hild could see the fear in the men below: How many did they face? Who were they?

One man leading a baggage horse turned and ran downstream. Bryhtsige ran, light as a deer, aimed, and threw. His spear caught the light as it arced up, and up, and the man looked back with a cry and tried to dodge, but his horse went the other way and the man fell with a wail into the water.

She whistled. Another rain of stones and two more spears, and when all nine of her people were gathered they looked at what they had done.

All along the burn horses were down or riderless. Cadwallon was on foot, sword drawn, five men about him.

He was pointing and giving orders, but over the rush of the burn and scream of horses and curses of wounded men she could not hear him.

She still could not see his face, but now that he was on foot it was plain, with that great barrel chest and the spindly legs of men as they aged, that he was past his prime.

Another order, and men were slapping horses, loosing them to run.

"The gold!" Aldnoth and Oeric both started forward but Hild called them back sharply. The gold could wait.

But while they were watching the horses, two men slipped away on foot in the other direction. She nodded at Bryhtsige and Leofdæg; they would not get far.

Eleven men left.

Cadwallon and his guard of four stepped forward. "Yffing!"

The call floated up the hill.

"Come and fight, Yffing!"

Hild unstopped her water bottle, drank. He was uninjured, but he was old, and she had the high ground. She reslung her bottle.

The sun was high. It would be light for a long time. If they were the only people in the world, Cadwallon would have no chance of escaping—

"Yffing!"

—but a mile away or less there were scores, perhaps still even hundreds of men, though she did not know what banners they rode under or where, exactly, they were.

"Again," she said.

And again the rain of stones, and then again from another direction, and this time when they were done there were nine men standing though one on a single leg, leaning on his spear. Now they had just one stone each and no more throwing spears. But they still had the high ground and the men below were moving slowly.

"Yffing, come and fight, man to man!"

His voice was thin, the peevish voice of an old, desperate man. He was afraid.

He was going to die on an unknown hillside at the hands of an unknown foe, and lie, unmarked and unsung, a pile of bones gnawed on by foxes. But it would have to be soon, for who knew what or who might appear as the sun fattened in the sky and the heat built.

"I need blood," she said.

She rode alone from the brow of the hill and paused in the full sun. Her face was painted with blood in a red boar mask, her furs around her like huge bristles. Flýte, too, wore blood. If she was Yffing she was Yffe from the underworld, Yffe heaved from the barrow or hauled from the grave. Baedd Coch. She moved one step forward, two. She said nothing.

Another step. Every eye below was fastened on her. She loomed tall as a giant. She did not even draw blade. What need did Baedd Coch have for a blade? One man crossed himself. She was too far away to see his eyes but she fixed her bloody gaze on his face, took another step. They were riveted. One more step.

And the day split open, red with screams and stones, raining upon them, and men masked in blood thundered down, sweeping in from every direction, spear in one hand and sword in the other, a thrust, a slash and away; then forming up behind the giant in a spear head thundering straight for Cadwallon. He broke, turned, and plunged into the burn, two of his guard backing into the water behind him, facing her. The water, she saw, was lower than it had been.

She broke one man's head with her staff, then leapt from Flýte's back over the head of the other and into the water after Cadwallon. Behind her she heard the familiar disciplined sweep, clash, stab, and cry of men fighting in threes, and she set it all aside. It was just her and this man who had killed Honey, killed Cian, Cadwallon Bradawc who stretched children out like deer and flayed them. Who burnt and destroyed because his heart was a hollow howling hole.

The water was cold and fierce. Up to mid-thigh. Like walking through freezing sand. But she would catch him. She would kill him. She had sworn it.

She drew her seax.

Closer, just three strides behind him now and he was struggling. He was waist-deep, grey-streaked hair wet and matted, gold-plated back heaving with effort. She could smell the fear stink on him.

"Cadwallon!"

He did not turn around, only struggled harder.

"Cadwallon Bradawc. Cadwallon Child Murderer. I am Hild Yffing, and I am come for you."

He stumbled—those thin, old-man's legs—then righted himself, then stumbled again and with a cry went down.

She strode forward, only it was deeper here, faster, and it was like fighting sullen stone. She forced her legs, inch by inch, leaning forward, panting. Cadwallon, facedown, water running fierce and wild over his golden back, flailed and splashed.

She stopped. Sheathed her seax. Put the iron tip of her staff against the base of his shaggy head and leaned on it with all her weight.

Wulf found her sitting on the bank, soaked from head to foot, a dead Cadwallon pulled half out of the water, staring at the sky.

"He has blue eyes," she said. "I didn't know that."

The sun was low and fat in the sky when Hild rode into Hagustaldesham under the great boar banner with threescore riders at her back, leading a great train of horse loaded with gold and spoil. They rode slowly, winding their way to the open ground where fires burned and meat roasted, and as they rode they sang the "Song of Baedd Coch," only now the song had more verses, and in this song Baedd Coch was the ruler of the whole isle.

Oswald and Oswiu, Rhoedd, Langwredd, the Bernician thegns, and Cormán waited to greet them under the rippling purple and gold raven banner. Beyond them she saw the Bryneich with Gwladus and Cuthred, Sintiadd and Morud, the traders of Rheged, and a small group of women, with Rhianmelldt at their centre.

She held up her hand. Her men halted; the singing wound to the end of the verse then her men burst into a chant of *Baedd Coch, Baedd Coch, Baedd Coch!*

Adair ab Beatan stamped his feet, *Baedd Coch, Baedd Coch!* And the Bryneich took it up, followed by Yrre and the younger Bernicians, until all but those under the raven banner were cheering.

She smelt the meat roasting, looked at the crowd, their upturned faces, red and smeared with joy, and thought, *This also is what it is to be king.* She had won the battle; she held the gold; the men were hers.

She slid from the saddle, walked the last five strides on her own. Stopped before Oswald and the raven banner.

Behind her the boar banner—smeared with mud and splashed with blood—flapped and slapped wetly in the wind.

She looked at Rhoedd, who bent his head a fraction, at the thegns, with their fists to their hearts, at Langwredd, who smiled: *Take it,* her eyes said. *Take it all.*

Her wyrd was balanced like a sword across her finger. One breath and it would tilt.

Oswald felt it, too. He was motionless, muscles coiled but arrested, waiting. He had worked his life to be king. He had fought for it. He would fight for it, like all kings. Because that's what kings did: They fought to be king, they fought as king, they fought to stay king. They could never let go, never rest because someone was always trying to be king in their place. Kings were never alone, never at peace. Never content. They murdered, they plotted, they fought, and the strongest, fastest, most cunning king won. And sooner or later they would fight someone stronger, or faster, or more cunning, and then they would die. It was how all kings ended: bleeding into the mud of the battlefield, whimpering in fear and pain.

"Yffing," he said.

"Oswald king," she said. A great weight seemed to lift from her shoulders and settle on his. She grinned. "I have your gold. Don't forget, some of it's mine. But you can have Cadwallon's golden armour."

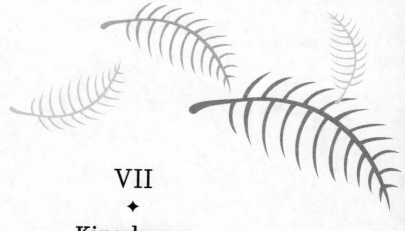

VII

◆

Kingshaper

Heavenfield—Hagustaldesham—Cetreht—York—Menewood

(*Meadmonath 634 to Hrethmonath 635, 33 weeks*)

36

✦

With the midday sun blazing from an enamel blue sky behind him, Cormán stood before the great cross they had raised just two days earlier. The priests had pulled off the mistletoe. He swept his gaze over the tenscore and more before him who had trooped there from Hagustaldesham, raised his hands, and began the Mass of Thanksgiving. Those who knew the rhythm of the thing knelt and responded and crossed themselves at the right moment but the rest, some still dripping with Tine water after their baptism, stood bemused—or sat, or lay propped against a friend, their bandages soaking through—while he shouted in Latin of God's will and Heaven's reward.

Hild leaned discreetly on the wall behind her, soaking up the sun. She watched a hen harrier following the contour of the wall over the rise and fall of hills, drifting low to surprise small mammals and birds. It was no doubt hungry; its eggs would be hatching or just-hatched on the south-facing slopes. She imagined the greyish-white eggs cracking and chicks opening bright pink mouths, newly alive in the world while all around them bodies rotted in the sun.

Cormán droned on. She had been up late into the night seeing to her men and horses, treating wounds, setting bones, speaking last words. Sitric had been the worst; he had not died until moonset, weeping for his little brother, and sometimes his mother, not knowing Hild, not able to leave a word for Grina. She ached to her bones, and longed for sleep, a good meal, and then to sleep again. Her arm itched. She would give a pound of gold for a long soak in a hot tub, followed by another nap.

Now he was giving some kind of homily, in Irish, pausing every now and again for Oswald to translate into Anglisc. It was a strange thing to see a king speak for a priest, even a bishop. They should have got Laisrén to do it. Or perhaps Oswald did it on purpose to convince his thegns and would-be thegns of the seriousness of his desire that they kneel to Christ.

Oswald must be tired, too, though she heard no hint of it in his voice. Perhaps his anger from this morning fuelled him. He had not been at all pleased that she would not share the spoil she had taken in the two months along the wall before the battle.

She had carefully not smiled when she shook her head and said, "No, Oswald king, that was not the bargain." And she nodded for Coelfrith to hand him the folded and sealed agreement signed at Urburg between her and Laisrén. He broke the seal with his deft fingers, and read—almost silently—his face turning to stone.

He had read it again, then beckoned to Laisrén for his copy. He read that, too, found it said the same thing, and handed the first back to Hild. "We will speak more of this after Mass."

She blinked awake; Cormán was giving the final blessing and people seemed to be limping forward and forming a line. She elbowed Gladmær, who was frankly snoring, and stood straighter.

"What are they doing?"

Bryhtsige said, "The shovel-jawed priest invited the wounded to come lay hands on the cross on Heaven's Field and be healed."

And lining them all up would give Oswald some time to think while they set up the boards for his first formal feast, and then the judging and divisions that would follow, and the inevitable quarrels that would follow that.

"Why are you smiling?" Gwladus said.

"I'm glad I'm not king."

Coelfrith had given her a rough accounting of their spoils, and back at Hagustaldesham, while they all drooled at the smell of roasting horse, Hild held her own informal gathering. She had started with threescore men, and lost only a dozen or so—most from the group she had left south of the Tine, who had met an overwhelming number of Cadwallon's men.

They had weighed the gold in one pile and silver in another, and a third was items too pretty to break. Then she had reserved half of each pile to herself.

From the rest, her people agreed between them that every surviving fighter would take an equal share, while Sintiadd, Morud, and Father Almund—to their everlasting delight—were each allotted a half share. The leaders of the three main bands were to receive double shares, along with each of the Fiercesomes. Further shares to favourites and to those left behind in Deira would be made from the lady's own share and at her pleasure.

Most of the fallen men had been professional fighters with no family, but the rest agreed that half the share of those who had died should go to the fallen's survivors.

Then they broached their last cask of Menewood mead to drink while they waited for the feast.

"Grina's going to be rich," Morud said.

Sintiadd snorted. "Not as rich as the Bryneich woman might have been if she dared make a claim."

Hild, sitting in the grass between Gwladus and Oeric, looked over to where Langwredd sat with her Bryneich, laughing, one hand cupped around the back of Cuthred's neck.

"Cat with the cream," Gwladus said.

Sintiadd had told Hild that while in Caer Luel with the children, Denw had confided that her mistress had not bled since Œstre Mass. No one knew who the father was, but it seemed she had chosen Cuthred for now. "Cuthred seems happy. I'm glad."

"It's good to be happy," Gwladus agreed. "What will the king do with her do you think?"

Oswald Lamnguin, king. It did not seem real. "Give her his blessing and install her at Din Baer." At least he would if he listened to her, and she had promised to uphold Langwredd's claim. "We'll see if she can hang on to the Bryneich on behalf of her young sons." If she did not, well, Langwredd and the Bryneich were no longer her problem but Oswald's.

"You're smiling again." Gwladus seemed to approve. "You'll let her take Cuthred?"

"I'll release him from his oath if that's what he wants." It would be a pity. He was shaping to be a good man, useful. There again, it would mean one less mouth to feed, something to think about now she owed tithes every year to a king, and had smaller borders to protect. "Though if I were Langwredd I'd choose someone older."

"Age doesn't matter. You're not older."

"Someone with more heft, then." In the distance, Cuthred looked up at Langwredd and said something, and she laughed, and kissed him, and they both smiled hugely, then wrapped themselves in each other's arms. It was hard not to smile along with them. "But there's a lot to be said for choosing one who makes one's heart sing."

"Who makes your heart sing?" Uinniau said as he joined them, hectic-cheeked and grinning. He plunked himself down by Gwladus and offered his leather bottle. "It's wine!" he said. "Good Gaulish wine from the Rheged traders back from Tinamutha." He took a deep pull. "So who is it that makes your heart sing?"

Gwladus took the bottle. "We were talking about the Bryneich princess there, who wants to be queen."

"What woman doesn't want to be a queen?"

Gwladus snorted and Hild laughed.

"Ah," he said. "Well, fine. And of course not my Begu. Now there's a woman who can make a heart sing! And soon, oh so very soon now, thanks to you, Hild Yffing, she can be mine! All mine! And in a year we'll be surrounded by fat babies! Oh, let's drink to that. Three times three!"

Laisrén was making his way towards them. Hild stood. "Save some of that wine for me."

"No!" said Uinniau cheerfully.

"I was talking to Gwladus, Winny. Because I don't doubt that priest is coming to collect us both."

Oswald Lamnguin, king of the north, sat on the closest thing to a throne his people could cobble together—a stool with an embroidered cushion that kept slipping, and a board behind him painted with both raven and boar, with all the banners planted behind that, hanging limply in the still air—while on a mixed circle of stools, stumps, and upturned barrels sat his chief people: Hild, with Coelfrith and the accounts he kept in his head, speaking for the British and Anglisc of Deira; Oswiu Iding; Rhoedd, with both Uinniau and Mot Oer, speaking for Rheged, for his kingdom was still his and would be, in name at least, until his death; Langwredd of the Bryneich, with young Adair ab Beatan looking both proud and solemn at the responsibility—though of course he had none, for Langwredd would want him only to agree to whatever she decided—for the British of Bernicia; Yrre of Melmin, looking scared, and speaking—for now, for Oswald was wary of those older thegns who had supported Edwin, and of their sons—for the Anglisc of Bernicia; Cormán, with Aidan, for the church; and Laisrén, though she was not sure of his position with Oswald.

"First," Oswald said. "An accounting." He was once again smooth-faced and even-voiced, the only sign of his fatigue being dark stubble on his chin and neck. It made him seem more human, less priestly. It was Laisrén who produced and read the lists, while Aidan, sitting behind Cormán with his tablet balanced on his knee, made notes. It took a long time.

The sun was a fat, rich yellow and hot on the back of Hild's shoulders rather than her head by the time they had agreed the weights and divisions of gold and silver. Few were happy, except Hild, for her bargain had been set and sealed before blood was spilled—and she had kept her side, and more; and no king could begin his reign as a bargain-breaker. It did not mean he was happy about it, and there would be more to come on the subject in private; kings always wanted more than their share.

Later, she knew, there would be fights among the Anglisc Bernicians when young Yrre came to them with the share to be further divided among the thegns and youngbloods. Perhaps a quarrel or two among the Bryneich, too, though Langwredd, through Cuthred, could probably call on the aid of others of Hild's men to sort any real problems. Perhaps he had been a wise choice after all.

It was halfway through gelotendæg by the time they got down to the real business.

The sun poured honey light over the meadow turning the Tine behind them to gold. It was hot, but now there was a breeze from the river to cool the feasting folk at their makeshift boards. It seemed Hild's was not the only group who had broached the casks early. As Oswald, sitting now on a chair raised on blocks, made proclamations and Aidan wrote them down, there were good-natured cheers and the occasional hoot.

He, Oswald Brightblade, heir to both Iding and Yffing, would be a good king, a strong king, a fine and fair king to all folk north of the Humbre.

From this place he would progress south to Deira, where he would make his esteemed cousin Oswine Yffing his underking of that region—

Puzzled silence from some quarters, boos from others. A few mutters: What about the lady? Cath Llew! Cath Llew eats poxy ravens!

—then progressing back north to overwinter in Bernicia, which was to be his own. Oswiu Iding, the king's brother and, until the king took himself a wife, the ætheling, would remove to Caer Luel with his new wife, Rhianmelldt of Rheged, there to remain until spring—

"Or til he's got his pretty new wife with child!" one wag shouted.

"Won't take long!" shouted another. And indeed, both Oswiu and Rhianmelldt were missing the feast.

—after which the ætheling would return to Oswald's side as his chief gesith.

Wulf nodded in approval. Dudda said, "We heard he had a good fight."

"Not as good as us," Gladmær said, admiring the gold on his arm—so many rings he could barely lift it.

"We had the lady," Oeric said.

"And God." Almund had not been there, but since Hild had taken him as her confessor he felt it his duty to remind her every now and again that she was mortal, though so far his tone was mild, even apologetic.

"Shh," Sintiadd said, for Oswald was speaking again.

Rhoedd, mighty king of Rheged, would remain so for the rest of his days, after which succession would pass to the children of Oswiu and Rhianmelldt.

Good-natured pounding of boards, for much of the wine they were drinking came courtesy of Rhoedd.

Though the king's cousin, Oswine Yffing, would be underking of Deira, Oswald's most esteemed cousin, the brave and cunning Hild Yffing, would have Elmet as her own, and not be subject to any but the king of the north.

A great roar of approval, hoots, scattered bits of song—Baedd Coch here, Cath Llew there. And Hild noted the slight tightening around Oswald's mouth.

He had to stop and wait for the noise to die down.

The good Langwredd, lady of the Bryneich, would repair to the stronghold of Din Baer, there to hold it in trust for Coledauc's sons, or until such time as Oswald chose.

Polite noises, but mostly it was a matter of indifference to the majority: Bernicia was wholly Oswald's, and who cared about a few ragtag Bryneich? Everyone knew they would just squabble and fight among themselves until there was nothing left, because that's what Bryneich did.

And finally, he charged Bishop Cormán to care for all their souls. Any among them who had not been baptised must do so before they left. And in due course there would be more to say about that—

"No doubt much more," Gwladus said.

Almund nodded.

—but, for now, each and every one of them must eat and drink as much as they were able, for he, Oswald, would be a good king, a strong king, a fine and fair king to all folk of the north. He would listen to them and guide them like a father, and bring peace and riches to the land!

Hild stood, put her fingers to her mouth, and split the air with a whistle. The noise stopped dead. She raised her cup. "To Oswald Brightblade, the wisdom of the raven and the courage of the boar, king of the north!"

"King of the north!"

Later, as the sky was turning to lilac, crickets were skricking, and even the river sounded relaxed, Hild sat in the grass among her core people, leaning back propped on her elbows, idly drinking, nibbling, watching Oswald walk from one group to another, talking. Every now and again one would nod, and clasp hands.

"He's recruiting," she said.

Coelfrith nodded. "He came to me."

"Did he?"

"I told him you held my oath."

Hild heard a hint of a question. "I'd release you, if that's what you want." He was still. "If you were a young, hungry gesith keen to make a name, I'd say go, with my blessing. Fighting for a king brings more chances for making a name." A better chance of being killed, too. "You're a good gesith, Coelfrith. Very good. But you're a better reeve. I've need of a reeve, and you're the best. I'd like you to stay. Will you?"

"I will. You will help me avenge my father."

Coelgar. "Yes. Though I won't lie: It will take some time. Meanwhile, I value you, as man, reeve, and gesith. Come talk to me if you ever get a better offer. I'll match it if I can." In terms of gold, she could. She was, for now, the richest lord in the north.

She sat up and turned to look at her other gesiths: Grimhun, her oldest

Hound; Oeric, the first who had ever sworn her an oath; her Fiercesomes, as much part of her as the five fingers of her right hand; Aldnoth, who had acquitted himself well for a youngster and would one day be a useful man; and Tole, who could put an arrow anywhere she chose and had somehow never gone back to the group of archers. "If any of you get offers, come and tell me so I can match them."

Dudda grinned. "We're already rich, lady."

"I'm not a king—"

Bryhtsige said, "If ever you want to be, you've only to say the word."

Nods here and there in the gathering gloom.

"Could a king give us this?" Leofdæg circled his finger to encompass their small group.

Wulf made an emphatic noise for their attention, then gestured rapidly: puppets, ugly, laughing, pushed away, clasped hands, whispers, awe, lady. And for once Dudda did not translate; he did not need to. Hild understood; they all understood. The Fiercesomes had been Edwin's ugly puppets. Shunned despite their strength and skills. Laughed at. Now they belonged. Now people looked at them and nodded and said, *They're the lady's men.* What more did they need?

And with a fierce bloom of heat under her breastbone she realised they had all been asked and all said no. They had refused a king, for her. "We—" She cleared her throat. "We leave in two days. We're travelling with the king. We'll talk more, then, of what you might need. For now, rest. Heal your wounds. Play—though, Dudda, try not to win everyone's gold."

"Even from the Bernician oafs?"

"Especially from the Bernician—our Bernician brothers." She grinned. "That is, you can win it all but then you have to lose most of it back. I don't want anyone killed over dice."

On her own or with her small band, Hild could have ridden from the wall to Cetreht in two days, one if she had no care for their mounts. But now she rode as part of a king's train, and though they rode on the wide war street, and though they did not creak along behind swaying wagons as they had with Edwin, it was a long, slow journey in the heat.

It was the night after the full moon when they came to Cetreht. Osthryth hosted the king with all the state that Craven, almost untouched by Cadwallon's ravages, could afford. As soon as it became apparent to Hild that they would be there for some time, she called Oeric and Aldnoth to her, charged them with messages, then went to find James.

James and Hild walked the banks of the Ur for miles, stopping to watch a kingfisher here, or an otter there. They sat on a gently sloping grassy bank and Hild watched the water, following the flow, the curling patterns each fall made, endlessly turning, turning.

"Was it very bad?"

"No. Hard, and messy. But not bad."

"And you killed him."

"I did." She thought maybe she should take her boots off and wade in that water.

"How did it feel?"

"I thought it would be an ending." She looked at the river flowing away from them. "But it's not."

37

S O NOW OSWALD WAS KING, crowned in the great stone church at York by Bishop Cormán, and knelt to in the great hall by Oswine Yffing. Oswine, in turn, was crowned—though not by Cormán, the mighty bishop, who distained a mere underking, but by Aidan—and was knelt to in turn by all the great and good of Deira, except Hild and the people of Elmet who knelt to no one but Oswald.

"Oswine doesn't seem to much mind," Hild told her mother as they walked through the garth. Here and there her mother tutted: Where there should have been herbs, there was crimson water figwort, humming with bees—a sign the drainage had not been properly attended to. And too many nettles.

It was hard to tell how her mother felt about the loss of Luftmær. She had lost weight and her face seemed sharper, younger. The death of Luftmær had cracked the shell of settledness that had grown about her the last year or two, and she seemed, now, more the Breguswith of their first years with Edwin than the thick-middled matron of married daughters.

"Why would Oswine mind when he has the whole of Deira to lord it over?"

"If he can hold on to it—though he listens to advice, at least." Hild did not voice her suspicion that this could eventually become a problem. It was clear to her that, from the moment Aidan had blessed the new underking, a mutual bond had sprung up—even James had noticed, or perhaps James especially had noticed—and Aidan was sharp-eyed with a bright mind. Oswine might become very well-advised indeed. "Has he approached you to run Deira's cloth trade yet?"

"No."

"He will."

"What would you have me say?"

Hild stopped, took her mother's hands in her own; they were rougher, harder than they had been. "Choose what would make you happy."

"Happy," Breguswith said. "I'm not sure what that means anymore."

"You will be."

Breguswith said nothing, just started walking again. "And you? I haven't seen Brona with you much the last few days."

"She's busy butchering. Kings and war bands eat a lot of meat. Here in York there's work enough for four, so she's busy." None of it was a lie, but it left a lot unsaid.

They were the same women they had been, and their bodies fit together the same—better, perhaps, for the absence. But now they were in York, where Brona had lived all her life, and it was different.

In Hild's apartments, Brona rolled on her belly, face dewy from their exertions. "Why didn't I come to the hall? Because I'd rather eat with Linnet in the alehouse, or share a skewer with the leather-workers at their stall than prance about like a pig in a dress and sit among the lords and ladies while you talk about things I don't understand."

"You understand well enough."

"You're right. I just don't—" She sighed, sat up. "Look, love, it was fine sitting with you at the board in Menewood, where ceorls sit with ladies and milkmaids with priests, but can you imagine me at your side here? With a king?"

"He's just my cousin."

"Yes. You're cousin to kings, sister to queens—"

"Does it matter?"

"—and I'm a butcher."

"And I'm a butcherbird!" Hild said lightly. Brona did not smile. "I'm sorry. I'm listening. I could find you something else—"

Brona was shaking her head. "I'm a butcher. It's what I do, it's who I am. I don't want anything else. It feels good to spend the day doing what I'm good at, talking to people who see me for who I am."

"But you're not just a butcher, you're—"

Brona held up her hand sharply. "Stop. Listen to me now and try to hear. There is no just in butcher. It's enough in itself."

"Well, of course it is. That's not what I meant."

"Then what did you mean?"

Hild moved closer, put her hands on Brona's warm thighs. "We have so much we could find out together, places we could go, people we could meet."

"Staying in one place can be interesting. Customers bring me curious things: the calf with the in-turned foot, the one-eyed sheep."

Hild herself liked to share curious things with Brona: how this bird nested here, and why. What the pattern on a leaf meant. Like Clut bringing a sparrow for Ceadwyn. Even the cat knew things were better with someone to share them. "We could live in Loidis; we'll need a butcher there as we grow."

"Loidis? You like to roam, always seeking the skyline. For you, even York isn't big enough. So why do you think you could stay in Loidis?"

Before Hild could think of what to say, Begu burst in, brilliant with excitement. "He's agreed—the king! And Aidan said he'd do it! He said the great church was the only fitting place for a prince of Rheged! And everyone's going to be there!" Her face stilled. "I just wish Fa could be here. He always liked Winny. You'll come, won't you? Both of you?" Then she seemed to take in their state of undress. "Oh! I'm sorry! Except—well, no, I'm not! I'm getting married and then I can be as shameless as you two. I can't wait!"

Oswald demanded that Hild show him something of Elmet. From York they toured Aberford. Heiu explained the collecting of fleeces and Laisrén questioned her closely about numbers and weights. Grimhun showed Oswald the beck and the dam, and, before Hild could stop him, the ingenious gate and toll mechanism for traders coming up Dere Street from the south.

"Though we've not had many," she said.

Oswald said to Laisrén, "See to it that you get more on this." Back to

Hild. "In York I was telling Oswine how much I admired his many berths and the ships in them, and he told me that was all your doing, that many of the ships are yours, and that you have many more at a place called Cnotinsleah. I would like to see Cnotinsleah. Now, today."

And so they did.

Grimhun had worked wonders here, too. A long house and gatehouse for guards; an alehouse, and those jetties. Hild's belly dropped when she saw seven ships berthed. Two were wide-bellied Frisians and one was Cenhelm's *Curlew*, but the other four were hers, including the *Seadragon* and the *Dolphin*.

Oswald was expressionless. He looked at them a long time. "How many ships have you in total?"

"Six." The *Dolphin* was just a small boat.

"And the men to sail them?"

She nodded.

"They were Edwin king's ships, Northumbre ships." It was not a question. "And now they are mine."

"They weren't part of the agreement."

"Only kings need war boats. I will have them."

She had more men and more gold than this king. If she wanted to fight him, she would win. But she did not want to be king. Elmet was enough. And Elmet in the best of times could barely find use for three ships—trading ships at that.

"I'll sell you three ships."

"You will give me them all and their men."

"Four, with their men."

"Five, and their men."

"Five and their men, but I choose which ship I keep, and I choose the men to sail her. And I trade tithe-free at royal wīcs." The *Seadragon* and the *Dolphin* were more than she needed, and now she would not have to carry the upkeep of the other five. She began to understand Edwin's satisfaction at always making a bargain work for him in the end.

They locked gazes, then Oswald nodded and held out his arm. "You bargain like a Frisian."

"You must not know any Frisians. The Frisian who captains that one"—she nodded at Bavo's ship—"always gets the better of me. He's a most useful man. I'll introduce you."

———

Oswald did not seem much interested in the new Loidis, perhaps because she was not, either.

They led their horses along the Hol Beck and she pointed out where the beavers had once built their dam. "One day Loidis will be useful," she said. "Near the war street, near Cnotinsleah. It'll be the perfect catchment and hub for trade from the south of Elmet." When she had gathered the south into the fold.

"Tell me of the south."

She told him of Caer Daun and the trackless waste between the war street and Lindsey.

"I shall want Lindsey back before long."

"I've some ideas about that."

"Have you?"

He did not need to know of her oath to avenge the murder of Coelfrith's father—but she could see a way to arrange his goals to suit hers. So she spoke to him of Adlingfleot and Gole, the Treonte and the water road into the heart of Lindsey. He did not need to know, either, that on her way to deal with Blæcca she could stop and see Afanc, as she had promised, and so fold the people of the mire into Elmet. This was what it was like to think as a king: to make one throw win three gains. "That water road is open only in winter. But before then you could send ships down the coast to the Wash and blockade the Haven. You could squeeze Blæcca—no, you should kill Blæcca, and sooner rather than later."

He raised an eyebrow.

"Blæcca is Penda of Mercia's man in all but name."

Oswald nodded. She could not tell if this was news to him or not. Penda himself would have to be dealt with one day. Not this year, or even the next, but one day. But they could deal with Penda's underlings soon, especially those hard by Elmet's boundaries.

"The East Angles would not be happy to see us take Lindsey."

"Hereswith queen is my sister. She, too, will be threatened by Penda." Even if she did not believe it yet.

"Yes." He stared across the Yr, unseeing, then snapped back. He had made a decision. "Cousin, don't marry without my permission."

"I'll marry as and when I like." She took a breath. "But, cousin, be assured, I'm in no hurry. And if I should marry, there would be no more children."

He looked around. "Of the places in Elmet, where does your heart lie?"

She could not tell what he was thinking. "Why?"

"I would offer you a token of my goodwill, and give you that one place to be yours, wholly and forever, tithe-free."

Bocland. Hers forever. "Menewood."

"Show me."

Laisrén had told Aidan about the priest network based in Menewood, and of the harmony between the Roman and the British religious here—both without bishops. So Aiden wished to travel there with them. And of course James, if there was to be talk of the future of the church, wanted to be there. So it was that five of them—the three religious, Hild, and Oswald—stopped at the pollard.

"Here?" Oswald turned this way and that in his saddle. "It seems . . ."

"Wet?" She smiled slightly. Rhin had followed the instructions she had sent with Oeric and partially dammed the beck to flood the mouth of the valley.

Laisrén caught the smile. "My king, this is a ruse. Cleverly designed by the lady Hild to hide the valley's existence or at the very least render it unattractive for exploration. But this valley is a most pleasant place. Because of the lady's foresight and planning, it remained hidden and untouched, the last redoubt of Deira even as Cadwallon and Penda over-wintered in York."

"Then let's go see what makes this valley so special."

Hild dismounted. "It'll be easier on foot." She patted the tree as she went past.

"This is wonderful!" Aidan said as he looked at Ceadwin's painted walls. He saw Ceadwin did not understand. "Lovely fish!" he said in Anglisc.

"They're salmon," Ceadwin said, trying not to tower over them all and succeeding only in hunching like a nervous spider.

"So? A most . . ." He looked at Hild, switched to Irish. "How do you say *noble* in Anglisc?"

"He understands British very well. Most in Menewood do."

"A most noble fish," Aidan said in that language. "We eat many on Hii. And it must be such a gift to be able to reach so high to paint the clouds."

It was a hot sunny day and the church doors were wide open and together with the milky glow of the parchment windows the light and colour were, indeed, lovely. The altar now held a small but beautifully carved cross with the thinnest silver-gilt plaque inset, and a finely embroidered linen cloth that she could tell, from the preponderance of yellow in the pattern, had been stitched by Begu.

Rhin, who as usual had been working in rough clothes—for everyone in Menewood knew him—came in wearing his hastily donned skirts, just in time to hear Aidan say, "And a carved cross, what an interesting choice."

"Lady. Welcome home." A respectful bend of his head. "Brothers." Then he realised that one of the clean-shaven man before him was not tonsured. "My lord."

"Father Rhin. This is Oswald Lamnguin, our new king."

"Lord king!" He bowed.

"Cousin, this is Father Rhin who in my absence leads this valley. This is his church. I'll leave you with him to explain how we worship here. Rhin, tell them of our plans. Ceadwin, come with me, please."

She left them listening to Rhin telling them about her promise to provide proper cross and plate, and perhaps even glass for the windows, and hurried along the path towards the long house. "Where are the children?"

Fllur and the children were in the garth. Maer was explaining something to Clut the cat while Wilfrid ran up and down with a small sack of grain, flinging it everywhere shouting, "Chickie here! Chickie here!" while the chickens prudently ran out of his way.

"He can run," she said. Or almost run. A few steps, then a walk, and he did not stagger but walked smoothly, then a few more running steps. And he could carry something at the same time. And throw. "He's grown."

"Children do," Ceadwin said with a fond smile.

Fllur saw them. "Look who's here! It's Mor Hild." She put down her twine next to the bean scaffold she was building and stood. "Lady."

Maer looked up, smiled shyly. Wilfrid stopped dead and frowned.

Hild went to one knee and opened her arms. After a moment Maer ran and gave Hild a hug. "Mor Hild! Oof! Ow."

"Sorry." She took off the arm rings and stowed them in various pockets. They clicked and clanked. She took them out again. Maer looked at them round-eyed.

Hild smiled. "Do you like them?"

Maer nodded.

"Here." She chose the smallest and lightest, a wrist cuff, handed it to her.

Maer looked at Ceadwin, then Fllur for permission, then slid it reverently onto her arm. It went all the way up to her shoulder. She stared at it, fascinated.

"Later, you can tell me about your summer. First I want to hug Wilfrid."

Wilfrid clutched his bag of seed and stared at her with one eye, then the other, like a cross bird. "Mum-mor?"

Hild nodded and held out her arms again. He looked at her sideways. "Me milk."

"No milk, Wilfrid," she said. She had had no milk for half a year. She looked at Fllur.

She shook her head. "He's not asked for milk for two months. And then only when he fell and banged his knee. Wilfie, come and say hello to your mor."

Hild laid the other arm rings on the path. "Look at the pretty things." She picked up the big hinged cuff she wore around her biceps, carefully moved the clasp, opened it, then closed it again, and moved the clasp back over the stud.

Intrigued, he took two steps towards her. She had been gone four months; perhaps she seemed like a dream of another time.

Then he made up his mind. Stepped in, put his arms around her neck, and nuzzled her cheek. Her heart squeezed and she felt that faint echo in her breasts; she breathed in his smell. "Wilfrid." Wilfrid, whom she had fed from her body. Wilfrid, whom her body recognised as hers. "My Wilfrid."

"Mum-um Hild," he said. He fingered the end of her braid with his chubby hands. Nodded, satisfied. "My mor."

"Yes," she said. "Yes. Your mor."

Then he pointed to the cuffs. "Mine." And to the one on Maer's arm. "Mine."

"No," Maer said.

"Give me."

"Do you like this one?" Hild said.

He looked at it. "I want all."

A whole thought. While she was gone he had become a small person.

"You can play with this one for now." She handed it to him. It nearly over-balanced him.

He plunked down on his bottom and started investigating the clasp. It would keep him occupied for a while.

She said to Fllur, "The king's here."

Fllur turned white.

"No, no. Not Cadwallon. He's gone; he can never hurt you or anyone else ever again. It's the new king. Oswald. We'll need food and drink." She looked to Ceadwin. "You see to that. Fllur, take the children to Brona's house and see if you can clean them up a bit. Then bring them to the long house."

"And up there?" Oswald said.

"Horse pasture," she said. "A small one. We'll be keeping most at old Caer Loid."

"Another place I haven't seen."

"There's not much to see."

"Cadwallon destroyed it, my king," Laisrén said. "Though Rhin tells me Bishop Paulinus destroyed the churches first."

Oswald and Laisrén exchanged a glance she could not interpret.

"Let us go eat."

The food, while simple, and oddly served by whispering people not used to playing the role of housefolk, was plentiful and good.

Oswald commented on the mead.

"It's our pride," she said. "Perhaps you would like part of the Elmet tithe paid in mead. Or perhaps just the honey it comes from." Easier to transport. "Ah. Here they are."

Fllur led in the children. Hild smiled. Fllur nudged them.

"Greetings, Mor Hild," Maer said. Then curtseyed. "My lords."

"My mor!" Wilfrid said belligerently, pulled his hand from Fllur's, and walked over, for all the world a tiny prince, the massive arm ring over his shoulder like a baldric. He climbed into Hild's lap and glared possessively at the rest of the table.

Hild smoothed his hair.

Oswald looked from boy to woman to boy, and said with great satisfaction, "Ah. Where your heart lies indeed. Please introduce us."

"He's—this is Wilfrid. But he's not—"

"My mor!"

"Oh, indeed, little one," Oswald said, and tousled his hair. Such a big hand on such a small fragile head. "Would you like to come visit me, little man?"

Wilfrid pointed to Oswald's jewelled belt. "No. Give me that."

"No doubt your mother will give you many things as you grow." Oswald rested his hand on the head a moment, nodded at Hild's expression, the involuntary move she had made to her seax, then lifted it. "And the girl?"

"This is Maer. Cadwallon killed her parents, as he did Wilfrid's father."

She set Wilfrid down on the floor, gave him a push towards Fllur. "Go with Fllur, both of you."

Ceadwin scooped Wilfrid up, swung him through the air. "Let's leave your mor to talk to the nice men. We'll go see if the duck eggs have hatched!"

Oswald watched them all the way to the door, then turned back to the board, and, as though nothing had happened, asked what kind of flowers the bees used to make such fine honey.

On the ride back to Aberford, Oswald rode ahead with Laisrén and made it plain he would not welcome interruption. Hild rode between James and Aidan, barely hearing them while her thoughts ran back and forth like trapped squirrels.

At Aberford Gwladus saw her face but was wise enough not to ask. But all the way back to York she stuck to Hild's side.

Brona was in her butcher's shop when they got back, with no time to talk. "I'll be going til the last moment, maybe even longer."

"I'll see you at the feast, then?"

Brona gave her a short look. "You really think they'll invite the butcher to the king's farewell feast?"

"I'm inviting you."

"And where would I sit? At the high bench with the great and good? Or stuck down at the lower benches being grateful for a look from you?" She shook her head. "That came out wrong—I'm feeling harried. I'll come to you later, after."

In the apartments, Sintiadd brushed her hair. "Gwladus said to take particular care tonight."

Hild nodded.

"And she said to say she's made sure both her and your mother will be next to you."

She nodded again.

"Lady, did something happen?"

"I've been threatened and I'm trying to decide what to do about it."

"Who'd be foolish enough to try frighten you? May as well try to catch air in a net. You want me to have Wulf stand behind you at the feast?"

"It's not that kind of threat. But thank you." She made an effort. "So what sort of impression are we making?"

"Well, Gwladus suggested to your mother that she suggest to Oswine that Osthryth be cupbearer. So you need to look different." She bustled over to a small chest, and, with some effort, lifted out something that looked like an armoured throat and chest collar, only made of gold, with great rubies inset in a cross. Obviously heavy. And old. "It's one of the things we took from Cadwallon, though who knows where he dug it up from. Look. And this for your seax." A blue leather sheath with snakes entwined in silver and gold with tiny garnet eyes. She lifted out piece after piece, and Hild realised it was all heavy, all gold, all red or blue, and not a single women's piece.

"No veil band."

"Gwladus said not. She said to braid your hair with this." A thin rope of woven gold. "And she thought this for your head." A circlet of gold inset with lapis, beryl, and sapphire. It looked Roman. "No sleeves for your dress. Your furs—I saw to it that they were cleaned—instead of a wrap."

"It's too hot for furs."

"She said you'd say that. And to tell you it's only for the walk to your seat. She and your mother talked about it together, and she said to please just trust her, and to remember: You don't have to pretend anymore." She smiled. "Also, there's this." She held out her hand. On her palm was a tiny bottle with a jewelled stopper. "This was my idea."

"Is that . . ." She lifted Sintiadd's hand to her face, sniffed the stoppered bottle. "Oh!" Jessamine.

Sintiadd nodded. "The only drop to be had in the north. I got Bavo to find it. Well, I got that Dudda to get him to find it." She worked at the stopper. "Hard to get out—tight as a gnat's naughty. And you wouldn't believe how much it cost! There you go. No, don't put it on yet. Just as you leave."

"Shouldn't that be about now?"

"Oh, there's no rush. You know kings, they're always late."

As Sintiadd dressed her, piece by piece, Hild found she was regarding herself as though from a distance, like a child being dressed for something she did not understand; it was not until the heavy gorget went around her neck and weighed against her chest like a boulder that she understood why. She stood up and let Sintiadd dab her wrists and neck with the jessamine oil, then drape the furs around her shoulders and hand her her staff. Unlike every other thing she wore or carried, it had not been painted or polished or oiled. It had been left plain and hard, no doubt at Gwladus's behest, with a hint of rust that could have been blood on the iron heel: a brutal contrast to the wealth and splendour of her gold and furs.

The roar of voices and music from the hall hit her like an enemy charge as she stepped from her apartments.

Just as she had on that Modraniht thirteen years before, Hild walked to the curtain between the kitchens and the hall while the scop sang of the riches and bounty of Deira, the majesty of Bernicia, and the glory not of Edwin but Oswald—he was already there, then.

Osthryth stood just behind the curtain, adjusting her cuffs, picking up a great golden cup—nothing like the one Hild had once carried, but just as heavy—setting it down again, while a houseboy kept starting to lift the curtain, then letting it drop again when he realised it was another false start. He saw Hild, and his eyes went round.

Osthryth turned. "Oh. Thank the Christ! They told me I couldn't go in until everyone was seated. But I've been waiting for an age! You're the last one. Even the king's there. Hurry, hurry." She flicked back her veil, then changed her mind and brought it forward again.

"You look just right." She checked the cup, not overfull, and handed it to Osthryth. "Just walk slowly, look only at the high table, and all will be well. I'll go first."

She nodded to the houseboy, who bowed low and lifted the curtain, holding it open while bent almost to the ground. She stepped through as the scop's last chord still hung in the air.

Every head turned her way.

Unlike the seven-year-old girl stepping uncertainly into the light, she strode. She strode as, long ago, Dunad's men strode into the hall, cloaks swinging, with the head of Ceredig king in a box. She did not need to carry a head, they all knew she had killed Cadwallon, the man who had killed the overking. This giant, with the brutal iron-shod staff, the very staff that had killed a king-killer, wearing more gold than most kings could bear, who could call the raven and the boar, who wore the skin of Cath Llew, who could snap her fingers and command the swords of all the war bands of the north. She was Hild. Herself. And she would not be threatened.

Even without fire burning in the pits, it was hot. Skin gleaming, the scent of jessamine—the scent of access to the power over the sea, the power in Cent, in Frankia—trailing behind her, she strode up the long, long passageway between the two lines of benches to the high bench where the king sat in the centre, Oswine to his left, Prince Uinniau of Rheged and Begu, farther to his left, and an empty seat to his right. She stopped, rested her hand on her seax hilt, the seax all knew had been a gift of the prince of the Bryneich, the alliance she had made to make Oswald king. "Hail, Oswald king. Elmet salutes you."

In perfect silence she strode around behind the board, stepped over the bench to stand between her mother and Oswald king, slung her furs off her shoulders, and held them behind her. Someone took them. Then she unhooked her sheath and held that over her other shoulder. Her gold glimmered and gleamed in the torchlight, red and blue and gold, and wearing the ancient Christian symbol as though god and wyrd were her servants—her servants not her masters. Let them look. Let them see her bare arms and her diadem, let them see her strength, her wealth, and her power: Hild Yffing, king maker and king breaker. When she felt the hall balanced on the edge of standing and roaring her name, she sat.

Unseen behind the edge-cloth, her mother gripped her thigh and shook hard, once, twice, eyes savage with triumph.

Then, like a deer stepping from the shelter of the forest into the light, Osthryth made her entrance. Hild stood and clapped, then everyone was clapping and hooting with relief—this they understood; this was what women were supposed to do—and Osthryth blushed coral red.

As Oswald and Hild sat, he said, "You're late, cousin." Then Osthryth was standing before them with the ceremonial cup. The hall quieted.

"Oswald Iding, king of all north of the Humbre, on behalf of Deira, I Osthryth, daughter of Osric, salute you! I bid you drink."

Oswald stood, took the cup, lifted it two-handed to Osthryth, to Oswine, and drank deep.

Hild, at the king's right, was next. She stood in turn, raised the cup two-handed to Oswald, to Oswine, to Osthryth, and brought the cup of stinging white mead to her lips. Like Edwin king's chief gesith on the Modraniht feast so long ago, she drained it, lifted it, and turned it upside down. The crowd roared and stamped. She grinned at Oswald, and handed it back to Osthryth.

Oswald breathed out and his shoulders dropped a full fingerwidth: no one who drank a whole cup of white mead was planning to fight. If there was to be a challenge it would not be from her, or not today.

The food kept coming, remove after remove, each haunch or swan or sucking pig more elaborate than the last; Brona had butchered everything beautifully.

The roar of conversation rose and fell with toasts and songs, and, farther down the benches, boasting. The scop began a song of some Irish battle or other in which Oswald had turned the tide.

"Luftmær would have put that scop to shame," Breguswith said.

"He would."

Gwladus leaned forward so Hild could see and hear her over the noise. "I told her how he died—not like a scop but fighting alongside Oswiu."

"Fool," Breguswith said. "No one ever cared that a song be true, only that people could sing it and that the chorus made the hero feel ten feet tall. But still, I'd like to hear of his end."

"Oswiu or one of his men would have to tell it," Hild said. "And he won't be back for a while."

Oswald leaned forward and turned to them. "I would be most happy, Lady Breguswith, to send word to you when my brother rejoins the court."

He must hear like a fox.

"Thank you, lord king," her mother said.

Oswald smiled politely but pointedly until both Breguswith and Gwladus turned away.

"I would have your advice, cousin." He nodded at Uinniau. "What shall I do with the prince?"

"Do?"

"He can't live in Rheged. There must be no murmurs of the true prince to muddy the succession after Rhoedd."

"All Uinniau's wanted these last years is to marry his Begu."

"People change."

"Uinniau doesn't want to be king."

"To the folk it doesn't always matter what a prince wants. I want Lord Uinniau out of Rheged."

Out of sight, out of mind. Otherwise Oswald or Oswiu would have to kill him.

Just beyond Oswine, Uinniau and Begu were laughing at some jest the man next to Begu had told them—Laisrén, she realised. Begu, sensing her attention, looked up and waved. Hild smiled and lifted her cup.

"She's your gemæcce, I'm told." And she could guess who had told him. Laisrén was like Gwladus—he found out everything. "No doubt you would like her safe."

And no doubt you would like to keep your tripes. But perhaps that would be speaking too plainly. White mead was strong stuff.

"There might be a place," she said. *Onnen, forgive me.* "Begu was born at the Bay of the Beacon, on the coast between Hereteu and the Humbre's mouth. Do you know it? It's a fine trading harbour that brings rich tithes, held once by Mulstan, Begu's father, a loyal thegn of your father's. His widow holds it now, on behalf of Mulstan's children."

"Ah." He thought about it. "An elegant solution. Though as it's a Deiran port cousin Oswine will have to agree."

Or you could just kill him, too. She took her hand away from her cup. "He will if you ask it. He's fond of Uinniau."

She watched Uinniau, who was now talking to Oswine, who threw back his head and laughed with abandon.

Oswald was studying her, and perhaps he had drunk more than she knew because, for the first time, he was not taking care to guard his expression: He was puzzled.

"Who are you, Hild Yffing? You read and write, and your priests treat you like a bishop—for they are your priests, Roman and British, that's plain. But people call you seer and hægtes."

"I'm not a seer."

"Are you not? Then why do people whisper as you pass? Hægtes of the wood, Cath Llew, Baedd Coch, Butcherbird. A cat, a boar, a bird . . ."

"Don't forget freemartin."

"A cat, a boar, a bird, and a cow who would be a bull. A shapeshifter and wyrd-maker. A godmouth and a prince. Who is the real Hild Yffing?"

She did not bother to answer him. He seemed happy to keep talking and eventually he would answer his own questions.

"You're cousin to the kings of the north, and sister to the queen of the East Anglisc. Rich and powerful, loved and feared. You killed one king and made another. Will you kill another when it suits you?"

"You've nothing to fear from me. I don't want to be king."

"Not yet at least. But even if you never do, it doesn't matter. You have power and someone will always try find a way to use that power."

Hild thought: Someone like you. But she would let no one ever use her again.

"I'd rather bend your power to my own ends than have it used against me." Definitely too much to drink; his speech was becoming less deft. "Laisrén'd have me kill you, or at least strip your power."

"And will you?" He would be a fool to try and he did not seem a fool.

"No. Your power's not in your gold or your name. It's in you. I don't understand it. And I don't understand why you felt the need to put it about that you're a seer."

"It was a story started by a frightened mother to protect her child."

"So you don't believe you're a godmouth?"

"I am not a godmouth."

"Good. And you wear a cross. Very good. Tell me, do you believe in any God but Christ?"

"There's only one god." The pattern. But that was not what he was really asking. "I can't foretell the future. I'm not always right."

"Infab—infibil—always being right is God's domain. I don't need you to be right, not all the time. Most of the time though—you can do that. Yes, I think you can. You made me king, Hild Yffing. You, an Yffing, made an Iding king. And I don't know why. So why?"

"Because the people will accept you as a king for both Bernicia and Deira. And because I think you'll be a good king."

"A good king." He mused on that, and now she could see the slight red to his eyes; too much white mead and not enough sleep. "I want that. To be a good king. And kings have to use what power is to hand. And I can't take yours, so will you lend it to me?"

He held up his hand as though she were about to interrupt, and switched to Irish.

"You've pledged to build Elmet's borders and pay your tithes." In the tongue he spoke most he seemed sharper and less drunk. "From what I've seen and learnt, that's well in hand. But take the winter to make doubly sure of those borders. And in spring, come to me in Bebbanburg—and bring that boy of yours."

"Wilfrid's not my son." She spoke Anglisc, aware of Gwladus and Breguswith listening.

"Is he not? He calls you Mother. There are songs of you giving birth in a battle and raising him in the marsh and mere, nursing him on revenge like the monsters in song. You fed him from your body, and he looks not unlike the black Yffings." He nodded back at Oswine and Osthryth. "So what does it matter if he's not the child of your body? It does not. No. What matters is what others think he is: a male Yffing. I need him under my eye."

"Don't threaten me, cousin."

"No. No, no. I mean only you can't keep him under your eye. Not when you're travelling."

Travel.

"Ha!" He slapped the board. "Good. Oh, very good. I'd heard you like to travel. Yes. Oh, yes. So." And now he spoke Anglisc again. "My brother Oswiu will be my war chief, my sword-hand and fist. I need—"

She was tired of what others needed.

He caught her expression. "We could help each other, cousin. There's Lindsey and East Anglia. Cent and Frankia. Travel with my token, just for a little while."

He looked past her and smiled slightly. She turned to find Gwladus watching them. She turned back.

"Being Left Hand of the king would be no small thing."

Just for a little while . . . She would not be threatened but she could be tempted.

When Hild left the feast the butcher shop was closed. In her apartments she stayed awake half the night, but Brona did not come.

In the morning Brona was in her shop cutting away at half a bullock hanging from a great hook. When she saw Hild she put down her knife and wiped her hands on a cloth. "I did come by your apartment when I'd finished last night. You weren't there."

It must have been early, then, before the feast ended. "I waited. I missed you."

Brona said nothing, just picked up the knife again.

"Is that the one you used on the dead horse in Menewood? Do you remember? I don't think you liked me very much. You said—"

Brona rested the tip of the knife on the butcher block. "What do you want, Hild?"

You. But she did not say it. "In spring I might have to travel; I haven't decided. If I did, and if I asked it, would you come to Menewood, and would you be there when I got back?"

"It's too small for a butcher, and I find I'm not made to be left behind doing nothing but wait."

"You could come with me."

"Could I? Then I'd be just staying behind and waiting somewhere new where I don't know anybody and have nothing to do."

"It wouldn't be like that."

"What would it be like?"

Silence.

"You can't say." Now Brona sounded patient, as she did when she explained something to Maer. "You haven't thought about it. I want to make a life with someone who's thought about it and wants to make a life with me, is interested in what I do."

"I do want to—"

"Hush, Hild. Hush. You don't know what you want yet or where you belong. I do. I like York. I was born here; I grew up here; I have a place. Here I'm Brona the butcher. This is my home."

"So you'll be staying."

Brona nodded.

"I'll miss you." Was this all? "If I visit York, can I come see you?"

Brona nodded again, and her eyes were very bright. "Bring the children, too. And give them my love. And keep stretching that hip. Send that girl of yours to me and I'll teach her how to rub the muscles."

"I—yes, of course. Yes." There was nothing else to say. "Fare well, Brona the butcher."

"Walk in the light, Hild Yffing."

"Hild! There you are! What are you doing sitting in here all alone in the dark? Where's Gwladus? I have such news! We're to go to Mulstanton! Me and Winny—Oswine's given it to us!" She was brimming with excitement. "We're to go now, on the first ship; we're to take the tithes in hand first thing. Not that they need taking in hand because Onnen always—only, oh, what shall I say to Onnen? You'll come, too, won't you? You have to. You always know the right thing to say. She'll listen to you."

"I can't come with you."

"Why?"

"I might be able to visit in spring. We'll see."

"But you've sorted everything out—surely you can do what you want? And, really, it would be so much better if you could come and explain things to Onnen. You're so good at that. You could tell her she can stay there as long as she likes."

"It's your news to give." Hild would rather cut out her tongue than be the one to deliver that message. "But if you want my advice, leave her in charge for a while yet. Decide what portion—of land, or income, whatever you and Uinniau decide—what portion should go to the twins, in care of Onnen, then break the rest to her gently."

"See? I hadn't thought of that! Oh, you will come, won't you?"

"Gemæcce, I'll always come to you. No matter what. Who else will help you with all those fat babies?"

Begu laughed, a picture of such joy that Hild's heart ached. "Oh, and do you suppose your mother would want to come? I think that would comfort Onnen."

Hild stood with Oswine, Breguswith, Gwladus, and half of York as Oswald's train prepared to move out. Cormán strode about importantly, shaking holy water on people and declaiming in a mix of Latin and Irish. No one understood a word he said, and they ignored him. He grew more and more cross, and so louder and louder.

Oswald beckoned to Hild. She came to stand by his stirrup. He seemed relaxed now he had decided where she would fit in his plans.

"Cousin. I'll look for you in spring with that boy of yours. You can meet my sister. Æbbe won't be marrying Domnall Brecc. Though you knew that, didn't you?"

Hild nodded; it had never made sense.

He sighed. "What is that bishop doing? Where's Laisrén? Aidan? Aidan!" Aidan came running. "Go find Laisrén to translate for the bishop." He took his reins up as though to go back there and do it himself.

"Cousin." Hild laid a hand on his arm. "Would you take an early piece of advice?"

He raised his eyebrows.

"No king should have to speak for another, not even for one who is a speaker for god." He frowned. "Find a bishop who understands his flock, and in turn can make himself understood."

"Cormán was recommended by the abbot of Hii himself." He gave her a long, thoughtful look, then nodded. "But I'll consider it and give you my answer in Bebbanburg."

38

✦

THE WINTERFYLLETH SKY was a hard, bright blue. Between the beck and the great Yr, Hild followed the scent of late elderberries through the wood. The glittering light was dazzling, turning the hanging leaves to giant hands of flame and bronze and gold, unreal as a dream or hero song.

There: not only elderberries but blackberries. She settled on her hams and began stripping them; dropping most into her basket but not a few in her mouth. So far it had been an abundant autumn; this winter they would not want for much.

A great grey slow worm glided out from under a fallen leaf and through the grass. She watched it for a while. It was long, with many scars on its head and neck, and she realised she had seen this very one two years ago, just before she and Cian left Menewood to join Edwin at Aberford. Its tail was shorter now, and a different colour: Something had bitten it off, and the worm had grown another.

"Here, great worm." She moved the grass aside to show it the snail on the underside of leaf. "Something for your larder. Eat well, sleep well, and perhaps we'll meet again in the spring."

If she chose to stay.

On the way back she checked the hornbeam nuts; not yet ripe. A jackdaw looked at her from a branch higher up, grey irises pale against its dark feathers and the dark wood. He lifted his head just as Hild heard the *kyow-kyow* of his mate warning she was coming in. She landed and they bellied up next to each other. The female showed her nape and ruffled her head feathers and her mate ran his beak through them, preening and smoothing. They ignored Hild utterly.

Had Cian cared for her like that? She was not sure. She knew him better as childhood companion than husband. Had she admired him? Some of the time. She only knew his absence was like a missing rib, something she curled around protectively without realising.

At the long house Gwladus and Sintiadd were at the outdoor hearth, cutting mushrooms and puff balls into chunks and tossing them into the iron skillet on the flames. Her mouth watered at the scent of mushrooms and goose grease.

"No," Gwladus said, and slapped her hand away. "We're potting these. Find us more and you can eat some."

"I brought these." She held up the basket of berries.

"For the crock or to eat today? We've plenty in the crock."

The fruit leather they were making would be good this year. They had a fine mix of wildling apples, dansom, and crabapples, and it looked as though the sun would be with them another few days. It was one of the best autumns she could remember.

Or perhaps it was the peace, she thought, as she went inside and added the berries to the crock. Menewood was back to its accustomed size, with barely twoscore people. Breguswith was in Loidis, Begu in the Bay of the Beacon, Oeric and Grimhun and Heiu in Cnotinsleah. Here she had Fllur, Llweriadd, Sintiadd, Morud, and the children. Gwladus and Rhin and Ceadwin and Almund. Rulf and his apprentice and of course the Fiercesomes.

Wherever they were, her people were safe at last. She had made them safe.

In the garth, she dug the dirt, turning it over, forking in the byre-leavings and dung. She dug for a long time, forming row after row of good dark dirt ready for planting. Worms slid pinkly through the mounds; a beetle clambered to the top, waved its feelers into the nonexistent wind.

She began to sweat, but it was good sweat.

When she took a break she sat with her back against the enclosure fence, arms straight and hands flat on the dirt, face lifted to the sun, muscles tired and relaxed. That was something to thank Brona for: With

Sintiadd stretching her muscles most days, for the first time in nearly two years her hip and belly did not hurt.

Two years. Cian had been dead two years. Two years today she had torn into the Gwynedd line by Caer Daun and cut a path to her beloved and found only a dead puppet dressed as the Cian she had known. He had never known the peace of Menewood as she had; Menewood had always been her place alone. Caer Loid was their shared place. Caer Loid was gone. Menewood was still here.

Menewood had spoken to her from the moment she found it. Here, now, she could feel the life in its dirt, like a hum under her feet, her sit-bones, her hands. She watched an ant climb the leaves of the last turnips waiting to be pulled. Each leg was segmented, tiny hairs glinted on its abdomen, and its eyes seemed latticed and were grey as a sieve. Its hard casing gleamed the dark brown of burnt honey. A tiny thing but perfect in every way. Even the turnip stem with one leaf missing was exactly as it should be: perfect in its imperfection, beautiful, alive. The whole garth felt like a pool of life, endlessly renewed by the hidden font, the spring welling at the centre of all things.

Between her fingers she saw a speck of worm cast, the glitter of mica, and, there, by a log, a wood louse—so many legs it looked as though it swam as much as walked—moving into the cool dark realm under the bark. She dug her fingers in the dirt and felt each crumble and granule. Each was just the right shape to make the perfect space between it and the next, space enough for the worm to glide through and between. Each was just the right weight for the mole to move aside as it followed the worm. Just the right consistency to collect and hold water for the roots of growing things to absorb. It was as though this whole marvellous, interlocking puzzle were cut to fit together exactly, like the figures Cian had once carved, so long ago.

And it no longer mattered that there was no Cian; it mattered only to be here, to feel the life, the purpose in the life under her feet, under her own skin. She saw how each leaf hanging from the tree was designed to catch the right portion of light and gain the most shelter from the wind. She saw the same pattern in her skin and the weathering wood, and knew it was repeated in the wax honeycomb laid down by bees. It was the pattern of life, and built to a purpose. And that purpose was itself life. She had only to decide to live it.

Sunlight lay on her like a blessing.

The bark of the ancient pollard was damp, cool to the touch. No leaves yet, not even buds. But it was only Hrethmonath; they would come. Time out of mind this oak had stood here at the head of the valley, and every year, as the world turned from winter to summer, it unfurled with green as fresh as any sapling. Old trees and new alike knew how to do that, how to begin again. It was their pattern.

Hild settled with her back against the trunk, astride the crooked limb that grew west and north overlooking the valley—her valley—caught in the pause between winter and spring. Under the morning mist gleamed the system of beck and bog and pond that ran to join the river Yr. The Yr to the Use. The Use to the Humbre. The Humbre to the sea . . .

A water vole cut the pond at the point of a widening crease. Swimming home to safety, or away in search of adventure?

She watched it, trying to guess which way it might go. It would be her sign.

The vole waddled from the water, washed the root in its mouth, then wiped its whiskers with both paws at once, briskly, as if to say, *What next?* But instead of trundling towards the horizon it plopped back into the water and shot into a hole in the bank she had not noticed. Home. The vole had chosen home.

She laughed. Well. The vole's wyrd was not hers. She knew the rhythms of Menewood now: knew where the tawny owls nested and when they branched. She knew when the blackbirds came and where the rooks roosted. She knew when to tap the birch sap and when the vetch would speckle the pasture. Menewood would be safe in Rhin's hands; her wyrd now was to learn new places, new people, new patterns. She would take Gwladus and the Fiercesomes, Sintiadd and Morud, Oeric and Fllur and the children to Bebbanburg.

She leaned forward to the hedgepig Cian had carved, and cradled the small head in her palm. "Farewell," she said, and let go.

Author's Note

❖

HISTORICITY

Hild was real. Almost everything we know of her comes from a single document, the *Ecclesiastical History of the English People* (HE), written by Bede, a Christian monk, about fifty years after her death. If we are to believe Bede—who was a careful historian but writing with an agenda and within the cultural constraints of his time—Hild was born circa 614 CE, probably in the north of what is now England, and died in her bed sixty-six years later as the abbess of what is now Whitby. We know her mother was Breguswith and her father Hereric; Hereric was poisoned in Elmet (West Yorkshire) when Hild was three. When she was about thirteen she was baptised in York alongside her (great-) uncle Edwin Yffing,[1] king of Northumbria, and she was recruited into the church when she was thirty-three. Of the rest of the first half of her life—including the years covered in this book, January 632 to March 635—we know only that she was "living most nobly in the secular habit." We don't know where, or doing what, or with whom.[2]

However, during the second half of her life, as abbess, we know "her wisdom was so great that not only ordinary people, but even kings and princes sometimes asked for and"—the part that made me sit up and pay attention—"took her advice."[3] In other words,

---

[1] I use *Yffing* as a family name for Edwin's (and Hild's) dynasty but this is not how it would have been used in the seventh century. Similarly, I doubt anyone in Hild's early life used the world *Northumbria*.

[2] I suspect that while Bede admired what Hild achieved, he did not wholly approve of how she lived. The (very few) other women he bothers to name in HE are admired for being "holy virgins" or "consecrated virgins" or—in the case of one queen married more than once, the second time for twelve years—having "preserved the glory of perpetual virginity." Hild is a conspicuous exception.

[3] The original, "quaererent et invenīrent," translates literally as "would seek and would find." I read it as "would take," but it could equally be "would accept" or "would receive."

the powers-that-be of seventh-century Britain, who took and held power with the sword, regarded Hild as smart enough and knowledgeable enough of their arenas to offer them valuable counsel. We know she was also an efficient and well-respected facilitator and administrator (she hosted the history-changing Synod of Whitby); a teacher (she trained five bishops); a forward thinker (she saw the value in using vernacular literature to convey ideas); and made an indelible impression on others (she is still venerated as a patron saint of learning and education 1,350 years after her death). Finally, she possessed a determined sense of fairness: The community she ran held all possessions in common and all members were treated equally. As people rarely have complete personality changes in their early thirties, we can assume Hild had these qualities to a degree before she joined the church—and on that assumption rest the events of this book.

While we don't know much about Hild the person, we do know something of her contemporaries and the bloody events of their time. It would take more space than I have here to detail which specifics in this story are documented (or inferred from material finds) and which are purely fictional, but the broad outlines of wars and regime change are true.

The book's first main battle, usually referred to by historians as the Battle of Hatfield, is dated by Bede to October 12, 632.[4] Edwin of Northumbria and his son the ætheling Osfrith Yffing, are killed by the combined forces of Penda of Mercia and Cadwallon of Gwynedd at a place Bede names Hæðfeld, usually taken to refer to what is now Hatfield Chase near Doncaster. Eadfrith Yffing, another son and ætheling, is captured and later killed by Penda. Edwin and Osfrith are dismembered and their heads and limbs staked out on the battlefield. Over a year of chaos follows, with the thrones of Deira and Bernicia variously claimed by Osric Yffing (a cousin) and Eanfrid Iding (eldest son of a rival dynasty, living in exile among the Picts). Both are slaughtered by Cadwallon, who was "utterly barbarous in temperament and behaviour. He was set upon exterminating the entire English race in Britain, and spared neither women nor innocent children, putting them all to horrible deaths with ruthless savagery, and continuously ravaging about the whole country." This time "remains accursed and hateful to all good men . . . hence all those calculating the reigns of kings have agreed to expunge memory" of the whole thing from their kinglists.

The second main battle, often called the Battle of Heavenfield, occurred at an unknown date in 634. Oswald, son of Æthelfrith Iding (the king of Northumbria who was killed by Edwin), returned from exile in Dál Riata with a small band. The day before the battle he raised a cross at a place "called in English Hefenfeld." Then in a surprise attack Cadwallon died just south of Hadrian's Wall by Deniseburna, what is now Rowley Burn. Oswald became king of Northumbria.

Bede's version of Hæðfeld needs only a little fictional intervention to make sense. Essentially, the combined armies of Mercia and Gwynedd march up the most convenient Roman road from their respective territories to Edwin's—even two hundred years after the tax-and-maintenance structure of Roman occupation collapsed, these roads were the best routes for rapid troop movement—to invade. They are met by Edwin's army where the Roman road crosses from disputed territory at the edge of Lindsey and Mercia

---

[4] Dates are disputed, depending on the source, the calendar they used, and their translator. Some argue the year of Hatfield was 633 or even 634; some sources suggest the date of October 14.

into Edwin's territory. Edwin loses. Penda and Cadwallon march north to claim Northumbria.[5]

On the other hand, the Battle of Heavenfield/Deniseburna, as written, makes no sense to me whatsoever. According to Bede, Oswald Iding, half brother of Eanfrid Iding, "mustered an army small in numbers but strong in the faith of Christ; and despite Cadwallon's vast forces, which he boasted of as irresistible, the infamous British leader was killed at a place known by the English as Deniseburn." Oswald was an ætheling-in-exile in Dál Riata (what is now the western seaboard of Scotland and northeastern Ireland—a long, difficult journey to Hadrian's Wall). If he had a war band at all it would have been a small number of personal followers. Cadwallon, already a proven commander, had a victorious army and had been accumulating men and materiel for over a year; he was also based in territory he knew very well. How could Oswald travel so far and arrive not only in good enough shape to beat an enemy who heavily outnumbered him but also unnoticed enough for his attack to be a surprise?

There are accounts of Oswald and this battle not only from Bede but also Adomnán (writing a little before Bede), and the compiler of the ninth-century Historia Brittonum. They couldn't make the battle make sense either—or for some reason were offended by what really happened—because to differing degrees they all lean on divine intervention.

I prefer a more rational explanation: a combination of, one, a knowledgeable, observant, persuasive, and charismatic noble whose counsel on the dynamics of power, as we've established, was sought by kings, and, two, the fickleness of nature. In my version of history, the deciding factor at Deniseburna is not divine intervention but Hild and the weather.

Is this what really happened? It could have. It makes sense of all the disparate pieces we have and none of it contravenes what is known to be known.[6] But in the final analysis *Menewood* is fiction. I made it up.

NAMES

For a historical novelist, seventh-century Old English naming conventions are awkward.[7] Families, particularly dynastic families, had names that look and sound the same to modern sensibilities, which is why there are so many characters in this book whose names begin with Ea- or Æth- or Os- (the Yffings and part-Yffings alone could fill half a page: Osric, Oswald, Oswiu, Oswine, Osfrith, Osthryth . . .). Unless I want to change history there's only so much I can do about that. I've used a combination of fudging—for example, Eanfrith Iding becomes Eanfrid to help distinguish him from Eadfrith Yffing—and epithets

[5] The only thing that does not make sense to me is why Cadwallon stayed in Northumbria but Penda did not, and why he harrowed the north, destroying everything and making no apparent attempt to build a base of power.
[6] But, oh, we know so little! Having said that, if anyone tells you that they know—that it's perfectly obvious—that seventh-century women never were and never could have been warriors, feel free to laugh. The evidence that over the last ten thousand years women have hunted, and used weapons in armed combat, is so overwhelming that I wouldn't know where to start.
[7] Old English names are generally dithematic, built of two elements, a prefix and a suffix. Families, especially those with dynastic pretensions, often used the same prefix through generations. Family names in the sense we use them today did not arrive until the Normans in the eleventh century.

or bynames: Eadfrith Yffing becomes Honeytongue, and Eanfrid becomes the Iding. Osric Yffing becomes the craven of Craven and his son, Oswine, becomes the Reed.

Happily, some characters did have documented bynames; sometimes more than one, and in more than one language. Depending on who was doing the naming, these epithets could be admiring, disparaging, or fond. Many of the bynames in *Hild* and *Menewood* are invented, though some are not—just as some of the characters themselves are invented, though many are not.

PRONUNCIATION

Hild would have encountered at least four languages on a regular basis: Old Irish (Irish), Ancient British or Brittonic (British), Latin, and Old English (Anglisc).

I won't attempt to codify the pronunciation of Old Irish; it's defeated better than me.

Ancient British is easier. If you think of it in the same terms as modern Welsh you'll get a sense of how to proceed. Every letter is sounded; *c* is pronounced k, *dd* as th, *ff* as v, *rh* as hr, and u, *g*, and w can be . . . mercurial. So:

Cian: KEE-*an*
Gwladus: OO-*la-doose*
Arddun: AR-thun
Rhroedd: HRO-*eth*
Afanc: AV-*ank*
Uinniau: oo-IN-NI-*eye* (the short form sounds very like *Winny*)

Latin sounds much as it looks with the exception of *v*, which sounds like w. Consonants are hard (*g* as in *go*, and *c* as k).

Old English is a particular and deliberate tongue, with every consonant and vowel sounded, r's trilled, and diphthongs accented on the first element. Some simplified pronunciation guidelines include:

æ: like the *a* in *cat*
sc: sh, as in *ship*
g: sometimes y, as in *yes*
ic: usually as *itch*
f: sometimes as v, as in *very*
ð: th, as in *then*

So:

Gipswīc: Yips-witch
gesith: yeh-SEETH
gemæcce: yeh-MATCH-*eh*
thegn: thayn
ceorl: churl
ætheling: ATH-*ell-ing*
scop: SHOW-p
Anglisc: ANG-*glish*
Eanflæd: AY-*on-vlad*
seax: sax

Yffi: IFF-y
Hereric: herr-EHR-itch
Wilnoð: oo-ILL-noth

PLACES

Some of the place names used here are guesses based on back formations from, for example, toponyms or legend. While many are honest attempts, I cheerfully admit that a fair few are invented. You may have wondered why some are modern English (York) while others are based on Anglicised versions of Latin (Corabrig), and still others on an ancestral version of Old Welsh, the closest I can come to Brittonic (Calchfynydd). My reasoning is as mixed as the results. In at least one case I wanted readers to have one well-known locality they could find on a modern map (York), sometimes I just liked the Welsh version better than the Old English, and sometimes one version looked too similar to something else so to avoid confusion I switched languages. You may notice that some of the names and places used in Hild (for example, Catterick) have been replaced by better choices (such as Cetreht) in *Menewood*.

MORE INFORMATION

For more information on many things mentioned in this note, please visit my website, nicolagriffith.com/menewood/. There you'll find not only a comprehensive list of characters showing who was real and who was not but also larger-scale, detailed maps of many of the places mentioned in the story, plus a downloadable PDF of a good translation of the relevant remarks Bede made on Hild.[8]

There are many useful online articles about people, places, and events of the early seventh century, but there are many that are not reliable. In particular, when it comes to battles—which seem to bring out the fantasist in us all—proceed with caution and much cross-reference. One open-access site I can recommend is the peer-reviewed journal *The Heroic Age* (https://www.heroicage.org/); see in particular the early issues.

---

[8] Translated by Roy L. Liuzza and used with permission.

Glossary

æfen	6:00 p.m. to 9:00 p.m.
Ærra Geola	December
ætheling	male youth in the line of succession, prince
Anglisc	pertaining to Angles: the people, the language
Annwn	otherworld ruled by Arawn (British)
baldric	wide weapons belt worn cross-wise over shoulder
basilica	main hall of old Roman administration building
beck	stream or brook (here used mostly in Deira)
bee glue	propolis; dark brown resinous mixture made by honeybees from saliva, beeswax, and the goop exuded by tree buds, sap flows, etc.; hard and brittle until warmed, then sticky
bletting	sweetening and making edible fruit by leaving on the tree after it's ripe and picking immediately after a frost (which begins the chemical breakdown process), then putting in a dark, cool room until soft
Blodmonath	November
bocland	land held by charter—written in an official record, a book
British	Brittonic, language of the Britons; precursor of Welsh, Cornish, Breton
bulger	fungus, *Bulgaria inquinans*, grows in groups on felled/fallen oak
burn	hill stream (here used in more northerly parts of Northumbre)
Cath Llew	large cat; uncanny; lynx (British)
cefn	high ridge, rocky outcrop
ceorl	freeman
colewort	cabbage
cyrtel	loose, long-sleeved dress; informal
dryhten	absolute lord

ealdorman	lord (earl), often of region that used to be independent kingdom (e.g., Elmet and Craven)
ell	about thirty inches
Elmetsætne	people of Elmet
Eorðe	goddess (Anglisc)
etin	giant
fig (the)	haemorrhoids
freemartin	female calf masculinised in womb by male twin
gelotendæg	3:00 p.m. to 6:00 p.m.
gemæcce	formal female friendship/partnership, often political
gesith	member of king's personal war band, elite warrior, unmarried
green chop	human-harvested, extra-nutritious greenstuff for valuable livestock
hægtes	formidable woman, user of uncanny power, rider of the Hel Boundary
Harvestmonath	September (harvest month)
Hel	Anglisc hell, a cold place
hogget	sheep, aged one to two years old
Hrethmonath	March (windy month)
hythe	sheltered landing place—sand or mud; informal trading area
Idings	royal dynasty, Bernicia
ironglass	green crystals of ferrous sulphate
league	about three miles
Litha	June
mastfall	the fall of mast—tree nuts such as hazel, beech, oak—in autumn
mead	an alcoholic drink fermented from honey and flavoured with other ingredients
Meadmonath	July
middæg	middle of the day, noon to 3:00 p.m.
midniht	midnight to 3:00 a.m.
Modraniht	Night of the Mothers, one of twelve celebrated feasts of Yuletide
morgen	6:00 a.m. to 9:00 a.m.
night soil	human excrement
niht	9:00 p.m. to 12 midnight
nithing	oath-breaker, one who is shunned
North Folk	Anglisc of northern East Anglia
Northumbre	Bernicia and Deira
Œstre Mass	Easter Sunday
Œstremonath	April (Easter month)
Oiscingas	royal dynasty, Kent
overking	ruler powerful enough to demand tribute and/or tithes from smaller kingdoms
pace	two strides, about five feet
princeps	pretentious title used by those still aping Roman ways
principia	old Roman administrative building
redcrest	Roman
rig	ridge, either natural or built (e.g., the linear earthwork of the redcrest Rig)
rod	length measure, 16.5 feet

saes	British for "stranger," often Anglisc
scop	royal bard (Anglisc)
seax	large, single-edged blade; weapon
sidsa	magic
small beer	second or even third brewing, each progressively less alcoholic, from previously used malt
snakesteel	pattern-welded blade, usually a sword
snakestone	ammonite (fossil)
Solmonath	February (mud month)
South Folk	Anglisc of southern East Anglia
sprite	supernatural figure/spirit of water
taff	board game
thegn	lord, former gesith with a lifetime lease on land from the king
Thromilchi	May (three-milkings month)
tithe	tax in goods, bullion, or services levied by a lord (usually a king)
tree hay	chopped-up brush, used as winter fodder
tufa	royal standard on a pole, based on Roman legionary standard
tun	cask; a large unit of liquid measurement
úht	3:00 a.m to 6:00 a.m.
underking	ruler of a previously independent kingdom or people—for example, Deira and Bernicia (subordinate to the king of Northumbre)
undern	9:00 a.m. to 12 noon
wariangle	term used in Elmet and Craven for shrike, or butcherbird
war street	Roman road in good repair: ideal for large-scale troop movement
wealh	Anglisc for "stranger," root word of present-day "Welsh"
Weodmonath	August (weed month)
wey	a wool measure, perhaps 175 pounds
white mead	high-status mead of high alcohol content (created by freezing mead, discarding the frozen solids, and retaining the liquid)
wīc	royal trading centre, often a port; controlled and taxed
wight	supernatural figure/ghost (as it is used in *Hild* and *Menewood*—in Old English it means a creature of any kind, a living thing)
Winterfylleth	October
Woden	god, Anglisc
Wuffings	royal dynasty, East Angles
Wulfmonath	January
wyrd	fate
Yffings	royal dynasty, Deira
Yr Hen Ogledd	The Old North; British kingdoms of northern England, southern Scotland, and northern Wales
Yuletide	the twelve days of Christmas; also called Christmastide

Acknowledgements

Every time I start a novel I promise myself that this time I'll keep a list of names; I won't forget a single gift, joy, favour, or lesson that contributed to the book's existence. Every time, when I sit down to write these acknowledgements, I discover that instead of a single neatly organised and deeply rational list I've kept a dozen lists on different bits of paper in different rooms, and in different documents on different text editors on different devices, platforms, and cloud storage services. As with every time before this I remember that no list and too many lists are functional equivalents. And so, as with every other long-in-the-making book, this list of names is but a pale shadow of the thronging tribe of people and events that truly made *Menewood* possible.

My thanks to Beverly Marshall Saling, for whom I wrote Afanc, the little beaver of High Brune, in gratitude for her donation to a favourite nonprofit. To Robin Sloan for proselytizing the joy of big books like *Hild*—and Neal Stephenson, ditto. Clare Lees and Gillian Overing, whose *Double Agents: Women and Clerical Culture in Anglo-Saxon England* was my way into breaking open Bede (nearly fifteen years ago), and therefore to start treating history as what it really is—a story we tell to explain what we think we know about the past in light of our present. Megan Cavell and Jenny Neville for the riddles. Hana Videen for *The Wordhord*. Matt Hussey for inviting me to speak at IONA and introducing me to so many early medievalists—and Jay Paul Gates for introducing me to more. Alaric Hall for the ælfe and hægtessan; Karen Jolly for ways to think about medicine, belief, and culture. Catherine Karkov, Nick Higham, Max Adams, Alex Woolf, Susan Oosthuizen, and Andrew Breeze for their work—always thought-provoking. If I get things wrong here it's not their fault.

For practical help, Rob Hardy for digital Bede and perceptive reviews. Christina Fanciullo and so many other librarians and academics for the PDFs. Roy L. Liuzza for kind permission to host part of his translation of Bede on my website. Marko Zalad for notes on Roman roads in Yorkshire. Al Newham for circumstantial evidence of Hild's first religious foundation (I'll get to that . . .). Tenaya Jorgensen for the wonderful GIS mapping of

Hadrian's Wall and surrounding topography so I could check my theories about who could see what from where (all mistakes, of course, are mine). And to Kate Macdonald—she knows why.

Again, and still, whether their blogs are now archived or still extant, three of the old blogging crew—Jonathan Jarrett, Michelle Zeigler, and Guy Halsall—whose lengthy discussions, thorough footnotes, original thinking, and delightful asides (sometimes fruitfully infuriating) were my entry into current early medieval research. (And to other early medievalists: Blogs are great public engagement! And you get to own your own platform! one that no algorithm will cover up and no billionaire can shut down or ban you from on a whim! More, please.) To Farah Mendlesohn and Edward James for many things. Paul Morriss for archiving an old Yahoo! group for me. And many others (there are a surprising number of you) who wish to remain anonymous but who nevertheless gave me help with a variety of technology, access, and information when I needed it most.

Many thanks to Sean McDonald, my editor—patient with the overruns of time and words (and detours into two other books, not to mention a PhD) and always perceptive in his edits—his assistant editor, Ben Brooks, and everyone at Farrar, Straus and Giroux/MCD who has helped to bring this book into the world (Caitlin Cataffo, Molly Grote, Abby Kagan, Na Kim, Bri Panzica, Daniel del Valle, and Sarita Varma). I'm thrilled once again by the art of the fabulous Balbusso twins, Anna and Elena, whose vision of Hild continues to grow alongside the character. Thanks always and often to Stephanie Cabot, my agent—not only *also* patient and perceptive but kind—and all at both Susanna Lea Associates and the Gernert Company. I'm profoundly grateful to my fellow writers for their books, conversations—at book events, conferences, and conventions (virtual and in-person)—and mutual support, without which everything would be ten times harder and a hundred times more lonely.

It's been an interesting few years. I wish I could have spent more time with friends, but the conversations we did have—Zoom calls, texts, long emails, FaceTime, brief exchanges on social media, freezing in the January sleet over a cocktail, melting in the July heat trying to eat while being eaten in turn by hordes of mosquitoes—kept me anchored and were worth every minute. I really hope we can do more of it, and more often. And to my family, by blood and choice: You know who you are; you know how much I love you; I just wish we could spend more time together and more often. Soon.

And finally* to Kelley, the queen and companion of my world, for the love, comfort, joy, explorations, support, excitement, questions, conversation, bravery, persistence, and laughter that fill my life with delight.

* Oh, yes, and to Charlie and George, whose insistence on timely treats and helpful four-footed edits are nothing but a bleszdr67%^%eDW56,. . .. . %$`````````

A Note About the Author

Nicola Griffith is a dual UK/US citizen who lives in Seattle, Washington. She is the author of award-winning novels including *Spear*, *Hild*, and *Ammonite*, and has written for *Nature*, *New Scientist*, *The New York Times*, *The Guardian*, and other publications. She is the founder and cohost of #CripLit, holds a PhD from Anglia Ruskin University, and enjoys a ferocious bout of wheelchair boxing. She is married to the novelist and screenwriter Kelley Eskridge.